U0063710

Henry David Thoreau 著

潘慶舲 譯

WALDEN

瓦爾登湖

商務印書館

瓦爾登湖 *Walden*

作　　者：Henry David Thoreau

譯　　者：潘慶舲

責任編輯：黃家麗

封面設計：涂　慧

出　　版：商務印書館（香港）有限公司

　　　　　香港筲箕灣耀興道 3 號東滙廣場 8 樓

　　　　　http://www.commercialpress.com.hk

發　　行：香港聯合書刊物流有限公司

　　　　　香港新界荃灣德士古道 220-248 號荃灣工業中心 16 樓

印　　刷：美雅印刷製本有限公司

　　　　　九龍觀塘榮業街 6 號海濱工業大廈 4 樓 A

版　　次：2021 年 5 月第 1 版第 1 次印刷

　　　　　© 2021 商務印書館（香港）有限公司

　　　　　ISBN 978 962 07 0439 0

　　　　　Printed in Hong Kong

Publisher's Note 出版説明

　　不甘心隨波逐流，勇於選擇自己的生活方式，是作者梭羅花兩年多時間，獨居於瓦爾登（Walden）海岸的目的。春天，梭羅身處綠樹林蔭，他用木板和石灰建造小木屋，用最少和最必要的家具裝飾房屋，與小鳥為友，感受大自然帶來的滿足感。夏天，他種植了一大片豆田，學習如何自給自足，又在湖中沐浴，享受原始的森林生活。秋天，開始用柴火為壁爐照明，享受讀書之樂。冬天，暴風雪雖然猛烈，他仍在冰凍湖面上滑行，欣賞有冰柱的樹木。

　　閱讀梭羅的生活實錄，讀者可體會他的心路歷程和對人生的深度思考。梭羅自我總結説："我至少從我的試驗中悟出了這麼一點心得：一個人只要充滿自信，朝着他夢想指引的方向前進，努力去過他心中想像的那種生活，那他就會獲得平時意想不到的成功。"本書被譽為 19 世紀最重要的著作之一，影響延續至今，對現代讀者具啟示作用。

　　初、中級英語程度讀者使用本書時，先閱讀英文原文，如遇到理解障礙，則參考中譯作為輔助。在英文原文後附註解，標註古英語、非現代詞彙拼寫形式及語法；在譯文結束之前附註釋，以幫助讀者理解原文故事背景。如有餘力，讀者可在閱讀原文部份段落後，查閱相應中譯，揣摩同樣詞句在雙語中不同的表達。

商務印書館（香港）有限公司

編輯出版部

目　錄 Contents

1
Economy

When I wrote the following pages, or rather the bulk of them, I lived alone, in the woods, a mile from any neighbour, in a house which I had built myself, on the shore of Walden Pond, in Concord, Massachusetts, and earned my living by the labour of my hands only. I lived there two years and two months. At present I am a sojourner in civilized life again.

I should not obtrude my affairs so much on the notice of my readers if very particular inquiries had not been made by my townsmen concerning my mode of life, which some would call impertinent, though they do not appear to me at all impertinent, but, considering the circumstances, very natural and pertinent. Some have asked what I got to eat; if I did not feel lonesome; if I was not afraid; and the like. Others have been curious to learn what portion of my income I devoted to charitable purposes; and some, who have large families, how many poor children I maintained. I will therefore ask those of my readers who feel no particular interest in me to pardon me if I undertake to answer some of these questions in this book. In most books, the *I*, or first person, is omitted; in this it will be retained; that, in respect to egotism, is the main difference. We commonly do not remember that it is, after all, always the first person that is speaking. I should not talk so much about myself if there were anybody else whom I knew as well. Unfortunately, I am confined to this theme by the narrowness of my experience. Moreover, I, on my side, require of every writer, first or last, a simple and sincere account of his own life, and not merely what he has heard of other men's lives; some such account as he would send to his kindred from a distant land; for if he has lived sincerely, it must have been in a distant land to me. Perhaps these pages are more particularly addressed to poor students. As for the rest of my readers, they will accept such portions as apply to them. I trust that none will stretch the seams in putting on the coat, for it may do good service to him whom it fits.

I would fain say something, not so much concerning the Chinese and

Sandwich Islanders as you who read these pages, who are said to live in New England; something about your condition, especially your outward condition or circumstances in this world, in this town, what it is, whether it is necessary that it be as bad as it is, whether it cannot be improved as well as not. I have travelled a good deal in Concord; and everywhere, in shops, and offices, and fields, the inhabitants have appeared to me to be doing penance in a thousand remarkable ways. What I have heard of Bramins sitting exposed to four fires and looking in the face of the sun; or hanging suspended, with their heads downward, over flames; or looking at the heavens over their shoulders "until it becomes impossible for them to resume their natural position, while from the twist of the neck nothing but liquids can pass into the stomach;" or dwelling, chained for life, at the foot of a tree; or measuring with their bodies, like caterpillars, the breadth of vast empires; or standing on one leg on the tops of pillars, —even these forms of conscious penance are hardly more incredible and astonishing than the scenes which I daily witness. The twelve labours of Hercules were trifling in comparison with those which my neighbours have undertaken; for they were only twelve, and had an end; but I could never see that these men slew or captured any monster or finished any labour. They have no friend Iolaus to burn with a hot iron the root of the hydra's head, but as soon as one head is crushed, two spring up.

I see young men, my townsmen, whose misfortune it is to have inherited farms, houses, barns, cattle, and farming tools; for these are more easily acquired than got rid of. Better if they had been born in the open pasture and suckled by a wolf, that they might have seen with clearer eyes what field they were called to labour in. Who made them serfs of the soil? Why should they eat their sixty acres, when man is condemned to eat only his peck of dirt? Why should they begin digging their graves as soon as they are born? They have got to live a man's life, pushing all these things before them, and get on as well as they can. How many a poor immortal soul have I met well-nigh crushed and smothered under its load, creeping down the road of life, pushing before it a barn seventy-five feet by forty, its Augean stables never cleansed, and one hundred acres of land, tillage, mowing, pasture, and wood-lot! The portionless, who struggle with no such unnecessary inherited encumbrances, find it labour enough to subdue and cultivate a few cubic feet of flesh.

But men labour under a mistake. The better part of the man is soon ploughed into the soil for compost. By a seeming fate, commonly called necessity, they are employed, as it says in an old book, laying up treasures which moth and rust will corrupt and thieves break through and steal. It is a fool's life, as they will find when they get to the end of it, if not before. It is said that Deucalion and Pyrrha created men by throwing stones over their heads behind them:—

> Inde genus durum sumus, experiensque laborum,
> Et documenta damus quâ simus origine nati.
> Or, as Raleigh rhymes it in his sonorous way,—
> "From thence our kind hard-hearted is, enduring pain and care,
> Approving that our bodies of a stony nature are."

So much for a blind obedience to a blundering oracle, throwing the stones over their heads behind them, and not seeing where they fell.

Most men, even in this comparatively free country, through mere ignorance and mistake, are so occupied with the factitious cares and superfluously coarse labours of life that its finer fruits cannot be plucked by them. Their fingers, from excessive toil, are too clumsy and tremble too much for that. Actually, the labouring man has not leisure for a true integrity day by day; he cannot afford to sustain the manliest relations to men; his labour would be depreciated in the market. He has no time to be anything but a machine. How can he remember well his ignorance — which his growth requires — who has so often to use his knowledge? We should feed and clothe him gratuitously sometimes, and recruit him with our cordials, before we judge of him. The finest qualities of our nature, like the bloom on fruits, can be preserved only by the most delicate handling. Yet we do not treat ourselves nor one another thus tenderly.

Some of you, we all know, are poor, find it hard to live, are sometimes, as it were, gasping for breath. I have no doubt that some of you who read this book are unable to pay for all the dinners which you have actually eaten, or for the coats and shoes which are fast wearing or are already worn out, and have come to this page to spend borrowed or stolen time, robbing your creditors of an hour. It is very evident what mean and sneaking lives many of you live, for my sight has been whetted by experience; always on the limits, trying to get into business and trying to get out of debt, a very ancient slough, called by the Latins *æs alienum*, another's brass, for some of their coins were made of brass;

still living, and dying, and buried by this other's brass; always promising to pay, promising to pay, tomorrow, and dying today, insolvent; seeking to curry favour, to get custom, by how many modes, only not state-prison offences; lying, flattering, voting, contracting yourselves into a nutshell of civility, or dilating into an atmosphere of thin and vapourous generosity, that you may persuade your neighbour to let you make his shoes, or his hat, or his coat, or his carriage, or import his groceries for him; making yourselves sick, that you may lay up something against a sick day, something to be tucked away in an old chest, or in a stocking behind the plastering, or, more safely, in the brick bank; no matter where, no matter how much or how little.

I sometimes wonder that we can be so frivolous, I may almost say, as to attend to the gross but somewhat foreign form of servitude called Negro Slavery, there are so many keen and subtle masters that enslave both North and South. It is hard to have a Southern overseer; it is worse to have a Northern one; but worst of all when you are the slave-driver of yourself. Talk of a divinity in man! Look at the teamster on the highway, wending to market by day or night; does any divinity stir within him? His highest duty to fodder and water his horses! What is his destiny to him compared with the shipping interests? Does not he drive for Squire Make-a-stir? How godlike, how immortal, is he? See how he cowers and sneaks, how vaguely all the day he fears, not being immortal nor divine, but the slave and prisoner of his own opinion of himself, a fame won by his own deeds. Public opinion is a weak tyrant compared with our own private opinion. What a man thinks of himself, that it is which determines, or rather indicates, his fate. Self-emancipation even in the West Indian provinces of the fancy and imagination,—what Wilberforce is there to bring that about? Think, also, of the ladies of the land weaving toilet cushions against the last day, not to betray too green an interest in their fates! As if you could kill time without injuring eternity.

The mass of men lead lives of quiet desperation. What is called resignation is confirmed desperation. From the desperate city you go into the desperate country, and have to console yourself with the bravery of minks and muskrats. A stereotyped but unconscious despair is concealed even under what are called the games and amusements of mankind. There is no play in them, for this comes after work. But it is a characteristic of wisdom not to do desperate things.

When we consider what, to use the words of the catechism, is the chief end of man, and what are the true necessaries and means of life, it appears as if men had deliberately chosen the common mode of living because they preferred it to any other. Yet they honestly think there is no choice left. But alert and healthy natures remember that the sun rose clear. It is never too late to give up our prejudices. No way of thinking or doing, however ancient, can be trusted without proof. What everybody echoes or in silence passes by as true today may turn out to be falsehood tomorrow, mere smoke of opinion, which some had trusted for a cloud that would sprinkle fertilizing rain on their fields. What old people say you cannot do, you try and find that you can. Old deeds for old people, and new deeds for new. Old people did not know enough once, perchance, to fetch fresh fuel to keep the fire a-going; new people put a little dry wood under a pot, and are whirled round the globe with the speed of birds, in a way to kill old people, as the phrase is. Age is no better, hardly so well, qualified for an instructor as youth, for it has not profited so much as it has lost. One may almost doubt if the wisest man has learned anything of absolute value by living. Practically, the old have no very important advice to give the young, their own experience has been so partial, and their lives have been such miserable failures, for private reasons, as they must believe; and it may be that they have some faith left which belies that experience, and they are only less young than they were. I have lived some thirty years on this planet, and I have yet to hear the first syllable of valuable or even earnest advice from my seniors. They have told me nothing, and probably cannot tell me anything to the purpose. Here is life, an experiment to a great extent untried by me; but it does not avail me that they have tried it. If I have any experience which I think valuable, I am sure to reflect that this my Mentors said nothing about.

One farmer says to me, "You cannot live on vegetable food solely, for it furnishes nothing to make bones with;" and so he religiously devotes a part of his day to supplying his system with the raw material of bones; walking all the while he talks behind his oxen, which, with vegetable-made bones, jerk him and his lumbering plough along in spite of every obstacle. Some things are really necessaries of life in some circles, the most helpless and diseased, which in others are luxuries merely, and in others still are entirely unknown.

The whole ground of human life seems to some to have been gone over by their predecessors, both the heights and the valleys, and all things to have been cared for. According to Evelyn, "the wise Solomon prescribed ordinances for the very distances of trees; and the Roman prætors have decided how often you may go into your neighbour's land to gather the acorns which fall on it without trespass, and what share belongs to that neighbour." Hippocrates has even left directions how we should cut our nails; that is, even with the ends of the fingers, neither shorter nor longer. Undoubtedly the very tedium and ennui which presume to have exhausted the variety and the joys of life are as old as Adam. But man's capacities have never been measured; nor are we to judge of what he can do by any precedents, so little has been tried. Whatever have been thy failures hitherto, "be not afflicted, my child, for who shall assign to thee what thou hast left undone?"

We might try our lives by a thousand simple tests; as, for instance, that the same sun which ripens my beans illumines at once a system of earths like ours. If I had remembered this it would have prevented some mistakes. This was not the light in which I hoed them. The stars are the apexes of what wonderful triangles! What distant and different beings in the various mansions of the universe are contemplating the same one at the same moment! Nature and human life are as various as our several constitutions. Who shall say what prospect life offers to another? Could a greater miracle take place than for us to look through each other's eyes for an instant? We should live in all the ages of the world in an hour; ay, in all the worlds of the ages. History, Poetry, Mythology!—I know of no reading of another's experience so startling and informing as this would be.

The greater part of what my neighbours call good I believe in my soul to be bad, and if I repent of anything, it is very likely to be my good behaviour. What demon possessed me that I behaved so well? You may say the wisest thing you can, old man,—you who have lived seventy years, not without honour of a kind,—I hear an irresistible voice which invites me away from all that. One generation abandons the enterprises of another like stranded vessels.

I think that we may safely trust a good deal more than we do. We may waive just so much care of ourselves as we honestly bestow elsewhere. Nature is as well adapted to our weakness as to our strength. The incessant anxiety and strain of some is a well-nigh incurable form of disease. We are made to exaggerate the importance of what work we do; and yet how much is not done by us! Or, what if we had been taken sick? How vigilant we are! Determined not to live by faith if we can avoid it; all the day long on the alert, at night we unwillingly say our prayers and commit ourselves to uncertainties. So thoroughly and sincerely are we compelled to live, reverencing our life, and denying the possibility of change. This is the only way, we say; but there are as many ways as there can be drawn radii from one centre. All change is a miracle to contemplate; but it is a miracle which is taking place every instant. Confucius said, "To know that we know what we know, and that we do not know what we do not know, that is true knowledge." When one man has reduced a fact of the imagination to be a fact to his understanding, I foresee that all men will at length establish their lives on that basis.

Let us consider for a moment what most of the trouble and anxiety which I have referred to is about, and how much it is necessary that we be troubled, or at least, careful. It would be some advantage to live a primitive and frontier life, though in the midst of an outward civilization, if only to learn what are the gross necessaries of life and what methods have been taken to obtain them; or even to look over the old-day-books of the merchants, to see what it was that men most commonly bought at the stores, what they stored, that is, what are the grossest groceries. For the improvements of ages have had but little influence on the essential laws of man's existence; as our skeletons, probably, are not to be distinguished from those of our ancestors.

By the words, *necessary of life*, I mean whatever, of all that man obtains by his own exertions, has been from the first, or from long use has become, so important to human life that few, if any, whether from savageness, or poverty, or philosophy, ever attempt to do without it. To many creatures there is in this sense but one necessary of life, Food. To the bison of the prairie it is a few inches of palatable grass, with water to drink; unless he seeks the Shelter of the forest or the mountain's shadow. None of the brute creation requires more than Food and Shelter. The necessaries of life for man in this climate may, accurately enough, be distributed under the several heads of Food, Shelter, Clothing, and Fuel; for not till we have secured these are we prepared to entertain the true problems of life with freedom and a prospect of success. Man has invented, not only houses, but clothes and cooked food; and possibly from the accidental discovery of the warmth of fire, and the consequent use of it, at first a luxury, arose the present necessity to sit by it. We observe cats and dogs acquiring the same second nature. By proper Shelter and Clothing we legitimately retain our own internal heat; but with an excess of these, or of Fuel, that is, with an external heat greater than our own internal, may not cookery properly be said to begin? Darwin, the naturalist, says of the inhabitants of Tierra del Fuego, that while his own party, who were well clothed and sitting close to a fire, were far from too warm, these naked savages, who were farther off, were observed, to his great surprise, "to be streaming with perspiration at undergoing such a roasting." So, we are told, the New Hollander goes naked with impunity, while the European shivers in his clothes. Is it impossible to combine the hardiness of these savages with the intellectualness of the civilized man? According to Liebig, man's body is a stove, and Food the Fuel which keeps up the internal combustion in the lungs. In cold weather we eat more, in warm less. The animal heat is the result of a slow combustion, and disease and death take place when this is too rapid; or for want of Fuel, or from some defect in the draught, the fire goes out. Of course the vital heat is not to be confounded with fire; but so much for analogy. It appears, therefore, from the above list, that the expression, *animal life*, is nearly synonymous with the expression, *animal heat*; for while Food may be regarded as the Fuel which keeps up the fire within us,—and Fuel serves only to prepare that Food or to increase the warmth of our bodies by addition from without,—Shelter and Clothing also serve only to retain the *heat* thus generated and absorbed.

The grand necessity, then, for our bodies, is to keep warm, to keep the vital heat in us. What pains we accordingly take, not only with our Food, and Clothing, and Shelter, but with our beds, which are our nightclothes, robbing the nests and breasts of birds to prepare this shelter within a shelter, as the mole has its bed of grass and leaves at the end of its burrow! The poor man is wont to complain that this is a cold world; and to cold, no less physical than social, we refer directly a great part of our ails. The summer, in some climates, makes possible to man a sort of Elysian life. Fuel, except to cook his Food, is then unnecessary; the sun is his fire, and many of the fruits are sufficiently cooked by its rays; while Food generally is more various, and more easily obtained, and Clothing and Shelter are wholly or half unnecessary. At the present day, and in this country, as I find by my own experience, a few implements, a knife, an axe, a spade, a wheelbarrow, etc., and for the studious, lamplight, stationery, and access to a few books, rank next to necessaries, and can all be obtained at a trifling cost. Yet some, not wise, go to the other side of the globe, to barbarous and unhealthy regions, and devote themselves to trade for ten or twenty years, in order that they may live,—that is, keep comfortably warm,—and die in New England at last. The luxuriously rich are not simply kept comfortably warm, but unnaturally hot; as I implied before, they are cooked, of course *à la mode*.

Most of the luxuries, and many of the so called comforts of life, are not only not indispensable, but positive hindrances to the elevation of mankind. With respect to luxuries and comforts, the wisest have ever lived a more simple and meagre life than the poor. The ancient philosophers, Chinese, Hindoo, Persian, and Greek, were a class than which none has been poorer in outward riches, none so rich in inward. We know not much about them. It is remarkable that *we* know so much of them as we do. The same is true of the more modern reformers and benefactors of their race. None can be an impartial or wise observer of human life but from the vantage ground of what *we* should call voluntary poverty. Of a life of luxury the fruit is luxury, whether in agriculture, or commerce, or literature, or art. There are nowadays professors of philosophy, but not philosophers. Yet it is admirable to profess because it was once admirable to live. To be a philosopher is not merely to have subtle thoughts, nor even to found a school, but so to love wisdom as to live according to its dictates, a life of simplicity, independence, magnanimity, and trust. It is to solve some of the problems of life, not only theoretically, but practically. The success of great scholars and thinkers is commonly a courtier-like success, not kingly, not manly. They make shift to live merely by conformity, practically as their fathers did, and are in no sense the progenitors of a noble race of men. But why do men degenerate ever? What makes families run out? What is the nature of the luxury which enervates and destroys nations? Are we sure that there is none of it in our own lives? The philosopher is in advance of his age even in the outward form of his life. He is not fed, sheltered, clothed, warmed, like his contemporaries. How can a man be a philosopher and not maintain his vital heat by better methods than other men?

When a man is warmed by the several modes which I have described, what does he want next? Surely not more warmth of the same kind, as more and richer food, larger and more splendid houses, finer and more abundant clothing, more numerous incessant and hotter fires, and the like. When he has obtained those things which are necessary to life, there is another alternative than to obtain the superfluities; and that is, to adventure on life now, his vacation from humbler toil having commenced. The soil, it appears, is suited to the seed, for it has sent its radicle downward, and it may now send its shoot upward also with confidence. Why has man rooted himself thus firmly in the earth, but that he may rise in the same proportion into the heavens above?—

for the nobler plants are valued for the fruit they bear at last in the air and light, far from the ground, and are not treated like the humbler esculents, which, though they may be biennials, are cultivated only till they have perfected their root, and often cut down at top for this purpose, so that most would not know them in their flowering season.

I do not mean to prescribe rules to strong and valiant natures, who will mind their own affairs whether in heaven or hell, and perchance build more magnificently and spend more lavishly than the richest, without ever impoverishing themselves, not knowing how they live,—if, indeed, there are any such, as has been dreamed; nor to those who find their encouragement and inspiration in precisely the present condition of things, and cherish it with the fondness and enthusiasm of lovers,—and, to some extent, I reckon myself in this number; I do not speak to those who are well employed, in whatever circumstances, and they know whether they are well employed or not;—but mainly to the mass of men who are discontented, and idly complaining of the hardness of their lot or of the times, when they might improve them. There are some who complain most energetically and inconsolably of any, because they are, as they say, doing their duty. I also have in my mind that seemingly wealthy, but most terribly impoverished class of all, who have accumulated dross, but know not how to use it, or get rid of it, and thus have forged their own golden or silver fetters.

If I should attempt to tell how I have desired to spend my life in years past, it would probably surprise those of my readers who are somewhat acquainted with its actual history; it would certainly astonish those who know nothing about it. I will only hint at some of the enterprises which I have cherished.

In any weather, at any hour of the day or night, I have been anxious to improve the nick of time, and notch it on my stick too; to stand on the meeting of two eternities, the past and future, which is precisely the present moment; to toe that line. You will pardon some obscurities, for there are more secrets in my trade than in most men's, and yet not voluntarily kept, but inseparable from its very nature. I would gladly tell all that I know about it, and never paint "No Admittance" on my gate.

I long ago lost a hound, a bay horse, and a turtle dove, and am still on their trail. Many are the travellers I have spoken concerning them, describing their tracks and what calls they answered to. I have met one or two who had heard the hound, and the tramp of the horse, and even seen the dove disappear behind a cloud, and they seemed as anxious to recover them as if they had lost them themselves.

To anticipate, not the sunrise and the dawn merely, but, if possible, Nature herself! How many mornings, summer and winter, before yet any neighbour was stirring about his business, have I been about mine! No doubt, many of my townsmen have met me returning from this enterprise, farmers starting for Boston in the twilight, or woodchoppers going to their work.

It is true, I never assisted the sun materially in his rising, but, doubt not, it was of the last importance only to be present at it.

So many autumn, ay, and winter days, spent outside the town, trying to hear what was in the wind, to hear and carry it express! I well-nigh sunk all my capital in it, and lost my own breath into the bargain, running in the face of it. If it had concerned either of the political parties, depend upon it, it would have appeared in the Gazette with the earliest intelligence. At other times watching from the observatory of some cliff or tree, to telegraph any new arrival; or waiting at evening on the hill-tops for the sky to fall, that I might catch something, though I never caught much, and that, manna-wise, would dissolve again in the sun.

For a long time I was reporter to a journal, of no very wide circulation, whose editor has never yet seen fit to print the bulk of my contributions, and, as is too common with writers, I got only my labour for my pains. However, in this case my pains were their own reward.

For many years I was self-appointed inspector of snow storms and rain storms, and did my duty faithfully; surveyor, if not of highways, then of forest paths and all across-lot routes, keeping them open, and ravines bridged and passable at all seasons, where the public heel had testified to their utility.

I have looked after the wild stock of the town, which give a faithful herdsman a good deal of trouble by leaping fences; and I have had an eye to the unfrequented nooks and corners of the farm; though I did not always know whether Jonas or Solomon worked in a particular field today; that was none of my business. I have watered the red huckleberry, the sand cherry and the nettle-tree, the red pine and the black ash, the white grape and the yellow violet, which might have withered else in dry seasons.

In short, I went on thus for a long time, I may say it without boasting, faithfully minding my business, till it became more and more evident that my townsmen would not after all admit me into the list of town officers, nor make my place a sinecure with a moderate allowance. My accounts, which I can swear to have kept faithfully, I have, indeed, never got audited, still less accepted, still less paid and settled. However, I have not set my heart on that.

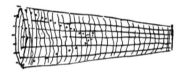

Not long since, a strolling Indian went to sell baskets at the house of a well-known lawyer in my neighbourhood. "Do you wish to buy any baskets?" he asked. "No, we do not want any," was the reply. "What!" exclaimed the Indian as he went out the gate, "do you mean to starve us?" Having seen his industrious white neighbours so well off,—that the lawyer had only to weave arguments, and by some magic wealth and standing followed, he had said to himself: I will go into business; I will weave baskets; it is a thing which I can do. Thinking that when he had made the baskets he would have done his part, and then it would be the white man's to buy them. He had not discovered that it was necessary for him to make it worth the other's while to buy them, or at least make him think that it was so, or to make something else which it would be worth his while to buy. I too had woven a kind of basket of a delicate texture, but I had not made it worth any one's while to buy them. Yet not the less, in my case, did I think it worth my while to weave them, and instead of studying how to make it worth men's while to buy my baskets, I studied rather how to avoid the necessity of selling them. The life which men praise and regard as successful is but one kind. Why should we exaggerate any one kind at the expense of the others?

Finding that my fellow-citizens were not likely to offer me any room in the court house, or any curacy or living anywhere else, but I must shift for myself, I turned my face more exclusively than ever to the woods, where I was better known. I determined to go into business at once, and not wait to acquire the usual capital, using such slender means as I had already got. My purpose in going to Walden Pond was not to live cheaply nor to live dearly there, but to transact some private business with the fewest obstacles; to be hindered from accomplishing which for want of a little common sense, a little enterprise and business talent, appeared not so sad as foolish.

I have always endeavoured to acquire strict business habits; they are indispensable to every man. If your trade is with the Celestial Empire, then some small counting house on the coast, in some Salem harbour, will be fixture enough. You will export such articles as the country affords, purely native products, much ice and pine timber and a little granite, always in native bottoms. These will be good ventures. To oversee all the details yourself in person; to be at once pilot and captain, and owner and underwriter; to buy and sell and keep the accounts; to read every letter received, and write or read every letter sent; to superintend the discharge of imports night and day; to be upon many parts of the coast almost at the same time;—often the richest freight will be discharged upon a Jersey shore;—to be your own telegraph, unweariedly sweeping the horizon, speaking all passing vessels bound coastwise; to keep up a steady despatch of commodities, for the supply of such a distant and exorbitant market; to keep yourself informed of the state of the markets, prospects of war and peace everywhere, and anticipate the tendencies of trade and civilization,—taking advantage of the results of all exploring expeditions, using new passages and all improvements in navigation;—charts to be studied, the position of reefs and new lights and buoys to be ascertained, and ever, and ever, the logarithmic tables to be corrected, for by the error of some calculator the vessel often splits upon a rock that should have reached a friendly pier,—there is the untold fate of La Prouse;—universal science to be kept pace with, studying the lives of all great discoverers and navigators, great adventurers and merchants, from Hanno and the Phoenicians down to our day; in fine, account of stock to be taken from time to time, to know how you stand. It is a labour to task the faculties of a man,—such problems of profit and loss, of interest, of tare and tret, and gauging of all kinds in it, as demand a universal knowledge.

I have thought that Walden Pond would be a good place for business, not solely on account of the railroad and the ice trade; it offers advantages which it may not be good policy to divulge; it is a good port and a good foundation. No Neva marshes to be filled; though you must everywhere build on piles of your own driving. It is said that a flood-tide, with a westerly wind, and ice in the Neva, would sweep St. Petersburg from the face of the earth.

As this business was to be entered into without the usual capital, it may not be easy to conjecture where those means, that will still be indispensable to every such undertaking, were to be obtained. As for Clothing, to come at once to the practical part of the question, perhaps we are led oftener by the love of novelty and a regard for the opinions of men, in procuring it, than by a true utility. Let him who has work to do recollect that the object of clothing is, first, to retain the vital heat, and secondly, in this state of society, to cover nakedness, and he may judge how much of any necessary or important work may be accomplished without adding to his wardrobe. Kings and queens who wear a suit but once, though made by some tailor or dressmaker to their majesties, cannot know the comfort of wearing a suit that fits. They are no better than wooden horses to hang the clean clothes on. Every day our garments become more assimilated to ourselves, receiving the impress of the wearer's character, until we hesitate to lay them aside, without such delay and medical appliances and some such solemnity even as our bodies. No man ever stood the lower in my estimation for having a patch in his clothes; yet I am sure that there is greater anxiety, commonly, to have fashionable, or at least clean and unpatched clothes, than to have a sound conscience. But even if the rent is not mended, perhaps the worst vice betrayed is improvidence. I sometimes try my acquaintances by such tests as this;—who could wear a patch, or two extra seams only, over the knee? Most behave as if they believed that their prospects for life would be ruined if they should do it. It would be easier for them to hobble to town with a broken leg than with a broken pantaloon. Often if an accident happens to a gentleman's legs, they can be mended; but if a similar accident happens to the legs of his pantaloons, there is no help for it; for he considers, not what is truly respectable, but what is respected. We know but few men, a great many coats and breeches. Dress a scarecrow in your last shift, you standing shiftless by, who would not soonest salute the scarecrow? Passing a cornfield the other day, close by a hat and coat on a stake, I recognized the owner of the farm. He was only a little more weather-beaten than when I saw him last. I have heard of a dog that barked at every stranger who approached his master's premises with clothes on, but was easily quieted by a naked thief. It is an interesting question how far men would retain their relative rank if they were divested of their clothes. Could you, in such a case, tell surely of any company of civilized men which belonged to the most respected class? When Madam Pfeiffer, in her adventurous travels round the world, from east to west, had got so near home as Asiatic Russia, she says that she felt the necessity of wearing other than a travelling dress, when she went to meet the authorities, for she "was now in a civilized country, where ... people are judged of by their clothes." Even in our democratic New England towns the accidental possession of wealth, and its manifestation in dress and equipage alone, obtain for the possessor almost universal respect. But they who yield such respect, numerous as they are, are so far heathen, and need to have a missionary sent to them. Besides, clothes introduced sewing, a kind of work which you may call endless; a woman's dress, at least, is never done.

A man who has at length found something to do will not need to get a new suit to do it in; for him the old will do, that has lain dusty in the garret for an indeterminate period. Old shoes will serve a hero longer than they have served his valet,—if a hero ever has a valet,—bare feet are older than shoes, and he can make them do. Only they who go to soirées and legislative balls must have new coats, coats to change as often as the man changes in them. But if my jacket and trousers, my hat and shoes, are fit to worship God in, they will do; will they not? Who ever saw his old clothes,—his old coat, actually worn out, resolved into its primitive elements, so that it was not a deed of charity to bestow it on some poor boy, by him perchance to be bestowed on some poorer still, or shall we say richer, who could do with less? I say, beware of all enterprises that require new clothes, and not rather a new wearer of clothes. If there is not a new man, how can the new clothes be made to fit? If you have any enterprise before you, try it in your old clothes. All men want, not something to *do with*, but something to *do*, or rather something to *be*. Perhaps we should never procure a new suit, however ragged or dirty the old, until we have so conducted, so enterprised or sailed in some way, that we feel like new men in the old, and that to retain it would be like keeping new wine in old bottles. Our moulting season, like that of the fowls, must be a crisis in our lives. The loon retires to solitary ponds to spend it. Thus also the snake casts its slough, and the caterpillar its wormy coat, by an internal industry and expansion; for clothes are but our outmost cuticle and mortal coil. Otherwise we shall be found sailing under false colours, and be inevitably cashiered at last by our own opinion, as well as that of mankind.

We don garment after garment, as if we grew like exogenous plants by addition without. Our outside and often thin and fanciful clothes are our epidermis or false skin, which partakes not of our life, and may be stripped off here and there without fatal injury; our thicker garments, constantly worn, are our cellular integument, or cortex; but our shirts are our liber or true bark, which cannot be removed without girdling and so destroying the man. I believe that all races at some seasons wear something equivalent to the shirt. It is desirable that a man be clad so simply that he can lay his hands on himself in the dark, and that he live in all respects so compactly and preparedly, that, if an enemy take the town, he can, like the old philosopher, walk out the gate empty-handed without anxiety. While one thick garment is, for most purposes, as good as three thin ones, and cheap clothing can be obtained at prices really to suit customers; while a thick coat can be bought for five dollars, which will last as many years, thick pantaloons for two dollars, cowhide boots for a dollar and a half a pair, a summer hat for a quarter of a dollar, and a winter cap for sixty-two and a half cents, or a better be made at home at a nominal cost, where is he so poor that, clad in such a suit, *of his own earning*, there will not be found wise men to do him reverence?

When I ask for a garment of a particular form, my tailoress tells me gravely, "They do not make them so now," not emphasizing the "They" at all, as if she quoted an authority as impersonal as the Fates, and I find it difficult to get made what I want, simply because she cannot believe that I mean what I say, that I am so rash. When I hear this oracular sentence, I am for a moment absorbed in thought, emphasizing to myself each word separately that I may come at the meaning of it, that I may find out by what degree of consanguinity *They* are related to *me*, and what authority they may have in an affair which affects me so nearly; and, finally, I am inclined to answer her with equal mystery, and without any more emphasis of the "they,"—"It is true, they did not make them so recently, but they do now." Of what use this measuring of me if she does not measure my character, but only the breadth of my shoulders, as it were a peg to hang the coat on? We worship not the Graces, nor the Parcæ, but Fashion. She spins and weaves and cuts with full authority. The head monkey at Paris puts on a traveller's cap, and all the monkeys in America do the same. I sometimes despair of getting anything quite simple and honest done in this world by the help of men. They would have to be passed through a powerful press first, to squeeze their old notions out of them, so that they would not soon get upon their legs again; and then there would be someone in the company with a maggot in his head, hatched from an egg deposited there nobody knows when, for not even fire kills these things, and you would have lost your labour. Nevertheless, we will not forget that some Egyptian wheat was handed down to us by a mummy.

On the whole, I think that it cannot be maintained that dressing has in this or any country risen to the dignity of an art. At present men make shift to wear what they can get. Like shipwrecked sailors, they put on what they can find on the beach, and at a little distance, whether of space or time, laugh at each other's masquerade. Every generation laughs at the old fashions, but follows religiously the new. We are amused at beholding the costume of Henry VIII, or Queen Elizabeth, as much as if it was that of the King and Queen of the Cannibal Islands. All costume off a man is pitiful or grotesque. It is only the serious eye peering from and the sincere life passed within it, which restrain laughter and consecrate the costume of any people. Let Harlequin be taken with a fit of the colic and his trappings will have to serve that mood too. When the soldier is hit by a cannon ball, rags are as becoming as purple.

The childish and savage taste of men and women for new patterns keeps how many shaking and squinting through kaleidoscopes that they may discover the particular figure which this generation requires today. The manufacturers have learned that this taste is merely whimsical. Of two patterns which differ only by a few threads more or less of a particular colour, the one will be sold readily, the other lie on the shelf, though it frequently happens that after the lapse of a season the latter becomes the most fashionable. Comparatively, tattooing is not the hideous custom which it is called. It is not barbarous merely because the printing is skin-deep and unalterable.

I cannot believe that our factory system is the best mode by which men may get clothing. The condition of the operatives is becoming every day more like that of the English; and it cannot be wondered at, since, as far as I have heard or observed, the principal object is, not that mankind may be well and honestly clad, but, unquestionably, that corporations may be enriched. In the long run men hit only what they aim at. Therefore, though they should fail immediately, they had better aim at something high.

As for a Shelter, I will not deny that this is now a necessary of life, though there are instances of men having done without it for long periods in colder countries than this. Samuel Laing says that "the Laplander in his skin dress, and in a skin bag which he puts over his head and shoulders, will sleep night after night on the snow ... in a degree of cold which would extinguish the life of one exposed to it in any woollen clothing." He had seen them asleep thus. Yet he adds, "They are not hardier than other people." But, probably, man did not live long on the earth without discovering the convenience which there is in a house, the domestic comforts, which phrase may have originally signified the satisfactions of the house more than of the family; though these must be extremely partial and occasional in those climates where the house is associated in our thoughts with winter or the rainy season chiefly, and two thirds of the year, except for a parasol, is unnecessary. In our climate, in the summer, it was formerly almost solely a covering at night. In the Indian gazettes a wigwam was the symbol of a day's march, and a row of them cut or painted on the bark of a tree signified that so many times they had camped. Man was not made so large limbed and robust but that he must seek to narrow his world, and wall in a space such as fitted him. He was at first bare and out of doors; but though this was pleasant enough in serene and warm weather, by daylight, the rainy season and the winter, to say nothing of the torrid sun, would perhaps have nipped his race in the bud if he had not made haste to clothe himself with the shelter of a house. Adam and Eve, according to the fable, wore the bower before other clothes. Man wanted a home, a place of warmth, or comfort, first of physical warmth, then the warmth of the affections.

We may imagine a time when, in the infancy of the human race, some enterprising mortal crept into a hollow in a rock for shelter. Every child begins the world again, to some extent, and loves to stay outdoors, even in wet and cold. It plays house, as well as horse, having an instinct for it. Who does not remember the interest with which when young he looked at shelving rocks, or any approach to a cave? It was the natural yearning of that portion of our most primitive ancestor which still survived in us. From the cave we have advanced to roofs of palm leaves, of bark and boughs, of linen woven and stretched, of grass and straw, of boards and shingles, of stones and tiles. At last, we know not what it is to live in the open air, and our lives are domestic in more senses than we think. From the hearth to the field is a great distance. It would be well perhaps if we were to spend more of our days and nights without any obstruction between us and the celestial bodies, if the poet did not speak so much from under a roof, or the saint dwell there so long. Birds do not sing in caves, nor do doves cherish their innocence in dovecots.

However, if one designs to construct a dwelling house, it behooves him to exercise a little Yankee shrewdness, lest after all he find himself in a workhouse, a labyrinth without a clue, a museum, an almshouse, a prison, or a splendid mausoleum instead. Consider first how slight a shelter is absolutely necessary. I have seen Penobscot Indians, in this town, living in tents of thin cotton cloth, while the snow was nearly a foot deep around them, and I thought that they would be glad to have it deeper to keep out the wind. Formerly, when how to get my living honestly, with freedom left for my proper pursuits, was a question which vexed me even more than it does now, for unfortunately I become somewhat callous, I used to see a large box by the railroad, six feet long by three wide, in which the labourers locked up their tools at night, and it suggested to me that every man who was hard pushed might get such a one for a dollar, and, having bored a few auger holes in it, to admit the air at least, get into it when it rained and at night, and hook down the lid, and so have freedom in his love, and in his soul be free. This did not appear the worst, nor by any means a despicable alternative. You could sit up as late as you pleased, and, whenever you got up, go abroad without any landlord or house-lord dogging you for rent. Many a man is harassed to death to pay the rent of a larger and more luxurious box who would not have frozen to death in such a box as this. I am far from jesting. Economy is a subject which admits of being treated with levity, but it cannot so be disposed of. A comfortable house for a rude and hardy race, that lived mostly out of doors, was once made here almost entirely of such materials as Nature furnished ready to their hands. Gookin, who was superintendent of the Indians subject to the Massachusetts Colony, writing in 1674, says, "The best of their houses are covered very neatly, tight and warm, with barks of trees, slipped from their bodies at those seasons when the sap is up, and made into great flakes, with pressure of weighty timber, when they are green.... The meaner sort are covered with mats which they make of a kind of bulrush, and are also indifferently tight and warm, but not so good as the former.... Some I have seen, sixty or a hundred feet long and thirty feet broad.... I have often lodged in their wigwams, and found them as warm as the best English houses." He adds that they were commonly carpeted and lined within with well-wrought embroidered mats, and were furnished with various utensils. The Indians had advanced so far as to regulate the effect of the wind by a mat suspended over the hole in the roof and moved by a string. Such a lodge was in the first instance constructed in a day or two at most, and taken down and put up in a few hours; and every family owned one, or its apartment in one.

In the savage state every family owns a shelter as good as the best, and sufficient for its coarser and simpler wants; but I think that I speak within bounds when I say that, though the birds of the air have their nests, and the foxes their holes, and the savages their wigwams, in modern civilized society not more than one half the families own a shelter. In the large towns and cities, where civilization especially prevails, the number of those who own a shelter is a very small fraction of the whole. The rest pay an annual tax for this outside garment of all, become indispensable summer and winter, which would buy a village of Indian wigwams, but now helps to keep them poor as long as they live. I do not mean to insist here on the disadvantage of hiring compared with owning, but it is evident that the savage owns his shelter because it costs so little, while the civilized man hires his commonly because he cannot afford to own it; nor can he, in the long run, any better afford to hire. But, answers one, by merely paying this tax the poor civilized man secures an abode which is a palace compared with the savage's. An annual rent from twenty-five to a hundred dollars, these are the country rates, entitles him to the benefit of the improvements of centuries, spacious apartments, clean paint and paper, Rumford fire-place, back plastering, Venetian blinds, copper pump, spring lock, a commodious cellar, and many other things. But how happens it that he who is said to enjoy these things is so commonly a *poor* civilized man, while the savage, who has them not, is rich as a savage? If it is asserted that civilization is a real advance in the condition of man,—and I think that it is, though only the wise improve their advantages,—it must be shown that it has produced better dwellings without making them more costly; and the cost of a thing is the amount of what I will call life which is required to be exchanged for it, immediately or in the long run. An average house in this neighbourhood costs perhaps eight hundred dollars, and to lay up this sum will take from ten to fifteen years of the labourer's life, even if he is not encumbered with a family;—estimating the pecuniary value of every man's labour at one dollar a day, for if some receive more, others receive less;—so that he must have spent more than half his life commonly before *his* wigwam will be earned. If we suppose him to pay a rent instead, this is but a doubtful choice of evils. Would the savage have been wise to exchange his wigwam for a palace on these terms?

It may be guessed that I reduce almost the whole advantage of holding this superfluous property as a fund in store against the future, so far as the individual is concerned, mainly to the defraying of funeral expenses. But perhaps a man is not required to bury himself. Nevertheless this points to an important distinction between the civilized man and the savage; and, no doubt, they have designs on us for our benefit, in making the life of a civilized people an *institution*, in which the life of the individual is to a great extent absorbed, in order to preserve and perfect that of the race. But I wish to show at what a sacrifice this advantage is at present obtained, and to suggest that we may possibly so live as to secure all the advantage without suffering any of the disadvantage. What mean ye by saying that the poor ye have always with you, or that the fathers have eaten sour grapes, and the children's teeth are set on edge?

"As I live, saith the Lord God, ye shall not have
occasion any more to use this proverb in Israel."
"Behold all souls are mine; as the soul of the father,
so also the soul of the son is mine: the soul that sinneth it shall die."

When I consider my neighbours, the farmers of Concord, who are at least as well off as the other classes, I find that for the most part they have been toiling twenty, thirty, or forty years, that they may become the real owners of their farms, which commonly they have inherited with encumbrances, or else bought with hired money,—and we may regard one third of that toil as the cost of their houses,—but commonly they have not paid for them yet. It is true, the encumbrances sometimes outweigh the value of the farm, so that the farm itself becomes one great encumbrance, and still a man is found to inherit it, being well acquainted with it, as he says. On applying to the assessors, I am surprised to learn that they cannot at once name a dozen in the town who own their farms free and clear. If you would know the history of these homesteads, inquire at the bank where they are mortgaged. The man who has actually paid for his farm with labour on it is so rare that every neighbour can point to him. I doubt if there are three such men in Concord. What has been said of the merchants, that a very large majority, even ninety-seven in a hundred, are sure to fail, is equally true of the farmers. With regard to the merchants, however, one of them says pertinently that a great part of their failures are not genuine pecuniary failures, but merely failures to fulfil their engagements, because it is inconvenient; that is, it is the moral character that breaks down. But this puts an infinitely worse face on the matter, and suggests, beside, that probably not even the other three succeed in saving their souls, but are perchance bankrupt in a worse sense than they who fail honestly. Bankruptcy and repudiation are the spring-boards from which much of our civilization vaults and turns its somersets, but the savage stands on the unelastic plank of famine. Yet the Middlesex Cattle Show goes off here with *éclat* annually, as if all the joints of the agricultural machine were suent.

The farmer is endeavouring to solve the problem of a livelihood by a formula more complicated than the problem itself. To get his shoestrings he speculates in herds of cattle. With consummate skill he has set his trap with a hair spring to catch comfort and independence, and then, as he turned away, got his own leg into it. This is the reason he is poor; and for a similar reason we are all poor in respect to a thousand savage comforts, though surrounded by luxuries. As Chapman sings,—

> "The false society of men—
> —for earthly greatness
> All heavenly comforts rarefies to air."

And when the farmer has got his house, he may not be the richer but the poorer for it, and it be the house that has got him. As I understand it, that was a valid objection urged by Momus against the house which Minerva made, that she "had not made it movable, by which means a bad neighbourhood might be avoided;" and it may still be urged, for our houses are such unwieldy property that we are often imprisoned rather than housed in them; and the bad neighbourhood to be avoided is our own scurvy selves. I know one or two families, at least, in this town, who, for nearly a generation, have been wishing to sell their houses in the outskirts and move into the village, but have not been able to accomplish it, and only death will set them free.

Granted that the *majority* are able at last either to own or hire the modern house with all its improvements. While civilization has been improving our houses, it has not equally improved the men who are to inhabit them. It has created palaces, but it was not so easy to create noblemen and kings. And *if the civilized man's pursuits are no worthier than the savage's, if he is employed the greater part of his life in obtaining gross necessaries and comforts merely, why should he have a better dwelling than the former?*

But how do the poor *minority* fare? Perhaps it will be found, that just in proportion as some have been placed in outward circumstances above the savage, others have been degraded below him. The luxury of one class is counterbalanced by the indigence of another. On the one side is the palace, on the other are the almshouse and "silent poor." The myriads who built the pyramids to be the tombs of the Pharaohs were fed on garlic, and they were not decently buried themselves. The mason who finishes the cornice of the palace returns at night perchance to a hut not so good as a wigwam. It is a mistake to suppose that, in a country where the usual evidences of civilization exist, the condition of a very large body of the inhabitants may not be as degraded as that of savages. I refer to the degraded poor, not now to the degraded rich. To know this I should not need to look farther than to the shanties which everywhere border our railroads, that last improvement in civilization; where I see in my daily walks human beings living in sties, and all winter with an open door, for the sake of light, without any visible, often imaginable, wood pile, and the forms of both old and young are permanently contracted by the long habit of shrinking from cold and misery, and the development of all their limbs and faculties is checked. It certainly is fair to look at that class by whose labour the works which distinguish this generation are accomplished. Such too, to a greater or less extent, is the condition of the operatives of every denomination in England, which is the great workhouse of the world. Or I could refer you to Ireland, which is marked as one of the white or enlightened spots on the map. Contrast the physical condition of the Irish with that of the North American Indian, or the South Sea Islander, or any other savage race before it was degraded by contact with the civilized man. Yet I have no doubt that that people's rulers are as wise as the average of civilized rulers. Their condition only proves what squalidness may consist with civilization. I hardly need refer now to the labourers in our Southern States who produce the staple exports of this country, and are themselves a staple production of the South.

But to confine myself to those who are said to be in *moderate* circumstances.

Most men appear never to have considered what a house is, and are actually though needlessly poor all their lives because they think that they must have such a life as their neighbours have. As if one were to wear any sort of coat which the tailor might cut out for him, or, gradually leaving off palmleaf hat or cap of woodchuck skin, complain of hard times because he could not afford to buy him a crown! It is possible to invent a house still more convenient and luxurious than we have, which yet all would admit that man could not afford to pay for. Shall we always study to obtain more of these things, and not sometimes to be content with less? Shall the respectable citizen thus gravely teach, by precept and example, the necessity of the young man's providing a certain number of superfluous glowshoes, and umbrellas, and empty guest chambers for empty guests, before he dies? Why should not our furniture be as simple as the Arab's or the Indian's? When I think of the benefactors of the race, whom we have apotheosized as messengers from heaven, bearers of divine gifts to man, I do not see in my mind any retinue at their heels, any car-load of fashionable furniture. Or what if I were to allow— would it not be a singular allowance?—that our furniture should be more complex than the Arab's, in proportion as we are morally and intellectually his superiors! At present our houses are cluttered and defiled with it, and a good housewife would sweep out the greater part into the dust hole, and not leave her morning's work undone. Morning work! By the blushes of Aurora and the music of Memnon, what should be man's *morning work* in this world? I had three pieces of limestone on my desk, but I was terrified to find that they required to be dusted daily, when the furniture of my mind was all undusted still, and I threw them out the window in disgust. How, then, could I have a furnished house? I would rather sit in the open air, for no dust gathers on the grass, unless where man has broken ground.

It is the luxurious and dissipated who set the fashions which the herd so diligently follow. The traveller who stops at the best houses, so called, soon discovers this, for the publicans presume him to be a Sardanapalus, and if he resigned himself to their tender mercies he would soon be completely emasculated. I think that in the railroad car we are inclined to spend more on luxury than on safety and convenience, and it threatens without attaining these to become no better than a modern drawing-room, with its divans, and ottomans, and sunshades, and a hundred other oriental things, which we are taking west with us, invented for the ladies of the harem and the effeminate natives of the Celestial Empire, which Jonathan should be ashamed to know the names of. I would rather sit on a pumpkin and have it all to myself, than be crowded on a velvet cushion. I would rather ride on earth in an ox cart, with a free circulation, than go to heaven in the fancy car of an excursion train and breathe a *malaria* all the way.

The very simplicity and nakedness of man's life in the primitive ages imply this advantage at least, that they left him still but a sojourner in nature. When he was refreshed with food and sleep, he contemplated his journey again. He dwelt, as it were, in a tent in this world, and was either threading the valleys, or crossing the plains, or climbing the mountain tops. But lo! Men have become the tools of their tools. The man who independently plucked the fruits when he was hungry has become a farmer; and he who stood under a tree for shelter, a housekeeper. We now no longer camp as for a night, but have settled down on earth and forgotten heaven. We have adopted Christianity merely as an improved method of *agri*-culture. We have built for this world a family mansion, and for the next a family tomb. The best works of art are the expression of man's struggle to free himself from this condition, but the effect of our art is merely to make this low state comfortable and that higher state to be forgotten. There is actually no place in this village for a work of *fine* art, if any had come down to us, to stand, for our lives, our houses and streets, furnish no proper pedestal for it. There is not a nail to hang a picture on, nor a shelf to receive the bust of a hero or a saint. When I consider how our houses are built and paid for, or not paid for, and their internal economy managed and sustained, I wonder that the floor does not give way under the visitor while he is admiring the gewgaws upon the mantel-piece, and let him through into the cellar, to some solid and honest though earthy foundation. I cannot but perceive that this so-called rich and refined life is a thing jumped at, and I do not get on in the enjoyment of the *fine* arts which adorn it, my attention being wholly occupied with the jump; for I remember that the greatest genuine leap, due to human muscles alone, on record, is that of certain wandering Arabs, who are said to have cleared twenty-five feet on level ground. Without factitious support, man is sure to come to earth again beyond that distance. The first question which I am tempted to put to the proprietor of such great impropriety is, who bolsters you? Are you one of the ninety-seven who fails, or the three who succeed? Answer me these questions, and then perhaps I may look at your baubles and find them ornamental. The cart before the horse is neither beautiful nor useful. Before we can adorn our houses with beautiful objects the walls must be stripped, and our lives must be stripped, and beautiful housekeeping and beautiful living be laid for a foundation: now, a taste for the beautiful is most cultivated out of doors, where there is no house and no housekeeper.

Old Johnson, in his "Wonder-Working Providence," speaking of the first settlers of this town, with whom he was contemporary, tells us that "they burrow themselves in the earth for their first shelter under some hillside, and, casting the soil aloft upon timber, they make a smoky fire against the earth, at the highest side." They did not "provide them houses," says he, "till the earth, by the Lord's blessing, brought forth bread to feed them," and the first year's crop was so light that "they were forced to cut their bread very thin for a long season." The secretary of the Province of New Netherland, writing in Dutch, in 1650, for the information of those who wished to take up land there, states more particularly that "those in New Netherland, and especially in New England, who have no means to build farmhouses at first according to their wishes, dig a square pit in the ground, cellar fashion, six or seven feet deep, as long and as broad as they think proper, case the earth inside with wood all round the wall, and line the wood with the bark of trees or something else to prevent the caving in of the earth; floor this cellar with plank, and wainscot it overhead for a ceiling, raise a roof of spars clear up, and cover the spars with bark or green sods, so that they can live dry and warm in these houses with their entire families for two, three, and four years, it being understood that partitions are run through those cellars which are adapted to the size of the family. The wealthy and principal men in New England, in the beginning of the colonies, commenced their first dwelling houses in this fashion for two reasons: firstly, in order not to waste time in building, and not to want food the next season; secondly, in order not to discourage poor labouring people whom they brought over in numbers from Fatherland. In the course of three or four years, when the country became adapted to agriculture, they built themselves handsome houses, spending on them several thousands."

In this course which our ancestors took there was a show of prudence at least, as if their principle were to satisfy the more pressing wants first. But are the more pressing wants satisfied now? When I think of acquiring for myself one of our luxurious dwellings, I am deterred, for, so to speak, the country is not yet adapted to *human* culture, and we are still forced to cut our *spiritual* bread far thinner than our forefathers did their wheaten. Not that all architectural ornament is to be neglected even in the rudest periods; but let our houses first be lined with beauty, where they come in contact with our lives, like the tenement of the shellfish, and not overlaid with it. But, alas! I have been inside one or two of them, and know what they are lined with.

Though we are not so degenerate but that we might possibly live in a cave or a wigwam or wear skins today, it certainly is better to accept the advantages, though so dearly bought, which the invention and industry of mankind offer. In such a neighbourhood as this, boards and shingles, lime and bricks, are cheaper and more easily obtained than suitable caves, or whole logs, or bark in sufficient quantities, or even well-tempered clay or flat stones. I speak understandingly on this subject, for I have made myself acquainted with it both theoretically and practically. With a little more wit we might use these materials so as to become richer than the richest now are, and make our civilization a blessing. The civilized man is a more experienced and wiser savage. But to make haste to my own experiment.

Near the end of March, 1845, I borrowed an axe and went down to the woods by Walden Pond, nearest to where I intended to build my house, and began to cut down some tall arrowy white pines, still in their youth, for timber. It is difficult to begin without borrowing, but perhaps it is the most generous course thus to permit your fellow-men to have an interest in your enterprise. The owner of the axe, as he released his hold on it, said that it was the apple of his eye; but I returned it sharper than I received it. It was a pleasant hillside where I worked, covered with pine woods, through which I looked out on the pond, and a small open field in the woods where pines and hickories were springing up. The ice in the pond was not yet dissolved, though there were some open spaces, and it was all dark coloured and saturated with water. There were some slight flurries of snow during the days that I worked there; but for the most part when I came out on to the railroad, on my way home, its yellow sand heap stretched away gleaming in the hazy atmosphere, and the rails shone in the spring sun, and I heard the lark and peewee and other birds already come to commence another year with us. They were pleasant spring days, in which the winter of man's discontent was thawing as well as the earth, and the life that had lain torpid began to stretch itself. One day, when my axe had come off and I had cut a green hickory for a wedge, driving it with a stone, and had placed the whole to soak in a pond hole in order to swell the wood, I saw a striped snake run into the water, and he lay on the bottom, apparently without inconvenience, as long as I stayed there, or more than a quarter of an hour; perhaps because he had not yet fairly come out of the torpid state. It appeared to me that for a like reason men remain in their present low and primitive condition; but if they should feel the influence of the spring of springs arousing them, they would of necessity rise to a higher and more ethereal life. I had previously seen the snakes in frosty mornings in my path with portions of their bodies still numb and inflexible, waiting for the sun to thaw them. On the 1st of April it rained and melted the ice, and in the early part of the day, which was very foggy, I heard a stray goose groping about over the pond and cackling as if lost, or like the spirit of the fog.

So I went on for some days cutting and hewing timber, and also studs and rafters, all with my narrow axe, not having many communicable or scholar-like thoughts, singing to myself,—

> Men say they know many things;
> But lo! They have taken wings,—
> The arts and sciences,
> And a thousand appliances;
> The wind that blows
> Is all that anybody knows.

I hewed the main timbers six inches square, most of the studs on two sides only, and the rafters and floor timbers on one side, leaving the rest of the bark on, so that they were just as straight and much stronger than sawed ones. Each stick was carefully mortised or tenoned by its stump, for I had borrowed other tools by this time. My days in the woods were not very long ones; yet I usually carried my dinner of bread and butter, and read the newspaper in which it was wrapped, at noon, sitting amid the green pine boughs which I had cut off, and to my bread was imparted some of their fragrance, for my hands were covered with a thick coat of pitch. Before I had done I was more the friend than the foe of the pine tree, though I had cut down some of them, having become better acquainted with it. Sometimes a rambler in the wood was attracted by the sound of my axe, and we chatted pleasantly over the chips which I had made.

By the middle of April, for I made no haste in my work, but rather made the most of it, my house was framed and ready for the raising. I had already bought the shanty of James Collins, an Irishman who worked on the Fitchburg Railroad, for boards. James Collins' shanty was considered an uncommonly fine one. When I called to see it he was not at home. I walked about the outside, at first unobserved from within, the window was so deep and high. It was of small dimensions, with a peaked cottage roof, and not much else to be seen, the dirt being raised five feet all around as if it were a compost heap. The roof was the soundest part, though a good deal warped and made brittle by the sun. Door-sill there was none, but a perennial passage for the hens under the door board. Mrs. C. came to the door and asked me to view it from the inside. The hens were driven in by my approach. It was dark, and had a dirt floor for the most part, dank, clammy, and aguish, only here a board and there a board which would not bear removal. She lighted a lamp to show me the inside of the roof and the walls, and also that the board floor extended under the bed, warning me not to step into the cellar, a sort of dust hole two feet deep. In her own words, they were "good boards overhead, good boards all around, and a good window,"—of two whole squares originally, only the cat had passed out that way lately. There was a stove, a bed, and a place to sit, an infant in the house where it was born, a silk parasol, gilt-framed looking-glass, and a patent new coffee mill nailed to an oak sapling, all told. The bargain was soon concluded, for James had in the meanwhile returned. I, to pay four dollars and twenty-five cents tonight, he to vacate at five tomorrow morning, selling to nobody else meanwhile: I to take possession at six. It were well, he said, to be there early, and anticipate certain indistinct but wholly unjust claims on the score of ground rent and fuel. This he assured me was the only encumbrance. At six I passed him and his family on the road. One large bundle held their all,—bed, coffee-mill, looking-glass, hens,—all but the cat; she took to the woods and became a wild cat, and, as I learned afterward, trod in a trap set for woodchucks, and so became a dead cat at last.

I took down this dwelling the same morning, drawing the nails, and removed it to the pond side by small cart-loads, spreading the boards on the grass there to bleach and warp back again in the sun. One early thrush gave me a note or two as I drove along the woodland path. I was informed treacherously by a young Patrick that neighbour Seeley, an Irishman, in the intervals of the carting, transferred the still tolerable, straight, and drivable nails, staples, and spikes to his pocket, and then stood when I came back to pass the time of day, and look freshly up, unconcerned, with spring thoughts, at the devastation; there being a dearth of work, as he said. He was there to represent spectatordom, and help make this seemingly insignificant event one with the removal of the gods of Troy.

I dug my cellar in the side of a hill sloping to the south, where a woodchuck had formerly dug his burrow, down through sumach and blackberry roots, and the lowest stain of vegetation, six feet square by seven deep, to a fine sand where potatoes would not freeze in any winter. The sides were left shelving, and not stoned; but the sun having never shone on them, the sand still keeps its place. It was but two hours' work. I took particular pleasure in this breaking of ground, for in almost all latitudes men dig into the earth for an equable temperature. Under the most splendid house in the city is still to be found the cellar where they store their roots as of old, and long after the superstructure has disappeared posterity remark its dent in the earth. The house is still but a sort of porch at the entrance of a burrow.

At length, in the beginning of May, with the help of some of my acquaintances, rather to improve so good an occasion for neighbourliness than from any necessity, I set up the frame of my house. No man was ever more honoured in the character of his raisers than I. They are destined, I trust, to assist at the raising of loftier structures one day. I began to occupy my house on the 4th of July, as soon as it was boarded and roofed, for the boards were carefully feather-edged and lapped, so that it was perfectly impervious to rain; but before boarding I laid the foundation of a chimney at one end, bringing two cartloads of stones up the hill from the pond in my arms. I built the chimney after my hoeing in the fall, before a fire became necessary for warmth, doing my cooking in the meanwhile out of doors on the ground, early in the morning: which mode I still think is in some respects more convenient and agreeable than the usual one. When it stormed before my bread was baked, I fixed a few boards over the fire, and sat under them to watch my loaf, and passed some pleasant hours in that way. In those days, when my hands were much employed, I read but little, but the least scraps of paper which lay on the ground, my holder, or tablecloth, afforded me as much entertainment, in fact answered the same purpose as the Iliad.

It would be worth the while to build still more deliberately than I did, considering, for instance, what foundation a door, a window, a cellar, a garret, have in the nature of man, and perchance never raising any superstructure until we found a better reason for it than our temporal necessities even. There is some of the same fitness in a man's building his own house that there is in a bird's building its own nest. Who knows but if men constructed their dwellings with their own hands, and provided food for themselves and families simply and honestly enough, the poetic faculty would be universally developed, as birds universally sing when they are so engaged? But alas! We do like cowbirds and cuckoos, which lay their eggs in nests which other birds have built, and cheer no traveller with their chattering and unmusical notes. Shall we forever resign the pleasure of construction to the carpenter? What does architecture amount to in the experience of the mass of men? I never in all my walks came across a man engaged in so simple and natural an occupation as building his house. We belong to the community. It is not the tailor alone who is the ninth part of a man; it is as much the preacher, and the merchant, and the farmer. Where is this division of labour to end? And what object does it finally serve? No doubt another *may* also think for me; but it is not therefore desirable that he should do so to the exclusion of my thinking for myself.

True, there are architects so called in this country, and I have heard of one at least possessed with the idea of making architectural ornaments have a core of truth, a necessity, and hence a beauty, as if it were a revelation to him. All very well perhaps from his point of view, but only a little better than the common dilettantism. A sentimental reformer in architecture, he began at the cornice, not at the foundation. It was only how to put a core of truth within the ornaments, that every sugarplum, in fact, might have an almond or caraway seed in it,—though I hold that almonds are most wholesome without the sugar,—and not how the inhabitant, the indweller, might build truly within and without, and let the ornaments take care of themselves. What reasonable man ever supposed that ornaments were something outward and in the skin merely,—that the tortoise got his spotted shell, or the shellfish its mother-o'-pearl tints, by such a contract as the inhabitants of Broadway their Trinity Church? But a man has no more to do with the style of architecture of his house than a tortoise with that of its shell: nor need the soldier be so idle as to try to paint the precise *colour* of his virtue on his standard. The enemy will find it out. He may turn pale when the trial comes. This man seemed to me to lean over the cornice, and timidly whisper his half truth to the rude occupants who really knew it better than he. What of architectural beauty I now see, I know has gradually grown from within outward, out of the necessities and character of the indweller, who is the only builder,—out of some unconscious truthfulness, and nobleness, without ever a thought for the appearance; and whatever additional beauty of this kind is destined to be produced will be preceded by a like unconscious beauty of life. The most interesting dwellings in this country, as the painter knows, are the most unpretending, humble log huts and cottages of the poor commonly; it is the life of the inhabitants whose shells they are, and not any peculiarity in their surfaces merely, which makes them *picturesque*; and equally interesting will be the citizen's suburban box, when his life shall be as simple and as agreeable to the imagination, and there is as little straining after effect in the style of his dwelling. A great proportion of architectural ornaments are literally hollow, and a September gale would strip them off, like borrowed plumes, without injury to the substantials. They can do without *architecture* who have no olives nor wines in the cellar. What if an equal ado were made about the ornaments of style in literature, and the architects of our bibles spent as much time about their cornices as the architects of our churches do? So are made the *belles-lettres* and the *beaux-arts* and their professors. Much it concerns a man, forsooth, how a few sticks are slanted over him or under him, and what colours are daubed upon his box. It would signify somewhat, if, in any earnest sense, *he* slanted them and daubed it; but the spirit having departed out of the tenant, it is of a piece with constructing his own coffin,—the architecture of the grave, and "carpenter," is but another name for "coffin-maker." One man says, in his despair or indifference to life, take up a handful of the earth at your feet, and paint your house that colour. Is he thinking of his last and narrow house? Toss up a copper for it as well. What an abundance of leisure he must have! Why do you take up a handful of dirt? Better paint your house your own complexion; let it turn pale or blush for you. An enterprise to improve the style of cottage architecture! When you have got my ornaments ready, I will wear them.

Before winter I built a chimney, and shingled the sides of my house, which were already impervious to rain, with imperfect and sappy shingles made of the first slice of the log, whose edges I was obliged to straighten with a plane.

I have thus a tight shingled and plastered house, ten feet wide by fifteen long, and eight-feet posts, with a garret and a closet, a large window on each side, two trap doors, one door at the end, and a brick fireplace opposite. The exact cost of my house, paying the usual price for such materials as I used, but not counting the work, all of which was done by myself, was as follows; and I give the details because very few are able to tell exactly what their houses cost, and fewer still, if any, the separate cost of the various materials which compose them:—

Boards,	$ 8.03½,	
mostly shanty boards.		
Refuse shingles for roof and sides,	4.00	
Laths,	1.25	
Two second-hand windows with glass,	2.43	
One thousand old brick,	4.00	
Two casks of lime,	2.40	That was high.
Hair,	0.31	More than I needed.
Mantle-tree iron,	0.15	
Nails,	3.90	
Hinges and screws,	0.14	
Latch,	0.10	
Chalk,	0.01	
Transportation,	1.40	I carried a good part — on my back.
In all	$28.12½	

These are all the materials, excepting the timber, stones, and sand, which I claimed by squatter's right. I have also a small wood-shed adjoining, made chiefly of the stuff which was left after building the house.

I intend to build me a house which will surpass any on the main street in Concord in grandeur and luxury, as soon as it pleases me as much and will cost me no more than my present one.

I thus found that the student who wishes for a shelter can obtain one for a lifetime at an expense not greater than the rent which he now pays annually. If I seem to boast more than is becoming, my excuse is that I brag for humanity rather than for myself; and my shortcomings and inconsistencies do not affect the truth of my statement. Notwithstanding much cant and hypocrisy,— chaff which I find it difficult to separate from my wheat, but for which I am as sorry as any man,—I will breathe freely and stretch myself in this respect, it is such a relief to both the moral and physical system; and I am resolved that I will not through humility become the devil's attorney. I will endeavour to speak a good word for the truth. At Cambridge College the mere rent of a student's room, which is only a little larger than my own, is thirty dollars each year, though the corporation had the advantage of building thirty-two side by side and under one roof, and the occupant suffers the inconvenience of many and noisy neighbours, and perhaps a residence in the fourth story. I cannot but think that if we had more true wisdom in these respects, not only less education would be needed, because, forsooth, more would already have been acquired, but the pecuniary expense of getting an education would in a great measure vanish. Those conveniences which the student requires at Cambridge or elsewhere cost him or somebody else ten times as great a sacrifice of life as they would with proper management on both sides. Those things for which the most money is demanded are never the things which the student most wants. Tuition, for instance, is an important item in the term bill, while for the far more valuable education which he gets by associating with the most cultivated of his contemporaries no charge is made. The mode of founding a college is, commonly, to get up a subscription of dollars and cents, and then following blindly the principles of a division of labour to its extreme, a principle which should never be followed but with circumspection,—to call in a contractor who makes this a subject of speculation, and he employs Irishmen or other operatives actually to lay the foundations, while the students that are to be are said to be fitting themselves for it; and for these oversights successive generations have to pay. I think that it would be *better than this*, for the students, or those who desire to be benefitted by it, even to lay the foundation themselves. The student who secures his coveted leisure and retirement by systematically shirking any labour necessary to man obtains but an ignoble and unprofitable leisure, defrauding himself of the experience which alone can make leisure fruitful. "But," says one, "you do not mean that the students should go to work with their hands instead of their heads?" I do not mean that exactly, but I mean something which he might think a good deal like that; I mean that they should not *play* life, or *study* it merely, while the community supports them at this expensive game, but earnestly *live* it from beginning to end. How could youths better learn to live than by at once trying the experiment of living? Me thinks this would exercise their minds as much as mathematics. If I wished a boy to know something about the arts and sciences, for instance, I would not pursue the common course, which is merely to send him into the neighbourhood of some professor, where anything is professed and practised but the art of life;—to survey the world through a telescope or a microscope, and never with his natural eye; to study chemistry, and not learn how his bread is made, or mechanics, and not learn how it is earned; to discover new satellites to Neptune, and not detect the motes in his eyes, or to what vagabond he is a satellite himself; or to be devoured by the monsters that swarm all around him, while contemplating the monsters in a drop of vinegar. Which would have advanced the most at the end of a month,—the boy who had made his own jackknife from the ore which he had dug and smelted, reading as much as would be necessary for this,—or the boy who had attended the lectures on metallurgy at the Institute in the meanwhile, and had received a Rogers' penknife from his father? Which would be most likely to cut his fingers?... To my astonishment I was informed on leaving college that I had studied navigation!—why, if I had taken one turn down the harbour I should have known more about it. Even the *poor* student studies and is taught only *political* economy, while that economy of living which is synonymous with philosophy is not even sincerely professed in our colleges. The consequence is, that while he is reading Adam Smith, Ricardo, and Say, he runs his father in debt irretrievably.

As with our colleges, so with a hundred "modern improvements;" there is an illusion about them; there is not always a positive advance. The devil goes on exacting compound interest to the last for his early share and numerous succeeding investments in them. Our inventions are wont to be pretty toys, which distract our attention from serious things. They are but improved means to an unimproved end, an end which it was already but too easy to arrive at; as railroads lead to Boston or New York. We are in great haste to construct a magnetic telegraph from Maine to Texas; but Maine and Texas, it may be, have nothing important to communicate. Either is in such a predicament as the man who was earnest to be introduced to a distinguished deaf woman, but when he was presented, and one end of her ear trumpet was put into his hand, had nothing to say. As if the main object were to talk fast and not to talk sensibly. We are eager to tunnel under the Atlantic and bring the old world some weeks nearer to the new; but perchance the first news that will leak through into the broad, flapping American ear will be that the Princess Adelaide has the whooping cough. After all, the man whose horse trots a mile in a minute does not carry the most important messages; he is not an evangelist, nor does he come round eating locusts and wild honey. I doubt if Flying Childers ever carried a peck of corn to mill.

One says to me, "I wonder that you do not lay up money; you love to travel; you might take the cars and go to Fitchburg today and see the country." But I am wiser than that. I have learned that the swiftest traveller is he that goes afoot. I say to my friend, "Suppose we try who will get there first." The distance is thirty miles; the fare ninety cents. That is almost a day's wages. I remember when wages were sixty cents a day for labourers on this very road. Well, I start now on foot, and get there before night; I have travelled at that rate by the week together. You will in the meanwhile have earned your fare, and arrive there some time tomorrow, or possibly this evening, if you are lucky enough to get a job in season. Instead of going to Fitchburg, you will be working here the greater part of the day. And so, if the railroad reached round the world, I think that I should keep ahead of you; and as for seeing the country and getting experience of that kind, I should have to cut your acquaintance altogether.

Such is the universal law, which no man can ever outwit, and with regard to the railroad even we may say it is as broad as it is long. To make a railroad round the world available to all mankind is equivalent to grading the whole surface of the planet. Men have an indistinct notion that if they keep up this activity of joint stocks and spades long enough all will at length ride somewhere, in next to no time, and for nothing; but though a crowd rushes to the depot, and the conductor shouts "All aboard!" when the smoke is blown away and the vapour condensed, it will be perceived that a few are riding, but the rest are run over,—and it will be called, and will be, "A melancholy accident." No doubt they can ride at last who shall have earned their fare, that is, if they survive so long, but they will probably have lost their elasticity and desire to travel by that time. This spending of the best part of one's life earning money in order to enjoy a questionable liberty during the least valuable part of it, reminds me of the Englishman who went to India to make a fortune first, in order that he might return to England and live the life of a poet. He should have gone up garret at once. "What!" exclaim a million Irishmen starting up from all the shanties in the land, "is not this railroad which we have built a good thing?" Yes, I answer, *comparatively* good, that is, you might have done worse; but I wish, as you are brothers of mine, that you could have spent your time better than digging in this dirt.

Before I finished my house, wishing to earn ten or twelve dollars by some honest and agreeable method, in order to meet my unusual expenses, I planted about two acres and a half of light and sandy soil near it chiefly with beans, but also a small part with potatoes, corn, peas, and turnips. The whole lot contains eleven acres, mostly growing up to pines and hickories, and was sold the preceding season for eight dollars and eight cents an acre. One farmer said that it was "good for nothing but to raise cheeping squirrels on." I put no manure whatever on this land, not being the owner, but merely a squatter, and not expecting to cultivate so much again, and I did not quite hoe it all once. I got out several cords of stumps in ploughing, which supplied me with fuel for a long time, and left small circles of virgin mould, easily distinguishable through the summer by the greater luxuriance of the beans there. The dead and for the most part unmerchantable wood behind my house, and the driftwood from the pond, have supplied the remainder of my fuel. I was obliged to hire a team and a man for the ploughing, though I held the plough myself. My farm outgoes for the first season were, for implements, seed, work, etc., 14.72^{1}/_{2}$. The seed corn was given me. This never costs anything to speak of, unless you plant more than enough. I got twelve bushels of beans, and eighteen bushels of potatoes, beside some peas and sweet corn. The yellow corn and turnips were too late to come to anything. My whole income from the farm was

$ 23.44

Deducting the outgoes, ... 14.72$^{1}/_{2}$
There are left, ... 8.71$^{1}/_{2}$

beside produce consumed and on hand at the time this estimate was made of the value of $4.50,—the amount on hand much more than balancing a little grass which I did not raise. All things considered, that is, considering the importance of a man's soul and of today, notwithstanding the short time occupied by my experiment, nay, partly even because of its transient character, I believe that that was doing better than any farmer in Concord did that year.

The next year I did better still, for I spaded up all the land which I required, about a third of an acre, and I learned from the experience of both years, not being in the least awed by many celebrated works on husbandry, Arthur Young among the rest, that if one would live simply and eat only the crop which he raised, and raise no more than he ate, and not exchange it for an insufficient quantity of more luxurious and expensive things, he would need to cultivate only a few rods of ground, and that it would be cheaper to spade up that than to use oxen to plough it, and to select a fresh spot from time to time than to manure the old, and he could do all his necessary farm work as it were with his left hand at odd hours in the summer; and thus he would not be tied to an ox, or horse, or cow, or pig, as at present. I desire to speak impartially on this point, and as one not interested in the success or failure of the present economical and social arrangements. I was more independent than any farmer in Concord, for I was not anchored to a house or farm, but could follow the bent of my genius, which is a very crooked one, every moment. Beside being better off than they already, if my house had been burned or my crops had failed, I should have been nearly as well off as before.

I am wont to think that men are not so much the keepers of herds as herds are the keepers of men, the former are so much the freer. Men and oxen exchange work; but if we consider necessary work only, the oxen will be seen to have greatly the advantage, their farm is so much the larger. Man does some of his part of the exchange work in his six weeks of haying, and it is no boy's play. Certainly no nation that lived simply in all respects, that is, no nation of philosophers, would commit so great a blunder as to use the labour of animals. True, there never was and is not likely soon to be a nation of philosophers, nor am I certain it is desirable that there should be. However, I should never have broken a horse or bull and taken him to board for any work he might do for me, for fear I should become a horse-man or a herds-man merely; and if society seems to be the gainer by so doing, are we certain that what is one man's gain is not another's loss, and that the stable-boy has equal cause with his master to be satisfied? Granted that some public works would not have been constructed without this aid, and let man share the glory of such with the ox and horse; does it follow that he could not have accomplished works yet more worthy of himself in that case? When men begin to do, not merely unnecessary or artistic, but luxurious and idle work, with their assistance, it is inevitable that a few do all the exchange work with the oxen, or, in other words, become the slaves of the strongest. Man thus not only works for the animal within him, but, for a symbol of this, he works for the animal without him. Though we have many substantial houses of brick or stone, the prosperity of the farmer is still measured by the degree to which the barn overshadows the house. This town is said to have the largest houses for oxen, cows, and horses hereabouts, and it is not behindhand in its public buildings;

but there are very few halls for free worship or free speech in this county. It should not be by their architecture, but why not even by their power of abstract thought, that nations should seek to commemorate themselves? How much more admirable the Bhagvat-Geeta than all the ruins of the East! Towers and temples are the luxury of princes. A simple and independent mind does not toil at the bidding of any prince. Genius is not a retainer to any emperor, nor is its material silver, or gold, or marble, except to a trifling extent. To what end, pray, is so much stone hammered? In Arcadia, when I was there, I did not see any hammering stone. Nations are possessed with an insane ambition to perpetuate the memory of themselves by the amount of hammered stone they leave. What if equal pains were taken to smooth and polish their manners? One piece of good sense would be more memorable than a monument as high as the moon. I love better to see stones in place. The grandeur of Thebes was a vulgar grandeur. More sensible is a rod of stone wall that bounds an honest man's field than a hundred-gated Thebes that has wandered farther from the true end of life. The religion and civilization which are barbaric and heathenish build splendid temples; but what you might call Christianity does not. Most of the stone a nation hammers goes toward its tomb only. It buries itself alive. As for the Pyramids, there is nothing to wonder at in them so much as the fact that so many men could be found degraded enough to spend their lives constructing a tomb for some ambitious booby, whom it would have been wiser and manlier to have drowned in the Nile, and then given his body to the dogs. I might possibly invent some excuses for them and him, but I have no time for it. As for the religion and love of art of the builders, it is much the same all the world over, whether the building be an Egyptian temple or the United States Bank. It costs more than it comes to. The mainspring is vanity, assisted by the love of garlic and bread and butter. Mr. Balcom, a promising young architect, designs it on the back of his Vitruvius, with hard pencil and ruler, and the job is let out to Dobson & Sons, stonecutters. When the thirty centuries begin to look down on it, mankind begin to look up at it. As for your high towers and monuments, there was a crazy fellow once in this town who undertook to dig through to China, and he got so far that, as he said, he heard the Chinese pots and kettles rattle; but I think that I shall not go out of my way to admire the hole which he made. Many are concerned about the monuments of the West and the East,—to know who built them. For my part, I should like to know who in those days did not build them,—who were above such trifling. But to proceed with my statistics.

By surveying, carpentry, and day-labour of various other kinds in the village in the meanwhile, for I have as many trades as fingers, I had earned $13.34. The expense of food for eight months, namely, from July 4th to March 1st, the time when these estimates were made, though I lived there more than two years,—not counting potatoes, a little green corn, and some peas, which I had raised, nor considering the value of what was on hand at the last date, was

Rice,	....	$ 1.73 $^1/_2$
Molasses,	....	173 Cheapest form of the saccharine.
Rye meal,	....	1.04 $^3/_4$
Indian meal,	....	0.99 $^3/_4$ Cheaper than rye.
Pork,	....	0.22

Flour,	....	0.88	Costs more than Indian meal, both money and trouble.
Sugar,	....	0.80	
Lard,	....	0.65	
Apples,	....	0.25	
Dried apple,	....	0.22	
Sweet potatoes,	....	0.10	
One pumpkin,	....	0.06	
One watermelon,	....	0.02	
Salt,	....	0.03	

Yes, I did eat $8.74, all told; but I should not thus unblushingly publish my guilt, if I did not know that most of my readers were equally guilty with myself, and that their deeds would look no better in print. The next year I sometimes caught a mess of fish for my dinner, and once I went so far as to slaughter a woodchuck which ravaged my bean-field,—effect his transmigration, as a Tartar would say,—and devour him, partly for experiment's sake; but though it afforded me a momentary enjoyment, notwithstanding a musky flavour, I saw that the longest use would not make that a good practice, however it might seem to have your woodchucks ready dressed by the village butcher.

Clothing and some incidental expenses within the same dates, though little can be inferred from this item, amounted to

		$ 8.40¾
Oil and some household utensils,	....	2.00

So that all the pecuniary outgoes, excepting for washing and mending, which for the most part were done out of the house, and their bills have not yet been received,—and these are all and more than all the ways by which money necessarily goes out in this part of the world,—were

House,	....	$28.12½
Farm one year,	....	14.72½
Food eight months,	....	8.74
Clothing, etc., eight months,	....	8.40¾
Oil, etc., eight months,	....	2.00
In all,	....	$61.99¾

I address myself now to those of my readers who have a living to get. And to meet this I have for farm produce sold

		$23.44
Earned by day-labour	....	13.34
In all	....	$36.78

which subtracted from the sum of the outgoes leaves a balance of $25.21¾ on the one side,—this being very nearly the means with which I started, and the measure of expenses to be incurred,—and on the other, beside the leisure and independence and health thus secured, a comfortable house for me as long as I choose to occupy it.

These statistics, however accidental and therefore uninstructive they may appear, as they have a certain completeness, have a certain value also. Nothing was given me of which I have not rendered some account. It appears from the above estimate, that my food alone cost me in money about twenty-seven cents a week. It was, for nearly two years after this, rye and Indian meal without yeast, potatoes, rice, a very little salt pork, molasses, and salt, and my drink water. It was fit that I should live on rice, mainly, who love so well the philosophy of India. To meet the objections of some inveterate cavillers, I may as well state, that if I dined out occasionally, as I always had done, and I trust shall have opportunities to do again, it was frequently to the detriment of my domestic arrangements. But the dining out, being, as I have stated, a constant element, does not in the least affect a comparative statement like this.

I learned from my two years' experience that it would cost incredibly little trouble to obtain one's necessary food, even in this latitude; that a man may use as simple a diet as the animals, and yet retain health and strength. I have made a satisfactory dinner, satisfactory on several accounts, simply off a dish of purslane (*Portulaca oleracea*) which I gathered in my cornfield, boiled and salted. I give the Latin on account of the savouriness of the trivial name. And pray what more can a reasonable man desire, in peaceful times, in ordinary noons, than a sufficient number of ears of green sweet-corn boiled, with the addition of salt? Even the little variety which I used was a yielding to the demands of appetite, and not of health. Yet men have come to such a pass that they frequently starve, not for want of necessaries, but for want of luxuries; and I know a good woman who thinks that her son lost his life because he took to drinking water only.

The reader will perceive that I am treating the subject rather from an economic than a dietetic point of view, and he will not venture to put my abstemiousness to the test unless he has a well-stocked larder.

Bread I at first made of pure Indian meal and salt, genuine hoe-cakes, which I baked before my fire out of doors on a shingle or the end of a stick of timber sawed off in building my house; but it was wont to get smoked and to have a musky flavour. I tried flour also; but have at last found a mixture of rye and Indian meal most convenient and agreeable. In cold weather it was no little amusement to bake several small loaves of this in succession, tending and turning them as carefully as an Egyptian his hatching eggs. They were a real cereal fruit which I ripened, and they had to my senses a fragrance like that of other noble fruits, which I kept in as long as possible by wrapping them in cloth. I made a study of the ancient and indispensable art of bread-making, consulting such authorities as offered, going back to the primitive days and first invention of the unleavened kind, when from the wildness of nuts and meats men first reached the mildness and refinement of this diet, and travelling gradually down in my studies through that accidental souring of the dough which, it is supposed, taught the leavening process, and through the various fermentations thereafter, till I came to "good, sweet, wholesome bread," the staff of life. Leaven, which some deem the soul of bread, the *spiritus* which fills its cellular tissue, which is religiously preserved like the vestal fire,—some precious bottle-full, I suppose, first brought over in the Mayflower, did the business for America, and its influence is still rising, swelling, spreading, in cerealian billows over the land,—this seed I regularly and faithfully procured from the village, till at length one morning I forgot the rules, and scalded my yeast; by which accident I discovered that even this was not indispensable,—for my discoveries were not by the synthetic but analytic process,—and I have gladly omitted it since, though most housewives earnestly assured me that safe and wholesome bread without yeast might not be, and elderly people prophesied a speedy decay of the vital forces. Yet I find it not to be an essential ingredient, and after going without it for a year am still in the land of the living; and I am glad to escape the trivialness of carrying a bottle-full in my pocket, which would sometimes pop and discharge its contents to my discomfiture. It is simpler and more respectable to omit it. Man is an animal who more than any other can adapt himself to all climates and circumstances. Neither did I put any sal soda, or other acid or alkali, into my bread. It would seem that I made it according to the recipe which Marcus Porcius Cato gave about two centuries before Christ. "Panem depsticium sic facito. Manus mortariumque bene lavato. Farinam in mortarium indito, aquæ paulatim addito, subigitoque pulchre. Ubi bene subegeris, defingito, coquitoque sub testu." Which I take to mean—"Make kneaded bread thus. Wash your hands and trough well. Put the meal into the trough, add water gradually, and knead it thoroughly. When you have kneaded it well, mould it, and bake it under a cover," that is, in a baking kettle. Not a word about leaven. But I did not always use this staff of life. At one time, owing to the emptiness of my purse, I saw none of it for more than a month.

Every New Englander might easily raise all his own breadstuffs in this land of rye and Indian corn, and not depend on distant and fluctuating markets for them. Yet so far are we from simplicity and independence that, in Concord, fresh and sweet meal is rarely sold in the shops, and hominy and corn in a still coarser form are hardly used by any. For the most part the farmer gives to his cattle and hogs the grain of his own producing, and buys flour, which is at least no more wholesome, at a greater cost, at the store. I saw that I could easily raise my bushel or two of rye and Indian corn, for the former will grow on the poorest land, and the latter does not require the best, and grind them in a hand-mill, and so do without rice and pork; and if I must have some concentrated sweet, I found by experiment that I could make a very good molasses either of pumpkins or beets, and I knew that I needed only to set out a few maples to obtain it more easily still, and while these were growing I could use various substitutes beside those which I have named. "For," as the Forefathers sang,—

"we can make liquor to sweeten our lips
Of pumpkins and parsnips and walnut-tree chips."

Finally, as for salt, that grossest of groceries, to obtain this might be a fit occasion for a visit to the seashore, or, if I did without it altogether, I should probably drink the less water. I do not learn that the Indians ever troubled themselves to go after it.

Thus I could avoid all trade and barter, so far as my food was concerned, and having a shelter already, it would only remain to get clothing and fuel. The pantaloons which I now wear were woven in a farmer's family,—thank Heaven there is so much virtue still in man; for I think the fall from the farmer to the operative as great and memorable as that from the man to the farmer;—and in a new country, fuel is an encumbrance. As for a habitat, if I were not permitted still to squat, I might purchase one acre at the same price for which the land I cultivated was sold—namely, eight dollars and eight cents. But as it was, I considered that I enhanced the value of the land by squatting on it.

There is a certain class of unbelievers who sometimes ask me such questions as, if I think that I can live on vegetable food alone; and to strike at the root of the matter at once,—for the root is faith,—I am accustomed to answer such, that I can live on board nails. If they cannot understand that, they cannot understand much that I have to say. For my part, I am glad to hear of experiments of this kind being tried; as that a young man tried for a fortnight to live on hard, raw corn on the ear, using his teeth for all mortar. The squirrel tribe tried the same and succeeded. The human race is interested in these experiments, though a few old women who are incapacitated for them, or who own their thirds in mills, may be alarmed.

My furniture, part of which I made myself, and the rest cost me nothing of which I have not rendered an account, consisted of a bed, a table, a desk, three chairs, a looking-glass three inches in diameter, a pair of tongs and andirons, a kettle, a skillet, and a frying-pan, a dipper, a wash-bowl, two knives and forks, three plates, one cup, one spoon, a jug for oil, a jug for molasses, and a japanned lamp. None is so poor that he need sit on a pumpkin. That is shiftlessness. There is a plenty of such chairs as I like best in the village garrets to be had for taking them away. Furniture! Thank God, I can sit and I can stand without the aid of a furniture warehouse. What man but a philosopher would not be ashamed to see his furniture packed in a cart and going up country exposed to the light of heaven and the eyes of men, a beggarly account of empty boxes? That is Spaulding's furniture. I could never tell from inspecting such a load whether it belonged to a so called rich man or a poor one; the owner always seemed poverty-stricken. Indeed, the more you have of such things the poorer you are. Each load looks as if it contained the contents of a dozen shanties; and if one shanty is poor, this is a dozen times as poor. Pray, for what do we *move* ever but to get rid of our furniture, our *exuviæ*; at last to go from this world to another newly furnished, and leave this to be burned? It is the same as if all these traps were buckled to a man's belt, and he could not move over the rough country where our lines are cast without dragging them,—dragging his trap. He was a lucky fox that left his tail in the trap. The muskrat will gnaw his third leg off to be free. No wonder man has lost his elasticity. How often he is at a dead set! "Sir, if I may be so bold, what do you mean by a dead set?" If you are a seer, whenever you meet a man you will see all that he owns, ay, and much that he pretends to disown, behind him, even to his kitchen furniture and all the trumpery which he saves and will not burn, and he will appear to be harnessed to it and making what headway he can. I think that the man is at a dead set who has got through a knot hole or gateway where his sledge load of furniture cannot follow him. I cannot but feel compassion when I hear some trig, compact-looking man, seemingly free, all girded and ready, speak of his "furniture," as whether it is insured or not.

"But what shall I do with my furniture?" My gay butterfly is entangled in a spider's web then. Even those who seem for a long while not to have any, if you inquire more narrowly you will find some stored in somebody's barn. I look upon England today as an old gentleman who is travelling with a great deal of baggage, trumpery which has accumulated from long housekeeping, which he has not the courage to burn; great trunk, little trunk, bandbox, and bundle. Throw away the first three at least. It would surpass the powers of a well man nowadays to take up his bed and walk, and I should certainly advise a sick one to lay down his bed and run. When I have met an immigrant tottering under a bundle which contained his all — looking like an enormous wen which had grown out of the nape of his neck — I have pitied him, not because that was his all, but because he had all *that* to carry. If I have got to drag my trap, I will take care that it be a light one and do not nip me in a vital part. But perchance it would be wisest never to put one's paw into it.

I would observe, by the way, that it costs me nothing for curtains, for I have no gazers to shut out but the sun and moon, and I am willing that they should look in. The moon will not sour milk nor taint meat of mine, nor will the sun injure my furniture or fade my carpet; and if he is sometimes too warm a friend, I find it still better economy to retreat behind some curtain which nature has provided, than to add a single item to the details of housekeeping. A lady once offered me a mat, but as I had no room to spare within the house, nor time to spare within or without to shake it, I declined it, preferring to wipe my feet on the sod before my door. It is best to avoid the beginnings of evil.

Not long since I was present at the auction of a deacon's effects, for his life had not been ineffectual:—

"The evil that men do lives after them."

As usual, a great proportion was trumpery which had begun to accumulate in his father's day. Among the rest was a dried tapeworm. And now, after lying half a century in his garret and other dust holes, these things were not burned; instead of a *bonfire*, or purifying destruction of them, there was an *auction*, or increasing of them. The neighbours eagerly collected to view them, bought them all, and carefully transported them to their garrets and dust holes, to lie there till their estates are settled, when they will start again. When a man dies he kicks the dust.

The customs of some savage nations might, perchance, be profitably imitated by us, for they at least go through the semblance of casting their slough annually; they have the idea of the thing, whether they have the reality or not. Would it not be well if we were to celebrate such a "busk," or "feast of first fruits," as Bartram describes to have been the custom of the Mucclasse Indians? "When a town celebrates the busk," says he, "having previously provided themselves with new clothes, new pots, pans, and other household utensils and furniture, they collect all their worn out clothes and other despicable things, sweep and cleanse their houses, squares, and the whole town, of their filth, which with all the remaining grain and other old provisions they cast together into one common heap, and consume it with fire. After having taken medicine, and fasted for three days, all the fire in the town is extinguished. During this fast they abstain from the gratification of every appetite and passion whatever. A general amnesty is proclaimed; all malefactors may return to their town."

"On the fourth morning, the high priest, by rubbing dry wood together, produces new fire in the public square, from whence every habitation in the town is supplied with the new and pure flame."

They then feast on the new corn and fruits, and dance and sing for three days, "and the four following days they receive visits and rejoice with their friends from neighbouring towns who have in like manner purified and prepared themselves."

The Mexicans also practised a similar purification at the end of every fifty-two years, in the belief that it was time for the world to come to an end.

I have scarcely heard of a truer sacrament, that is, as the dictionary defines it, "outward and visible sign of an inward and spiritual grace," than this, and I have no doubt that they were originally inspired directly from Heaven to do thus, though they have no biblical record of the revelation.

For more than five years I maintained myself thus solely by the labour of my hands, and I found, that by working about six weeks in a year, I could meet all the expenses of living. The whole of my winters, as well as most of my summers, I had free and clear for study. I have thoroughly tried school-keeping, and found that my expenses were in proportion, or rather out of proportion, to my income, for I was obliged to dress and train, not to say think and believe, accordingly, and I lost my time into the bargain. As I did not teach for the good of my fellow-men, but simply for a livelihood, this was a failure.

I have tried trade; but I found that it would take ten years to get under way in that, and that then I should probably be on my way to the devil. I was actually afraid that I might by that time be doing what is called a good business. When formerly I was looking about to see what I could do for a living, some sad experience in conforming to the wishes of friends being fresh in my mind to tax my ingenuity, I thought often and seriously of picking huckleberries; that surely I could do, and its small profits might suffice,—for my greatest skill has been to want but little,—so little capital it required, so little distraction from my wonted moods, I foolishly thought. While my acquaintances went unhesitatingly into trade or the professions, I contemplated this occupation as most like theirs; ranging the hills all summer to pick the berries which came in my way, and thereafter carelessly dispose of them; so, to keep the flocks of Admetus. I also dreamed that I might gather the wild herbs, or carry evergreens to such villagers as loved to be reminded of the woods, even to the city, by hay-cart loads. But I have since learned that trade curses everything it handles; and though you trade in messages from heaven, the whole curse of trade attaches to the business.

As I preferred some things to others, and especially valued my freedom, as I could fare hard and yet succeed well, I did not wish to spend my time in earning rich carpets or other fine furniture, or delicate cookery, or a house in the Grecian or the Gothic style just yet. If there are any to whom it is no interruption to acquire these things, and who know how to use them when acquired, I relinquish to them the pursuit. Some are "industrious," and appear to love labour for its own sake, or perhaps because it keeps them out of worse mischief; to such I have at present nothing to say. Those who would not know what to do with more leisure than they now enjoy, I might advise to work twice as hard as they do,—work till they pay for themselves, and get their free papers. For myself I found that the occupation of a day-labourer was the most independent of any, especially as it required only thirty or forty days in a year to support one. The labourer's day ends with the going down of the sun, and he is then free to devote himself to his chosen pursuit, independent of his labour; but his employer, who speculates from month to month, has no respite from one end of the year to the other.

In short, I am convinced, both by faith and experience, that to maintain one's self on this earth is not a hardship but a pastime, if we will live simply and wisely; as the pursuits of the simpler nations are still the sports of the more artificial. It is not necessary that a man should earn his living by the sweat of his brow, unless he sweats easier than I do.

One young man of my acquaintance, who has inherited some acres, told me that he thought he should live as I did, *if he had the means*. I would not have any one adopt *my* mode of living on any account; for, beside that before he has fairly learned it I may have found out another for myself, I desire that there may be as many different persons in the world as possible; but I would have each one be very careful to find out and pursue *his own way*, and not his father's or his mother's or his neighbour's instead. The youth may build or plant or sail, only let him not be hindered from doing that which he tells me he would like to do. It is by a mathematical point only that we are wise, as the sailor or the fugitive slave keeps the polestar in his eye; but that is sufficient guidance for all our life. We may not arrive at our port within a calculable period, but we would preserve the true course.

Undoubtedly, in this case, what is true for one is truer still for a thousand, as a large house is not proportionally more expensive than a small one, since one roof may cover, one cellar underlie, and one wall separate several apartments. But for my part, I preferred the solitary dwelling. Moreover, it will commonly be cheaper to build the whole yourself than to convince another of the advantage of the common wall; and when you have done this, the common partition, to be much cheaper, must be a thin one, and that other may prove a bad neighbour, and also not keep his side in repair. The only cooperation which is commonly possible is exceedingly partial and superficial; and what little true cooperation there is, is as if it were not, being a harmony inaudible to men. If a man has faith, he will cooperate with equal faith everywhere; if he has not faith, he will continue to live like the rest of the world, whatever company he is joined to. To cooperate in the highest as well as the lowest sense, means *to get our living together*. I heard it proposed lately that two young men should travel together over the world, the one without money, earning his means as he went, before the mast and behind the plough, the other carrying a bill of exchange in his pocket. It was easy to see that they could not long be companions or cooperate, since one would not *operate* at all. They would part at the first interesting crisis in their adventures. Above all, as I have implied, the man who goes alone can start today; but he who travels with another must wait till that other is ready, and it may be a long time before they get off.

But all this is very selfish, I have heard some of my townsmen say. I confess that I have hitherto indulged very little in philanthropic enterprises. I have made some sacrifices to a sense of duty, and among others have sacrificed this pleasure also. There are those who have used all their arts to persuade me to undertake the support of some poor family in the town; and if I had nothing to do,—for the devil finds employment for the idle,—I might try my hand at some such pastime as that. However, when I have thought to indulge myself in this respect, and lay their Heaven under an obligation by maintaining certain poor persons in all respects as comfortably as I maintain myself, and have even ventured so far as to make them the offer, they have one and all unhesitatingly preferred to remain poor. While my townsmen and women are devoted in so many ways to the good of their fellows, I trust that one at least may be spared to other and less humane pursuits. You must have a genius for charity as well as for anything else. As for Doing-good, that is one of the professions which are full. Moreover, I have tried it fairly, and, strange as it may seem, am satisfied that it does not agree with my constitution. Probably I should not consciously and deliberately forsake my particular calling to do the good which society demands of me, to save the universe from annihilation; and I believe that a like but infinitely greater steadfastness elsewhere is all that now preserves it. But I would not stand between any man and his genius; and to him who does this work, which I decline, with his whole heart and soul and life, I would say, Persevere, even if the world call it doing evil, as it is most likely they will.

I am far from supposing that my case is a peculiar one; no doubt many of my readers would make a similar defence. At doing something,—I will not engage that my neighbours shall pronounce it good,—I do not hesitate to say that I should be a capital fellow to hire; but what that is, it is for my employer to find out. What *good* I do, in the common sense of that word, must be aside from my main path, and for the most part wholly unintended. Men say, practically, Begin where you are and such as you are, without aiming mainly to become of more worth, and with kindness aforethought go about doing good. If I were to preach at all in this strain, I should say rather, Set about being good. As if the sun should stop when he had kindled his fires up to the splendour of a moon or a star of the sixth magnitude, and go about like a Robin Goodfellow, peeping in at every cottage window, inspiring lunatics, and tainting meats, and making darkness visible, instead of steadily increasing his genial heat and beneficence till he is of such brightness that no mortal can look him in the face, and then, and in the meanwhile too, going about the world in his own orbit, doing it good, or rather, as a truer philosophy has discovered, the world going about him getting good. When Phaeton, wishing to prove his heavenly birth by his beneficence, had the sun's chariot but one day, and drove out of the beaten track, he burned several blocks of houses in the lower streets of heaven, and scorched the surface of the earth, and dried up every spring, and made the great desert of Sahara, till at length Jupiter hurled him headlong to the earth with a thunderbolt, and the sun, through grief at his death, did not shine for a year.

There is no odour so bad as that which arises from goodness tainted. It is human, it is divine, carrion. If I knew for a certainty that a man was coming to my house with the conscious design of doing me good, I should run for my life, as from that dry and parching wind of the African deserts called the simoom, which fills the mouth and nose and ears and eyes with dust till you are suffocated, for fear that I should get some of his good done to me,—some of its virus mingled with my blood. No,—in this case I would rather suffer evil the natural way. A man is not a good *man* to me because he will feed me if I should be starving, or warm me if I should be freezing, or pull me out of a ditch if I should ever fall into one. I can find you a Newfoundland dog that will do as much. Philanthropy is not love for one's fellow-man in the broadest sense. Howard was no doubt an exceedingly kind and worthy man in his way, and has his reward; but, comparatively speaking, what are a hundred Howards to *us*, if their philanthropy do not help *us* in our best estate, when we are most worthy to be helped? I never heard of a philanthropic meeting in which it was sincerely proposed to do any good to me, or the like of me.

The Jesuits were quite balked by those Indians who, being burned at the stake, suggested new modes of torture to their tormentors. Being superior to physical suffering, it sometimes chanced that they were superior to any consolation which the missionaries could offer; and the law to do as you would be done by fell with less persuasiveness on the ears of those who, for their part, did not care how they were done by, who loved their enemies after a new fashion, and came very near freely forgiving them all they did.

Be sure that you give the poor the aid they most need, though it be your example which leaves them far behind. If you give money, spend yourself with it, and do not merely abandon it to them. We make curious mistakes sometimes. Often the poor man is not so cold and hungry as he is dirty and ragged and gross. It is partly his taste, and not merely his misfortune. If you give him money, he will perhaps buy more rags with it. I was wont to pity the clumsy Irish labourers who cut ice on the pond, in such mean and ragged clothes, while I shivered in my more tidy and somewhat more fashionable garments, till, one bitter cold day, one who had slipped into the water came to my house to warm him, and I saw him strip off three pairs of pants and two pairs of stockings ere he got down to the skin, though they were dirty and ragged enough, it is true, and that he could afford to refuse the *extra* garments which I offered him, he had so many *intra* ones. This ducking was the very thing he needed. Then I began to pity myself, and I saw that it would be a greater charity to bestow on me a flannel shirt than a whole slop-shop on him. There are a thousand hacking at the branches of evil to one who is striking at the root, and it may be that he who bestows the largest amount of time and money on the needy is doing the most by his mode of life to produce that misery which he strives in vain to relieve. It is the pious slave-breeder devoting the proceeds of every tenth slave to buy a Sunday's liberty for the rest. Some show their kindness to the poor by employing them in their kitchens. Would they not be kinder if they employed themselves there? You boast of spending a tenth part of your income in charity; maybe you should spend the nine tenths so, and done with it. Society recovers only a tenth part of the property then. Is this owing to the generosity of him in whose possession it is found, or to the remissness of the officers of justice?

Philanthropy is almost the only virtue which is sufficiently appreciated by mankind. Nay, it is greatly overrated; and it is our selfishness which overrates it. A robust poor man, one sunny day here in Concord, praised a fellow-townsman to me, because, as he said, he was kind to the poor; meaning himself. The kind uncles and aunts of the race are more esteemed than its true spiritual fathers and mothers. I once heard a reverend lecturer on England, a man of learning and intelligence, after enumerating her scientific, literary, and political worthies, Shakespeare, Bacon, Cromwell, Milton, Newton, and others, speak next of her Christian heroes, whom, as if his profession required it of him, he elevated to a place far above all the rest, as the greatest of the great. They were Penn, Howard, and Mrs. Fry. Every one must feel the falsehood and cant of this. The last were not England's best men and women; only, perhaps, her best philanthropists.

I would not subtract anything from the praise that is due to philanthropy, but merely demand justice for all who by their lives and works are a blessing to mankind. I do not value chiefly a man's uprightness and benevolence, which are, as it were, his stem and leaves. Those plants of whose greenness withered we make herb tea for the sick, serve but a humble use, and are most employed by quacks. I want the flower and fruit of a man; that some fragrance be wafted over from him to me, and some ripeness flavour our intercourse. His goodness must not be a partial and transitory act, but a constant superfluity, which costs him nothing and of which he is unconscious. This is a charity that hides a multitude of sins. The philanthropist too often surrounds mankind with the remembrance of his own castoff griefs as an atmosphere, and calls it sympathy. We should impart our courage, and not our despair, our health and ease, and not our disease, and take care that this does not spread by contagion. From what southern plains comes up the voice of wailing? Under what latitudes reside the heathen to whom we would send light? Who is that intemperate and brutal man whom we would redeem? If anything ail a man, so that he does not perform his functions, if he has a pain in his bowels even,—for that is the seat of sympathy,—he forthwith sets about reforming—the world. Being a microcosm himself, he discovers, and it is a true discovery, and he is the man to make it,—that the world has been eating green apples; to his eyes, in fact, the globe itself is a great green apple, which there is danger awful to think of that the children of men will nibble before it is ripe; and straightway his drastic philanthropy seeks out the Esquimau and the Patagonian, and embraces the populous Indian and Chinese villages; and thus, by a few years of philanthropic activity, the powers in the meanwhile using him for their own ends, no doubt, he cures himself of his dyspepsia, the globe acquires a faint blush on one or both of its cheeks, as if it were beginning to be ripe, and life loses its crudity and is once more sweet and wholesome to live. I never dreamed of any enormity greater than I have committed. I never knew, and never shall know, a worse man than myself.

I believe that what so saddens the reformer is not his sympathy with his fellows in distress, but, though he be the holiest son of God, is his private ail. Let this be righted, let the spring come to him, the morning rise over his couch, and he will forsake his generous companions without apology. My excuse for not lecturing against the use of tobacco is, that I never chewed it; that is a penalty which reformed tobacco-chewers have to pay; though there are things enough I have chewed, which I could lecture against. If you should ever be betrayed into any of these philanthropies, do not let your left hand know what your right hand does, for it is not worth knowing. Rescue the drowning and tie your shoestrings. Take your time, and set about some free labour.

Our manners have been corrupted by communication with the saints. Our hymn-books resound with a melodious cursing of God and enduring him forever. One would say that even the prophets and redeemers had rather consoled the fears than confirmed the hopes of man. There is nowhere recorded a simple and irrepressible satisfaction with the gift of life, any memorable praise of God. All health and success does me good, however far off and withdrawn it may appear; all disease and failure helps to make me sad and does me evil, however much sympathy it may have with me or I with it. If, then, we would indeed restore mankind by truly Indian, botanic, magnetic, or natural means, let us first be as simple and well as Nature ourselves, dispel the clouds which hang over our own brows, and take up a little life into our pores. Do not stay to be an overseer of the poor, but endeavour to become one of the worthies of the world.

I read in the Gulistan, or Flower Garden, of Sheik Sadi of Shiraz, that "They asked a wise man, saying: Of the many celebrated trees which the Most High God has created lofty and umbrageous, they call none azad, or free, excepting the cypress, which bears no fruit; what mystery is there in this? He replied, Each has its appropriate produce, and appointed season, during the continuance of which it is fresh and blooming, and during their absence dry and withered; to neither of which states is the cypress exposed, being always flourishing; and of this nature are the azads, or religious independents.—Fix not thy heart on that which is transitory; for the Dijlah, or Tigris, will continue to flow through Bagdad after the race of caliphs is extinct; if thy hand has plenty, be liberal as the date tree; but if it affords nothing to give away, be an azad, or free man, like the cypress."

COMPLEMENTAL VERSES

The Pretensions of Poverty
"Thou dost presume too much, poor needy wretch,
To claim a station in the firmament
Because thy humble cottage, or thy tub,
Nurses some lazy or pedantic virtue
In the cheap sunshine or by shady springs,
With roots and pot-herbs; where thy right hand,
Tearing those humane passions from the mind,
Upon whose stocks fair blooming virtues flourish,
Degradeth nature, and benumbeth sense,
And, Gorgon-like, turns active men to stone.
We not require the dull society
Of your necessitated temperance,
Or that unnatural stupidity
That knows nor joy nor sorrow; nor your forc'd
Falsely exalted passive fortitude
Above the active. This low abject brood,
That fix their seats in mediocrity,
Become your servile minds; but we advance
Such virtues only as admit excess,
Brave, bounteous acts, regal magnificence,
All-seeing prudence, magnanimity
That knows no bound, and that heroic virtue
For which antiquity hath left no name,
But patterns only, such as Hercules,
Achilles, Theseus. Back to thy loath'd cell;
And when thou seest the new enlightened sphere,
Study to know but what those worthies were."

T. CAREW

2
Where I Lived, and What I Lived for

At a certain season of our life we are accustomed to consider every spot as the possible site of a house. I have thus surveyed the country on every side within a dozen miles of where I live. In imagination I have bought all the farms in succession, for all were to be bought, and I knew their price. I walked over each farmer's premises, tasted his wild apples, discoursed on husbandry with him, took his farm at his price, at any price, mortgaging it to him in my mind; even put a higher price on it,—took everything but a deed of it,—took his word for his deed, for I dearly love to talk,—cultivated it, and him too to some extent, I trust, and withdrew when I had enjoyed it long enough, leaving him to carry it on. This experience entitled me to be regarded as a sort of real-estate broker by my friends. Wherever I sat, there I might live, and the landscape radiated from me accordingly. What is a house but a *sedes*, a seat?—better if a country seat. I discovered many a site for a house not likely to be soon improved, which some might have thought too far from the village, but to my eyes the village was too far from it. Well, there I might live, I said; and there I did live, for an hour, a summer and a winter life; saw how I could let the years run off, buffet the winter through, and see the spring come in. The future inhabitants of this region, wherever they may place their houses, may be sure that they have been anticipated. An afternoon sufficed to lay out the land into orchard, woodlot, and pasture, and to decide what fine oaks or pines should be left to stand before the door, and whence each blasted tree could be seen to the best advantage; and then I let it lie, fallow perchance, for a man is rich in proportion to the number of things which he can afford to let alone.

My imagination carried me so far that I even had the refusal of several farms,—the refusal was all I wanted,—but I never got my fingers burned by actual possession. The nearest that I came to actual possession was when I bought the Hollowell place, and had begun to sort my seeds, and collected materials with which to make a wheelbarrow to carry it on or off with; but before the owner gave me a deed of it, his wife—every man has such a wife—changed her mind and wished to keep it, and he offered me ten dollars to release him. Now, to speak the truth, I had but ten cents in the world, and it surpassed my arithmetic to tell, if I was that man who had ten cents, or who had a farm, or ten dollars, or all together. However, I let him keep the ten dollars and the farm too, for I had carried it far enough; or rather, to be generous, I sold him the farm for just what I gave for it, and, as he was not a rich man, made him a present of ten dollars, and still had my ten cents, and seeds, and materials for a wheelbarrow left. I found thus that I had been a rich man without any damage to my poverty. But I retained the landscape, and I have since annually carried off what it yielded without a wheelbarrow. With respect to landscapes,—

> "I am monarch of all I *survey*,
> My right there is none to dispute."

I have frequently seen a poet withdraw, having enjoyed the most valuable part of a farm, while the crusty farmer supposed that he had got a few wild apples only. Why, the owner does not know it for many years when a poet has put his farm in rhyme, the most admirable kind of invisible fence, has fairly impounded it, milked it, skimmed it, and got all the cream, and left the farmer only the skimmed milk.

The real attractions of the Hollowell farm, to me, were: its complete retirement, being, about two miles from the village, half a mile from the nearest neighbour, and separated from the highway by a broad field; its bounding on the river, which the owner said protected it by its fogs from frosts in the spring, though that was nothing to me; the gray colour and ruinous state of the house and barn, and the dilapidated fences, which put such an interval between me and the last occupant; the hollow and lichen-covered apple trees, gnawed by rabbits, showing what kind of neighbours I should have; but above all, the recollection I had of it from my earliest voyages up the river, when the house was concealed behind a dense grove of red maples, through which I heard the house-dog bark. I was in haste to buy it, before the proprietor finished getting out some rocks, cutting down the hollow apple trees, and grubbing up some young birches which had sprung up in the pasture, or, in short, had made any more of his improvements. To enjoy these advantages I was ready to carry it on; like Atlas, to take the world on my shoulders,—I never heard what compensation he received for that,—and do all those things which had no other motive or excuse but that I might pay for it and be unmolested in my possession of it; for I knew all the while that it would yield the most abundant crop of the kind I wanted if I could only afford to let it alone. But it turned out as I have said.

All that I could say, then, with respect to farming on a large scale, (I have always cultivated a garden,) was, that I had had my seeds ready. Many think that seeds improve with age. I have no doubt that time discriminates between the good and the bad; and when at last I shall plant, I shall be less likely to be disappointed. But I would say to my fellows, once for all, As long as possible live free and uncommitted. It makes but little difference whether you are committed to a farm or the county jail.

Old Cato, whose "De Re Rusticâ" is my "Cultivator," says, and the only translation I have seen makes sheer nonsense of the passage, "When you think of getting a farm, turn it thus in your mind, not to buy greedily; nor spare your pains to look at it, and do not think it enough to go round it once. The oftener you go there the more it will please you, if it is good." I think I shall not buy greedily, but go round and round it as long as I live, and be buried in it first, that it may please me the more at last.

The present was my next experiment of this kind, which I purpose to describe more at length; for convenience, putting the experience of two years into one. As I have said, I do not propose to write an ode to dejection, but to brag as lustily as chanticleer in the morning, standing on his roost, if only to wake my neighbours up.

When first I took up my abode in the woods, that is, began to spend my nights as well as days there, which, by accident, was on Independence Day, or the Fourth of July, 1845, my house was not finished for winter, but was merely a defence against the rain, without plastering or chimney, the walls being of rough, weather-stained boards, with wide chinks, which made it cool at night. The upright white hewn studs and freshly planed door and window casings gave it a clean and airy look, especially in the morning, when its timbers were saturated with dew, so that I fancied that by noon some sweet gum would exude from them. To my imagination it retained throughout the day more or less of this auroral character, reminding me of a certain house on a mountain which I had visited the year before. This was an airy and unplastered cabin, fit to entertain a travelling god, and where a goddess might trail her garments. The winds which passed over my dwelling were such as sweep over the ridges of mountains, bearing the broken strains, or celestial parts only, of terrestrial music. The morning wind forever blows, the poem of creation is uninterrupted; but few are the ears that hear it. Olympus is but the outside of the earth everywhere.

The only house I had been the owner of before, if I except a boat, was a tent, which I used occasionally when making excursions in the summer, and this is still rolled up in my garret; but the boat, after passing from hand to hand, has gone down the stream of time. With this more substantial shelter about me, I had made some progress toward settling in the world. This frame, so slightly clad, was a sort of crystallization around me, and reacted on the

builder. It was suggestive somewhat as a picture in outlines. I did not need to go outdoors to take the air, for the atmosphere within had lost none of its freshness. It was not so much within doors as behind a door where I sat, even in the rainiest weather. The Harivansa says, "An abode without birds is like a meat without seasoning." Such was not my abode, for I found myself suddenly neighbour to the birds; not by having imprisoned one, but having caged myself near them. I was not only nearer to some of those which commonly frequent the garden and the orchard, but to those wilder and more thrilling songsters of the forest which never, or rarely, serenade a villager,—the wood-thrush, the veery, the scarlet tanager, the field-sparrow, the whip-poorwill, and many others.

I was seated by the shore of a small pond, about a mile and a half south of the village of Concord and somewhat higher than it, in the midst of an extensive wood between that town and Lincoln, and about two miles south of that our only field known to fame, Concord Battle Ground; but I was so low in the woods that the opposite shore, half a mile off, like the rest, covered with wood, was my most distant horizon. For the first week, whenever I looked out on the pond it impressed me like a tarn high up on the side of a mountain, its bottom far above the surface of other lakes, and, as the sun arose, I saw it throwing off its nightly clothing of mist, and here and there, by degrees, its soft ripples or its smooth reflecting surface was revealed, while the mists, like ghosts, were stealthily withdrawing in every direction into the woods, as at the breaking up of some nocturnal conventicle. The very dew seemed to hang upon the trees later into the day than usual, as on the sides of mountains.

This small lake was of most value as a neighbour in the intervals of a gentle rain storm in August, when, both air and water being perfectly still, but the sky overcast, mid-afternoon had all the serenity of evening, and the wood-thrush sang around, and was heard from shore to shore. A lake like this is never smoother than at such a time; and the clear portion of the air above it being shallow and darkened by clouds, the water, full of light and reflections, becomes a lower heaven itself so much the more important. From a hill top near by, where the wood had been recently cut off, there was a pleasing vista southward across the pond, through a wide indentation in the hills which form the shore there, where their opposite sides sloping toward each other suggested a stream flowing out in that direction through a wooded valley, but stream there was none. That way I looked between and over the near green hills to some distant and higher ones in the horizon, tinged with blue. Indeed, by standing on tiptoe I could catch a glimpse of some of the peaks of the still bluer and more distant mountain ranges in the north-west, those true-blue coins from heaven's own mint, and also of some portion of the village. But in other directions, even from this point, I could not see over or beyond the woods which surrounded me. It is well to have some water in your neighbourhood, to give buoyancy to and float the earth. One value even of the smallest well is, that when you look into it you see that earth is not continent but insular. This is as important as that it keeps butter cool. When I looked across the pond from this peak toward the Sudbury meadows, which in time of flood I distinguished elevated perhaps by a mirage in their seething valley, like a coin in a basin, all the earth beyond the pond appeared like a thin crust insulated and floated even by this small sheet of intervening water, and I was reminded that this on which I dwelt was but *dry land*.

Though the view from my door was still more contracted, I did not feel crowded or confined in the least. There was pasture enough for my imagination. The low shrub-oak plateau to which the opposite shore arose, stretched away toward the prairies of the West and the steppes of Tartary, affording ample room for all the roving families of men. "There are none happy in the world but beings who enjoy freely a vast horizon,"—said Damodara, when his herds required new and larger pastures.

Both place and time were changed, and I dwelt nearer to those parts of the universe and to those eras in history which had most attracted me. Where I lived was as far off as many a region viewed nightly by astronomers. We are wont to imagine rare and delectable places in some remote and more celestial corner of the system, behind the constellation of Cassiopeia's Chair, far from noise and disturbance. I discovered that my house actually had its site in such a withdrawn, but forever new and unprofaned, part of the universe. If it were worth the while to settle in those parts near to the Pleiades or the Hyades, to Aldebaran or Altair, then I was really there, or at an equal remoteness from the life which I had left behind, dwindled and twinkling with as fine a ray to my nearest neighbour, and to be seen only in moonless nights by him. Such was that part of creation where I had squatted;—

> "There was a shepherd that did live,
> And held his thoughts as high

As were the mounts whereon his flocks
Did hourly feed him by."

What should we think of the shepherd's life if his flocks always wandered to higher pastures than his thoughts?

Every morning was a cheerful invitation to make my life of equal simplicity, and I may say innocence, with Nature herself. I have been as sincere a worshipper of Aurora as the Greeks. I got up early and bathed in the pond; that was a religious exercise, and one of the best things which I did. They say that characters were engraven on the bathing tub of King Tching-thang to this effect: "Renew thyself completely each day; do it again, and again, and forever again." I can understand that. Morning brings back the heroic ages. I was as much affected by the faint hum of a mosquito making its invisible and unimaginable tour through my apartment at earliest dawn, when I was sitting with door and windows open, as I could be by any trumpet that ever sang of fame. It was Homer's requiem; itself an Iliad and Odyssey in the air, singing its own wrath and wanderings. There was something cosmical about it; a standing advertisement, till forbidden, of the everlasting vigour and fertility of the world. The morning, which is the most memorable season of the day, is the awakening hour. Then there is least somnolence in us; and for an hour, at least, some part of us awakes which slumbers all the rest of the day and night. Little is to be expected of that day, if it can be called a day, to which we are not awakened by our Genius, but by the mechanical nudgings of some servitor, are not awakened by our own newly-acquired force and aspirations from within, accompanied by the undulations of celestial music, instead of factory bells, and a fragrance filling the air—to a higher life than we fell asleep from; and thus the darkness bear its fruit, and prove itself to be good, no less than the light. That man who does not believe that each day contains an earlier, more sacred, and auroral hour than he has yet profaned, has despaired of life, and is pursuing a descending and darkening way. After a partial cessation of his sensuous life, the soul of man, or its organs rather, are reinvigorated each day, and his Genius tries again what noble life it can make. All memorable events, I should say, transpire in morning time and in a morning atmosphere. The Vedas say, "All intelligences awake with the morning." Poetry and art, and the fairest and most memorable of the actions of men, date from such an hour. All poets and heroes, like Memnon, are the children of Aurora, and emit their music at sunrise. To him whose elastic and vigourous thought keeps pace with the sun, the day is a perpetual morning. It matters not what the clocks say or the attitudes and labours of men. Morning is when I am awake and there is a dawn in me. Moral reform is the effort to throw off sleep. Why is it that men give so poor an account of their day if they have not been slumbering? They are not such poor calculators. If they had not been overcome with drowsiness, they would have performed something. The millions are awake enough for physical labour; but only one in a million is awake enough for effective intellectual exertion, only one in a hundred millions to a poetic or divine life. To be awake is to be alive. I have never yet met a man who was quite awake. How could I have looked him in the face?

We must learn to reawaken and keep ourselves awake, not by mechanical aids, but by an infinite expectation of the dawn, which does not forsake us in our soundest sleep. I know of no more encouraging fact than the unquestionable ability of man to elevate his life by a conscious endeavour. It is something to be able to paint a particular picture, or to carve a statue, and so to make a few objects beautiful; but it is far more glorious to carve and paint the very atmosphere and medium through which we look, which morally we can do. To affect the quality of the day, that is the highest of arts. Every man is tasked to make his life, even in its details, worthy of the contemplation of his most elevated and critical hour. If we refused, or rather used up, such paltry information as we get, the oracles would distinctly inform us how this might be done.

I went to the woods because I wished to live deliberately, to front only the essential facts of life, and see if I could not learn what it had to teach, and not, when I came to die, discover that I had not lived. I did not wish to live what was not life, living is so dear; nor did I wish to practise resignation, unless it was quite necessary. I wanted to live deep and suck out all the marrow of life, to live so sturdily and Spartan-like as to put to rout all that was not life, to cut a broad swath and shave close, to drive life into a corner, and reduce it to its lowest terms, and, if it proved to be mean, why then to get the whole and genuine meanness of it, and publish its meanness to the world; or if it were sublime, to know it by experience, and be able to give a true account of it in my next excursion. For most men, it appears to me, are in a strange uncertainty about it, whether it is of the devil or of God, and have *somewhat hastily* concluded that it is the chief end of man here to "glorify God and enjoy him forever."

Still we live meanly, like ants; though the fable tells us that we were long ago changed into men; like pygmies we fight with cranes; it is error upon error, and clout upon clout, and our best virtue has for its occasion a superfluous and evitable wretchedness. Our life is frittered away by detail. An honest man has hardly need to count more than his ten fingers, or in extreme cases he may add his ten toes, and lump the rest. Simplicity, simplicity, simplicity! I say, let your affairs be as two or three, and not a hundred or a thousand; instead of a million count half a dozen, and keep your accounts on your thumb-nail. In the midst of the chopping sea of civilized life, such are the clouds and storms and quicksands and thousand-and-one items to be allowed for, that a man has to live, if he would not founder and go to the bottom and not make his port at all, by dead reckoning, and he must be a great calculator indeed who succeeds. Simplify, simplify. Instead of three meals a day, if it be necessary eat but one; instead of a hundred dishes, five; and reduce other things in proportion. Our life is like a German Confederacy, made up of petty states, with its boundary forever fluctuating, so that even a German cannot tell you how it is bounded at any moment. The nation itself, with all its so called internal improvements, which, by the way, are all external and superficial, is just such an unwieldy and overgrown establishment, cluttered with furniture and tripped up by its own traps, ruined by luxury and heedless expense, by want of calculation and a worthy aim, as the million households in the land; and the only cure for it, as for them, is in a rigid economy, a stern and more than Spartan simplicity of life and elevation of purpose. It lives too fast. Men think that it is essential that the *Nation* have commerce, and export ice, and talk through a telegraph, and ride thirty miles an hour, without a doubt, whether *they* do or not; but whether we should live like baboons or like men, is a little uncertain. If we do not get out sleepers, and forge rails, and devote days and nights to the work, but go to tinkering upon our *lives* to improve *them*, who will build railroads? And if railroads are not built, how shall we get to heaven in season? But if we stay at home and mind our business, who will want railroads? We do not ride on the railroad; it rides upon us. Did you ever think what those sleepers are that underlie the railroad? Each one is a man, an Irishman, or a Yankee man. The rails are laid on them, and they are covered with sand, and the cars run smoothly over them. They are sound sleepers, I assure you. And every few years a new lot is laid down and run over; so that, if some have the pleasure of riding on a rail, others have the misfortune to be ridden upon. And when they run over a man that is walking in his sleep, a supernumerary sleeper in the wrong position, and wake him up, they suddenly stop the cars, and make a hue and cry about it, as if this were an exception. I am glad to know that it takes a gang of men for every five miles to keep the sleepers down and level in their beds as it is, for this is a sign that they may sometime get up again.

Why should we live with such hurry and waste of life? We are determined to be starved before we are hungry. Men say that a stitch in time saves nine, and so they take a thousand stitches today to save nine tomorrow. As for *work*, we haven't any of any consequence. We have the Saint Vitus' dance, and cannot possibly keep our heads still. If I should only give a few pulls at the parish bell-rope, as for a fire, that is, without setting the bell, there is hardly a man on his farm in the outskirts of Concord, notwithstanding that press of engagements which was his excuse so many times this morning, nor a boy, nor a woman, I might almost say, but would forsake all and follow that sound, not mainly to save property from the flames, but, if we will confess the truth, much more to see it burn, since burn it must, and we, be it known, did not set it on fire,—or to see it put out, and have a hand in it, if that is done as handsomely; yes, even if it were the parish church itself. Hardly a man takes a half hour's nap after dinner, but when he wakes he holds up his head and asks, "What's the news?" as if the rest of mankind had stood his sentinels. Some give directions to be waked every half hour, doubtless for no other purpose; and then, to pay for it, they tell what they have dreamed. After a night's sleep the news is as indispensable as the breakfast. "Pray tell me anything new that has happened to a man anywhere on this globe,"—and he reads it over his coffee and rolls, that a man has had his eyes gouged out this morning on the Wachito River; never dreaming the while that he lives in the dark unfathomed mammoth cave of this world, and has but the rudiment of an eye himself.

For my part, I could easily do without the post-office. I think there are very few important communications made through it. To speak critically, I never received more than one or two letters in my life—I wrote this some years ago—that were worth the postage. The penny-post is, commonly, an institution through which you seriously offer a man that penny for his thoughts which is so often safely offered in jest. And I am sure that I never read any memorable news in a newspaper. If we read of one man robbed, or murdered, or killed by accident, or one house burned, or one vessel wrecked, or one steamboat blown up, or one cow run over on the Western Railroad, or one mad dog killed, or one lot of grasshoppers in the winter—we never need read of another. One is enough. If you are acquainted with the principle, what do you care for a myriad instances and applications? To a philosopher all *news*, as it is called, is gossip, and they who edit and read it are old women over their tea. Yet not a few are greedy after this gossip. There was such a rush, as I hear, the other day at one of the offices to learn the foreign news by the last arrival, that several large squares of plate glass belonging to the establishment were broken by the pressure,—news which I seriously think a ready wit might write a twelvemonth, or twelve years, beforehand with sufficient accuracy. As for Spain, for instance, if you know how to throw in Don Carlos and the Infanta, and Don Pedro and Seville and Granada, from time to time in the right proportions,—they may have changed the names a little since I saw the papers,—and serve up a bull-fight when other entertainments fail, it will be true to the letter, and give us as good an idea of the exact state or ruin of things in Spain as the most succinct and lucid reports under this head in the newspapers: and as for England, almost the last significant scrap of news from that quarter was the revolution of 1649; and if you have learned the history of her crops for an average year, you never need attend to that thing again, unless your speculations are of a merely pecuniary character. If one may judge who rarely looks into the newspapers, nothing new does ever happen in foreign parts, a French revolution not excepted.

What news! How much more important to know what that is which was never old! "Kieou-he-yu (great dignitary of the state of Wei) sent a man to Khoung-tseu to know his news. Khoung-tseu caused the messenger to be seated near him, and questioned him in these terms: What is your master doing? The messenger answered with respect: My master desires to diminish the number of his faults, but he cannot come to the end of them. The messenger being gone, the philosopher remarked: What a worthy messenger! What a worthy messenger!" The preacher, instead of vexing the ears of drowsy farmers on their day of rest at the end of the week,—for Sunday is the fit conclusion of an ill-spent week, and not the fresh and brave beginning of a new one,—with this one other draggletail of a sermon, should shout with thundering voice,—"Pause! Avast! Why so seeming fast, but deadly slow?"

Shams and delusions are esteemed for soundest truths, while reality is fabulous. If men would steadily observe realities only, and not allow themselves to be deluded, life, to compare it with such things as we know, would be like a fairy tale and the Arabian Nights' Entertainments. If we respected only what is inevitable and has a right to be, music and poetry would resound along the streets. When we are unhurried and wise, we perceive that only great and worthy things have any permanent and absolute existence,— that petty fears and petty pleasures are but the shadow of the reality. This is always exhilarating and sublime. By closing the eyes and slumbering, and consenting to be deceived by shows, men establish and confirm their daily life of routine and habit everywhere, which still is built on purely illusory foundations. Children, who play life, discern its true law and relations more clearly than men, who fail to live it worthily, but who think that they are wiser by experience, that is, by failure. I have read in a Hindoo book, that "there was a king's son, who, being expelled in infancy from his native city, was brought up by a forester, and, growing up to maturity in that state, imagined himself to belong to the barbarous race with which he lived. One of his father's ministers having discovered him, revealed to him what he was, and the misconception of his character was removed, and he knew himself to be a prince. So soul," continues the Hindoo philosopher, "from the circumstances in which it is placed, mistakes its own character, until the truth is revealed to it by some holy teacher, and then it knows itself to be *Brahme*." I perceive that we inhabitants of New England live this mean life that we do because our vision does not penetrate the surface of things. We think that that *is* which *appears* to be. If a man should walk through this town and see only the reality, where, think you, would the "Mill-dam" go to? If he should give us an account of the realities he beheld there, we should not recognize the place in his description. Look at a meeting-house, or a court-house, or a jail, or a shop, or a dwelling-house, and say what that thing really is before a true gaze, and they would all go to pieces in your account of them. Men esteem truth remote, in the outskirts of the system, behind the farthest star, before Adam and after the last man. In eternity there is indeed something true and sublime. But all these times and places and occasions are now and here. God himself culminates in the present moment, and will never be more divine in the lapse of all the ages. And we are enabled to apprehend at all what is sublime and noble only by the perpetual instilling and drenching of the reality that surrounds us. The universe constantly and obediently answers to our conceptions; whether we travel fast or slow, the track is laid for us. Let us spend our lives in conceiving then. The poet or the artist never yet had so fair and noble a design but some of his posterity at least could accomplish it.

Let us spend one day as deliberately as Nature, and not be thrown off the track by every nutshell and mosquito's wing that falls on the rails. Let us rise early and fast, or break fast, gently and without perturbation; let company come and let company go, let the bells ring and the children cry,—determined to make a day of it. Why should we knock under and go with the stream? Let us not be upset and overwhelmed in that terrible rapid and whirlpool called a dinner, situated in the meridian shallows. Weather this danger and you are safe, for the rest of the way is down hill. With unrelaxed nerves, with morning vigour, sail by it, looking another way, tied to the mast like Ulysses. If the engine whistles, let it whistle till it is hoarse for its pains. If the bell rings, why should we run? We will consider what kind of music they are like. Let us settle ourselves, and work and wedge our feet downward through the mud and slush of opinion, and prejudice, and tradition, and delusion, and appearance, that alluvion which covers the globe, through Paris and London, through New York and Boston and Concord, through church and state, through poetry and philosophy and religion, till we come to a hard bottom and rocks in place, which we can call *reality*, and say, this is, and no mistake; and then begin, having a *point d'appui*, below freshet and frost and fire, a place where you might found a wall or a state, or set a lamp-post safely, or perhaps a gauge, not a Nilometer, but a Realometer, that future ages might know how deep a freshet of shams and appearances had gathered from time to time. If you stand right fronting and face to face to a fact, you will see the sun glimmer on both its surfaces, as if it were a cimeter, and feel its sweet edge dividing you through the heart and marrow, and so you will happily conclude your mortal career. Be it life or death, we crave only reality. If we are really dying, let us hear the rattle in our throats and feel cold in the extremities; if we are alive, let us go about our business.

Time is but the stream I go a-fishing in. I drink at it; but while I drink I see the sandy bottom and detect how shallow it is. Its thin current slides away, but eternity remains. I would drink deeper; fish in the sky, whose bottom is pebbly with stars. I cannot count one. I know not the first letter of the alphabet. I have always been regretting that I was not as wise as the day I was born. The intellect is a cleaver; it discerns and rifts its way into the secret of things. I do not wish to be any more busy with my hands than is necessary. My head is hands and feet. I feel all my best faculties concentrated in it. My instinct tells me that my head is an organ for burrowing, as some creatures use their snout and fore-paws, and with it I would mine and burrow my way through these hills. I think that the richest vein is somewhere hereabouts; so by the divining rod and thin rising vapours I judge; and here I will begin to mine.

3
Reading

With a little more deliberation in the choice of their pursuits, all men would perhaps become essentially students and observers, for certainly their nature and destiny are interesting to all alike. In accumulating property for ourselves or our posterity, in founding a family or a state, or acquiring fame even, we are mortal; but in dealing with truth we are immortal, and need fear no change nor accident. The oldest Egyptian or Hindoo philosopher raised a corner of the veil from the statue of the divinity; and still the trembling robe remains raised, and I gaze upon as fresh a glory as he did, since it was I in him that was then so bold, and it is he in me that now reviews the vision. No dust has settled on that robe; no time has elapsed since that divinity was revealed. That time which we really improve, or which is improvable, is neither past, present, nor future.

My residence was more favourable, not only to thought, but to serious reading, than a university; and though I was beyond the range of the ordinary circulating library, I had more than ever come within the influence of those books which circulate round the world, whose sentences were first written on bark, and are now merely copied from time to time on to linen paper. Says the poet Mîr Camar Uddîn Mast, "Being seated, to run through the region of the spiritual world; I have had this advantage in books. To be intoxicated by a single glass of wine; I have experienced this pleasure when I have drunk the liquor of the esoteric doctrines." I kept Homer's Iliad on my table through the summer, though I looked at his page only now and then. Incessant labour with my hands, at first, for I had my house to finish and my beans to hoe at the same time, made more study impossible. Yet I sustained myself by the prospect of such reading in future. I read one or two shallow books of travel in the intervals of my work, till that employment made me ashamed of myself, and I asked where it was then that I lived.

The student may read Homer or Æschylus in the Greek without danger of dissipation or luxuriousness, for it implies that he in some measure emulate their heroes, and consecrate morning hours to their pages. The heroic books, even if printed in the character of our mother tongue, will always be in a language dead to degenerate times; and we must labouriously seek the meaning of each word and line, conjecturing a larger sense than common use permits out of what wisdom and valour and generosity we have. The modern cheap and fertile press, with all its translations, has done little to bring us nearer to the heroic writers of antiquity. They seem as solitary, and the letter in which they are printed as rare and curious, as ever. It is worth the expense of youthful days and costly hours, if you learn only some words of an ancient language, which are raised out of the trivialness of the street, to be perpetual suggestions and provocations. It is not in vain that the farmer remembers and repeats the few Latin words which he has heard. Men sometimes speak as if the study of the classics would at length make way for more modern and practical studies; but the adventurous student will always study classics, in whatever language they may be written and however ancient they may be. For what are the classics but the noblest recorded thoughts of man? They are the only oracles which are not decayed, and there are such answers to the most modern inquiry in them as Delphi and Dodona never gave. We might as well omit to study Nature because she is old. To read well, that is, to read true books in a true spirit, is a noble exercise, and one that will task the reader more than any exercise which the customs of the day esteem. It requires a training such as the athletes underwent, the steady intention almost of the whole life to this object. Books must be read as deliberately and reservedly as they were written. It is not enough even to be able to speak the language of that nation by which they are written, for there is a memorable interval between the spoken and the written language, the language heard and the language read. The one is commonly transitory, a sound, a tongue, a dialect merely, almost brutish, and we learn it unconsciously, like the brutes, of our mothers. The other is the maturity and experience of that; if that is our mother tongue, this is our father tongue, a reserved and select expression, too significant to be heard by the ear, which we must be born again in order to speak. The crowds of men who merely *spoke* the Greek and Latin tongues in the Middle Ages were not entitled by the accident of birth to *read* the works of genius written in those languages; for these were not written in that Greek or Latin which they knew, but in the select language of literature. They had not learned the nobler dialects of

Greece and Rome, but the very materials on which they were written were waste paper to them, and they prized instead a cheap contemporary literature. But when the several nations of Europe had acquired distinct though rude written languages of their own, sufficient for the purposes of their rising literatures, then first learning revived, and scholars were enabled to discern from that remoteness the treasures of antiquity. What the Roman and Grecian multitude could not *hear*, after the lapse of ages a few scholars *read*, and a few scholars only are still reading it. However much we may admire the orator's occasional bursts of eloquence, the noblest written words are commonly as far behind or above the fleeting spoken language as the firmament with its stars is behind the clouds. *There* are the stars, and they who can may read them. The astronomers forever comment on and observe them. They are not exhalations like our daily colloquies and vapourous breath. What is called eloquence in the forum is commonly found to be rhetoric in the study. The orator yields to the inspiration of a transient occasion, and speaks to the mob before him, to those who can *hear* him; but the writer, whose more equable life is his occasion, and who would be distracted by the event and the crowd which inspire the orator, speaks to the intellect and health of mankind, to all in any age who can *understand* him.

No wonder that Alexander carried the Iliad with him on his expeditions in a precious casket. A written word is the choicest of relics. It is something at once more intimate with us and more universal than any other work of art. It is the work of art nearest to life itself. It may be translated into every language, and not only be read but actually breathed from all human lips;— not be represented on canvas or in marble only, but be carved out of the breath of life itself. The symbol of an ancient man's thought becomes a modern man's speech. Two thousand summers have imparted to the monuments of Grecian literature, as to her marbles, only a maturer golden and autumnal tint, for they have carried their own serene and celestial atmosphere into all lands to protect them against the corrosion of time. Books are the treasured wealth of the world and the fit inheritance of generations and nations. Books, the oldest and best, stand naturally and rightfully on the shelves of every cottage. They have no cause of their own to plead, but while they enlighten and sustain the reader his common sense will not refuse them. Their authors are a natural and irresistible aristocracy in every society, and, more than kings or emperors, exert an influence on mankind. When the illiterate and perhaps scornful trader has earned by enterprise and industry his coveted leisure and independence, and is admitted to the circles of wealth and fashion, he turns inevitably at last to those still higher but yet inaccessible circles of intellect and genius, and is sensible only of the imperfection of his culture and the vanity and insufficiency of all his riches, and further proves his good sense by the pains which be takes to secure for his children that intellectual culture whose want he so keenly feels; and thus it is that he becomes the founder of a family.

Those who have not learned to read the ancient classics in the language in which they were written must have a very imperfect knowledge of the history of the human race; for it is remarkable that no transcript of them has ever been made into any modern tongue, unless our civilization itself may be regarded as such a transcript. Homer has never yet been printed in English, nor Æschylus, nor Virgil even,—works as refined, as solidly done, and as beautiful almost as the morning itself; for later writers, say what we will of their genius, have rarely, if ever, equalled the elabourate beauty and finish and the lifelong and heroic literary labours of the ancients. They only talk of forgetting them who never knew them. It will be soon enough to forget them when we have the learning and the genius which will enable us to attend to and appreciate them. That age will be rich indeed when those relics which we call Classics, and the still older and more than classic but even less known Scriptures of the nations, shall have still further accumulated, when the Vaticans shall be filled with Vedas and Zendavestas and Bibles, with Homers and Dantes and Shakespeares, and all the centuries to come shall have successively deposited their trophies in the forum of the world. By such a pile we may hope to scale heaven at last.

The works of the great poets have never yet been read by mankind, for only great poets can read them. They have only been read as the multitude read the stars, at most astrologically, not astronomically. Most men have learned to read to serve a paltry convenience, as they have learned to cipher in order to keep accounts and not be cheated in trade; but of reading as a noble intellectual exercise they know little or nothing; yet this only is reading, in a high sense, not that which lulls us as a luxury and suffers the nobler faculties to sleep the while, but what we have to stand on tip-toe to read and devote our most alert and wakeful hours to.

I think that having learned our letters we should read the best that is in literature, and not be forever repeating our a-b-abs, and words of one syllable, in the fourth or fifth classes, sitting on the lowest and foremost form all our lives. Most men are satisfied if they read or hear read, and perchance have been convicted by the wisdom of one good book, the Bible, and for the rest of their lives vegetate and dissipate their faculties in what is called easy reading. There is a work in several volumes in our Circulating Library entitled "Little Reading," which I thought referred to a town of that name which I had not been to. There are those who, like cormorants and ostriches, can digest all sorts of this, even after the fullest dinner of meats and vegetables, for they suffer nothing to be wasted. If others are the machines to provide this provender, they are the machines to read it. They read the nine thousandth tale about Zebulon and Sephronia, and how they loved as none had ever loved before, and neither did the course of their true love run smooth,—at any rate, how it did run and stumble, and get up again and go on! how some poor unfortunate got up on to a steeple, who had better never have gone up as far as the belfry; and then, having needlessly got him up there, the happy novelist rings the bell for all the world to come together and hear, O dear! How he did get down again! For my part, I think that they had better metamorphose all such aspiring heroes of universal noveldom into man weathercocks, as they used to put heroes among the constellations, and let them swing round there till they are rusty, and not come down at all to bother honest men with their pranks. The next time the novelist rings the bell I will not stir though the meeting-house burn down. "The Skip of the Tip-Toe-Hop, a Romance of the Middle Ages, by the celebrated author of 'Tittle-Tol-Tan,' to appear in monthly parts; a great rush; don't all come together." All this they read with saucer eyes, and erect

and primitive curiosity, and with unwearied gizzard, whose corrugations even yet need no sharpening, just as some little four-year-old bencher his two-cent gilt-covered edition of Cinderella,—without any improvement, that I can see, in the pronunciation, or accent, or emphasis, or any more skill in extracting or inserting the moral. The result is dulness of sight, a stagnation of the vital circulations, and a general deliquium and sloughing off of all the intellectual faculties. This sort of gingerbread is baked daily and more sedulously than pure wheat or rye-and-Indian in almost every oven, and finds a surer market.

The best books are not read even by those who are called good readers. What does our Concord culture amount to? There is in this town, with a very few exceptions, no taste for the best or for very good books even in English literature, whose words all can read and spell. Even the college-bred and so called liberally educated men here and elsewhere have really little or no acquaintance with the English classics; and as for the recorded wisdom of mankind, the ancient classics and Bibles, which are accessible to all who will know of them, there are the feeblest efforts anywhere made to become acquainted with them. I know a woodchopper, of middle age, who takes a French paper, not for news as he says, for he is above that, but to "keep himself in practice," he being a Canadian by birth; and when I ask him what he considers the best thing he can do in this world, he says, beside this, to keep up and add to his English. This is about as much as the college bred generally do or aspire to do, and they take an English paper for the purpose. One who has just come from reading perhaps one of the best English books will find how many with whom he can converse about it? Or suppose he comes from reading a Greek or Latin classic in the original, whose praises are familiar even to the so called illiterate; he will find nobody at all to speak to, but must keep silence about it. Indeed, there is hardly the professor in our colleges, who, if he has mastered the difficulties of the language, has proportionally mastered the difficulties of the wit and poetry of a Greek poet, and has any sympathy to impart to the alert and heroic reader; and as for the sacred Scriptures, or Bibles of mankind, who in this town can tell me even their titles? Most men do not know that any nation but the Hebrews have had a scripture. A man, any man, will go considerably out of his way to pick up a silver dollar; but here are golden words, which the wisest men of antiquity have uttered, and whose worth the wise of every succeeding age have assured us of;—and yet we learn to read only as far as Easy Reading, the primers and class-books, and when we leave school, the "Little Reading," and story-books, which are for boys and beginners; and our reading, our conversation and thinking, are all on a very low level, worthy only of pygmies and manikins.

I aspire to be acquainted with wiser men than this our Concord soil has produced, whose names are hardly known here. Or shall I hear the name of Plato and never read his book? As if Plato were my townsman and I never saw him, — my next neighbour and I never heard him speak or attended to the wisdom of his words. But how actually is it? His Dialogues, which contain what was immortal in him, lie on the next shelf, and yet I never read them. We are under-bred and low-lived and illiterate; and in this respect I confess I do not make any very broad distinction between the illiterateness of my townsman who cannot read at all, and the illiterateness of him who has learned to read only what is for children and feeble intellects. We should be as good as the worthies of antiquity, but partly by first knowing how good they were. We are a race of tit-men, and soar but little higher in our intellectual flights than the columns of the daily paper.

It is not all books that are as dull as their readers. There are probably words addressed to our condition exactly, which, if we could really hear and understand, would be more salutary than the morning or the spring to our lives, and possibly put a new aspect on the face of things for us. How many a man has dated a new era in his life from the reading of a book! The book exists for us perchance which will explain our miracles and reveal new ones. The at present unutterable things we may find somewhere uttered. These same questions that disturb and puzzle and confound us have in their turn occurred to all the wise men; not one has been omitted; and each has answered them, according to his ability, by his words and his life. Moreover, with wisdom we shall learn liberality. The solitary hired man on a farm in the outskirts of Concord, who has had his second birth and peculiar religious experience, and is driven as he believes into the silent gravity and exclusiveness by his faith, may think it is not true; but Zoroaster, thousands of years ago, travelled the same road and had the same experience; but he, being wise, knew it to be universal, and treated his neighbours accordingly, and is even said to have invented and established worship among men. Let him humbly commune with Zoroaster then, and, through the liberalizing influence of all the worthies, with Jesus Christ himself, and let "our church" go by the board.

We boast that we belong to the Nineteenth Century and are making the most rapid strides of any nation. But consider how little this village does for its own culture. I do not wish to flatter my townsmen, nor to be flattered by them, for that will not advance either of us. We need to be provoked — goaded like oxen, as we are, into a trot. We have a comparatively decent system of common schools, schools for infants only; but excepting the half-starved Lyceum in the winter, and latterly the puny beginning of a library suggested by the State, no school for ourselves. We spend more on almost any article of bodily aliment or ailment than on our mental aliment. It is time that we had uncommon schools, that we did not leave off our education when we begin to be men and women. It is time that villages were universities, and their elder inhabitants the fellows of universities, with leisure — if they are, indeed, so well off — to pursue liberal studies the rest of their lives. Shall the world be confined to one Paris or one Oxford forever? Cannot students be boarded here and get a liberal education under the skies of Concord? Can we not hire some Abelard to lecture to us? Alas! What with foddering the cattle and tending the store, we are kept from school too long, and our education is sadly neglected. In this country, the village should in some respects take the place of the nobleman of Europe. It should be the patron of the fine arts. It is rich enough. It wants only the magnanimity and refinement. It can spend money enough on such things as farmers and traders value, but it is thought Utopian to propose spending money for things which more intelligent men know to be of far more worth. This town has spent seventeen thousand dollars on a town-house, thank fortune or politics, but probably it will not spend so much on living wit, the true meat to put into that shell, in a hundred years. The one hundred and twenty-five dollars annually subscribed for a Lyceum in the winter is better spent than any other equal sum raised in the town. If we live in the Nineteenth Century, why should we not enjoy the advantages which the Nineteenth Century offers? Why should our life be in any respect provincial? If we will read newspapers, why not skip the gossip of Boston and take the best newspaper in the world at once? — not be sucking the pap of "neutral family" papers, or browsing "Olive Branches" here in New England. Let the reports of all the learned societies come to us, and we will see if they know anything. Why should we leave it to Harper & Brothers and Redding & Co. to select our reading? As the nobleman of cultivated taste surrounds himself with whatever conduces to his culture — genius — learning — wit — books — paintings — statuary — music — philosophical instruments, and the like; so let the village do — not stop short at a pedagogue, a parson, a sexton, a parish library, and three selectmen, because our Pilgrim forefathers got through a cold winter once on a bleak rock with these. To act collectively is according to the spirit of our institutions; and I am confident that, as our circumstances are more flourishing, our means are greater than the nobleman's. New England can hire all the wise men in the world to come and teach her, and board them round the while, and not be provincial at all. That is the uncommon school we want. Instead of noblemen, let us have noble villages of men. If it is necessary, omit one bridge over the river, go round a little there, and throw one arch at least over the darker gulf of ignorance which surrounds us.

4
Sounds

But while we are confined to books, though the most select and classic, and read only particular written languages, which are themselves but dialects and provincial, we are in danger of forgetting the language which all things and events speak without metaphor, which alone is copious and standard. Much is published, but little printed. The rays which stream through the shutter will be no longer remembered when the shutter is wholly removed. No method nor discipline can supersede the necessity of being forever on the alert. What is a course of history or philosophy, or poetry, no matter how well selected, or the best society, or the most admirable routine of life, compared with the discipline of looking always at what is to be seen? Will you be a reader, a student merely, or a seer? Read your fate, see what is before you, and walk on into futurity.

I did not read books the first summer; I hoed beans. Nay, I often did better than this. There were times when I could not afford to sacrifice the bloom of the present moment to any work, whether of the head or hands. I love a broad margin to my life. Sometimes, in a summer morning, having taken my accustomed bath, I sat in my sunny doorway from sunrise till noon, rapt in a revery, amidst the pines and hickories and sumachs, in undisturbed solitude and stillness, while the birds sing around or flitted noiseless through the house, until by the sun falling in at my west window, or the noise of some traveller's wagon on the distant highway, I was reminded of the lapse of time. I grew in those seasons like corn in the night, and they were far better than any work of the hands would have been. They were not time subtracted from my life, but so much over and above my usual allowance. I realized what the Orientals mean by contemplation and the forsaking of works. For the most part, I minded not how the hours went. The day advanced as if to light some work of mine; it was morning, and lo, now it is evening, and nothing memorable is accomplished. Instead of singing like the birds, I silently smiled at my incessant good fortune. As the sparrow had its trill, sitting on the hickory before my door, so had I my chuckle or suppressed warble which he might hear out of my nest. My days were not days of the week, bearing the stamp of any heathen deity, nor were they minced into hours and fretted by the ticking of a clock; for I lived like the Puri Indians, of whom it is said that "for yesterday, today, and tomorrow they have only one word, and they express the variety of meaning by pointing backward for yesterday forward for tomorrow, and overhead for the passing day." This was sheer idleness to my fellow-townsmen, no doubt; but if the birds and flowers had tried me by their standard, I should not have been found wanting. A man must find his occasions in himself, it is true. The natural day is very calm, and will hardly reprove his indolence.

I had this advantage, at least, in my mode of life, over those who were obliged to look abroad for amusement, to society and the theatre, that my life itself has become my amusement and never ceased to be novel. It was a drama of many scenes and without an end. If we were always, indeed, getting our living, and regulating our lives according to the last and best mode we had learned, we should never be troubled with ennui. Follow your genius closely enough, and it will not fail to show you a fresh prospect every hour. Housework was a pleasant pastime. When my floor was dirty, I rose early, and, setting all my furniture out of doors on the grass, bed and bedstead making but one budget, dashed water on the floor, and sprinkled white sand from the pond on it, and then with a broom scrubbed it clean and white; and by the time the villagers had broken their fast the morning sun had dried my house sufficiently to allow me to move in again, and my meditations were almost uninterupted. It was pleasant to see my whole household effects out on the

grass, making a little pile like a gypsy's pack, and my three-legged table, from which I did not remove the books and pen and ink, standing amid the pines and hickories. They seemed glad to get out themselves, and as if unwilling to be brought in. I was sometimes tempted to stretch an awning over them and take my seat there. It was worth the while to see the sun shine on these things, and hear the free wind blow on them; so much more interesting most familiar objects look out of doors than in the house. A bird sits on the next bough, life-everlasting grows under the table, and blackberry vines run round its legs; pine cones, chestnut burs, and strawberry leaves are strewn about. It looked as if this was the way these forms came to be transferred to our furniture, to tables, chairs, and bedsteads — because they once stood in their midst.

My house was on the side of a hill, immediately on the edge of the larger wood, in the midst of a young forest of pitch pines and hickories, and half a dozen rods from the pond, to which a narrow footpath led down the hill. In my front yard grew the strawberry, blackberry, and life-everlasting, johnswort and goldenrod, shrub oaks and sand cherry, blueberry and groundnut. Near the end of May, the sand cherry (Cerasus pumila) adorned the sides of the path with its delicate flowers arranged in umbels cylindrically about its short stems, which last, in the fall, weighed down with goodsized and handsome cherries, fell over in wreaths like rays on every side. I tasted them out of compliment to Nature, though they were scarcely palatable. The sumach (Rhus glabra) grew luxuriantly about the house, pushing up through the embankment which I had made, and growing five or six feet the first season. Its broad pinnate tropical

leaf was pleasant though strange to look on. The large buds, suddenly pushing out late in the spring from dry sticks which had seemed to be dead, developed themselves as by magic into graceful green and tender boughs, an inch in diameter; and sometimes, as I sat at my window, so heedlessly did they grow and tax their weak joints, I heard a fresh and tender bough suddenly fall like a fan to the ground, when there was not a breath of air stirring, broken off by its own weight. In August, the large masses of berries, which, when in flower, had attracted many wild bees, gradually assumed their bright velvety crimson hue, and by their weight again bent down and broke the tender limbs.

As I sit at my window this summer afternoon, hawks are circling about my clearing; the tantivy of wild pigeons, flying by two and threes athwart my view, or perching restless on the white pine boughs behind my house, gives a voice to the air; a fish hawk dimples the glassy surface of the pond and brings up a fish; a mink steals out of the marsh before my door and seizes a frog by the shore; the sedge is bending under the weight of the reed-birds flitting hither and thither; and for the last half-hour I have heard the rattle of railroad cars, now dying away and then reviving like the beat of a partridge, conveying travellers from Boston to the country. For I did not live so out of the world as that boy who, as I hear, was put out to a farmer in the east part of the town, but ere long ran away and came home again, quite down at the heel and homesick. He had never seen such a dull and out-of-the-way place; the folks were all gone off; why, you couldn't even hear the whistle! I doubt if there is such a place in Massachusetts now:—

> "In truth, our village has become a butt
> For one of those fleet railroad shafts, and o'er
> Our peaceful plain its soothing sound is — Concord."

The Fitchburg Railroad touches the pond about a hundred rods south of where I dwell. I usually go to the village along its causeway, and am, as it were, related to society by this link. The men on the freight trains, who go over the whole length of the road, bow to me as to an old acquaintance, they pass me so often, and apparently they take me for an employee; and so I am. I too would fain be a track-repairer somewhere in the orbit of the earth.

The whistle of the locomotive penetrates my woods summer and winter, sounding like the scream of a hawk sailing over some farmer's yard, informing me that many restless city merchants are arriving within the circle of the town, or adventurous country traders from the other side. As they come under one horizon, they shout their warning to get off the track to the other, heard sometimes through the circles of two towns. Here come your groceries, country; your rations, countrymen! Nor is there any man so independent on his farm that he can say them nay. And here's your pay for them! Screams the countryman's whistle; timber like long battering-rams going twenty miles an hour against the city's walls, and chairs enough to seat all the weary and heavy-laden that dwell within them. With such huge and lumbering civility the country hands a chair to the city. All the Indian huckleberry hills are stripped, all the cranberry meadows are raked into the city. Up comes the cotton, down goes the woven cloth; up comes the silk, down goes the woollen; up come the books, but down goes the wit that writes them.

When I meet the engine with its train of cars moving off with planetary motion — or, rather, like a comet, for the beholder knows not if with that velocity and with that direction it will ever revisit this system, since its orbit does not look like a returning curve — with its steam cloud like a banner streaming behind in golden and silver wreaths, like many a downy cloud which I have seen, high in the heavens, unfolding its masses to the light — as if this traveling demigod, this cloud-compeller, would ere long take the sunset sky for the livery of his train; when I hear the iron horse make the hills echo with his snort like thunder, shaking the earth with his feet, and breathing fire and smoke from his nostrils (what kind of winged horse or fiery dragon they will put into the new Mythology I don't know), it seems as if the earth had got a race now worthy to inhabit it. If all were as it seems, and men made the elements their servants for noble ends! If the cloud that hangs over the engine were the perspiration of heroic deeds, or as beneficent as that which floats over the farmer's fields, then the elements and Nature herself would cheerfully accompany men on their errands and be their escort.

I watch the passage of the morning cars with the same feeling that I do the rising of the sun, which is hardly more regular. Their train of clouds stretching far behind and rising higher and higher, going to heaven while the cars are going to Boston, conceals the sun for a minute and casts my distant field into the shade, a celestial train beside which the petty train of cars which hugs the earth is but the barb of the spear. The stabler of the iron horse was up early this winter morning by the light of the stars amid the mountains, to fodder and harness his steed. Fire, too, was awakened thus early to put the vital heat in him and get him off. If the enterprise were as innocent as it is early! If the snow lies deep, they strap on his snowshoes, and, with the giant plough, plough a furrow from the mountains to the seaboard, in which the cars, like a following drill-barrow, sprinkle all the restless men and floating merchandise in the country for seed. All day the fire-steed flies over the country, stopping only that his master may rest, and I am awakened by his tramp and defiant snort at midnight, when in some remote glen in the woods he fronts the elements incased in ice and snow; and he will reach his stall only with the morning star, to start once more on his travels without rest or slumber. Or perchance, at evening, I hear him in his stable blowing off the superfluous energy of the day, that he may calm his nerves and cool his liver and brain for a few hours of iron slumber. If the enterprise were as heroic and commanding as it is protracted and unwearied!

Far through unfrequented woods on the confines of towns, where once only the hunter penetrated by day, in the darkest night dart these bright saloons without the knowledge of their inhabitants; this moment stopping at some brilliant station-house in town or city, where a social crowd is gathered, the next in the Dismal Swamp, scaring the owl and fox. The startings and arrivals of the cars are now the epochs in the village day. They go and come with such regularity and precision, and their whistle can be heard so far, that the farmers set their clocks by them, and thus one well-conducted institution regulates a whole country. Have not men improved somewhat in punctuality since the railroad was invented? Do they not talk and think faster in the depot than they did in the stage-office? There is something electrifying in the atmosphere of the former place. I have been astonished at the miracles it has wrought; that some of my neighbours, who, I should have prophesied, once for all, would never get to Boston by so prompt a conveyance, are on hand when the bell rings. To do things "railroad fashion" is now the byword; and it is worth the while to be warned so often and so sincerely by any power to get off its track. There is no stopping to read the riot act, no firing over the heads of the mob, in this case. We have constructed a fate, an Atropos, that never turns aside. (Let that be the name of your engine.) Men are advertised that at a certain hour and minute these bolts will be shot toward particular points of the compass; yet it interferes with no man's business, and the children go to school on the other track. We live the steadier for it. We are all educated thus to be sons of Tell. The air is full of invisible bolts. Every path but your own is the path of fate. Keep on your own track, then.

What recommends commerce to me is its enterprise and bravery. It does not clasp its hands and pray to Jupiter. I see these men every day go about their business with more or less courage and content, doing more even than they suspect, and perchance better employed than they could have consciously devised. I am less affected by their heroism who stood up for half an hour in the front line at Buena Vista, than by the steady and cheerful valour of the men who inhabit the snowplough for their winter quarters; who have not merely the three-o'-clock-in-the-morning courage, which Bonaparte thought was the rarest, but whose courage does not go to rest so early, who go to sleep only when the storm sleeps or the sinews of their iron steed are frozen. On this morning of the Great Snow, perchance, which is still raging and chilling men's blood, I hear the muffled tone of their engine bell from out the fog bank of their chilled breath, which announces that the cars are coming, without long delay, notwithstanding the veto of a New England northeast snow-storm, and I behold the ploughmen covered with snow and rime, their heads peering, above the mould-board which is turning down other than daisies and the nests of field mice, like bowlders of the Sierra Nevada, that occupy an outside place in the universe.

Commerce is unexpectedly confident and serene, alert, adventurous, and unwearied. It is very natural in its methods withal, far more so than many fantastic enterprises and sentimental experiments, and hence its singular success. I am refreshed and expanded when the freight train rattles past me, and I smell the stores which go dispensing their odours all the way from Long Wharf to Lake Champlain, reminding me of foreign parts, of coral reefs, and Indian oceans, and tropical climes, and the extent of the globe. I feel more like a citizen of the world at the sight of the palm-leaf which will cover so many flaxen New England heads the next summer, the Manilla hemp and cocoanut husks, the old junk, gunny bags, scrap iron, and rusty nails. This carload of torn sails is more legible and interesting now than if they should be wrought into paper and printed books. Who can write so graphically the history of the storms they have weathered as these rents have done? They are proof-sheets which need no correction. Here goes lumber from the Maine woods, which did not go out to sea in the last freshet, risen four dollars on the thousand because of what did go out or was split up; pine, spruce, cedar

— first, second, third, and fourth qualities, so lately all of one quality, to wave over the bear, and moose, and caribou. Next rolls Thomaston lime, a prime lot, which will get far among the hills before it gets slacked. These rags in bales, of all hues and qualities, the lowest condition to which cotton and linen descend, the final result of dress — of patterns which are now no longer cried up, unless it be in Milwaukee, as those splendid articles, English, French, or American prints, ginghams, muslins, etc., gathered from all quarters both of fashion and poverty, going to become paper of one colour or a few shades only, on which, forsooth, will be written tales of real life, high and low, and founded on fact! This closed car smells of salt fish, the strong New England and commercial scent, reminding me of the Grand Banks and the fisheries. Who has not seen a salt fish, thoroughly cured for this world, so that nothing can spoil it, and putting, the perseverance of the saints to the blush? With which you may sweep or pave the streets, and split your kindlings, and the teamster shelter himself and his lading against sun, wind, and rain behind it — and the trader, as a Concord trader once did, hang it up by his door for a sign when he commences business, until at last his oldest customer cannot tell surely whether it be animal, vegetable, or mineral, and yet it shall be as pure as a snowflake, and if it be put into a pot and boiled, will come out an excellent dun-fish for a Saturday's dinner. Next Spanish hides, with the tails still preserving their twist and the angle of elevation they had when the oxen that wore them were careering over the pampas of the Spanish Main — a type of all obstinacy, and evincing how almost hopeless and incurable are all constitutional vices. I confess, that practically speaking, when I have learned a man's real disposition, I have no hopes of changing it for the better or worse in this state of existence. As the Orientals say, "A cur's tail may be warmed, and pressed, and bound round with ligatures, and after a twelve years' labour bestowed upon it, still it will retain its natural form." The only effectual cure for such inveteracies as these tails exhibit is to make glue of them, which I believe is what is usually done with them, and then they will stay put and stick. Here is a hogshead of molasses or of brandy directed to John Smith, Cuttingsville, Vermont, some trader among the Green Mountains, who imports for the farmers near his clearing, and now perchance stands over his bulkhead and thinks of the last arrivals on the coast, how they may affect the price for him, telling his customers this moment, as he has told them twenty times before this morning, that he expects some by the next train of prime quality. It is advertised in the Cuttingsville Times.

While these things go up other things come down. Warned by the whizzing sound, I look up from my book and see some tall pine, hewn on far northern hills, which has winged its way over the Green Mountains and the Connecticut, shot like an arrow through the township within ten minutes, and scarce another eye beholds it; going

"to be the mast
Of some great ammiral."

And hark! Here comes the cattle-train bearing the cattle of a thousand hills, sheepcots, stables, and cow-yards in the air, drovers with their sticks, and shepherd boys in the midst of their flocks, all but the mountain pastures, whirled along like leaves blown from the mountains by the September gales. The air is filled with the bleating of calves and sheep, and the hustling of oxen, as if a pastoral valley were going by. When the old bell-wether at the head rattles his bell, the mountains do indeed skip like rams and the little hills like lambs. A carload of drovers, too, in the midst, on a level with their droves now, their vocation gone, but still clinging to their useless sticks as their badge of office. But their dogs, where are they? It is a stampede to them; they are quite thrown out; they have lost the scent. Methinks I hear them barking behind the Peterboro' Hills, or panting up the western slope of the Green Mountains. They will not be in at the death. Their vocation, too, is gone. Their fidelity and sagacity are below par now. They will slink back to their kennels in disgrace, or perchance run wild and strike a league with the wolf and the fox. So is your pastoral life whirled past and away. But the bell rings, and I must get off the track and let the cars go by;—

What's the railroad to me?
I never go to see
Where it ends.
It fills a few hollows,
And makes banks for the swallows,
It sets the sand a-blowing,
And the blackberries a-growing,

but I cross it like a cart-path in the woods. I will not have my eyes put out and my ears spoiled by its smoke and steam and hissing.

Now that the cars are gone by and all the restless world with them, and the fishes in the pond no longer feel their rumbling, I am more alone than ever. For the rest of the long afternoon, perhaps, my meditations are interrupted only by the faint rattle of a carriage or team along the distant highway.

Sometimes, on Sundays, I heard the bells, the Lincoln, Acton, Bedford, or Concord bell, when the wind was favourable, a faint, sweet, and, as it were, natural melody, worth importing into the wilderness. At a sufficient distance over the woods this sound acquires a certain vibratory hum, as if the pine needles in the horizon were the strings of a harp which it swept. All sound heard at the greatest possible distance produces one and the same effect, a vibration of the universal lyre, just as the intervening atmosphere makes a distant ridge of earth interesting to our eyes by the azure tint it imparts to it. There came to me in this case a melody which the air had strained, and which had conversed with every leaf and needle of the wood, that portion of the sound which the elements had taken up and modulated and echoed from vale to vale. The echo is, to some extent, an original sound, and therein is the magic and charm of it. It is not merely a repetition of what was worth repeating in the bell, but partly the voice of the wood; the same trivial words and notes sung by a wood-nymph.

At evening, the distant lowing of some cow in the horizon beyond the woods sounded sweet and melodious, and at first I would mistake it for the voices of certain minstrels by whom I was sometimes serenaded, who might be straying over hill and dale; but soon I was not unpleasantly disappointed when it was prolonged into the cheap and natural music of the cow. I do not mean to be satirical, but to express my appreciation of those youths' singing, when I state that I perceived clearly that it was akin to the music of the cow, and they were at length one articulation of Nature.

Regularly at half-past seven, in one part of the summer, after the evening train had gone by, the whip-poor-wills chanted their vespers for half an hour, sitting on a stump by my door, or upon the ridge-pole of the house. They would begin to sing almost with as much precision as a clock, within five minutes of a particular time, referred to the setting of the sun, every evening. I had a rare opportunity to become acquainted with their habits. Sometimes I heard four or five at once in different parts of the wood, by accident one a bar behind another, and so near me that I distinguished not only the cluck after each note, but often that singular buzzing sound like a fly in a spider's web, only proportionally louder. Sometimes one would circle round and round me in the woods a few feet distant as if tethered by a string, when probably I was near its eggs. They sang at intervals throughout the night, and were again as musical as ever just before and about dawn.

When other birds are still, the screech owls take up the strain, like mourning women their ancient u-lu-lu. Their dismal scream is truly Ben Jonsonian. Wise midnight hags! It is no honest and blunt tu-whit tu-who of the poets, but, without jesting, a most solemn graveyard ditty, the mutual consolations of suicide lovers remembering the pangs and the delights of supernal love in the infernal groves. Yet I love to hear their wailing, their doleful responses, trilled along the woodside; reminding me sometimes of music and singing birds; as if it were the dark and tearful side of music, the regrets and sighs that would fain be sung. They are the spirits, the low spirits and melancholy forebodings, of fallen souls that once in human shape night-walked the earth and did the deeds of darkness, now expiating their sins with their wailing hymns or threnodies in the scenery of their transgressions. They give me a new sense of the variety and capacity of that nature which is our common dwelling. Oh-o-o-o-o that I never had been bor-r-r-r-n! sighs one on this side of the pond, and circles with the restlessness of despair to some new perch on the gray oaks. Then — that I never had been bor-r-r-r-n! echoes another on the farther side with tremulous sincerity, and — bor-r-r-r-n! comes faintly from far in the Lincoln woods.

I was also serenaded by a hooting owl. Near at hand you could fancy it the most melancholy sound in Nature, as if she meant by this to stereotype and make permanent in her choir the dying moans of a human being — some poor weak relic of mortality who has left hope behind, and howls like an animal, yet with human sobs, on entering the dark valley, made more awful by a certain gurgling melodiousness — I find myself beginning with the letters gl when I try to imitate it — expressive of a mind which has reached the gelatinous, mildewy stage in the mortification of all healthy and courageous thought. It reminded me of ghouls and idiots and insane howlings. But now one answers from far woods in a strain made really melodious by distance — Hoo hoo hoo, hoorer hoo; and indeed for the most part it suggested only pleasing associations, whether heard by day or night, summer or winter.

I rejoice that there are owls. Let them do the idiotic and maniacal hooting for men. It is a sound admirably suited to swamps and twilight woods which no day illustrates, suggesting a vast and undeveloped nature which men have not recognized. They represent the stark twilight and unsatisfied thoughts which all have. All day the sun has shone on the surface of some savage swamp, where the single spruce stands hung with usnea lichens, and small hawks circulate above, and the chickadee lisps amid the evergreens, and the partridge and rabbit skulk beneath; but now a more dismal and fitting day dawns, and a different race of creatures awakes to express the meaning of Nature there.

Late in the evening I heard the distant rumbling of wagons over bridges — a sound heard farther than almost any other at night — the baying of dogs, and sometimes again the lowing of some disconsolate cow in a distant barnyard. In the meanwhile all the shore rang with the trump of bullfrogs, the sturdy spirits of ancient wine-bibbers and wassailers, still unrepentant, trying to sing a catch in their Stygian lake — if the Walden nymphs will pardon the comparison, for though there are almost no weeds, there are frogs there — who would fain keep up the hilarious rules of their old festal tables, though their voices have waxed hoarse and solemnly grave, mocking at mirth, and the wine has lost its flavour, and become only liquor to distend their paunches, and sweet intoxication never comes to drown the memory of the past, but mere saturation and waterloggedness and distention. The most aldermanic, with his chin upon a heart-leaf, which serves for a napkin to his drooling chaps, under this northern shore quaffs a deep draught of the once scorned water, And passes round the cup with the ejaculation tr-r-r-oonk, tr-r-r—oonk, tr-r-r-oonk! and straightway comes over the water from some distant cove the same password repeated, where the next in seniority and girth has gulped down to his mark; and when this observance has made the circuit of the shores, then ejaculates the master of ceremonies, with satisfaction, tr-r-r-oonk! And each in his turn repeats the same down to the least distended, leakiest, and flabbiest paunched, that there be no mistake; and then the howl goes round again and again, until the sun disperses the morning mist, and only the patriarch is not under the pond, but vainly bellowing troonk from time to time, and pausing for a reply.

I am not sure that I ever heard the sound of cock-crowing from my clearing, and I thought that it might be worth the while to keep a cockerel for his music merely, as a singing bird. The note of this once wild Indian pheasant is certainly the most remarkable of any bird's, and if they could be naturalized without being domesticated, it would soon become the most famous sound in our woods, surpassing the clangor of the goose and the hooting of the owl; and then imagine the cackling of the hens to fill the pauses when their lords' clarions rested! No wonder that man added this bird to his tame stock — to say nothing of the eggs and drumsticks. To walk in a winter morning in a wood where these birds abounded, their native woods, and hear the wild cockerels crow on the trees, clear and shrill for miles over the resounding earth, drowning the feebler notes of other birds — think of it! It would put nations on the alert. Who would not be early to rise, and rise earlier and earlier every successive day of his life, till he became unspeakably healthy, wealthy, and wise? This foreign bird's note is celebrated by the poets of all countries along with the notes of their native songsters. All climates agree with brave Chanticleer. He is more indigenous even than the natives. His health is ever good, his lungs are sound, his spirits never flag. Even the sailor on the Atlantic and Pacific is awakened by his voice; but its shrill sound never roused me from my slumbers. I kept neither dog, cat, cow, pig, nor hens, so that you would have said there was a deficiency of domestic sounds; neither the churn, nor the spinning-wheel, nor even the singing of the kettle, nor the hissing of the urn, nor children crying, to comfort one. An old-fashioned man would have lost his senses or died of ennui before this. Not even rats in the wall, for they were starved out, or rather were never baited in — only squirrels on the roof and under the floor, a whip-poor-will on the ridge-pole, a blue jay screaming beneath the window, a hare or woodchuck under the house, a screech owl or a cat owl behind it, a flock of wild geese or a laughing loon on the pond, and a fox to bark in the night. Not even a lark or an oriole, those mild plantation birds, ever visited my clearing. No cockerels to crow nor hens to cackle in the yard. No yard! But unfenced nature reaching up to your very sills. A young forest growing up under your meadows, and wild sumachs and blackberry vines breaking through into your cellar; sturdy pitch pines rubbing and creaking against the shingles for want of room, their roots reaching quite under the house. Instead of a scuttle or a blind blown off in the gale — a pine tree snapped off or torn up by the roots behind your house for fuel. Instead of no path to the front-yard gate in the Great Snow — no gate — no front-yard — and no path to the civilized world.

5
Solitude

This is a delicious evening, when the whole body is one sense, and imbibes delight through every pore. I go and come with a strange liberty in Nature, a part of herself. As I walk along the stony shore of the pond in my shirt-sleeves, though it is cool as well as cloudy and windy, and I see nothing special to attract me, all the elements are unusually congenial to me. The bullfrogs trump to usher in the night, and the note of the whip-poor-will is borne on the rippling wind from over the water. Sympathy with the fluttering alder and poplar leaves almost takes away my breath; yet, like the lake, my serenity is rippled but not ruffled. These small waves raised by the evening wind are as remote from storm as the smooth reflecting surface. Though it is now dark, the wind still blows and roars in the wood, the waves still dash, and some creatures lull the rest with their notes. The repose is never complete. The wildest animals do not repose, but seek their prey now; the fox, and skunk, and rabbit, now roam the fields and woods without fear. They are Nature's watchmen — links which connect the days of animated life.

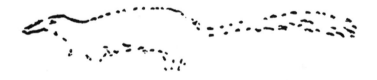

When I return to my house I find that visitors have been there and left their cards, either a bunch of flowers, or a wreath of evergreen, or a name in pencil on a yellow walnut leaf or a chip. They who come rarely to the woods take some little piece of the forest into their hands to play with by the way, which they leave, either intentionally or accidentally. One has peeled a willow wand, woven it into a ring, and dropped it on my table. I could always tell if visitors had called in my absence, either by the bended twigs or grass, or the print of their shoes, and generally of what sex or age or quality they were by some slight trace left, as a flower dropped, or a bunch of grass plucked and thrown away, even as far off as the railroad, half a mile distant, or by the lingering odour of a cigar or pipe. Nay, I was frequently notified of the passage of a traveller along the highway sixty rods off by the scent of his pipe.

There is commonly sufficient space about us. Our horizon is never quite at our elbows. The thick wood is not just at our door, nor the pond, but somewhat is always clearing, familiar and worn by us, appropriated and fenced in some way, and reclaimed from Nature. For what reason have I this vast range and circuit, some square miles of unfrequented forest, for my privacy, abandoned to me by men? My nearest neighbour is a mile distant, and no house is visible from any place but the hill-tops within half a mile of my own. I have my horizon bounded by woods all to myself; a distant view of the railroad where it touches the pond on the one hand, and of the fence which skirts the woodland road on the other. But for the most part it is as solitary where I live as on the prairies. It is as much Asia or Africa as New England. I have, as it were, my own sun and moon and stars, and a little world all to myself. At night there was never a traveller passed my house, or knocked at my door, more than if I were the first or last man; unless it were in the spring, when at long intervals some came from the village to fish for pouts — they plainly fished much more in the Walden Pond of their own natures, and baited their hooks with darkness — but they soon retreated, usually with light baskets, and left "the world to darkness and to me," and the black kernel of the night was never profaned by any human neighbourhood. I believe that men are generally still a little afraid of the dark, though the witches are all hung, and Christianity and candles have been introduced.

Yet I experienced sometimes that the most sweet and tender, the most innocent and encouraging society may be found in any natural object, even for the poor misanthrope and most melancholy man. There can be no very black melancholy to him who lives in the midst of Nature and has his senses still. There was never yet such a storm but it was AEolian music to a healthy and innocent ear. Nothing can rightly compel a simple and brave man to a vulgar sadness. While I enjoy the friendship of the seasons I trust that nothing can make life a burden to me. The gentle rain which waters my beans and keeps me in the house today is not drear and melancholy, but good for me too. Though it prevents my hoeing them, it is of far more worth than my hoeing. If it should continue so long as to cause the seeds to rot in the ground and destroy the potatoes in the low lands, it would still be good for the grass on the uplands, and, being good for the grass, it would be good for me. Sometimes, when I compare myself with other men, it seems as if I were more favoured by the gods than they, beyond any deserts that I am conscious of; as if I had a warrant and surety at their hands which my fellows have not, and were especially guided and guarded. I do not flatter myself, but if it be possible they flatter me. I have never felt lonesome, or in the least oppressed by a sense of solitude, but once, and that was a few weeks after I came to the woods, when, for an hour, I doubted if the near neighbourhood of man was not essential to a serene and healthy life. To be alone was something unpleasant. But I was at the same time conscious of a slight insanity in my mood, and seemed to foresee my recovery. In the midst of a gentle rain while these thoughts prevailed, I was suddenly sensible of such sweet and beneficent society in Nature, in the very pattering of the drops, and in every sound and sight around my house, an infinite and unaccountable friendliness all at once like an atmosphere sustaining me, as made the fancied advantages of human neighbourhood insignificant, and I have never thought of them since. Every little pine needle expanded and swelled with sympathy and befriended me. I was so distinctly made aware of the presence of something kindred to me, even in scenes which

we are accustomed to call wild and dreary, and also that the nearest of blood to me and humanest was not a person nor a villager, that I thought no place could ever be strange to me again.

> "Mourning untimely consumes the sad;
> Few are their days in the land of the living,
> Beautiful daughter of Toscar."

Some of my pleasantest hours were during the long rain-storms in the spring or fall, which confined me to the house for the afternoon as well as the forenoon, soothed by their ceaseless roar and pelting; when an early twilight ushered in a long evening in which many thoughts had time to take root and unfold themselves. In those driving northeast rains which tried the village houses so, when the maids stood ready with mop and pail in front entries to keep the deluge out, I sat behind my door in my little house, which was all entry, and thoroughly enjoyed its protection. In one heavy thunder-shower the lightning struck a large pitch pine across the pond, making a very conspicuous and perfectly regular spiral groove from top to bottom, an inch or more deep, and four or five inches wide, as you would groove a walking-stick. I passed it again the other day, and was struck with awe on looking up and beholding that mark, now more distinct than ever, where a terrific and resistless bolt came down out of the harmless sky eight years ago. Men frequently say to me, "I should think you would feel lonesome down there, and want to be nearer to folks, rainy and snowy days and nights especially." I am tempted to reply to such — This whole earth which we inhabit is but a point in space. How far apart, think you, dwell the two most distant inhabitants of yonder star, the breadth of whose disk cannot be appreciated by our instruments? Why should I feel lonely? Is not our planet in the Milky Way? This which you put seems to me not to be the most important question. What sort of space is that which separates a man from his fellows and makes him solitary? I have found that no exertion of the legs can bring two minds much nearer to one another. What do we want most to dwell near to? Not to many men surely, the depot, the post-office, the bar-room, the meeting-house, the school-house, the grocery, Beacon Hill, or the Five Points, where men most congregate, but to the perennial source of our life, whence in all our experience we have found that to issue, as the willow stands near the water and sends out its roots in that direction.

This will vary with different natures, but this is the place where a wise man will dig his cellar.... I one evening overtook one of my townsmen, who has accumulated what is called "a handsome property" — though I never got a fair view of it — on the Walden road, driving a pair of cattle to market, who inquired of me how I could bring my mind to give up so many of the comforts of life. I answered that I was very sure I liked it passably well; I was not joking. And so I went home to my bed, and left him to pick his way through the darkness and the mud to Brighton — or Bright-town — which place he would reach some time in the morning.

Any prospect of awakening or coming to life to a dead man makes indifferent all times and places. The place where that may occur is always the same, and indescribably pleasant to all our senses. For the most part we allow only outlying and transient circumstances to make our occasions. They are, in fact, the cause of our distraction. Nearest to all things is that power which fashions their being. Next to us the grandest laws are continually being executed. Next to us is not the workman whom we have hired, with whom we love so well to talk, but the workman whose work we are.

"How vast and profound is the influence of the subtile powers of Heaven and of Earth!"

"We seek to perceive them, and we do not see them; we seek to hear them, and we do not hear them; identified with the substance of things, they cannot be separated from them."

"They cause that in all the universe men purify and sanctify their hearts, and clothe themselves in their holiday garments to offer sacrifices and oblations to their ancestors. It is an ocean of subtile intelligences. They are everywhere, above us, on our left, on our right; they environ us on all sides."

We are the subjects of an experiment which is not a little interesting to me. Can we not do without the society of our gossips a little while under these circumstances — have our own thoughts to cheer us? Confucius says truly, "Virtue does not remain as an abandoned orphan; it must of necessity have neighbours."

With thinking we may be beside ourselves in a sane sense. By a conscious effort of the mind we can stand aloof from actions and their consequences; and all things, good and bad, go by us like a torrent. We are not wholly involved in Nature. I may be either the driftwood in the stream, or Indra in the sky looking down on it. I may be affected by a theatrical exhibition; on the other hand, I may not be affected by an actual event which appears to concern me much more. I only know myself as a human entity; the scene, so to speak, of thoughts and affections; and am sensible of a certain doubleness by which I can stand as remote from myself as from another. However intense my experience, I am conscious of the presence and criticism of a part of me, which, as it were, is not a part of me, but spectator, sharing no experience, but taking note of it, and that is no more I than it is you. When the play, it may be the tragedy, of life is over, the spectator goes his way. It was a kind of fiction, a work of the imagination only, so far as he was concerned. This doubleness may easily make us poor neighbours and friends sometimes.

I find it wholesome to be alone the greater part of the time. To be in company, even with the best, is soon wearisome and dissipating. I love to be alone. I never found the companion that was so companionable as solitude. We are for the most part more lonely when we go abroad among men than when we stay in our chambers. A man thinking or working is always alone, let him be where he will. Solitude is not measured by the miles of space that intervene between a man and his fellows. The really diligent student in one of the crowded hives of Cambridge College is as solitary as a dervish in the desert. The farmer can work alone in the field or the woods all day, hoeing or chopping, and not feel lonesome, because he is employed; but when he comes home at night he cannot sit down in a room alone, at the mercy of his thoughts, but must be where he can "see the folks," and recreate, and, as he thinks, remunerate himself for his day's solitude; and hence he wonders how the student can sit alone in the house all night and most of the day without ennui and "the blues"; but he does not realize that the student, though in the house, is still at work in his field, and chopping in his woods, as the farmer in his, and in turn seeks the same recreation and society that the latter does, though it may be a more condensed form of it.

Society is commonly too cheap. We meet at very short intervals, not having had time to acquire any new value for each other. We meet at meals three times a day, and give each other a new taste of that old musty cheese that we are. We have had to agree on a certain set of rules, called etiquette and politeness, to make this frequent meeting tolerable and that we need not come to open war. We meet at the post-office, and at the sociable, and about the fireside every night; we live thick and are in each other's way, and stumble over one another, and I think that we thus lose some respect for one another. Certainly less frequency would suffice for all important and hearty communications. Consider the girls in a factory — never alone, hardly in their dreams. It would be better if there were but one inhabitant to a square mile, as where I live. The value of a man is not in his skin, that we should touch him.

I have heard of a man lost in the woods and dying of famine and exhaustion at the foot of a tree, whose loneliness was relieved by the grotesque visions with which, owing to bodily weakness, his diseased imagination surrounded him, and which he believed to be real. So also, owing to bodily and mental health and strength, we may be continually cheered by a like but more normal and natural society, and come to know that we are never alone.

I have a great deal of company in my house; especially in the morning, when nobody calls. Let me suggest a few comparisons, that someone may convey an idea of my situation. I am no more lonely than the loon in the pond that laughs so loud, or than Walden Pond itself. What company has that lonely lake, I pray? And yet it has not the blue devils, but the blue angels in it, in the azure tint of its waters. The sun is alone, except in thick weather, when there sometimes appear to be two, but one is a mock sun. God is alone — but the devil, he is far from being alone; he sees a great deal of company; he is legion. I am no more lonely than a single mullein or dandelion in a pasture, or a bean leaf, or sorrel, or a horse-fly, or a bumblebee. I am no more lonely than the Mill Brook, or a weathercock, or the north star, or the south wind, or an April shower, or a January thaw, or the first spider in a new house.

I have occasional visits in the long winter evenings, when the snow falls fast and the wind howls in the wood, from an old settler and original proprietor, who is reported to have dug Walden Pond, and stoned it, and fringed it with pine woods; who tells me stories of old time and of new eternity; and between us we manage to pass a cheerful evening with social mirth and pleasant views of things, even without apples or cider — a most wise and humorous friend, whom I love much, who keeps himself more secret than ever did Goffe or Whalley; and though he is thought to be dead, none can show where he is buried. An elderly dame, too, dwells in my neighbourhood, invisible to most persons, in whose odourous herb garden I love to stroll sometimes, gathering simples and listening to her fables; for she has a genius of unequalled fertility, and her memory runs back farther than mythology, and she can tell me the original of every fable, and on what fact every one is founded, for the incidents occurred when she was young. A ruddy and lusty old dame, who delights in all weathers and seasons, and is likely to outlive all her children yet.

The indescribable innocence and beneficence of Nature — of sun and wind and rain, of summer and winter — such health, such cheer, they afford forever! And such sympathy have they ever with our race, that all Nature would be affected, and the sun's brightness fade, and the winds would sigh humanely, and the clouds rain tears, and the woods shed their leaves and put on mourning in midsummer, if any man should ever for a just cause grieve. Shall I not have intelligence with the earth? Am I not partly leaves and vegetable mould myself?

What is the pill which will keep us well, serene, contented? Not my or thy great-grandfather's, but our great-grandmother Nature's universal, vegetable, botanic medicines, by which she has kept herself young always, outlived so many old Parrs in her day, and fed her health with their decaying fatness. For my panacea, instead of one of those quack vials of a mixture dipped from Acheron and the Dead Sea, which come out of those long shallow black-schooner looking wagons which we sometimes see made to carry bottles, let me have a draught of undiluted morning air. Morning air! If men will not drink of this at the fountainhead of the day, why, then, we must even bottle up some and sell it in the shops, for the benefit of those who have lost their subscription ticket to morning time in this world. But remember, it will not keep quite till noonday even in the coolest cellar, but drive out the stopples long ere that and follow westward the steps of Aurora. I am no worshipper of Hygeia, who was the daughter of that old herb-doctor AEsculapius, and who is represented on monuments holding a serpent in one hand, and in the other a cup out of which the serpent sometimes drinks; but rather of Hebe, cup-bearer to Jupiter, who was the daughter of Juno and wild lettuce, and who had the power of restoring gods and men to the vigour of youth. She was probably the only thoroughly sound-conditioned, healthy, and robust young lady that ever walked the globe, and wherever she came it was spring.

6
Visitors

I think that I love society as much as most, and am ready enough to fasten myself like a bloodsucker for the time to any full-blooded man that comes in my way. I am naturally no hermit, but might possibly sit out the sturdiest frequenter of the bar-room, if my business called me thither.

I had three chairs in my house; one for solitude, two for friendship, three for society. When visitors came in larger and unexpected numbers there was but the third chair for them all, but they generally economized the room by standing up. It is surprising how many great men and women a small house will contain. I have had twenty-five or thirty souls, with their bodies, at once under my roof, and yet we often parted without being aware that we had come very near to one another. Many of our houses, both public and private, with their almost innumerable apartments, their huge halls and their cellars for the storage of wines and other munitions of peace, appear to be extravagantly large for their inhabitants. They are so vast and magnificent that the latter seem to be only vermin which infest them. I am surprised when the herald blows his summons before some Tremont or Astor or Middlesex House, to see come creeping out over the piazza for all inhabitants a ridiculous mouse, which soon again slinks into some hole in the pavement.

One inconvenience I sometimes experienced in so small a house, the difficulty of getting to a sufficient distance from my guest when we began to utter the big thoughts in big words. You want room for your thoughts to get into sailing trim and run a course or two before they make their port. The bullet of your thought must have overcome its lateral and ricochet motion and fallen into its last and steady course before it reaches the ear of the hearer, else it may plough out again through the side of his head. Also, our sentences wanted room to unfold and form their columns in the interval. Individuals, like nations, must have suitable broad and natural boundaries, even a considerable neutral ground, between them. I have found it a singular luxury to talk across the pond to a companion on the opposite side. In my house we were so near that we could not begin to hear — we could not speak low enough to be heard; as when you throw two stones into calm water so near that they break each other's undulations. If we are merely loquacious and loud talkers, then we can afford to stand very near together, cheek by jowl, and feel each other's breath; but if we speak reservedly and thoughtfully, we want to be farther apart, that all animal heat and moisture may have a chance to evapourate. If we would enjoy the most intimate society with that in each of us which is without, or above, being spoken to, we must not only be silent, but commonly so far apart bodily that we cannot possibly hear each other's voice in any case. Referred to this standard, speech is for the convenience of those who are hard of hearing; but there are many fine things which we cannot say if we have to shout. As the conversation began to assume a loftier and grander tone, we gradually shoved our chairs farther apart till they touched the wall in opposite corners, and then commonly there was not room enough.

My "best" room, however, my withdrawing room, always ready for company, on whose carpet the sun rarely fell, was the pine wood behind my house. Thither in summer days, when distinguished guests came,

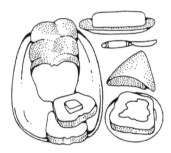

I took them, and a priceless domestic swept the floor and dusted the furniture and kept the things in order.

If one guest came he sometimes partook of my frugal meal, and it was no interruption to conversation to be stirring a hasty-pudding, or watching the rising and maturing of a loaf of bread in the ashes, in the meanwhile. But if twenty came and sat in my house there was nothing said about dinner, though there might be bread enough for two, more than if eating were a forsaken habit; but we naturally practised abstinence; and this was never felt to be an offence against hospitality, but the most proper and considerate course. The waste and decay of physical life, which so often needs repair, seemed miraculously retarded in such a case, and the vital vigour stood its ground. I could entertain thus a thousand as well as twenty; and if any ever went away disappointed or hungry from my house when they found me at home, they may depend upon it that I sympathized with them at least. So easy is it, though many housekeepers doubt it, to establish new and better customs in the place of the old. You need not rest your reputation on the dinners you give. For my own part, I was never so effectually deterred from frequenting a man's house, by any kind of Cerberus whatever, as by the parade one made about dining me, which I took to be a very polite and roundabout hint never to trouble him so again. I think I shall never revisit those scenes. I should be proud to have for the motto of my cabin those lines of Spenser which one of my visitors inscribed on a yellow walnut leaf for a card:—

> "Arrived there, the little house they fill,
> Ne looke for entertainment where none was;
> Rest is their feast, and all things at their will:
> The noblest mind the best contentment has."

When Winslow, afterward governor of the Plymouth Colony, went with a companion on a visit of ceremony to Massasoit on foot through the woods, and arrived tired and hungry at his lodge, they were well received by the king, but nothing was said about eating that day. When the night arrived, to quote their own words — "He laid us on the bed with himself and his wife, they at the one end and we at the other, it being only planks laid a foot from the ground and a thin mat upon them. Two more of his chief men, for want of room, pressed by and upon us; so that we were worse weary of our lodging than of our journey." At one o'clock the next day Massasoit "brought two fishes that he had shot," about thrice as big as a bream. "These being boiled, there were at least forty looked for a share in them; the most eat of them. This meal only we had in two nights and a day; and had not one of us bought a partridge, we had taken our journey fasting." Fearing that they would be light-headed for want of food and also sleep, owing to "the savages' barbarous singing, (for they use to sing themselves asleep,)" and that they might get home while they had strength to travel, they departed. As for lodging, it is true they were but poorly entertained, though what they found an inconvenience was no doubt intended for an honour; but as far as eating was concerned, I do not see how the Indians could have done better. They had nothing to eat themselves, and they were wiser than to think that apologies could supply the place of food to their guests; so they drew their belts tighter and said nothing about it. Another time when Winslow visited them, it being a season of plenty with them, there was no deficiency in this respect.

As for men, they will hardly fail one anywhere. I had more visitors while I lived in the woods than at any other period in my life; I mean that I had some. I met several there under more favourable circumstances than I could anywhere else. But fewer came to see me on trivial business. In this respect, my company was winnowed by my mere distance from town. I had withdrawn so far within the great ocean of solitude, into which the rivers of society empty, that for the most part, so far as my needs were concerned, only the finest sediment was deposited around me. Beside, there were wafted to me evidences of unexplored and uncultivated continents on the other side.

Who should come to my lodge this morning but a true Homeric or Paphlagonian man — he had so suitable and poetic a name that I am sorry I cannot print it here — a Canadian, a woodchopper and post-maker, who can hole fifty posts in a day, who made his last supper on a woodchuck which his dog caught. He, too, has heard of Homer, and, "if it were not for books," would "not know what to do rainy days," though perhaps he has not read one wholly through for many rainy seasons. Some priest who could pronounce the Greek itself taught him to read his verse in the Testament in his native parish far away; and now I must translate to him, while he holds the book, Achilles' reproof to Patroclus for his sad countenance. —

> "Why are you in tears, Patroclus, like a young girl?"
> "Or have you alone heard some news from Phthia?
> They say that Menoetius lives yet, son of Actor,
> And Peleus lives, son of AEacus, among the Myrmidons,
> Either of whom having died, we should greatly grieve."

He says, "That's good." He has a great bundle of white oak bark under his arm for a sick man, gathered this Sunday morning. "I suppose there's no harm in going after such a thing today," says he. To him Homer was a great writer, though what his writing was about he did not know. A more simple and natural man it would be hard to find. Vice and disease, which cast such a sombre moral hue over the world, seemed to have hardly any existance for him. He was about twenty-eight years old, and had left Canada and his father's house a dozen years before to work in the States, and earn money to buy a farm with at last, perhaps in his native country. He was cast in the coarsest mould; a stout but sluggish body, yet gracefully carried, with a thick sunburnt neck, dark bushy hair, and dull sleepy blue eyes, which were occasionally lit up with expression. He wore a flat gray cloth cap, a dingy wool-coloured greatcoat, and cowhide boots. He was a great consumer of meat, usually carrying his dinner to his work a couple of miles past my house — for he chopped all summer — in a tin pail; cold meats, often cold woodchucks, and coffee in a stone bottle which dangled by a string from his belt; and sometimes he offered me a drink. He came along early, crossing my bean-field, though without anxiety or haste to get to his work, such as Yankees exhibit. He wasn't a-going to hurt himself. He didn't care if he only earned his board. Frequently he would leave his dinner in the bushes, when his dog had caught a woodchuck by the way, and go back a mile and a half to dress it and leave it in the cellar of the house where he boarded, after deliberating first for half an hour whether he could not sink it in the pond safely till nightfall — loving to dwell long upon these themes. He would say, as he went by in the morning, "How thick the pigeons are! If working every day were not my trade, I could get all the meat I should want by hunting-pigeons, woodchucks, rabbits, partridges — by gosh! I could get all I should want for a week in one day."

He was a skilful chopper, and indulged in some flourishes and ornaments in his art. He cut his trees level and close to the ground, that the sprouts which came up afterward might be more vigourous and a sled might slide over the stumps; and instead of leaving a whole tree to support his corded wood, he would pare it away to a slender stake or splinter which you could break off with your hand at last.

He interested me because he was so quiet and solitary and so happy withal; a well of good humor and contentment which overflowed at his eyes. His mirth was without alloy. Sometimes I saw him at his work in the woods, felling trees, and he would greet me with a laugh of inexpressible satisfaction, and a salutation in Canadian French, though he spoke English as well. When I approached him he would suspend his work, and with half-suppressed mirth lie along the trunk of a pine which he had felled, and, peeling off the inner bark, roll it up into a ball and chew it while he laughed and talked. Such an exuberance of animal spirits had he that he sometimes tumbled down and rolled on the ground with laughter at anything which made him think and tickled him. Looking round upon the trees he would exclaim — "By George! I can enjoy myself well enough here chopping; I want no better sport." Sometimes, when at leisure, he amused himself all day in the woods with a pocket pistol, firing salutes to himself at regular intervals as he walked. In the winter he had a fire by which at noon he warmed his coffee in a kettle; and as he sat on a log to eat his dinner the chickadees would sometimes come round and alight on his arm and peck at the potato in his fingers; and he said that he "liked to have the little fellers about him."

In him the animal man chiefly was developed. In physical endurance and contentment he was cousin to the pine and the rock. I asked him once if he was not sometimes tired at night, after working all day; and he answered, with a sincere and serious look, "Gorrappit, I never was tired in my life." But the intellectual and what is called spiritual man in him were slumbering as in an infant. He had been instructed only in that innocent and ineffectual way in which the Catholic priests teach the aborigines, by which the pupil is never educated to the degree of consciousness, but only to the degree of trust and reverence, and a child is not made a man, but kept a child. When Nature made him, she gave him a strong body and contentment for his portion, and propped him on every side with reverence and reliance, that he might live out his threescore years and ten a child. He was so genuine and unsophisticated that no introduction would serve to introduce him, more than if you introduced a woodchuck to your neighbour. He had got to find him out as you did. He would not play any part. Men paid him wages for work, and so helped to feed and clothe him; but he never exchanged opinions with them. He was so simply and naturally humble — if he can be called humble who never aspires — that humility was no distinct quality in him, nor could he conceive of it. Wiser men were demigods to him. If you told him that such a one was coming, he did as if he thought that anything so grand would expect nothing of himself, but take all the responsibility on itself, and let him be forgotten still. He never heard the sound of praise. He particularly reverenced the writer and the preacher. Their performances were miracles. When I told him that I wrote considerably, he thought for a long time that it was merely the handwriting which I meant, for he could write a remarkably good hand himself. I sometimes found the name of his native parish handsomely written in the snow by the highway, with the proper French accent, and knew that he had passed. I asked him if he ever wished to write his thoughts. He said that he had read and written letters for those who could not, but he never tried to write thoughts — no, he could not, he could not tell what to put first, it would kill him, and then there was spelling to be attended to at the same time!

I heard that a distinguished wise man and reformer asked him if he did not want the world to be changed; but he answered with a chuckle of surprise in his Canadian accent, not knowing that the question had ever been entertained before, "No, I like it well enough." It would have suggested many things to a philosopher to have dealings with him. To a stranger he appeared to know nothing of things in general; yet I sometimes saw in him a man whom I had not seen before, and I did not know whether he was as wise as Shakespeare or as simply ignorant as a child, whether to suspect him of a fine poetic consciousness or of stupidity. A townsman told me that when he met him sauntering through the village in his small close-fitting cap, and whistling to himself, he reminded him of a prince in disguise.

His only books were an almanac and an arithmetic, in which last he was considerably expert. The former was a sort of cyclopaedia to him, which he supposed to contain an abstract of human knowledge, as indeed it does to a considerable extent. I loved to sound him on the various reforms of the day, and he never failed to look at them in the most simple and practical light. He had never heard of such things before. Could he do without factories? I asked. He had worn the home-made Vermont gray, he said, and that was good. Could he dispense with tea and coffee? Did this country afford any beverage beside water? He had soaked hemlock leaves in water and drank it, and thought that was better than water in warm weather. When I asked him if he could do without money, he showed the convenience of money in such a way as to suggest and coincide with the most philosophical accounts of the origin of this institution, and the very derivation of the word pecunia. If an ox were his property, and he wished to get needles and thread at the store, he thought it would be inconvenient and impossible soon to go on mortgaging some portion of the creature each time to that amount. He could defend many institutions better than any philosopher, because, in describing them as they concerned him, he gave the true reason for their prevalence, and speculation had not suggested to him any other. At another time, hearing Plato's definition of a man — a biped without feathers — and that one exhibited a cock plucked and called it Plato's man, he thought it an important difference that the knees bent the wrong way. He would sometimes exclaim, "How I love to talk! By George, I could talk all day!" I asked him once, when I had not seen him for many months, if he had got a new idea this summer. "Good Lord" — said he, "a man that has to work as I do, if he does not forget the ideas he has had, he will do well. May be the man you hoe with is inclined to race; then, by gorry, your mind must be there; you think of weeds." He would sometimes ask me first on such occasions, if I had made any improvement. One winter day I asked him if he was always satisfied with himself, wishing to suggest a substitute within him for the priest without, and some higher motive for living. "Satisfied!" said he; "some men are satisfied with one thing, and some with another. One man, perhaps, if he has got enough, will be satisfied to sit all day with his back to the fire and his belly to the table, by George!" Yet I never, by any manoeuvring, could get him to take the spiritual view of things; the highest that he appeared to conceive of was a simple expediency, such as you might expect an animal to appreciate; and this, practically, is true of most men. If I suggested any improvement in his mode of life, he merely answered, without expressing any regret, that it was too late. Yet he thoroughly believed in honesty and the like virtues.

There was a certain positive originality, however slight, to be detected in him, and I occasionally observed that he was thinking for himself and expressing his own opinion, a phenomenon so rare that I would any day walk ten miles to observe it, and it amounted to the re-origination of many of the institutions of society. Though he hesitated, and perhaps failed to express himself distinctly, he always had a presentable thought behind. Yet his thinking was so primitive and immersed in his animal life, that, though more promising than a merely learned man's, it rarely ripened to anything which can be reported. He suggested that there might be men of genius in the lowest grades of life, however permanently humble and illiterate, who take their own view always, or do not pretend to see at all; who are as bottomless even as Walden Pond was thought to be, though they may be dark and muddy.

Many a traveller came out of his way to see me and the inside of my house, and, as an excuse for calling, asked for a glass of water. I told them that I drank at the pond, and pointed thither, offering to lend them a dipper.

Far off as I lived, I was not exempted from the annual visitation which occurs, methinks, about the first of April, when everybody is on the move; and I had my share of good luck, though there were some curious specimens among my visitors. Half-witted men from the almshouse and elsewhere came to see me; but I endeavoured to make them exercise all the wit they had, and make their confessions to me; in such cases making wit the theme of our conversation; and so was compensated. Indeed, I found some of them to be wiser than the so-called overseers of the poor and selectmen of the town, and thought it was time that the tables were turned. With respect to wit, I learned that there was not much difference between the half and the whole. One day, in particular, an inoffensive, simple-minded pauper, whom with others I had often seen used as fencing stuff, standing or sitting on a bushel in the fields to keep cattle and himself from straying, visited me, and expressed a wish to live as I did. He told me, with the utmost simplicity and truth, quite superior, or rather inferior, to anything that is called humility, that he was "deficient in intellect." These were his words. The Lord had made him so, yet he supposed the Lord cared as much for him as for another. "I have always been so," said he, "from my childhood; I never had much mind; I was not like other children; I am weak in the head. It was the Lord's will, I suppose." And there he was to prove the truth of his words. He was a metaphysical puzzle to me. I have rarely met a fellowman on such promising ground — it was so simple and sincere and so true all that he said. And, true enough, in proportion as he appeared to humble himself was he exalted. I did not know at first but it was the result of a wise policy. It seemed that from such a basis of truth and frankness as the poor weak-headed pauper had laid, our intercourse might go forward to something better than the intercourse of sages.

I had some guests from those not reckoned commonly among the town's poor, but who should be; who are among the world's poor, at any rate; guests who appeal, not to your hospitality, but to your hospitality; who earnestly wish to be helped, and preface their appeal with the information that they are resolved, for one thing, never to help themselves. I require of a visitor that he be not actually starving, though he may have the very best appetite in the world, however he got it. Objects of charity are not guests. Men who did not know when their visit had terminated, though I went about my business again, answering them from greater and greater remoteness. Men of almost every degree of wit called on me in the migrating season. Some who had more wits than they knew what to do with; runaway slaves with plantation manners, who listened from time to time, like the fox in the fable, as if they heard the hounds a-baying on their track, and looked at me beseechingly, as much as to say, —

"O Christian, will you send me back?

One real runaway slave, among the rest, whom I helped to forward toward the north star. Men of one idea, like a hen with one chicken, and that a duckling; men of a thousand ideas, and unkempt heads, like those hens which are made to take charge of a hundred chickens, all in pursuit of one bug, a score of them lost in every morning's dew — and become frizzled and mangy in consequence; men of ideas instead of legs, a sort of intellectual centipede that made you crawl all over. One man proposed a book in which visitors should write their names, as at the White Mountains; but, alas! I have too good a memory to make that necessary.

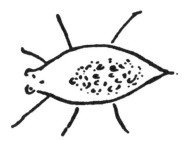

I could not but notice some of the peculiarities of my visitors. Girls and boys and young women generally seemed glad to be in the woods. They looked in the pond and at the flowers, and improved their time. Men of business, even farmers, thought only of solitude and employment, and of the great distance at which I dwelt from something or other; and though they said that they loved a ramble in the woods occasionally, it was obvious that they did not. Restless committed men, whose time was an taken up in getting a living or keeping it; ministers who spoke of God as if they enjoyed a monopoly of the subject, who could not bear all kinds of opinions; doctors, lawyers, uneasy housekeepers who pried into my cupboard and bed when I was out — how came Mrs. — to know that my sheets were not as clean as hers? — young men who had ceased to be young, and had concluded that it was safest to follow the beaten track of the professions — all these generally said that it was not possible to do so much good in my position. Ay! There was the rub. The old and infirm and the timid, of whatever age or sex, thought most of sickness, and sudden accident and death; to them life seemed full of danger — what danger is there if you don't think of any? — and they thought that a prudent man would carefully select the safest position, where Dr. B. might be on hand at a moment's warning. To them the village was literally a community, a league for mutual defence, and you would suppose that they would not go a-huckleberrying without a medicine chest. The amount of it is, if a man is alive, there is always danger that he may die, though the danger must be allowed to be less in proportion as he is dead-and-alive to begin with. A man sits as many risks as he runs. Finally, there were the self-styled reformers, the greatest bores of all, who thought that I was forever singing,—

This is the house that I built;

This is the man that lives in the house that I built;

but they did not know that the third line was,

These are the folks that worry the man

That lives in the house that I built.

I did not fear the hen-harriers, for I kept no chickens; but I feared the men-harriers rather.

I had more cheering visitors than the last. Children come a-berrying, railroad men taking a Sunday morning walk in clean shirts, fishermen and hunters, poets and philosophers; in short, all honest pilgrims, who came out to the woods for freedom's sake, and really left the village behind, I was ready to greet with — "Welcome, Englishmen! Welcome, Englishmen!" for I had had communication with that race.

7
The Bean-Field

Meanwhile my beans, the length of whose rows, added together, was seven miles already planted, were impatient to be hoed, for the earliest had grown considerably before the latest were in the ground; indeed they were not easily to be put off. What was the meaning of this so steady and self-respecting, this small Herculean labour, I knew not. I came to love my rows, my beans, though so many more than I wanted. They attached me to the earth, and so I got strength like Antaeus. But why should I raise them? Only Heaven knows. This was my curious labour all summer — to make this portion of the earth's surface, which had yielded only cinquefoil, blackberries, johnswort, and the like, before, sweet wild fruits and pleasant flowers, produce instead this pulse. What shall I learn of beans or beans of me? I cherish them, I hoe them, early and late I have an eye to them; and this is my day's work. It is a fine broad leaf to look on. My auxiliaries are the dews and rains which water this dry soil, and what fertility is in the soil itself, which for the most part is lean and effete. My enemies are worms, cool days, and most of all woodchucks. The last have nibbled for me a quarter of an acre clean. But what right had I to oust johnswort and the rest, and break up their ancient herb garden? Soon, however, the remaining beans will be too tough for them, and go forward to meet new foes.

When I was four years old, as I well remember, I was brought from Boston to this my native town, through these very woods and this field, to the pond. It is one of the oldest scenes stamped on my memory. And now to-night my flute has waked the echoes over that very water. The pines still stand here older than I; or, if some have fallen, I have cooked my supper with their stumps, and a new growth is rising all around, preparing another aspect for new infant eyes. Almost the same johnswort springs from the same perennial root in this pasture, and even I have at length helped to clothe that fabulous landscape of my infant dreams, and one of the results of my presence and influence is seen in these bean leaves, corn blades, and potato vines.

I planted about two acres and a half of upland; and as it was only about fifteen years since the land was cleared, and I myself had got out two or three cords of stumps, I did not give it any manure; but in the course of the summer it appeared by the arrowheads which I turned up in hoeing, that an extinct nation had anciently dwelt here and planted corn and beans ere white men came to clear the land, and so, to some extent, had exhausted the soil for this very crop.

Before yet any woodchuck or squirrel had run across the road, or the sun had got above the shrub oaks, while all the dew was on, though the farmers warned me against it — I would advise you to do all your work if possible while the dew is on — I began to level the ranks of haughty weeds in my bean-field and throw dust upon their heads. Early in the morning I worked barefooted, dabbling like a plastic artist in the dewy and crumbling sand, but later in the day the sun blistered my feet. There the sun lighted me to hoe beans, pacing slowly backward and forward over that yellow gravelly upland, between the long green rows, fifteen rods, the one end terminating in a shrub oak copse where I could rest in the shade, the other in a blackberry field where the green berries deepened their tints by the time I had made another bout. Removing the weeds, putting fresh soil about the bean stems, and encouraging this weed which I had sown, making the yellow soil express its summer thought in bean leaves and blossoms rather than in wormwood and piper and millet grass, making the earth say beans instead of grass — this was my daily work. As I had little aid from horses or cattle, or hired men or boys, or improved implements of husbandry, I was much slower, and became much more intimate with my beans than usual. But labour of the hands, even when pursued to the verge of drudgery, is perhaps never the worst form of idleness. It has a constant and imperishable moral, and to the scholar it yields a classic result. A very agricola labouriosus was I to travellers bound westward through Lincoln and Wayland to nobody knows where; they sitting at their ease in gigs, with elbows on knees, and reins loosely hanging in festoons; I the home-staying, labourious native of the soil. But soon my homestead was out of their sight and thought. It was the only open and cultivated field for a great distance on either side of the road, so they made the most of it; and sometimes the man in the field heard more of travellers' gossip and comment than was meant for his ear: "Beans so late! peas so late!" — for I continued to plant when others had begun to hoe — the ministerial husbandman had not suspected it. "Corn, my boy, for fodder; corn for fodder." "Does he live there?" asks the black bonnet of the gray coat; and the hard-featured farmer reins up his grateful dobbin to inquire what you are doing where he sees no manure in the furrow, and recommends a little chip dirt, or any little waste stuff, or it may be ashes or plaster. But here were two acres and a half of furrows, and only a hoe for cart and two hands to draw it — there being an aversion to other carts and horses — and chip dirt far away. Fellow-travellers as they rattled by compared it aloud with the fields which they had passed, so that I came to know how I stood in the agricultural world. This was one field not in Mr. Coleman's report. And, by the way, who estimates the value of the crop which nature yields in the still wilder fields unimproved by man? The crop of English hay is carefully weighed, the moisture calculated, the silicates and the potash; but in all dells and pond-holes in the woods and pastures and swamps grows a rich and various crop only unreaped by man. Mine was, as it were, the connecting link between wild and cultivated fields; as some states are civilized, and others half-civilized, and others savage or barbarous, so my field was, though not in a bad sense, a half-cultivated field. They were beans cheerfully returning to their wild and primitive state that I cultivated, and my hoe played the Rans des Vaches for them.

Near at hand, upon the topmost spray of a birch, sings the brown thrasher — or red mavis, as some love to call him — all the morning, glad of your society, that would find out another farmer's field if yours were not here.

While you are planting the seed, he cries — "Drop it, drop it — cover it up, cover it up — pull it up, pull it up, pull it up." But this was not corn, and so it was safe from such enemies as he. You may wonder what his rigmarole, his amateur Paganini performances on one string or on twenty, have to do with your planting, and yet prefer it to leached ashes or plaster. It was a cheap sort of top dressing in which I had entire faith.

As I drew a still fresher soil about the rows with my hoe, I disturbed the ashes of unchronicled nations who in primeval years lived under these heavens, and their small implements of war and hunting were brought to the light of this modern day. They lay mingled with other natural stones, some of which bore the marks of having been burned by Indian fires, and some by the sun, and also bits of pottery and glass brought hither by the recent cultivators of the soil. When my hoe tinkled against the stones, that music echoed to the woods and the sky, and was an accompaniment to my labour which yielded an instant and immeasurable crop. It was no longer beans that I hoed, nor I that hoed beans; and I remembered with as much pity as pride, if I remembered at all, my acquaintances who had gone to the city to attend the oratorios. The nighthawk circled overhead in the sunny afternoons — for I sometimes made a day of it — like a mote in the eye, or in heaven's eye, falling from time to time with a swoop and a sound as if the heavens were rent, torn at last to very rags and tatters, and yet a seamless cope remained; small imps that fill the air and lay their eggs on the ground on bare sand or rocks on the tops of hills, where few have found them; graceful and slender like ripples caught up from the pond, as leaves are raised by the wind to float in the heavens; such kindredship is in nature. The hawk is aerial brother of the wave which he sails over and surveys, those his perfect air-inflated wings answering to the elemental unfledged pinions of the sea. Or sometimes I watched a pair of hen-hawks circling high in the sky, alternately soaring and descending, approaching, and leaving one another, as if they were the embodiment of my own thoughts. Or I was attracted by the passage of wild pigeons from this wood to that, with a slight quivering winnowing sound and carrier haste; or from under a rotten stump my hoe turned up a sluggish portentous and outlandish spotted salamander, a trace of Egypt and the Nile, yet our contemporary. When I paused to lean on my hoe, these sounds and sights I heard and saw anywhere in the row, a part of the inexhaustible entertainment which the country offers.

On gala days the town fires its great guns, which echo like popguns to these woods, and some waifs of martial music occasionally penetrate thus far. To me, away there in my bean-field at the other end of the town, the big guns sounded as if a puffball had burst; and when there was a military turnout of which I was ignorant, I have sometimes had a vague sense all the day of some sort of itching and disease in the horizon, as if some eruption would break out there soon, either scarlatina or canker-rash, until at length some more favourable puff of wind, making haste over the fields and up the Wayland road, brought me information of the "trainers." It seemed by the distant hum as if somebody's bees had swarmed, and that the neighbours, according to Virgil's advice, by a faint tintinnabulum upon the most sonorous of their domestic utensils, were endeavouring to call them down into the hive again. And when the sound died quite away, and the hum had ceased, and the most favourable breezes told no tale, I knew that they had got the last drone of them all safely into the Middlesex hive, and that now their minds were bent on the honey with which it was smeared.

I felt proud to know that the liberties of Massachusetts and of our fatherland were in such safe keeping; and as I turned to my hoeing again I was filled with an inexpressible confidence, and pursued my labour cheerfully with a calm trust in the future.

When there were several bands of musicians, it sounded as if all the village was a vast bellows and all the buildings expanded and collapsed alternately with a din. But sometimes it was a really noble and inspiring strain that reached these woods, and the trumpet that sings of fame, and I felt as if I could spit a Mexican with a good relish — for why should we always stand for trifles? — and looked round for a woodchuck or a skunk to exercise my chivalry upon. These martial strains seemed as far away as Palestine, and reminded me of a march of crusaders in the horizon, with a slight tantivy and tremulous motion of the elm tree tops which overhang the village. This was one of the great days; though the sky had from my clearing only the same everlastingly great look that it wears daily, and I saw no difference in it.

It was a singular experience that long acquaintance which I cultivated with beans, what with planting, and hoeing, and harvesting, and threshing, and picking over and selling them — the last was the hardest of all — I might add eating, for I did taste. I was determined to know beans. When they were growing, I used to hoe from five o'clock in the morning till noon, and commonly spent the rest of the day about other affairs. Consider the intimate and curious acquaintance one makes with various kinds of weeds — it will bear some iteration in the account, for there was no little iteration in the labour — disturbing their delicate organizations so ruthlessly, and making such invidious distinctions with his hoe, levelling whole ranks of one species, and sedulously cultivating another. That's Roman wormwood — that's pigweed — that's sorrel — that's piper-grass — have at him, chop him up, turn his roots upward to the sun, don't let him have a fibre in the shade, if you do he'll turn himself t' other side up and be as green as a leek in two days. A long war, not with cranes, but with weeds, those Trojans who had sun and rain and dews on their side. Daily the beans saw me come to their rescue armed with a hoe, and thin the ranks of their enemies, filling up the trenches with weedy dead. Many a lusty crest — waving Hector, that towered a whole foot above his crowding comrades, fell before my weapon and rolled in the dust.

Those summer days which some of my contemporaries devoted to the fine arts in Boston or Rome, and others to contemplation in India, and others to trade in London or New York, I thus, with the other farmers of New England, devoted to husbandry. Not that I wanted beans to eat, for I am by nature a Pythagorean, so far as beans are concerned, whether they mean porridge or voting, and exchanged them for rice; but, perchance, as some must work in fields if only for the sake of tropes and expression, to serve a parable-maker one day. It was on the whole a rare amusement, which, continued too long, might have become a dissipation. Though I gave them no manure, and did not hoe them all once, I hoed them unusually well as far as I went, and was paid for it in the end, "there being in truth," as Evelyn says, "no compost or laetation whatsoever comparable to this continual motion, repastination, and turning of the mould with the spade." "The earth," he adds elsewhere, "especially if fresh, has a certain magnetism in it, by which it attracts the salt, power, or virtue (call it either) which gives it life, and is the logic of all the labour and stir we keep about it, to sustain us; all dungings and other sordid temperings being but the vicars succedaneous to this improvement." Moreover, this being one of those "worn-out and exhausted lay fields which enjoy their sabbath," had perchance, as Sir Kenelm Digby thinks likely, attracted "vital spirits" from the air. I harvested twelve bushels of beans.

But to be more particular, for it is complained that Mr. Coleman has reported chiefly the expensive experiments of gentlemen farmers, my outgoes were,—

For a hoe .... $ 0.54
Ploughing, harrowing, and furrowing .... 7.50 Too much.
Beans for seed .... 3.12+
Potatoes for seed 1.33
Peas for seed 0.40
Turnip seed 0.06
White line for crow fence 0.02
Horse cultivator and boy three hours 1.00
Horse and cart to get crop 0.75
In all .... $14.72+
My income was (patrem familias vendacem,
non emacem esse oportet), from
Nine bushels and twelve quarts of beans sold .. $16.94
Five " large potatoes 2.50
Nine " small 2.25
Grass 1.00
Stalks 0.75
In all $23.44
Leaving a pecuniary profit,
as I have elsewhere said, of .... $ 8.71+

This is the result of my experience in raising beans: Plant the common small white bush bean about the first of June, in rows three feet by eighteen inches apart, being careful to select fresh round and unmixed seed. First look out for worms, and supply vacancies by planting anew. Then look out for woodchucks, if it is an exposed place, for they will nibble off the earliest tender leaves almost clean as they go; and again, when the young tendrils make their appearance, they have notice of it, and will shear them off with both buds and young pods, sitting erect like a squirrel. But above all harvest as early as possible, if you would escape frosts and have a fair and salable crop; you may save much loss by this means.

This further experience also I gained: I said to myself, I will not plant beans and corn with so much industry another summer, but such seeds, if the seed is not lost, as sincerity, truth, simplicity, faith, innocence, and the like, and see if they will not grow in this soil, even with less toil and manurance, and sustain me, for surely it has not been exhausted for these crops. Alas! I said this to myself; but now another summer is gone, and another, and another, and I am obliged to say to you, Reader, that the seeds which I planted, if indeed they were the seeds of those virtues, were wormeaten or had lost their vitality, and so did not come up. Commonly men will only be brave as their fathers were brave, or timid. This generation is very sure to plant corn and beans each new year precisely as the Indians did centuries ago and taught the first settlers to do, as if there were a fate in it. I saw an old man the other day, to my astonishment, making the holes with a hoe for the seventieth time at least, and not for himself to lie down in! But why should not the New Englander try new adventures, and not lay so much stress on his grain, his potato and grass crop, and his orchards — raise other crops than these? Why concern ourselves so much about our beans for seed, and not be concerned at all about a new generation of men? We should really be fed and cheered if when we met a man we were sure to see that some of the qualities which I have named, which we all prize more than those other productions, but which are for the most part broadcast and floating in the air, had taken root and grown in him. Here comes such a subtile and ineffable quality, for instance, as truth or justice, though the slightest amount or new variety of it, along the road. Our ambassadors should be instructed to send home such seeds as these, and Congress help to distribute them over all the land. We should never stand upon ceremony with sincerity. We should never cheat and insult and banish one another by our meanness, if there were present the kernel of worth and friendliness. We should not meet thus in haste. Most men I do not meet at all, for they seem not to have time; they are busy about their beans. We would not deal with a man thus plodding ever, leaning on a hoe or a spade as a staff between his work, not as a mushroom, but partially risen out of the earth, something more than erect, like swallows alighted and walking on the ground:—

"And as he spake, his wings would now and then

Spread, as he meant to fly, then close again —"

so that we should suspect that we might be conversing with an angel. Bread may not always nourish us; but it always does us good, it even takes stiffness out of our joints, and makes us supple and buoyant, when we knew not what ailed us, to recognize any generosity in man or Nature, to share any unmixed and heroic joy.

Ancient poetry and mythology suggest, at least, that husbandry was once a sacred art; but it is pursued with irreverent haste and heedlessness by us, our object being to have large farms and large crops merely. We have no festival, nor procession, nor ceremony, not excepting our cattle-shows and so-called Thanksgivings, by which the farmer expresses a sense of the sacredness of his calling, or is reminded of its sacred origin. It is the premium and the feast which tempt him. He sacrifices not to Ceres and the Terrestrial Jove, but to the infernal Plutus rather. By avarice and selfishness, and a grovelling habit, from which none of us is free, of regarding the soil as property, or the means of acquiring property chiefly, the landscape is deformed, husbandry is degraded with us, and the farmer leads the meanest of lives. He knows Nature but as a robber. Cato says that the profits of agriculture are particularly pious or just (maximeque pius quaestus), and according to Varro the old Romans "called the same earth Mother and Ceres, and thought that they who cultivated it led a pious and useful life, and that they alone were left of the race of King Saturn."

We are wont to forget that the sun looks on our cultivated fields and on the prairies and forests without distinction. They all reflect and absorb his rays alike, and the former make but a small part of the glorious picture which he beholds in his daily course. In his view the earth is all equally cultivated like a garden. Therefore we should receive the benefit of his light and heat with a corresponding trust and magnanimity. What though I value the seed of these beans, and harvest that in the fall of the year? This broad field which I have looked at so long looks not to me as the principal cultivator, but away from me to influences more genial to it, which water and make it green. These beans have results which are not harvested by me. Do they not grow for woodchucks partly? The ear of wheat (in Latin spica, obsoletely speca, from spe, hope) should not be the only hope of the husbandman; its kernel or grain (granum from gerendo, bearing) is not all that it bears. How, then, can our harvest fail? Shall I not rejoice also at the abundance of the weeds whose seeds are the granary of the birds? It matters little comparatively whether the fields fill the farmer's barns. The true husbandman will cease from anxiety, as the squirrels manifest no concern whether the woods will bear chestnuts this year or not, and finish his labour with every day, relinquishing all claim to the produce of his fields, and sacrificing in his mind not only his first but his last fruits also.

8
The Village

After hoeing, or perhaps reading and writing, in the forenoon, I usually bathed again in the pond, swimming across one of its coves for a stint, and washed the dust of labour from my person, or smoothed out the last wrinkle which study had made, and for the afternoon was absolutely free. Every day or two I strolled to the village to hear some of the gossip which is incessantly going on there, circulating either from mouth to mouth, or from newspaper to newspaper, and which, taken in homoeopathic doses, was really as refreshing in its way as the rustle of leaves and the peeping of frogs. As I walked in the woods to see the birds and squirrels, so I walked in the village to see the men and boys; instead of the wind among the pines I heard the carts rattle. In one direction from my house there was a colony of muskrats in the river meadows; under the grove of elms and buttonwoods in the other horizon was a village of busy men, as curious to me as if they had been prairie-dogs, each sitting at the mouth of its burrow, or running over to a neighbour's to gossip. I went there frequently to observe their habits. The village appeared to me a great news room; and on one side, to support it, as once at Redding & Company's on State Street, they kept nuts and raisins, or salt and meal and other groceries. Some have such a vast appetite for the former commodity, that is, the news, and such sound digestive organs, that they can sit forever in public avenues without stirring, and let it simmer and whisper through them like the Etesian winds, or as if inhaling ether, it only producing numbness and insensibility to pain — otherwise it would often be painful to bear — without affecting the consciousness. I hardly ever failed, when I rambled through the village, to see a row of such worthies, either sitting on a ladder sunning themselves, with their bodies inclined forward and their eyes glancing along the line this way and that, from time to time, with a voluptuous expression, or else leaning against a barn with their hands in their pockets, like caryatides, as if to prop it up. They, being commonly out of doors, heard whatever was in the wind. These are the coarsest mills, in which all gossip is first rudely digested or cracked up before it is emptied into finer and more delicate hoppers within doors. I observed that the vitals of the village were the grocery, the bar-room, the post-office, and the bank; and, as a necessary part of the machinery, they kept a bell, a big gun, and a fire-engine, at convenient places; and the houses were so arranged as to make the most of mankind, in lanes and fronting one another, so that every traveller had to run the gauntlet, and every man, woman, and child might get a lick at him. Of course, those who were stationed nearest to the head of the line, where they could most see and be seen, and have the first blow at him, paid the highest prices for their places; and the few straggling inhabitants in the outskirts, where long gaps in the line began to occur, and the traveller could get over walls or turn aside into cow-paths, and so escape, paid a very slight ground or window tax. Signs were hung out on all sides to allure him; some to catch him by the appetite, as the tavern and victualling cellar; some by the fancy, as the dry goods store and the jeweller's; and others by the hair or the feet or the skirts, as the barber, the shoemaker, or the tailor. Besides, there was a still more terrible standing invitation to call at every one of these houses, and company expected about these times. For the most part I escaped wonderfully from these dangers, either by proceeding at once boldly and without deliberation to the goal, as is recommended to

those who run the gauntlet, or by keeping my thoughts on high things, like Orpheus, who, "loudly singing the praises of the gods to his lyre, drowned the voices of the Sirens, and kept out of danger." Sometimes I bolted suddenly, and nobody could tell my whereabouts, for I did not stand much about gracefulness, and never hesitated at a gap in a fence. I was even accustomed to make an irruption into some houses, where I was well entertained, and after learning the kernels and very last sieveful of news — what had subsided, the prospects of war and peace, and whether the world was likely to hold together much longer — I was let out through the rear avenues, and so escaped to the woods again.

It was very pleasant, when I stayed late in town, to launch myself into the night, especially if it was dark and tempestuous, and set sail from some bright village parlor or lecture room, with a bag of rye or Indian meal upon my shoulder, for my snug harbour in the woods, having made all tight without and withdrawn under hatches with a merry crew of thoughts, leaving only my outer man at the helm, or even tying up the helm when it was plain sailing. I had many a genial thought by the cabin fire "as I sailed." I was never cast away nor distressed in any weather, though I encountered some severe storms. It is darker in the woods, even in common nights, than most suppose. I frequently had to look up at the opening between the trees above the path in order to learn my route, and, where there was no cart-path, to feel with my feet the faint track which I had worn, or steer by the known relation of particular trees which I felt with my hands, passing between two pines for instance, not more than eighteen inches apart, in the midst of the woods, invariably, in the darkest night. Sometimes, after coming home thus late in a dark and muggy night, when my feet felt the path which my eyes could not see, dreaming and absent-minded all the way, until I was aroused by having to raise my hand to lift the latch, I have not been able to recall a single step of my walk, and I have thought that perhaps my body would find its way home if its master should forsake it, as the hand finds its way to the mouth without assistance. Several times, when a visitor chanced to stay into evening, and it proved a dark night, I was obliged to conduct him to the cart-path in the rear of the house, and then point out to him the direction he was to pursue, and in keeping which he was to be guided rather by his feet than his eyes. One very dark night I directed thus on their way two young men who had been fishing in the pond. They lived about a mile off through the woods, and were quite used to the route. A day or two after one of them told me that they wandered about the greater part of the night, close by their own premises, and did not get home till toward morning, by which time, as there had been several heavy showers in the meanwhile, and the leaves were very wet, they were drenched to their skins. I have heard of many going astray even in the village streets, when the darkness was so thick that you could cut it with a knife, as the saying is. Some who live in the outskirts, having come to town a-shopping in their wagons, have been obliged to put up for the night; and gentlemen and ladies making a call have gone half a mile out of their way, feeling the sidewalk only with their feet, and not knowing when they turned. It is a surprising and memorable, as well as valuable experience, to be lost in the woods any time. Often in a snow-storm, even by day, one will come out upon a well-known road and yet find it impossible to tell which way leads to the village. Though he knows that he has travelled it a thousand times, he cannot recognize a feature in it, but it is as strange to him as if it were a road in Siberia. By night, of course, the perplexity is infinitely greater. In our most trivial walks, we are constantly, though unconsciously, steering like pilots by certain well-known beacons and headlands, and if we go beyond our usual course we still carry in our minds the bearing of some neighbouring cape; and not till we are completely lost, or turned round — for a man needs only to be turned round once with his eyes shut in this world to be lost — do we appreciate the vastness and strangeness of nature. Every man has to learn the points of compass again as often as be awakes, whether from sleep or any abstraction. Not till we are lost, in other words not till we have lost the world, do we begin to find ourselves, and realize where we are and the infinite extent of our relations.

One afternoon, near the end of the first summer, when I went to the village to get a shoe from the cobbler's, I was seized and put into jail, because, as I have elsewhere related, I did not pay a tax to, or recognize the authority of, the State which buys and sells men, women, and children, like cattle, at the door of its senate-house. I had gone down to the woods for other purposes. But, wherever a man goes, men will pursue and paw him with their dirty institutions, and, if they can, constrain him to belong to their desperate odd-fellow society. It is true, I might have resisted forcibly with more or less effect, might have run "amok" against society; but I preferred that society should run "amok" against me, it being the desperate party. However, I was released the next day, obtained my mended shoe, and returned to the woods in season to get my dinner of huckleberries on Fair Haven Hill. I was never molested by any person but those who represented the State. I had no lock nor bolt but for the desk which held my papers, not even a nail to put over my latch or windows. I never fastened my door night or day, though I was to be absent several days; not even when the next fall I spent a fortnight in the woods of Maine. And yet my house was more respected than if it had been surrounded by a file of soldiers. The tired rambler could rest and warm himself by my fire, the literary amuse himself with the few books on my table, or the curious, by opening my closet door, see what was left of my dinner, and what prospect I had of a supper. Yet, though many people of every class came this way to the pond, I suffered no serious inconvenience from these sources, and I never missed anything but one small book, a volume of Homer, which perhaps was improperly gilded, and this I trust a soldier of our camp has found by this time. I am convinced, that if all men were to live as simply as I then did, thieving and robbery would be unknown. These take place only in communities where some have got more than is sufficient while others have not enough. The Pope's Homers would soon get properly distributed.

"Nec bella fuerunt,
Faginus astabat dum scyphus ante dapes."

"Nor wars did men molest,
When only beechen bowls were in request."

"You who govern public affairs, what need have you to employ punishments?
Love virtue, and the people will be virtuous.
The virtues of a superior man are like the wind;
the virtues of a common man are like the grass
— I the grass, when the wind passes over it, bends."

9
The Ponds

Sometimes, having had a surfeit of human society and gossip, and worn out all my village friends, I rambled still farther westward than I habitually dwell, into yet more unfrequented parts of the town, "to fresh woods and pastures new," or, while the sun was setting, made my supper of huckleberries and blueberries on Fair Haven Hill, and laid up a store for several days. The fruits do not yield their true flavour to the purchaser of them, nor to him who raises them for the market. There is but one way to obtain it, yet few take that way. If you would know the flavour of huckleberries, ask the cowboy or the partridge. It is a vulgar error to suppose that you have tasted huckleberries who never plucked them. A huckleberry never reaches Boston; they have not been known there since they grew on her three hills. The ambrosial and essential part of the fruit is lost with the bloom which is rubbed off in the market cart, and they become mere provender. As long as Eternal Justice reigns, not one innocent huckleberry can be transported thither from the country's hills.

Occasionally, after my hoeing was done for the day, I joined some impatient companion who had been fishing on the pond since morning, as silent and motionless as a duck or a floating leaf, and, after practising various kinds of philosophy, had concluded commonly, by the time I arrived, that he belonged to the ancient sect of Coenobites. There was one older man, an excellent fisher and skilled in all kinds of woodcraft, who was pleased to look upon my house as a building erected for the convenience of fishermen; and I was equally pleased when he sat in my doorway to arrange his lines. Once in a while we sat together on the pond, he at one end of the boat, and I at the other; but not many words passed between us, for he had grown deaf in his later years, but he occasionally hummed a psalm, which harmonized well enough with my philosophy. Our intercourse was thus altogether one of unbroken harmony, far more pleasing to remember than if it had been carried on by speech. When, as was commonly the case, I had none to commune with, I used to raise the echoes by striking with a paddle on the side of my boat, filling the surrounding woods with circling and dilating sound, stirring them up as the keeper of a menagerie his wild beasts, until I elicited a growl from every wooded vale and hillside.

    In warm evenings I frequently sat in the boat playing the flute, and saw the perch, which I seem to have charmed, hovering around me, and the moon travelling over the ribbed bottom, which was strewed with the wrecks of the forest. Formerly I had come to this pond adventurously, from time to time, in dark summer nights, with a companion, and, making a fire close to the water's edge, which we thought attracted the fishes, we caught pouts with a bunch of worms strung on a thread, and when we had done, far in the night, threw the burning brands high into the air like skyrockets, which, coming down into the pond, were quenched with a loud hissing, and we were suddenly groping in total darkness. Through this, whistling a tune, we took our way to the haunts of men again. But now I had made my home by the shore.

Sometimes, after staying in a village parlor till the family had all retired, I have returned to the woods, and, partly with a view to the next day's dinner, spent the hours of midnight fishing from a boat by moonlight, serenaded by owls and foxes, and hearing, from time to time, the creaking note of some unknown bird close at hand. These experiences were very memorable and valuable to me — anchored in forty feet of water, and twenty or thirty rods from the shore, surrounded sometimes by thousands of small perch and shiners, dimpling the surface with their tails in the moonlight, and communicating by a long flaxen line with mysterious nocturnal fishes which had their dwelling forty feet below, or sometimes dragging sixty feet of line about the pond as I drifted in the gentle night breeze, now and then feeling a slight vibration along it, indicative of some life prowling about its extremity, of dull uncertain blundering purpose there, and slow to make up its mind. At length you slowly raise, pulling hand over hand, some horned pout squeaking and squirming to the upper air. It was very queer, especially in dark nights, when your thoughts had wandered to vast and cosmogonal themes in other spheres, to feel this faint jerk, which came to interrupt your dreams and link you to Nature again. It seemed as if I might next cast my line upward into the air, as well as downward into this element, which was scarcely more dense. Thus I caught two fishes as it were with one hook.

The scenery of Walden is on a humble scale, and, though very beautiful, does not approach to grandeur, nor can it much concern one who has not long frequented it or lived by its shore; yet this pond is so remarkable for its depth and purity as to merit a particular description. It is a clear and deep green well, half a mile long and a mile and three quarters in circumference, and contains about sixty-one and a half acres; a perennial spring in the midst of pine and oak woods, without any visible inlet or outlet except by the clouds and evapouration. The surrounding hills rise abruptly from the water to the height of forty to eighty feet, though on the southeast and east they attain to about one hundred and one hundred and fifty feet respectively, within a quarter and a third of a mile. They are exclusively woodland. All our Concord waters have two colours at least; one when viewed at a distance, and another, more proper, close at hand. The first depends more on the light, and follows the sky. In clear weather, in summer, they appear blue at a little distance, especially if agitated, and at a great distance all appear alike. In stormy weather they are sometimes of a dark slate-colour. The sea, however, is said to be blue one day and green another without any perceptible change in the atmosphere. I have seen our river, when, the landscape being covered with snow, both water and ice were almost as green as grass. Some consider blue "to be the colour of pure water, whether liquid or solid." But, looking directly down into our waters from a boat, they are seen to be of very different colours. Walden is blue at one time and green at another, even from the same point of view. Lying between the earth and the heavens, it partakes of the colour of both. Viewed from a hilltop it reflects the colour of the sky; but near at hand it is of a yellowish tint next the shore where you can see the sand, then a light green, which gradually deepens to a uniform dark green in the body of the pond. In some lights, viewed even from a hilltop, it is of a vivid green next the shore. Some have referred this to the reflection of the verdure; but it is equally green there against the railroad sandbank, and in the spring, before the leaves are expanded, and it may be simply the result of the prevailing blue mixed with the yellow of the sand. Such is the colour of its iris. This is that portion, also, where in the spring, the ice being warmed by the heat of the sun reflected from the bottom, and also transmitted through the earth, melts first and forms a narrow canal about the still frozen middle. Like the rest of our waters, when much agitated, in clear weather, so that the surface of the waves may reflect the sky at the right angle, or because there is more light mixed with it, it appears at a little distance of a darker blue than the sky itself; and at such a time, being on its surface, and looking with divided vision, so as to see the reflection, I have discerned a matchless and indescribable light blue, such as watered or changeable silks and sword blades suggest, more cerulean than the sky itself, alternating with the original dark green on the opposite sides of the waves, which last appeared but muddy in comparison. It is a vitreous greenish blue, as I remember it, like those patches of the winter sky seen through cloud vistas in the west before sundown. Yet a single glass of its water held up to the light is as colourless as an equal quantity of air. It is well known that a large plate of glass will have a green tint, owing, as the makers say, to its "body," but a small piece of the same will be colourless. How large a body of Walden water would be required to reflect a green tint I have never proved. The water of our river is black or a very dark brown to one looking directly down on it, and, like that of most ponds, imparts to the body of one bathing in it a yellowish tinge; but this water is of such crystalline purity that the body of the bather appears of an alabaster whiteness, still more unnatural, which, as the limbs are magnified and distorted withal, produces a monstrous effect, making fit studies for a Michael Angelo.

The water is so transparent that the bottom can easily be discerned at the depth of twenty-five or thirty feet. Paddling over it, you may see, many feet beneath the surface, the schools of perch and shiners, perhaps only an inch long, yet the former easily distinguished by their transverse bars, and you think that they must be ascetic fish that find a subsistence there. Once, in the winter, many years ago, when I had been cutting holes through the ice in order to catch pickerel, as I stepped ashore I tossed my axe back on to the ice, but, as if some evil genius had directed it, it slid four or five rods directly into one of the holes, where the water was twenty-five feet deep. Out of curiosity, I lay down on the ice and looked through the hole, until I saw the axe a little on one side, standing on its head, with its helve erect and gently swaying to and fro with the pulse of the pond; and there it might have stood erect and swaying till in the course of time the handle rotted off, if I had not disturbed it. Making another hole directly over it with an ice chisel which I had, and cutting down the longest birch which I could find in the neighbourhood with my knife, I made a slip-noose, which I attached to its end, and, letting it down carefully, passed it over the knob of the handle, and drew it by a line along the birch, and so pulled the axe out again.

The shore is composed of a belt of smooth rounded white stones like paving-stones, excepting one or two short sand beaches, and is so steep that in many places a single leap will carry you into water over your head; and were it not for its remarkable transparency, that would be the last to be seen of its bottom till it rose on the opposite side. Some think it is bottomless. It is nowhere muddy, and a casual observer would say that there were no weeds at all in it; and of noticeable plants, except in the little meadows recently overflowed, which do not properly belong to it, a closer scrutiny does not detect a flag nor a bulrush, nor even a lily, yellow or white, but only a few small heart-leaves and potamogetons, and perhaps a water-target or two; all which however a bather might not perceive; and these plants are clean and bright like the element they grow in. The stones extend a rod or two into the water, and then the bottom is pure sand, except in the deepest parts, where there is usually a little sediment, probably from the decay of the leaves which have been wafted on to it so many successive falls, and a bright green weed is brought up on anchors even in midwinter.

We have one other pond just like this, White Pond, in Nine Acre Corner, about two and a half miles westerly; but, though I am acquainted with most of the ponds within a dozen miles of this centre I do not know a third of this pure and well-like character. Successive nations perchance have drank at, admired, and fathomed it, and passed away, and still its water is green and pellucid as ever. Not an intermitting spring! Perhaps on that spring morning when Adam and Eve were driven out of Eden Walden Pond was already in existence, and even then breaking up in a gentle spring rain accompanied with mist and a southerly wind, and covered with myriads of ducks and geese, which had not heard of the fall, when still such pure lakes sufficed them. Even then it had commenced to rise and fall, and had clarified its waters and coloured them

of the hue they now wear, and obtained a patent of Heaven to be the only Walden Pond in the world and distiller of celestial dews. Who knows in how many unremembered nations' literatures this has been the Castalian Fountain? Or what nymphs presided over it in the Golden Age? It is a gem of the first water which Concord wears in her coronet.

Yet perchance the first who came to this well have left some trace of their footsteps. I have been surprised to detect encircling the pond, even where a thick wood has just been cut down on the shore, a narrow shelf-like path in the steep hillside, alternately rising and falling, approaching and receding from the water's edge, as old probably as the race of man here, worn by the feet of aboriginal hunters, and still from time to time unwittingly trodden by the present occupants of the land. This is particularly distinct to one standing on the middle of the pond in winter, just after a light snow has fallen, appearing as a clear undulating white line, unobscured by weeds and twigs, and very obvious a quarter of a mile off in many places where in summer it is hardly distinguishable close at hand. The snow reprints it, as it were, in clear white type alto-relievo. The ornamented grounds of villas which will one day be built here may still preserve some trace of this.

The pond rises and falls, but whether regularly or not, and within what period, nobody knows, though, as usual, many pretend to know. It is commonly higher in the winter and lower in the summer, though not corresponding to the general wet and dryness. I can remember when it was a foot or two lower, and also when it was at least five feet higher, than when I lived by it. There is a narrow sand-bar running into it, with very deep water on one side, on which I helped boil a kettle of chowder, some six rods from the main shore, about the year 1824, which it has not been possible to do for twenty-five years; and, on the other hand, my friends used to listen with incredulity when I told them, that a few years later I was accustomed to fish from a boat in a secluded cove in the woods, fifteen rods from the only shore they knew, which place was long since converted into a meadow. But the pond has risen steadily for two years, and now, in the summer of '52, is just five feet higher than when I lived there, or as high as it was thirty years ago, and fishing goes on again in the meadow. This makes a difference of level, at the outside, of six or seven feet; and yet the water shed by the surrounding hills is insignificant in amount, and this overflow must be referred to causes which affect the deep springs. This same summer the pond has begun to fall again.

It is remarkable that this fluctuation, whether periodical or not, appears thus to require many years for its accomplishment. I have observed one rise and a part of two falls, and I expect that a dozen or fifteen years hence the water will again be as low as I have ever known it. Flint's Pond, a mile eastward, allowing for the disturbance occasioned by its inlets and outlets, and the smaller intermediate ponds also, sympathize with Walden, and recently attained their greatest height at the same time with the latter. The same is true, as far as my observation goes, of White Pond.

This rise and fall of Walden at long intervals serves this use at least; the water standing at this great height for a year or more, though it makes it difficult to walk round it, kills the shrubs and trees which have sprung up about its edge since the last rise — pitch pines, birches, alders, aspens, and others — and, falling again, leaves an unobstructed shore; for, unlike many ponds and all waters which are subject to a daily tide, its shore is cleanest when the water is lowest. On the side of the pond next my house a row of pitch pines, fifteen feet high, has been killed and tipped over as if by a lever, and thus a stop put to their encroachments; and their size indicates how many years have elapsed since the last rise to this height. By this fluctuation the pond asserts its title to a shore, and thus the shore is shorn, and the trees cannot hold it by right of possession. These are the lips of the lake, on which no beard grows. It licks its chaps from time to time. When the water is at its height, the alders, willows, and maples send forth a mass of fibrous red roots several feet long from all sides of their stems in the water, and to the height of three or four feet from the ground, in the effort to maintain themselves; and I have known the high blueberry bushes about the shore, which commonly produce no fruit, bear an abundant crop under these circumstances.

Some have been puzzled to tell how the shore became so regularly paved. My townsmen have all heard the tradition — the oldest people tell me that they heard it in their youth — that anciently the Indians were holding a pow-wow upon a hill here, which rose as high into the heavens as the pond now sinks deep into the earth, and they used much profanity, as the story goes, though this vice is one of which the Indians were never guilty, and while they were thus engaged the hill shook and suddenly sank, and only one old squaw, named Walden, escaped, and from her the pond was named. It has been conjectured that when the hill shook these stones rolled down its side and became the present shore. It is very certain, at any rate, that once there was no pond here, and now there is one; and this Indian fable does not in any respect conflict with the account of that ancient settler whom I have mentioned, who remembers so well when he first came here with his divining-rod, saw a thin vapour rising from the sward, and the hazel pointed steadily downward, and he concluded to dig a well here. As for the stones, many still think that they are hardly to be accounted for by the action of the waves on these hills; but I observe that the surrounding hills are remarkably full of the same kind of stones, so that they have been obliged to pile them up in walls on both sides of the railroad cut nearest the pond; and, moreover, there are most stones where the shore is most abrupt; so that, unfortunately, it is no longer a mystery to me. I detect the paver. If the name was not derived from that of some English locality — Saffron Walden, for instance — one might suppose that it was called originally Walled-in Pond.

The pond was my well ready dug. For four months in the year its water is as cold as it is pure at all times; and I think that it is then as good as any, if not the best, in the town. In the winter, all water which is exposed to the air is colder than springs and wells which are protected from it. The temperature of the pond water which had stood in the room where I sat from five o'clock in the afternoon till noon the next day, the sixth of March, 1846, the thermometer having been up to 65x or 70x some of the time, owing partly to the sun on the roof, was 42x, or one degree colder than the water of one of the coldest wells in the village just drawn. The temperature of the Boiling Spring the same day was 45x, or the warmest of any water tried, though it is the coldest that I know of in summer, when, beside, shallow and stagnant surface water is not mingled with it. Moreover, in summer, Walden never becomes so warm as most water which is exposed to the sun, on account of its depth. In the warmest weather I usually placed a pailful in my cellar, where it became cool in the night, and remained so during the day; though I also resorted to a spring in the neighbourhood. It was as good when a week old as the day it was dipped, and

had no taste of the pump. Whoever camps for a week in summer by the shore of a pond, needs only bury a pail of water a few feet deep in the shade of his camp to be independent of the luxury of ice.

There have been caught in Walden pickerel, one weighing seven pounds — to say nothing of another which carried off a reel with great velocity, which the fisherman safely set down at eight pounds because he did not see him — perch and pouts, some of each weighing over two pounds, shiners, chivins or roach (Leuciscus pulchellus), a very few breams, and a couple of eels, one weighing four pounds — I am thus particular because the weight of a fish is commonly its only title to fame, and these are the only eels I have heard of here; — also, I have a faint recollection of a little fish some five inches long, with silvery sides and a greenish back, somewhat dace-like in its character, which I mention here chiefly to link my facts to fable. Nevertheless, this pond is not very fertile in fish. Its pickerel, though not abundant, are its chief boast. I have seen at one time lying on the ice pickerel of at least three different kinds: a long and shallow one, steel-coloured, most like those caught in the river; a bright golden kind, with greenish reflections and remarkably deep, which is the most common here; and another, golden-coloured, and shaped like the last, but peppered on the sides with small dark brown or black spots, intermixed with a few faint blood-red ones, very much like a trout. The specific name reticulatus would not apply to this; it should be guttatus rather. These are all very firm fish, and weigh more than their size promises. The shiners, pouts, and perch also, and indeed all the fishes which inhabit this pond, are much cleaner, handsomer, and firmer-fleshed than those in the river and most other ponds, as the water is purer, and they can easily be distinguished from them. Probably many ichthyologists would make new varieties of some of them. There are also a clean race of frogs and tortoises, and a few mussels in it; muskrats and minks leave their traces about it, and occasionally a travelling mud-turtle visits it. Sometimes, when I pushed off my boat in the morning, I disturbed a great mud-turtle which had secreted himself under the boat in the night. Ducks and geese frequent it in the spring and fall, the white-bellied swallows (Hirundo bicolour) skim over it, and the peetweets (Totanus macularius) "teeter" along its stony shores all summer. I have sometimes disturbed a fish hawk sitting on a white pine over the water; but I doubt if it is ever profaned by the wind of a gull, like Fair Haven. At most, it tolerates one annual loon. These are all the animals of consequence which frequent it now.

You may see from a boat, in calm weather, near the sandy eastern shore, where the water is eight or ten feet deep, and also in some other parts of the pond, some circular heaps half a dozen feet in diameter by a foot in height, consisting of small stones less than a hen's egg in size, where all around is bare sand. At first you wonder if the Indians could have formed them on the ice for any purpose, and so, when the ice melted, they sank to the bottom; but they are too regular and some of them plainly too fresh for that. They are similar to those found in rivers; but as there are no suckers nor lampreys here, I know not by what fish they could be made. Perhaps they are the nests of the chivin. These lend a pleasing mystery to the bottom.

The shore is irregular enough not to be monotonous. I have in my mind's eye the western, indented with deep bays, the bolder northern, and the beautifully scalloped southern shore, where successive capes overlap each other and suggest unexplored coves between. The forest has never so good a setting, nor is so distinctly beautiful, as when seen from the middle of a small lake amid hills which rise from the water's edge; for the water in which it is reflected not only makes the best foreground in such a case, but, with its winding shore, the most natural and agreeable boundary to it. There is no rawness nor imperfection in its edge there, as where the axe has cleared a part, or a cultivated field abuts on it. The trees have ample room to expand on the water side, and each sends forth its most vigourous branch in that direction. There Nature has woven a natural selvage, and the eye rises by just gradations from the low shrubs of the shore to the highest trees. There are few traces of man's hand to be seen. The water laves the shore as it did a thousand years ago.

A lake is the landscape's most beautiful and expressive feature. It is earth's eye; looking into which the beholder measures the depth of his own nature. The fluviatile trees next the shore are the slender eyelashes which fringe it, and the wooded hills and cliffs around are its overhanging brows.

Standing on the smooth sandy beach at the east end of the pond, in a calm September afternoon, when a slight haze makes the opposite shore-line indistinct, I have seen whence came the expression, "the glassy surface of a lake." When you invert your head, it looks like a thread of finest gossamer stretched across the valley, and gleaming against the distant pine woods, separating one stratum of the atmosphere from another. You would think that you could walk dry under it to the opposite hills, and that the swallows which skim over might perch on it. Indeed, they sometimes dive below this line, as it were by mistake, and are undeceived. As you look over the pond westward you are obliged to employ both your hands to defend your eyes against the reflected as well as the true sun, for they are equally bright; and if, between the two, you survey its surface critically, it is literally as smooth as glass, except where the skater insects, at equal intervals scattered over its whole extent, by their motions in the sun produce the finest imaginable sparkle on it, or, perchance, a duck plumes itself, or, as I have said, a swallow skims so low as to touch it. It may be that in the distance a fish describes an arc of three or four feet in the air, and there is one bright flash where it emerges, and another where it strikes the water; sometimes the whole silvery arc is revealed; or here and there, perhaps, is a thistle-down floating on its surface, which the fishes dart at and so dimple it again. It is like molten glass cooled but not congealed, and the few motes in it are pure and beautiful like the imperfections in glass. You may often detect a yet smoother and darker water, separated from the rest as if by an invisible cobweb, boom of the water nymphs, resting on it. From a hilltop you can see a fish leap in almost any part; for not a pickerel or shiner picks an insect from this smooth surface but it manifestly disturbs the equilibrium of the whole lake. It is wonderful with what elabourateness this simple fact is advertised — this piscine murder will out — and from my distant perch I distinguish the circling undulations when they are half a dozen rods in diameter. You can even detect a water-bug (Gyrinus) ceaselessly progressing over the smooth surface a quarter of a mile off; for they furrow the water slightly, making a conspicuous ripple bounded by two diverging lines, but the skaters glide over it without rippling it perceptibly. When the surface is considerably agitated there are no skaters nor water-bugs on it, but apparently, in calm days, they leave their havens and adventurously glide forth from the shore by short impulses till they completely cover it. It is a soothing employment, on one of those fine days in the fall when all the warmth of the sun is fully appreciated, to sit on a stump on such a height as this, overlooking the pond, and study the dimpling circles which are incessantly inscribed on its otherwise invisible surface amid the reflected skies and trees. Over this great expanse there is no disturbance but it is thus at once gently smoothed away and assuaged, as, when a vase of water is jarred, the trembling circles seek the shore and all is smooth again. Not a fish can leap or an insect fall on the pond but it is thus reported in circling dimples, in lines of beauty, as it were the constant welling up of its fountain, the gentle pulsing of its life, the heaving of its breast. The thrills of joy and thrills of pain are undistinguishable. How peaceful the phenomena of the lake! Again the works of man shine as in the spring. Ay, every leaf and twig and stone and cobweb sparkles now at mid-afternoon as when covered with dew in a spring morning. Every motion of an oar or an insect produces a flash of light; and if an oar falls, how sweet the echo!

In such a day, in September or October, Walden is a perfect forest mirror, set round with stones as precious to my eye as if fewer or rarer. Nothing so fair, so pure, and at the same time so large, as a lake, perchance, lies on the surface of the earth. Sky water. It needs no fence. Nations come and go without defiling it. It is a mirror which no stone can crack, whose quicksilver will never wear off, whose gilding Nature continually repairs; no storms, no dust, can dim its surface ever fresh; — a mirror in which all impurity presented to it sinks, swept and dusted by the sun's hazy brush — this the light dust-cloth — which retains no breath that is breathed on it, but sends its own to float as clouds high above its surface, and be reflected in its bosom still.

A field of water betrays the spirit that is in the air. It is continually receiving new life and motion from above. It is intermediate in its nature between land and sky. On land only the grass and trees wave, but the water itself is rippled by the wind. I see where the breeze dashes across it by the streaks or flakes of light. It is remarkable that we can look down on its surface. We shall, perhaps, look down thus on the surface of air at length, and mark where a still subtler spirit sweeps over it.

The skaters and water-bugs finally disappear in the latter part of October, when the severe frosts have come; and then and in November, usually, in a calm day, there is absolutely nothing to ripple the surface. One November afternoon, in the calm at the end of a rain-storm of several days' duration, when the sky was still completely overcast and the air was full of mist, I observed that the pond was remarkably smooth, so that it was difficult to distinguish its surface; though it no longer reflected the bright tints of October, but the sombre November colours of the surrounding hills. Though I passed over it as gently as possible, the slight undulations produced by my boat extended almost as far as I could see, and gave a ribbed appearance to the reflections. But, as I was looking over the surface, I saw here and there at a distance a faint glimmer, as if some skater insects which had escaped the frosts might be collected there, or, perchance, the surface, being so smooth, betrayed where a spring welled up from the bottom. Paddling gently to one of these places, I was surprised to find myself surrounded by myriads of small perch, about five inches long, of a rich bronze colour in the green water, sporting there, and constantly rising to the surface and dimpling it, sometimes leaving bubbles on it. In such transparent and seemingly bottomless water, reflecting the clouds, I seemed to be floating through the air as in a balloon, and their swimming impressed me as a kind of flight or hovering, as if they were a compact flock of birds passing just beneath my level on the right or left, their fins, like sails, set all around them. There were many such schools in the pond, apparently improving the short season before winter would draw an icy shutter over their broad skylight, sometimes giving to the surface an appearance as if a slight breeze struck it, or a few rain-drops fell there. When I approached carelessly and alarmed them, they made a sudden splash and rippling with their tails, as if one had struck the water with a brushy bough, and instantly took refuge in the depths. At length the wind rose, the mist increased, and the waves began to run, and the perch leaped much higher than before, half out of water, a hundred black points, three inches long, at once above the surface. Even as late as the fifth of December, one year, I saw some dimples on the surface, and thinking it was going to rain hard immediately, the air being fun of mist, I made haste to take my place at the oars and row homeward; already the rain seemed rapidly increasing, though I felt none on my cheek, and I anticipated a thorough soaking. But suddenly the dimples ceased, for they were produced by the perch, which the noise of my oars had seared into the depths, and I saw their schools dimly disappearing; so I spent a dry afternoon after all.

An old man who used to frequent this pond nearly sixty years ago, when it was dark with surrounding forests, tells me that in those days he sometimes saw it all alive with ducks and other water-fowl, and that there were many eagles about it. He came here a-fishing, and used an old log canoe which he found on the shore. It was made of two white pine logs dug out and pinned together, and was cut off square at the ends. It was very clumsy, but lasted a great many years before it became water-logged and perhaps sank to the bottom. He did not know whose it was; it belonged to the pond. He used to make a cable for his anchor of strips of hickory bark tied together. An old man, a potter, who lived by the pond before the Revolution, told him once that there was an iron chest at the bottom, and that he had seen it. Sometimes it would come floating up to the shore; but when you went toward it, it would go back into deep water and disappear. I was pleased to hear of the old log canoe, which took the place of an Indian one of the same material but more graceful construction, which perchance had first been a tree on the bank, and then, as it were, fell into the water, to float there for a generation, the most proper vessel for the lake. I remember that when I first looked into these depths there were many large trunks to be seen indistinctly lying on the bottom, which had either been blown over formerly, or left on the ice at the last cutting, when wood was cheaper; but now they have mostly disappeared.

When I first paddled a boat on Walden, it was completely surrounded by thick and lofty pine and oak woods, and in some of its coves grape-vines had run over the trees next the water and formed bowers under which a boat could pass. The hills which form its shores are so steep, and the woods on them were then so high, that, as you looked down from the west end, it had the appearance of an amphitheatre for some land of sylvan spectacle. I have spent many an hour, when I was younger, floating over its surface as the zephyr willed, having paddled my boat to the middle, and lying on my back across the seats, in a summer forenoon, dreaming awake, until I was aroused by the boat touching the sand, and I arose to see what shore my fates had impelled me to; days when idleness was the most attractive and productive industry. Many a forenoon have I stolen away, preferring to spend thus the most valued part of the day; for I was rich, if not in money, in sunny hours and summer days, and spent them lavishly; nor do I regret that I did not waste more of them in the workshop or the teacher's desk. But since I left those shores the woodchoppers have still further laid them waste, and now for many a year there will be no more rambling through the aisles of the wood, with occasional vistas through which you see the water. My Muse may be excused if she is silent henceforth. How can you expect the birds to sing when their groves are cut down?

Now the trunks of trees on the bottom, and the old log canoe, and the dark surrounding woods, are gone, and the villagers, who scarcely know where it lies, instead of going to the pond to bathe or drink, are thinking to bring its water, which should be as sacred as the Ganges at least, to the village in a pipe, to wash their dishes with! — to earn their Walden by the turning of a cock or drawing of a plug! That devilish Iron Horse, whose ear-rending neigh is heard throughout the town, has muddied the Boiling Spring with his foot, and he it is that has browsed off all the woods on Walden shore, that Trojan horse, with a thousand men in his belly, introduced by mercenary Greeks! Where is the country's champion, the Moore of Moore Hill, to meet him at the Deep Cut and thrust an avenging lance between the ribs of the bloated pest?

Nevertheless, of all the characters I have known, perhaps Walden wears best, and best preserves its purity. Many men have been likened to it, but few deserve that honour. Though the woodchoppers have laid bare first this shore and then that, and the Irish have built their sties by it, and the railroad has infringed on its border, and the ice-men have skimmed it once, it is itself unchanged, the same water which my youthful eyes fell on; all the change is in me. It has not acquired one permanent wrinkle after all its ripples. It is perennially young, and I may stand and see a swallow dip apparently to pick an insect from its surface as of yore. It struck me again tonight, as if I had not seen it almost daily for more than twenty years — Why, here is Walden, the same woodland lake that I discovered so many years ago; where a forest was cut down last winter another is springing up by its shore as lustily as ever; the same thought is welling up to its surface that was then; it is the same liquid joy and happiness to itself and its Maker, ay, and it may be to me. It is the work of a brave man surely, in whom there was no guile! He rounded this water with his hand, deepened and clarified it in his thought, and in his will bequeathed it to Concord. I see by its face that it is visited by the same reflection; and I can almost say, Walden, is it you?

It is no dream of mine,
To ornament a line;
I cannot come nearer to God and Heaven

Than I live to Walden even.
I am its stony shore,
And the breeze that passes o'er;
In the hollow of my hand
Are its water and its sand,
And its deepest resort
Lies high in my thought.

The cars never pause to look at it; yet I fancy that the engineers and firemen and brakemen, and those passengers who have a season ticket and see it often, are better men for the sight. The engineer does not forget at night, or his nature does not, that he has beheld this vision of serenity and purity once at least during the day. Though seen but once, it helps to wash out State Street and the engine's soot. One proposes that it be called "God's Drop."

I have said that Walden has no visible inlet nor outlet, but it is on the one hand distantly and indirectly related to Flint's Pond, which is more elevated, by a chain of small ponds coming from that quarter, and on the other directly and manifestly to Concord River, which is lower, by a similar chain of ponds through which in some other geological period it may have flowed, and by a little digging, which God forbid, it can be made to flow thither again. If by living thus reserved and austere, like a hermit in the woods, so long, it has acquired such wonderful purity, who would not regret that the comparatively impure waters of Flint's Pond should be mingled with it, or itself should ever go to waste its sweetness in the ocean wave?

Flint's, or Sandy Pond, in Lincoln, our greatest lake and inland sea, lies about a mile east of Walden. It is much larger, being said to contain one hundred and ninety-seven acres, and is more fertile in fish; but it is comparatively shallow, and not remarkably pure. A walk through the woods thither was often my recreation. It was worth the while, if only to feel the wind blow on your cheek freely, and see the waves run, and remember the life of mariners. I went a-chestnutting there in the fall, on windy days, when the nuts were dropping into the water and were washed to my feet; and one day, as I crept along its sedgy shore, the fresh spray blowing in my face, I came upon the mouldering wreck of a boat, the sides gone, and hardly more than the impression of its flat bottom left amid the rushes; yet its model was sharply defined, as if it were a large decayed pad, with its veins. It was as impressive a wreck as one could imagine on the seashore, and had as good a moral. It is by this time mere vegetable mould and undistinguishable pond shore, through which rushes and flags have pushed up. I used to admire the ripple marks on the sandy bottom, at the north end of this pond, made firm and hard to the feet of the wader by the pressure of the water, and the rushes which grew in Indian file, in waving lines, corresponding to these marks, rank behind rank, as if the waves had planted them. There also I have found, in considerable quantities, curious balls, composed apparently of fine grass or roots, of pipewort perhaps, from half an inch to four inches in diameter, and perfectly spherical. These wash back and forth in shallow water on a sandy bottom, and are sometimes cast on the shore. They are either solid grass, or have a little sand in the middle. At first you would say that they were formed by the action of the waves, like a pebble; yet the smallest are made of equally coarse materials, half an inch long, and they are produced only at one season of the year. Moreover, the waves, I suspect, do not so much construct as wear down a material which has already acquired consistency. They preserve their form when dry for an indefinite period.

Flint's Pond! Such is the poverty of our nomenclature. What right had the unclean and stupid farmer, whose farm abutted on this sky water, whose shores he has ruthlessly laid bare, to give his name to it? Some skin-flint, who loved better the reflecting surface of a dollar, or a bright cent, in which he could see his own brazen face; who regarded even the wild ducks which settled in it as trespassers; his fingers grown into crooked and bony talons from the long habit of grasping harpy-like; — so it is not named for me. I go not there to see him nor to hear of him; who never saw it, who never bathed in it, who never loved it, who never protected it, who never spoke a good word for it, nor thanked God that He had made it. Rather let it be named from the fishes that swim in it, the wild fowl or quadrupeds which frequent it, the wild flowers which grow by its shores, or some wild man or child the thread of whose history is interwoven with its own; not from him who could show no title to it but the deed which a like-minded neighbour or legislature gave him — him who thought only of its money value; whose presence perchance cursed all the shores; who exhausted the land around it, and would fain have exhausted the waters within it; who regretted only that it was not English hay or cranberry meadow — there was nothing to redeem it, forsooth, in his eyes — and would have drained and sold it for the mud at its bottom. It did not turn his mill, and it was no privilege to him to behold it. I respect not his labours, his farm where everything has its price, who would carry the landscape, who would carry his God, to market, if he could get anything for him; who goes to market for his god as it is; on whose farm nothing grows free, whose fields bear no crops, whose meadows no flowers, whose trees no fruits, but dollars; who loves not the beauty of his fruits, whose fruits are not ripe for him till they are turned to dollars. Give me the poverty that enjoys true wealth. Farmers are respectable and interesting to me in proportion as they are poor — poor farmers. A model farm! Where the house stands like a fungus in a muckheap, chambers for men horses, oxen, and swine, cleansed and uncleansed, all contiguous to one another! Stocked with men! A great grease-spot, redolent of manures and buttermilk! Under a high state of cultivation, being manured with the hearts and brains of men! As if you were to raise your potatoes in the churchyard! Such is a model farm.

No, no; if the fairest features of the landscape are to be named after men, let them be the noblest and worthiest men alone. Let our lakes receive as true names at least as the Icarian Sea, where "still the shore" a "brave attempt resounds."

Goose Pond, of small extent, is on my way to Flint's; Fair Haven, an expansion of Concord River, said to contain some seventy acres, is a mile southwest; and White Pond, of about forty acres, is a mile and a half beyond Fair Haven. This is my lake country. These, with Concord River, are my water privileges; and night and day, year in year out, they grind such grist as I carry to them.

Since the wood-cutters, and the railroad, and I myself have profaned Walden, perhaps the most attractive, if not the most beautiful, of all our lakes, the gem of the woods, is White Pond; — a poor name from its commonness, whether derived from the remarkable purity of its waters or the colour of its sands. In these as in other respects, however, it is a lesser twin of Walden. They are so much alike that you would say they must be connected under ground. It has the same stony shore, and its waters are of the same hue. As at Walden, in sultry dog-day weather, looking down through the woods on some of its bays which are not so deep but that the reflection from the bottom tinges them, its waters are of a misty bluish-green or glaucous colour. Many years since I used to go there to collect the sand by cartloads, to make sandpaper with, and I have continued to visit it ever since. One who frequents it proposes to call it Virid Lake. Perhaps it might be called Yellow Pine Lake, from the following circumstance. About fifteen years ago you could see the top of a pitch pine, of the kind called yellow pine hereabouts, though it is not a distinct species, projecting above the surface in deep water, many rods from the shore. It was even supposed by some that the pond had sunk, and this was one of the primitive forest that formerly stood there. I find that even so long ago as 1792, in a "Topographical Description of the Town of Concord," by one of its citizens, in the Collections of the Massachusetts Historical Society, the author, after speaking of Walden and White Ponds, adds, "In the middle of the latter may be seen, when the water is very low, a tree which appears as if it grew in the place where it now stands, although the roots are fifty feet below the surface of the water; the top of this tree is broken off, and at that place measures fourteen inches in diameter." In the spring of '49 I talked with the man who lives nearest the pond in Sudbury, who told me that it was he who got out this tree ten or fifteen years before. As near as he could remember, it stood twelve or fifteen rods from the shore, where the water was thirty or forty feet deep. It was in the winter, and he had been getting out ice in the forenoon, and had resolved that in the afternoon, with the aid of his neighbours, he would take out the old yellow pine. He sawed a channel in the ice toward the shore, and hauled it over and along and out on to the ice with oxen; but, before he had gone far in his work, he was surprised to find that it was wrong end upward, with the stumps of the branches pointing down, and the small end firmly fastened in the sandy bottom. It was about a foot in diameter at the big end, and he had expected to get a good saw-log, but it was so rotten as to be fit only for fuel, if for that. He had some of it in his shed then. There were marks of an axe and of woodpeckers on the butt. He thought that it might have been a dead tree on the shore, but was finally blown over into the pond, and after the top had become water-logged, while the butt-end was still dry and light, had drifted out and sunk wrong end up. His father, eighty years old, could not remember when it was not there. Several pretty large logs may still be seen lying on the bottom, where, owing to the undulation of the surface, they look like huge water snakes in motion.

This pond has rarely been profaned by a boat, for there is little in it to tempt a fisherman. Instead of the white lily, which requires mud, or the common sweet flag, the blue flag (Iris versicolour) grows thinly in the pure water, rising from the stony bottom all around the shore, where it is visited by hummingbirds in June; and the colour both of its bluish blades and its flowers and especially their reflections, is in singular harmony with the glaucous water.

White Pond and Walden are great crystals on the surface of the earth, Lakes of Light. If they were permanently congealed, and small enough to be clutched, they would, perchance, be carried off by slaves, like precious stones, to adorn the heads of emperors; but being liquid, and ample, and secured to us and our successors forever, we disregard them, and run after the diamond of Kohinoor. They are too pure to have a market value; they contain no muck. How much more beautiful than our lives, how much more transparent than our characters, are they! We never learned meanness of them. How much fairer than the pool before the farmers door, in which his ducks swim! Hither the clean wild ducks come. Nature has no human inhabitant who appreciates her. The birds with their plumage and their notes are in harmony with the flowers, but what youth or maiden conspires with the wild luxuriant beauty of Nature? She flourishes most alone, far from the towns where they reside. Talk of heaven! Ye disgrace earth.

10
Baker Farm

Sometimes I rambled to pine groves, standing like temples, or like fleets at sea, full-rigged, with wavy boughs, and rippling with light, so soft and green and shady that the Druids would have forsaken their oaks to worship in them; or to the cedar wood beyond Flint's Pond, where the trees, covered with hoary blue berries, spiring higher and higher, are fit to stand before Valhalla, and the creeping juniper covers the ground with wreaths full of fruit; or to swamps where the usnea lichen hangs in festoons from the white spruce trees, and toadstools, round tables of the swamp gods, cover the ground, and more beautiful fungi adorn the stumps, like butterflies or shells, vegetable winkles; where the swamp-pink and dogwood grow, the red alderberry glows like eyes of imps, the waxwork grooves and crushes the hardest woods in its folds, and the wild holly berries make the beholder forget his home with their beauty, and he is dazzled and tempted by nameless other wild forbidden fruits, too fair for mortal taste. Instead of calling on some scholar, I paid many a visit to particular trees, of kinds which are rare in this neighbourhood, standing far away in the middle of some pasture, or in the depths of a wood or swamp, or on a hilltop; such as the black birch, of which we have some handsome specimens two feet in diameter; its cousin, the yellow birch, with its loose golden vest, perfumed like the first; the beech, which has so neat a bole and beautifully lichen-painted, perfect in all its details, of which, excepting scattered specimens, I know but one small grove of sizable trees left in the township, supposed by some to have been planted by the pigeons that were once baited with beechnuts near by; it is worth the while to see the silver grain sparkle when you split this wood; the bass; the hornbeam; the Celtis occidentalis, or false elm, of which we have but one well-grown; some taller mast of a pine, a shingle tree, or a more perfect hemlock than usual, standing like a pagoda in the midst of the woods; and many others I could mention. These were the shrines I visited both summer and winter.

Once it chanced that I stood in the very abutment of a rainbow's arch, which filled the lower stratum of the atmosphere, tinging the grass and leaves around, and dazzling me as if I looked through coloured crystal. It was a lake of rainbow light, in which, for a short while, I lived like a dolphin. If it had lasted longer it might have tinged my employments and life. As I walked on the railroad causeway, I used to wonder at the halo of light around my shadow, and would fain fancy myself one of the elect. One who visited me declared that the shadows of some Irishmen before him had no halo about them, that it was only natives that were so distinguished. Benvenuto Cellini tells us in his memoirs, that, after a certain terrible dream or vision which he had during his confinement in the castle of St. Angelo a resplendent light appeared over the shadow of his head at morning and evening, whether he was in Italy or France, and it was particularly conspicuous when the grass was moist with dew. This was probably the same phenomenon to which I have referred, which is especially observed in the morning, but also at other times, and even by moonlight. Though a constant one, it is not commonly noticed, and, in the case of an excitable imagination like Cellini's, it would be basis enough for superstition. Beside, he tells us that he showed it to very few. But are they not indeed distinguished who are conscious that they are regarded at all?

I set out one afternoon to go a-fishing to Fair Haven, through the woods, to eke out my scanty fare of vegetables. My way led through Pleasant Meadow, an adjunct of the Baker Farm, that retreat of which a poet has since sung, beginning,—

> "Thy entry is a pleasant field,
> Which some mossy fruit trees yield
> Partly to a ruddy brook,
> By gliding musquash undertook,
> And mercurial trout,
> Darting about."

I thought of living there before I went to Walden. I "hooked" the apples, leaped the brook, and scared the musquash and the trout. It was one of those afternoons which seem indefinitely long before one, in which many events may happen, a large portion of our natural life, though it was already half spent when I started. By the way there came up a shower, which compelled me to stand half an hour under a pine, piling boughs over my head, and wearing my handkerchief for a shed; and when at length I had made one cast over the pickerelweed, standing up to my middle in water, I found myself suddenly in the shadow of a cloud, and the thunder began to rumble with such emphasis that I could do no more than listen to it. The gods must be proud, thought I, with such forked flashes to rout a poor unarmed fisherman. So I made haste for shelter to the nearest hut, which stood half a mile from any road, but so much the nearer to the pond, and had long been uninhabited:—

> "And here a poet builded,
> In the completed years,
> For behold a trivial cabin
> That to destruction steers."

So the Muse fables. But therein, as I found, dwelt now John Field, an Irishman, and his wife, and several children, from the broad-faced boy who assisted his father at his work, and now came running by his side from the bog to escape the rain, to the wrinkled, sibyl-like, cone-headed infant that sat upon its father's knee as in the palaces of nobles, and looked out from its home in the midst of wet and hunger inquisitively upon the stranger, with the privilege of infancy, not knowing but it was the last of a noble line, and the hope and cynosure of the world, instead of John Field's poor starveling brat. There we sat together under that part of the roof which leaked the least, while it showered and thundered without. I had sat there many times of old before the ship was built that floated his family to America. An honest, hard-working, but shiftless man plainly was John Field; and his wife, she too was brave to cook so many successive dinners in the recesses of that lofty stove; with round greasy face and bare breast, still thinking to improve her condition one day; with the never absent mop in one hand, and yet no effects of it visible anywhere. The chickens, which had also taken shelter here from the rain, stalked about the room like members of the family, too humanized, methought, to roast well. They stood and looked in my eye or pecked at my shoe significantly. Meanwhile my host told me his story, how hard he worked "bogging" for a neighbouring farmer, turning up a meadow with a spade or bog hoe at the rate of ten dollars an acre and the use of the land with manure for one year, and his little broad-faced son worked cheerfully at his father's side the while, not knowing how poor a bargain the latter had made. I tried to help him with my experience, telling him that he was one of my nearest neighbours, and that I too, who came a-fishing here, and looked like a loafer, was getting my living like himself; that I lived in a tight, light, and clean house, which hardly cost more than the annual rent of such a ruin as his commonly amounts to; and how, if he chose, he might in a month or two build himself a palace of his own; that I did not use tea, nor coffee, nor butter, nor milk, nor fresh meat, and so did not have to work to get them; again, as I did not work hard, I did not have to eat hard, and it cost me but a trifle for my food; but as he began with tea, and coffee, and butter, and milk, and beef, he had to work hard to pay for them, and when he had worked hard he had to eat hard again to repair the waste of his system — and so it was as broad as it was long, indeed it was broader than it was long, for he was discontented and wasted his life into the bargain; and yet he had rated it as a gain in coming to America, that here you could get tea, and coffee, and meat every day. But the only true America is that country where you are at liberty to pursue such a mode of life as may enable you to do without these, and where the state does not endeavour to compel you to sustain the slavery and war and other superfluous expenses which directly or indirectly result from the use of such things. For I purposely talked to him as if he were a philosopher, or desired to be one. I should be glad if all the meadows on the earth were left in a wild state, if that were the consequence of men's beginning to redeem themselves. A man will not need to study history to find out what is best for his own culture. But alas! The culture of an Irishman is an enterprise to be undertaken with a sort of moral bog hoe. I told him, that as he worked so hard at bogging, he required thick boots and stout clothing, which yet were soon soiled and worn out, but I wore light shoes and thin clothing, which cost not half so much, though he might think that I was dressed like a gentleman (which, however, was not the case), and in an hour or two, without labour, but as a recreation, I could, if I wished, catch as many fish as I should want for two days, or earn enough money to support me a week. If he and his family would live simply, they might all go a-huckleberrying in the summer for their amusement. John heaved a sigh at this, and his wife stared with arms a-kimbo, and both appeared to be wondering if they had capital enough to begin such a course with, or arithmetic enough to carry it through. It was sailing by dead reckoning to them, and they saw not clearly how to make their port so; therefore I suppose they still take life bravely, after their fashion, face to face, giving it tooth and nail, not having skill to split its massive columns with any fine entering wedge, and rout it in detail; — thinking to deal with it roughly, as one should handle a thistle. But they fight at an overwhelming disadvantage — living, John Field, alas! Without arithmetic, and failing so.

"Do you ever fish?" I asked. "Oh yes, I catch a mess now and then when I am lying by; good perch I catch. — "What's your bait?" "I catch shiners with fishworms, and bait the perch with them." "You'd better go now, John," said his wife, with glistening and hopeful face; but John demurred.

The shower was now over, and a rainbow above the eastern woods promised a fair evening; so I took my departure. When I had got without I asked for a drink, hoping to get a sight of the well bottom, to complete my survey of the premises; but there, alas! Are shallows and quicksands, and rope broken withal, and bucket irrecoverable. Meanwhile the right culinary vessel was selected, water was seemingly distilled, and after consultation and long delay passed out to the thirsty one — not yet suffered to cool, not yet to settle. Such gruel sustains life here, I thought; so, shutting my eyes, and excluding the motes by a skilfully directed undercurrent, I drank to genuine hospitality the heartiest draught I could. I am not squeamish in such cases when manners are concerned.

As I was leaving the Irishman's roof after the rain, bending my steps again to the pond, my haste to catch pickerel, wading in retired meadows, in sloughs and bog-holes, in forlorn and savage places, appeared for an instant trivial to me who had been sent to school and college; but as I ran down the hill toward the reddening west, with the rainbow over my shoulder, and some faint tinkling sounds borne to my ear through the cleansed air, from I know not what quarter, my Good Genius seemed to say — Go fish and hunt far and wide day by day — farther and wider — and rest thee by many brooks and hearth-sides without misgiving. Remember thy Creator in the days of thy youth. Rise free from care before the dawn, and seek adventures. Let the noon find thee by other lakes, and the night overtake thee everywhere at home. There are no larger fields than these, no worthier games than may here be played. Grow wild according to thy nature, like these sedges and brakes, which will never become English bay. Let the thunder rumble; what if it threaten ruin to farmers' crops? That is not its errand to thee. Take shelter under the cloud, while they flee to carts and sheds. Let not to get a living be thy trade, but thy sport. Enjoy the land, but own it not. Through want of enterprise and faith men are where they are, buying and selling, and spending their lives like serfs.

> O Baker Farm!
> "Landscape where the richest element
> Is a little sunshine innocent." ...
> "No one runs to revel
> On thy rail-fenced lea." ...
> "Debate with no man hast thou,
> With questions art never perplexed,
> As tame at the first sight as now,
> In thy plain russet gabardine dressed." ...
> "Come ye who love,

> And ye who hate,
> Children of the Holy Dove,
> And Guy Faux of the state,
> And hang conspiracies
> From the tough rafters of the trees!"

Men come tamely home at night only from the next field or street, where their household echoes haunt, and their life pines because it breathes its own breath over again; their shadows, morning and evening, reach farther than their daily steps. We should come home from far, from adventures, and perils, and discoveries every day, with new experience and character.

Before I had reached the pond some fresh impulse had brought out John Field, with altered mind, letting go "bogging" ere this sunset. But he, poor man, disturbed only a couple of fins while I was catching a fair string, and he said it was his luck; but when we changed seats in the boat luck changed seats too. Poor John Field! — I trust he does not read this, unless he will improve by it — thinking to live by some derivative old-country mode in this primitive new country — to catch perch with shiners. It is good bait sometimes, I allow. With his horizon all his own, yet he a poor man, born to be poor, with his inherited Irish poverty or poor life, his Adam's grandmother and boggy ways, not to rise in this world, he nor his posterity, till their wading webbed bog-trotting feet get talaria to their heels.

11
Higher Laws

As I came home through the woods with my string of fish, trailing my pole, it being now quite dark, I caught a glimpse of a woodchuck stealing across my path, and felt a strange thrill of savage delight, and was strongly tempted to seize and devour him raw; not that I was hungry then, except for that wildness which he represented. Once or twice, however, while I lived at the pond, I found myself ranging the woods, like a half-starved hound, with a strange abandonment, seeking some kind of venison which I might devour, and no morsel could have been too savage for me. The wildest scenes had become unaccountably familiar. I found in myself, and still find, an instinct toward a higher, or, as it is named, spiritual life, as do most men, and another toward a primitive rank and savage one, and I reverence them both. I love the wild not less than the good. The wildness and adventure that are in fishing still recommended it to me. I like sometimes to take rank hold on life and spend my day more as the animals do. Perhaps I have owed to this employment and to hunting, when quite young, my closest acquaintance with Nature. They early introduce us to and detain us in scenery with which otherwise, at that age, we should have little acquaintance. Fishermen, hunters, woodchoppers, and others, spending their lives in the fields and woods, in a peculiar sense a part of Nature themselves, are often in a more favourable mood for observing her, in the intervals of their pursuits, than philosophers or poets even, who approach her with expectation. She is not afraid to exhibit herself to them. The traveller on the prairie is naturally a hunter, on the head waters of the Missouri and Columbia a trapper, and at the Falls of St. Mary a fisherman. He who is only a traveller learns things at second-hand and by the halves, and is poor authority. We are most interested when science reports what those men already know practically or instinctively, for that alone is a true humanity, or account of human experience.

They mistake who assert that the Yankee has few amusements, because

he has not so many public holidays, and men and boys do not play so many games as they do in England, for here the more primitive but solitary amusements of hunting, fishing, and the like have not yet given place to the former. Almost every New England boy among my contemporaries shouldered a fowling-piece between the ages of ten and fourteen; and his hunting and fishing grounds were not limited, like the preserves of an English nobleman, but were more boundless even than those of a savage. No wonder, then, that he did not oftener stay to play on the common. But already a change is taking place, owing, not to an increased humanity, but to an increased scarcity of game, for perhaps the hunter is the greatest friend of the animals hunted, not excepting the Humane Society.

Moreover, when at the pond, I wished sometimes to add fish to my fare for variety. I have actually fished from the same kind of necessity that the first fishers did. Whatever humanity I might conjure up against it was all factitious, and concerned my philosophy more than my feelings. I speak of fishing only now, for I had long felt differently about fowling, and sold my gun before

I went to the woods. Not that I am less humane than others, but I did not perceive that my feelings were much affected. I did not pity the fishes nor the worms. This was habit. As for fowling, during the last years that I carried a gun my excuse was that I was studying ornithology, and sought only new or rare birds. But I confess that I am now inclined to think that there is a finer way of studying ornithology than this. It requires so much closer attention to the habits of the birds, that, if for that reason only, I have been willing to omit the gun. Yet notwithstanding the objection on the score of humanity, I am compelled to doubt if equally valuable sports are ever substituted for these; and when some of my friends have asked me anxiously about their boys, whether they should let them hunt, I have answered, yes — remembering that it was one of the best parts of my education — make them hunters, though sportsmen only at first, if possible, mighty hunters at last, so that they shall not find game large enough for them in this or any vegetable wilderness — hunters as well as fishers of men. Thus far I am of the opinion of Chaucer's nun, who

"yave not of the text a pulled hen
That saith that hunters ben not holy men."

There is a period in the history of the individual, as of the race, when the hunters are the "best men," as the Algonquins called them. We cannot but pity the boy who has never fired a gun; he is no more humane, while his education has been sadly neglected. This was my answer with respect to those youths who were bent on this pursuit, trusting that they would soon outgrow it. No humane being, past the thoughtless age of boyhood, will wantonly murder any creature which holds its life by the same tenure that he does. The hare in its extremity cries like a child. I warn you, mothers, that my sympathies do not always make the usual philanthropic distinctions.

Such is oftenest the young man's introduction to the forest, and the most original part of himself. He goes thither at first as a hunter and fisher, until at last, if he has the seeds of a better life in him, he distinguishes his proper objects, as a poet or naturalist it may be, and leaves the gun and fishpole behind. The mass of men are still and always young in this respect. In some countries a hunting parson is no uncommon sight. Such a one might make a good shepherd's dog, but is far from being the Good Shepherd. I have been surprised to consider that the only obvious employment, except wood-chopping, ice-cutting, or the like business, which ever to my knowledge detained at Walden Pond for a whole half-day any of my fellow-citizens, whether fathers or children of the town, with just one exception, was fishing. Commonly they did not think that they were lucky, or well paid for their time, unless they got a long string of fish, though they had the opportunity of seeing the pond all the while. They might go there a thousand times before the sediment of fishing would sink to the bottom and leave their purpose pure; but no doubt such a clarifying process would be going on all the while. The Governor and his Council faintly remember the pond, for they went a-fishing there when they were boys; but now they are too old and dignified to go a-fishing, and so they know it no more forever. Yet even they expect to go to heaven at last. If the legislature regards it, it is chiefly to regulate the number of hooks to be used there; but they know nothing about the hook of hooks with which to angle for the pond itself, impaling the legislature for a bait. Thus, even in civilized communities, the embryo man passes through the hunter stage of development.

I have found repeatedly, of late years, that I cannot fish without falling a little in self-respect. I have tried it again and again. I have skill at it, and, like many of my fellows, a certain instinct for it, which revives from time to time, but always when I have done I feel that it would have been better if I had not fished. I think that I do not mistake. It is a faint intimation, yet so are the first streaks of morning. There is unquestionably this instinct in me which belongs to the lower orders of creation; yet with every year I am less a fisherman, though without more humanity or even wisdom; at present I am no fisherman at all. But I see that if I were to live in a wilderness I should again be tempted to become a fisher and hunter in earnest. Beside, there is something essentially unclean about this diet and all flesh, and I began to see where housework commences, and whence the endeavour, which costs so much, to wear a tidy and respectable appearance each day, to keep the house sweet and free from all ill odours and sights. Having been my own butcher and scullion and cook, as well as the gentleman for whom the dishes were served up, I can speak from an unusually complete experience. The practical objection to animal food in my case was its uncleanness; and besides, when I had caught and cleaned and cooked and eaten my fish, they seemed not to have fed me essentially. It was insignificant and unnecessary, and cost more than it came to. A little bread or a few potatoes would have done as well, with less trouble and filth. Like many of my contemporaries, I had rarely for many years used animal food, or tea, or coffee, etc.; not so much because of any ill effects which I had traced to them, as because they were not agreeable to my imagination. The repugnance to animal food is not the effect of experience, but is an instinct. It appeared more beautiful to live low and fare hard in many respects; and though I never did so, I went far enough to please my imagination. I believe that every man who has ever been earnest to preserve his higher or poetic faculties in the best condition has been particularly inclined to abstain from animal food, and from much food of any kind. It is a significant fact, stated by entomologists — I find it in Kirby and Spence — that "some insects in their perfect state, though furnished with organs of feeding, make no use of them"; and they lay it down as "a general rule, that almost all insects in this state eat much less than in that of larvae. The voracious caterpillar when transformed into a butterfly ... and the gluttonous maggot when become a fly" content themselves with a drop or two of honey or some other sweet liquid. The abdomen under the wings of the butterfly still represents the larva. This is the tidbit which tempts his insectivorous fate. The gross feeder is a man in the larva state; and there are whole nations in that condition, nations without fancy or imagination, whose vast abdomens betray them.

It is hard to provide and cook so simple and clean a diet as will not offend the imagination; but this, I think, is to be fed when we feed the body; they should both sit down at the same table. Yet perhaps this may be done. The fruits eaten temperately need not make us ashamed of our appetites, nor interrupt the worthiest pursuits. But put an extra condiment into your dish, and it will poison you. It is not worth the while to live by rich cookery. Most men would feel shame if caught preparing with their own hands precisely such a dinner, whether of animal or vegetable food, as is every day prepared for them by others. Yet till this is otherwise we are not civilized, and, if gentlemen and ladies, are not true men and women. This certainly suggests what change is to be made. It may be vain to ask why the imagination will not be reconciled to flesh and fat. I am satisfied that it is not. Is it not a reproach that man is a carnivorous animal? True, he can and does live, in a great measure, by preying on other animals; but this is a miserable way — as any one who will go to snaring rabbits, or slaughtering lambs, may learn — and he will be regarded as a benefactor of his race who shall teach man to confine himself to a more innocent and wholesome diet. Whatever my own practice may be, I have no doubt that it is a part of the destiny of the human race, in its gradual improvement, to leave off eating animals, as surely as the savage tribes have left off eating each other when they came in contact with the more civilized. If one listens to the faintest but constant suggestions of his genius, which are certainly true, he sees not to what extremes, or even insanity, it may lead him; and yet that way, as he grows more resolute and faithful, his road lies. The faintest assured objection which one healthy man feels will at length prevail over the arguments and customs of mankind. No man ever followed his genius till it misled him. Though the result were bodily weakness, yet perhaps no one can say that the consequences were to be regretted, for these were a life in conformity to higher principles. If the day and the night are such that you greet them with joy, and life emits a fragrance like flowers and sweet-scented herbs, is more elastic, more starry, more immortal — that is your success. All nature is your congratulation, and you have cause momentarily to bless yourself. The greatest gains and values are farthest from being appreciated. We easily come to doubt if they exist. We soon forget them. They are the highest reality. Perhaps the facts most astounding and most real are never communicated by man to man. The true harvest of my daily life is somewhat as intangible and indescribable as the tints of morning or evening. It is a little star-dust caught, a segment of the rainbow which I have clutched.

Yet, for my part, I was never unusually squeamish; I could sometimes eat a fried rat with a good relish, if it were necessary. I am glad to have drunk water so long, for the same reason that I prefer the natural sky to an opium-eater's heaven. I would fain keep sober always; and there are infinite degrees of drunkenness. I believe that water is the only drink for a wise man; wine is not so noble a liquor; and think of dashing the hopes of a morning with a cup of warm coffee, or of an evening with a dish of tea! Ah, how low I fall when I am tempted by them! Even music may be intoxicating. Such apparently slight causes destroyed Greece and Rome, and will destroy England and America. Of all ebriosity, who does not prefer to be intoxicated by the air he breathes? I have found it to be the most serious objection to coarse labours long continued, that they compelled me to eat and drink coarsely also. But to tell the truth, I find myself at present somewhat less particular in these respects. I carry less religion to the table, ask no blessing; not because I am wiser than I was, but, I am obliged to confess, because, however much it is to be regretted, with years I have grown more coarse and indifferent. Perhaps these questions are entertained only in youth, as most believe of poetry. My practice is "nowhere," my opinion is here. Nevertheless I am far from regarding myself as one of those privileged ones to whom the Ved refers when it says, that "he who has true faith in the Omnipresent Supreme Being may eat all that exists," that is, is not bound to inquire what is his food, or who prepares it; and even in their case it is to be observed, as a Hindoo commentator has remarked, that the Vedant limits this privilege to "the time of distress."

Who has not sometimes derived an inexpressible satisfaction from his food in which appetite had no share? I have been thrilled to think that I owed a mental perception to the commonly gross sense of taste, that I have been inspired through the palate, that some berries which I had eaten on a hillside had fed my genius. "The soul not being mistress of herself," says Thseng-tseu, "one looks, and one does not see; one listens, and one does not hear; one eats, and one does not know the savour of food." He who distinguishes the true savour of his food can never be a glutton; he who does not cannot be otherwise. A puritan may go to his brown-bread crust with as gross an appetite as ever an alderman to his turtle. Not that food which entereth into the mouth defileth a man, but the appetite with which it is eaten. It is neither the quality nor the quantity, but the devotion to sensual savours; when that which is eaten is not a viand to sustain our animal, or inspire our spiritual life, but food for the worms that possess us. If the hunter has a taste for mud-turtles, muskrats, and other such savage tidbits, the fine lady indulges a taste for jelly made of a calf's foot, or for sardines from over the sea, and they are even. He goes to the mill-pond, she to her preserve-pot. The wonder is how they, how you and I, can live this slimy, beastly life, eating and drinking.

Our whole life is startlingly moral. There is never an instant's truce between virtue and vice. Goodness is the only investment that never fails. In the music of the harp which trembles round the world it is the insisting on this which thrills us. The harp is the travelling patterer for the Universe's Insurance Company, recommending its laws, and our little goodness is all the assessment that we pay. Though the youth at last grows indifferent, the laws of the universe are not indifferent, but are forever on the side of the most sensitive. Listen to every zephyr for some reproof, for it is surely there, and he is unfortunate who does not hear it. We cannot touch a string or move a stop but the charming moral transfixes us. Many an irksome noise, go a long way off, is heard as music, a proud, sweet satire on the meanness of our lives.

We are conscious of an animal in us, which awakens in proportion as our higher nature slumbers. It is reptile and sensual, and perhaps cannot be wholly expelled; like the worms which, even in life and health, occupy our bodies. Possibly we may withdraw from it, but never change its nature. I fear that it may enjoy a certain health of its own; that we may be well, yet not pure. The other day I picked up the lower jaw of a hog, with white and sound teeth and tusks, which suggested that there was an animal health and vigour distinct from the spiritual. This creature succeeded by other means than temperance and purity. "That in which men differ from brute beasts," says Mencius, "is a thing very inconsiderable; the common herd lose it very soon; superior men preserve it carefully." Who knows what sort of life would result if we had attained to purity? If I knew so wise a man as could teach me purity I would go to seek him forthwith. "A command over our passions, and over the external senses of the body, and good acts, are declared by the Ved to be indispensable in the mind's approximation to God." Yet the spirit can for the time pervade and control every member and function of the body, and transmute what in form is the grossest sensuality into purity and devotion. The generative energy, which, when we are loose, dissipates and makes us unclean, when we are continent invigorates and inspires us. Chastity is the flowering of man; and what are called Genius, Heroism, Holiness, and the like, are but various fruits which succeed it. Man flows at once to God when the channel of purity is open. By turns our purity inspires and our impurity casts us down. He is blessed who is assured that the animal is dying out in him day by day, and the divine being established. Perhaps there is none but has cause for shame on account of the inferior and brutish nature to which he is allied. I fear that we are such gods or demigods only as fauns and satyrs, the divine allied to beasts, the creatures of appetite, and that, to some extent, our very life is our disgrace.—

> "How happy's he who hath due place assigned
> To his beasts and disafforested his mind!
>
> . . .

Can use this horse, goat, wolf, and ev'ry beast,
And is not ass himself to all the rest!
Else man not only is the herd of swine,
But he's those devils too which did incline
Them to a headlong rage, and made them worse."

All sensuality is one, though it takes many forms; all purity is one. It is the same whether a man eat, or drink, or cohabit, or sleep sensually. They are but one appetite, and we only need to see a person do any one of these things to know how great a sensualist he is. The impure can neither stand nor sit with purity. When the reptile is attacked at one mouth of his burrow, he shows himself at another. If you would be chaste, you must be temperate. What is chastity? How shall a man know if he is chaste? He shall not know it. We have heard of this virtue, but we know not what it is. We speak conformably to the rumor which we have heard. From exertion come wisdom and purity; from sloth ignorance and sensuality. In the student sensuality is a sluggish habit of mind. An unclean person is universally a slothful one, one who sits by a stove, whom the sun shines on prostrate, who reposes without being fatigued. If you would avoid uncleanness, and all the sins, work earnestly, though it be at cleaning a stable. Nature is hard to be overcome, but she must be overcome. What avails it that you are Christian, if you are not purer than the heathen, if you deny yourself no more, if you are not more religious? I know of many systems of religion esteemed heathenish whose precepts fill the reader with shame, and provoke him to new endeavours, though it be to the performance of rites merely.

I hesitate to say these things, but it is not because of the subject — I care not how obscene my words are — but because I cannot speak of them without betraying my impurity. We discourse freely without shame of one form of sensuality, and are silent about another. We are so degraded that we cannot speak simply of the necessary functions of human nature. In earlier ages, in some countries, every function was reverently spoken of and regulated by law. Nothing was too trivial for the Hindoo lawgiver, however offensive it may be to modern taste. He teaches how to eat, drink, cohabit, void excrement and urine, and the like, elevating what is mean, and does not falsely excuse himself by calling these things trifles.

Every man is the builder of a temple, called his body, to the god he worships, after a style purely his own, nor can he get off by hammering marble instead. We are all sculptors and painters, and our material is our own flesh and blood and bones. Any nobleness begins at once to refine a man's features, any meanness or sensuality to imbrute them.

John Farmer sat at his door one September evening, after a hard day's work, his mind still running on his labour more or less. Having bathed, he sat down to re-create his intellectual man. It was a rather cool evening, and some of his neighbours were apprehending a frost. He had not attended to the train of his thoughts long when he heard someone playing on a flute, and that sound harmonized with his mood. Still he thought of his work; but the burden of his thought was, that though this kept running in his head, and he found himself planning and contriving it against his will, yet it concerned him very little. It was no more than the scurf of his skin, which was constantly shuffled off. But the notes of the flute came home to his ears out of a different sphere from that he worked in, and suggested work for certain faculties which slumbered in him. They gently did away with the street, and the village, and the state in which he lived. A voice said to him — Why do you stay here and live this mean moiling life, when a glorious existence is possible for you? Those same stars twinkle over other fields than these. — But how to come out of this condition and actually migrate thither? All that he could think of was to practise some new austerity, to let his mind descend into his body and redeem it, and treat himself with ever increasing respect.

12
Brute Neighbours

Sometimes I had a companion in my fishing, who came through the village to my house from the other side of the town, and the catching of the dinner was as much a social exercise as the eating of it.

Hermit. I wonder what the world is doing now. I have not heard so much as a locust over the sweet-fern these three hours. The pigeons are all asleep upon their roosts — no flutter from them. Was that a farmer's noon horn which sounded from beyond the woods just now? The hands are coming in to boiled salt beef and cider and Indian bread. Why will men worry themselves so? He that does not eat need not work. I wonder how much they have reaped. Who would live there where a body can never think for the barking of Bose? And oh, the housekeeping! to keep bright the devil's door-knobs, and scour his tubs this bright day! Better not keep a house. Say, some hollow tree; and then for morning calls and dinner-parties! Only a woodpecker tapping. Oh, they swarm; the sun is too warm there; they are born too far into life for me. I have water from the spring, and a loaf of brown bread on the shelf. — Hark! I hear a rustling of the leaves. Is it some ill-fed village hound yielding to the instinct of the chase? Or the lost pig which is said to be in these woods, whose tracks I saw after the rain? It comes on apace; my sumachs and sweetbriers tremble. — Eh, Mr. Poet, is it you? How do you like the world today?

Poet. See those clouds; how they hang! That's the greatest thing I have seen today. There's nothing like it in old paintings, nothing like it in foreign lands — unless when we were off the coast of Spain. That's a true Mediterranean sky. I thought, as I have my living to get, and have not eaten today, that I might go a-fishing. That's the true industry for poets. It is the only trade I have learned. Come, let's along.

Hermit. I cannot resist. My brown bread will soon be gone. I will go with you gladly soon, but I am just concluding a serious meditation. I think that I am near the end of it. Leave me alone, then, for a while. But that we may not be delayed, you shall be digging the bait meanwhile. Angleworms are rarely to be met with in these parts, where the soil was never fattened with manure; the race is nearly extinct. The sport of digging the bait is nearly equal to that of catching the fish, when one's appetite is not too keen; and this you may have all to yourself today. I would advise you to set in the spade down yonder among the ground-nuts, where you see the johnswort waving. I think that I may warrant you one worm to every three sods you turn up, if you look well in among the roots of the grass, as if you were weeding. Or, if you choose to go farther, it will not be unwise, for I have found the increase of fair bait to be very nearly as the squares of the distances.

Hermit alone. Let me see; where was I? Methinks I was nearly in this frame of mind; the world lay about at this angle. Shall I go to heaven or a-fishing? If I should soon bring this meditation to an end, would another so sweet occasion be likely to offer? I was as near being resolved into the essence of things as ever I was in my life. I fear my thoughts will not come back to me. If it would do any good, I would whistle for them. When they make us an offer, is it wise to say, We will think of it? My thoughts have left no track, and I cannot find the path again. What was it that I was thinking of? It was a very hazy day. I will just try these three sentences of Confutsee; they may fetch that state about again. I know not whether it was the dumps or a budding ecstasy. Mem. There never is but one opportunity of a kind.

Poet. How now, Hermit, is it too soon? I have got just thirteen whole ones, beside several which are imperfect or undersized; but they will do for the smaller fry; they do not cover up the hook so much. Those village worms are quite too large; a shiner may make a meal off one without finding the skewer.

Hermit. Well, then, let's be off. Shall we to the Concord? There's good sport there if the water be not too high.

Why do precisely these objects which we behold make a world? Why has man just these species of animals for his neighbours; as if nothing but a mouse could have filled this crevice? I suspect that Pilpay & Co. have put animals to their best use, for they are all beasts of burden, in a sense, made to carry some portion of our thoughts.

The mice which haunted my house were not the common ones, which are said to have been introduced into the country, but a wild native kind not found in the village. I sent one to a distinguished naturalist, and it interested him much. When I was building, one of these had its nest underneath the house, and before I had laid the second floor, and swept out the shavings, would come out regularly at lunch time and pick up the crumbs at my feet. It probably had never seen a man before; and it soon became quite familiar, and would run over my shoes and up my clothes. It could readily ascend the sides of the room by short impulses, like a squirrel, which it resembled in its motions. At length, as I leaned with my elbow on the bench one day, it ran up my clothes, and along my sleeve, and round and round the paper which held my dinner, while I kept the latter close, and dodged and played at bopeep with it; and when at last I held still a piece of cheese between my thumb and finger, it came and nibbled it, sitting in my hand, and afterward cleaned its face and paws, like a fly, and walked away.

A phoebe soon built in my shed, and a robin for protection in a pine which grew against the house. In June the partridge (Tetrao umbellus), which is so shy a bird, led her brood past my windows, from the woods in the rear to the front of my house, clucking and calling to them like a hen, and in all her behaviour proving herself the hen of the woods. The young suddenly disperse on your approach, at a signal from the mother, as if a whirlwind had swept them away, and they so exactly resemble the dried leaves and twigs that many a traveler has placed his foot in the midst of a brood, and heard the whir of the old bird as she flew off, and her anxious calls and mewing, or seen her trail her wings to attract his attention, without suspecting their neighbourhood. The parent will sometimes roll and spin round before you in such a dishabille, that you cannot, for a few moments, detect what kind of creature it is. The young squat still and flat, often running their heads under a leaf, and mind only their mother's directions given from a distance, nor will your approach make them run again and betray themselves.

You may even tread on them, or have your eyes on them for a minute, without discovering them. I have held them in my open hand at such a time, and still their only care, obedient to their mother and their instinct, was to squat there without fear or trembling. So perfect is this instinct, that once, when I had laid them on the leaves again, and one accidentally fell on its side, it was found with the rest in exactly the same position ten minutes afterward. They are not callow like the young of most birds, but more perfectly developed and precocious even than chickens. The remarkably adult yet innocent expression of their open and serene eyes is very memorable. All intelligence seems reflected in them. They suggest not merely the purity of infancy, but a wisdom clarified by experience. Such an eye was not born when the bird was, but is coeval with the sky it reflects. The woods do not yield another such a gem. The traveller does not often look into such a limpid well. The ignorant or reckless sportsman often shoots the parent at such a time, and leaves these innocents to fall a prey to some prowling beast or bird, or gradually mingle with the decaying leaves which they so much resemble. It is said that when hatched by a hen they will directly disperse on some alarm, and so are lost, for they never hear the mother's call which gathers them again. These were my hens and chickens.

It is remarkable how many creatures live wild and free though secret in the woods, and still sustain themselves in the neighbourhood of towns, suspected by hunters only. How retired the otter manages to live here! He grows to be four feet long, as big as a small boy, perhaps without any human being getting a glimpse of him. I formerly saw the raccoon in the woods behind where my house is built, and probably still heard their whinnering at night. Commonly I rested an hour or two in the shade at noon, after planting, and ate my lunch, and read a little by a spring which was the source of a swamp and of a brook, oozing from under Brister's Hill, half a mile from my field. The approach to this was through a succession of descending grassy hollows, full of young pitch pines, into a larger wood about the swamp. There, in a very secluded and shaded spot, under a spreading white pine, there was yet a clean, firm sward to sit on. I had dug out the spring and made a well of clear gray water, where I could dip up a pailful without roiling it, and thither I went for this purpose almost every day in midsummer, when the pond was warmest. Thither, too, the woodcock led her brood, to probe the mud for worms, flying but a foot above them down the bank, while they ran in a troop beneath; but at last, spying me, she would leave her young and circle round and round me, nearer and nearer till within four or five feet, pretending broken wings and legs, to attract my attention, and get off her young, who would already have taken up their march, with faint, wiry peep, single file through the swamp, as she directed. Or I heard the peep of the young when I could not see the parent bird. There too the turtle doves sat over the spring, or fluttered from bough to bough of the soft white pines over my head; or the red squirrel, coursing down the nearest bough, was particularly familiar and inquisitive. You only need sit still long enough in some attractive spot in the woods that all its inhabitants may exhibit themselves to you by turns.

I was witness to events of a less peaceful character. One day when I went out to my wood-pile, or rather my pile of stumps, I observed two large ants, the one red, the other much larger, nearly half an inch long, and black, fiercely contending with one another. Having once got hold they never let go, but struggled and wrestled and rolled on the chips incessantly. Looking farther, I was surprised to find that the chips were covered with such combatants, that it was not a duellum, but a bellum, a war between two races of ants, the red always pitted against the black, and frequently two red ones to one black. The legions of these Myrmidons covered all the hills and vales in my wood-yard, and the ground was already strewn with the dead and dying, both red and black. It was the only battle which I have ever witnessed, the only battle-field I ever trod while the battle was raging; internecine war; the red republicans on the one hand, and the black imperialists on the other. On every side they were engaged in deadly combat, yet without any noise that I could hear, and human soldiers never fought so resolutely. I watched a couple that were fast locked in each other's embraces, in a little sunny valley amid the chips, now at noonday prepared to fight till the sun went down, or life went out. The smaller red champion had fastened himself like a vice to his adversary's front, and through all the tumblings on that field never for an instant ceased to gnaw at one of his feelers near the root, having already caused the other to go by the board; while the stronger black one dashed him from side to side, and, as I saw on looking nearer, had already divested him of several of his members. They fought with more pertinacity than bulldogs. Neither manifested the least disposition to retreat. It was evident that their battle-cry was "Conquer or die." In the meanwhile there came along a single red ant on the hillside of this valley, evidently full of excitement, who either had despatched his foe, or had not yet taken part in the battle; probably the latter, for he had lost none of his limbs; whose mother had charged him to return with his shield or upon it. Or perchance he was some Achilles, who had nourished his wrath apart, and had now come to avenge or rescue his Patroclus. He saw this unequal combat from afar — for the blacks were nearly twice the size of the red — he drew near with rapid pace till he stood on his guard within half an inch of the combatants; then, watching his opportunity, he sprang upon the black warrior, and commenced his operations near the root of his right fore leg, leaving the foe to select among his own members; and so there were three united for life, as if a new kind of attraction had been invented which put all other locks and cements to shame. I should not have wondered by this time to find that they had their respective musical bands stationed on some eminent chip, and playing their national airs the while, to excite the slow and cheer the dying combatants. I was myself excited somewhat even as if they had been men. The more you think of it, the less the difference. And certainly there is not the fight recorded in Concord history, at least, if in the history of America, that will bear a moment's comparison with this, whether for the numbers engaged in it, or for the patriotism and heroism displayed. For numbers and for carnage it was an Austerlitz or Dresden. Concord Fight! Two killed on the patriots' side, and Luther Blanchard wounded! Why here every ant was a Buttrick — "Fire! for God's sake fire!" — and thousands shared the fate of Davis and Hosmer. There was not one hireling there. I have no doubt that it was a principle they fought for, as much as our ancestors, and not to avoid a three-penny tax on their tea; and the results of this battle will be as important and memorable to those whom it concerns as those of the battle of Bunker Hill, at least.

I took up the chip on which the three I have particularly described were struggling, carried it into my house, and placed it under a tumbler on my window-sill, in order to see the issue. Holding a microscope to the first-mentioned red ant, I saw that, though he was assiduously gnawing at the near fore leg of his enemy, having severed his remaining feeler, his own breast was all torn away, exposing what vitals he had there to the jaws of the black warrior, whose breastplate was apparently too thick for him to pierce; and the dark carbuncles of the sufferer's eyes shone with ferocity such as war only could excite. They struggled half an hour longer under the tumbler, and when I looked again the black soldier had severed the heads of his foes from their bodies, and the still living heads were hanging on either side of him like ghastly trophies at his saddle-bow, still apparently as firmly fastened as ever, and he was endeavouring with feeble struggles, being without feelers and with only the remnant of a leg, and I know not how many other wounds, to divest himself of them; which at length, after half an hour more, he accomplished. I raised the glass, and he went off over the window-sill in that crippled state. Whether he finally survived that combat, and spent the remainder of his days in some Hotel des Invalides, I do not know; but I thought that his industry would not be worth much thereafter. I never learned which party was victorious, nor the cause of the war; but I felt for the rest of that day as if I had had my feelings excited and harrowed by witnessing the struggle, the ferocity and carnage, of a human battle before my door.

Kirby and Spence tell us that the battles of ants have long been celebrated and the date of them recorded, though they say that Huber is the only modern author who appears to have witnessed them. "AEneas Sylvius," say they, "after giving a very circumstantial account of one contested with great obstinacy by a great and small species on the trunk of a pear tree," adds that "this action was fought in the pontificate of Eugenius the Fourth, in the presence of Nicholas Pistoriensis, an eminent lawyer, who related the whole, history of the battle with the greatest fidelity." A similar engagement between great and small ants is recorded by Olaus Magnus, in which the small ones, being victorious, are said to have buried the bodies of their own soldiers, but left those of their giant enemies a prey to the birds. This event happened previous to the expulsion of the tyrant Christiern the Second from Sweden." The battle which I witnessed took place in the Presidency of Polk, five years before the passage of Webster's Fugitive-Slave Bill.

Many a village Bose, fit only to course a mud-turtle in a victualling cellar, sported his heavy quarters in the woods, without the knowledge of his master, and ineffectually smelled at old fox burrows and woodchucks' holes; led perchance by some slight cur which nimbly threaded the wood, and might still inspire a natural terror in its denizens; — now far behind his guide, barking like a canine bull toward some small squirrel which had treed itself for scrutiny, then, cantering off, bending the bushes with his weight, imagining that he is on the track of some stray member of the jerbilla family. Once I was surprised to see a cat walking along the stony shore of the pond, for they rarely wander so far from home. The surprise was mutual. Nevertheless the most domestic cat, which has lain on a rug all her days, appears quite at home in the woods, and, by her sly and stealthy behaviour, proves herself more native there than the regular inhabitants. Once, when berrying, I met with a cat with young kittens in the woods, quite wild, and they all, like their mother, had their backs up and were fiercely spitting at me. A few years before I lived in the woods there was what was called a "winged cat" in one of the farm-houses in Lincoln nearest the pond, Mr. Gilian Baker's. When I called to see her in June, 1842, she was gone a-hunting in the woods, as was her wont (I am not sure whether it was a male or female, and so use the more common pronoun), but her mistress told me that she came into the neighbourhood a little more than a year before, in April, and was finally taken into their house; that she was of a dark brownish-gray colour, with a white spot on her throat, and white feet, and had a large bushy tail like a fox; that in the winter the fur grew thick and flatted out along her sides, forming stripes ten or twelve inches long by two and a half wide, and under her chin like a muff, the upper side loose, the under matted like felt, and in the spring these appendages dropped off. They gave me a pair of her "wings," which I keep still. There is no appearance of a membrane about them. Some thought it was part flying squirrel or some other wild animal, which is not impossible, for, according to naturalists, prolific hybrids have been produced by the union of the marten and domestic cat. This would have been the right kind of cat for me to keep, if I had kept any; for why should not a poet's cat be winged as well as his horse?

In the fall the loon (Colymbus glacialis) came, as usual, to moult and bathe in the pond, making the woods ring with his wild laughter before I had risen. At rumor of his arrival all the Mill-dam sportsmen are on the alert, in gigs and on foot, two by two and three by three, with patent rifles and conical balls and spy-glasses. They come rustling through the woods like autumn leaves, at least ten men to one loon. Some station themselves on this side of the pond, some on that, for the poor bird cannot be omnipresent; if he dive here he must come up there. But now the kind October wind rises, rustling the leaves and rippling the surface of the water, so that no loon can be heard or seen, though his foes sweep the pond with spy-glasses, and make the woods resound with their discharges. The waves generously rise and dash angrily, taking sides with all water-fowl, and our sportsmen must beat a retreat to town and shop and unfinished jobs. But they were too often successful. When I went to get a pail of water early in the morning I frequently saw this stately bird sailing out of my cove within a few rods. If I endeavoured to overtake him in a boat, in order to see how he would manoeuvre, he would dive and be completely lost, so that I did not discover him again, sometimes, till the latter part of the day. But I was more than a match for him on the surface. He commonly went off in a rain.

As I was paddling along the north shore one very calm October afternoon, for such days especially they settle on to the lakes, like the milkweed down, having looked in vain over the pond for a loon, suddenly one, sailing out from the shore toward the middle a few rods in front of me, set up his wild laugh and betrayed himself. I pursued with a paddle and he dived, but when he came up I was nearer than before. He dived again, but I miscalculated the direction he would take, and we were fifty rods apart when he came to the surface this time, for I had helped to widen the interval; and again he laughed long and loud, and with more reason than before. He manoeuvred so cunningly that I could not get within half a dozen rods of him. Each time, when he came to the surface, turning his head this way and that, he cooly surveyed the water and the land, and apparently chose his course so that he might come up where there was the widest expanse of water and at the greatest distance from the boat. It was surprising how quickly he made up his mind and put his resolve into execution. He led me at once to the widest part of the pond, and could not be driven from it. While he was thinking one thing in his brain, I was endeavouring to divine his thought in mine. It was a pretty game, played on the smooth surface of the pond, a man against a loon. Suddenly your adversary's checker disappears beneath the board, and the problem is to place yours nearest to where his will appear again. Sometimes he would come up unexpectedly on the opposite side of me, having apparently passed directly under the boat. So long-winded was he and so unweariable, that when he had swum farthest he would immediately plunge again, nevertheless; and then no wit could divine where in the deep pond, beneath the smooth surface, he might be speeding his way like a fish, for he had time and ability to visit the bottom of the pond in its deepest part. It is said that loons have been caught in the New York lakes eighty feet beneath the surface, with hooks set for trout — though Walden is deeper than that. How surprised must the fishes be to see this ungainly visitor from another sphere speeding his way amid their schools! Yet he appeared to know his course as surely under water as on the surface, and swam much faster there. Once or twice I saw a ripple where he approached the surface, just put his head out to reconnoitre, and instantly dived again. I found that it was as well for me to rest on my oars and wait his reappearing as to endeavour to calculate where he would rise; for again and again, when I was straining my eyes over the surface one way, I would suddenly be startled by his unearthly laugh behind me. But why, after displaying so much cunning, did he invariably betray himself the moment he came up by that loud laugh? Did not his white breast enough betray him? He was indeed a silly loon, I thought. I could commonly hear the splash of the water when he came up, and so also detected him. But after an hour he seemed as fresh as ever, dived as willingly, and swam yet farther than at first. It was surprising to see how serenely he sailed off with unruffled breast when he came to the surface, doing all the work with his webbed feet beneath. His usual note was this demoniac laughter, yet somewhat like that of a water-fowl; but occasionally, when he had balked me most successfully and come up a long way off, he uttered a long-drawn unearthly howl, probably more like that of a wolf than any bird; as when a beast puts his muzzle to the ground and deliberately howls. This was his looning — perhaps the wildest sound that is ever heard here, making the woods ring far and wide. I concluded that he laughed in derision of my efforts, confident of his own resources. Though the sky was by this time overcast, the pond was so smooth that I could see where he broke the surface when I did not hear him. His white breast, the stillness of the air, and the smoothness of the water were all against him. At length having come up fifty rods off, he uttered one of those prolonged howls, as if calling on the god of loons to aid him, and immediately there came a wind from the east and rippled the surface, and filled the whole air with misty rain, and I was impressed as if it were the prayer of the loon answered, and his god was angry with me; and so I left him disappearing far away on the tumultuous surface.

For hours, in fall days, I watched the ducks cunningly tack and veer and hold the middle of the pond, far from the sportsman; tricks which they will have less need to practise in Louisiana bayous. When compelled to rise they would sometimes circle round and round and over the pond at a considerable height, from which they could easily see to other ponds and the river, like black motes in the sky; and, when I thought they had gone off thither long since, they would settle down by a slanting flight of a quarter of a mile on to a distant part which was left free; but what beside safety they got by sailing in the middle of Walden I do not know, unless they love its water for the same reason that I do.

13
House-Warming

In October I went a-graping to the river meadows, and loaded myself with clusters more precious for their beauty and fragrance than for food. There, too, I admired, though I did not gather, the cranberries, small waxen gems, pendants of the meadow grass, pearly and red, which the farmer plucks with an ugly rake, leaving the smooth meadow in a snarl, heedlessly measuring them by the bushel and the dollar only, and sells the spoils of the meads to Boston and New York; destined to be jammed, to satisfy the tastes of lovers of Nature there. So butchers rake the tongues of bison out of the prairie grass, regardless of the torn and drooping plant. The barberry's brilliant fruit was likewise food for my eyes merely; but I collected a small store of wild apples for coddling, which the proprietor and travellers had overlooked. When chestnuts were ripe I laid up half a bushel for winter. It was very exciting at that season to roam the then boundless chestnut woods of Lincoln — they now sleep their long sleep under the railroad — with a bag on my shoulder, and a stick to open burs with in my hand, for I did not always wait for the frost, amid the rustling of leaves and the loud reproofs of the red squirrels and the jays, whose half-consumed nuts I sometimes stole, for the burs which they had selected were sure to contain sound ones. Occasionally I climbed and shook the trees. They grew also behind my house, and one large tree, which almost overshadowed it, was, when in flower, a bouquet which scented the whole neighbourhood, but the squirrels and the jays got most of its fruit; the last coming in flocks early in the morning and picking the nuts out of the burs before they fell, I relinquished these trees to them and visited the more distant woods composed wholly of chestnut. These nuts, as far as they went, were a good substitute for bread. Many other substitutes might, perhaps, be found. Digging one day for fishworms, I discovered the ground-nut (Apios tuberosa) on its string, the potato of the aborigines, a sort of fabulous fruit, which I had begun to doubt if I had ever dug and eaten in childhood, as I had told, and had not dreamed it. I had often since seen its crumpled red velvety blossom supported by the stems of other plants without knowing it to be the same. Cultivation has well-nigh exterminated it. It has a sweetish taste, much like that of a frost-bitten potato, and I found it better boiled than roasted. This tuber seemed like a faint promise of Nature to rear her own children and feed them simply here at some future period. In these days of fatted cattle and waving grain-fields this humble root, which was once the totem of an Indian tribe, is quite forgotten, or known only by its flowering vine; but let wild Nature reign here once more, and the tender and luxurious English grains will probably disappear before a myriad of foes, and without the care of man the crow may carry back even the last seed of corn to the great cornfield of the Indian's God in the southwest, whence he is said to have brought it; but the now almost exterminated ground-nut will perhaps revive and flourish in spite of frosts and wildness, prove itself indigenous, and resume its ancient importance and dignity as the diet of the hunter tribe. Some Indian Ceres or Minerva must have been the inventor and bestower of it; and when the reign of poetry commences here, its leaves and string of nuts may be represented on our works of art.

Already, by the first of September, I had seen two or three small maples turned scarlet across the pond, beneath where the white stems of three aspens diverged, at the point of a promontory, next the water. Ah, many a tale their colour told! And gradually from week to week the character of each tree came out, and it admired itself reflected in the smooth mirror of the lake. Each morning the manager of this gallery substituted some new picture, distinguished by more brilliant or harmonious colouring, for the old upon the walls.

The wasps came by thousands to my lodge in October, as to winter quarters, and settled on my windows within and on the walls overhead, sometimes deterring visitors from entering. Each morning, when they were numbed with cold, I swept some of them out, but I did not trouble myself much to get rid of them; I even felt complimented by their regarding my house as a desirable shelter. They never molested me seriously, though they bedded with me; and they gradually disappeared, into what crevices I do not know, avoiding winter and unspeakable cold.

Like the wasps, before I finally went into winter quarters in November, I used to resort to the northeast side of Walden, which the sun, reflected from the pitch pine woods and the stony shore, made the fireside of the pond; it is so much pleasanter and wholesomer to be warmed by the sun while you can be, than by an artificial fire. I thus warmed myself by the still glowing embers which the summer, like a departed hunter, had left.

When I came to build my chimney I studied masonry. My bricks, being second-hand ones, required to be cleaned with a trowel, so that I learned more than usual of the qualities of bricks and trowels. The mortar on them was fifty years old, and was said to be still growing harder; but this is one of those sayings which men love to repeat whether they are true or not. Such sayings themselves grow harder and adhere more firmly with age, and it would take many blows with a trowel to clean an old wiseacre of them. Many of the villages of Mesopotamia are built of second-hand bricks of a very good quality, obtained from the ruins of Babylon, and the cement on them is older and probably harder still. However that may be, I was struck by the peculiar toughness of the steel which bore so many violent blows without being worn out. As my bricks had been in a chimney before, though I did not read the name of Nebuchadnezzar on them, I picked out its many fireplace bricks as I could find, to save work and waste, and I filled the spaces between the bricks about the fireplace with stones from the pond shore, and also made my mortar with the white sand from the same place. I lingered most about the fireplace, as the most vital part of the house. Indeed, I worked so deliberately, that though I commenced at the ground in the morning, a course of bricks raised a few inches above the floor served for my pillow at night; yet I did not get a stiff neck for it that I remember; my stiff neck is of older date. I took a poet to board for a fortnight about those times, which caused me to be put to it for room. He brought his own knife, though I had two, and we used to scour them by thrusting them into the earth. He shared with me the labours of cooking. I was pleased to see my work rising so square and solid by degrees, and reflected, that, if it proceeded slowly, it was calculated to endure a long time. The chimney is to some extent an independent structure, standing on the ground, and rising through the house to the heavens; even after the house is burned it still stands sometimes, and its importance and independence are apparent. This was toward the end of summer. It was now November.

The north wind had already begun to cool the pond, though it took many weeks of steady blowing to accomplish it, it is so deep. When I began to have a fire at evening, before I plastered my house, the chimney carried smoke particularly well, because of the numerous chinks between the boards. Yet I passed some cheerful evenings in that cool and airy apartment, surrounded by the rough brown boards full of knots, and rafters with the bark on high overhead. My house never pleased my eye so much after it was plastered, though I was obliged to confess that it was more comfortable. Should not every apartment in which man dwells be lofty enough to create some obscurity overhead, where flickering shadows may play at evening about the rafters? These forms are more agreeable to the fancy and imagination than fresco paintings or other the most expensive furniture. I now first began to inhabit my house, I may say, when I began to use it for warmth as well as shelter. I had got a couple of old fire-dogs to keep the wood from the hearth, and it did me good to see the soot form on the back of the chimney which I had built, and I poked the fire with more right and more satisfaction than usual. My dwelling was small, and I could hardly entertain an echo in it; but it seemed larger for being a single apartment and remote from neighbours. All the attractions of a house were concentrated in one room; it was kitchen, chamber, parlor, and keeping-room; and whatever satisfaction parent or child, master or servant, derive from living in a house, I enjoyed it all. Cato says, the master of a family (patremfamilias) must have in his rustic villa "cellam oleariam, vinariam, dolia multa, uti lubeat caritatem expectare, et rei, et virtuti, et gloriae erit," that is, "an oil and wine cellar, many casks, so that it may be pleasant to expect hard times; it will be for his advantage, and virtue, and glory." I had in my cellar a firkin of potatoes, about two quarts of peas with the weevil in them, and on my shelf a little rice, a jug of molasses, and of rye and Indian meal a peck each.

I sometimes dream of a larger and more populous house, standing in a golden age, of enduring materials, and without gingerbread work, which shall still consist of only one room, a vast, rude, substantial, primitive hall, without ceiling or plastering, with bare rafters and purlins supporting a sort of lower heaven over one's head — useful to keep off rain and snow, where the king and queen posts stand out to receive your homage, when you have done reverence to the prostrate Saturn of an older dynasty on stepping over the sill; a cavernous house, wherein you must reach up a torch upon a pole to see the roof; where some may live in the fireplace, some in the recess of a window, and some on settles, some at one end of the hall, some at another, and some aloft on rafters with the spiders, if they choose; a house which you have got into when you have opened the outside door, and the ceremony is over; where the weary traveller may wash, and eat, and converse, and sleep, without further journey; such a shelter as you would be glad to reach in a tempestuous night, containing all the essentials of a house, and nothing for house-keeping; where you can see all the treasures of the house at one view, and everything hangs upon its peg, that a man should use; at once kitchen, pantry, parlor, chamber, storehouse, and garret; where you can see so necessary a thing, as a barrel or a ladder, so convenient a thing as a cupboard, and hear the pot boil, and pay your respects to the fire that cooks your dinner, and the oven that bakes your bread, and the necessary furniture and utensils are the chief ornaments; where the washing is not put out, nor the fire, nor the mistress, and perhaps you are sometimes requested to move from off the trap-door, when the cook would descend into the cellar, and so learn whether the ground is solid or hollow beneath you without stamping. A house whose inside is as open and manifest as a bird's nest, and you cannot go in at the front door and out at the back without seeing some of its inhabitants; where to be a guest is to be presented with the freedom of the house, and not to be carefully excluded from seven eighths of it, shut up in a particular cell, and told to make yourself at home there — in solitary confinement. Nowadays the host does not admit you to his hearth, but has got the mason to build one for yourself somewhere in his alley, and hospitality is the art of keeping you at the greatest distance. There is as much secrecy about the cooking as if he had a design to poison you. I am aware that I have been on many a man's premises, and might have been legally ordered off, but I am not aware that I have been in many men's houses. I might visit in my old clothes a king and queen who lived simply in such a house as I have described, if I were going their way; but backing out of a modern palace will be all that I shall desire to learn, if ever I am caught in one.

It would seem as if the very language of our parlors would lose all its nerve and degenerate into palaver wholly, our lives pass at such remoteness from its symbols, and its metaphors and tropes are necessarily so far fetched, through slides and dumb-waiters, as it were; in other words, the parlor is so far from the kitchen and workshop. The dinner even is only the parable of a dinner, commonly. As if only the savage dwelt near enough to Nature and Truth to borrow a trope from them. How can the scholar, who dwells away in the North West Territory or the Isle of Man, tell what is parliamentary in the kitchen?

However, only one or two of my guests were ever bold enough to stay and eat a hasty-pudding with me; but when they saw that crisis approaching they beat a hasty retreat rather, as if it would shake the house to its foundations. Nevertheless, it stood through a great many hasty-puddings.

I did not plaster till it was freezing weather. I brought over some whiter and cleaner sand for this purpose from the opposite shore of the pond in a boat, a sort of conveyance which would have tempted me to go much farther if necessary. My house had in the meanwhile been shingled down to the ground on every side. In lathing I was pleased to be able to send home each nail with a single blow of the hammer, and it was my ambition to transfer the plaster from the board to the wall neatly and rapidly. I remembered the story of a conceited fellow, who, in fine clothes, was wont to lounge about the village once, giving advice to workmen. Venturing one day to substitute deeds for words, he turned up his cuffs, seized a plasterer's board, and having loaded his trowel without mishap, with a complacent look toward the lathing overhead, made a bold gesture thitherward; and straightway, to his complete discomfiture, received the whole contents in his ruffled bosom. I admired anew the economy and convenience of plastering, which so effectually shuts out the cold and takes a handsome finish, and I learned the various casualties to which the plasterer is liable. I was surprised to see how thirsty the bricks were which drank up all the moisture in my plaster before I had smoothed it, and how many pailfuls of water it takes to christen a new hearth. I had the previous winter made a small quantity of lime by burning the shells of the Unio fluviatilis, which our river affords, for the sake of the experiment; so that I knew where my materials came from. I might have got good limestone within a mile or two and burned it myself, if I had cared to do so.

The pond had in the meanwhile skimmed over in the shadiest and shallowest coves, some days or even weeks before the general freezing. The first ice is especially interesting and perfect, being hard, dark, and transparent, and affords the best opportunity that ever offers for examining the bottom where it is shallow; for you can lie at your length on ice only an inch thick, like a skater insect on the surface of the water, and study the bottom at your leisure, only two or three inches distant, like a picture behind a glass, and the water is necessarily always smooth then. There are many furrows in the sand where some creature has travelled about and doubled on its tracks; and, for wrecks, it is strewn with the cases of caddis-worms made of minute grains of white quartz. Perhaps these have creased it, for you find some of their cases in the furrows, though they are deep and broad for them to make. But the ice itself is the object of most interest, though you must improve the earliest opportunity to study it. If you examine it closely the morning after it freezes, you find that the greater part of the bubbles, which at first appeared to be within it, are against its under surface, and that more are continually rising from the bottom; while the ice is as yet comparatively solid and dark, that is, you see the water through it. These bubbles are from an eightieth to an eighth of an inch in diameter, very clear and beautiful, and you see your face reflected in them through the ice. There may be thirty or forty of them to a square inch. There are also already within the ice narrow oblong perpendicular bubbles about half an inch long, sharp cones with the apex upward; or oftener, if the ice is quite fresh, minute spherical bubbles one directly above another, like a string of beads. But these within the ice are not so numerous nor obvious as those beneath. I sometimes used to cast on stones to try the strength of the ice, and those which broke through carried in air with them, which formed very large and conspicuous white bubbles beneath. One day when I came to the same place forty-eight hours afterward, I found that those large bubbles were still perfect, though an inch more of ice had formed, as I could see distinctly by the seam in the edge of a cake. But as the last two days had been very warm, like an Indian summer, the ice was not now transparent, showing the dark green colour of the water, and the bottom, but opaque and whitish or gray, and though twice as thick was hardly stronger than before, for the air bubbles had greatly expanded under this heat and run together, and lost their regularity; they were no longer one directly over another, but often like silvery coins poured from a bag, one overlapping another, or in thin flakes, as if occupying slight cleavages. The beauty of the ice was gone, and it was too late to study the bottom. Being curious to know what position my great bubbles occupied with regard to the new ice, I broke out a cake containing a middling sized one, and turned it bottom upward. The new ice had formed around and under the bubble, so that it was included between the two ices. It was wholly in the lower ice, but close against the upper, and was flattish, or perhaps slightly lenticular, with a rounded edge, a quarter of an inch deep by four inches in diameter; and I was surprised to find that directly under the bubble the ice was melted with great regularity in the form of a saucer reversed, to the height of five eighths of an inch in the middle, leaving a thin partition there between the water and the bubble, hardly an eighth of an inch thick; and in many places the small bubbles in this partition had burst out downward, and probably there was no ice at all under the largest bubbles, which were a foot in diameter. I inferred that the infinite number of minute bubbles which I had first seen against the under surface of the ice were now frozen in likewise, and that each, in its degree, had operated like a burning-glass on the ice beneath to melt and rot it. These are the little air-guns which contribute to make the ice crack and whoop.

At length the winter set in good earnest, just as I had finished plastering, and the wind began to howl around the house as if it had not had permission to do so till then. Night after night the geese came lumbering in the dark with a clangor and a whistling of wings, even after the ground was covered with snow, some to alight in Walden, and some flying low over the woods toward Fair Haven, bound for Mexico. Several times, when returning from the village at ten or eleven o'clock at night, I heard the tread of a flock of geese, or else ducks, on the dry leaves in the woods by a pond-hole behind my dwelling, where they had come up to feed, and the faint honk or quack of their leader as they hurried off. In 1845 Walden froze entirely over for the first time on the night of the 22nd of December, Flint's and other shallower ponds and the river having been frozen ten days or more; in '46, the 16th; in '49, about the 31st; and in '50, about the 27th of December; in '52, the 5th of January; in '53, the 31st of December. The snow had already covered the ground since the 25th of November, and surrounded me suddenly with the scenery of winter. I withdrew yet farther into my shell, and endeavoured to keep a bright fire both within my house and within my breast. My employment out of doors now was to collect the dead wood in the forest, bringing it in my hands or on my shoulders, or sometimes trailing a dead pine tree under each arm to my shed. An old forest fence which had seen its best days was a great haul for me. I sacrificed it to Vulcan, for it was past serving the god Terminus. How much more interesting an event is that man's supper who has just been forth in the snow to hunt, nay, you might say, steal, the fuel to cook it with! His bread and meat are sweet. There are enough fagots and waste wood of all kinds in the forests of most of our towns to support many fires, but which at present warm none, and, some think, hinder the growth of the young wood. There was also the driftwood of the pond. In the course of the summer I had discovered a raft of pitch pine logs with the bark on, pinned together by the Irish when the railroad was built. This I hauled up partly on the shore. After soaking two years and then lying high six months it was perfectly sound, though waterlogged past drying. I amused myself one winter day with sliding this piecemeal across the pond, nearly half a mile, skating behind with one end of a log fifteen feet long on my shoulder, and the other on the ice; or I tied several logs together with a birch withe, and then, with a longer birch or alder which had a book at the end, dragged them across. Though completely waterlogged and almost as heavy as lead, they not only burned long, but made a very hot fire; nay, I thought that they burned better for the soaking, as if the pitch, being confined by the water, burned longer, as in a lamp.

Gilpin, in his account of the forest borderers of England, says that "the encroachments of trespassers, and the houses and fences thus raised on the borders of the forest," were "considered as great nuisances by the old forest law, and were severely punished under the name of purprestures, as tending ad terrorem ferarum — ad nocumentum forestae, etc.," to the frightening of the game and the detriment of the forest. But I was interested in the preservation of the venison and the vert more than the hunters or woodchoppers, and as much as though I had been the Lord Warden himself; and if any part was burned, though I burned it myself by accident, I grieved with a grief that lasted longer and was more inconsolable than that of the proprietors; nay, I grieved when it was cut down by the proprietors themselves. I would that our farmers when they cut down a forest felt some of that awe which the old Romans did when they came to thin, or let in the light to, a consecrated grove (lucum conlucare), that is, would believe that it is sacred to some god. The Roman made an expiatory offering, and prayed, Whatever god or goddess thou art to whom this grove is sacred, be propitious to me, my family, and children, etc.

It is remarkable what a value is still put upon wood even in this age and in this new country, a value more permanent and universal than that of gold. After all our discoveries and inventions no man will go by a pile of wood. It is as precious to us as it was to our Saxon and Norman ancestors. If they made their bows of it, we make our gun-stocks of it. Michaux, more than thirty years ago, says that the price of wood for fuel in New York and Philadelphia "nearly equals, and sometimes exceeds, that of the best wood in Paris, though this immense capital annually requires more than three hundred thousand cords, and is surrounded to the distance of three hundred miles by cultivated plains." In this town the price of wood rises almost steadily, and the only question is, how much higher it is to be this year than it was the last. Mechanics and tradesmen who come in person to the forest on no other errand, are sure to attend the wood auction, and even pay a high price for the privilege of gleaning after the woodchopper. It is now many years that men have resorted to the forest for fuel and the materials of the arts: the New Englander and the New Hollander, the Parisian and the Celt, the farmer and Robin Hood, Goody Blake and Harry Gill; in most parts of the world the prince and the peasant, the scholar and the savage, equally require still a few sticks from the forest to warm them and cook their food. Neither could I do without them.

Every man looks at his wood-pile with a kind of affection. I love to have mine before my window, and the more chips the better to remind me of my pleasing work. I had an old axe which nobody claimed, with which by spells in winter days, on the sunny side of the house, I played about the stumps which I had got out of my bean-field. As my driver prophesied when I was ploughing, they warmed me twice — once while I was splitting them, and again when they were on the fire, so that no fuel could give out more heat. As for the axe, I was advised to get the village blacksmith to "jump" it; but I jumped him, and, putting a hickory helve from the woods into it, made it do. If it was dull, it was at least hung true.

A few pieces of fat pine were a great treasure. It is interesting to remember how much of this food for fire is still concealed in the bowels of the earth. In previous years I had often gone prospecting over some bare hillside, where a pitch pine wood had formerly stood, and got out the fat pine roots. They are almost indestructible. Stumps thirty or forty years old, at least, will still be sound at the core, though the sapwood has all become vegetable mould, as appears by the scales of the thick bark forming a ring level with the earth four or five inches distant from the heart. With axe and shovel you explore this mine, and follow the marrowy store, yellow as beef tallow, or as if you had struck on a vein of gold, deep into the earth. But commonly I kindled my fire with the dry leaves of the forest, which I had stored up in my shed before the snow came. Green hickory finely split makes the woodchopper's kindlings, when he has a camp in the woods. Once in a while I got a little of this. When the villagers were lighting their fires beyond the horizon, I too gave notice to the various wild inhabitants of Walden vale, by a smoky streamer from my chimney, that I was awake.—

Light-winged Smoke, Icarian bird,
Melting thy pinions in thy upward flight,
Lark without song, and messenger of dawn,
Circling above the hamlets as thy nest;
Or else, departing dream, and shadowy form
Of midnight vision, gathering up thy skirts;
By night star-veiling, and by day
Darkening the light and blotting out the sun;
Go thou my incense upward from this hearth,
And ask the gods to pardon this clear flame.

Hard green wood just cut, though I used but little of that, answered my purpose better than any other. I sometimes left a good fire when I went to take a walk in a winter afternoon; and when I returned, three or four hours afterward, it would be still alive and glowing. My house was not empty though I was gone. It was as if I had left a cheerful housekeeper behind. It was I and Fire that lived there; and commonly my housekeeper proved trustworthy.

One day, however, as I was splitting wood, I thought that I would just look in at the window and see if the house was not on fire; it was the only time I remember to have been particularly anxious on this score; so I looked and saw that a spark had caught my bed, and I went in and extinguished it when it had burned a place as big as my hand. But my house occupied so sunny and sheltered a position, and its roof was so low, that I could afford to let the fire go out in the middle of almost any winter day.

The moles nested in my cellar, nibbling every third potato, and making a snug bed even there of some hair left after plastering and of brown paper; for even the wildest animals love comfort and warmth as well as man, and they survive the winter only because they are so careful to secure them. Some of my friends spoke as if I was coming to the woods on purpose to freeze myself. The animal merely makes a bed, which he warms with his body, in a sheltered place; but man, having discovered fire, boxes up some air in a spacious apartment, and warms that, instead of robbing himself, makes that his bed, in which he can move about divested of more cumbrous clothing, maintain a kind of summer in the midst of winter, and by means of windows even admit the light, and with a lamp lengthen out the day. Thus he goes a step or two beyond instinct, and saves a little time for the fine arts. Though, when I had been exposed to the rudest blasts a long time, my whole body began to grow torpid, when I reached the genial atmosphere of my house I soon recovered my faculties and prolonged my life. But the most luxuriously housed has little to boast of in this respect, nor need we trouble ourselves to speculate how the human race may be at last destroyed. It would be easy to cut their threads any time with a little sharper blast from the north. We go on dating from Cold Fridays and Great Snows; but a little colder Friday, or greater snow would put a period to man's existence on the globe.

The next winter I used a small cooking-stove for economy, since I did not own the forest; but it did not keep fire so well as the open fireplace. Cooking was then, for the most part, no longer a poetic, but merely a chemic process. It will soon be forgotten, in these days of stoves, that we used to roast potatoes in the ashes, after the Indian fashion. The stove not only took up room and scented the house, but it concealed the fire, and I felt as if I had lost a companion. You can always see a face in the fire. The labourer, looking into it at evening, purifies his thoughts of the dross and earthiness which they have accumulated during the day. But I could no longer sit and look into the fire, and the pertinent words of a poet recurred to me with new force.—

"Never, bright flame, may be denied to me
Thy dear, life imaging, close sympathy.
What but my hopes shot upward e'er so bright?
What but my fortunes sunk so low in night?
Why art thou banished from our hearth and hall,
Thou who art welcomed and beloved by all?
Was thy existence then too fanciful
For our life's common light, who are so dull?
Did thy bright gleam mysterious converse hold
With our congenial souls? secrets too bold?
Well, we are safe and strong, for now we sit
Beside a hearth where no dim shadows flit,
Where nothing cheers nor saddens, but a fire
Warms feet and hands — nor does to more aspire;
By whose compact utilitarian heap
The present may sit down and go to sleep,
Nor fear the ghosts who from the dim past walked,
And with us by the unequal light of the old wood fire talked."

14
Former Inhabitants and Winter Visitors

I weathered some merry snow-storms, and spent some cheerful winter evenings by my fireside, while the snow whirled wildly without, and even the hooting of the owl was hushed. For many weeks I met no one in my walks but those who came occasionally to cut wood and sled it to the village. The elements, however, abetted me in making a path through the deepest snow in the woods, for when I had once gone through the wind blew the oak leaves into my tracks, where they lodged, and by absorbing the rays of the sun melted the snow, and so not only made a my bed for my feet, but in the night their dark line was my guide. For human society I was obliged to conjure up the former occupants of these woods. Within the memory of many of my townsmen the road near which my house stands resounded with the laugh and gossip of inhabitants, and the woods which border it were notched and dotted here and there with their little gardens and dwellings, though it was then much more shut in by the forest than now. In some places, within my own remembrance, the pines would scrape both sides of a chaise at once, and women and children who were compelled to go this way to Lincoln alone and on foot did it with fear, and often ran a good part of the distance. Though mainly but a humble route to neighbouring villages, or for the woodman's team, it once amused the traveller more than now by its variety, and lingered

longer in his memory. Where now firm open fields stretch from the village to the woods, it then ran through a maple swamp on a foundation of logs, the remnants of which, doubtless, still underlie the present dusty highway, from the Stratton, now the Alms-House Farm, to Brister's Hill.

East of my bean-field, across the road, lived Cato Ingraham, slave of Duncan Ingraham, Esquire, gentleman, of Concord village, who built his slave a house, and gave him permission to live in Walden Woods; — Cato, not Uticensis, but Concordiensis. Some say that he was a Guinea Negro. There are a few who remember his little patch among the walnuts, which he let grow up till he should be old and need them; but a younger and whiter speculator got them at last. He too, however, occupies an equally narrow house at present. Cato's half-obliterated cellar-hole still remains, though known to few, being concealed from the traveller by a fringe of pines. It is now filled with the smooth sumach (Rhus glabra), and one of the earliest species of goldenrod (Solidago stricta) grows there luxuriantly.

Here, by the very corner of my field, still nearer to town, Zilpha, a coloured woman, had her little house, where she spun linen for the townsfolk, making the Walden Woods ring with her shrill singing, for she had a loud and notable voice. At length, in the war of 1812, her dwelling was set on fire by English soldiers, prisoners on parole, when she was away, and her cat and dog and hens were all burned up together. She led a hard life, and somewhat inhumane. One old frequenter of these woods remembers, that as he passed her house one noon he heard her muttering to herself over her gurgling pot — "Ye are all bones, bones!" I have seen bricks amid the oak copse there.

Down the road, on the right hand, on Brister's Hill, lived Brister Freeman, "a handy Negro," slave of Squire Cummings once — there where grow still the apple trees which Brister planted and tended; large old trees now, but their fruit still wild and ciderish to my taste. Not long since I read his epitaph in the old Lincoln burying-ground, a little on one side, near the unmarked graves of some British grenadiers who fell in the retreat from Concord — where he is styled "Sippio Brister" — Scipio Africanus he had some title to be called — "a man of colour," as if he were discoloured. It also told me, with staring emphasis, when he died; which was but an indirect way of informing me that he ever lived. With him dwelt Fenda, his hospitable wife, who told fortunes, yet pleasantly — large, round, and black, blacker than any of the children of night, such a dusky orb as never rose on Concord before or since.

Farther down the hill, on the left, on the old road in the woods, are marks of some homestead of the Stratton family; whose orchard once covered all the slope of Brister's Hill, but was long since killed out by pitch pines, excepting a few stumps, whose old roots furnish still the wild stocks of many a thrifty village tree.

Nearer yet to town, you come to Breed's location, on the other side of the way, just on the edge of the wood; ground famous for the pranks of a demon not distinctly named in old mythology, who has acted a prominent and astounding part in our New England life, and deserves, as much as any mythological character, to have his biography written one day; who first comes in the guise of a friend or hired man, and then robs and murders the whole family — New-England Rum. But history must not yet tell the tragedies enacted here; let time intervene in some measure to assuage and lend an azure tint to them. Here the most indistinct and dubious tradition says that once a tavern stood; the well the same, which tempered the traveller's beverage and refreshed his steed. Here then men saluted one another, and heard and told the news, and went their ways again.

Breed's hut was standing only a dozen years ago, though it had long been unoccupied. It was about the size of mine. It was set on fire by mischievous boys, one Election night, if I do not mistake. I lived on the edge of the village then, and had just lost myself over Davenant's "Gondibert," that winter that I laboured with a lethargy — which, by the way, I never knew whether to regard as a family complaint, having an uncle who goes to sleep shaving himself, and is obliged to sprout potatoes in a cellar Sundays, in order to keep awake and keep the Sabbath, or as the consequence of my attempt to read Chalmers' collection of English poetry without skipping. It fairly overcame my Nervii. I had just sunk my head on this when the bells rung fire, and in hot haste the engines rolled that way, led by a straggling troop of men and boys, and I among the foremost, for I had leaped the brook. We thought it was far south over the woods — we who had run to fires before — barn, shop, or dwelling-house, or all together. "It's Baker's barn," cried one. "It is the Codman place," affirmed another. And then fresh sparks went up above the wood, as if the roof fell in, and we all shouted "Concord to the rescue!" Wagons shot past with furious speed and crushing loads, bearing, perchance, among the rest, the agent of the Insurance Company, who was bound to go however far; and ever and anon the engine bell tinkled behind, more slow and sure; and rearmost of all, as it was afterward whispered, came they who set the fire and gave the alarm. Thus we kept on like true idealists, rejecting the evidence of our senses, until at a turn in the road we heard the crackling and actually felt the heat of the fire from over the wall, and realized, alas! That we were there. The very nearness of the fire but cooled our ardor. At first we thought to throw a frog-pond on to it; but concluded to let it burn, it was so far gone and so worthless. So we stood round our engine, jostled one another, expressed our sentiments through speaking-trumpets, or in lower tone referred to the great conflagrations which the world has witnessed, including Bascom's shop, and, between ourselves, we thought that, were we there in season with our "tub," and a full frog-pond by, we could turn that threatened last and universal one into another flood. We finally retreated without doing any mischief — returned to sleep and "Gondibert." But as for "Gondibert," I would except that passage in the preface about wit being the soul's powder — "but most of mankind are strangers to wit, as Indians are to powder."

It chanced that I walked that way across the fields the following night, about the same hour, and hearing a low moaning at this spot, I drew near in the dark, and discovered the only survivor of the family that I know, the heir of both its virtues and its vices, who alone was interested in this burning, lying on his stomach and looking over the cellar wall at the still smouldering cinders beneath, muttering to himself, as is his wont. He had been working far off in the river meadows all day, and had improved the first moments that he could call his own to visit the home of his fathers and his youth. He gazed into the cellar from all sides and points of view by turns, always lying down to it, as if there was some treasure, which he remembered, concealed between the stones, where there was absolutely nothing but a heap of bricks and ashes. The house being gone, he looked at what there was left. He was soothed by the sympathy which my mere presence, implied, and showed me, as well as the darkness permitted, where the well was covered up; which, thank Heaven, could never be burned; and he groped long about the wall to find the well-sweep which his father had cut and mounted, feeling for the iron hook or staple by which a burden had been fastened to the heavy end — all that he could now cling to — to convince me that it was no common "rider." I felt it, and still remark it almost daily in my walks, for by it hangs the history of a family.

Once more, on the left, where are seen the well and lilac bushes by the wall, in the now open field, lived Nutting and Le Grosse. But to return toward

Lincoln.

Farther in the woods than any of these, where the road approaches nearest to the pond, Wyman the potter squatted, and furnished his townsmen with earthenware, and left descendants to succeed him. Neither were they rich in worldly goods, holding the land by sufferance while they lived; and there often the sheriff came in vain to collect the taxes, and "attached a chip," for form's sake, as I have read in his accounts, there being nothing else that he could lay his hands on. One day in midsummer, when I was hoeing, a man who was carrying a load of pottery to market stopped his horse against my field and inquired concerning Wyman the younger. He had long ago bought a potter's wheel of him, and wished to know what had become of him. I had read of the potter's clay and wheel in Scripture, but it had never occurred to me that the pots we use were not such as had come down unbroken from those days, or grown on trees like gourds somewhere, and I was pleased to hear that so fictile an art was ever practiced in my neighbourhood.

The last inhabitant of these woods before me was an Irishman, Hugh Quoil (if I have spelt his name with coil enough), who occupied Wyman's tenement — Col. Quoil, he was called. Rumor said that he had been a soldier at Waterloo. If he had lived I should have made him fight his battles over again. His trade here was that of a ditcher. Napoleon went to St. Helena; Quoil came to Walden Woods. All I know of him is tragic. He was a man of manners, like one who had seen the world, and was capable of more civil speech than you could well attend to. He wore a greatcoat in midsummer, being affected with the trembling delirium, and his face was the colour of carmine. He died in the road at the foot of Brister's Hill shortly after I came to the woods, so that I have not remembered him as a neighbour. Before his house was pulled down, when his comrades avoided it as "an unlucky castle," I visited it. There lay his old clothes curled up by use, as if they were himself, upon his raised plank bed. His pipe lay broken on the hearth, instead of a bowl broken at the fountain. The last could never have been the symbol of his death, for he confessed to me that, though he had heard of Brister's Spring, he had never seen it; and soiled cards, kings of diamonds, spades, and hearts, were scattered over the floor. One black chicken which the administrator could not catch, black as night and as silent, not even croaking, awaiting Reynard, still went to roost in the next apartment. In the rear there was the dim outline of a garden, which had been planted but had never received its first hoeing, owing to those terrible shaking fits, though it was now harvest time. It was overrun with Roman wormwood and beggar-ticks, which last stuck to my clothes for all fruit. The skin of a woodchuck was freshly stretched upon the back of the house, a trophy of his last Waterloo; but no warm cap or mittens would he want more.

Now only a dent in the earth marks the site of these dwellings, with buried cellar stones, and strawberries, raspberries, thimble-berries, hazel-bushes, and sumachs growing in the sunny sward there; some pitch pine or gnarled oak occupies what was the chimney nook, and a sweet-scented black birch, perhaps, waves where the door-stone was. Sometimes the well dent is visible, where once a spring oozed; now dry and tearless grass; or it was covered deep — not to be discovered till some late day — with a flat stone under the sod, when the last of the race departed. What a sorrowful act must that be — the covering up of wells! Coincident with the opening of wells of tears. These cellar dents, like deserted fox burrows, old holes, are all that is left where once were the stir and bustle of human life, and "fate, free will, foreknowledge absolute," in some form and dialect or other were by turns discussed. But all I can learn of their conclusions amounts to just this, that "Cato and Brister pulled wool"; which is about as edifying as the history of more famous schools of philosophy.

Still grows the vivacious lilac a generation after the door and lintel and the sill are gone, unfolding its sweet-scented flowers each spring, to be plucked by the musing traveller; planted and tended once by children's hands, in front-yard plots — now standing by wallsides in retired pastures, and giving place to new-rising forests; — the last of that stirp, sole survivor of that family. Little did the dusky children think that the puny slip with its two eyes only, which they stuck in the ground in the shadow of the house and daily watered, would root itself so, and outlive them, and house itself in the rear that shaded it, and grown man's garden and orchard, and tell their story faintly to the lone wanderer a half-century after they had grown up and died — blossoming as fair, and smelling as sweet, as in that first spring. I mark its still tender, civil, cheerful lilac colours.

But this small village, germ of something more, why did it fail while Concord keeps its ground? Were there no natural advantages — no water privileges, forsooth? Ay, the deep Walden Pond and cool Brister's Spring — privilege to drink long and healthy draughts at these, all unimproved by these men but to dilute their glass. They were universally a thirsty race. Might not the basket, stable-broom, mat-making, corn-parching, linen-spinning, and pottery business have thrived here, making the wilderness to blossom like the rose, and a numerous posterity have inherited the land of their fathers? The sterile soil would at least have been proof against a low-land degeneracy. Alas! How little does the memory of these human inhabitants enhance the beauty of the landscape! Again, perhaps, Nature will try, with me for a first settler, and my house raised last spring to be the oldest in the hamlet.

I am not aware that any man has ever built on the spot which I occupy. Deliver me from a city built on the site of a more ancient city, whose materials are ruins, whose gardens cemeteries. The soil is blanched and accursed there, and before that becomes necessary the earth itself will be destroyed. With such reminiscences I repeopled the woods and lulled myself asleep.

At this season I seldom had a visitor. When the snow lay deepest no wanderer ventured near my house for a week or fortnight at a time, but there I lived as snug as a meadow mouse, or as cattle and poultry which are said to have survived for a long time buried in drifts, even without food; or like that early settler's family in the town of Sutton, in this State, whose cottage was completely covered by the great snow of 1717 when he was absent, and an Indian found it only by the hole which the chimney's breath made in the drift, and so relieved the family. But no friendly Indian concerned himself about me; nor needed he, for the master of the house was at home. The Great Snow! How cheerful it is to hear of! When the farmers could not get to the woods and swamps with their teams, and were obliged to cut down the shade trees before their houses, and, when the crust was harder, cut off the trees in the swamps, ten feet from the ground, as it appeared the next spring.

In the deepest snows, the path which I used from the highway to my house, about half a mile long, might have been represented by a meandering dotted line, with wide intervals between the dots. For a week of even weather I took exactly the same number of steps, and of the same length, coming and going, stepping deliberately and with the precision of a pair of dividers in my own deep tracks — to such routine the winter reduces us — yet often they were filled with heaven's own blue. But no weather interfered fatally with my walks, or rather my going abroad, for I frequently tramped eight or ten miles through the deepest snow to keep an appointment with a beech tree, or a yellow birch, or an old acquaintance among the pines; when the ice and snow causing their limbs to droop, and so sharpening their tops, had changed the pines into fir trees; wading to the tops of the highest hills when the show was nearly two feet deep on a level, and shaking down another snow-storm on my head at every step; or sometimes creeping and floundering thither on my hands and knees, when the hunters had gone into winter quarters. One afternoon I amused myself by watching a barred owl (Strix nebulosa) sitting on one of the lower dead limbs of a white pine, close to the trunk, in broad daylight, I standing within a rod of him. He could hear me when I moved and cronched the snow with my feet, but could not plainly see me. When I made most noise he would stretch out his neck, and erect his neck feathers, and open his eyes wide; but their lids soon fell again, and he began to nod. I too felt a slumberous influence after watching him half an hour, as he sat thus with his eyes half open, like a cat, winged brother of the cat. There was only a narrow slit left between their lids, by which be preserved a pennisular relation to me; thus, with half-shut eyes, looking out from the land of dreams, and endeavouring to realize me, vague object or mote that interrupted his visions. At length, on some louder noise or my nearer approach, he would grow uneasy and sluggishly turn about on his perch, as if impatient at having his dreams disturbed; and when he launched himself off and flapped through the pines, spreading his wings to unexpected breadth, I could not hear the slightest sound from them. Thus, guided amid the pine boughs rather by a delicate sense of their neighbourhood than by sight, feeling his twilight way, as it were, with his sensitive pinions, he found a new perch, where he might in peace await the dawning of his day.

As I walked over the long causeway made for the railroad through the meadows, I encountered many a blustering and nipping wind, for nowhere has it freer play; and when the frost had smitten me on one cheek, heathen as I was, I turned to it the other also. Nor was it much better by the carriage road from Brister's Hill. For I came to town still, like a friendly Indian, when the contents of the broad open fields were all piled up between the walls of the Walden road, and half an hour sufficed to obliterate the tracks of the last traveller. And when I returned new drifts would have formed, through which I floundered, where the busy northwest wind had been depositing the powdery snow round a sharp angle in the road, and not a rabbit's track, nor even the fine print, the small type, of a meadow mouse was to be seen. Yet I rarely failed to find, even in midwinter, some warm and springly swamp where the grass and the skunk-cabbage still put forth with perennial verdure, and some hardier bird occasionally awaited the return of spring.

Sometimes, notwithstanding the snow, when I returned from my walk at evening I crossed the deep tracks of a woodchopper leading from my door, and found his pile of whittlings on the hearth, and my house filled with the odour of his pipe. Or on a Sunday afternoon, if I chanced to be at home, I heard the cronching of the snow made by the step of a long-headed farmer, who from far through the woods sought my house, to have a social "crack"; one of the few of his vocation who are "men on their farms"; who donned a frock instead of a professor's gown, and is as ready to extract the moral out of church or state as to haul a load of manure from his barn-yard. We talked of rude and simple times, when men sat about large fires in cold, bracing weather, with clear heads; and when other dessert failed, we tried our teeth on many a nut which wise squirrels have long since abandoned, for those which have the thickest shells are commonly empty.

The one who came from farthest to my lodge, through deepest snows and most dismal tempests, was a poet. A farmer, a hunter, a soldier, a reporter, even a philosopher, may be daunted; but nothing can deter a poet, for he is actuated by pure love. Who can predict his comings and goings? His business calls him out at all hours, even when doctors sleep. We made that small house ring with boisterous mirth and resound with the murmur of much sober talk, making amends then to Walden vale for the long silences. Broadway was still and deserted in comparison. At suitable intervals there were regular salutes of laughter, which might have been referred indifferently to the last-uttered or the forth-coming jest. We made many a "bran new" theory of life over a thin dish of gruel, which combined the advantages of conviviality with the clear-headedness which philosophy requires.

I should not forget that during my last winter at the pond there was another welcome visitor, who at one time came through the village, through snow and rain and darkness, till he saw my lamp through the trees, and shared with me some long winter evenings. One of the last of the philosophers — Connecticut gave him to the world — he peddled first her wares, afterwards, as he declares, his brains. These he peddles still, prompting God and disgracing man, bearing for fruit his brain only, like the nut its kernel. I think that he must be the man of the most faith of any alive. His words and attitude always suppose a better state of things than other men are acquainted with, and he will be the last man to be disappointed as the ages revolve. He has no venture in the present. But though comparatively disregarded now, when his day comes, laws unsuspected by most will take effect, and masters of families and rulers will come to him for advice.

"How blind that cannot see serenity!"

A true friend of man; almost the only friend of human progress. An Old Mortality, say rather an Immortality, with unwearied patience and faith making plain the image engraven in men's bodies, the God of whom they are but defaced and leaning monuments. With his hospitable intellect he embraces children, beggars, insane, and scholars, and entertains the thought of all, adding to it commonly some breadth and elegance. I think that he should keep a caravansary on the world's highway, where philosophers of all nations might put up, and on his sign should be printed, "Entertainment for man, but not for his beast. Enter ye that have leisure and a quiet mind, who earnestly seek the right road." He is perhaps the sanest man and has the fewest crotchets of any I chance to know; the same yesterday and tomorrow. Of yore we had sauntered and talked, and effectually put the world behind us; for he was pledged to no institution in it, freeborn, ingenuus. Whichever way we turned, it seemed that the heavens and the earth had met together, since he enhanced the beauty of the landscape. A blue-robed man, whose fittest roof is the overarching sky which reflects his serenity. I do not see how he can ever die; Nature cannot spare him.

Having each some shingles of thought well dried, we sat and whittled them, trying our knives, and admiring the clear yellowish grain of the pumpkin pine. We waded so gently and reverently, or we pulled together so smoothly, that the fishes of thought were not scared from the stream, nor feared any angler on the bank, but came and went grandly, like the clouds which float through the western sky, and the mother-o'-pearl flocks which sometimes form and dissolve there. There we worked, revising mythology, rounding a fable here and there, and building castles in the air for which earth offered no worthy foundation. Great Looker! Great Expecter! To converse with whom was a New England Night's Entertainment. Ah! Such discourse we had, hermit and philosopher, and the old settler I have spoken of — we three — it expanded and racked my little house; I should not dare to say how many pounds' weight there was above the atmospheric pressure on every circular inch; it opened its seams so that they had to be calked with much dulness thereafter to stop the consequent leak; — but I had enough of that kind of oakum already picked.

There was one other with whom I had "solid seasons," long to be remembered, at his house in the village, and who looked in upon me from time to time; but I had no more for society there.

There too, as everywhere, I sometimes expected the Visitor who never comes. The Vishnu Purana says, "The house-holder is to remain at eventide in his courtyard as long as it takes to milk a cow, or longer if he pleases, to await the arrival of a guest." I often performed this duty of hospitality, waited long enough to milk a whole herd of cows, but did not see the man approaching from the town.

15
Winter Animals

When the ponds were firmly frozen, they afforded not only new and shorter routes to many points, but new views from their surfaces of the familiar landscape around them. When I crossed Flint's Pond, after it was covered with snow, though I had often paddled about and skated over it, it was so unexpectedly wide and so strange that I could think of nothing but Baffin's Bay. The Lincoln hills rose up around me at the extremity of a snowy plain, in which I did not remember to have stood before, and the fishermen, at an indeterminable distance over the ice, moving slowly about with their wolfish dogs, passed for sealers, or Esquimaux, or in misty weather loomed like fabulous creatures, and I did not know whether they were giants or pygmies. I took this course when I went to lecture in Lincoln in the evening, travelling in no road and passing no house between my own hut and the lecture room. In Goose Pond, which lay in my way, a colony of muskrats dwelt, and raised their cabins high above the ice, though none could be seen abroad when I crossed it. Walden, being like the rest usually bare of snow, or with only shallow and interrupted drifts on it, was my yard where I could walk freely when the snow was nearly two feet deep on a level elsewhere and the villagers were confined to their streets. There, far from the village street, and except at very long intervals, from the jingle of sleigh-bells, I slid and skated, as in a vast moose-yard well trodden, overhung by oak woods and solemn pines bent down with snow or bristling with icicles.

For sounds in winter nights, and often in winter days, I heard the forlorn but melodious note of a hooting owl indefinitely far; such a sound as the frozen earth would yield if struck with a suitable plectrum, the very lingua vernacula of Walden Wood, and quite familiar to me at last, though I never saw the bird while it was making it. I seldom opened my door in a winter evening without hearing it; Hoo hoo hoo, hoorer, hoo, sounded sonorously, and the first three syllables accented somewhat like how der do; or sometimes hoo, hoo only. One night in the beginning of winter, before the pond froze over, about nine o'clock, I was startled by the loud honking of a goose, and, stepping to the door, heard the sound of their wings like a tempest in the woods as they flew low over my house. They passed over the pond toward Fair Haven, seemingly deterred from settling by my light, their commodoure honking all the while with a regular beat. Suddenly an unmistakable cat-owl from very near me, with the most harsh and tremendous voice I ever heard from any inhabitant of the woods, responded at regular intervals to the goose, as if determined to expose and disgrace this intruder from Hudson's Bay by exhibiting a greater compass and volume of voice in a native, and boo-hoo him out of Concord horizon. What do you mean by alarming the citadel at this time of night consecrated to me? Do you think I am ever caught napping at such an hour, and that I have not got lungs and a larynx as well as yourself? Boo-hoo, boo-hoo, boo-hoo! It was one of the most thrilling discords I ever heard. And yet, if you had a discriminating ear, there were in it the elements of a concord such as these plains never saw nor heard.

I also heard the whooping of the ice in the pond, my great bed-fellow in that part of Concord, as if it were restless in its bed and would fain turn over, were troubled with flatulency and had dreams; or I was waked by the cracking of the ground by the frost, as if someone had driven a team against my door, and in the morning would find a crack in the earth a quarter of a mile long and a third of an inch wide.

Sometimes I heard the foxes as they ranged over the snow-crust, in moonlight nights, in search of a partridge or other game, barking raggedly and demoniacally like forest dogs, as if labouring with some anxiety, or seeking expression, struggling for light and to be dogs outright and run freely in the streets; for if we take the ages into our account, may there not be a civilization going on among brutes as well as men? They seemed to me to be rudimental, burrowing men, still standing on their defence, awaiting their transformation. Sometimes one came near to my window, attracted by my light, barked a vulpine curse at me, and then retreated.

Usually the red squirrel (Sciurus Hudsonius) waked me in the dawn, coursing over the roof and up and down the sides of the house, as if sent out of the woods for this purpose. In the course of the winter I threw out half a bushel of ears of sweet corn, which had not got ripe, on to the snow-crust by my door, and was amused by watching the motions of the various animals which were baited by it. In the twilight and the night the rabbits came regularly and made a hearty meal. All day long the red squirrels came and went, and afforded me much entertainment by their manoeuvres. One would approach at first warily through the shrub oaks, running over the snow-crust by fits and starts like a leaf blown by the wind, now a few paces this way, with wonderful speed and waste of energy, making inconceivable haste with his "trotters," as if it were for a wager, and now as many paces that way, but never getting on more than half a rod at a time; and then suddenly pausing with a ludicrous expression and a gratuitous somerset, as if all the eyes in the universe were eyed on him — for all the motions of a squirrel, even in the most solitary recesses of the forest, imply spectators as much as those of a dancing girl — wasting more time in delay and circumspection than would have sufficed to walk the whole distance — I never saw one walk — and then suddenly, before you could say Jack Robinson, he would be in the top of a young pitch pine, winding up his clock and chiding all imaginary spectators, soliloquizing and talking to all the universe at the same time — for no reason that I could ever detect, or he himself was aware of, I suspect. At length he would reach the corn, and selecting a suitable ear, frisk about in the same uncertain trigonometrical way to the topmost stick of my wood-pile, before my window, where he looked me in the face, and there sit for hours, supplying himself with a new ear from time to time, nibbling at first voraciously and throwing the half-naked cobs about; till at length he grew more dainty still and played with his food, tasting only the inside of the kernel, and the ear, which was held balanced over the stick by one paw, slipped from his careless grasp and fell to the ground, when he would look over at it with a ludicrous expression of uncertainty, as if suspecting that it had life, with a mind not made up whether to get it again, or a new one, or be off; now thinking of corn, then listening to hear what was in the wind. So the little impudent fellow would waste many an ear in a forenoon; till at last, seizing some longer and plumper one, considerably bigger than himself, and skilfully balancing it, he would set out with it to the woods, like a tiger with a buffalo, by the same zig-zag course and frequent pauses, scratching along with it as if it were too heavy for him and falling all the while, making its fall a diagonal between

a perpendicular and horizontal, being determined to put it through at any rate; — a singularly frivolous and whimsical fellow; — and so he would get off with it to where he lived, perhaps carry it to the top of a pine tree forty or fifty rods distant, and I would afterwards find the cobs strewn about the woods in various directions.

At length the jays arrive, whose discordant screams were heard long before, as they were warily making their approach an eighth of a mile off, and in a stealthy and sneaking manner they flit from tree to tree, nearer and nearer, and pick up the kernels which the squirrels have dropped. Then, sitting on a pitch pine bough, they attempt to swallow in their haste a kernel which is too big for their throats and chokes them; and after great labour they disgorge it, and spend an hour in the endeavour to crack it by repeated blows with their bills. They were manifestly thieves, and I had not much respect for them; but the squirrels, though at first shy, went to work as if they were taking what was their own.

Meanwhile also came the chickadees in flocks, which, picking up the crumbs the squirrels had dropped, flew to the nearest twig and, placing them under their claws, hammered away at them with their little bills, as if it were an insect in the bark, till they were sufficiently reduced for their slender throats. A little flock of these titmice came daily to pick a dinner out of my woodpile, or the crumbs at my door, with faint flitting lisping notes, like the tinkling of icicles in the grass, or else with sprightly day day day, or more rarely, in spring-like days, a wiry summery phe-be from the woodside. They were so familiar that at length one alighted on an armful of wood which I was carrying in, and pecked at the sticks without fear. I once had a sparrow alight upon my shoulder for a moment while I was hoeing in a village garden, and I felt that I was more distinguished by that circumstance than I should have been by any epaulet I could have worn. The squirrels also grew at last to be quite familiar, and occasionally stepped upon my shoe, when that was the nearest way.

When the ground was not yet quite covered, and again near the end of winter, when the snow was melted on my south hillside and about my wood-pile, the partridges came out of the woods morning and evening to feed there. Whichever side you walk in the woods the partridge bursts away on whirring wings, jarring the snow from the dry leaves and twigs on high, which comes sifting down in the sunbeams like golden dust, for this brave bird is not to be scared by winter. It is frequently covered up by drifts, and, it is said, "sometimes plunges from on wing into the soft snow, where it remains concealed for a day or two." I used to start them in the open land also, where they had come out of the woods at sunset to "bud" the wild apple trees. They will come regularly every evening to particular trees, where the cunning sportsman lies in wait for them, and the distant orchards next the woods suffer thus not a little. I am glad that the partridge gets fed, at any rate. It is Nature's own bird which lives on buds and diet drink.

In dark winter mornings, or in short winter afternoons, I sometimes heard a pack of hounds threading all the woods with hounding cry and yelp, unable to resist the instinct of the chase, and the note of the hunting-horn at intervals, proving that man was in the rear. The woods ring again, and yet no fox bursts forth on to the open level of the pond, nor following pack pursuing their Actaeon. And perhaps at evening I see the hunters returning with a single brush trailing from their sleigh for a trophy, seeking their inn. They tell me that if the fox would remain in the bosom of the frozen earth he would be safe, or if be would run in a straight line away no foxhound could overtake him; but, having left his pursuers far behind, he stops to rest and listen till they come up, and when he runs he circles round to his old haunts, where the hunters await him. Sometimes, however, he will run upon a wall many rods, and then leap off far to one side, and he appears to know that water will not retain his scent. A hunter told me that he once saw a fox pursued by hounds burst out on to Walden when the ice was covered with shallow puddles, run part way across, and then return to the same shore. Ere long the hounds arrived, but here they lost the scent. Sometimes a pack hunting by themselves would pass my door, and circle round my house, and yelp and hound without regarding me, as if afflicted by a species of madness, so that nothing could divert them from the pursuit. Thus they circle until they fall upon the recent trail of a fox, for a wise hound will forsake everything else for this. One day a man came to my hut from Lexington to inquire after his hound that made a large track, and had been hunting for a week by himself. But I fear that he was not the wiser for all I told him, for every time I attempted to answer his questions he interrupted me by asking, "What do you do here?" He had lost a dog, but found a man.

One old hunter who has a dry tongue, who used to come to bathe in Walden once every year when the water was warmest, and at such times looked in upon me, told me that many years ago he took his gun one afternoon and went out for a cruise in Walden Wood; and as he walked the Wayland road he heard the cry of hounds approaching, and ere long a fox leaped the wall into the road, and as quick as thought leaped the other wall out of the road, and his swift bullet had not touched him. Some way behind came an old hound and her three pups in full pursuit, hunting on their own account, and disappeared again in the woods. Late in the afternoon, as he was resting in the thick woods south of Walden, he heard the voice of the hounds far over toward Fair Haven still pursuing the fox; and on they came, their hounding cry which made all the woods ring sounding nearer and nearer, now from Well Meadow, now from the Baker Farm. For a long time he stood still and listened to their music, so sweet to a hunter's ear, when suddenly the fox appeared, threading the solemn aisles with an easy coursing pace, whose sound was concealed by a sympathetic rustle of the leaves, swift and still, keeping the round, leaving his pursuers far behind; and, leaping upon a rock amid the woods, he sat erect and listening, with his back to the hunter. For a moment compassion restrained the latter's arm; but that was a short-lived mood, and as quick as thought can follow thought his piece was levelled, and whang! — the fox, rolling over the rock, lay dead on the ground. The hunter still kept his place and listened to the hounds. Still on they came, and now the near woods resounded through all their aisles with their demoniac cry. At length the old hound burst into view with muzzle to the ground, and snapping the air as if possessed, and ran directly to the rock; but, spying the dead fox, she suddenly ceased her hounding as if struck dumb with amazement, and walked round and round him in silence; and one by one her pups arrived, and, like their mother, were sobered into silence by the mystery. Then the hunter came forward and stood in their midst, and the mystery was solved. They waited in silence while he skinned the fox, then followed the brush a while, and at length turned off into the woods again. That evening a Weston squire came to the Concord hunter's cottage to inquire for his hounds, and told how for a week they had been hunting on their own account from Weston woods. The Concord hunter told him what he knew and offered him the skin; but the other declined it and departed. He did not find his hounds that night, but the next day learned that they had crossed the river and put up at a farmhouse for the night, whence, having been well fed, they took their departure early in the morning.

The hunter who told me this could remember one Sam Nutting, who used to hunt bears on Fair Haven Ledges, and exchange their skins for rum in Concord village; who told him, even, that he had seen a moose there. Nutting had a famous foxhound named Burgoyne — he pronounced it Bugine — which my informant used to borrow. In the "Wast Book" of an old trader of this town, who was also a captain, town-clerk, and representative, I find the following entry. Jan. 18th, 1742-3, "John Melven Cr. by 1 Grey Fox 0—2—3";

they are not now found here; and in his ledger, Feb, 7th, 1743, Hezekiah Stratton has credit "by 1/2 a Catt skin 0—1—4+"; of course, a wild-cat, for Stratton was a sergeant in the old French war, and would not have got credit for hunting less noble game. Credit is given for deerskins also, and they were daily sold. One man still preserves the horns of the last deer that was killed in this vicinity, and another has told me the particulars of the hunt in which his uncle was engaged. The hunters were formerly a numerous and merry crew here. I remember well one gaunt Nimrod who would catch up a leaf by the roadside and play a strain on it wilder and more melodious, if my memory serves me, than any hunting-horn.

At midnight, when there was a moon, I sometimes met with hounds in my path prowling about the woods, which would skulk out of my way, as if afraid, and stand silent amid the bushes till I had passed.

Squirrels and wild mice disputed for my store of nuts. There were scores of pitch pines around my house, from one to four inches in diameter, which had been gnawed by mice the previous winter — a Norwegian winter for them, for the snow lay long and deep, and they were obliged to mix a large proportion of pine bark with their other diet. These trees were alive and apparently flourishing at midsummer, and many of them had grown a foot, though completely girdled; but after another winter such were without exception dead. It is remarkable that a single mouse should thus be allowed a whole pine tree for its dinner, gnawing round instead of up and down it; but perhaps it is necessary in order to thin these trees, which are wont to grow up densely.

The hares (Lepus Americanus) were very familiar. One had her form under my house all winter, separated from me only by the flooring, and she startled me each morning by her hasty departure when I began to stir — thump, thump, thump, striking her head against the floor timbers in her hurry. They used to come round my door at dusk to nibble the potato parings which I had thrown out, and were so nearly the colour of the ground that they could hardly be distinguished when still. Sometimes in the twilight I alternately lost and recovered sight of one sitting motionless under my window. When I opened my door in the evening, off they would go with a squeak and a bounce. Near at hand they only excited my pity. One evening one sat by my door two paces from me, at first trembling with fear, yet unwilling to move; a poor wee thing, lean and bony, with ragged ears and sharp nose, scant tail and slender paws. It looked as if Nature no longer contained the breed of nobler bloods, but stood on her last toes. Its large eyes appeared young and unhealthy, almost dropsical. I took a step, and lo, away it scud with an elastic spring over the snow-crust, straightening its body and its limbs into graceful length, and soon put the forest between me and itself — the wild free venison, asserting its vigour and the dignity of Nature. Not without reason was its slenderness. Such then was its nature. (Lepus, levipes, light-foot, some think.)

What is a country without rabbits and partridges? They are among the most simple and indigenous animal products; ancient and venerable families known to antiquity as to modern times; of the very hue and substance of Nature, nearest allied to leaves and to the ground — and to one another; it is either winged or it is legged. It is hardly as if you had seen a wild creature when a rabbit or a partridge bursts away, only a natural one, as much to be expected as rustling leaves. The partridge and the rabbit are still sure to thrive, like true natives of the soil, whatever revolutions occur. If the forest is cut off, the sprouts and bushes which spring up afford them concealment, and they become more numerous than ever. That must be a poor country indeed that does not support a hare. Our woods teem with them both, and around every swamp may be seen the partridge or rabbit walk, beset with twiggy fences and horse-hair snares, which some cow-boy tends.

16
The Pond in Winter

After a still winter night I awoke with the impression that some question had been put to me, which I had been endeavouring in vain to answer in my sleep, as what — how — when — where? But there was dawning Nature, in whom all creatures live, looking in at my broad windows with serene and satisfied face, and no question on her lips. I awoke to an answered question, to Nature and daylight. The snow lying deep on the earth dotted with young pines, and the very slope of the hill on which my house is placed, seemed to say, Forward! Nature puts no question and answers none which we mortals ask. She has long ago taken her resolution. "O Prince, our eyes contemplate with admiration and transmit to the soul the wonderful and varied spectacle of this universe. The night veils without doubt a part of this glorious creation; but day comes to reveal to us this great work, which extends from earth even into the plains of the ether."

Then to my morning work. First I take an axe and pail and go in search of water, if that be not a dream. After a cold and snowy night it needed a divining-rod to find it. Every winter the liquid and trembling surface of the pond, which was so sensitive to every breath, and reflected every light and shadow, becomes solid to the depth of a foot or a foot and a half, so that it will support the heaviest teams, and perchance the snow covers it to an equal depth, and it is not to be distinguished from any level field. Like the marmots in the surrounding hills, it closes its eyelids and becomes dormant for three months or more. Standing on the snow-covered plain, as if in a pasture amid the hills, I cut my way first through a foot of snow, and then a foot of ice, and open a window under my feet, where, kneeling to drink, I look down into the quiet parlor of the fishes, pervaded by a softened light as through a window of ground glass, with its bright sanded floor the same as in summer; there a perennial waveless serenity reigns as in the amber twilight sky, corresponding to the cool and even temperament of the inhabitants. Heaven is under our feet is well as over our heads.

Early in the morning, while all things are crisp with frost, men come with fishing-reels and slender lunch, and let down their fine lines through the snowy field to take pickerel and perch; wild men, who instinctively follow other fashions and trust other authorities than their townsmen, and by their goings and comings stitch towns together in parts where else they would be ripped. They sit and eat their luncheon in stout fear-naughts on the dry oak leaves on the shore, as wise in natural lore as the citizen is in artificial. They never consulted with books, and know and can tell much less than they have done. The things which they practice are said not yet to be known. Here is one fishing for pickerel with grown perch for bait. You look into his pail with wonder as into a summer pond, as if he kept summer locked up at home, or knew where she had retreated. How, pray, did he get these in midwinter? Oh, he got worms out of rotten logs since the ground froze, and so he caught them. His life itself passes deeper in nature than the studies of the naturalist penetrate; himself a subject for the naturalist. The latter raises the moss and bark gently with his knife in search of insects; the former lays open logs to their core with his axe, and moss and bark fly far and wide. He gets his living by barking trees. Such a man has some right to fish, and I love to see nature carried out in him. The perch swallows the grub-worm, the pickerel swallows the perch, and the fisherman swallows the pickerel; and so all the chinks in the scale of being are filled.

When I strolled around the pond in misty weather I was sometimes amused by the primitive mode which some ruder fisherman had adopted. He would perhaps have placed alder branches over the narrow holes in the ice, which were four or five rods apart and an equal distance from the shore, and having fastened the end of the line to a stick to prevent its being pulled through, have passed the slack line over a twig of the alder, a foot or more above the ice, and tied a dry oak leaf to it, which, being pulled down, would show when he had a bite. These alders loomed through the mist at regular intervals as you walked half way round the pond.

Ah, the pickerel of Walden! When I see them lying on the ice, or in the well which the fisherman cuts in the ice, making a little hole to admit the water, I am always surprised by their rare beauty, as if they were fabulous fishes, they are so foreign to the streets, even to the woods, foreign as Arabia to our Concord life. They possess a quite dazzling and transcendent beauty which separates them by a wide interval from the cadaverous cod and haddock whose fame is trumpeted in our streets. They are not green like the pines, nor gray like the stones, nor blue like the sky; but they have, to my eyes, if possible, yet rarer colours, like flowers and precious stones, as if they were the pearls, the animalized nuclei or crystals of the Walden water. They, of course, are Walden all over and all through; are themselves small Waldens in the animal kingdom, Waldenses. It is surprising that they are caught here — that in this deep and capacious spring, far beneath the rattling teams and chaises and tinkling sleighs that travel the Walden road, this great gold and emerald fish swims. I never chanced to see its kind in any market; it would be the cynosure of all eyes there. Easily, with a few convulsive quirks, they give up their watery ghosts, like a mortal translated before his time to the thin air of heaven.

As I was desirous to recover the long lost bottom of Walden Pond, I surveyed it carefully, before the ice broke up, early in '46, with compass and chain and sounding line. There have been many stories told about the bottom, or rather no bottom, of this pond, which certainly had no foundation for themselves. It is remarkable how long men will believe in the bottomlessness of a pond without taking the trouble to sound it. I have visited two such Bottomless Ponds in one walk in this neighbourhood. Many have believed that Walden reached quite through to the other side of the globe. Some who have lain flat on the ice for a long time, looking down through the illusive medium, perchance with watery eyes into the bargain, and driven to hasty conclusions by the fear of catching cold in their breasts, have seen vast holes "into which a load of hay might be driven," if there were anybody to drive it, the undoubted source of the Styx and entrance to the Infernal Regions from these parts. Others have gone down from the village with a "fifty-six" and a wagon load of inch rope, but yet have failed to find any bottom; for while the "fifty-six" was resting by the way, they were paying out the rope in the vain attempt to fathom their truly immeasurable capacity for marvellousness. But I can assure my readers that Walden has a reasonably tight bottom at a not unreasonable, though at an unusual, depth. I fathomed it easily with a cod-line and a stone weighing about a pound and a half, and could tell accurately when the stone left the bottom, by having to pull so much harder before the water got underneath to help me. The greatest depth was exactly one hundred and two feet; to which may be added the five feet which it has risen since, making one hundred and seven. This is a remarkable depth for so small an area; yet not an inch of it can be spared by the imagination. What if all ponds were shallow? Would it not react on the minds of men? I am thankful that this pond was made deep and pure for a symbol. While men believe in the infinite some ponds will be thought to be bottomless.

A factory-owner, hearing what depth I had found, thought that it could not be true, for, judging from his acquaintance with dams, sand would not lie at so steep an angle. But the deepest ponds are not so deep in proportion to their area as most suppose, and, if drained, would not leave very remarkable valleys. They are not like cups between the hills; for this one, which is so unusually deep for its area, appears in a vertical section through its centre not deeper than a shallow plate. Most ponds, emptied, would leave a meadow no more hollow than we frequently see. William Gilpin, who is so admirable in all that relates to landscapes, and usually so correct, standing at the head of Loch Fyne, in Scotland, which he describes as "a bay of salt water, sixty or seventy fathoms deep, four miles in breadth," and about fifty miles long, surrounded by mountains, observes, "If we could have seen it immediately after the diluvian crash, or whatever convulsion of nature occasioned it, before the waters gushed in, what a horrid chasm must it have appeared!

> "So high as heaved the tumid hills, so low
> Down sunk a hollow bottom broad and deep,
> Capacious bed of waters."

But if, using the shortest diameter of Loch Fyne, we apply these proportions to Walden, which, as we have seen, appears already in a vertical section only like a shallow plate, it will appear four times as shallow. So much for the increased horrors of the chasm of Loch Fyne when emptied. No doubt many a smiling valley with its stretching cornfields occupies exactly such a "horrid chasm," from which the waters have receded, though it requires the insight and the far sight of the geologist to convince the unsuspecting inhabitants of this fact. Often an inquisitive eye may detect the shores of a primitive lake in the low horizon hills, and no subsequent elevation of the plain have been necessary to conceal their history. But it is easiest, as they who work on the highways know, to find the hollows by the puddles after a shower. The amount of it is, the imagination give it the least license, dives deeper and soars higher than Nature goes. So, probably, the depth of the ocean will be found to be very inconsiderable compared with its breadth.

As I sounded through the ice I could determine the shape of the bottom with greater accuracy than is possible in surveying harbours which do not freeze over, and I was surprised at its general regularity. In the deepest part there are several acres more level than almost any field which is exposed to the sun, wind, and plough. In one instance, on a line arbitrarily chosen, the depth did not vary more than one foot in thirty rods; and generally, near the middle, I could calculate the variation for each one hundred feet in any direction beforehand within three or four inches. Some are accustomed to speak of deep and dangerous holes even in quiet sandy ponds like this, but the effect of water under these circumstances is to level all inequalities. The regularity of the bottom and its conformity to the shores and the range of the neighbouring hills were so perfect that a distant promontory betrayed itself in the soundings quite across the pond, and its direction could be determined by observing the opposite shore. Cape becomes bar, and plain shoal, and valley and gorge deep water and channel.

When I had mapped the pond by the scale of ten rods to an inch, and put down the soundings, more than a hundred in all, I observed this remarkable coincidence. Having noticed that the number indicating the greatest depth was apparently in the centre of the map, I laid a rule on the map lengthwise, and then breadthwise, and found, to my surprise, that the line of greatest length intersected the line of greatest breadth exactly at the point of greatest depth, notwithstanding that the middle is so nearly level, the outline of the pond far from regular, and the extreme length and breadth were got by measuring into the coves; and I said to myself, Who knows but this hint would conduct to the deepest part of the ocean as well as of a pond or puddle? Is not this the rule also for the height of mountains, regarded as the opposite of valleys? We know that a hill is not highest at its narrowest part.

Of five coves, three, or all which had been sounded, were observed to have a bar quite across their mouths and deeper water within, so that the bay tended to be an expansion of water within the land not only horizontally but vertically, and to form a basin or independent pond, the direction of the two capes showing the course of the bar. Every harbour on the sea-coast, also, has its bar at its entrance. In proportion as the mouth of the cove was wider compared with its length, the water over the bar was deeper compared with that in the basin. Given, then, the length and breadth of the cove, and the character of the surrounding shore, and you have almost elements enough to make out a formula for all cases.

In order to see how nearly I could guess, with this experience, at the deepest point in a pond, by observing the outlines of a surface and the character of its shores alone, I made a plan of White Pond, which contains about forty-one acres, and, like this, has no island in it, nor any visible inlet or outlet; and as the line of greatest breadth fell very near the line of least breadth, where two opposite capes approached each other and two opposite bays receded, I ventured to mark a point a short distance from the latter line, but still on the line of greatest length, as the deepest. The deepest part was found to be within one hundred feet of this, still farther in the direction to which I had inclined, and was only one foot deeper, namely, sixty feet. Of course, a stream running through, or an island in the pond, would make the problem much more complicated.

If we knew all the laws of Nature, we should need only one fact, or the description of one actual phenomenon, to infer all the particular results at that point. Now we know only a few laws, and our result is vitiated, not, of course, by any confusion or irregularity in Nature, but by our ignorance of essential elements in the calculation. Our notions of law and harmony are commonly confined to those instances which we detect; but the harmony which results from a far greater number of seemingly conflicting, but really concurring, laws, which we have not detected, is still more wonderful. The particular laws are as our points of view, as, to the traveller, a mountain outline varies with every step, and it has an infinite number of profiles, though absolutely but one form. Even when cleft or bored through it is not comprehended in its entireness.

What I have observed of the pond is no less true in ethics. It is the law of average. Such a rule of the two diameters not only guides us toward the sun in the system and the heart in man, but draws lines through the length and breadth of the aggregate of a man's particular daily behaviours and waves of life into his coves and inlets, and where they intersect will be the height or depth of his character. Perhaps we need only to know how his shores trend and his adjacent country or circumstances, to infer his depth and concealed bottom. If he is surrounded by mountainous circumstances, an Achillean shore, whose peaks overshadow and are reflected in his bosom, they suggest a corresponding depth in him. But a low and smooth shore proves him shallow on that side. In our bodies, a bold projecting brow falls off to and indicates a corresponding depth of thought. Also there is a bar across the entrance of our every cove, or particular inclination; each is our harbour for a season, in which we are detained and partially land-locked. These inclinations are not whimsical usually, but their form, size, and direction are determined by the promontories of the shore, the ancient axes of elevation. When this bar is gradually increased by storms, tides, or currents, or there is a subsidence of the waters, so that it reaches to the surface, that which was at first but an inclination in the shore in which a thought was harboured becomes an individual lake, cut off from the ocean, wherein the thought secures its own conditions — changes, perhaps, from salt to fresh, becomes a sweet sea, dead sea, or a marsh. At the advent of each individual into this life, may we not suppose that such a bar has risen to the surface somewhere? It is true, we are such poor navigators that our thoughts, for the most part, stand off and on upon a harbourless coast, are conversant only with the bights of the bays of poesy, or steer for the public ports of entry, and go into the dry docks of science, where they merely refit for this world, and no natural currents concur to individualize them.

As for the inlet or outlet of Walden, I have not discovered any but rain and snow and evapouration, though perhaps, with a thermometer and a line, such places may be found, for where the water flows into the pond it will probably be coldest in summer and warmest in winter. When the ice-men were at work here in '46-7, the cakes sent to the shore were one day rejected by those who were stacking them up there, not being thick enough to lie side by side with the rest; and the cutters thus discovered that the ice over a small space was two or three inches thinner than elsewhere, which made them think that there was an inlet there. They also showed me in another place what they thought was a "leach-hole," through which the pond leaked out under a hill into a neighbouring meadow, pushing me out on a cake of ice to see it. It was a small cavity under ten feet of water; but I think that I can warrant the pond not to need soldering till they find a worse leak than that. One has suggested, that if such a "leach-hole" should be found, its connection with the meadow, if any existed, might be proved by conveying some, coloured powder or sawdust to the mouth of the hole, and then putting a strainer over the spring in the meadow, which would catch some of the particles carried through by the current.

While I was surveying, the ice, which was sixteen inches thick, undulated under a slight wind like water. It is well known that a level cannot be used on ice. At one rod from the shore its greatest fluctuation, when observed by means of a level on land directed toward a graduated staff on the ice, was three quarters of an inch, though the ice appeared firmly attached to the shore. It was probably greater in the middle. Who knows but if our instruments were delicate enough we might detect an undulation in the crust of the earth? When two legs of my level were on the shore and the third on the ice, and the sights were directed over the latter, a rise or fall of the ice of an almost infinitesimal amount made a difference of several feet on a tree across the pond. When I began to cut holes for sounding there were three or four inches of water on the ice under a deep snow which had sunk it thus far; but the water began immediately to run into these holes, and continued to run for two days in deep streams, which wore away the ice on every side, and contributed essentially, if not mainly, to dry the surface of the pond; for, as the water ran in, it raised and floated the ice. This was somewhat like cutting a hole in the bottom of a ship to let the water out. When such holes freeze, and a rain succeeds, and finally a new freezing forms a fresh smooth ice over all, it is beautifully mottled internally by dark figures, shaped somewhat like a spider's web, what you may call ice rosettes, produced by the channels worn by the water flowing from all sides to a centre. Sometimes, also, when the ice was covered with shallow puddles, I saw a double shadow of myself, one standing on the head of the other, one on the ice, the other on the trees or hillside.

While yet it is cold January, and snow and ice are thick and solid, the prudent landlord comes from the village to get ice to cool his summer drink; impressively, even pathetically, wise, to foresee the heat and thirst of July now in January — wearing a thick coat and mittens! When so many things are not provided for. It may be that he lays up no treasures in this world which will cool his summer drink in the next. He cuts and saws the solid pond, unroofs the house of fishes, and carts off their very element and air, held fast by chains and stakes like corded wood, through the favouring winter air, to wintry cellars, to underlie the summer there. It looks like solidified azure, as, far off, it is drawn through the streets. These ice-cutters are a merry race, full of jest and sport, and when I went among them they were wont to invite me to saw pit-fashion with them, I standing underneath.

In the winter of '46-7 there came a hundred men of Hyperborean extraction swoop down on to our pond one morning, with many carloads of ungainly-looking farming tools — sleds, ploughs, drill-barrows, turf-knives, spades, saws, rakes, and each man was armed with a double-pointed pike-staff, such as is not described in the New-England Farmer or the Cultivator. I did not know whether they had come to sow a crop of winter rye, or some other kind of grain recently introduced from Iceland. As I saw no manure, I judged that they meant to skim the land, as I had done, thinking the soil was deep and had lain fallow long enough. They said that a gentleman farmer, who was behind the scenes, wanted to double his money, which, as I understood, amounted to half a million already; but in order to cover each one of his dollars with another, he took off the only coat, ay, the skin itself, of Walden Pond in the midst of a hard winter. They went to work at once, ploughing, barrowing, rolling, furrowing, in admirable order, as if they were bent on making this a model farm; but when I was looking sharp to see what kind of seed they dropped into the furrow, a gang of fellows by my side suddenly began to hook up the virgin mould itself, with a peculiar jerk, clean down to the sand, or rather the water — for it was a very springy soil — indeed all the terra firma there was — and haul it away on sleds, and then I guessed that they must be cutting peat in a bog. So they came and went every day, with a peculiar shriek from the locomotive, from and to some point of the polar regions, as it seemed to me, like a flock of arctic snow-birds. But sometimes Squaw Walden had her revenge, and a hired man, walking behind his team, slipped through a crack in the ground down toward Tartarus, and he who was so brave before suddenly became but the ninth part of a man, almost gave up his animal heat, and was glad to take refuge in my house, and acknowledged that there was some virtue in a stove; or sometimes the frozen soil took a piece of steel out of a ploughshare, or a plough got set in the furrow and had to be cut out.

To speak literally, a hundred Irishmen, with Yankee overseers, came from Cambridge every day to get out the ice. They divided it into cakes by methods too well known to require description, and these, being sledded to the shore, were rapidly hauled off on to an ice platform, and raised by grappling irons and block and tackle, worked by horses, on to a stack, as surely as so many barrels of flour, and there placed evenly side by side, and row upon row, as if they formed the solid base of an obelisk designed to pierce the clouds. They told me that in a good day they could get out a thousand tons, which was the yield of about one acre. Deep ruts and "cradle-holes" were worn in the ice, as on terra firma, by the passage of the sleds over the same track, and the horses invariably ate their oats out of cakes of ice hollowed out like buckets. They stacked up the cakes thus in the open air in a pile thirty-five feet high on one side and six or seven rods square, putting hay between the outside layers to exclude the air; for when the wind, though never so cold, finds a passage through, it will wear large cavities, leaving slight supports or studs only here and there, and finally topple it down. At first it looked like a vast blue fort or Valhalla; but when they began to tuck the coarse meadow hay into the crevices, and this became covered with rime and icicles, it looked like a venerable moss-grown and hoary ruin, built of azure-tinted marble, the abode of Winter, that old man we see in the almanac — his shanty, as if he had a design to estivate with us. They calculated that not twenty-five per cent of this would reach its destination, and that two or three per cent would be wasted in the cars. However, a still greater part of this heap had a different destiny from what was intended; for, either because the ice was found not to keep so well as was expected, containing more air than usual, or for some other reason, it never got to market. This heap, made in the winter of '46-7 and estimated to contain ten thousand tons, was finally covered with hay and boards; and though it was unroofed the following July, and a part of it carried off, the rest remaining exposed to the sun, it stood over that summer and the next winter, and was not quite melted till September, 1848. Thus the pond recovered the greater part.

Like the water, the Walden ice, seen near at hand, has a green tint, but at a distance is beautifully blue, and you can easily tell it from the white ice of the river, or the merely greenish ice of some ponds, a quarter of a mile off. Sometimes one of those great cakes slips from the ice-man's sled into the village street, and lies there for a week like a great emerald, an object of interest to all passers. I have noticed that a portion of Walden which in the state of water was green will often, when frozen, appear from the same point of view blue. So the hollows about this pond will, sometimes, in the winter, be filled with a greenish water somewhat like its own, but the next day will have frozen blue. Perhaps the blue colour of water and ice is due to the light and air they contain, and the most transparent is the bluest. Ice is an interesting subject for contemplation. They told me that they had some in the ice-houses at Fresh Pond five years old which was as good as ever. Why is it that a bucket of water soon becomes putrid, but frozen remains sweet forever? It is commonly said that this is the difference between the affections and the intellect.

Thus for sixteen days I saw from my window a hundred men at work like busy husbandmen, with teams and horses and apparently all the implements of farming, such a picture as we see on the first page of the almanac; and as often as I looked out I was reminded of the fable of the lark and the reapers, or the parable of the sower, and the like; and now they are all gone, and in thirty days more, probably, I shall look from the same window on the pure sea-green Walden water there, reflecting the clouds and the trees, and sending up its evapourations in solitude, and no traces will appear that a man has ever stood there. Perhaps I shall hear a solitary loon laugh as he dives and plumes himself, or shall see a lonely fisher in his boat, like a floating leaf, beholding his form reflected in the waves, where lately a hundred men securely laboured.

Thus it appears that the sweltering inhabitants of Charleston and New Orleans, of Madras and Bombay and Calcutta, drink at my well. In the morning I bathe my intellect in the stupendous and cosmogonal philosophy of the Bhagvat-Geeta, since whose composition years of the gods have elapsed, and in comparison with which our modern world and its literature seem puny and trivial; and I doubt if that philosophy is not to be referred to a previous state of existence, so remote is its sublimity from our conceptions. I lay down the book and go to my well for water, and lo! There I meet the servant of the Bramin, priest of Brahma and Vishnu and Indra, who still sits in his temple on the Ganges reading the Vedas, or dwells at the root of a tree with his crust and water jug. I meet his servant come to draw water for his master, and our buckets as it were grate together in the same well. The pure Walden water is mingled with the sacred water of the Ganges. With favouring winds it is wafted past the site of the fabulous islands of Atlantis and the Hesperides, makes the periplus of Hanno, and, floating by Ternate and Tidore and the mouth of the Persian Gulf, melts in the tropic gales of the Indian seas, and is landed in ports of which Alexander only heard the names.

17
Spring

The opening of large tracts by the ice-cutters commonly causes a pond to break up earlier; for the water, agitated by the wind, even in cold weather, wears away the surrounding ice. But such was not the effect on Walden that year, for she had soon got a thick new garment to take the place of the old. This pond never breaks up so soon as the others in this neighbourhood, on account both of its greater depth and its having no stream passing through it to melt or wear away the ice. I never knew it to open in the course of a winter, not excepting that of '52-3, which gave the ponds so severe a trial. It commonly opens about the first of April, a week or ten days later than Flint's Pond and Fair Haven, beginning to melt on the north side and in the shallower parts where it began to freeze. It indicates better than any water hereabouts the absolute progress of the season, being least affected by transient changes of temperature. A severe cold of a few days duration in March may very much retard the opening of the former ponds, while the temperature of Walden increases almost uninterruptedly. A thermometer thrust into the middle of Walden on the 6th of March, 1847, stood at 32x, or freezing point; near the shore at 33x; in the middle of Flint's Pond, the same day, at 32+x; at a dozen rods from the shore, in shallow water, under ice a foot thick, at 36x. This difference of three and a half degrees between the temperature of the deep water and the shallow in the latter pond, and the fact that a great proportion of it is comparatively shallow, show why it should break up so much sooner than Walden. The ice in the shallowest part was at this time several inches thinner than in the middle. In midwinter the middle had been the warmest and the ice thinnest there. So, also, every one who has waded about the shores of the pond in summer must have perceived how much warmer the water is close to the shore, where only three or four inches deep, than a little distance out, and on the surface where it is deep, than near the bottom. In spring the sun not only exerts an influence through the increased temperature of the air and earth, but its heat passes through ice a foot or more thick, and is reflected from the bottom in shallow water, and so also warms the water and melts the under side of the ice, at the same time that it is melting it more directly above, making it uneven, and causing the air bubbles which it contains to extend themselves upward and downward until it is completely honeycombed, and at last disappears suddenly in a single spring rain. Ice has its grain as well as wood, and when a cake begins to rot or "comb," that is, assume the appearance of honeycomb, whatever may be its position, the air cells are at right angles with what was the water surface. Where there is a rock or a log rising near to the surface the ice over it is much thinner, and is frequently quite dissolved by this reflected heat; and I have been told that in the experiment at Cambridge to freeze water in a shallow wooden pond, though the cold air circulated underneath, and so had access to both sides, the reflection of the sun from the bottom more than counterbalanced this advantage. When a warm rain in the middle of the winter melts off the snow-ice from Walden, and leaves a hard dark or transparent ice on the middle, there will be a strip of rotten though thicker white ice, a rod or more wide, about the shores, created by this reflected heat. Also, as I have said, the bubbles themselves within the ice operate as burning-glasses to melt the ice beneath.

The phenomena of the year take place every day in a pond on a small scale. Every morning, generally speaking, the shallow water is being warmed more rapidly than the deep, though it may not be made so warm after all, and every evening it is being cooled more rapidly until the morning. The day is an epitome of the year. The night is the winter, the morning and evening are the spring and fall, and the noon is the summer. The cracking and booming of the ice indicate a change of temperature. One pleasant morning after a cold night, February 24th, 1850, having gone to Flint's Pond to spend the day, I noticed with surprise, that when I struck the ice with the head of my axe, it resounded like a gong for many rods around, or as if I had struck on a tight drum-head. The pond began to boom about an hour after sunrise, when it felt the influence of the sun's rays slanted upon it from over the hills; it stretched itself and yawned like a waking man with a gradually increasing tumult, which was kept up three or four hours. It took a short siesta at noon, and boomed once more toward night, as the sun was withdrawing his influence. In the right stage of the weather a pond fires its evening gun with great regularity. But in the middle of the day, being full of cracks, and the air also being less elastic, it had completely lost its resonance, and probably fishes and muskrats could not then have been stunned by a blow on it. The fishermen say that the "thundering of the pond" scares the fishes and prevents their biting. The pond does not thunder every evening, and I cannot tell surely when to expect its thundering; but though I may perceive no difference in the weather, it does. Who would have suspected so large and cold and thick-skinned a thing to be so sensitive? Yet it has its law to which it thunders obedience when it should as surely as the buds expand in the spring. The earth is all alive and covered with papillae. The largest pond is as sensitive to atmospheric changes as the globule of mercury in its tube.

One attraction in coming to the woods to live was that I should have leisure and opportunity to see the Spring come in. The ice in the pond at length begins to be honeycombed, and I can set my heel in it as I walk. Fogs and rains and warmer suns are gradually melting the snow; the days have grown sensibly longer; and I see how I shall get through the winter without adding to my wood-pile, for large fires are no longer necessary. I am on the alert for the first signs of spring, to hear the chance note of some arriving bird, or the striped squirrel's chirp, for his stores must be now nearly exhausted, or see the woodchuck venture out of his winter quarters. On the 13th of March, after I had heard the bluebird, song sparrow, and red-wing, the ice was still nearly a foot thick. As the weather grew warmer it was not sensibly worn away by the water, nor broken up and floated off as in rivers, but, though it was completely melted for half a rod in width about the shore, the middle was

merely honeycombed and saturated with water, so that you could put your foot through it when six inches thick; but by the next day evening, perhaps, after a warm rain followed by fog, it would have wholly disappeared, all gone off with the fog, spirited away. One year I went across the middle only five days before it disappeared entirely. In 1845 Walden was first completely open on the 1st of April; in '46, the 25th of March; in '47, the 8th of April; in '51, the 28th of March; in '52, the 18th of April; in '53, the 23rd of March; in '54, about the 7th of April.

Every incident connected with the breaking up of the rivers and ponds and the settling of the weather is particularly interesting to us who live in a climate of so great extremes. When the warmer days come, they who dwell near the river hear the ice crack at night with a startling whoop as loud as artillery, as if its icy fetters were rent from end to end, and within a few days see it rapidly going out. So the alligator comes out of the mud with quakings of the earth. One old man, who has been a close observer of Nature, and seems as thoroughly wise in regard to all her operations as if she had been put upon the stocks when he was a boy, and he had helped to lay her keel — who has come to his growth, and can hardly acquire more of natural lore if he should live to the age of Methuselah — told me — and I was surprised to hear him express wonder at any of Nature's operations, for I thought that there were no secrets between them — that one spring day he took his gun and boat, and thought that he would have a little sport with the ducks. There was ice still on the meadows, but it was all gone out of the river, and he dropped down without obstruction from Sudbury, where he lived, to Fair Haven Pond, which he found, unexpectedly, covered for the most part with a firm field of ice. It was a warm day, and he was surprised to see so great a body of ice remaining. Not seeing any ducks, he hid his boat on the north or back side of an island in the pond, and then concealed himself in the bushes on the south side, to await them. The ice was melted for three or four rods from the shore, and there was a smooth and warm sheet of water, with a muddy bottom, such as the ducks love, within, and he thought it likely that some would be along pretty soon. After he had lain still there about an hour he heard a low and seemingly very distant sound, but singularly grand and impressive, unlike anything he had ever heard, gradually swelling and increasing as if it would have a universal and memorable ending, a sullen rush and roar, which seemed to him all at once like the sound of a vast body of fowl coming in to settle there, and, seizing his gun, he started up in haste and excited; but he found, to his surprise, that the whole body of the ice had started while he lay there, and drifted in to the shore, and the sound he had heard was made by its edge grating on the shore — at first gently nibbled and crumbled off, but at length heaving up and scattering its wrecks along the island to a considerable height before it came to a standstill.

At length the sun's rays have attained the right angle, and warm winds blow up mist and rain and melt the snowbanks, and the sun, dispersing the mist, smiles on a checkered landscape of russet and white smoking with incense, through which the traveller picks his way from islet to islet, cheered by the music of a thousand tinkling rills and rivulets whose veins are filled with the blood of winter which they are bearing off. Few phenomena gave me more delight than to observe the forms which thawing sand and clay assume in flowing down the sides of a deep cut on the railroad through which I passed on my way to the village, a phenomenon not very common on so large a scale, though the number of freshly exposed banks of the right material must have been greatly multiplied since railroads were invented. The material was sand of every degree of fineness and of various rich colours, commonly mixed with a little clay. When the frost comes out in the spring, and even in a thawing day in the winter, the sand begins to flow down the slopes like lava, sometimes bursting out through the snow and overflowing it where no sand was to be seen before. Innumerable little streams overlap and interlace one with another, exhibiting a sort of hybrid product, which obeys half way the law of currents, and half way that of vegetation. As it flows it takes the forms of sappy leaves or vines, making heaps of pulpy sprays a foot or more in depth, and resembling, as you look down on them, the laciniated, lobed, and imbricated thalluses of some lichens; or you are reminded of coral, of leopard's paws or birds' feet, of brains or lungs or bowels, and excrements of all kinds. It is a truly grotesque vegetation, whose forms and colour we see imitated in bronze, a sort of architectural foliage more ancient and typical than acanthus, chiccory, ivy, vine, or any vegetable leaves; destined perhaps, under some circumstances, to become a puzzle to future geologists. The whole cut impressed me as if it were a cave with its stalactites laid open to the light. The various shades of the sand are singularly rich and agreeable, embracing the different iron colours, brown, gray, yellowish, and reddish. When the flowing mass reaches the drain at the foot of the bank it spreads out flatter into strands, the separate streams losing their semi-cylindrical form and gradually becoming more flat and broad, running together as they are more moist, till they form an almost flat sand, still variously and beautifully shaded, but in which you can trace the original forms of vegetation; till at length, in the water itself, they are converted into banks, like those formed off the mouths of rivers, and the forms of vegetation are lost in the ripple marks on the bottom.

The whole bank, which is from twenty to forty feet high, is sometimes overlaid with a mass of this kind of foliage, or sandy rupture, for a quarter of a mile on one or both sides, the produce of one spring day. What makes this sand foliage remarkable is its springing into existence thus suddenly. When I see on the one side the inert bank — for the sun acts on one side first — and on the other this luxuriant foliage, the creation of an hour, I am affected as if in a peculiar sense I stood in the labouratory of the Artist who made the world and me — had come to where he was still at work, sporting on this bank, and with excess of energy strewing his fresh designs about. I feel as if I were nearer to the vitals of the globe, for this sandy overflow is something such a foliaceous mass as the vitals of the animal body. You find thus in the very sands an anticipation of the vegetable leaf. No wonder that the earth expresses itself outwardly in leaves, it so labours with the idea inwardly. The atoms have already learned this law, and are pregnant by it. The overhanging leaf sees here its prototype. Internally, whether in the globe or animal body, it is a moist thick lobe, a word especially applicable to the liver and lungs and the leaves of fat (jnai, labour, lapsus, to flow or slip downward, a lapsing; jiais, globus, lobe, globe; also lap, flap, and many other words); externally a dry thin leaf, even as the f and v are a pressed and dried b. The radicals of lobe are lb, the soft mass of the b (single lobed, or B, double lobed), with the liquid l behind it pressing it forward. In globe, glb, the guttural g adds to the meaning the capacity of the throat. The feathers and wings of birds are still drier and thinner leaves. Thus, also, you pass from the lumpish grub in the earth to the airy and fluttering butterfly. The very globe continually transcends and translates itself, and becomes winged in its orbit. Even ice begins with delicate crystal leaves, as if it had flowed into moulds which the fronds of waterplants have impressed on the watery mirror. The whole tree itself is but one leaf, and rivers are still vaster leaves whose pulp is intervening earth, and towns and cities are the ova of insects in their axils.

When the sun withdraws the sand ceases to flow, but in the morning the streams will start once more and branch and branch again into a myriad of others. You here see perchance how blood-vessels are formed. If you look closely you observe that first there pushes forward from the thawing mass a stream of softened sand with a drop-like point, like the ball of the finger, feeling its way slowly and blindly downward, until at last with more heat and moisture, as the sun gets higher, the most fluid portion, in its effort to obey the law to which the most inert also yields, separates from the latter and forms for itself a meandering channel or artery within that, in which is seen a little silvery stream glancing like lightning from one stage of pulpy leaves or branches to another, and ever and anon swallowed up in the sand. It is wonderful how rapidly yet perfectly the sand organizes itself as it flows, using the best material its mass affords to form the sharp edges of its channel. Such are the sources of rivers. In the silicious matter which the water deposits is perhaps the bony system, and in the still finer soil and organic matter the fleshy fibre or cellular tissue. What is man but a mass of thawing clay? The ball of the human finger is but a drop congealed. The fingers and toes flow to their extent from the thawing mass of the body. Who knows what the human body would expand and flow out to under a more genial heaven? Is not the hand a spreading palm leaf with its lobes and veins? The ear may be regarded, fancifully, as a lichen, umbilicaria, on the side of the head, with its lobe or drop. The lip — labium, from labour (?) — laps or lapses from the sides of the cavernous mouth. The nose is a manifest congealed drop or stalactite. The chin is a still larger drop, the confluent dripping of the face. The cheeks are a slide from the brows into the valley of the face, opposed and diffused by the cheek bones. Each rounded lobe of the vegetable leaf, too, is a thick and now loitering drop, larger or smaller; the lobes are the fingers of the leaf; and as many lobes as it has, in so many directions it tends to flow, and more heat or other genial influences would have caused it to flow yet farther.

Thus it seemed that this one hillside illustrated the principle of all the operations of Nature. The Maker of this earth but patented a leaf. What Champollion will decipher this hieroglyphic for us, that we may turn over a new leaf at last? This phenomenon is more exhilarating to me than the luxuriance and fertility of vineyards. True, it is somewhat excrementitious in its character, and there is no end to the heaps of liver, lights, and bowels, as if the globe were turned wrong side outward; but this suggests at least that Nature has some bowels, and there again is mother of humanity. This is the frost coming out of the ground; this is Spring. It precedes the green and flowery spring, as mythology precedes regular poetry. I know of nothing more purgative of winter fumes and indigestions. It convinces me that Earth is still in her swaddling-clothes, and stretches forth baby fingers on every side. Fresh curls spring from the baldest brow. There is nothing inorganic. These foliaceous heaps lie along the bank like the slag of a furnace, showing that Nature is "in full blast" within. The earth is not a mere fragment of dead history, stratum upon stratum like the leaves of a book, to be studied by geologists and antiquaries chiefly, but living poetry like the leaves of a tree, which precede flowers and fruit — not a fossil earth, but a living earth; compared with whose great central life all animal and vegetable life is merely parasitic. Its throes will heave our exuviae from their graves. You may melt your metals and cast them into the most beautiful moulds you can; they will never excite me like the forms which this molten earth flows out into. And not only it, but the institutions upon it are plastic like clay in the hands of the potter.

Ere long, not only on these banks, but on every hill and plain and in every hollow, the frost comes out of the ground like a dormant quadruped from its burrow, and seeks the sea with music, or migrates to other climes in clouds. Thaw with his gentle persuasion is more powerful than Thor with his hammer. The one melts, the other but breaks in pieces.

When the ground was partially bare of snow, and a few warm days had dried its surface somewhat, it was pleasant to compare the first tender signs of the infant year just peeping forth with the stately beauty of the withered vegetation which had withstood the winter — life-everlasting, goldenrods, pinweeds, and graceful wild grasses, more obvious and interesting frequently than in summer even, as if their beauty was not ripe till then; even cotton-grass, cat-tails, mulleins, johnswort, hard-hack, meadow-sweet, and other strong-stemmed plants, those unexhausted granaries which entertain the earliest birds — decent weeds, at least, which widowed Nature wears. I am particularly attracted by the arching and sheaf-like top of the wool-grass; it brings back the summer to our winter memories, and is among the forms which art loves to copy, and which, in the vegetable kingdom, have the same relation to types already in the mind of man that astronomy has. It is an antique style, older than Greek or Egyptian. Many of the phenomena of Winter are suggestive of an inexpressible tenderness and fragile delicacy. We are accustomed to hear this king described as a rude and boisterous tyrant; but with the gentleness of a lover he adorns the tresses of Summer.

At the approach of spring the red squirrels got under my house, two at a time, directly under my feet as I sat reading or writing, and kept up the queerest chuckling and chirruping and vocal pirouetting and gurgling sounds that ever were heard; and when I stamped they only chirruped the louder, as if past all fear and respect in their mad pranks, defying humanity to stop them. No, you don't — chickaree — chickaree. They were wholly deaf to my arguments, or failed to perceive their force, and fell into a strain of invective that was irresistible.

The first sparrow of spring! The year beginning with younger hope than ever! The faint silvery warblings heard over the partially bare and moist fields from the bluebird, the song sparrow, and the red-wing, as if the last flakes of winter tinkled as they fell! What at such a time are histories, chronologies, traditions, and all written revelations? The brooks sing carols and glees to the spring. The marsh hawk, sailing low over the meadow, is already seeking the first slimy life that awakes. The sinking sound of melting snow is heard in all dells, and the ice dissolves apace in the ponds. The grass flames up on the hillsides like a spring fire — "et primitus oritur herba imbribus primoribus evocata" — as if the earth sent forth an inward heat to greet the returning sun; not yellow but green is the colour of its flame; — the symbol of perpetual youth, the grass-blade, like a long green ribbon, streams from the sod into the summer, checked indeed by the frost, but anon pushing on again, lifting its spear of last year's hay with the fresh life below. It grows as steadily as the rill oozes out of the ground. It is almost identical with that, for in the growing days of June, when the rills are dry, the grass-blades are their channels, and

from year to year the herds drink at this perennial green stream, and the mower draws from it betimes their winter supply. So our human life but dies down to its root, and still puts forth its green blade to eternity.

Walden is melting apace. There is a canal two rods wide along the northerly and westerly sides, and wider still at the east end. A great field of ice has cracked off from the main body. I hear a song sparrow singing from the bushes on the shore — olit, olit, olit — chip, chip, chip, che char — che wiss, wiss, wiss. He too is helping to crack it. How handsome the great sweeping curves in the edge of the ice, answering somewhat to those of the shore, but more regular! It is unusually hard, owing to the recent severe but transient cold, and all watered or waved like a palace floor. But the wind slides eastward over its opaque surface in vain, till it reaches the living surface beyond. It is glorious to behold this ribbon of water sparkling in the sun, the bare face of the pond full of glee and youth, as if it spoke the joy of the fishes within it, and of the sands on its shore — a silvery sheen as from the scales of a leuciscus, as it were all one active fish. Such is the contrast between winter and spring. Walden was dead and is alive again. But this spring it broke up more steadily, as I have said.

The change from storm and winter to serene and mild weather, from dark and sluggish hours to bright and elastic ones, is a memorable crisis which all things proclaim. It is seemingly instantaneous at last. Suddenly an influx of light filled my house, though the evening was at hand, and the clouds of winter still overhung it, and the eaves were dripping with sleety rain. I looked out the window, and lo! Where yesterday was cold gray ice there lay the transparent pond already calm and full of hope as in a summer evening, reflecting a summer evening sky in its bosom, though none was visible overhead, as if it had intelligence with some remote horizon. I heard a robin in the distance, the first I had heard for many a thousand years, methought, whose note I shall not forget for many a thousand more — the same sweet and powerful song as of yore. O the evening robin, at the end of a New England summer day! If I could ever find the twig he sits upon! I mean he; I mean the twig. This at least is not the Turdus migratorius. The pitch pines and shrub oaks about my house, which had so long drooped, suddenly resumed their several characters, looked brighter, greener, and more erect and alive, as if effectually cleansed and restored by the rain. I knew that it would not rain any more. You may tell by looking at any twig of the forest, ay, at your very wood-pile, whether its winter is past or not. As it grew darker, I was startled by the honking of geese flying low over the woods, like weary travellers getting in late from Southern lakes, and indulging at last in unrestrained complaint and mutual consolation. Standing at my door, I could bear the rush of their wings; when, driving toward my house, they suddenly spied my light, and with hushed clamor wheeled and settled in the pond. So I came in, and shut the door, and passed my first spring night in the woods.

In the morning I watched the geese from the door through the mist, sailing in the middle of the pond, fifty rods off, so large and tumultuous that Walden appeared like an artificial pond for their amusement. But when I stood on the shore they at once rose up with a great flapping of wings at the signal of their commander, and when they had got into rank circled about over my head, twenty-nine of them, and then steered straight to Canada, with a regular honk from the leader at intervals, trusting to break their fast in muddier pools. A "plump" of ducks rose at the same time and took the route to the north in the wake of their noisier cousins.

For a week I heard the circling, groping clangor of some solitary goose in the foggy mornings, seeking its companion, and still peopling the woods with the sound of a larger life than they could sustain. In April the pigeons were seen again flying express in small flocks, and in due time I heard the martins twittering over my clearing, though it had not seemed that the township contained so many that it could afford me any, and I fancied that they were peculiarly of the ancient race that dwelt in hollow trees ere white men came. In almost all climes the tortoise and the frog are among the precursors and heralds of this season, and birds fly with song and glancing plumage, and plants spring and bloom, and winds blow, to correct this slight oscillation of the poles and preserve the equilibrium of nature.

As every season seems best to us in its turn, so the coming in of spring is like the creation of Cosmos out of Chaos and the realization of the Golden Age.—

> "Eurus ad Auroram Nabathaeaque regna recessit,
> Persidaque, et radiis juga subdita matutinis."

> "The East-Wind withdrew to Aurora and the Nabathean kingdom,
> And the Persian, and the ridges placed under the morning rays.

Man was born. Whether that Artificer of things,
The origin of a better world, made him from the divine seed;
Or the earth, being recent and lately sundered from the high Ether, retained
some seeds of cognate heaven."

A single gentle rain makes the grass many shades greener. So our prospects brighten on the influx of better thoughts. We should be blessed if we lived in the present always, and took advantage of every accident that befell us, like the grass which confesses the influence of the slightest dew that falls on it; and did not spend our time in atoning for the neglect of past opportunities, which we call doing our duty. We loiter in winter while it is already spring. In a pleasant spring morning all men's sins are forgiven. Such a day is a truce to vice. While such a sun holds out to burn, the vilest sinner may return. Through our own recovered innocence we discern the innocence of our neighbours. You may have known your neighbour yesterday for a thief, a drunkard, or a sensualist, and merely pitied or despised him, and despaired of the world; but the sun shines bright and warm this first spring morning, recreating the world, and you meet him at some serene work, and see how it is exhausted and debauched veins expand with still joy and bless the new day, feel the spring influence with the innocence of infancy, and all his faults are forgotten. There is not only an atmosphere of good will about him, but even a savour of holiness groping for expression, blindly and ineffectually perhaps, like a new-born instinct, and for a short hour the south hill-side echoes to no vulgar jest. You see some innocent fair shoots preparing to burst from his gnarled rind and try another year's life, tender and fresh as the youngest plant. Even he has entered into the joy of his Lord. Why the jailer does not leave open his prison doors — why the judge does not dismis his case — why the preacher does not dismiss his congregation! It is because they do not obey the hint which God gives them, nor accept the pardon which he freely offers to all.

"A return to goodness produced each day in the tranquil and beneficent breath of the morning, causes that in respect to the love of virtue and the hatred of vice, one approaches a little the primitive nature of man, as the sprouts of the forest which has been felled. In like manner the evil which one does in the interval of a day prevents the germs of virtues which began to spring up again from developing themselves and destroys them.

"After the germs of virtue have thus been prevented many times from developing themselves, then the beneficent breath of evening does not suffice to preserve them. As soon as the breath of evening does not suffice longer to preserve them, then the nature of man does not differ much from that of the brute. Men seeing the nature of this man like that of the brute, think that he has never possessed the innate faculty of reason. Are those the true and natural sentiments of man?"

> "The Golden Age was first created, which without any avenger
> Spontaneously without law cherished fidelity and rectitude.
> Punishment and fear were not; nor were threatening words read
> On suspended brass; nor did the suppliant crowd fear
> The words of their judge; but were safe without an avenger.
> Not yet the pine felled on its mountains had descended
> To the liquid waves that it might see a foreign world,
> And mortals knew no shores but their own.
>
> . . .
>
> There was eternal spring, and placid zephyrs with warm
> Blasts soothed the flowers born without seed."

On the 29th of April, as I was fishing from the bank of the river near the Nine-Acre-Corner bridge, standing on the quaking grass and willow roots, where the muskrats lurk, I heard a singular rattling sound, somewhat like that of the sticks which boys play with their fingers, when, looking up, I observed a very slight and graceful hawk, like a nighthawk, alternately soaring like a ripple and tumbling a rod or two over and over, showing the under side of its wings, which gleamed like a satin ribbon in the sun, or like the pearly inside of a shell. This sight reminded me of falconry and what nobleness and poetry are associated with that sport. The Merlin it seemed to me it might be called: but I care not for its name. It was the most ethereal flight I had ever witnessed. It did not simply flutter like a butterfly, nor soar like the larger hawks, but it sported with proud reliance in the fields of air; mounting again and again with its strange chuckle, it repeated its free and beautiful fall, turning over and over like a kite, and then recovering from its lofty tumbling, as if it had never set its foot on terra firma. It appeared to have no companion in the universe

— sporting there alone — and to need none but the morning and the ether with which it played. It was not lonely, but made all the earth lonely beneath it. Where was the parent which hatched it, its kindred, and its father in the heavens? The tenant of the air, it seemed related to the earth but by an egg hatched some time in the crevice of a crag; — or was its native nest made in the angle of a cloud, woven of the rainbow's trimmings and the sunset sky, and lined with some soft midsummer haze caught up from earth? Its eyry now some cliffy cloud.

Beside this I got a rare mess of golden and silver and bright cupreous fishes, which looked like a string of jewels. Ah! I have penetrated to those meadows on the morning of many a first spring day, jumping from hummock to hummock, from willow root to willow root, when the wild river valley and the woods were bathed in so pure and bright a light as would have waked the dead, if they had been slumbering in their graves, as some suppose. There needs no stronger proof of immortality. All things must live in such a light. O Death, where was thy sting? O Grave, where was thy victory, then?

Our village life would stagnate if it were not for the unexplored forests and meadows which surround it. We need the tonic of wildness — to wade sometimes in marshes where the bittern and the meadow-hen lurk, and hear the booming of the snipe; to smell the whispering sedge where only some wilder and more solitary fowl builds her nest, and the mink crawls with its belly close to the ground. At the same time that we are earnest to explore and learn all things, we require that all things be mysterious and unexplorable, that land and sea be infinitely wild, unsurveyed and unfathomed by us because unfathomable. We can never have enough of nature. We must be refreshed by the sight of inexhaustible vigour, vast and titanic features, the sea-coast with its wrecks, the wilderness with its living and its decaying trees, the thunder-cloud, and the rain which lasts three weeks and produces freshets. We need to witness our own limits transgressed, and some life pasturing freely where we never wander. We are cheered when we observe the vulture feeding on the carrion which disgusts and disheartens us, and deriving health and strength from the repast. There was a dead horse in the hollow by the path to my house, which compelled me sometimes to go out of my way, especially in the night when the air was heavy, but the assurance it gave me of the strong appetite and inviolable health of Nature was my compensation for this. I love to see that Nature is so rife with life that myriads can be afforded to be sacrificed and suffered to prey on one another; that tender organizations can be so serenely squashed out of existence like pulp — tadpoles which herons gobble up, and tortoises and toads run over in the road; and that sometimes it has rained flesh and blood! With the liability to accident, we must see how little account is to be made of it. The impression made on a wise man is that of universal innocence. Poison is not poisonous after all, nor are any wounds fatal. Compassion is a very untenable ground. It must be expeditious. Its pleadings will not bear to be stereotyped.

Early in May, the oaks, hickories, maples, and other trees, just putting out amidst the pine woods around the pond, imparted a brightness like sunshine to the landscape, especially in cloudy days, as if the sun were breaking through mists and shining faintly on the hillsides here and there. On the third or fourth of May I saw a loon in the pond, and during the first week of the month I heard the whip-poor-will, the brown thrasher, the veery, the wood pewee, the chewink, and other birds. I had heard the wood thrush long before. The phoebe had already come once more and looked in at my door and window, to see if my house was cavern-like enough for her, sustaining herself on humming wings with clinched talons, as if she held by the air, while she surveyed the premises. The sulphur-like pollen of the pitch pine soon covered the pond and the stones and rotten wood along the shore, so that you could have collected a barrelful. This is the "sulphur showers" we hear of. Even in Calidas' drama of Sacontala, we read of "rills dyed yellow with the golden dust of the lotus." And so the seasons went rolling on into summer, as one rambles into higher and higher grass.

Thus was my first year's life in the woods completed; and the second year was similar to it. I finally left Walden September 6th, 1847.

18
Conclusion

To the sick the doctors wisely recommend a change of air and scenery. Thank Heaven, here is not all the world. The buckeye does not grow in New England, and the mockingbird is rarely heard here. The wild goose is more of a cosmopolite than we; he breaks his fast in Canada, takes a luncheon in the Ohio, and plumes himself for the night in a southern bayou. Even the bison, to some extent, keeps pace with the seasons cropping the pastures of the Colourado only till a greener and sweeter grass awaits him by the Yellowstone. Yet we think that if rail fences are pulled down, and stone walls piled up on our farms, bounds are henceforth set to our lives and our fates decided. If you are chosen town clerk, forsooth, you cannot go to Tierra del Fuego this summer: but you may go to the land of infernal fire nevertheless. The universe is wider than our views of it.

Yet we should oftener look over the tafferel of our craft, like curious passengers, and not make the voyage like stupid sailors picking oakum. The other side of the globe is but the home of our correspondent. Our voyaging is only great-circle sailing, and the doctors prescribe for diseases of the skin merely. One hastens to southern Africa to chase the giraffe; but surely that is not the game he would be after. How long, pray, would a man hunt giraffes if he could? Snipes and woodcocks also may afford rare sport; but I trust it would be nobler game to shoot one's self.—

> "Direct your eye right inward, and you'll find
> A thousand regions in your mind
> Yet undiscovered. Travel them, and be
> Expert in home-cosmography."

What does Africa — what does the West stand for? Is not our own interior white on the chart? Black though it may prove, like the coast, when discovered. Is it the source of the Nile, or the Niger, or the Mississippi, or a

Northwest Passage around this continent, that we would find? Are these the problems which most concern mankind? Is Franklin the only man who is lost, that his wife should be so earnest to find him? Does Mr. Grinnell know where he himself is? Be rather the Mungo Park, the Lewis and Clark and Frobisher, of your own streams and oceans; explore your own higher latitudes — with shiploads of preserved meats to support you, if they be necessary; and pile the empty cans sky-high for a sign. Were preserved meats invented to preserve meat merely? Nay, be a Columbus to whole new continents and worlds within you, opening new channels, not of trade, but of thought. Every man is the lord of a realm beside which the earthly empire of the Czar is but a petty state, a hummock left by the ice. Yet some can be patriotic who have no self-respect, and sacrifice the greater to the less. They love the soil which makes their graves, but have no sympathy with the spirit which may still animate their clay. Patriotism is a maggot in their heads. What was the meaning of that South-Sea Exploring Expedition, with all its parade and expense, but an indirect recognition of the fact that there are continents and seas in the moral world to which every man is an isthmus or an inlet, yet unexplored by him, but that it is easier to sail many thousand miles through cold and storm and cannibals, in a government ship, with five hundred men and boys to assist one, than it is to explore the private sea, the Atlantic and Pacific Ocean of one's being alone.

> "Erret, et extremos alter scrutetur Iberos.
> Plus habet hic vitae, plus habet ille viae."

> Let them wander and scrutinize the outlandish Australians.
> I have more of God, they more of the road.

It is not worth the while to go round the world to count the cats in Zanzibar. Yet do this even till you can do better, and you may perhaps find some "Symmes' Hole" by which to get at the inside at last. England and France, Spain and Portugal, Gold Coast and Slave Coast, all front on this private sea; but no bark from them has ventured out of sight of land, though it is without doubt the direct way to India. If you would learn to speak all tongues and conform to the customs of all nations, if you would travel farther than all travellers, be naturalized in all climes, and cause the Sphinx to dash her head against a stone, even obey the precept of the old philosopher, and Explore thyself. Herein are demanded the eye and the nerve. Only the defeated and deserters go to the wars, cowards that run away and enlist. Start now on that farthest western way, which does not pause at the Mississippi or the Pacific, nor conduct toward a wornout China or Japan, but leads on direct, a tangent to this sphere, summer and winter, day and night, sun down, moon down, and at last earth down too.

It is said that Mirabeau took to highway robbery "to ascertain what degree of resolution was necessary in order to place one's self in formal opposition to the most sacred laws of society." He declared that "a soldier who fights in the ranks does not require half so much courage as a footpad" — "that honour and religion have never stood in the way of a well-considered and a firm resolve." This was manly, as the world goes; and yet it was idle, if not desperate. A saner man would have found himself often enough "in formal opposition" to what are deemed "the most sacred laws of society," through obedience to yet more sacred laws, and so have tested his resolution without going out of his way. It is not for a man to put himself in such an attitude to society, but to maintain himself in whatever attitude he find himself through obedience to the laws of his being, which will never be one of opposition to a just government, if he should chance to meet with such.

I left the woods for as good a reason as I went there. Perhaps it seemed to me that I had several more lives to live, and could not spare any more time for that one. It is remarkable how easily and insensibly we fall into a particular route, and make a beaten track for ourselves. I had not lived there a week before my feet wore a path from my door to the pond-side; and though it is five or six years since I trod it, it is still quite distinct. It is true, I fear, that others may have fallen into it, and so helped to keep it open. The surface of the earth is soft and impressible by the feet of men; and so with the paths which the mind travels. How worn and dusty, then, must be the highways of the world, how deep the ruts of tradition and conformity! I did not wish to take a cabin passage, but rather to go before the mast and on the deck of the world, for there I could best see the moonlight amid the mountains. I do not wish to go below now.

I learned this, at least, by my experiment: that if one advances confidently in the direction of his dreams, and endeavours to live the life which he has imagined, he will meet with a success unexpected in common hours. He will put some things behind, will pass an invisible boundary; new, universal, and more liberal laws will begin to establish themselves around and within him; or the old laws be expanded, and interpreted in his favour in a more liberal sense, and he will live with the license of a higher order of beings. In proportion as he simplifies his life, the laws of the universe will appear less complex, and solitude will not be solitude, nor poverty poverty, nor weakness weakness. If you have built castles in the air, your work need not be lost; that is where they should be. Now put the foundations under them.

It is a ridiculous demand which England and America make, that you shall speak so that they can understand you. Neither men nor toadstools grow so. As if that were important, and there were not enough to understand you without them. As if Nature could support but one order of understandings, could not sustain birds as well as quadrupeds, flying as well as creeping things, and hush and whoa, which Bright can understand, were the best English. As if there were safety in stupidity alone. I fear chiefly lest my expression may not be extravagant enough, may not wander far enough beyond the narrow limits of my daily experience, so as to be adequate to the truth of which I have been convinced. Extravagance! It depends on how you are yarded. The migrating buffalo, which seeks new pastures in another latitude, is not extravagant like the cow which kicks over the pail, leaps the cowyard fence, and runs after her calf, in milking time. I desire to speak somewhere without bounds; like a man in a waking moment, to men in their waking moments; for I am convinced that I cannot exaggerate enough even to lay the foundation of a true expression. Who that has heard a strain of music feared then lest he should speak extravagantly any more forever? In view of the future or possible, we should live quite laxly and undefined in front, our outlines dim and misty on that side; as our shadows reveal an insensible perspiration toward the sun. The volatile truth of our words should continually betray the inadequacy of the residual statement. Their truth is instantly translated; its literal monument alone remains. The words which express our faith and piety are not definite; yet they are significant and fragrant like frankincense to superior natures.

Why level downward to our dullest perception always, and praise that as common sense? The commonest sense is the sense of men asleep, which they express by snoring. Sometimes we are inclined to class those who are once-and-a-half-witted with the half-witted, because we appreciate only a third part of their wit. Some would find fault with the morning red, if they ever got up early enough. "They pretend," as I hear, "that the verses of Kabir have four different senses; illusion, spirit, intellect, and the exoteric doctrine of the

Vedas"; but in this part of the world it is considered a ground for complaint if a man's writings admit of more than one interpretation. While England endeavours to cure the potato-rot, will not any endeavour to cure the brain-rot, which prevails so much more widely and fatally?

I do not suppose that I have attained to obscurity, but I should be proud if no more fatal fault were found with my pages on this score than was found with the Walden ice. Southern customers objected to its blue colour, which is the evidence of its purity, as if it were muddy, and preferred the Cambridge ice, which is white, but tastes of weeds. The purity men love is like the mists which envelop the earth, and not like the azure ether beyond.

Some are dinning in our ears that we Americans, and moderns generally, are intellectual dwarfs compared with the ancients, or even the Elizabethan men. But what is that to the purpose? A living dog is better than a dead lion. Shall a man go and hang himself because he belongs to the race of pygmies, and not be the biggest pygmy that he can? Let every one mind his own business, and endeavour to be what he was made.

Why should we be in such desperate haste to succeed and in such desperate enterprises? If a man does not keep pace with his companions, perhaps it is because he hears a different drummer. Let him step to the music which he hears, however measured or far away. It is not important that he should mature as soon as an apple tree or an oak. Shall he turn his spring into summer? If the condition of things which we were made for is not yet, what were any reality which we can substitute? We will not be shipwrecked on a vain reality. Shall we with pains erect a heaven of blue glass over ourselves, though when it is done we shall be sure to gaze still at the true ethereal heaven far above, as if the former were not?

There was an artist in the city of Kouroo who was disposed to strive after perfection. One day it came into his mind to make a staff. Having considered that in an imperfect work time is an ingredient, but into a perfect work time does not enter, he said to himself, It shall be perfect in all respects, though I should do nothing else in my life. He proceeded instantly to the forest for wood, being resolved that it should not be made of unsuitable material; and as he searched for and rejected stick after stick, his friends gradually deserted him, for they grew old in their works and died, but he grew not older by a moment. His singleness of purpose and resolution, and his elevated piety, endowed him, without his knowledge, with perennial youth. As he made no compromise with Time, Time kept out of his way, and only sighed at a distance because he could not overcome him. Before he had found a stock in all respects suitable the city of Kouroo was a hoary ruin, and he sat on one of its mounds to peel the stick. Before he had given it the proper shape the dynasty of the Candahars was at an end, and with the point of the stick he wrote the name of the last of that race in the sand, and then resumed his work. By the time he had smoothed and polished the staff Kalpa was no longer the pole-star; and ere he had put on the ferule and the head adorned with precious stones, Brahma had awoke and slumbered many times. But why do I stay to mention these things? When the finishing stroke was put to his work, it suddenly expanded before the eyes of the astonished artist into the fairest of all the creations of Brahma. He had made a new system in making a staff, a world with full and fair proportions; in which, though the old cities and dynasties had passed away, fairer and more glorious ones had taken their places. And now he saw by the heap of shavings still fresh at his feet, that, for him and his work, the former lapse of time had been an illusion, and that no more time had elapsed than is required for a single scintillation from the brain of Brahma to fall on and inflame the tinder of a mortal brain. The material was pure, and his art was pure; how could the result be other than wonderful?

No face which we can give to a matter will stead us so well at last as the truth. This alone wears well. For the most part, we are not where we are, but in a false position. Through an infinity of our natures, we suppose a case, and put ourselves into it, and hence are in two cases at the same time, and it is doubly difficult to get out. In sane moments we regard only the facts, the case that is. Say what you have to say, not what you ought. Any truth is better than make-believe. Tom Hyde, the tinker, standing on the gallows, was asked if he had anything to say. "Tell the tailors," said he, "to remember to make a knot in their thread before they take the first stitch." His companion's prayer is forgotten.

However mean your life is, meet it and live it; do not shun it and call it hard names. It is not so bad as you are. It looks poorest when you are richest. The fault-finder will find faults even in paradise. Love your life, poor as it is. You may perhaps have some pleasant, thrilling, glorious hours, even in a poorhouse. The setting sun is reflected from the windows of the almshouse as brightly as from the rich man's abode; the snow melts before its door as early in the spring. I do not see but a quiet mind may live as contentedly there, and have as cheering thoughts, as in a palace. The town's poor seem to me often to live the most independent lives of any. Maybe they are simply great enough to receive without misgiving. Most think that they are above being supported by the town; but it oftener happens that they are not above supporting themselves by dishonest means, which should be more disreputable. Cultivate poverty like a garden herb, like sage. Do not trouble yourself much to get new things, whether clothes or friends. Turn the old; return to them. Things do not change; we change. Sell your clothes and keep your thoughts. God will see that you do not want society. If I were confined to a corner of a garret all my days, like a spider, the world would be just as large to me while I had my thoughts about me. The philosopher said: "From an army of three divisions one can take away its general, and put it in disorder; from the man the most abject and vulgar one cannot take away his thought." Do not seek so anxiously to be developed, to subject yourself to many influences to be played on; it is all dissipation. Humility like darkness reveals the heavenly lights. The shadows of poverty and meanness gather around us, "and lo! Creation widens to our view." We are often reminded that if there were bestowed on us the wealth of Croesus, our aims must still be the same, and our means essentially the same. Moreover, if you are restricted in your range by poverty, if you cannot buy books and newspapers, for instance, you are but confined to the most significant and vital experiences; you are compelled to deal with the material which yields the most sugar and the most starch. It is life near the bone where it is sweetest. You are defended from being a trifler. No man loses ever on a lower level by magnanimity on a higher. Superfluous wealth can buy superfluities only. Money is not required to buy one necessary of the soul.

I live in the angle of a leaden wall, into whose composition was poured a little alloy of bell-metal. Often, in the repose of my mid-day, there reaches my ears a confused tintinnabulum from without. It is the noise of my contemporaries. My neighbours tell me of their adventures with famous gentlemen and ladies, what notabilities they met at the dinner-table; but I am no more interested in such things than in the contents of the Daily Times. The interest and the conversation are about costume and manners chiefly; but a goose is a goose still, dress it as you will. They tell me of California and Texas, of England and the Indies, of the Hon. Mr. — of Georgia or of Massachusetts, all transient and fleeting phenomena, till I am ready to leap from their court-yard like the Mameluke bey. I delight to come to my bearings — not walk in procession with pomp and parade, in a conspicuous place, but to walk even with the Builder of the universe, if I may — not to live in this restless, nervous, bustling, trivial Nineteenth Century, but stand or sit thoughtfully while it goes by. What are men celebrating? They are all on a committee of arrangements, and hourly expect a speech from somebody. God is only the president of the day, and Webster is his orator. I love to weigh, to settle, to gravitate toward that which most strongly and rightfully attracts me — not hang by the beam of the scale and try to weigh less — not suppose a case, but take the case that is; to travel the only path I can, and that on which no power can resist me. It affords me no satisfaction to commerce to spring an arch before I have got a solid foundation. Let us not play at kittly-benders. There is a solid bottom everywhere. We read that the traveller asked the boy if the swamp before him had a hard bottom. The boy replied that it had. But presently the traveller's horse sank in up to the girths, and he observed to the boy, "I thought you said that this bog had a hard bottom." "So it has," answered the latter, "but you have not got half way to it yet." So it is with the bogs and quicksands of society; but he is an old boy that knows it. Only what is thought, said, or done at a certain rare coincidence is good. I would not be one of those who will foolishly drive a nail into mere lath and plastering; such a deed would keep me awake nights. Give me a hammer, and let me feel for the furring. Do not depend on the putty. Drive a nail home and clinch it so faithfully that you can wake up in the night and think of your work with satisfaction — a work at which you would not be ashamed to invoke the Muse. So will help you God, and so only. Every nail driven should be as another rivet in the machine of the universe, you carrying on the work.

Rather than love, than money, than fame, give me truth. I sat at a table where were rich food and wine in abundance, and obsequious attendance, but sincerity and truth were not; and I went away hungry from the inhospitable board. The hospitality was as cold as the ices. I thought that there was no need of ice to freeze them. They talked to me of the age of the wine and the fame of the vintage; but I thought of an older, a newer, and purer wine, of a more glorious vintage, which they had not got, and could not buy. The style, the house and grounds and "entertainment" pass for nothing with me. I called on the king, but he made me wait in his hall, and conducted like a man incapacitated for hospitality. There was a man in my neighbourhood who lived in a hollow tree. His manners were truly regal. I should have done better had I called on him.

How long shall we sit in our porticoes practising idle and musty virtues, which any work would make impertinent? As if one were to begin the day with long-suffering, and hire a man to hoe his potatoes; and in the afternoon go forth to practise Christian meekness and charity with goodness aforethought! Consider the China pride and stagnant self-complacency of mankind. This generation inclines a little to congratulate itself on being the last of an illustrious line; and in Boston and London and Paris and Rome, thinking of its long descent, it speaks of its progress in art and science and literature with satisfaction. There are the Records of the Philosophical Societies, and the public Eulogies of Great Men! It is the good Adam contemplating his own virtue. "Yes, we have done great deeds, and sung divine songs, which shall never die" — that is, as long as we can remember them. The learned societies and great men of Assyria — where are they? What youthful philosophers and experimentalists we are! There is not one of my readers who has yet lived a whole human life. These may be but the spring months in the life of the race. If we have had the seven-years' itch, we have not seen the seventeen-year locust yet in Concord. We are acquainted with a mere pellicle of the globe on which we live. Most have not delved six feet beneath the surface, nor leaped as many above it. We know not where we are. Beside, we are sound asleep nearly half our time. Yet we esteem ourselves wise, and have an established order on the surface. Truly, we are deep thinkers, we are ambitious spirits! As I stand over the insect crawling amid the pine needles on the forest floor, and endeavouring to conceal itself from my sight, and ask myself why it will cherish those humble thoughts, and hide its head from me who might, perhaps, be its benefactor, and impart to its race some cheering information, I am reminded of the greater Benefactor and Intelligence that stands over me the human insect.

There is an incessant influx of novelty into the world, and yet we tolerate incredible dulness. I need only suggest what kind of sermons are still listened to in the most enlightened countries. There are such words as joy and sorrow, but they are only the burden of a psalm, sung with a nasal twang, while we believe in the ordinary and mean. We think that we can change our clothes only. It is said that the British Empire is very large and respectable, and that the United States are a first-rate power. We do not believe that a tide rises and falls behind every man which can float the British Empire like a chip, if he should ever harbour it in his mind. Who knows what sort of seventeen-year locust will next come out of the ground? The government of the world I live in was not framed, like that of Britain, in after-dinner conversations over the wine.

The life in us is like the water in the river. It may rise this year higher than man has ever known it, and flood the parched uplands; even this may be the eventful year, which will drown out all our muskrats. It was not always dry land where we dwell. I see far inland the banks which the stream anciently washed, before science began to record its freshets. Every one has heard the story which has gone the rounds of New England, of a strong and beautiful bug which came out of the dry leaf of an old table of apple-tree wood, which had stood in a farmer's kitchen for sixty years, first in Connecticut, and afterward in Massachusetts — from an egg deposited in the living tree many years earlier still, as appeared by counting the annual layers beyond it; which was heard gnawing out for several weeks, hatched perchance by the heat of an urn. Who does not feel his faith in a resurrection and immortality strengthened by hearing of this? Who knows what beautiful and winged life, whose egg has been buried for ages under many concentric layers of woodenness in the dead dry life of society, deposited at first in the alburnum of the green and living tree, which has been gradually converted into the semblance of its well-seasoned tomb — heard perchance gnawing out now for years by the astonished family of man, as they sat round the festive board — may unexpectedly come forth from amidst society's most trivial and handselled furniture, to enjoy its perfect summer life at last!

I do not say that John or Jonathan will realize all this; but such is the character of that morrow which mere lapse of time can never make to dawn. The light which puts out our eyes is darkness to us. Only that day dawns to which we are awake. There is more day to dawn. The sun is but a morning star.

瓦爾登湖

Preface to the Chinese Translation
中文譯本序

我無意寫一首悶悶不樂的頌歌，但我要像破曉晨雞般在棲木上引吭啼唱，只要能喚醒我的左鄰右里就可以了。

—— 梭羅

人與自然和美共存的讚歌

19世紀初葉，年輕的美國剛擺脫戰爭創傷，元氣得以恢復，國內經濟迅速發展，儼然躋身一流經濟大國。與此同時，日新月異的科學發明與大規模開發自然環境，一方面使美國人過上了空前富裕舒適的物質生活，另一方面由於掠奪性開發自然，嚴重破壞了生態環境，導致原先純樸恬淡的鄉村生活銷聲匿跡。這時候，一位獨具慧眼、頗有憂患意識的偉大先驅，大聲疾呼人與大自然要和諧共處 —— 他就是新英格蘭著名作家、美國生態文學批評的始祖亨利・大衛・梭羅。

亨利・大衛・梭羅 (Henry David Thoreau) 1817 年 7 月 12 日生於美國馬薩諸塞州康科德鎮一個商人家庭。康科德鎮的風景如畫，梭羅喜歡經常到野外去，獨自徘徊在樹木花草、鳥獸魚蟲之間，與大自然結下了不解之緣。1833 年他進入哈佛大學，是班級優等生；1837 年畢業後返回故鄉任教兩年 (1838—1840)，還當過鄉村土地測量員。但他畢生非常喜愛漫步、觀察與思考，寫下了大量日記，其中積累了他日後進行創作的豐富素材。他與大作家愛默生 (Ralph Waldo Emerson, 1803—1882) 很投契，於 1841—1843 年住在愛默生家裏，成為他的門生兼助手。於是，他棄教從文，在愛默生的激勵下，開始寫詩與論說文，起初給超驗主義雜誌《日晷》寫文章、隨後為其他報刊撰稿。

1845 年，他在離康科德 2 英里遠的瓦爾登湖畔（愛默生擁有的土地上，事前徵得老師同意）親手搭建一間小木屋，在那裏度過了兩年多的時光，其間完成了《康科德河與梅里麥克河上一週》和《瓦爾登湖》兩部作品（均在他生前出版）。1847 年梭羅返回康科德居住，其後就在故鄉從事寫作、講學及觀察、研究當地動植物，偶然也出門作短途旅行，以廣見聞，為日後創作打下堅實基礎。不過有時，他還得到父親的鉛筆工廠去賺點錢維持生活。1862 年 5 月 6 日，梭羅因患肺結核不幸去世，年僅 44 歲。他生前一直默默無聞，並不被同時代的人賞識。直到 20 世紀，人們才從他的不朽傑作中開始普遍認識他。實際上，他真正的聲名日隆，還是在 20 世紀 30 年代以後。

1846 年 2 月 4 日，梭羅在獨居瓦爾登湖畔期間，曾經給康科德鎮的人做過一次學術性的演講，題為《托馬斯‧卡萊爾及其作品》。演講結束後，鎮裏的居民如實相告，他們根本不愛聽他說的題目，他們很想聽聽他談談個人在湖畔林居生活的所見所聞。於是，在 1847 年 2 月 10 日，他以《我的個人經歷》為題，在康科德再次登台演講，這次受到聽眾們的熱烈歡迎，這令他喜出望外。聽眾們甚至要求他在一週後再講一遍，希望他的講稿還可以進一步增補內容。因此，這次演講以及後來類似的演說，就成為本書的雛形，並於 1847 年 9 月完成初稿，1849 年打算出書，可萬萬沒想到會受到挫折。因此，他不得不用五年時間，將此書反覆修改、增補、潤飾，前後計有 8 次之多，終於使它成為結構緊湊、文采斐然的一部文學作品。在 19 世紀美國文學中，本書被公認為最受讀者歡迎的非虛構作品，直至今日已有 200 種以上不同的版本，同時也有不計其數的外國語言的譯本。

本書乃是梭羅本人入住瓦爾登湖畔林居的實錄。此書一開始，作者就聲明是為了"鎮上人們想細緻入微探聽我的生活方式"而寫的。他選擇湖畔為未來住所，就地取材，親自搭建小木屋，恰巧於 1845 年美國獨立紀念日入住，種莊稼、栽菜蔬，過着獨立不羈、悠閒自在的生活。當時在美國，就有人拿這本書當作 19 世紀笛福的《魯賓遜漂流記》來閱讀欣賞。奢望此書中風光旖旎的田園魅力，能誘惑數以百計的讀者退隱山林，或者傍湖築舍，競相仿效這位賢哲的生活模式。一般說來，這種趣事是人們都始料不及的，殊不知梭羅彷彿料事如神似的，他在書中語重心長奉勸讀者，說不希望有任何人採取他的生活方式。因為人們很容易看此書為逃避現實的隱士幽居勝地或者世外桃源，事實上，這恰恰有違梭羅的初衷。梭羅在書中開宗明義說，他之所以入住瓦爾登，是要探索生活的真諦，思考人與大自然這個重大問題，顯然不是消極出世的，而是積極入世的。實際上，梭羅入住之後，並不是孤獨，與人老死不相往來，恰好相反，他一方面經常出門走訪，回康科德演講，另一方面，也有各種各樣的來客專程前來登門造訪，有的還冒着大風雪趕來，與作者傾心交談，所以說，梭羅始終置身於這個社會大家庭中。再有很重要的一點是《魯賓遜漂流記》畢竟是笛福的虛構小說，而此書乃是名副其實的非虛構作品，兩者不可同日而語。

在某種程度上說，本書就像是康科德地方誌中的動植物篇。誠然，梭羅一生中大多數時間在康科德與瓦爾登湖邊度過，始終致力於觀察與研究飛禽走獸、草木花果，以及一年四季的變化進程。從他寫到的草木、禽獸，如按生物綱、目、科分類粗略估算一下，動輒數以百計，他還給它們分別標上拉丁文（或希臘文）學名，追述淵源、觀察研究之精準、地道，與博物學家相比，也毫不遜色。更有甚者，梭羅還運用他的生花妙筆，將他的心得體會點染在自己的描述中，從而被譽為此書中的精華所在。難怪19世紀美國書評家奉勸過讀者，不妨跳過此書中頗有哲學意味的片段，直接品味賞析描寫大自然的篇章。誠然，說梭羅是描寫大自然的高手，他實在當之無愧，他在促進生態文學創作發展方面，確實功不可沒。雖說在他之前，美國也有過許多專門描述大自然的作家，但他們僅僅報導科學界的一些發現，顯得相當單調乏味，所以，能以神來之筆描寫大自然而形成獨具一格的文學佳構，那毫無疑問，梭羅堪稱箇中翹楚。美國有的批評家曾經舉例指出，單單從此書中有關潛水鳥的描寫，若與約翰·奧杜龐所著《美國鳥類》一書中潛水鳥章節作一比較，顯然大有天淵之別，後者純屬科技性的報導，前者則是藝術作品。同樣，我在譯書過程中也覺得，梭羅不論是描寫紅黑螞蟻大戰，還是對灰背隼、紅松鼠、獵狐犬等的描寫，都是如此繪聲繪色、引人入勝，真可以說是曠世罕見的華章。

作為藝術品，本書在美國已被公認為現代美國散文的最早範本。它的風格，若與它同時代的作品相比，比方說具有寫作天才的霍桑、梅爾維爾、愛默生等人的作品，都是迥然不同。那主要是因為梭羅這種獨特的體裁，頗具20世紀散文風格。當然，它的主題，顯而易見，寫的十之八九是19世紀的人和事，然而妙就妙在，作者對字句文體的選擇似乎有些超前，頗具20世紀的風格。句子寫得率真簡潔，一掃維多利亞時期那種漫無邊際的文風，而且用字極其精當，富有實體感，幾乎不用模糊抽象的字形容。因此，梭羅這篇寫於19世紀的散文，除文體多變外，實際上與20世紀海明威或亨利·米勒的散文並沒有多大差異。

寫作手法上，梭羅在書中也有不少獨創之處，特別是比喻的運用，幾乎達到了極致。讀者可以發現各類著名比喻語之實例，包括從音節的調配到意重語輕的反語法，或者比較通俗的從明喻到雙關語等等。讀過本書的人都知道，梭羅特別喜愛使用雙關語，在全書中俯拾即是，我覺得讀者如果有興趣，不妨試着編成目錄手冊，的確引人入勝。精彩絕妙的雙關語，我在這裏只是隨手拿來一兩個，僅供讀者細細玩味。梭羅寫到一個在瓦爾登湖沒有釣到魚的漁夫，管他叫做修道士（Coenobites），作者在此不僅暗示此漁夫乃虔誠宗教人士，而且我們要是稍加留意，聽一聽"修道士"這個英文詞彙的發音，立刻會發覺，其實，梭羅是在說："你看，沒有魚來上釣。（See, no bites.）"再說，他寫到作為資本主義物質文明的標誌——鐵路時，既表示鐵路開通有利於人際往來、城鄉交流，但對鐵路建設破壞自然生態等等，卻又深表不滿，就借"枕木"這個雙關語寫道："如果一些人快快樂樂乘坐火車在鐵軌上駛過，那肯定有另一些人遭遇不幸，在下面被碾壓過去。"他說"躺在鐵路底下的枕木"，"就是一個人，一個愛爾蘭人，或者說一個北方佬"，"他們可睡得很酣。"作者在這裏通過英文枕木（sleeper）這個雙關語，比喻那些為修造鐵路賣命而又昏睡不醒、毫無覺悟的人。對於這些勞工，梭羅確實滿懷同情，真可以說，哀其不幸，怒其昏睡不醒。總之，梭羅筆下那麼多的雙關語，我在譯述時不由得一一加注，我想，說不定讀者也會感興趣。

從書中的雙關語，我們不禁聯想到梭羅那種獨特的幽默感。儘管當時文壇上很有權威的洛厄爾撰文說梭羅沒有幽默感，但不少批評家卻反駁道，缺乏幽默感的倒是洛厄爾，而絕不是梭羅，因為人們在閱讀本書時會發現字裏行間都閃耀着梭羅的智慧光芒。他的幽默不見得都是喧嘩的，就像喜劇性那樣俗不可耐。梭羅的幽默感飽含着一種批評性的、亦莊亦諧的韻味，它不僅使讀者看在眼裏，心情輕鬆，乃至於忍俊不禁，而且還像斯威夫特、伏爾泰、馬克·吐溫或蕭伯納的幽默，發人深省。比方說，19世紀上半葉，新生的美國立國不久，人們總是覺得自己脫不掉鄉下人的土氣，一切的時尚緊跟在歐洲後面，特別是以英國、法國馬首是瞻，甚至東施效顰，也屢見不鮮。因此，梭羅就在書中寫出了"巴黎的猴王戴了一頂旅行帽，全美國的猴子便群起仿效"。讀者不難揣想，美國人讀到這類詼諧字句，肯定暗自發笑，毋庸否認，這笑聲裏面還包含着梭羅當他們為猴羣的默認呢。總之，像上面這樣涉筆成趣、詼諧幽默的詞句，在書中可謂比比皆是。梭羅就是通過它們來揭示：我們人類是何等愚蠢啊。

梭羅還擅長誇張手法。最好的實例就是當年他在本書初次問世時，扉頁上所寫的題詞："我無意寫一首悶悶不樂的頌歌，我要像破曉晨雞在棲木上引吭啼唱，只要能喚醒我的左鄰右里就好。"不言而喻，作者旨在說明自己不願做甚麼悶悶不樂的哀歎，他要使自己寫在書中的切身感受能對人們多少有些裨益。反過來說，作者寫在書裏的是一首精神抖擻、樂觀向上、歌唱生活的歡樂頌。這是全書的宗旨，氣勢豪邁，而又言簡意賅，原本印在卷首，意在引人注目。不知何故，後來數以百計的版本上幾乎全給刪去了，依我看，這顯然違背了作者的初衷。

梭羅還在書中談天說地、縱古攬今時，一邊立論公允、痛斥時弊，一邊又提出不少積極性的批評與建議，其內容十分廣泛，涉及飲食文化、住房建築、生態環境、學校教育、農貿漁獵等等。他反對當時嚴重脫離實際、費用高昂、培養年輕學子的學院式教育，提倡"與同時代中最有教養的人交遊，從而得到更有價值的教育，那是根本不需要付甚麼錢的"。顯然，這是梭羅根據自己追隨愛默生、獲益匪淺的可貴經驗而得出的結論，十分精彩有力，至今仍然啟迪後人。他一貫主張生活簡樸、社會公正，在書中這麼寫道："我深信如果人人都像我當時那樣過簡樸的生活，那麼，偷竊和搶劫也不會發生。這樣的事之所以發生，蓋因社會上存在貧富不均。"寥寥數語就一針見血觸及當時美國社會上貧富懸殊的要害。梭羅還根據個人耕作體驗，認為"一年裏面只要工作六週，就足夠生活開支"，或者換句話說，一週之中只要工作一天，剩下六天時間，完全可以自由自在，安心讀書，思考問題，或者從事藝術創作等等。要知道，一週以內，人們六天工作，一天是安息日，這本來就是上帝的安排。梭羅身為基督徒，卻大唱反調，主張工作一天，休息六天，豈不是大逆不道嗎？反正在本書中，讀者時不時碰到類似上述的叛逆言論，如果說梭羅是一個社會批評家，也一點不過份。

梭羅在書中用很大篇幅談到人與自然和諧相處，人與草木鳥獸和諧相處，有許許多多精彩片段，恕不一一列舉。我打算日後另撰專文予以介紹。這裏着重提一下，梭羅還主張社會內部各族羣之間和諧相處。遠古以來，北美大陸的主人、原住民是各部落的印第安人，歐洲殖民者到達“新大陸”後，不僅肆意殘殺無辜的印第安人，使其瀕臨種族滅絕的境況，而且徹底毀掉了悠久的印第安文化與生活方式，還對印第安人持極端歧視的態度。殊不知梭羅乃是狷介之士，卻反其道而行。他在書中常常寫到印第安人的種種美德，甚至說，即使是“野蠻民族”，美國人也“不妨學一學，也許大有裨益”，具體來說，就是要學習各部落印第安人和墨西哥人的風俗文化，比如，“第一批果實節”、“除舊祭祀活動”，好像是在“蛻皮求新”，“淨化自己處世理念”等等，試想遠在一個半世紀以前，梭羅就具有上述真知灼見，確實值得世人稱道。

梭羅從年輕時起即好學不倦，博覽羣書。古希臘羅馬文學、東方哲學和德國古典哲學對他都有影響，但是，愛默生的《論自然》等著述中的超驗主義思想卻給他較深的影響。超驗主義思想的基本出發點，就是反對權威，崇尚直覺；其核心是主張人能超越感覺和理性而直接認識真理。無奈梭羅是一個富有詩人氣質而又注重實踐的哲學家。他和愛默生雖然是師生關係，在哲學思想上有很多相同之處，但他們的思想觀點卻是和而不同。這主要是因為他們兩人的個性與作風畢竟大異其趣，結果反而使他們日益疏遠，越到後來，越難接近。愛默生偏重於哲理的思辨，而梭羅則力求將自己相信的哲理付諸實踐，就是說要身體力行。有趣的是，以愛默生為代表的康科德派文人，雖然也在小溪農莊和花果園地建立了一些公社，希望實現他們的理想，一邊耕地，一邊談論哲學。可惜這兩個烏托邦社會都失敗了。但是，梭羅主張人應該過一種有深刻內容的返璞歸真的生活；他抱着堅強的意志入住湖畔林居，本書是根據個人生活體驗寫成的不朽之作，就是他通過自己身體力行而結出的豐碩成果，並且贏得超驗主義聖經的美譽。

不言而喻，梭羅曾經從東方哲學思想中取得不少滋養與借鑒，從而豐富了自己獨特的思想見解。值得注意的是梭羅對中國文化，尤其是儒家思想情有獨鍾。他在書中旁徵博引孔子、孟子等先秦賢哲儒家經典言論，總共有九處之多。博大精深的儒家經典，崇尚自然、天人合一、民胞物與、仁者樂山、智者樂水，不僅成了梭羅在闡發自己的思想論點時有力的支柱，而且不經意間還擴大了現代美國文化的思想視野。就讀者來說，讀到梭羅如此熱衷向美國人介紹孔孟之道、老莊思想，我想也一定會很感興趣。經過梭羅引經據典並進行了新的詮釋，難道不是在重新發掘和激活中國傳統文化，尤其是儒家文化固有的獨特魅力和活力，從而順勢融合到美國文化，乃至於全球文化嗎？

梭羅根據自己深信的超驗主義觀點，在書中就自然界四季更迭和精神復甦作出了極其精彩的描述。從章節上看，本書是以春天開端，依次經歷夏天、秋天和冬天，最後仍然以春天告終，好像生命輪迴的寫照，既是終點又是起點，生生不息復甦。梭羅在書末講到一個在新英格蘭廣泛流傳的故事：從一個蟄伏 60 年之久的蟲卵裏，孵化出一隻健壯美麗的小蟲，再次強調世上任何力量扼殺不了生命的復甦，同樣也表達了他無比樂觀的人生態度。梭羅在結尾時寫下的雋語箴言，直至今日，依然令人對未來充滿希望："遮蓋我們眼睛的亮光，對我們無異於黑暗。唯有我們清醒的時候，天光才大亮。天光大亮的日子多着呢。"

隨着歲月流逝，本書越來越受世人的無比崇敬，曾被譽為"塑造讀者人生的 25 本書之一"（美國國會圖書館評語），"美國文學中無可爭議的 6 本或 8 本傳世佳作之一"（美國著名批評家約瑟夫‧伍德‧克魯奇評語）。美國批評家伊拉‧布魯克甚至還說過："在過去 100 年裏，此書已經成為美國文化中純潔天堂的同義詞。"不用說，英國著名作家喬治·愛略特更是慧眼識珠，遠在當年《西敏寺週報》上就撰文指出：此書是一本超凡入聖的好書。嚴重的污染使人們喪失了田園的寧靜，所以，梭羅這本書便被整個世界閱讀和懷念。走筆至此，我突然記起此書於 1848 年問世之後，恩格斯於 1873—1886 年寫成的《自然辯證法·序言》中，也曾告誡過世人這一段名言："我們不要過份陶醉於我們對自然界的勝利。對於每一次這樣的勝利，自然界都報復了我們。"（《馬克思恩格斯選集·第三卷》，人民出版社，1972 年版，第 517 頁）此外，還有不久前有識之士在深圳舉辦自然論壇，在特意向廣大讀者鄭重推薦的"十大自然讀物"的書中，本書名列榜首，足見它確實是舉世公認的一部不朽名著。說真的，梭羅寫在書裏的一字一句，對上至國家決策人、下至草根百姓來說，都是恆久不變的警世箴言。我想，不管怎麼說，當前全球生態環境仍在不斷惡化，天上罕見一片藍天、一絲和風，地上難覓一方淨土、一泓清水，社會上貧富越來越懸殊，種種破壞自然生態環境的奇談怪論依然甚囂塵上，只要以上現象還沒有得到全部徹底根除，在各個不同國家、各個不同民族，人們總要回首前塵，帶着無限眷戀的心情，緬懷崇尚人與自然和諧的先驅，研讀梭羅的這部不朽經典，從中不斷給自己汲取靈感、力量和希望。

潘慶舲

2007 年 1 月識於上海聖約翰名邸

2013 年 5 月稍有增補

1
省儉有方

寫下面這些篇章，或者說寫這裏面大部份篇章時，我正一個人住在馬薩諸塞州康科德[1]的瓦爾登湖畔樹林，我親手搭建的一間小木屋裏，離左鄰右里一英里，僅憑一雙手養活自己。我在那裏住了兩年零兩個月。如今，我又是文明生活中的匆匆過客了。

要不是我的鄉友們仔細探聽我的生活方式，我本來不想向讀者多講自己的私事，儘管有人會認為我的生活方式不合常理，可在我看來並不盡然；而且，考慮到當時情況，我反而覺得非常合理。有人問我吃些甚麼，是不是感到孤獨，害不害怕，以及諸如此類的問題。另一些人則好奇想知道我收入中有多少捐給慈善事業了。還有一些拖男帶女的人問我助養了多少個貧困兒童。因此，我在本書中對其中某些問題作出回答，要請那些對我並不特別感興趣的人多多包涵。大多數書裏，都不使用第一人稱"我"這個字。在這本書裏，"我"將保留第一人稱。"我"字用得特別多，也成了本書的一大特色。其實，不管哪本書，說到底，都是第一人稱在說這說那，不過我們往往忘了它。要是我既有自知之明又有知人之深，那我必定不會大談特談我自己的。不幸的是，我閱歷疏淺，只能局限於這一個主題。再說，我還要求每個作家，樸實無華、真心誠意寫自己的生活，不僅僅是寫他聽說過的別人的生活；還要寫一些就像他從遠方寄給親人那樣的書簡。因為只要他真心誠意融入生活，一定是在離我十分遙遠的地方。本書這些篇章，也許對清貧學子特別適合。至於其他讀者，他們也會擇善而從。我相信，沒有人會穿上撐破線縫的衣服，因為衣服只有合身，穿着才舒服。

　　我想要說的事情，倒不是關於中國人和桑威奇羣島人 [2]，而是關於你們，閱讀以下這些篇章的讀者，據說都是住在新英格蘭的人 [3]，有關你們的生存狀況，特別是你們在當今世界上的外部狀況或者現實環境，你們這個鎮究竟是甚麼樣，是不是非得壞成目前這個樣，還能不能改善。我在康科德去過許多地方，所到之處，不管是商店、辦公室、田野，依我看，居民們都在用上千種驚人的方式苦修贖罪。我聽說過婆羅門教的信徒在烈火中打坐，兩眼直望太陽；或是身體倒懸在烈焰之上；或是側轉腦袋仰望穹蒼，直到他們的身體無法恢復自然姿態，食道扭曲不能吞嚥流質以外的食物；又或者棲身在一棵樹底下，今生今世將自己跟鏈子拴在一起；或者像毛毛蟲，用自己的身體丈量各大帝國的疆土；或者用一條腿站在立柱頂上 —— 即使是這些有意識的贖罪苦行，也不見得比我每天見到的情景更不可置信，更令人觸目驚心。赫拉克勒斯是古希臘和古羅馬神話中的神，力大無比，曾不畏艱難，完成了十二件苦差事。但是，他的十二件苦差與我鄰居們所受的困苦相比，簡直是小巫見大巫。畢竟赫拉克勒斯只有十二件苦差，做完了總算結束；可是我從沒見過我鄰居們捕殺過任何妖魔鬼怪，或者服完任何苦役。他們沒有像伊俄拉斯（古希臘神話中英雄人物，赫拉克勒斯的姪子，車夫與助手，幫助赫拉克勒斯完成第二件苦差，即殺死九頭水蛇和與前者結盟的螃蟹，）這樣的朋友用通紅的烙鐵燒掉九頭蛇的蛇頭。不過九頭蛇嘛，一個蛇頭剛除掉，兩個蛇頭馬上又長出來了。

　　我看到年輕人，亦即我的鄉友們，他們繼承了農場、房子、穀倉、牲畜以及各種農具，因為這些家產來得容易，但要捨棄卻很難，這是他們的不幸。他們還不如出生在空曠的牧場上，讓狼餵養成人為好，他們就可以雙眼更清楚看到他們應召去工作的田地是怎樣的。誰讓他們成為土地的奴隸？為甚麼有人只好含垢忍辱，有人就可以坐吃他們六十英畝

[4] 的收成？為甚麼他們一生下來就要開始給自己挖墳墓？他們本該像常人那樣過日子，推着他們眼前的一切，盡可能過好他們的日子。我碰到過許多可憐蟲，他們幾乎被沉重的負擔壓垮了，連氣都透不過來，在生活道路上爬行，推動一座七十五英尺長四十英尺寬的穀倉、從來不打掃的奧吉厄斯的牛棚[5]，祖傳一百英畝的土地還要耕種、除草、放牧、護林！沒有繼承祖產的人，固然不被繼承而來的拖累折磨，但他們卻要拼命工作，才能培育自己幾立方英尺的血肉之軀。

可是人們常在誤導下辛勤勞作。人的音容才智很快被犁入泥土中，化成肥料。正如古書裏所説，受一種似是而非、通稱必然的命運支配。人們累積的財寶會遭到蟲咬、鏽壞，而且誘賊入屋偷竊[6]，這是一個笨蛋的一生，他們要是生前也許還不明白，那麼在臨終前一定會明白。據説，丟卡利翁和庇娜是從頭頂向身後扔石頭才創造了人類。源自古希臘神話，丟卡利翁（普羅米修斯之子）與妻子庇娜逃脱了宙斯所發的洪水，夫婦兩人從肩頭向身後扔石頭（即指大地母親的骨頭），石頭變成男男女女，從而重新創造了人類。—— Inde genus durum sumus, experiensque laborum, Et documenta damus qu simus origine nati.[7]

或者有如羅利[8]鏗然吟詠過的詩句 —— 從此人心堅硬，任勞任怨，證明我們的軀體源自岩石。如此盲從荒謬的神諭，將石頭從頭頂往身後扔去，也不看看它們都掉落在甚麼地方。

大多數人，即使在這個相對自由的國家，僅僅因為無知和誤導，要應對的是虛假的憂慮，沒完沒了的粗重工作，卻採擷不到更美好的生命果實。他們的手指，由於操勞過度，極其粗笨，而且一直顫抖，實在沒法摘果子了。説真的，勞動的人沒閒暇休息，使身體得以日漸復原。他無法保持最灑脱的人際關係，他的勞動到了市場上就不免貶值。他除了做一部機器以外，哪有空去做其他甚麼事情。他怎麼會記得自己是無知呢 —— 他正是靠了無知才成長起來 —— 儘管他時不時讓自己的知識派上用場。有時我們應該免費讓他得到溫飽，並用我們的補品使他恢復健康，然後才好對他評頭品足。我們天性中最優秀的品質，好像水果外皮的粉霜，只有精心加以呵護才保得住。可是，我們不管對待自己，還是對待別人，都失去了這樣的溫情柔意。

我們全都知道，你們之中有些人很窮，覺得生活艱難，有時甚至連氣都喘不過來。我毫不懷疑在讀者之中，有些人進餐後並不是都付得出錢來，或者說衣鞋快要穿爛，或者早已穿爛了也沒有錢買新的。即使如此，你們還忙裏偷閒，來閱讀這幾頁文字，這一點時間還是從你們的債主那處偷來的。你們之中許多人，一望可知，過的是多麼卑微、鬼鬼祟祟的日子，反正我看得一清二楚。你們總是身陷困厄，很想做一點事來還債，你們深陷在一個非常古老的泥坑，拉丁文叫做 aes alienum，亦即是指別人的銅錢，因為他們的錢幣是用銅鑄成的；你們生前，臨終，直至最後入土，用的都是別人的銅錢；你們總是說好還債，滿口答應還債，明天就還，直到今天死了，債並沒有償還；你們竭力討好求寵、獲得惠顧，並且還使盡渾身解數，只圖自己不吃官司坐大牢；你們撒謊，阿諛奉承，選舉投票，甘願被那套繁文縟節框住，或是大吹大擂，營造一種薄弱的慷慨模樣，以圖說服你的鄰居讓你給他們做鞋子、製帽子、縫衣服、造馬車或者給他們代買食品雜貨，想着日後會生病而儲下點甚麼，不料倒弄到自己累得病倒了。你塞一點錢到一個舊箱裏，或在泥灰牆後面一個襪筒裏藏起這錢來，或用更保險的方式，塞它進磚櫃裏，根本不管藏在哪裏，也不管積攢多少。

有時候，我暗自納悶，我們怎能如此輕率 —— 我幾乎要說 —— 致力於推行那種萬惡不赦、外國引進的所謂 "黑奴制"，有那麼多心思精明城府深的奴隸主在奴役南方和北方的奴隸。南方監工良心固然壞，北方監工良心卻更壞，但是話又說回來，良心最壞的還是你成為你自己的奴隸監工。胡說甚麼 —— 人的神聖！看一看大路上的車日以繼夜趕往市場，難道他心裏還有甚麼神性在激盪嗎？他最高職責是給馱馬餵料添水！跟他運貨的盈利相比，他的命運算得上甚麼？他還不是在給一個富有的鄉紳趕車嗎？他要甚麼神性呢？他要甚麼永垂不朽？照他那副畏畏縮縮、鬼鬼祟祟的樣子，整天不清楚自己為甚麼營營役役，哪有甚麼不朽和神性。他不過是以奴隸和囚犯自居，以自己做的工作賺個好口碑罷了。與我們的自知之明相比，公眾輿論只是一個輕弱無力的暴君。一個人如何看待自己，這是決定了，或者換句話説，揭示了他的命運。甚至在西印度羣島各省談論空想的自我解放 —— 又怎會有威爾伯福斯[9]呢？不妨再想一想，這塊國土的女士們，她們編織梳粧用的墊子，為世界末日作準備，對她們自己的命運卻漠不關心！彷彿你儘管消磨大量時光，卻似乎對永生絲毫無損。

人們在絕望中默默過日子。所謂聽天由命，就是一種根深蒂固的絕望。你從絕望之城走向絕望之鄉，還要拿水貂和麝鼠的勇氣來安慰自己。甚至在人類所謂的遊戲和娛樂下，都隱藏着一種陳舊和下意識的絕望。不過，不做絕望的事才是智慧的一種特徵。

我們使用教理問答式的語言，思考甚麼是人生的宗旨，甚麼是真正的生活必需品和生活資料時，彷彿人們已經深思熟慮選擇了這種生活的共同方式，因為他們就是喜歡這種方式，而其他的則一概不喜歡。其實，他們心裏也明白，除此之外別無選擇。不過，神志清健的人都知道日出山河清；拋棄我們的偏見，從來不算為時太晚。任何一種思考方式或者行為方式，不管它有多麼古老，如無確證都是不可信的。今天人人附和或者予以默認的真理，明天卻有可能成為謬論。而這種謬論只不過是縹緲煙霧，不過有人卻堅信，那是雨雲，會向他們的農田灑甘霖田。老人説你不能做的事，你不妨試一試，也許發現你是能做的。老人有老辦法，新人有新招數。古人也許不知道添上燃料，火苗就滅不了；新人會在火車鍋爐底下放上一點乾柴，還可以像鳥兒似的繞着地球轉！正如一句老話：氣死老人家。其實，老年人未必比年輕人更有資格做導師，因為老年人一生中獲益也不見得比失去的更多。人們幾乎可以質疑，即使是最聰明的人從生活中又能感悟出多少具有絕對價值的東西呢？說實話，老年人沒有甚麼至關緊要的忠告給年輕人，他們自己的經驗都不夠完美，他們一生中又遭到如此慘敗，他們必須承認那都是咎由自取；也許他們還有一些有悖於那種經驗的信心，可惜他們已經不再年輕了。我在這個星球上已生活了三十多年，還沒有聽到我的長輩說過一句話可謂有價值的忠告。他們甚麼都沒有告訴過我，也許他們對我說不出甚麼深入中肯的話。這就是生活，一個在很大程度上我還沒有嘗試過的實驗；他們倒是嘗試過了，但對我絲毫無益。如果說我有甚麼自以為有價值的經驗，我一定會想，這可是我的賢師們都還沒有說過的。

有一個農夫對我說："你不能光吃蔬菜過活，因為蔬菜對骨頭毫無營養可言。"於是，他虔誠奉獻一部份時間，給自己的骨骼系統提供滋養；他一邊說，一邊跟在耕牛後面，而他的那頭耕牛就靠蔬菜長成的骨頭，卻不顧一切障礙，用力拖着他和他的耕犁往前趕。有些東西在某些人的生活圈子裏，那些最無助、病得最重的人，確實是生命的必需品，但換一個角度，卻成了奢侈品，要是再換一個角度，則完全成了未知之物。

整個人生活領域，不論山巔還是峽谷，在有些人看來，已被前人涉足過，所有問題也都被關注過。按照約翰·伊夫林[10]的說法："聰明的所羅門曾經下令，規定樹與樹之間應有的距離；羅馬地方官也曾規定過，你可以多少次到鄰居的地上，去拾落下來的橡果而不算非法侵入，多少橡果應歸鄰居所有。"希波克拉底[11]甚至給我們留下了剪指甲的方法，就是說我們的指甲應剪得不可過長，也不可過短，與手指頭並齊。有人認為如此枯燥無聊會將生活的多樣化和歡樂消耗殆盡，這種看法毫無疑問如同亞當[12]一樣古老。然而，人的各種能量從來還沒有被估量過；我們也不應該根據任何先例來判斷人的能量，嘗試過的事的確太少了。不管你到今日經歷過多大失敗，"別難過，我的孩子，有誰會指派你去做你未竟之事呢？"

我們可以通過成千種簡單的測試來考驗我們的生命：比方說，這是同一個太陽，它使我種的豆子成熟，同時也照亮了就像我們地球一樣的整個太陽系。這點我只要記住了，就可以少犯一些錯誤。但我在鋤豆子地時卻沒有這種想法。星星是許多神奇的三角形的頂點！宇宙間形形色色的宿或宮中，有多少相距很遠的不同物種，卻會在同一個時刻思考着同一個事物！如同我們的各種體制一樣，大自然和人生也是變化莫測。有誰能說清楚別人的一生會有甚麼前景嗎？我們在一瞬間彼此兩眼對望，難道說還有甚麼比這更偉大的奇蹟嗎？我們應該在一個小時內經歷這個世界上所有的時代；是的，經歷所有時代中所有的世界。歷史、詩歌、神話——我可不知道閱讀別人的經驗，還會有甚麼能像閱讀歷史、詩歌、神話那樣令人驚訝而又增長見聞呢？

凡是我的鄰居說是好的，大部份在我心目中卻認為是壞的，如果說我有甚麼要反思，也許恰恰是我的正派作風。是哪個惡魔纏住了我，使我的所作所為這樣正派？老人啊，那些最睿智的話你儘管說好了——你畢竟活了七十歲，活得還算體面——可我卻聽到一種不可抗拒的聲音，要跟這一切離得遠遠的。一代人拋棄上一代努力的成果，就像拋棄擱淺了的船。

我想，我們可以確實相信，比我們實際上相信還要多得多的事物。我們對自己的關懷能放棄多少，就能在別處誠心誠意給予他人多少。大自然既能適應我們的長處，也能適應我們的弱點。有些人不斷緊張焦慮，成了一種接近不治的痼疾。我們生來就愛誇大我們所做的工作的重要性，可是又有多少工作我們還沒有去做？或者換句話說，我們萬一病倒了，又該怎麼辦？我們該有多麼小心謹慎！我們決心不靠信教過活，只要能不信教的話；白日裏總是提心吊膽，晚上我們口不對心禱告，託付自己給未定之天。我們如此徹底真誠被迫着過活，既要崇敬自己的生命，又要否認變革的可能性。我們説：這就是唯一的生活方式；但既然從一個中心可以畫出許多半徑來，同樣，生活方式也可以有許多種。一切變革都是奇蹟，值得思考；而奇蹟是分分秒秒都在發生的。孔子説過："知之為知之，不知為不知，是知也。"[13]。有一個人將想像的事實歸納為自己所理解的事實時，我敢預言説，所有人最終都會在那個基礎上打造他們的生活。

讓我們略費片刻思考一下，我在前文提及的麻煩和焦慮，十之八九是些甚麼，有多少需要我們煩心，或者至少還要小心應對。我們儘管置身於一種徒有其表的文明之中，若能過上一種原生態的、開拓疆土的生活，還是頗有裨益，即使僅僅為了明白大量生活必需品是些甚麼，要用甚麼方法方可獲得這些必需品；或者，甚至只需要翻一翻商人的舊賬簿，看看人們在商店裏買得最多的是甚麼，商店裏存貨是甚麼，也就是説，存量最大的雜貨是甚麼。因為，時代固然在進步，但它對人類生存的基本法則並沒有多大影響；就像我們的骨骼同我們祖先的骨骼相比，大抵也沒有多大差別。

據我看，生活必需品，是指人通過自己的努力所獲得的一切，或者換句話説，它從一開始（或者經過長期使用）就對人類生活變得如此密不可分，因此，沒有哪個人，不管是出於野蠻、貧困還是哲學上的緣故，試圖不靠它獨自過活，即使有這樣的人，那也是寥寥無幾。許多人認為，從這個意義上講的生活必需品只有一種，那就是 —— 食物。對大草原上的美洲野牛來説，那就是幾英寸長、可咀嚼的青草，可飲用的水，此外還要在森林裏或者山陰處尋覓棲身之地。野獸需要的，不外乎是食物和棲身之地。在這個氣候區，人的生活必需品可以極精確分為幾大類：食物、住所、衣服和燃料；因為只有獲得以上這些東西，我們才可以自由考慮真正的人生問題，並有望取得成功。人類發明不僅有房子，還有衣服、熟食；也許是偶然發現烤火可以取暖，後來使用了火，最初被看成是一種奢侈品，到目前圍火取暖也成為一種必需品了。我們已看到貓狗也都獲得了這種第二天性。我們只要住處合宜，穿着適當，就能合理保持體內的熱量；可是，如果說我們住處過暖，穿着過厚，或者燃料消耗過多，也就是說，外部的熱量大大超過我們體內的熱量，那豈不是說在烘烤人體了嗎？自然科學家達爾文談到火地島：位於南美洲南部，以火地島為主的島羣，分屬阿根廷與智利的原住民說，他自己那一夥人穿得很厚實，圍坐在火堆邊一點也不覺得熱，那時一絲不掛的野蠻人在離火堆很遠的地方等着，達爾文因發現他們竟被"烘烤得汗流浹背"而感到很驚訝。同樣，據說新荷蘭人赤身裸體走來走去，若無其事似的，而歐洲人穿了衣服還冷得瑟瑟發抖。這些野蠻人的體質鐵硬，和文明人的資質聰明，難道不可互相結合在一起嗎？根據李比希[14]的說法，人體是一座火爐，食物即是維持肺內消耗的燃料。我們冷天吃得多些，熱天就吃得少些。動物體內的熱量是內部消耗緩慢的結果，內耗太快，就會出現疾病和死亡；或者換句話說，由於缺乏燃料，通風裝置出了毛病，火就會熄滅。當然，生命的體溫與火不能混為一談，但作為比喻也就只好到此為止。因此，從前文所述來看，動物生命和動物體溫幾乎可作同義詞用；因為食物可以被看成維持我們體內之火不熄的燃料 —— 而燃料只不過用來煮熟食物，或者說從體外來增加我們的體溫 —— 此外，住處和衣服也只是保持由此產生和吸收的熱量。

因此，就人體來說，最大的必需品就是保暖，保持生命的熱量。我們為此就要何等含辛茹苦，不僅為了獲取食物、衣服和住所，而且還要尋覓牀鋪，也就是我們的睡衣，從鳥巢和飛鳥的胸脯上掠奪羽毛來打造這個住所裏面的棲身之地，就像鼯鼠在地洞盡頭拿雜草和樹葉建窩一樣！窮人動不動就發牢騷，說這是一個寒冷的世界；我們的大部份疾病，不論生理上的也好，社會上的也好，我們乾脆都歸罪於飽受風寒。在一些氣候區，夏天會給予人們一種天上樂園似的生活。那時節，燃料除了煮熟食物以外，也就不是必需品了，太陽就像是一團火，許多果實給太陽的光線煮熟了；一般來說，食物的種類繁多，而且又是唾手可得，衣服和住所已是完全用不着，或者說部份用不着。現在這個國家，根據我的親身經歷，我覺得只要有幾件工具：一把刀、一柄斧頭、一把鐵鍬和一輛手推車等，就可以過日子了。對於好學之士，另添一盞燈、一些文具，再加上幾本書，這些均屬次要的必需品，稍微花上幾個銅錢就能獲得。但是，有些人不太聰明，跑到地球的另一邊，到了蠻荒和骯髒的地區，一直費盡心思做了一二十年的生意，為了謀生 —— 就是說，為了追求舒適溫暖 —— 可是到頭來還是魂歸新英格蘭。奢侈的富人不只是得到令人舒適的暖和，而是熱得太過反常；正如我前文所說的，他們肉體是在烘烤，不用說，是很切合時尚的方式，原文為法文 La Mode。

　　絕大多數奢侈品，以及許多所謂使生活舒適的物品，不僅是非必要的，而且還對人類進步帶來極大妨礙。就奢侈和舒適來說，最聰明的人的生活，甚至比窮人過得還要簡單、樸素。古代哲學家，不論在中國、印度、波斯還是希臘，都是同一種類型的人，從外表看，他們比誰都窮，從內心看，他們卻比誰都富。我們對他們了解得不夠，難能可貴的是，我們對他們的認識也不少。近代改革家和他們的民族救星，他們也都是這樣。一個人唯有站在我們稱之為甘於清貧的有利地位上，方能成為人類生活的公正、睿智的觀察家。不論在農業、商業、文學或藝術中，奢侈生活結出的果實也都是奢侈。現時哲學教授比比皆是，但哲學家卻一個也沒有。然而，教授是令人豔羨的，因為教授的生活曾經令人豔羨。做一個哲學家，不僅要有奧博的思想，或建立一個學派，而且還要熱愛智慧，按照智慧的要求，過一種簡樸、獨立、豁達大度與富有信心的生活。不僅要從理論上，而且還要在實踐中，解決生活中的一些問題。大學問家和大思想家的成功，不是帝王式的，也不是壯漢式的，通常都是侍臣式的成功。他們一味隨流徇俗，應對生活變化，他們的所作所為，實際上跟父輩們如出一轍，根本成不了甚麼頂天立地的人類始祖。那麼，為甚麼人類一直在退化呢？是甚麼使得許多家族沒落？奢侈導致國家衰亡，那它的實質又是甚麼？在我們自己的生活中，我們敢不敢說一點都沒有奢侈味道？即使在生活的外部形式上，哲學家也是處於時代前列。他不像他的同時代人那樣飲食、居住、穿着和取暖。一個人既然做了哲學家，怎能沒有比別人更好的方法來維持自己生命的熱量呢？

一個人從我所描述的多種模式中得到了溫暖，接下來他還想要些甚麼呢？當然不會是更多同樣的溫暖，更多更豐盛的食物，更大更華麗的房子，更精美更大量的衣着，更多更持久更旺盛的爐火。他獲得了這些生活必需品之後，就不會再要那些剩餘品，而要選擇另外的東西了；那就是說，要擺脫卑微的勞動，開始度假，親歷生活中的奇遇。這裏泥土看來對種子是很適宜的，因為泥土已使胚根向下延伸，隨後又充滿信心使嫩莖不斷朝上茁壯成長。人既然在大地上牢牢紮了根，為甚麼就不能同樣恰如其份升高到天空中去呢？——因為這是名貴植物的價值，是由遠離地面、最終在空氣和陽光下結出的果實來評定的，跟比較低等的菜蔬不可相提並論。那些菜蔬，哪怕是兩年生的品種，也僅僅被栽培到根鬚長好為止，而上面的枝葉通常都給剪去，因此，到了開花季節，人們多半認不得它們了。

我不打算給那些堅強勇敢的人釐定甚麼規章，不論在天堂還是在地獄，他們都會專心於自己的事情；或許他們的住宅造得比富豪更豪華，揮霍得也更驚人，卻並沒有因此而赤貧如洗，真不知道他們究竟如何生活的——如果就像人們所夢想那樣，確實有過這樣的人的話；再說，我也不打算給下面那些人釐定甚麼規章，他們是從各種事物現狀中得到鼓勵和靈感，他們以戀人般的狂熱珍惜喜愛現狀——在某種程度上說，我想，我自己就是屬於這類人；我也不想對那些不管在甚麼情況下都能安居樂業的人說些甚麼，反正他們都知道自己是不是安居樂業，——我主要是向那些心懷不滿的人說話，他們原本可以改善自己的生活，但他們總是徒然訴苦，說自己命運不濟，時世艱難。有些人對任何事情都叫苦不迭，使人沒法給予安慰，因為據他們自己所說，他們這是在盡他們的職責。在我心目中還有一種人，他們看上去很富有，實際上卻是各類人當中最窮的人，他們儘管攢下了一點破銅爛鐵甚麼的，卻不知道如何使用它，也不知道如何擺脫它，就這樣拿金銀給他們自己打造了一副鐐銬。

我要是試圖說一說，過去幾年裏，我是如何希望打發自己的生活，也許會讓多少有所了解實際情況的讀者感到驚喜，當然也會讓全然不了解的人吃驚，我只是稍微談一談我心愛的事情。

不管天色陰晴，也不管白晝黑夜，我任何時候都渴望及時改善自己現在的境況，並在自己的手杖上刻下記號；站在過去與未來這兩個永恆的真理的交匯點上，也就是此時此刻；腳尖抵着那條線。請原諒我說話有些晦澀，因為我的行業秘密要比大多數人的行業多得多，不是我存心要保密，而是我這個行業離不開這個特點。我很樂意說出我所知道的一切，絕不會在我門上寫下"不准入內"的字樣。

很久以前，我丟失了一條獵犬，一匹栗色馬和一隻斑鳩[15]約。我至今還在追尋牠們，我跟許多觀光客說過牠們，描述過牠們的蹤跡，以及牠們對怎樣的叫喚聲會作出回應。我碰到過一兩個人，他們聽到過那條獵犬的吠聲，也聽到過馬蹄聲，甚至還看到過斑鳩消失在浮雲後面；而且，他們看來也焦急想找牠們回來，好像是他們自己丟失了似的。

殷切期望着，不僅觀看日出和黎明，如有可能，還可一睹大自然本色！無論寒冬酷暑多少個清晨，左鄰右里還沒有起來忙這忙那以前，我早就開始忙自己的事了。我有很多鄉友們，有些是天亮時趕往波士頓的農夫，也有些是出門做事的樵夫，他們都碰到過我一大早已完成工作回來。

説真的，太陽冉冉升起，我從來沒具體出過力，但是千萬別懷疑，只要趕在日出之時到達現場，其意義就非同小可。

有多少個秋天，是的，還有多少個冬天，我是在鎮外度過的，試圖聆聽風中有甚麼好聽的，聽後準確無誤將它播放出去！我為此幾乎投入了我所有資金，為了這筆生意，我頂着風東奔西跑，累得連氣都喘不過來。要是風中有涉及兩黨政治的信息，那它肯定成為最新要聞刊登在《新聞報》上了。其他時候，守望在懸崖或者大樹旁的觀測臺上，用電報發佈新來的人的信息；或者傍晚時份在山巔上等待暮色徐徐降臨，也許我會捕捉到一點甚麼——儘管我捕捉到的從來就不多——何況這不多的東西如同“天糧”[16]似的會在陽光下消融殆盡。有過很長一段時間，我是一家發行量不很大的雜誌《日晷》[17]撰稿的記者，編輯也從來不覺得我寫的大量稿子可以刊用，反正作家們對此都有同感，我費煞思量去寫作，換來的只是痛苦。不過，就這件事來説，痛苦只是它自身的回報而已。

許多年來，我自我指派為暴風雪和暴風雨的督察員，而且忠於職守；我還兼任測量員，測量公路以外的森林小道和所有交叉通道，確保它們暢通無阻；此外，我還測量過四季通行的峽谷橋樑，反正公眾接踵而至，足以證實它們具有很高的利用率。

我還看守過鎮上未馴化的牲畜，因為牠們常常跑過圍柵逃脱，讓一個恪守職責的牧人吃足苦頭；我對農場裏罕至的各個角落也很注意；雖然我並不知道約那斯或者所羅門均為《聖經》中的人物。今天有沒有在哪一個特定的地方做工，反正那跟我毫不相干。我給紅色的越橘、沙地櫻桃樹、蕁麻、紅松和黑楊，還有白葡萄藤和黃色紫羅蘭都澆過水，要不然它們在天氣乾燥的季節裏就會枯萎。

總而言之，我就這樣做過很長時間，全副心思放在我的工作上，可是，我的鄉友們根本不歸我入本鎮公職人員之列，也不讓我掛個閒職，拿一點菲薄的津貼。我做的賬目可以說非常準確可靠，但從來沒有人來核查過，更不用說獲得同意，付了款，就結清了賬，好在我也沒有放這件事在心上。

此後沒多久，一個四處流浪的印第安人到我住處附近一個知名律師家兜售籃子。"你們想買籃子嗎？"他問。回答是："不，我們不要。""天哪！"印第安人出門時大聲叫道，"你們是存心讓我們餓死嗎？"看到他的勤奮的白人鄰居日子過得如此興旺——當律師只需要編好論據，就像變魔術似的，財富和地位就跟着來了——這個印第安人自言自語道：我要做點生意，我要編籃子，做這些籃子我一定行。他滿以為籃子編好了，自己也就大功告成了，隨後該是白人向他買籃子。他沒有察覺到他必須將籃子編得讓別人值得買；或至少讓別人認為值得買，要不然他還不如去編其他讓人感到值得購買的東西。我自己也編過一個質地精美的籃子，但我沒法做到讓人一看就感到值得買。我思考的，不是如何讓人感到值得來買籃子，我琢磨的是如何避免籃子編好後非得賣掉不可。人們讚賞並認為成功的生活，也只不過是生活中的一種罷了。我們為甚麼要誇大一種生活，貶低另一種生活呢？

我發覺我的鄉友們不大可能在縣府大樓裏給我一個職位，也不會給我一個助理牧師職位，或者其他甚麼工作，於是，我只好自謀出路，我要比平日更專注，讓自己的心思轉向樹林，反正那裏的一草一木我全都熟悉。我決定立即開業，不必再等到籌措足夠資金，不妨就先動用我手邊已有的那麼一點微薄的積蓄。我到瓦爾登湖的目的，不是因為那處生活費用便宜或者昂貴，而是去經營一些私人業務，在那裏麻煩可以減到最少；要不然，由於缺乏業務常識，又沒有做生意的才幹而一事無成，難免做出慘不忍睹的傻事來。

我一直竭盡全力，要使自己獲得嚴格的經商習慣；這些習慣對每個人都是不可或缺的。如果說你的生意是跟天朝帝國：指舊時中國打交道，那麼，在塞勒姆：美國馬薩諸塞州東北部一港口城市。在海濱某處設置小小一間賬房，有這麼一個固定機構也就夠了。你可以出口國內生產的各種產品，比方說，純正的土產品，還有許多冰柱啦、松木啦、一點花崗岩啦，常用本國貨船運走。這些都是賺錢的買賣；事無大小，你都要親自過問；你又是一身兼數職，兼任領航員和船長，貨主和保險商；你要買進、賣出，兼管記賬，收到的信函要一一過目，發出的信件要自己擬寫或者審閱；日以繼夜地監督進口物品卸貨；幾乎與此同時，你要到沿海各地露露面 —— 因為裝貨最多的大船往往都在美國東北部新澤西海岸卸貨的 —— 自己樂此不疲充當電報員，發送到天涯海角，同時還要跟駛往海岸的所有船隻通話；要給一個遙遠而需求不斷增長的海外市場源源不絕發送貨物；你自己要熟悉市場行情，了解各處戰爭與和平的前景，預測貿易和文明的趨向 —— 利用所有探險活動的成果，使用新的航道和所有一切先進航海技術 —— 要研究海圖，認準各處暗礁、新燈塔和浮標的位置，對數圖表要不斷校正，因為萬一計算出了差錯，本應抵達友好碼頭的船隻往往會被礁石撞得粉碎，再有就是拉·貝魯斯[18]的未知命運 —— 要緊緊跟上宇宙科學的發展，要研究從漢諾[19]紀和腓尼基人直到我們當代所有偉大的發現者和航海家、偉大的冒險家和商人的一生；最後，艙裏的貨物要時不時記清楚，你才可知道自己如何給貨船取特定航向。反正以下所述的種種問題，都會讓你累得筋疲力盡，真是苦不堪言，還有就是利潤啦、虧損啦、利息啦、淨重計算啦，諸如此類的問題，全都要有精確數字來測定，那就非得具備廣博的知識不可。

我已想過瓦爾登湖將會成為做買賣的好地方，不單單因為有鐵路和採冰業；它還有諸多有利條件，洩露它們出來，恐怕也不是上策罷；它是一個良好的港口，具備良好基礎。沒有涅瓦河[20]那樣的沼澤地需要填埋，儘管你還要到處打樁加固。據說涅瓦河只要發了大水，再加上西風和冰塊助虐，就會從地球上沖走了聖彼得堡。

通常必備的資金還沒有到位，我倒是先做起生意來了，因此，我打從哪裏可以獲得像每一個這樣的企業至今仍然不可或缺的資金，這個也許很不容易加以揣測吧。先說衣服，一下子就觸及問題的實質。也許我們購置衣服時常常被愛好新奇、別人對它的看法所誤導，就不太考慮衣服是不是實用。讓那些有工作做的人記住穿衣服的目的，首先，是保證維持生命的體溫，其次是在大庭廣眾遮蓋起一絲不掛的身體來，然後他就可以作出判斷，不用給衣櫃裏增添甚麼衣服，就能完成多少必須的或重要的工作。國王和皇后有御用男女裁縫給他們製衣，但每套衣服通共只穿一次，所以體會不到穿上合身衣服的樂趣。他們比披上乾淨衣服的特洛伊木馬好不了多少。我們穿的衣服天長日久，已與我們融為一體，而且由此凸現出穿衣人的性格，直到我們捨不得丟棄它們，而且如此一本正經，就像捨不得丟棄我們自己的軀體一樣，所以總是一再拖延，彷彿想給它療救一下似的。有人穿了帶補丁的衣服，在我的心目中，並不是低人一等；但我也相信，一般人更急於求得的是時髦的衣服，至少要乾乾淨淨，沒有補丁，至於他們有沒有健全的良心，就不是這般放在心上了。其實，即使衣服破了沒給縫補，從而暴露出最大的缺點，也不過是為人隨便罷了。有時候，我就用以下這種方法來測試我的朋友們——有誰肯穿一條膝蓋上有補丁的，或者只是多了兩條線縫的褲子？大多數人似乎都相信他們要是這樣穿了，就會完全毀了自己的前程。他們寧可跛着一條腿進城，也不肯穿破褲子出門去。一位紳士要是在一場事故中腿受傷了，通常總有辦法給予療救。但是，如果他的褲腿在同樣的事故中給扯破了，卻是無法補救；因為他考慮的，不是真正令人可敬的東西，而是受到人們尊敬的東西。我們認識的人屈指可數，認識的衣服和褲子卻是不計其數。你給稻草人穿上你最時髦的一套內衣，你懶洋洋站在一邊，有誰不馬上向稻草人致敬？那天，我路過一塊玉米田，在那根穿衣戴帽的椿桿旁，一眼就認出了農場的主人。同我上次見到他時相比，他由於飽經風霜，似乎顯得更憔悴。我聽說有一隻狗，只要見到衣冠整齊的陌生人走近主人家門口，就會向着他大聲吠叫，但牠卻很容易被一個赤身裸體的小偷蒙混得一聲不吭。人們要是被剝去了衣服，還能在多大程度上保住各自相對的身份地位，這是一個很有意思的問題。如果說人人身上被剝去了衣服，你能肯定說出哪一輩文明人是屬於最尊貴的階層嗎？菲菲夫人 [21] 在她周遊世界、從東向西的探險之旅中，差不多快要抵達亞洲境內的俄羅斯，即將晉謁當地長官時，她說，她覺得自己非得脫去旅行服，另換衣服不可，因為她"現時是在一個文明的國度，在那裏，人們是根據衣着打扮來評定人的"。甚至在我們這個民主的新英格蘭各城鎮，誰只要不經意間發了大財，衣着奢華，寶馬香車，照樣也會贏得幾乎眾人的尊敬。不過，那些這樣令人尊敬的人，儘管人數極多，但都是不信上帝的人，說真的，應該送一名傳教士給他們才對。再說，衣服是一針一針縫起來的，你會說，那是沒完沒了的工作；反正一個女人的衣服，也是一輩子都做不完的。

　　一個終於找到了工作的人，上班時用不着穿甚麼新衣服；對他來說，有一身舊衣服就行了，即使是那套舊衣服在閣樓裏已放了不知多久，積滿了塵土。英雄穿舊鞋子的時間，要比英雄的僕人穿舊鞋子的時間長得多 —— 如果說英雄也有過僕人的話 —— 光着腳的歷史要比穿鞋子的歷史更久遠，反正英雄光着腳走路也行。唯有那些赴晚宴和進入議會大廳的人非穿新衣服不可，而且他們還要一套又一套不斷變換衣服，如同那些場合裏的人換了一批又一批。不過，如果說我的外衣和褲子、帽子和鞋子，一一穿戴起來，才適合給上帝做禮拜的話，那麼，這些衣物也好給上帝做禮拜，可不是嗎？有誰見過自己的舊衣服 —— 他的舊外衣，實實在在給他穿爛了，變成原先一匹布，就算送給某個窮孩子都稱不上甚麼行善不行善，說不定那個窮孩子還會拿去轉送給某個比他更窮的人，或者也可以説比這窮孩子還要富的人，因為他沒有這破衣服也照樣過日子？我説，要小心提防的，不是單單穿新衣服的人，而是所有需要穿新衣服的企業。要是沒有新人，怎能給他裁製合身的新衣服呢？如果説你有甚麼事要做，不妨還是穿上舊衣服去試試看。人之所求，不是做事情時要穿甚麼，而是要做甚麼，或者換句話説，要成為甚麼。不論舊衣服有多破、多髒，也許我們根本不該置備甚麼新衣服，我們還是這樣我行我素，或者慘淡經營，或者揚帆遠航，直到那時我們才覺得自己好像新人穿舊衣，依然故我，無異於新酒裝在舊瓶子裏。人的換衣季節，猶如飛禽更換羽毛，必定是人生中的一個轉折點。潛水鳥隱沒在人煙罕至的湖邊換羽毛。蛇蜕皮，蛹出繭，也是如此，全靠體內奮力苦鬥，往外擴展；因為在我們看來，衣服至多只不過是外層薄膜和塵世煩惱罷了。要不然我們就會被發覺扯着虛假的船旗在航行，到頭來將無可避免被全人類以及自己的看法所唾棄。

我們穿上一件又一件衣服，好像我們是外長植物，靠外部添加而成長。穿在我們外面的，通常很薄的奇裝異服，是我們的表皮，或者説，假的肌膚，並不是我們生命的組成部份，即使在這裏那裏給剥下來，都不會造成致命傷；我們經常穿着厚一些的衣服，是我們的細胞外膜，或者説皮層；不過，我們穿的襯衫，卻是我們的韌皮，或者説真正的樹皮，一剥下來，肯定連皮帶肉，以致身亡。我相信，所有物種到了某些季節，都會穿上某種類似襯衫的東西。可取的辦法有如下述：一個人穿着力求簡單，就算在黑暗中兩手總能摸到自己，而且，他的生活不論從哪個方面來説都是如此充實，有備無患，哪怕是敵人攻佔了城市，他也能像古代哲學家一樣，從容不迫，空手徒步出城。一件厚衣服等於三件薄的衣服一樣派用場，顧客可按照自己能接受的價格買到便宜的衣服。厚外衣好幾年都穿不破，五塊錢可買到一件，兩塊錢可買一條厚實的長褲，一塊半錢買一雙牛皮靴，兩角半買一頂夏天的遮陽帽，六角兩分半買一頂冬天的帽子，或者換句話說，只花很少的錢在家就可以製作一頂質地更好的帽子。有一個人窮雖窮，但一穿上用自己的辛苦錢準備的行裝，難道說還會沒有聰明人去向他表示敬意嗎？

我要訂造一件款式特別的衣服，女裁縫聽了以後一本正經告訴我："現在的人不流行這個啦。"話音裏根本沒有強調"人"，彷彿她引用的有如命運三女神那樣毫無人情味的權威似的。我發現很難得到我要的款式，僅僅因為女裁縫不相信我說的話是真的，好像只不過是隨便說說而已。我聽了這神諭一般的話，一時間陷入沉思，稍後才使這句話逐個字顯得特別清晰，好讓我悟出箇中含意，以便發現別人和我有多大血緣關係，在一件跟我如此密切相關的事情上，別人究竟擁有多大權威；最後，我決定同樣神神秘秘回答她，對"別人"兩字同樣根本沒有加以強調，說："不錯，前一陣子別人不流行這個，可是現在別人又流行啦。"她要是沒有量過我的特色，單單量了一下我的肩寬，彷彿我是一顆掛衣服的釘子，這樣量法又有甚麼用處呢？我們崇拜的不是美惠[22]三女神，也不是珀爾茜古羅馬神話中的命運三女神的總稱。三女神，而是時髦這位女神。她紡線、織布、剪裁，具有百份之百的權威。巴黎的猴王戴上了一頂旅行帽，全美國的猴子便羣起仿效。有時候，我感到絕望，在這人世間原本一些非常簡單樸實的事情都要靠人幫助方能完成。人們不得不首先經過一部強而有力的壓榨機，從裏面擠壓出他們的舊觀念來，他們兩腿再也不能馬上直立起來，那時候，人羣中就會有人生出怪念頭來，從一個不知何時就存在那裏的卵子裏面孵化出來，即使烈火也都燒不盡它們，而你的一切辛苦全都白廢了。不管怎麼說，我們可別忘了，埃及有一種麥子是從一具木乃伊那裏一直傳到了我們手裏。

本國或者別國的服裝已經達到了一種藝術上的尊貴地位，上述這種說法，從整體上看，我認為是不能成立的。現在，人們還是能尋找到甚麼就穿甚麼。如同擱淺船上的水手，他們在沙灘上能找到甚麼就穿甚麼，越過時空間距之後，不免彼此嘲笑對方身上化裝舞會似的服飾。每一代人都在嘲笑舊的時尚，同時又在虔誠緊追新的時尚。我們見到亨利八世[23] 或者英國女王伊麗莎白一世[24] 的衣服，不免覺得好笑，彷彿這些都是食人島上島王和島后的衣服。反正衣服一離開了特定身份的人，就會顯得可憐兮兮，或者稀奇古怪。唯有以嚴肅的眼光凝視穿衣人的真誠生活，才能抑制住嘲笑並對人們所穿的衣服肅然起敬。喜劇丑角在表演一陣陣急腹痛時，他的穿著打扮也不得不表達出這種痛苦的神態。士兵被炮彈打中，他那身上炸爛了的軍服會頓時變成高貴的帝王紫袍。在古羅馬，紫色被公認為高貴的象徵。

如今，男男女女都喜愛新款式。這種既幼稚又原始的趣味，使多少人搖着萬花筒，眯起眼睛，不斷窺看，能不能從裏面發現今天這一代人所需求的那種獨特的圖樣。那些製造商早就知道人們這種趣味是反覆無常的。兩種款式，不同之處僅僅是有幾根線條在色彩上多少有點不一樣，可是一款立刻賣掉了，而另一款卻在貨架上無人問津，怎料過了一個季節，無人問津的衣服反而成了最時髦的熱門貨，反正這類事屢見不鮮。相比之下，紋身還算不上是人們所說的那麼可怕的陋習。其實，總不能因為刺花是在表皮且不會改變，便讓紋身跟野蠻劃上等號。

我不相信，我們的工廠制度是人們有衣可穿的最佳模式。技工們的情況日復一日更像英國的情況；這不足為奇，因為據我所見所聞，原來他們的主要目的，並不是讓人們穿得既好而又體面，而是，毫無疑問，為了公司要多多賺錢。從長遠看，人們只好迎合他們所制定的目標。因此，儘管暫時不會得逞，他們還是覺得目標不妨定高一些。

至於住處，我並不否認，現在它已成為一種生活必需品，儘管有例子說明，在比我們這裏更寒冷的地區，人們長期以來居無定所，也照樣能生活下去。塞繆爾・萊恩[25] 説："拉普蘭人指居住在北歐，比如挪威、瑞典和芬蘭一帶的人。身穿皮衣，頭和肩套在皮袋裏，就這樣一夜又一

夜睡在雪地上 —— 寒冷的程度會使身歷其境的穿毛衣的人都給凍死。"
他看過他們就這樣睡在雪地裏。但萊恩還補充說:"其實,他們並不比
別人更健壯。"不過,也許人類在地球上生活了沒有多久,就發現住在
房子裏有諸多便利,以及家庭生活的舒適,這句話的原意可能表示對房
子感到滿意,而不是對家庭生活覺得滿意。然而,在某些氣候區,一提
到房子,就會使我們聯想到冬天和雨季;一年裏面有三份之二的時間,
用不着房子,只要一把遮陽傘就夠了。上述說法非常片面,間中適用而
已。在我們的氣候區,從前到了夏季,差不多只蓋一點被單之類就能過
夜。在印第安人的記事裏,一座棚屋象徵着一整天的行程,樹皮上刻畫
的一排棚屋,說明他們露宿已有過多少次了。人生下來肢體並不粗壯、
身材魁梧,所以,他要設法縮小自己的活動天地,用牆板圍造一個與自
己相宜的空間。人類早先赤身裸體,都在戶外過活,大白天,趕上寧靜
而又暖和的天氣,的確非常令人愉快;可是遇到雨季和冬天,姑且不說
那大太陽,要不是人類趕快用房子遮蔽起自己來,也許早在萌芽狀態就
給消滅了。根據傳說,亞當和夏娃穿衣服以前就是用樹葉遮蔽身體。每
個人都想有個家,一個溫暖的或者舒適的地方,先是生理上的溫暖,然
後才是感情上的溫暖。

　　我們可以想像那個時候,人類還處在嬰兒期,有些頗有魄力的人爬
進岩洞裏尋找庇護。從某種程度上說,每個孩子都是在開始重演這個創
世紀的歷程,喜歡留在戶外,哪怕是雨天和冷天。孩子玩造房子,騎木
馬遊戲,都是出於本能。有誰會不記得小時候窺探一座疊岩,或者走近
一個岩洞時引起的極大興趣呢?這是一種與生俱來的渴望,我們最原始
的祖先遺留它的一部份在我們體內。從岩洞開始,我們逐漸進步,依次
使用棕櫚葉屋頂、樹皮和樹枝屋頂、編織可撐開的亞麻屋頂、雜草和稻
草屋頂、木板和木瓦屋頂、一直到石塊和磚瓦屋頂。最後,我們反而不
知道甚麼叫露天生活,我們的生活比我們所想到的有更多家庭情調。從

圍爐走到田野，畢竟相距太遠了。如果説我們在未來的日日夜夜裏沒有任何遮擋隔開我們和天體，如果説詩人不是在屋頂底下那麼高談闊論，或者説聖人沒有在屋子裏住得那麼長久，也許這樣就會更好。鳥兒在岩洞裏不會歌唱，鴿子在鴿棚裏不會覺得自己天真可愛。

　　但是話又説回來，要是有人設計建造一所住宅，他就要像我們新英格蘭人那樣精明一點，免得日後發現自己置身於一間感化院中，一座走不出去的迷宮中、一座博物館中、一所濟貧院中、一座監獄中或者一座壯麗的陵墓中。先要想一想，這樣的棲息處是不是非造不可。我看過來自佩諾勃斯科特河的印第安人，就在這個鎮上，住在薄棉布的帳篷裏面，而四周的積雪差不多有一英尺深了。於是我揣測猜想，也許他們想大雪下得更深，好給他們擋擋風。我如何獲得體面的生活，讓我自由從事正當的探索研究，這個問題在過去一直使我煩惱不已，可是現在呢，多虧我對它變得有點麻木不仁了；過去，我常看見鐵路旁邊有一個大箱子，六英尺長、三英尺寬，夜裏工人們就在裏面鎖着自己的工具。這使我想到：每個生活艱難的人，不妨花一塊錢，買這麼一個箱子，在上面鑿幾個窟窿通通氣，到了下雨和過夜的時候鑽進去，隨手合上箱蓋，這樣一來，他就有了愛他所愛的自由，心靈也獲得了自由。看來這不見得是個壞主意，一定不會遭人白眼的。你可以隨心所欲，徹夜不眠，而且，不管甚麼時候你起身外出，也不會有哪個房東或者旅店老闆盯住你要房租。為了給一個更大、更豪華的箱子付房租，許多人一直被困擾得快死了，而在這麼一個小箱子裏面，他們萬萬不會凍死的。我這話可不是在開玩笑。經濟學是一門科學，儘管一直被人輕視，但是決不能就這樣被去掉。一個長年累月在露天過活的體質健壯的民族，從前在這裏造過一所舒適的房子，幾乎全部採用大自然提供的現成材料。馬薩諸塞殖民地主管印第安人事務的負責人古金，曾在 1674 年寫道："他們最好的房子，房頂都用樹皮覆蓋得非常整齊、緊密而又暖和；那些樹皮是在樹汁充沛的季節從樹幹上剝下來，趁樹皮還發綠時，在沉重的原木壓力下，壓它們成很大的薄片……稍微差一些的房子，覆蓋在房頂上的是一種燈芯草編成的草席，同樣也很緊密、很暖和，只是不如前一種好看……我還見到過，有些房子，六十或者一百英尺長，三十英尺寬，……我晚上常住在他們的棚屋裏，覺得就像在最好的英式住宅裏一樣暖和。"他還補充寫道，那些房子裏面常鋪鑲花的草席子在地上和牆上，各式器皿一應俱全。印第安人已經相當先進，在屋頂上開了洞孔，掛上一張草席子，用一根繩子牽拉，調節通風狀態。這樣的棚屋最多一兩天就能造好，幾個鐘頭內保證拆掉；每家都有這樣一座棚屋，或者在這樣的棚屋裏面擁有一個單間。

在原始的狀態中，每家都擁有一個說得上最好的住處，滿足他們比較粗陋而又簡單的需求；不過，我認為，我說下面這些話還是很有分寸的：雖然空中的鳥有窩，[26]"耶穌說，狐狸有洞，天空的飛鳥有窩，人子卻沒有枕頭的地方。"，狐狸有洞，野蠻人有棚屋，然而，在現代文明社會裏，居有其所的家庭卻不到一半。在文明特別發達的大城市裏，擁有住房的人只佔全體居民的極小一部份。絕大多數人為這件遮蔽身體的外套每年都要支付房租，不管寒來暑往，那是不可或缺的，而這筆錢原本可以買一個村裏面的印第安人棚屋，如今卻讓他們一輩子捱窮受苦。在這裏，我無意比較租房和買房之間孰優孰劣，但很明顯，野蠻人擁有房子，是因為它的造價很低，而文明人通常租房子住，是因為他們買不起房子；從長遠看，即使租房住，也未必一直租得起。但是有人回答說，貧窮的文明人只要付了這麼一份租金，就有了房子住，這種房子同原始人棚屋相比，不僅是皇宮。一年的房租是二十五塊錢到一百塊錢，這是鄉下的價格，卻讓他得到了經歷幾個世紀改進後的成果，其中有寬敞的房間、潔淨的塗料和牆紙，拉姆福德[27]式壁爐，抹上灰泥的頂板，軟百葉窗簾，銅質水泵，彈簧鎖，偌大的地下室，以及許多其他東西。可是，據説享受這些玩意的人，通常是貧窮的文明人，而享受不到這些玩意的野蠻人，卻像野蠻人那樣的富有，這究竟是怎麼一回事呢？如果説這是指文明使人類生活條件獲得真正的改善 —— 我認為這話是很對的，雖然只是聰明的人使他們的有利條件得到改善 —— 那麼，它必須説明：文明不會使房價太貴就可以造出質量較好的住房；所謂物價，就是用於交換物品的，我稱之為生命的量，一就立即支付，一就以後支付。附近這一帶，一所普通房子造價，大約要八百塊錢，要儲蓄這筆錢，需要一個勞動者付出十年到十五年的生命代價，而且此人還要沒有家室的拖累 —— 按每個勞動者一天一塊錢的價格來計算，反正有人收入多了，別人就會收入少了 —— 因此，通常他必須花掉大半輩子的生命，才賺得到他的一座印第安人棚屋。如果我們假定説他不買房子而租房，那也只不過是在兩件壞事當中作出了一種令人可疑的選擇。野蠻人懂不懂得在這些條件下，拿他的棚屋去換取一座皇宮呢？

擁有這多餘財產，最大好處就是儲蓄資金，以防未來不時之需。我認為，就個人而言，主要夠他支付自己的喪葬費罷了。也許人們猜想，我對儲蓄的最大好處幾乎説得一無是處。不過話又説回來，其實一個人也許用不着自己來埋藏自己。不管怎麼説，這可指出了文明人和野蠻人之間一個重大區別；他們為了保存文明種族，使文明種族達到完善，就給文明人的生活設計了一套制度。這無疑是為我們的利益着想，無奈個人的生活卻在很大程度上受到損害。不過，我倒是想指出，我們為了得到現時這種好處，已經作出了多大犧牲；我由此還想到，我們原本不必遭受任何損失，照樣也可以得到所有好處。你們説窮人總是和你在一起，[28]"因為常有窮人和你們同在。"，或者説父輩們吃過酸葡萄，孩子們牙齒還在發酸，這話究竟是甚麼意思？

"主耶和華説，我指我的永生起誓，你們在以色列中必不再有用這俗語的因由。"

"看啊，世人都是屬我的；為父的怎樣屬我，為子的也照樣屬我。犯罪的他必死亡。"[29] 我一想到我的鄰居，康科德的農夫們，他們的境況至少和其他階級的人一樣好，我卻發現他們裏面十之八九已經辛苦了二十年、三十年，乃至於四十年，不外乎是為了成為他們農場的真正主人，這些農場通常都附帶抵押權而繼承下來，要不然就靠借貸買下來的 —— 我們不妨將他們工作的三份之一當作置房費 —— 但是這筆錢他們通常還沒有償還呢。不錯，那些抵押權有時超過了農場的價值，結果農場本身成了一大累贅，而到頭來總要有一個人來接受它，因為正如這個人所說，他對農場太熟悉了。我向評估官諮詢時，吃驚地發現他們不能一下子舉出鎮上十來個無任何負擔而擁有農場的人的名字。如果你要了解這些農場的詳細情況，不妨去銀行問一問有關抵押的情況就可以了。依靠在農場工作、真的能支付農場債務的人是如此少，就算有的話，任何一個鄰居都可以說出來這個人的姓名。康科德能否找得出兩三個這樣的人，我表示懷疑。人們談論商人時說過，絕大多數，甚至百份之九十七的商人，肯定要破產的，農場主人也同樣如此。不過，說到商人，他們之中有一個人倒是說到了重點上，他說他們的破產，八成並不是真正的虧本，而僅僅是由於諸多麻煩事，沒有履行承諾之故；這也就是說，信譽道德垮掉了。可是，這麼一來，問題簡直糟透了，而且還會使人聯想到，即使是百份之三的人，說不定也拯救不了自己的靈魂，他們的破產，很可能比那些老老實實破產的人更要糟糕。破產和拒付債務都是一塊塊跳板，我們的文明有很大一部份是從這些跳板上用力騰躍，又不斷在向上跑，而野蠻人卻依然站在饑荒這塊沒有彈性的木板上。不過，一年一度在這裏舉行的米德爾塞克斯牛展評選，照例是興高采烈，彷彿農業這部機器所有環節都運轉自如。

農場主人一直在想辦法來解決生活問題，無奈採用的方式卻比問題本身更複雜。為了得到一點蠅頭薄利，他居然投資牲畜生意。他憑藉嫻熟的技巧，用細如髮絲的套索設置一個陷阱，捕捉舒適又獨立的生活，不料他一轉身，自己的一條腿反而掉進了陷阱。他的窮根就在這裏；而且，出於相同的原因，儘管我們被各種奢侈品所包圍，但是如果跟野蠻人的成千種舒適相比，我們都是一貧如洗的。正如查普曼[30]

　　—— 這虛偽的人類社會 ——
　　　—— 為了塵世的宏偉[31]

　　天上種種安樂像空氣般稀薄。農夫得到他的房子，但並沒有因此變得更富有，倒是反而更窮了，惹他發火的恰好是他的房子。按照我所理解的來看，莫摩斯[32] 所造房子的理由 - 是言之鑿鑿，令人信服；他說密涅瓦"沒有造它成一座可以移動的房子，如果可以移動，就能躲開壞鄰居"。這種反對意見成立，因為我們的房子其實一點也不實用，與其說我們住在裏面，還不如說被關押在裏面；要躲開的壞鄰居，恰恰是我們自己可鄙的"自我"。我知道在這個鎮上，至少有一兩戶人，他們差不多盼了一代人的時間都想賣掉郊區的房子，遷到村裏去，無奈一直未能如願以償，唯有一瞑不視之時，方能徹底解脫。

　　就算大多數人最終能夠擁有，或者說租用具備各種改進設施後的現代化房子吧。文明雖然一直使我們的房子得到改善，但它並沒有使住在房子裏面的人同樣得到改善。文明打造了一座座皇宮，但要打造貴族和國王，可不是那麼容易。如果文明人的追求並不比野蠻人的追求更有價值，如果文明人所花去的一生中大部份時間，只是去獲得那些粗劣的必需品和舒適的生活享受。那麼，他為甚麼非得擁有比野蠻人更好的住所呢？

　　但是，那些貧窮的少數人又如何過日子呢？也許人們會發現，有一些人的外部境遇比野蠻人好，其他一些人的外部境遇。則成正比地比野蠻人差。一個階級的奢侈和另一個階級的窮苦，是互為消長的。一邊是宮殿聳立，另一邊則是濟貧院和"沉默的窮人"。修建金字塔亦即各法老陵墓的百萬勞工，只能靠大蒜過活，死後也不見得會殮葬得像模像樣。石匠給宮殿修飛簷添彩，夜晚也許就回到遠不如印第安人棚屋的窩裏。有人以為，在一個文明國度裏，絕大多數居民的生活狀況，可能不至於降低到如同野蠻人的生活狀況那樣，這就大錯特錯了。我說的是那些落魄的窮人，此刻還沒有談到那些落魄的富人。要了解這一點，用不着往遠處看，只需看看我們鐵路邊上到處都有的簡陋小木屋，那些毫無文明改進的地方；我每天散步時都看到，人們都擠在小窩棚裏，整個冬天門都敞着，為了透進一點陽光，看不到有甚麼取暖火堆，那只是存在於他們的想像之中。無論是老年人還是年輕人，他們的軀體由於長期捱凍受苦習慣性捲縮在一起，且永遠變了形，他們的四肢和官能也得不到正常發展。當然應該平等看待這個階級，正是由於他們的辛勤勞動，許多使這一代人享有盛名的工程才得以完成。在英國這一世界特大濟貧院裏，名目繁多的技工們的狀況，多少也是如此。要不然，我就給你說一說愛爾蘭的情況吧，愛爾蘭這個地方，在地圖上標出為白人居住的開明地區。不妨比較一下愛爾蘭人的身體狀況和北美洲印第安人、南太平洋島民或任何與文明人沒有接觸，並未退化的野蠻民族的身體狀況。但我毫不懷疑，，野蠻人的統治者和文明人的統治者是同樣聰明的。他們的狀況只能說明，何等骯髒的東西是可以和文明並存。現在我幾乎不必提到我們南方各州的勞工，這個國家的主要出口產品都是他們生產的，而他們自己卻成了南方的一種主要產品。不過，別扯遠了，我還是只談談那些屬於中產的人吧。

大多數人好像從來沒有思考過，一所房子究竟是甚麼樣子，他們原本不應該窮，實際上卻窮了一輩子，僅僅是因為他們心裏總想得到一所跟鄰居一個樣的房子。好像一個人只能穿裁縫給他量體製作的衣服，或者，由於逐步拋掉了棕櫚葉帽子或土撥鼠皮帽子，他就抱怨時世艱難，因為他實在沒錢買一頂皇冠！要造一幢比我們住的房子更方便、更豪華的房子是有可能的，但是大家承認那樣的房子誰都買不起。難道說我們應該總是琢磨如何尋找到更多的這類東西，而不是有時候應該滿足於少尋找一些東西嗎？那些可敬的公民，竟然如此一本正經來言傳身教，開導年輕人要在老死之前多多置備些富餘的烏亮的皮鞋啦、雨傘啦，還有空蕩蕩的客房，來招待空想中的客人，這樣行不行呢？我們的家具為甚麼不可以簡單一些，就像阿拉伯人或者印度人的家具那樣呢？我們將民族的救星尊稱為來自天國的使者，給人類帶來神聖的禮物，我想到他們時腦海裏卻怎麼也想不出他們身後還緊跟着甚麼隨從啦，或者甚麼滿載時髦家具的車輛啦。或者，有人說，既然我們在道德上和智力上比阿拉伯人高出一籌，那麼，我們的家具就應該比他們的更為複雜，我要是同意了以上說法 —— 這種同意的說法豈不是很怪嗎？ —— 那又會怎麼樣呢？目前，我們的房子裏面堆滿了家具，簡直髒亂不堪，一個好主婦寧願讓大量家具堆成垃圾堆，早上的工作萬萬不可擱在一邊不做。早上的工作啊！在奧羅拉古羅馬神話中的曙光女神。燦爛的霞光裏，在門農埃及底庇斯附近阿孟霍特普三世的巨大石雕像，相傳日出前會發出豎琴聲，公元 170 年經羅馬皇帝修復後卻不再發聲。美妙的琴聲裏，世人們早上的工作該做些甚麼？我的案頭上有三塊石灰石，每天尚且還需要給它們撣去塵埃，而我腦海裏的家具至今還沒有撣去塵埃，於是我在一氣之下扔它們到窗外去了。那麼，我怎麼能擁有一座帶家具的房子呢？我寧可坐在露天，反正草地上不會塵土成堆，除非人們已在那裏破了土。

貪圖奢侈，揮霍成性，正是驕奢淫逸之徒開創的新時尚，眾百姓卻趨之若鶩，唯恐落人之後。在一所人們所說最佳的旅店下榻的一個觀光客，很快發現果然名不虛傳，因為店主們當他為薩達那珀勒斯傳說中的古亞述末代國王，約在公元前 700 年，以窮奢極侈、驕橫不可一世著稱於世。他要是接受了他們的盛情款待，沒多久他的陽剛之氣肯定消失殆盡。我認為我們在火車車廂裏，總是喜歡花更多錢在奢侈的設施上，而不是花在安全和方便上，結果安全和方便付之闕如，車廂反而成了現代化客廳，裏面有長沙發，土耳其式睡榻，遮陽窗簾，還有上百種其他富有東方情調的玩意，全部照搬到我們西方來了，其實，原先都是為天朝帝國的後宮嬪妃和六宮粉黛發明的。約拿單，《聖經》中的人物，掃羅的兒子，大衛的朋友。要是聽到了這些名字，肯定羞慚得無地自容。我寧願坐在一隻南瓜上，為我一人所獨佔，也不樂意跟眾人一起擠坐在一個有天鵝絨坐墊的椅子上。我寧願坐在一輛牛車上走天下，來去自由，也不願意乘甚麼花哨的觀光遊覽列車飛向天空，一路上呼吸着污濁的空氣。

在蠻荒時代，人們生活極其簡單，而且赤身裸體，那至少有一個好處，他依然是大自然中匆匆過客。他吃飽睡足，振作精神之後，心裏就琢磨自己重新上路。可以說，他住在這個塵寰的帳篷裏，不是穿過峽谷，就是越過平原，或者攀登山巔。可是，看吧！人們已經成為他們的工具的工具了。從前肚子餓了獨自摘果子的人，如今成了一個農夫，而原先站在樹底下庇蔭的人，如今卻成了一個管家[33]。現在我們不再撐起帳篷過夜，無非是安居在大地上，遺忘了天堂。我們信奉基督教，無非當它是改良農業的一種方法而已。我們已經為塵世修建宅第，並為陰曹冥府修造墳墓。最美好的藝術作品裏表達的，都是人類為自己擺脫上述這種精神狀態而進行的搏鬥，可是我們的藝術效果只是使這種低迷的精神狀態變得安逸，而完全忘掉較為高昂的精神狀態。在這個村裏，美術作品實際上沒有立足之地，就算有甚麼作品已經傳下來了，我們的生活、我們的房子和街市，也沒法給它配置合適的底座。我們這裏連掛一張畫的釘子都沒有，安裝英雄或聖人的胸像的台架也沒有。我一想到我們的房子是如何修造的，款項已付清或者還沒有付清，它們內部經濟又是如何管理和如何支撐，就暗自納悶，客人在讚賞壁爐上那些華而不實的擺設時，虧得地板倒是沒有塌下去，讓他打從地下室，一直落到某塊碩骨鐵硬的宅基地上。我不能不看到，這種所謂富有和優雅的生活，好像讓人越級攀升的階梯，我根本也欣賞不了那些點綴生活的藝術品，我已全神貫注在人們跳躍的高度上了；因為我記得，僅僅由於人的肌肉能達到的最高跳高紀錄，還是某些流浪的阿拉伯人保持的，據說他們從平地跳過了二十五英尺高。如果沒有人給予支持的話，即使跳到這樣的高度，一定還會回落的。我首先要問問舉止如此不合適的業主，是誰在支持你？你是百份之九十七個失敗者裏面的一個，還是百份之三個成功者裏面的一個？請回答我以上這些問題，隨後，也許我會看一看你那些華而不實的玩意，發現它們原來是一些裝飾品罷了。車子套在馬前頭，既不美觀，也沒有用處。我們用漂亮的飾物裝飾房子前，務必剝掉房子牆壁的一層皮，也剝掉我們生命的一層皮，此外還要有出色的家政和美好的生活作為基礎；如今，審美觀大抵都是在戶外培育，那裏既沒有房子，也沒有管家。

　　老約翰遜[34] 在他的《神奇的造化》一書中，談到了這個城鎮的最早移民，原來他與他們都是同時代人，他告訴我們："他們在某個小山坡上挖土修窯洞，作為自己最早的棲身之處，堆泥土在原木上，再生起煙火烘烤泥土。"他還說，那時候他們還沒有給自己造房子，直到托上帝的福，讓大地給他們帶來麵包，來養活他們。怎知道，第一年收成不大好，"有好長一段歲月，他們不得不減少自己口糧。"好長一段時間，新尼德蘭州北美原荷蘭殖民地的稱謂，即今日的紐約州等地區。秘書，用荷蘭文所寫的、給希望移民到那處的人提供的信息中，特別詳細介紹説："在新尼德蘭的那些人，尤其是在新英格蘭那些人，最初沒法按照他們的心願修造農舍，他們只好在地上挖一個方形坑，像地窖一樣，六七英尺深，長和寬只要他們合意就行，坑內四壁圍上木板，又給襯上樹皮或者其他甚麼材料，以防泥土從縫隙滲進來；就在這種地窖裏，地面鋪了木板，頂上用護壁板作天花板，架起一個圓桿屋頂，再在圓桿上覆蓋樹皮或者綠草皮，這樣他們就可一家人住在裏面，既乾爽而又暖和地過上兩三年或者四年，而且，地窖裏面還按照家庭人口多少，分隔成一些小小單位，這也是不難理解的。新英格蘭有錢有勢的人物，在殖民地初創時期，開始時也都住在這種樣式的房子裏，是有以下兩個原因：首先，不用為修造房子浪費了時間，導致下一個季節糧食短缺；其次，不要讓他們從本國帶來的大批貧窮勞工感到灰心喪志。過了三四年，這裏周圍已適宜耕種了，他們才花上好幾千塊錢，給自己修造漂亮的房子。"

我們祖先採取這種做法，說明他們至少是小心謹慎的，好像他們的原則就是首先滿足當前最緊迫的需求。可是現在，最緊迫的需求得到滿足了嗎？一想到要為自己找一棟豪宅，我就嚇住了，因為，可以這麼說，這個國家與人類文化還是不相適應，我們至今還不得不將我們的精神麵包削得更薄，甚至削得比我們祖先削過的全麥麵包還要薄得多。這倒不是，即使在初創時期，所有建築裝飾可以置之不顧，而是說讓我們跟自己的生活息息相關的房子先裝飾得美一些，有如貝類動物的內壁，可又不要有過之而無不及。可是，老天哪！我去過一兩處這樣的房子，才知道他們室內裝潢究竟是甚麼樣。

今天，我們固然沒有退化到再去住窯洞，或者住棚屋，或者去穿獸皮，但是接受人類的發明和工業提供的、也是來之不易的種種好處，那當然是再好不過了。在我們這一帶，現在木板、木瓦、石灰和磚塊，比適宜居住的窯洞要便宜得多，也更容易尋找到；整根原木、大批量樹皮，甚至高質量黏土或平坦的石板也都不難得到。我談這個問題還算通情達理吧，因為我對它很熟悉，既有理論，也有實踐。只要動一點腦筋，我們就可以將這些材料利用得更好，比時下那些富豪更富有，使我們的文明成為一種福祉。文明人無非是一個更有經驗、更聰明的野蠻人罷了。不過，還是讓我趕緊做我自己的試驗吧。

1845 年快到 3 月底的時候，我借了一柄斧頭，來到瓦爾登湖畔樹林裏，就在離我打算修造房子的最近處，開始砍了一些雖然高大但尚屬幼齡的箭矢形白松，作為造房用的木材。開了工就很難不向人借這借那，不過，這麼一來，讓你的同胞們在你的慘淡經營中沾一點光，這也不失為最慷慨大方的善舉吧。斧頭的主人遞斧頭給我的時候說，那是他的寶貝呢，怎料我歸還他時，那斧頭比我剛借到時還要鋒利。我是在景色宜人的山坡上工作，那處滿山坡全是松樹林，透過松樹林我望得見瓦爾登湖，還有一小塊林中空地，在那裏，松樹和山核桃樹像雨後春筍似的冒了出來。湖裏的冰柱還沒有融化，雖然有好幾處化開了的窟窿，全是黑黝黝的顏色，濕漉漉的樣子。我在那裏工作的日子裏，稀疏的雪花還飄過幾次；不過，在我出了樹林、打從鐵路走回家的路上，只見大部份地方還是綿延不絕的黃沙堆，在灰濛濛的雲氣暮靄裏微微閃光，鐵路道軌則在春天豔陽之下閃閃發亮，我聽到雲雀、小鷚和其他鳥兒在歌唱，跟我們在一起迎接新的一年了。在春回大地的日子裏，令人不快的冬天正在跟凍土一起消融，而蟄伏的生命則開始自我舒展。有一天，我的斧頭從柄上脫落下來，我砍了一段碧綠的山核桃樹枝做楔子，用石塊嵌楔子入斧頭眼，稍後連柄帶斧一起浸泡在湖水裏，以便木頭發脹，這時，我看見一條花蛇躥入水中，潛伏在湖底，顯然毫無不適之感，竟然跟我留在那裏的時間一樣長或者大約有一刻多鐘；也許牠還沒有從蟄伏狀態中完全甦醒過來吧。依我看，人們之所以滯留在目前低級和原始的狀態，也出於同樣的原因吧。不過，如果說他們感受到萬木之春的影響，使自己奮發起來，那麼，他們必然會崛起，到達飄飄欲仙的人生最高境界。前一陣子，我在霜凍的清晨看過小徑上有好幾條蛇，蛇體有些部份依然麻木欠靈活，等待太陽出來融化牠們。4 月 1 日下了雨，冰柱融化了，在濃霧彌漫的前半天，我聽到一隻失羣的孤雁在湖上四處摸索哀鳴，好像是迷了路，或者說又像是濃霧中的精靈。

就這樣，我連續工作了幾天，砍伐樹木，切削立柱和橡子，全靠我這柄小斧頭，既沒有多少可以告知各位，也沒有甚麼學者式的思想，只是獨自哼唱──人們都說自己是見多識廣；

> 看啊，他們長出了翅膀──
>
> 藝術呀，科學呀，
>
> 還有上千種技藝呀，
>
> 其實，只是一陣吹過的風，
>
> 才是他們見識的全部。

主要木材我砍成六英寸，以這個長度為邊的正方形，大多數立柱只砍兩邊，橡子和地板木料只砍一面，其他幾面保留樹皮，這麼一來，它們跟鋸過的木料一樣平直，而且還要結實。這時，我還借到了一些其他工具，所以，每一根木料都精心地開了榫眼，削好榫頭。我在樹林裏度過的白晝時間不是很長；我常常帶着麵包牛油當午餐，正午時份，坐在我砍下來的碧綠松樹丫枝上，讀讀原來包裝麵包牛油的報紙，連麵包上也散發着松香味，因為我雙手給塗上了厚厚一層的松脂。完工以前，我就成了松樹的朋友，而不是仇敵，儘管我在松樹林裏砍過了一些樹木，卻跟松樹越發熟悉了。有時候，我的丁丁伐木聲吸引了林中閒遊的人過來，就會在我砍下的碎木屑堆頭上跟我愉快閒聊。

我做事不是性急慌忙，而是全力以赴，到了 4 月中旬，我的房子框架已做好，可以立起來了。我已經買下了在菲奇伯格鐵路工作的愛爾蘭人詹姆斯·科林斯的小木屋，裏面的木板還可以利用。詹姆斯·科林斯的小木屋，人們都說是一所不同凡響的好房子。我去看房子時，他並不在家。我在屋外轉了一圈，起初並沒有被屋裏面的人發現，因為窗子很深而又高。這所小木屋不算大，有一個尖屋頂，其他也沒有甚麼好看的，四周堆着五英尺高的垃圾，好像是一堆堆積肥。屋頂不少地方已被太陽曬得翹裂而且發脆，但它還是屋子裏面最完好的材料。門檻沒有了，不過，門板下面有一條常年可供母雞們進出的通道。科林斯太太來到大門口，請我到小木屋裏面去看看。我一走近小木屋，倒趕母雞們進屋子裏去了。屋子裏面光線很暗，地板八成都很髒，冷冰冰，潮膩膩，陰濕發黏，不由得令人渾身寒戰，裏邊木板東一塊、西一塊的，好像已經不起挪動了。她點燃了一盞燈，給我看看屋頂裏面和四壁內牆，還有一直延伸到牀底下的地板，她提醒我可別踩到地窖裏面去，其實，那是一個有兩英尺深的垃圾洞。拿她自己的話來說，小木屋的“頂上木板是好的、四壁木板是好的，還有窗子也是好的”——原來是兩個方框，近來只有貓咪從這裏進進出出。屋子裏有一個火爐，一張牀，一個可以坐坐的地方，一個在這屋子裏面出生的嬰兒，一把絲綢遮陽傘，一塊鍍金邊框的鏡子，一隻釘在橡木上新穎的咖啡磨，這些就是他們的全部家當了。這筆買賣很快就成交，因為詹姆斯這時也回來了。當天晚上，我付給他四塊兩毛五分錢，他呢，應該在次天清晨撤離，不得再賣房子給別人：六點鐘，小木屋產權歸我所有。他關照我說，最好還是趁早搬過來，以免有人在地租和燃料上提出數目不清而又蠻不講理的要求。他還向我保證說，唯一的麻煩就只有這一個。六點鐘，我在路上就碰到他們一家人。那一大堆東西——牀、咖啡磨、鏡子和母雞——他們的全部家當都在這裏，唯獨貓咪沒見到，原來牠直奔樹林成了野貓，後來我聽說，那貓咪踩進了誘捕土撥鼠的陷阱，最終成了一隻死貓。

當天早上，我就拆卸這個小木屋，拔下木料上的釘子，隨後一小車、一小車運到了湖邊，鋪木板在草地上，以便在陽光下曬白、復原。我駕車經過林間小道時，一隻早起的畫眉向我鳴叫了一兩聲。一個名叫帕特立克的年輕人悄悄告訴我，說鄰居愛爾蘭人西萊，在我木板裝車的間隙，趁機將仍然好用、筆筆直的、可以再派用場的釘子、U 形釘和牆頭釘通通裝進自己口袋裏去;等我回過去接班時,心裏不免悵然,既感慨又滿不在乎,望着那一片廢墟似的場景,這時,他就站在一旁,說:沒甚麼工作可做啦。此時此刻,他正代表大夥作壁上觀,使這種看似區區小事,倒是很像特洛伊城眾神[35] 在大撤離。

我在南邊的山坡上給自己挖了一個地窖,以前土撥鼠曾在這裏挖過洞穴;我刨去漆樹和黑莓的根,一直挖到幾乎見不到植物痕跡的地方,亦即六英尺,以這個長度為邊的正方形、七英尺深的一塊優質沙土上,日後不管冬天有多冷,馬鈴薯也不會給凍壞。地窖四壁裝上擱板,所以沒有砌上石塊;反正陽光照不到地窖,沙土始終保持不變。這項工作只不過花了兩個小時。我對這種破土挖洞的工作感到特別開心,因為差不多在所有的緯度上,人們只要動工挖洞,都會得到同樣的溫度。在大城市豪宅裏至今仍有地窖,他們在裏面儲存一些塊根植物,有如古人那樣,即使在上層建築消失之後,後人還會在黃土裏發現它遺留的凹痕。所謂房子,只不過是通往地洞的一道門廊罷了。

最後,到了 5 月初,我在一些朋友幫助下 —— 其實並沒甚麼必要,只不過借此改善一下鄰里關係 —— 豎起了房子的框架。這些朋友均為美國著名作家、詩人,如:愛默生、阿爾科特和 W・E・錢功等。前來相助,就拿他們的聲名來説,我已感到無上榮幸。我相信,他們會出力相助修建許多更為高大的建築。7 月 4 日,我開始住進我的房子了,當時木板安裝才不久,屋頂也剛剛竣工,反正木板上下嵌邊,都是精心製作,緊密扣在一起,防雨是萬無一失的。鑲嵌木板前,我已經在屋子的一端砌好煙囪的底座,所用的石塊有兩小車左右,全憑我的兩隻胳臂從湖邊往山上搬過來的。入秋後鋤過莊稼,趕在非生火取暖不可之前,我就造好煙囪,因為前一陣子,我一大早起來,就在露天做飯:這種方式,我至今依然認為,從某些方面來説,比通常的方式要更方便,更合心。要是我的麵包還沒有烤好前碰上颶風下雨,我就會拿幾塊木板,架在火堆上遮擋一下，自己則坐在木板下面看我的麵包，就這樣，我度過了多麼開心的時光。在那些日子裏，我手上的工作很多，書讀得很少，不過，只要在地上有零星碎紙片甚麼的，甚至我的布襯墊或者枱布，都會帶給我實際上不遜於閱讀《伊利亞特》時一樣多的樂趣。

我造房子固然很細心，不過要是更細心一些，也許更好，比方說，一道門，一扇窗，一個地窖，一間閣樓，從人的生理需要方面來看，要考慮到有甚麼樣的基礎，而且，我們在找到除了滿足暫時需要以外更好的理由之前，也許永遠不會修建甚麼上層建築物[36]了。人給自己造房子和鳥兒築巢，都是同樣合情合理。有誰知道，要是人們都用自己的雙手給自己造住房，這樣簡單樸實為自己和家人提供食物，那麼，富有詩情畫意的才能就會得到普遍發展，這好像鳥兒忙碌時引吭高唱、響徹雲霄一樣。可是，天哪！我們倒是很像牛鸝和杜鵑，牠們總是到其他鳥兒築好的窩裏去產卵，那嘰嘰喳喳的刺耳噪聲，讓路過的遊客聽了大為掃興。難道我們就這樣永遠讓營造的樂趣給木匠師傅嗎？在人類經驗中，建築算得上甚麼呢？我那麼多次散步中，從來沒碰到過某某人在從事像給自己造房子這麼簡單而又自然的工作呢。我們全都歸屬於社會。縫縫補補不是只有裁縫可做；傳教士、商人和農夫，同樣也可以做嘛。這種分工究竟要分到怎樣才算盡呢？到了最後又會有甚麼結果？毫無疑問，別人也可以代我來思考吧；但是，如果說他思考是為了不讓我自己思考，那就不可取了。

誠然，這個國家有所謂的建築師，至少我聽說過有一位建築師，此人有一種想法，建築裝飾要具有一個真理的核心，一種必要性，因此才有一種美，彷彿這是神靈給予他的啟示。也許從他的觀點看來，全都美得很，其實，他比半瓶子醋的業餘愛好者只不過稍微高明一點罷了。作為建築學領域裏一位多愁善感的改革者，他不是從基礎上，而是從飛簷上入手。照他的設想，只不過是琢磨如何以真理為核心裝進各種裝飾裏面，好比每塊糖裏面實際上都有一顆杏仁或者一顆葛縷子——儘管我覺得，沒有糖衣的杏仁更有利於健康——但他並沒有想到居民，亦即住在裏面的人，如何使房子真正造得裏裏外外都很好，而讓各種裝飾順其自然就可以了。哪個有理性的人，會認為裝飾只是表面的東西——好比烏龜有斑紋外殼，殼類動物有珠母的光澤，都要像百老匯的居民有他們的三一教堂一樣，需要甚麼立約規定呢？不過，一個人跟他的房子的建築風格無關，如同烏龜跟牠的硬殼無關一樣；一個士兵也不見得那麼無聊，在軍旗上塗他那驍勇無敵的確切色彩，敵人自會發現。一到緊張關頭，他便會急赤白臉。據我看，這個建築師彷彿從飛簷上俯下身來，對住在裏面的老百姓怯生生嘀咕着半真半假的話，其實後者卻比他知道得還要多呢。我現在見到的所謂建築學上的美，是從內部逐漸向外部形成的，是迎合了居住者的各種需要和性格，因為只有居住者才是獨一無二的建築師——它來自不知不覺的真實與高貴，對於外表從來不予考慮；如果說此外還有甚麼類似這種的美註定產生的話，那麼此前必定有過一種同樣不知不覺的生命之美。這個國家最耐人尋味的住宅，正如畫家都知道，通常是窮人那些毫無虛飾的簡陋木屋和農舍；這些木屋和農舍之所以別具風姿，不是在外表上有甚麼與眾不同的特色，而是因為住在外表好似貝殼的房子裏面的居民生活；同樣有趣的，還有市民建在郊外的那些箱子形狀的木屋，他們的生活有如想像一樣簡單而普通，他們並沒有竭力追求甚麼住房的風格效果。絕大多數的建築裝飾都是形同虛設，9月間的一場大風就會使它們如同借來的羽毛[37]，喻指借來的漂亮衣服或不屬本人的榮耀，一樣通通給剝光了，對住房實體則絲毫無損。地窖裏既沒有橄欖、又沒有美酒的人，就算不懂建築藝術也無所謂。如果說在文學作品裏也同樣竭力追求甚麼裝飾風格，那結果會是怎樣？如果說我們的《聖經》設計師，就像我們教堂的建築師那樣，花大量時間在飛簷上，那結果又會是怎樣呢？純文學和藝術學以及它們的教授，都是這麼打造出來的。不用說，誰都很關心的是，這幾根木條究竟斜放在他上頭還是底下，他那箱子形狀房子應該塗上甚麼色彩。說真的，要是他斜放那些木條子，給房子塗色，那是很有道理的；但是，如果說精神一離開居民的軀體，那它也就無異於給自己打造棺材的材料——亦即造墓工程；而“木匠”不外乎是“做棺材的人”的另一種叫法。有人說，你要是感到絕望或者對生活非常冷漠時，不妨從你腳下抓起一把泥土，給你房子塗成黃土色。他就想到了他那最終的狹窄的房子，可不是嗎？不妨拋一枚銅幣，碰碰運氣吧。想必他有的是許多許多閒暇時間！為甚麼你只抓起一把泥土？最好還是用你的膚色粉刷自己的房子吧；讓它顏色蒼白或者為你感到羞愧。改進村舍建築風格的一大創舉！等你為我的住房裝飾準備妥當了，我一定會採用它們的。

趕在入冬之前，我已造好煙囪，房子兩側原先擋不住雨水，這時已釘上從原木上砍下來的薄片，這些薄片很不齊整，樹汁又多，我不得不用鉋子削平它們的兩邊。

就這樣，我有了一所嚴絲密縫、塗抹灰泥的木板房子，七英尺寬，十五英尺長，立柱有八英尺高，一個小閣樓，一間盥洗室，每一邊有一個大窗子，兩個活動天窗，房子一端有一扇大門，大門對面有一個磚砌的壁爐。我造房的確切費用支出，只是按我採用的這些材料的通常價格，人工不算在內，因為造房的工作是由我自己做的，現將清單開列如下：我之所以列舉得鉅細無遺，是因為很少有人說得出自己造房究竟花了多少錢，即使有的話，能單獨列出造房的各種各樣材料費用，一一加以說明，這樣的人也是極少的——

木板 8.035 元（大多數採用舊棚屋木板）

屋頂與兩側使用的舊牆板 4.00 元

板條 1.25 元

2 扇舊玻璃窗 2.43 元

1,000 塊舊磚 4.00 元

2 桶石灰 2.40 元（買貴了）

發毛織物 0.31 元（買多了）

壁爐架鐵料 0.15 元

釘子 3.90 元

鉸鏈和螺絲釘 0.14 元

門閂 0.10 元

粉筆 0.01 元

搬運費 1.40 元

（大多數自己馱）

總計 28.125 元。

　　造房的所有用料有如上述，不過，原木、石料和沙不包括在內，因為這幾項材料我是按照政府公地上造房定居者應享受的權利取得的。我還搭了一小間雜物屋，主要利用造房剩餘材料蓋成的。

　　我打算給自己造一幢房子，論宏偉豪華，要蓋過康科德的那條大街上任何一幢房子，只要它能像現時這個木屋那樣使我喜歡，而造價卻不超過前者的話。

　　由此我發現，要想得到一個住處的學生，只要支付還不到現在每年所付房租的費用，就可獲得一所他終生受用的房子。如果說我這話好像言過其實，那麼我的理由是：我是為人類，而不是為自己誇耀；而且我的缺點和前後不一致並不會影響我的論述的真實性。儘管我有不少虛假和偽善之處──那就像糠秕很難跟麥子分離一樣，我和別人一樣為此感到遺憾──可是就這件事來說，我還是要自由呼吸，挺直自己的腰板，這對身心來說都是一種莫大欣慰。我已決定絕不低聲下氣，絕不變成魔鬼的代理人。我將竭盡全力為真理說一句好話。在劍橋學院，學生住宿的房間只比我自己那個木屋稍微大一點，每年租金卻高達三十塊錢，而那家公司佔盡便宜，在一個屋頂底下並排修建了三十二個房間，由於鄰居眾多又嘈雜，所以，居住者都覺得諸多不便，也許還不得不去住四層樓。我不禁想到，如果我們在這些方面有更多的真知灼見，不僅教育的需求可以減少，因為，說真的，人們已經獲得更多的教育，而且受教育要繳費這種現象多半也會消失。在劍橋或者其他甚麼學校，學生為了得到這些便利，他們或者甚麼其他人就要付出很大的生命代價，不過雙方要是處理得當，那只要付出十份之一也就夠了。那些最花錢的東西，絕不是學生最需要的東西。比方說，學費是一學期收費賬單上重要的一項，可是，與同時代人中最有教養的人交遊，從而得到更有價值的教育，那是根本不需要付錢的。[39] 建立一所學院的方式，通常是靠募捐，收進美元和分幣，然而極端盲目來遵循分工的原則——其實，這種原則非要謹慎從事不可——招來了一個承包商，不料這個承包商當它投機生意來做，僱了一些愛爾蘭人或者甚麼其他的技工，果真奠基開工了，而來校上學的學生據說就不得不將就着住了進去；為了這些失誤，一代又一代的人不得不掏錢繳學費。我認為，如果學生或者說那些渴望從上學中受益的人，哪怕他們自己動手奠基動工，也會比上面這種做法好得多。學生經常逃避人人必不可缺的任何勞動，得到了他所垂涎的閒暇和休息，他得到的只是一種可恥而無益的空閒，而唯有讓這種空閒結出碩果的經歷，卻沒有得到。"可是，"有人說，"你這不是說學生不該用腦袋，而是應該用雙手去做事吧？"我的本意確實不是這樣。我是說學生不妨多多思考一下；我的本意是說他們不應該拿生活當作遊戲，或者僅僅拿生活來研究一番，而同時在這場昂貴的遊戲中還要這個社會大家庭供養他們。他們應該自始至終認真體驗生活。青年人要是不趕快投入生活實踐，怎能學會活得更好？我想，這就很像學習數學一樣訓練他們的心智。比方說，我要是希望一個孩子學一點藝術和科學，我就不願走舊路，那不外乎送他到鄰近某某教授那裏去，在那裏甚麼都教，甚麼都練，唯獨生活藝術不教不練——教他從望遠鏡和顯微鏡下觀察世界，從來不教他用肉眼來看世上萬物；學了化學，卻不懂得麵包是如何做成的；學了力學，卻不懂得這是如何得來的。發現了海王星周圍幾顆新衛星，卻沒有發現自己眼睛裏的微塵，或者說沒有發現自己成了一顆甚麼漂泊無定的衛星；或者說他在一滴醋酸裏觀察各種怪物，卻反而被他周圍的怪物吞噬了。一個孩子一邊從書本裏盡量找到他所需要的知識，一邊自己挖掘鐵礦石，加以熔煉，終於給自己打造了一把摺刀——而另一個孩子在大學裏聽有關冶金學的講座，同時又收到了父親給他的一把羅傑斯牌摺刀，一個月之後，這兩個孩子面究竟是哪一個進步得更快呢？哪一個孩子的手指最有可能給摺刀刮破呢？……讓我大吃一驚的是，我離開大學時就被告知，說我已經學過航海學了！——可以了，我只要到港口去兜個圈，肯定學到更多的航海知識。政治經濟學，就算可憐的大學生都學過了，但只是被教過罷了，而生活經濟學，那是哲學的同義語，甚至從來沒有在我們學院裏教授過。結果是學生一面在學亞當·斯密 [40]、李嘉圖 [41] 和薩伊 [42] 的政治經濟學，一面卻使他父親陷入無法擺脫的債務之中。

我們的大學是這樣，一百項“現代化改進設施”也是這樣。對它們抱有幻想，但並不是總有積極進展。魔鬼因為他很早就向那些設施入了股，後來又不斷增資，所以不斷在索取福利，一直到最後。我們的發明常常是一些漂亮的玩具，使我們分心，不能專注於嚴肅的事物。它們不外乎是對毫無改進的目標提供一些改進的手段，其實，這個是早已達到而且很容易達到的，正如通往波士頓或者紐約的鐵路那樣。我們匆匆從緬因州興建了一條磁性電報線路直達得克薩斯州，可是緬因州和得克薩斯州之間，說不定根本沒有甚麼重要信息需要溝通。這就好比一個男人，趕着想見一個耳聾的貴婦，可是一等到他被引見給這位貴婦，她的助聽器一端也放在他手裏了，他卻發現自己無話可說，你倒説説，大家尷尬不尷尬。彷彿主要目的，是要趕快説出話來而不是要説得合情合理。我們急於在大西洋底下修建隧道，讓舊世界縮短幾個星期時間到達新世界，殊不知傳入美國人的偌大耳朵裏的第一條消息，也許就是阿黛萊德公主得了百日咳。反正騎着馬一分鐘跑一英里的人，不會帶來最重要的消息；他可不是一個福音傳道者，他跑來跑去也用不着吃蝗蟲和野蜜 [43]。《聖經·新約全書·馬太福音》第 3 章 1 太福節説：約翰在曠野裏傳道，他"身穿駱駝毛的衣服，腰束皮帶，吃的是蝗蟲、野蜜"。我懷疑，飛童指當時英國跑得最快的一匹有名的賽馬，有沒有帶過一粒穀子到磨坊去。

有人跟我説："我煩惱你怎麼不積攢一些錢；你喜歡旅遊；你不妨搭乘汽車，今天就去菲奇伯格見見世面。"可我想的卻比這聰明。我知道最快的旅遊者是安步當車的人。我跟我的朋友説，我們不妨試一試，看看誰先到達那裏。這段路程是三十英里；車費是九角錢。這差不多是一天的工資。我記得工人在這條路上工作，一天只賺六角錢。好了，我現在開始步行，天黑之前到達那裏；一個星期以來，我一直保持這個速度行走。這個時候，你是在賺車資，明天某個時間才能到達，或者説今天晚上也會到達，要是你運氣好及時找到工作的話。其實，你並沒有去菲奇伯格，而是你這一天絕大部份時間都在這裏工作。所以説，就算這條鐵路繞着全世界一周，我想，我總得趕在你前頭；至於見見世面，多一點這方面的閲歷，那我也只好跟你完全斷絕往來了。

這是普遍的法則，沒有哪個人曾智取它，至於鐵路嘛，我們甚至可以説，反正它有多廣就有多長。要想給人類修建一條環球鐵路，無異於鏟平這個星球的全個表面。人們模模糊糊覺得，彷彿只要堅持這種合股經營方式，用鐵鍬不停挖下去，要不了多長時間，最後大家可以分文不花來乘火車，到達任何一個地方；不料，人們一窩蜂擁向火車站，乘務員高喊"大家上車吧"，這時火車黑煙四起，蒸汽密集噴發，才發現只有少數人登上了火車，其餘的人卻通通被火車碾壓過去了——這將被稱為而且確實也是"一次令人為之惻隱的意外事故"。毫無疑問，賺到了車資的人，最後還是趕得上火車的，也就是說，如果他們還能活到那時候的話。不過話又說回來，他們到時候也許早就心情不佳，遊興闌珊。耗費生命中最美好的時光去賺錢，為了享受最不寶貴的時間裏那一點可疑的自由，這使我想起了那個英國人，他最先跑到印度去發財，為了日後可以回英國，過上一種詩人般的生活。其實，他應該馬上住上小閣樓去。"甚麼？"一百多萬愛爾蘭人從四面八方的窩棚裏大聲驚呼道，"我們修造的這條鐵路，難道不是一個好東西嗎？"是的，我回答說，是比較好，要不然你們會做得更差呢；不過，既然你們是我的弟兄們，我希望你們過的日子能比這挖土工作來得更美好。

　　我的房子落成之前，我希望通過誠實而又愉快的方式，賺到十塊或者十二塊錢，來應付我的額外開支，於是，我在房子附近大約二英畝半沙土地上種了點東西，主要是豆子，也種了一點馬鈴薯，還有玉米、豌豆和蘿蔔。整塊地總共十一英畝，大抵種植松樹和山核桃樹，上一個季度，一英畝賣到八塊零八分錢。一位農場主人說，這塊地"沒有甚麼用處，只好養幾隻嘰嘰叫的松鼠"。我沒有給這塊地施過肥，因為我不是這塊地的主人，僅僅是個合法定居者，我也不指望再耕種這麼多的地，就沒有一下子鋤完這塊地。我在犁地時挖出了好幾堆樹樁頭，供我燃用了好長時間，於是留下了小小幾圈有待開墾的肥沃土地，夏天裏一眼就能看出來，因為那處的豆子長得份外茂盛。我房子後面那些枯死、多半賣不掉的樹木，以及從湖上漂過來的木材，提供了我尚待補足的燃料。我還租了一套馬匹犁地，僱了一個短工幫我耕地，雖然仍由我親自扶犁。在頭一個季度，我的農場開支，例如農具、種子等等，是十四塊七角二分錢。玉米種子是別人送給我的。這實在也值不了多少錢，除非你種得太多。我收穫了十二蒲式耳 [44] 豆子，十八蒲式耳馬鈴薯，此外還有一些豌豆和甜玉米。黃玉米和蘿蔔種得太晚了，一無所得。我的農場全部收入是——，

十八蒲式元

扣除支出費用 14.725 元

結餘 8.715 元

除了我消費掉的和手頭還存有的農產品以外，當時估算約值四塊半錢——我手頭的這筆錢，已超過了我沒有種植的那一點菜蔬。經過全面考慮，那就是說，我考慮到人的靈魂和今天的重要性，儘管我的實驗只佔用了很短時間，不，也許正是由於時間很短，我相信，我當年的收成要比康科德任何一個農場主人的都好。

第二年，我做得更開心了，因為我完全鏟平了所需的土地，約有三份之一英畝。我根本沒有被許多有關耕作的名著嚇倒，其中包括亞瑟・楊 [45] 的著作，我從兩年來的經驗中認識到，一個人要是過簡樸日子，只吃自己種的糧食，而且吃多少種多少，不拿糧食貪得無厭去交換更奢侈、更昂貴的物品，那麼，他只需要種一兩平方桿度量單位，[46] 的地就夠了。這麼一點土地，用鐵鍬翻地要比用牛耕地更便宜，每次可更換一塊新地，省得給舊地不斷施肥，所有必要的農耕工作，他只要在夏天抽空做一點就可以了。這麼一來，他就不會像今日那樣被一頭公牛、一匹馬、一頭母牛或者一頭豬拴在一起了。我希望就這個問題說話時力求不帶偏見，因為不管它成功也好、失敗也好，我對目前經濟和社會措施都不感興趣。我比康科德任何一個農人更要特立獨行，因為我不管怎樣沒有給鎖定在哪一所房子裏面或者哪一個農場上，而是可以隨着自

己的悟性行事，悟性是瞬息萬變的呢。再說，我的日子已經比他們好多了，萬一我的房子着火了，或者說我收成欠佳了，我的日子還可以像往昔一樣過得很不賴。

我常常這樣想，不是人在放牛，而是牛在牧人，反正前者有更多自由。人與牛是在交換勞動。如果說我們考慮的只是必不可缺的勞動，那麼，牛就具有很大優勢，牠們的農場也是大得多。人做的一部份交換勞動，就是在六個星期裏割草曬乾，這可不是兒戲呢。當然，沒有一個生活全面簡單的民族，亦即沒有一個賢哲民族，會犯下如此大錯，竟讓牲畜去勞動。說真的，過去從來沒有過，將來也未必很快會有那麼一個賢哲民族，是不是一定要有，我也說不定。不管怎麼說，我絕不會馴養一匹馬或者一頭牛，讓牠替我做任何牠可以做的工作，唯恐自己會成為一名馬夫或者牛倌；如果這樣做了，社會好像成了贏家，難道我們能肯定說，一個人是贏家並不意味着另一個人是輸家，小馬倌跟他的主人一樣有理由感到滿意嗎？就算有些公共設施沒有牛馬的幫助便不能完成，還讓人們與牛馬一起沾沾自喜，難道我們可以得出結論說，人們就不可能做出更令人稱道的事情來嗎？人們在牛馬的幫助下開始從事不僅僅毫無必要或者毫無藝術感，而且又奢侈、又懶散的工作，那就有少數人無可避免去跟牛馬交換勞動，或者換句話說，少數人便成了最強者的奴隸。就這樣，人不僅給他內心的獸性工作，而且作為這方面的一種象徵，還要給他身外的獸性工作。雖說我們已經有了許多磚塊或石塊砌成的房子，但是一個農人的富有與否，仍然要看他的穀倉在多大程度上蓋過了他住的房子。據說這一帶最大的房子都辟為耕牛、奶牛和馬匹的廄舍，而且比城鎮裏的公共建築也毫不遜色；可是，這個縣裏可供信仰自由或言論自由的廳堂卻絕無僅有。國家為何偏偏不是用抽象的思維能力，而是要靠大興土木來給自己豎立紀念碑呢？一部《福者之歌》[47]比東方各國的所有廢墟還要令人讚歎不已！塔樓和廟宇是王孫公子們的奢侈品。

一顆單純的獨立心靈不會聽從任何王孫公子的旨意去做苦工。天才不是給予任何皇帝的訂金，連那有形的金子、銀子或者大理石也不是，即使是的話，也是微乎其微。請問，開鑿這麼多的石頭到底是為了甚麼？我在奧卡狄亞，古希臘一高原地區，後來在詩歌中常比喻為簡樸的田園牧歌式生活。就沒有看到有任何人在開鑿岩石。許多國家都像瘋了似的，癡心妄想留下大量石雕，讓自己永垂不朽。要是他們付出同樣的心血來打磨自己的風度，那又會是甚麼樣呢？理智要比一座高得可攀月的紀念碑更值得流傳下去。我偏偏喜歡岩石留在原地不動。底比斯，埃及尼羅河畔一古城，以石雕聞名，是世界著名古跡之一。它的宏偉是一種庸俗的宏偉。一座有一百個城門的底比斯城，早就遠離了人生的真正目標，遠不如圍繞老實人的田地的一桿長石頭牆那麼合情合理。野蠻的異教徒的宗教和文明修建了許多華麗的寺院；而被你們稱之為基督教的卻沒修建些甚麼。一個國家所開鑿的岩石，十之八九只供它的墳墓使用。它活埋了自己。說到金字塔，它們原本說不上是甚麼奇蹟不奇蹟，不過令人吃驚的倒是在於：有那麼多人竟然如此忍辱負重，不惜耗盡自己的性命，為某個野心勃勃的傻瓜修造墳墓，其實，這個傻瓜還不如淹死在尼羅河裏，隨後扔他的屍體餵狗，反而顯得更聰明些、更有幾分鬍眉漢的氣派。也許我還可以給他們和他尋找一些藉口，可惜我沒有這閒工夫。至於那些建築師的宗教信仰和藝術愛好，倒是全世界都一樣的，不管他們修造的是埃及神廟，還是美國銀行。成本總是超過實用價值。主要動力是虛榮，對大蒜、麵包、牛油的熱愛則出力相助。年輕有為的建築師，巴爾科姆先生，悉心追隨維特魯威 [48] 他用硬鉛筆和直尺設計了一張圖紙，隨後交它給多布森父子採石公司。當三十個世紀開始俯視它時，人類則開始仰視它。說到你們那些高樓和紀念碑，這個鎮上有過一個瘋瘋癲癲的傢伙，要開挖一條通往中國的隧道，他已挖得很深很深，據他所說，他已經聽到了中國的水鍋和茶壺裏煮沸的響聲；不過我想，我可不會一反常態去讚賞他挖的那個窟窿。許多人都關注着東方和西方的那些紀念碑——要想知道是誰造的。而我呢，倒是很想知道當時是誰不肯造的——是誰不屑於做這般區區小事。不過算了，還是回到我的各項統計上來吧。

當時，我在村裏又做測量，又做過木工和各種各樣打雜的工作，反正我做過的工作跟我的手指頭一樣多，就這樣，我共賺到了十三塊三角四分錢。八個月的伙食費，就是說，從 7 月 4 日到翌年 3 月 1 日，根據這八個月的時間估算，儘管我在那裏住了兩年多——至於我自己種的馬鈴薯、一點嫩玉米和豌豆都不算在內——結賬當天留在手上的存貨的價值也不算在內，

合計：大米 1.735 元

糖蜜 1.73 元（最便宜的一種糖精）

黑麥 1.0475 元

印第安粗玉米粉 0.99 元（比黑麥便宜）

豬肉 0.22 元

麵粉 0.88 元

（比印第安粗玉米粉貴，而且麻煩）

糖 0.80 元

豬油 0.65 元

蘋果 0.25 元

蘋果乾 0.22 元

甘薯 0.10 元

一個南瓜 0.06 元

一個西瓜 0.02 元

鹽 0.03 元

所有試驗均告失敗。是的，我總共吃掉八塊七角四分錢；不過，我不應該這樣不知羞恥來公佈我的罪過，如果說我不知道我的讀者裏面大多數人跟我有同樣的罪過，他們的行為公之於眾，恐怕還不見得會比我的好吧。第二年，我有時就捉幾條魚來充當正餐，有一次我甚至還宰了一隻糟蹋過我豆子地的土撥鼠——就像韃靼人所說，讓牠的靈魂轉世——並吃掉了牠，部份是為了進行實驗；儘管它有一股麝香味道，牠還是讓我瞬間一飽口福；不過，我知道，長期享受這種野味是不可取的，哪怕你請村裏的屠夫預先將土撥鼠加工處理過也不行。

同一時期內，衣服和其他零星費用，儘管數目不大，卻有：8.4075 元。

油和一些家庭用具 2.00 元，除了洗衣和縫補費用，因為這些工作多半到外頭去請人代勞，賬單還沒有收到——這些費用都是世界上這塊地必須開支的（即使稍微有些超支）——全部錢財支出是：房子 28.125 元。

農場的一年開支 14.725 元

八個月內食物 8.74 元

八個月內衣服及其他開支 8.4075 元

八個月內油及其他開支 2.00 元

總計 61.9975 元。

現在，我是跟那些要謀生的讀者說幾句話。為了支付以上開銷，我出售了農場上的產品，收入計有：23.44 元。

打短工賺得 13.34 元

共計 36.78 元。

從支出中減去此數，還差二十五塊兩角一點七五分——這跟我啟動時的那點錢相差無幾，也就是我原本準備開支的金額，這是一方面——而另一方面，我從中獲得閒暇、獨立和健康，此外還擁有一座舒適的房子，我樂意住多久就住多久。

這些統計資料看上去未免瑣碎，好像沒有多大意思，不過因為相當完整，也就有了一定價值。但凡我開支過的，我全都入了賬。從上述賬目中可以看出，單是食物一項，每星期就要花掉我大約兩角七分錢。在此之後近兩年裏面，我的食物不外乎是黑麥和不發酵的印第安粗玉米粉、馬鈴薯、大米、少量的鹹肉、糖蜜、鹽和飲用水。像我這種對印度哲學精神情有獨鍾的人，以大米為主食，自然非常合適。為了應對一些只愛吹毛求疵的人的反對，我也不妨在此聲明，要是我偶然在外頭用餐——正如過去我常在外頭用餐那樣，相信以後有機會我還會外出用餐——那往往有損於我的家用開支安排。不過我已經說過了，在外頭用餐是常有的事，對這麼一個比較聲明，絲毫不發生影響。

我從兩年的經歷中知道，即使在這個緯度上，獲得一個人所必需的食物，一點也不費事，真是令人難以置信；一個人飲食可以像動物一樣簡單，但仍然保持健康，孔武有力。我只是從玉米地裏摘來一些馬齒莧 [49]，煮熟加鹽，權當一頓正餐，各方面都讓我感到滿意。我之所以附上它的拉丁文學名，是因為它名字雖俗，但味道可不錯。請問，在和平的歲月裏，日常的中午時份，除了品嚐相當豐盛的煮熟加鹽的嫩甜玉米，一個通情達理的人還會要求甚麼？就算我稍微變換一些花樣，也不外乎遷就一下口味，並不是為了健康的緣故。但是，人們免不了經常捱餓，不是因為短缺必需品，而是因為缺乏奢侈品；我還認識一個心地善良的婦人，她認為自己兒子之所以一命嗚呼乃是他只喝白開水的緣故。

讀者也許會看出來，我是從經濟的視角，而不是從美食的角度來處置這個問題。讀者也不會貿然拿我這種節食方法來做試驗，除非他是一個胖子。

最初我用純質印第安粗玉米粉加鹽做麵包，地地道道的鋤頭玉米餅因原先將餅放在鋤頭上烤熟而得名，我放它們在一塊牆面板上，或者一根我造房子時鋸下來的木棍上，然後移到戶外的火堆上去烘烤；但是時常給烤糊了，還帶着一股松樹味道。我也使用過麵粉；到頭來我卻發現黑麥摻上印第安粗玉米粉一起烘烤是最方便的，口味也最好。天冷的時候，連續烘烤幾個這樣的小麵包，就像埃及人一邊小心侍候、一邊翻轉正在孵化中的雞蛋一樣，倒不失為一件趣事。它們是我烘烤成熟的真正穀物果實，在我的五種官能中，它們如同其他高貴果實似的具有一種芳香，我用一塊布包起它們，盡可能長時間保存着這種芳香。我研究了不可或缺的古代麵包的製作工藝，向有關權威人士求教，一直追溯到原始時代，首次發明未經發酵的食品，那時人類從啖食堅果生肉的野蠻狀態，首次達到了麵包這種食物的味道和優雅境界。隨後，我從循序漸進的研究中，了解到據說就是那個偶然間發酵的麵團教會了人們發酵的過程，自此以後經過各種發酵作用，我終於讀到了"優質、味甜和有益於健康的麵包"，這一生命的支柱。有人認為酵母是麵包的靈魂，填充麵包細胞組織的精神，像女灶神維斯太的聖火一樣，以虔誠的方式保存下來 —— 我在想這好幾瓶珍貴的酵母，最初還是"五月花"號，[50] 帶來的，為美國立下了大功，它的影響至今仍然在上升、膨脹，波及四方，就像這片國土上麥浪在起伏蕩漾 —— 這酵母，我是從村裏定期取得，準確可靠，直到有一天早上，我不知怎的忘了慣例，用開水燙壞了我的酵母；從這個意外事故中，我發現其實酵母有沒有也無所謂 —— 因為我的發現是分析的經過，而不是綜合的過程 —— 自此以後，我就乾脆省掉了酵母，儘管大多數主婦滿懷熱忱勸說過我，不經過發酵，恐怕麵包不太安全，而且還不利於健康；而老人們則預言說體力很快會衰退的。但我發現酵母並不是必不可缺的成份，不用酵母，我照樣過了一年，如今還不是在這塊充滿活力之地好好活着。我很高興總算用不着口袋裏總裝着一個瓶子，有時它會砰的一聲爆裂，瓶子裏面的東西全給抖出來，讓我好不尷尬。省掉了酵母，這樣就更簡便，質量反而更好。人這種動物，與其他動物相比，更能適應各種各樣的氣候和環境。我也沒有給麵包裏放過甚麼鹽、蘇打，或者其他酸性和鹼性的東西。看來我是根據基督出生前大約兩個世紀的馬庫斯‧波修斯‧卡托[51]的配方做麵包。"Manus mortariutmque bene lavato. Farinam in mortarium indito, aquae paulatim addito, subigitoque pulchre. Ubi bene subegeris, defingito, coquitoque sub testu." 這段拉丁文，我的理解是："揉麵製作麵包是這樣的。洗淨你的手和揉麵長槽。投粗麵粉入長槽。逐漸加水，揉得要透徹。揉好後捏成麵包的形狀，最後蓋上蓋子烘烤。"也就是說，在小烘鍋裏烘烤。全文沒有一個字提到發酵的。不過，我也不總是使用這生命的支柱。有過一陣子，由於囊中羞澀，我有一個多月沒有見到過麵包。

在這塊適宜種植黑麥和印第安粗玉米的土地上，每個新英格蘭人都毫不費力生產出自己所需的麵包原料，而不依靠價格波動的遠方市場來獲取原料。無奈我們如今生活既不簡樸，又缺乏獨立性，在康科德，新鮮香甜的玉米粉在商店裏幾乎很少出售。玉米片和更粗一點的玉米，差不多沒有人食用了。農場主人都用自己生產的部份穀物餵牲畜和豬，自己卻出了高昂的代價，到商店裏購買未必有益健康的麵粉。我想，我毫不費力可種上一兩蒲式耳黑麥和印第安玉米，因為前者在最貧瘠的地裏都能生長，後者也用不着肥沃的土地。只要用手磨碾碎了它們，沒有大米，沒有豬肉，也照樣過日子；如果說我一定要用一些濃縮的甜味素，我通過實驗發現從南瓜或甜菜面就可以熬出一種非常好的糖蜜來；我還知道，我只要栽幾棵槭樹，也就更容易得到這種糖蜜；哪怕這幾種菜蔬還在生長期間，我也可以利用各種替代品，取代我上面提到的那些東西。"因為，"有如祖先們歌唱的——我們可以用南瓜、防風和核桃樹葉釀成美酒，滋潤我們的雙唇。據稱選自約翰‧華爾納‧巴伯爾的《歷史詩選》(1839 年版)。最後，說到鹽，雜貨裏面的大路貨。要想尋找鹽，不妨借此機會到海邊去走走，或者換句話說，完全不用鹽，也許我還很少喝水呢。反正我沒聽說過，印第安人會費煞苦心去尋找鹽。

就這樣，我避免一切買賣與物物交換，至少食物一項是這樣。幸好我已有了一個安身之處，剩下來的就是穿着和燃料這兩項了。我現在穿的這條褲子，是在一個農人家庭裏織成的 —— 謝天謝地，人身上依然還有那麼多的美德呢；因為我覺得，農人一下子降為技工，就像人降為農人，兩者同樣偉大，令人難忘。新來乍到鄉間，燃料是一件夠你傷腦筋的事。至於棲息之地，如果不讓我繼續住在依法可以佔用的公地，那我不妨按我耕種過的那塊土地出讓價格 —— 即八塊八角錢，另外購置一英畝地。事實上，我倒是覺得，我在這裏居住後，使這塊土地反而增值了。

有一批不肯輕信的人，有時會問我諸如此類的問題，比方說，我是不是覺得自己光吃蔬菜就能活下去；為了立時揭示事物的實質 —— 因為實質就是信念 —— 我慣常這樣回答說：我只靠木板上的釘子，照樣也能活下去。他們如果連這話都聽不懂，那不管我說多少，反正他們還是聽不懂。聽說有個年輕人做過半個月試驗，拿他的牙齒當研缽，光啃連皮帶穗的玉米過日子。松鼠族做過同樣的試驗，獲得成功。人類對此試驗很感興趣，雖然有少數幾個老婦人對此類試驗力不從心，或者說在磨坊裏擁有三份之一產權，她們會感到擔心。

我的家具 —— 部份是我自己打造的，其餘部份沒花過多少錢，所以也沒有記賬 —— 包括一張牀、一張桌子、一張寫字枱，三把椅子、一塊直徑三英寸的鏡子、一把火鉗、一個壁爐柴架、一把水壺、一個長柄平底鍋、一個煎鍋、一把長柄勺、一個臉盆、兩副刀叉、三個盤子、一隻杯、一把勺、一個油罐、一個糖罐以及一盞塗上日本油漆的燈。沒有人會窮得只好坐在一個南瓜上。那就是苟且偷安。村裏的閣樓上，有許許多多我喜歡的椅子，只要你喜歡，儘管拿走就是了。家具！謝天謝地，我能坐，我也能站，用不着家具公司來幫忙。可是有人看見自己的家具——不外乎是一些少得可憐的空箱——裝在馬車上，串鄉走村，暴露在光天化日，眾目睽睽之下，除了聖哲以外，誰會不羞慚得無地自容呢？這莫非是斯波爾丁[52]看過這麼一車家具，我看不出它是屬於一個所謂富人的呢，還是屬於窮人的；這些家具的主人彷彿總是窮困潦倒似的。說真的，反正這樣的東西，你越多，你就越窮。每一車裝的好像都是十幾個窩棚裏面的東西；一個窩棚如果說是窮的，那它豈不是窮十幾倍。我們既然總是在搬家，為甚麼不扔掉我們的家具，扔掉我們的蛻皮；最後離開這個界域，到另一個置備新家具的界域，而通通燒掉老家具呢？這就像有人在自己腰帶上扣了所有圈套，只要他搬家經過我們撒下繩索的荒野時，不能不拽動那些繩索，從而給拽進了自己的圈套裏去。他是一隻走運的狐狸，尾巴給掐斷在陷阱裏。麝鼠為了逃命，就會咬斷自己的第三條腿。難怪人已失去了自己的靈活性。有多少次他走上了絕路啊！"先生，恕我太魯莽，你說的絕路是甚麼意思？"如果説你是一個預言家，不管甚麼時候碰到一個人，你都會看出他所擁有的一切，還有許多他佯裝不是自己的東西，甚至他廚房裏的用具和破爛的零星雜物，他都要留着，捨不得燒掉，彷彿他被拴在它們的軛上，用力拖着它們往前趕路。有一個人從一個節孔或者一道門穿過去，而他身後的一車子家具卻穿不過去，我說，此時此刻，這個人就是走上絕路了。我聽說有個衣冠楚楚、外表壯碩的人，看上去很自由，萬事齊備，沒承望他說到自己"家具"不知道有沒有買保險，就在這時，我不由得憐憫起他。"我的家具該怎麼辦呢？"於是，我的快活的蝴蝶，就這樣被蜘蛛網糾纏在一起了。甚至還有這樣一些人，多年來好像並沒有甚麼家具，不過你要是細問一下，你就會發現，他在某某人的穀倉裏面儲存好些家庭用具。我看當今英格蘭就像一個垂垂老去的紳士，帶着許許多多行李外出旅行，全是長年累月節儉持家積下來的破爛玩意，就是沒有勇氣全部燒掉它們；大箱，小箱，手提箱，還有大大小小的包裹。至少前面三樣東西該扔掉吧。今日就算身體不錯的人，恐怕也不會拿了褲子[53]來到處閒逛，因此，我當然要勸告有病的人不妨丟下褲子，迅速小跑吧。我碰到過一個移民，扛着他那全部家當的包裹 —— 看上去好像他脖子根後面長出來的一大巨瘤 —— 跌跌撞撞似的走着。我覺得他怪可憐的，倒不是因為他總共只有這麼一點，而是因為他還要抬着那個玩意。如果我也非得拖着圈套走路不可，那我就會小心留神，拖一個輕一點的，別讓它夾住我的要害部位。但是，千萬別讓你的手掌進入圈套，也許這才叫做最聰明。

順便提一下，我不會花錢去買甚麼窗簾的，因為除了太陽和月亮，我覺得不需要在屋子外頭擋住喜歡偷窺的人；我倒是樂意他們往裏面看一看。月亮不會使我的牛奶發酸，也不會讓我的肉發臭，而太陽也不會損壞我的家具，或者使我的地毯褪色，如果說這位朋友有時候太熱情了，那我覺得躲到大自然提供的簾子後面去，從開支上來說倒是更值得，不必在家用賬上另添一筆費用。有一次，一位太太要送我一塊草墊，無奈我屋裏面找不到讓它鋪開的空間，也沒時間在屋裏屋外去打掃它，我就只好謝絕了，寧可在我門前的草地上擦擦自己的鞋底。最好是在邪惡一露頭之前就避而遠之。

過後不久，我參加了一次教會執事動產的拍賣，因為他的生命並沒有白活 —— 人們做了惡事，死後免不了遭人唾罵。[54]大部份東西照例都是很寒酸，打從他父親在世時就開始積存下來。這裏面居然還有一條乾絛蟲。在他的閣樓和其他垃圾堆裏躺了半個世紀之後，這些東西並沒有給燒掉；豈止沒有付之一炬，或者說火化銷毀掉，如今還拿來拍賣，換句話說，讓它們的生命得以延續下去。街坊四鄰匆匆聚攏來看看這些玩意，一口氣全給買下來，隨後小心翼翼搬它們進自家的閣樓和垃圾堆，讓它們躺在那裏，直到各自家產進行清理時，它們另一次搬家又開始了。人死了，不外乎踢起某些家產上的灰塵。

某些野蠻民族的風俗，我們不妨學一學，也許大有裨益，因為他們至少每年從表面上看彷彿總要舉行蛻皮求新似的活動；這是他們的處世理念，不管他們實際上有沒有做到。正如巴特拉姆[55]描述穆克拉斯族印第安人的風俗那樣，我們倘能也有類似除舊祭祀活動，或者換句話說，舉辦第一批果實節[56]，豈不是很好嗎？"一個小鎮節慶活動，"巴特拉姆這麼說道，"大家早就給自己準備好新衣服、新壺、新罐、新盤子，以及其他家用器皿和家具，通通收攏穿過的舊衣服和其他廢物，打掃和清理他們的房子、廣場和整個小鎮，一把扔這些舊東西（包括所有餘糧以及其他舊物）到一個公共的堆物垛上付之一炬。隨後大家服藥禁食三天，全鎮禁絕煙火。禁食期間，他們一概不進食，清心寡慾。這時大赦令宣佈，所有罪犯都可以回到小鎮上來——

"到了第四天早上，大祭司兩手摩擦着乾燥的木頭，在公共廣場上燃起新的火焰，鎮上每戶人都從這裏取得了新生、純潔的火種。"

隨後，他們品嚐新的玉米和水果，一連三天載歌載舞，"後四天，他們接待毗鄰鎮上的朋友來訪，共慶節日，因為這些朋友也按同樣的方式淨化自己並且準備就緒。"

墨西哥人每過五十二年也會在年底進行一次同樣的淨化活動，他們相信大千世界每過五十二年就會暫告一段落。

我幾乎從未聽説過比這更真誠的聖禮，也就是説，如同字典上釐定的，"一種內在的心靈美轉為外在的可見到的神跡。"我一點都不懷疑，他們這種做法原先是由天意直接傳授，雖然他們沒有一部像《聖經》那樣的書籍來記述這種啟示。

五年多來，我就這樣光靠雙手工作，養活了我自己，而且我還發現一年裏面只要工作六個星期，就足夠支付我所有的生活開支。整個冬天，還有大部份夏天，我自由自在，安心讀書。我全力以赴辦過私學，發現我的各項支出與我的收入基本相抵，或者略有超支，因為我不得不穿衣服、坐火車，更不用説還要有相應的思考和信仰，結果我的時間都耗費在這件事上。我教書不是為了我的同胞受益，而是為了自己謀生，所以這次辦學失敗了。我還試過做生意，但我發現，要想經商發財，就得花上十年時間，到了那時，也許我正在趕去見魔鬼的路上。説真的，我發愁的是，到了那時候，我也許正在做所謂的好生意。從前，我在到處尋找甚麼謀生之道時，由於依照朋友的願望，腦海裏不時浮現一些可悲的經歷，已使我耗盡精力，於是，我常常認真思想還不如去撿漿果算了；反正這工作我肯定做得來，而且，那一點蠅頭小利對於我也足夠了 —— 因為我的最大本領是需求很少 —— 這只需要一點資金，對我素常的情緒又極少抵觸，我就這麼帶點傻氣在思考着。我的朋友一點不猶豫，做起了生意或者就業了，而我想自己這個職業倒是很像他們的行業；整個夏天，我漫遊於羣山之間，路見漿果就撿起來，之後又隨意扔掉它們，好像在看守阿德墨托斯古希臘神話中的塞薩利國王，曾去海外尋找金羊毛的阿爾戈英雄之一，阿波羅替他看管過羊羣。我還夢想自己不妨採集野草，或者用乾草車輛運些常青樹給喜愛樹木的村民，甚至於運到城裏去。但是從這以後，我才明白，商業詛咒它經管的每一件事，就算你經營的是天堂的福音，還是躲不開商業對它的全部詛咒。

由於我非常喜愛某些事物，特別珍惜和重視個人自由，而且我能吃苦，又能獲取成功，所以，我並不希望浪費時光，去賺取華麗的地毯或者其他優質家具，或者味美可口的烹調術，或者修造一幢古希臘式或哥德式的房子。這些東西要是有人唾手可得，得到之後還懂得如何使用它們的話，那我乾脆讓他們去追求算了。有些人是"勤勞的"，似乎天生熱愛勞動，或者也許因為勞動使他們避免去做更要不得的壞事；對諸如此類的人，目前我還是無話可説。至於那些有了比現在更多的閒暇，卻不懂得如何安排的人，也許我會奉勸他們要比過去更努力工作——一直工作到他們能養活自己，獲得他們的自由身份證件。至於我自己，我發現，所有職業中，打短工的人是最獨立不羈，特別是短工這個職業，一年裏面只要三四十天，就可以養活自己了。夕陽西下時，打短工的工作也告結束，隨後他就自由自在，專心從事自己喜愛的、但跟白天工作毫不相干的事；可是他的僱主要做投機買賣，從這一個月到下一個月，反正一年到頭連氣都喘不過來。

總之，根據信仰和經驗，我確信，一個人在這個世界上謀生，只要生活得簡樸和聰明，並不是一件苦事，而是一種消遣；有如生活較為簡樸的民族，其追求至今還是不大自然的體育運動。一個人要謀生，其實用不着汗流浹背，除非他比我還容易出汗。

我認識一個繼承過好幾英畝地的年輕人，他跟我說他覺得自己應該像我這樣生活，如果說他有辦法的話。我並不願意有人採用我的生活方式，不管出於甚麼理由；因為在他還沒有學會我的生活方式以前，也許我已經尋找到另一種生活方式；我倒是希望在這個世界上，各不相同的人越多越好；但我又希望，每個人都要小心謹慎，尋找和追求他自己的方式，而不是他父親的、他母親的或者他鄰居的方式。年輕人可以造房子，可以種植，可以航海，只要不阻撓他去做他告訴我他喜歡做的事就行了。僅僅從精確的視點來看，我們是聰明的，如同水手或者逃亡的奴隸兩眼盯着北極星一樣；這一點就足以引導我們一輩子了。也許我們在預定期間到達不了我們的港口，可是我們也不會偏離正確的航線。

在這裏，但凡適用於一個人的，無疑更適用於一千個人，比方說，一所大房子，按比例來說，並不比一個小房子造價更昂貴，因為一個屋頂可以覆蓋幾個房間，底下合用一個地窖，一堵牆可分隔出幾個房間來，不過，我個人偏愛離羣獨居。再說，與其說服別人相信合用一堵牆的好處，你還不如自己動手造房子，通常會更便宜。你要是跟別人合用一堵牆，固然更便宜，但是合用這堵隔牆一定很薄，説不定你的鄰居人品不好，到時候他那半邊牆壞了，也不會去修繕的。通常可行的那種合作，也是極其有限，而且是表面上的；就算有那麼一點真正的合作，表面上也看不出來，是要有一種聽不見的和諧。如果説一個人有信心，那他不論到哪裏都會跟同樣有信心的人合作；如果説他沒有信心，那他會像世界上其他的人一樣，繼續過自己的日子，不管他跟甚麼人做伴。合作無非就是讓我們生活在一起。最近我聽説，有兩個年輕人打算結伴環球旅行，一個人沒錢，一路上就在桅桿前和犁耙後面賺錢，而另一個人口袋裏裝着一張旅行支票。他們不論結伴也好、合作也好，一眼就看出來，都不會持久的，因為其中一個人根本甚麼事都做不了。他們在路上碰到第一個令人關注的危機時，就會散夥。最重要的是，我在上面説過的，單獨出去旅行的人可以今天説走就走，而結伴旅行卻要等到另一個人準備就緒，也許還要等上很長時間才能上路。

不過，這一切都是非常自私的，我就聽到過我鎮上有些人這樣説。我承認直到現在為止，我很少致力於慈善事業。我有一種責任感，為此我作出了一些犧牲，其中包括行善樂趣。有人施盡所有花招，勸我資助鎮上一些窮困家庭；如果説我沒有甚麼事可做 —— 因為魔鬼只給閒人找事做 —— 也許我會試着做諸如此類的娛樂消遣。可是，每當我想到自己要肆意從事這方面活動，讓某些窮人在各方面過得像我自己過的日子一樣舒適，當他們享受天堂般的生活為一種義務，乃至於已經向他們提供了幫助，沒想到他們一點不猶豫，一致表示寧願繼續貧困下去。我們鎮上的男男女女已在想盡辦法，竭力為自己的同伴們謀福祉，我相信，這至少可以使人不去做沒有人情味的事情。從事慈善事業，如同從事其他事情一樣，非得具備天資不可。至於“做好事”，那是一種充滿激情的職業。況且，我不管怎樣也嘗試過呢。看來也許很奇怪，這種事不合我的脾性，因此我倒是對自己覺得很滿意。也許我不應該故意迴避自己這種特殊的職責，即社會要求我去做的拯救宇宙、使它免遭毀滅的好事。我相信在其他地方，確實有一種類似的，卻無限堅定的力量，至今仍在保護這個宇宙。不過，我不會阻攔任何一個人去發揮他的天才。這種事我自己是不做的，但是有人全心全意，終其一生去做，我就會對他說，哪怕世人叫它做壞事，他們很可能會有這樣看法，可你們也一定要堅持下去。

我絕對不是說我的情況特殊。毫無疑問，我的讀者裏面有許多人都會作出類似的辯白。在做某件事的時候 —— 我不敢保證說我的左鄰右里會叫做好事 —— 毫不猶豫我會說自己是一個首屈一指的僱工；但我為甚麼是首屈一指的僱工，這就要我的僱主去發現。我做甚麼好事，通常對"好"這個字的理解來說，一定是我的份外事，而且十之八九完全是我無意之中做的。人們幾乎都這樣說，你就照現在的樣子，從自己身邊開始，別指望成為更有價值的人，而首先要有一顆善心，才會去做好事。如果我完全仿效這種論調說教，還不如乾脆這麼說："去吧，先開始做個好人吧。"好像太陽用自己的火焰照亮了月球或者一顆六等星後，應該停下來，如同羅賓·古德費洛 [57] 一樣，窺探每個村舍的窗，使人瘋瘋癲癲，叫肉食變味，使黑暗變得可以看得見東西；而不是漸漸增加它那宜人的熱量和恩澤，直到它變得如此光芒四射，沒有人能夠仰望它的臉，隨後，也就是說，與此同時，行走在自己的軌道上，繞着地球做好事，或說得更準確些，正如一種更為真實的哲學思想發現的，地球繞着太陽周轉，從而得到了恩澤。法厄同 [58] 一心想以惠澤世人來證明自己是天神出身，就駕着太陽神的四馬金車出遊，僅僅走了一天，即越出軌道，燒掉了天堂下面好幾排街上的房子，烤焦了大地表層，燒乾了每個春天，打造了撒哈拉大沙漠，直到最後朱庇特 [59] 一聲霹靂把他擊斃在地上，而太陽為他的死哀慟逾恆，整整一年沒有發光。

行善走了味，那才是奇臭難聞。有如人的腐屍，神的腐屍一樣。如果我確實知道有人要到我家來特意為我做好事，那我肯定要逃命了，就像躲避非洲沙漠裏所謂西蒙風[60]，乾熱灼人，刮得你嘴巴裏、鼻子裏、耳朵裏、眼睛裏全是沙土，直到把你窒息至死，我唯恐他向着我做起好事來──它的病毒會跟我的血液摻雜在一起。不──要是真的這樣，我寧可遭災受難，反而來得自然呢。如果有這麼一個人，儘管我肚子餓了，他會來餵飽我，我快凍死了，他來溫暖我，我要是掉進水溝，他會拉我上來，但我並不認為他就是好人。我不妨就找一條紐芬蘭狗給你看，牠也樣樣做得到呢。從廣義上說，慈善並不是泛愛同胞。霍華德[61]從他個人的作為來說，無疑是極其善良而備受尊敬的人，而且，他的善行也已得到了善報；但是，相比較而言，在我們最值得接受幫助的時候，霍華德的慈善行為要是落實不到我們擁有最好的財產的這些人身上，就算有上百個霍華德，對我們來說，又有甚麼用處呢？我從來沒有聽說過，有哪個慈善大會曾誠心誠意提議給我，或像我這樣的人去做點好事。

耶穌會會士已被印第安人所挫敗，這些印第安人在被綁住活活燒死之際，竟向行刑者提出了一些新的折磨方式。他們雖然肉體受苦但並不屈服，有時候他們對傳教士所給予的安慰也無動於衷。你們應該奉行的法則是，行刑時在他們耳邊少說規勸之類的話，至於他們如何被折磨至死，倒是他們自己都並不在乎。他們反而用一種新的方式去愛他們的仇敵，對後者所做的一切罪惡幾乎全給寬赦了。

窮人遠遠落在你們後面，對你們來說是一種儆醒勸誡，因此，你務必給窮人最需要的幫助。如果說你給錢，那你還要拿錢跟他們一起花掉，切不可把錢一扔給他們就完事了。有時候，我們會犯一些莫名其妙的錯誤。窮人儘管邋遢，衣衫襤褸，舉止粗俗，但有時候不見得都是處於饑寒交迫的境況。這多半由於他個人愛好，而並不單單是他的命運多舛所致。如果你給了他錢，也許他會拿這錢去買更多的破爛衣服。我素常憐憫那些笨手笨腳的愛爾蘭勞工，他們在湖上鑿取冰塊，身上穿着破衣爛衫，真的寒酸極了，而我儘管穿着比較乾淨、入時的衣服，還是給凍得瑟瑟發抖。後來，有一個砭人肌骨的大冷天，一個落水的愛爾蘭人來我家裏取暖，我看到他脫下了三條褲子、兩雙襪子，這才見到了皮膚，一點沒錯，儘管這些褲襪簡直骯髒破爛極了，可他還是拒絕了我要送給他的額外衣服，因為他已有那麼多裏面穿的衣服。看他求之若渴的正是這次落水啊。於是，我就開始可憐我自己，我覺得如果送我一件法蘭絨衫，要比送他一家廉價成衣店反而更功德無量。有上千個人在砍罪惡的枝椏，只有一個人砍掉了罪惡之根，也許就是這個在窮人身上花的時間和金錢最多的人，通過他的生活方式正在造的孽也最多，雖然他千方百計想要加以補救，但還是徒勞。正是假虔誠的蓄奴主拿出奴隸創造的利潤的十份之一，給其他奴隸購買星期日的自由。有的人僱用窮人幫廚，來顯示自己對窮人的慈悲心。要是他們親自下廚房工作，豈不是更慈悲嗎？你誇口説捐自己收入的十份之一給慈善事業，也許你應該捐出收入的十份之九去行善，善始善終嘛。即使這樣，社會收回來的也只有財富的十份之一。這歸咎於財富佔有者的慷慨大方呢，還是公正的官員們的粗心大意？

慈善事業幾乎可以説是人類讚賞備至的唯一美德。不，這的確對它估計過高了；而正是我們的自私才對它估計過高了。康科德一個陽光燦爛的日子裏，有一個粗壯的窮人，向我誇讚鎮上一個市民，因為正如他所説，這個市民對窮人很善良，而這個窮人就是他自己。人類裏面善良的大伯大嬸們，要比真正的聖靈父母更受尊敬。有一次，我聽到英格蘭的一個才學兼優的牧師在話説英國，他先是列舉了英國的科學、文學和政治領域的偉大人物，比方説，莎士比亞、培根、克倫威爾、彌爾頓以及牛頓等人，隨後，他説到了英國基督教的英雄們，好像他的職業要求他務必如是説似的，他一味抬高基督教的英雄們，使他們凌駕於上述所有的偉人之上，成為偉人中的偉人。這些基督徒英雄就是佩恩、霍華德和弗萊夫人。人們一定都會覺得他在胡扯。最後三位並不是英國的最佳男人和女人，也許只好算作英國的最佳慈善家罷了。

至於慈善事業應該得到的讚揚，我是不會加以貶損的。我僅僅是要求把公正給予所有用自己的生命和勞動為人類造福的人。我器重一個人並不是以他的正直與善行為主要依據，因為兩者不外乎是他的枝枝葉葉罷了。我們拿綠葉枯乾後的草木做成藥茶給病人喝，這種用處可說微乎其微，大抵被江湖醫生所利用。我要的是一個人好比能開花結果，讓芳香從他那裏向我飄過來，成熟果子就在我們的交往中芳香四溢。想必他的善良不是局部的、短暫的行為，而是持久的、綽綽有餘，對他絲毫無損，但也是無意識的行為。這是一種掩蓋萬惡的善行。慈善家總是念念不忘，要把自己一文不值的悲憫給芸芸眾生營造一種氣氛，美其名曰同情心。我們應該廣泛施予人們的是我們的勇氣，不是我們的絕望；是我們的健康和安適，不是我們的病疾，而且還要小心莫讓疾病通過感染四處蔓延。是從哪些南方平原上傳來了號哭聲？我們會給住在甚麼緯度上的異教徒送去光明嗎？誰是我們會去救贖的那個縱慾無度而又殘暴的人呢？如果有人得了病，他就不能履行自己的職責，如果他還感到腸裏疼痛 —— 這可很值得同情 —— 那他就要着手改造 —— 這個世界。作為宇宙的一個縮影，他發現，這是一個真正的發現，而且就是他發現的 —— 這個世界一直在吃青蘋果；事實上，在他的眼裏，地球本身就是一個巨大的青蘋果，想想該有多嚇人，人類的孩子在蘋果還沒有成熟前就去啃它多危險；他那些雷厲風行的慈善團體直接找到了愛斯基摩人和巴塔哥尼亞人 [62]，還體察了人口稠密的印度和中國的村舍；就這樣，經過好幾年慈善活動，有權有勢的人物卻利用他達到他們自己的目的，毫無疑問，他治好了自己的消化不良症，地球的單頰或雙頰都泛着淡淡的紅暈，好像它正在開始成熟，而生活的粗鄙狀態也已消失，重新恢復美麗健康的原貌。我從來沒有夢見過比我自己所犯更大的罪孽。我從來沒見過，今後也不會見到比我自己更壞的人。

我相信，令改革家這樣悲傷的，並不是他對苦難中的人們表示同情，而是他自己心存愧疚，儘管他是最神聖的上帝之子。讓這一切糾正過來吧，讓春天來到他身邊吧，曙光在他的臥榻上升起來，他將拋棄他慷慨的朋友們。我不反對吸煙的原因，是我從來不吸煙；吸煙的人終究會自食其果，哪怕他已經戒絕；儘管我自己嚐過其他東西也夠多的，我還是可以表示反對。如果說你不慎上當做過一些慈善活動，那就別讓你的左手知道你的右手做過些甚麼，因為就算知道了也沒有意思。救起溺水的人，繫好你的鞋帶。你還是悠閒着一點，去做一些自由的活動。

我們的風度因與聖者交遊而被毀掉了。我們從悅耳的讚美詩中，發出褻瀆上帝和永遠容忍他的迴響。也許有人會說，即使先知和救世主，也只是撫慰人們的恐懼，而不是肯定人們的希望。哪裏都沒有對生命禮物表示簡單而由衷的滿意，以及令人難忘的讚美上帝的記載。所有的成功和健康使我受益，儘管它看上去多麼遙遠而不可冀及；所有的失敗和病恙使我悲傷，讓我遭殃，儘管說不定它很同情我，或者我很同情它。如果說我們真的採用印第安人的、自然成長的、有魅力的，或者說合乎人性的方式來振興人類，那麼，先讓我們自己簡樸和美如同大自然一樣，驅散懸在我們額頭上的烏雲，給我們體內的毛孔注入一點生命活力。再也不要做濟貧院裏教會執事濟貧助理，要努力成為一個值得世人敬重的人。

我在設拉子[63]有舉世聞名的波斯帝國都城波斯波利斯遺跡。謝赫・薩迪[64]所寫的《薔薇園》裏讀到：有人問一位哲學家說：主造了那麼多高大、成蔭、有名的樹，為甚麼單單稱不結果實的柏樹為“自由樹”呢？他回答說：每種樹都有一定的季節，到了那季節，才會茂長，過了那季節，便會凋落。唯有柏樹，不為時間所限，四季常青，所以叫做自由。暫存的一切不要貪求。

哈里發的光榮已成虛無。

巴格達城外的江水萬古長流！

你應像棗樹一樣慷慨大度。

即使你是貧無所有，

也應像柏樹一樣無拘無束。[65]

你實在太放肆，

要求在穹蒼底下有一席之地，

你的破棚屋或者你的木桶

培養出一些懶惰或迂腐的德行，

在廉價的陽光下，或陰涼的泉水邊

啃野菜和蘱根；在那裏你的右手

從心坎上扯去人類的熱情，

美德之花在熱情中燦然開放，

你貶損了大自然，又讓感官麻木不仁，

像蛇髮女妖[66]誰見到她，立即化成頑石。那樣，將活人化成頑石。

我們並不需要這個沉悶的社會

你在那裏務必自我克制，

我們也不需要那種不自然的愚蠢

不知歡樂與悲傷；也不知道

你被迫使虛假消極的韌勁凌駕於

積極的韌勁之上。這低賤的一批人

固定他們的位置在平庸之輩，

成為你的奴性的心靈，可是我們

推崇這樣的美德，承認節制，

勇敢慷慨的行為，莊嚴宏偉，

縱覽一切的審慎，無邊無際的

寬宏大度，還有那種英雄的美德

自古以來沒有留下一個名稱，

只有一些典型，比如赫拉克勒斯，

阿喀琉斯[67]。忒修斯[68]。

回到你可憎的陋屋；

你看到了文明的新天地時，

仔細研究會知道最有價值的是甚麼。[69]

章註

1　馬薩諸塞州的康科德：(又譯麻省)的州府波士頓，位於美國東北部，北美移民最早登陸處。康科德是馬州東部 小鎮 梭羅的家鄉，也是超驗主義學派的活動中心。

2　桑威奇羣島人：即今日夏威夷羣島人。

3　新英格蘭的人：美國東北部 (包括馬薩諸塞州在內) 六州總稱，乃是英國清教徒最早移殖之地。

4　英畝：一英畝等於 40.47 公畝或 6.07 畝或 4047 平方米。

5　奧吉厄斯的牛棚：源自古希臘神話，傳說奧吉厄斯王牛棚裏有 300 頭牛，三十年沒有打掃過，後來赫拉克勒斯以河水打掃牛棚，一天就掃乾淨了。

6　詳見《聖經‧新約全書‧馬太福音》第 6 章 19 節："不要為自己積攢財寶在地上，地上有蟲子咬，能鏽壞，也有賊挖窟窿來偷。" 第 6 章 20 節："只要積攢財寶在天上，天上沒有蟲子咬，不能鏽壞，也沒有賊挖窟窿來偷。"

7　原文為拉丁文，引自古羅馬作家奧維德《變形記》第 1 卷第 414 行，意思是人從此成為堅硬物種，歷盡辛苦，以證明自己的出身來歷。

8　羅利：Sir Walter Raleigh，1552—1618，英國探險家、作家，早期美洲殖民者，頗具傳奇色彩，著有《世界史》。

9　威爾伯福斯：William Wilberforce，1759—1833，從事殖民地奴隸解放活動的英國人，被後人認為思想超前。

10　約翰‧伊夫林：John Evelyn，1620—1706，英國作家，皇家學會創始人之一，寫過有關美術、林學、宗教等著作 30 多部。他的《日記》一書見證了英國 60 年來的政治、社會和宗教生活實況。

11 希波克拉底：Hippocrates，公元前 460—公元前 370，古希臘著名醫生，被譽為 "醫學之父"。

12 亞當：Adam，《聖經》中的人物，相傳為人類始祖，詳見《聖經‧舊約全書‧創世記》。

13 引自《論語‧為政》。

14 李比希：Justus von Liebig，1803—1873，德國化學家，以發展基因理論聞名於世。

15 斑鳩：此處栗色馬與斑鳩，據研究者考證，是暗指已故的梭羅哥哥約翰與少女艾倫‧西華爾，梭羅、約翰同時愛戀着西華爾，但後來梭羅終身未娶。

16 天糧：manna，亦譯 "嗎哪"，古代以色列人抵達曠野獲得從天而降的糧食，故稱天糧，詳見《聖經‧舊約全書‧出埃及記》第 16 章。

17 《日暑》：原文為 Journal，意思是 "雜誌"、"日記"，雙關語。此處指作者自己寫的日記，也可能是為超驗主義會的雜誌。

18 拉‧貝魯斯：Jean Francois de La Perouse，1741—1788，法國航海家，1785 年受法王路易十六指派進行航海探險活動，在新赫布里底羣島以北美拉尼西亞的瓦尼科羅島被當地人殺害。

19 漢諾：Hanno，約生活在公元前 3 世紀後半葉，迦太基航海家，一生富有傳奇色彩。

20 涅瓦河：一條貫穿俄國聖彼得堡的著名大河。

21 菲菲夫人：Mrs. Ida Pfeiffer，1797—1858，奧地利旅行家兼作家。

22 美惠：古希臘神話中，司掌光明、歡樂和豐盛的三女神的總稱。

23 亨利八世：Henry VIII，英國國王，以暴虐和生活糜爛著稱，喜歡華麗服飾。

24 英國女王伊麗莎白一世：Elizabeth I，終身未嫁，以喜愛服飾華麗著稱。

25 塞繆爾‧萊恩，Samuel Laing，1780—1868，英國作家。

26 詳見《聖經‧新約全書‧馬太福音》第 8 章 20 節。

27 拉姆福德：Rumford，1753—1814，美國科學家，曾以發明通風良好的壁爐著稱。

28 詳見《聖經‧新約全書‧馬太福音》第 26 章 11 節。

29 這兩段話引自《聖經‧新約全書‧馬太福音》第 18 章 3 至 4 節。

30 查普曼：George Chapman，1559—1634，英國詩人、劇作家、翻譯家和傳教士，以翻譯荷馬史詩著稱於世。

31 此處引詩參見他寫的悲劇《愷撒與龐培》第 5 幕第 2 場。

32 莫摩斯（Momus），古希臘神話中的嘲弄與指責之神，反對密涅瓦（Minerva），古羅馬神話中的智慧女神。

33 一個管家：此處暗喻《聖經·舊約全書·創世記》中的亞當和夏娃。

34 老約翰遜：Edward Johnson，1598—1672，北美早期移民，歷史學家。

35 特洛伊城眾神：詳見古希臘詩人荷馬的史詩《伊利亞特》。

36 此處亦可指建築物、艦船、鐵路及橋樑等的上部結構或上部建築。

37 源自寒鴉向孔雀借羽毛的寓言。

38 劍橋學院：哈佛大學最早名為劍橋學院。"那家公司"指管理哈佛大學的董事會機構，一直沿襲至今。

39 梭羅一生追隨愛默生，獲益匪淺，在此説出了他的經驗之談。他在本節中談論教育的觀點十分精彩，至今仍發人深省。

40 亞當·斯密：Adam Smith，英國經濟學家，古典政治經濟學的代表人物，從人性出發，主張經濟自由，反對重商主義與國家干預，主要著作有《道德情操論》和《國富論》等。

41 李嘉圖：David Ricardo，英國經濟學家，古典政治經濟學的代表人物，主張自由貿易，提出勞動價值論，主要著作有《政治經濟學及賦税原理》和《論農業的保護》等。

42 薩伊：Jean Baptiste Say，法國早期庸俗政治經濟學的代表人物。

43 蝗蟲和野蜜：此處指施洗約翰。

44 蒲式耳：英美容量單位，在英國為 36.238 升，在美國為 35.238 升。

45 亞瑟·楊：Arthur Young，英國農業科學的先驅，著有許多關於農耕的書。

46 1 平方桿 = 30 平方碼。

47 《福者之歌》：印度古代敘事詩《摩呵婆羅多》中的一部份，以對話形式闡明印度教教義。

48 維特魯威：Marcus Vitruvius，公元前 1 世紀，古羅馬著名建築師，他的著作《建築十書》對文藝復興時期、巴洛克與新古典主義時期均產生了影響。

49 馬齒莧：拉丁文學名 Portulaca Oleracea。

50 "五月花"號：一艘最早前往北美殖民地的英國清教徒所搭乘的船。

51 馬庫斯·波修斯·卡托：Marcus Porcius Cato，公元前 234—公元前 149，古羅馬政治家、作家，著有《史源》和《鄉村篇》等，為拉丁文散文的開創者。

52 斯波爾丁：Gilbert R·Spaulding，美國某著名馬戲團班主，他在美國率先帶領馬戲團坐火車四處演出。梭羅本人家具簡陋，所以調侃説，那些家具像馬戲團變戲法所用的一箱子家當。

53 褥子：此處出典，詳見《聖經·新約全書·馬太福音》第 9 章 6 節：有人用褥子抬着一個癱子讓耶穌治療。耶穌對癱子説："起來，拿你的褥子回家去吧。"

54 人們做了惡事，死後免不了遭人唾罵：引自莎士比亞的名劇《裘力斯‧愷撒》第三幕第二場。朱生豪譯《莎士比亞全集》第 8 卷，第 262 頁，人民文學出版社。

55 巴特拉姆：William Bartram， 1739—1823，美國博物學家，著有《南北加洛拉納旅行記》。

56 果實節：第一批果實節，指一個季節中最早成熟並收穫的農產品，尤指用來祭神的瓜果。

57 羅賓‧古德費洛：英格蘭民間故事中只愛惡作劇的小精靈。

58 法厄同：古希臘神話中太陽神赫里阿斯的兒子，駕着其父的太陽車狂奔，差點焚燒整個世界，幸虧宙斯見狀，用雷將他擊斃，世界才倖免於難。

59 朱庇特：古羅馬神話中主宰一切的主神，統治眾神，其地位相當於古希臘神話中的宙斯。

60 西蒙風：非洲和阿拉伯沙漠的乾熱風。

61 霍華德：John Howard， 1726—1790，英國慈善家，因倡導監獄改革而聞名。

62 巴塔哥尼亞人：居住在阿根廷中部、南部潘帕斯草原和巴塔哥尼亞高原的印第安人。

63 設拉子：伊朗南部城市，古波斯文化中心，有許多大詩人陵墓，東北 60 公里處。

64 謝赫‧薩迪：Saadi，1213—1292，波斯著名詩人，代表作有《果園》與《薔薇園》，含有精深哲理性，在國內外產生深遠影響。此處借用著名翻譯家水建馥譯文，詳見《魯達基‧海亞姆‧薩迪‧哈菲茲作品選》，潘慶舲、水建馥、邢秉順譯，人民文學出版社 1998 年版，第 338 頁。

65 補充詩篇貧窮的托詞可憐的窮鬼。

66 蛇髮女妖：古希臘神話中三個蛇髮女妖之一，即戈爾戈（譯音），面目猙獰。

67 阿喀琉斯：希臘神話中英雄人物之一，出生後被其母手握腳跟，倒提着浸在冥河水中，除腳踵外，渾身刀槍不入。

68 忒修斯：希臘神話中羅馬國王，以殺死牛首人身的怪物米諾陶洛斯而聞名。

69 T‧卡魯托馬斯‧卡魯：Thomas Carew， 1595—1645，英國騎士派詩人，著有長詩《狂喜》和愛情詩《詩集》等。此處題名是梭羅加的。

2

我的住地；我的生活探索

到了我們一生中的某個時期，我們都慣常當每個地方為可以建房安家之處。就這樣，住地周圍方圓十多英里以內的鄉村我通通考察過了。我在想像中已經接二連三全部買下了那處的農場，因為所有的農場都要買下來，反正我心裏對它們的價格一清二楚。我到過每一個農場主人的場址，品嚐過他的野蘋果，跟他談過莊稼，由他開出個價錢，不管甚麼價錢，買下他的農場，在心裏再抵押農場給他，甚至價錢定得高一些——通通都買下來，只是沒有立契約——當他的話為契約，因為我平素最愛閒扯——我開耕了這些土地，從某種程度上說，也算是跟他培養感情，我想，等我閒扯夠了自己就離開，讓他繼續種下去。這番經歷使朋友們都看我為某種地產經銷商。其實，不管我坐在哪裏，我都可以過日子，那裏的風景因此還會為我熠熠生輝。何謂家宅，乃是拉丁文 Sede (椅子)，意即邸宅、別墅——如果是一座鄉村別墅就更好。我發現許多宅子的選址，似乎不大可能很快加以改進，也許有人會覺得它離村莊太遠，但我覺得倒是村莊離它太遠了。算了，我不妨就住在那裏：於是，我果真在那裏住上一個小時、一個夏天和一個冬天；看着我讓歲月如何流逝而去，熬過了嚴冬，轉瞬間春天就到了。這個地區未來的居民，不管他們的住房造在哪裏，都可以肯定那裏已有人捷足先登。只需要一個下午，肯定開闢這塊地為果園、林地和牧場，決定門前應該留下哪些優良的橡樹或者松樹，這麼一來，從哪一個角度來看，每一棵枯萎的樹木都會顯得最美；然後，我暫且放下不管，讓它閒置着，有時讓它休耕，因為一個人總有許許多多事情，反正越是放得下來，也就越是富有。

我神思逸飛未免太遠，乃至於被幾個農場拒絕了 —— 拒絕正是我求之不得呢 —— 但我從來沒有讓現實灼傷過自己的手指頭[1]。跡近現實佔有的那一次，是我購買霍爾維爾鄉間住宅的時候，我已開始選種，還備好材料，打造一輛手推車，用來裝卸種子；殊不知還沒等到業主將契約交給我，他的妻子 —— 每個男人照例都有這樣的妻子 —— 忽然變卦了，打算給自己留着，而他違了約就賠給我十塊錢。說真的，當時我身上竟然只有一角錢，這可叫我算不上來，鬧不清楚，我自己真的有一角錢，或者說有一個農場，或者說有十塊錢，或者說我擁有了這一切。不管怎麼說，我退回了他的十塊錢，連農場也還給他了，因為這事我已經做得十分純熟了；或者換句話說，我做得很漂亮大方，還按照我的買入價賣了農場給他。因為他不是很富裕，我還送給他十塊錢，但是我照舊擁有我的一角錢、種子以及打造手推車的木料。我因此發現我自己一直是個富人，又無損於我的貧窮。但是我留住了那裏的風景。而且打這以後，我每年都帶走它生產的果實，用不着手推車。至於風景 ——

> 我是眺望全景的皇帝，
> 我的權利毋庸爭議。[2]

我經常看到一個詩人，欣賞了農場裏令人叫絕的風景就離去了，而脾氣急躁的農場主人還以為他拿走的只是幾個野蘋果罷了。殊不知詩人已寫了詩吟詠他的農場，而農場主人多少年來都還蒙在鼓裏呢；這麼一道令人豔羨的無形柵籬，已經圈起了農場，擠出它的牛奶來，取其精華 —— 奶油，然後通通拿走，留給農場主人的是撇去了奶油的奶水。

依我看，霍爾維爾鄉間住宅的真正魅力，是它全然遁世隱退之勝地，離村莊兩英里遠，最近的鄰居也在半英里開外，一塊很大的地隔開了它和公路；它以一條河劃界，據農場主人説，春天河面上升起了大霧，霜凍也就不見影子，不過，這可跟我完全風馬牛不相及。農舍和穀倉都是破敗不堪；失修倒塌的柵籬，彷彿在我和早先的居民之間相隔了如此悠久歲月；那些蘋果樹早已中空，長滿苔蘚，還被兔子啃咬過；由此可見，與我比鄰而居的將會是甚麼人；不過，最主要的倒是我回憶到早年溯河而上時，望見那華屋依稀掩映在茂密的紅楓樹叢裏，還聽得到打從那裏傳過來的家犬的吠聲。我急急買下它，等不及業主搬走那些石塊，砍掉樹身早已中空的蘋果樹，連根鏟掉牧場上長出來的小白樺樹，總之，等不及業主進一步收拾妥當了。為了享有上述那些優點，我就索性一不做、二不休吧；如同阿特拉斯[3]一樣，整個世界扛到我肩膀上 —— 我從沒聽説過他得到了甚麼回報 —— 一切全由我自己操作，自然沒有其他甚麼動機和藉口，只等錢款付清，就可平平安安擁有霍爾維爾鄉間別墅。因為我一直知道，只要我讓它自由發展，它就會帶來我預期得到的最豐美的收成。但結果呢，如同我在前文所説的一樣。

因此，有關大規模耕作一事（至今我一直在侍弄着一個園子），我所能説説的只是，種子我早已準備好了。很多人以為種子放得越久越好。我並不懷疑時間是能分得出好與壞的，到了最後我真的要下種時，我想大概總不至於讓我大失所望吧。但是，我要告訴我的夥伴們：你們要盡可能長時間生活得自由自在，無牽無掛。你們捆住自己在農場上，無異於將自己投進大牢裏。

老卡托 —— 他的《鄉村篇》乃是我的"栽培者" —— 我見到以下這段話在他的唯一譯本裏簡直譯得不知所云 —— 其實，他是這樣説的："你想要購置一座農場，腦子裏務必多想想，切莫匆匆買下；也不要怕累、怕麻煩，不去多看看，更不要以為繞着它轉了一圈就夠了。如果説農場真是不錯的話，那裏你去得越是勤，你就會越是喜歡它。"我想，我不會匆匆買它下來，反正我能活多久，就繞着它轉多久，即使一瞑不視了，也要先掩埋在那裏，說不定最終它會使我獲得更多樂趣呢。

現在談的是我又一個這類實驗，我打算描述得更詳盡；為了方便起見，我這兩年的經驗以合二為一方式來寫。我已説過，我無意寫一首悶悶不樂的頌歌，而是要像破曉晨雞在棲木上引吭啼唱，只要能喚醒我的左鄰右里就好 [4]。

我住進樹林的第一天（也就是説，開始在樹林裏過日子），碰巧正是獨立日，亦即 1845 年 7 月 4 日，當時我的房子還沒有竣工，自然抵禦不了嚴冬，只能勉強用來遮擋一下風雨，既沒有抹泥灰，也沒有砌煙囪，牆壁採用的是飽經風雨侵蝕過的粗木板，縫隙很大，入夜以後就讓人感到冷絲絲的。經過劈削後筆直的白色立柱，以及剛剛刨過的門窗的框架，使小屋顯得潔淨又有一點透風，特別是大清早，木頭都吸足了露水，令我浮想聯翩，莫非到了正午時份，一些鮮美的樹膠會從木頭裏滲出來。在我的想像之中，屋裏整整一天或多或少都保留着黎明時那種氣氛，讓我回想到前年觀光過的一間山上小屋。那間小屋通風良好，又沒有抹過泥灰，適宜接待一位雲遊四方的神仙，在那裏女神也不妨拖曳長裙。打從我的屋頂吹過的風，有如橫掃山脊的風發出時斷時續的音調，或者説就是人間樂曲從天上落下的幾個片段。晨風不斷吹拂，創世記的詩篇從來沒有間斷過；可惜聽者寥寥無幾。奧林匹斯山 [5] 到處都有，但能悟出箇中奧妙之人卻屈指可數。

過去，除了一條小船，我擁有獨一無二的房子只是一個帳篷，夏日出遊時我偶然使用過，如今已經捲好，仍然放在我的閣樓上；但是那條小船幾經轉手，早已沉沒在時間的溪流裏了。今日有了這個頗具質感的棲身之處，我定居在世間也算有了些改善。這小屋雖説有點單薄，卻有一種氣氛環繞着我，而且還跟我這個營造氣氛的人息息相關。它還使人聯想到有點像一幅素描畫。我不必到門外去呼吸新鮮空氣，因為屋裏的空氣絲毫不失新鮮。我坐在門後與置身門外都差不多，即使在陰雨天也一樣。哈利梵薩印度成書於公元五世紀的古代梵文敘事詩《摩訶婆羅多》的附錄，記述毗瑟拿（Vishnu）的化身克利須那（Krishna）的事蹟和教義。說：「居無鳥，猶如食無味。」誠然，我的住所並非這樣，因為我發現自己突然與鳥兒們比鄰而居；這不是捉一隻鳥兒來，幽禁起牠，而是我讓自己關在屋子裏與鳥兒做伴。我跟牠們最接近的，不僅有常在花園和果園裏飛來飛去的鳥兒，而且還有更富有野趣、更扣人心弦的林中鳴禽——好像畫眉、鶇鳥、紅鶿、田雀、三聲夜鶯以及其他許多鳴禽，牠們從來沒有過，就算有過，也極其難得向村民們吟唱過甚麼小夜曲。

我住在一個小湖邊上，離康科德村以南大約一英里半，地勢比它稍高些，位於它和林肯[6]之間那一大片樹林裏，往南再走兩英里，乃是我們唯一的聞名遐邇的勝地——康科德戰場[7]；不過，我這裏的位置在樹林裏來說比較低，半英里開外的湖岸，如同其他地方一樣，都被樹木所掩蓋，卻成了我看得到的最遙遠的地平線。在頭一個星期裏，不管甚麼時候，我凝望小湖，在印象中都覺得它是一個山中之湖，高踞在山的一側，它的湖底遠遠高於其他湖泊。太陽冉冉升起時，我依稀看見它正在濛濛夜霧中卸粧，湖面上這裏那裏漸漸看得見微波粼粼，或者晶瑩如鏡的景象。這時，霧氣像幽靈似的悄悄旁溢，消失在樹林裏，如同夜間秘密集會正在散場一樣。霧水懸掛在樹梢頭，如同懸掛在山的兩側一樣，到了比往日更晚的時份，彷彿還遲遲不肯消退似的。

8月裏，和風細雨停歇時，小湖就成了我最珍貴的鄰居，這時，空氣和湖水平靜極了，可是天上卻烏雲密佈，下午才過了一半，儼然傍晚時份的寂靜，畫眉在四下裏啼唱，隔岸隱約可聞。如此的小湖，從來沒有比這個時刻更平靜了；小湖上空部份清朗的氣氛很稀薄，被烏雲所遮掩而黯然無光；水中卻浮光閃閃，倒影綽綽，自成一片下界天國，更值得珍視。從剛被砍掉樹木的附近一個小山上，舉目眺望小湖的南岸，真是景色宜人；山與山之間有一處凹口，十分開闊，於是形成湖岸，兩座小山坡向下傾斜，使人聯想到彷彿有一條溪澗，穿過樹木茂密的峽谷，朝那個方向傾瀉而下，其實，那裏並沒有甚麼溪澗。就這樣，我從鄰近碧綠羣山之間和之上，眺望地平線上呈現天藍色的遠方崇山峻嶺。真的，踮起了腳尖，我能望得到西北角一些更藍、更遠的山脈頂峯，那些純藍色恐怕都是渾然天成吧。此外，我還望得見村裏區區一隅。但是換個方向，即使還是這個視角，因為被四周樹木圍住，我就甚麼也看不到。最好你住的地方附近有水，因為它有浮力，使地面浮了起來。哪怕是小小的一口水井，也有這麼一點好處，當你俯瞰水井時，會發現地球並不是連綿的一大片，而是孤立的島嶼。這一發現如同井水可以冷藏牛油一樣重要。我從這個山巔舉目眺望小湖對岸，薩得伯里草地在發大水期間，我分明看得出草地驟然升高了，也許是雲蒸霞蔚的峽谷所呈現的海市蜃樓吧，猶如盆底一枚硬幣，小湖那一邊的大地看起來勝過薄薄的一層外殼，因為有一小片橫穿而過的澗水而形成孤島似的漂浮起來。這時，我才恍然大悟，我的住處原來就是乾旱地區。

從我的門口抬眼望去，視野雖窄，但我一點都沒有逼仄之感。我想像的駿馬仍有任意馳騁的天地。長滿低矮的橡樹叢的高地，從小湖對岸升起，一直逶迤到西部的原野和韃靼人[8]的大草原，給所有流浪的人提供了廣闊的天地。"人世間再也沒有人，比能夠自由欣賞遼闊地平線的人更快活。"——達摩達拉[9]就這樣說過，當時他的牛羊需要更大的新牧場。

地點和時間都已變換，我住的地方離宇宙那些最吸引我的區域，離歷史上最吸引我那些時代都更近了。我住的地方跟天文學家夜間觀測的許多區域一樣遙遠。我們習慣於想像：在天體的某個遙遠而神聖的角落，仙后座五亮星後面，遠離喧嘩和煩惱，總有一些罕見而令人愉快的地方。我發現我的小屋實際上就是這麼一個遁世之地，屬萬古常新、無玷污過的宇宙，其中一部份。如果説定居在這些地方，靠近昴星團或者畢星團，靠近牽牛星或者天鷹星，是頗有意思的話，那我就真的住在這種地方，或者換句話説，如同那些星座一樣，遠離我早已拋在後面的濁世塵俗，有如一縷微光閃爍不定，照着我最近的鄰居，僅僅在沒有月亮的夜晚方才看得見。我住的地方就是宇宙萬物中的一隅——

> 世上有過一個牧羊人，
> 他的思想就像高山那樣。
> 他在山上的一羣羊，
> 時時刻刻餵養他。[10]

如果説牧羊人的羊羣總是遊蕩在比自己思想還要高的牧場上，那麼，我們對牧羊人的生活該會作何感想呢？

每個早晨都是一份令人愉快的邀請書，使我的生活與大自然本身一樣簡樸，也許我可以説，跟大自然本身一樣純真。我一直崇拜曙光女神奧羅拉，論虔誠不下於希臘人。我很早起牀，在湖中洗澡；它如同洗滌靈魂一樣，也是我做得最好的一件事。據説，成湯王的浴盆上刻着如下文字："苟日新，日日新，又日新。"[11] 我懂得箇中深意。黎明帶回來了英雄時代。天剛濛濛亮，我坐在敞開着的門窗邊，一隻蚊在我屋子裏看不見也想不到為何到處飛呀飛，牠那微弱的嗡嗡聲，就像那歌頌美名的喇叭聲一樣，使我非常感動。這是荷馬的安魂曲；其本身乃是人們感悟中的《伊利亞特》和《奧德賽》，吟唱着它的憤怒與漂泊。其中不乏宇宙的情懷，總是宣揚着世人的無窮活力與生生不息，直到被禁止。早晨是一天中最耐人尋味的時段，是一覺醒來的時刻；那時候，我們一點沒有睡眼惺忪的樣子，至少在個多小時裏，我們不管白天黑夜裏常有昏昏沉沉的部份感覺也都甦醒過來了。如果説我們不是由我們自己的守護神喚醒的，而是由某個僕從用肘子給捅醒的，如果說我們不是由我們自己的新生力量與內心的渴望，以及天上的仙樂與空中的芳香，而是被工廠的上班鐘聲所喚醒 —— 反正沒有靈感的白晝是不會帶我們到比我們睡前生活層次更高些的地方去；那麼，這樣的白晝即使美其名曰白晝，也不會有多少期盼可言。倒是黑暗反而會結出果子來證明自己有能耐，一點也不比白晝遜色。一個人如果不相信每一天都有一個他還沒有濫用過的、更早更神聖的黎明時刻，那他對生命早已絕望，正在尋找一條沉淪黑暗的道路。感官的生活部份間歇之後，人的靈魂，或說得更準確一些，是人的器官每天都會散發出新的活力，他的守護神又會試探他能打造出何等高貴的生活。我敢說，凡是令人難忘的事情都在黎明時刻的氣氛裏發生。《吠陀經》[12]說：“萬知醒於晨。”詩歌與藝術，以及最優美、最難以忘懷的人類行為，都來自這樣一個時刻。所有詩人和英雄，如同門農[13]一樣，都是曙光女神奧羅拉的兒子，常在日出時份彈奏他們美妙的音樂。對那些擁有積極的彈性思維的晨型人來說，一天之中任何時間都是早晨。這跟座鐘報時、人們持甚麼態度和做甚麼工作都毫不相干。早晨就是我醒來時，心裏不覺有了一個黎明。德育改良就是力戒倦意。人們倘若不是昏睡不醒，那他們何至如此一事無成呢？但他們全都是精明人。他們要是沒有昏睡不醒的話，本來會做出一些事情來的。好幾百萬人能在非常清醒的狀態下從事體力勞動；但是一百萬人中，只有一個人能在非常清醒的狀態中，從事有成效的知識勞動，一億人中只有一個人能歡度富有詩意或神聖的生活[14]。清醒才是真正活着。我還從沒見到過一個非常清醒的人。如果見到了，我又該如何正視他呢？

　　我們必須學會自己甦醒，使自己保持清醒，不靠機械的幫助，而是寄厚望於黎明，就算我們在酣睡之際，黎明也不會拋棄我們。通過有意識的努力，人們毫無疑問有能力提高他們的生活質量，我沒有看到比這更令人振奮的事實。能繪製某一幅畫，或者塑造一座雕像，或者美化幾個事物，都是很了不起；不過，要是能塑造和描繪出那種恰到好處的藝術情調，可以使我們賞心悅目，那就更值得稱道。能影響當今上流人士，乃是藝術的最高境界。每個人都應該使自己的生活，乃至於它的細節，跟他在最莊嚴緊急之際的深思熟慮相匹配。如果說我們拒絕了，或者耗盡了我們所得到的這樣微不足道的信息，那麼，神諭就會清楚告訴我們如何做好這事。

我到樹林去，是因為我希望自己生活得有目的[15]，僅僅面對生活中的基本事實，看看我能不能學會生活要教給我的東西，免得我在彌留之際覺得自己虛度了一生。我不希望過算不上生活的那種生活，因為生活是那麼珍貴；我也不希望自己與世無爭，除非出於萬般無奈。我想生活得有深度，汲取生活中的全部精髓，堅強生活下去，像斯巴達人[16]一樣，摒棄所有一切算不上生活的東西，開闢一塊又寬又長的地，用心侍候它，讓生活處於區區一隅，使生活條件降到最低限度，如果說它被證明是毫無價值，那麼就要弄清楚整個毫無價值的真相，隨後昭告世人；或者如果說它是崇高的，那就以親身經歷去了解它，在我的下次出遊時能對它作出真實的描述。因為在我看來，大多數人對生活都不清不楚，搞不清楚是屬於魔鬼還是屬於上帝；他們卻又頗為草率，下結論認為人生主要目的，乃是"永遠崇拜上帝，熱愛上帝"[17]。

可是我們的生活仍然毫無價值，好像螞蟻似的；雖然古代寓言告訴我們，我們早已變成人了[18]；我們好像侏儒俾格米人一樣在跟天鶴[19]打仗；這真是錯上加錯，越抹越髒了。我們最優美的德行，這時卻成了多餘的本可避免的討厭鬼。我們的生活已被瑣碎事消耗掉了。一個誠實的人除了數數自己的十個手指頭以外，幾乎用不着再計算更多數字，或者說，在極端情況下至多再加上他的十隻腳趾頭，其餘不妨算統賬就算了。簡樸、簡樸、簡樸！[20]我說，最好你的事情只有兩三件，而不是一百件或者一千件，數到半打即可，為甚麼非要一百萬呢，不妨在你的大拇指甲上記賬就可以了。在這驚濤駭浪的文明生活的汪洋中，一個人要想生存，就要對這樣的烏雲密佈、暴風驟雨、流沙險灘、一千零一件[21]事情通通要考慮到，如果説他不是讓船沉沒，自己潛入海底，不通過船位推算抵達目的港的話；一個事業有成的人，必定是一個了不起的精明人。簡化，簡化吧！用不着一日三餐，必要時一餐就夠了；用不着上一百道菜，五道菜足矣；餘下的事按比例遞減。我們的生活像德意志聯邦，由許許多多大小公國組成，互相之間的邊界永遠在變動，即使德國人也不能隨時告訴你準確的邊界。這個國家儘管有其所謂的內部改進——順便説一下，全是外表的和膚淺的——它本身就是這麼一個難於操作、過份臃腫的龐大機構，裏面塞滿了附屬單位，從而落入了自己設置的陷阱，因為缺乏計算和崇高的目標，都給奢侈和揮霍毀掉了，就像國內上百萬的家庭一樣；對於一個國家，如同上百萬的家庭一樣，唯一療救的辦法就是推行嚴格的經濟措施，過一種比斯巴達人更簡樸的生活，並且提高生活的目的。當今生活太放蕩了。人們以為國家必須有商業，出口冰塊，通過電報對話，一小時驅車三十英里，毫不懷疑人們是不是都做得到。至於我們的生活過得應該是像狒狒呢，還是像人一樣，那反而説不定。如果説我們不是打造枕木[22]鐵路，鍛造鋼軌，日以繼夜工作，忙着改善生活，卻是徒勞無功，那麼，有誰會去修造鐵路呢？如果説鐵路沒有造好，我們又如何能及時到達天堂呢？不過話又説回來，如果我們守在家裏，只管自己的事，那麼，又有誰需要鐵路呢？我們並沒有乘坐鐵路，倒是鐵路在乘坐我們。難道你們沒有想到過：那些躺在鐵路底下的枕木是些甚麼嗎？每一根枕木就是一個人，一個愛爾蘭人，或者説一個北方佬，鐵軌就鋪在他們身上，他們身上又給黃沙所覆蓋，列車從他們身上平穩疾駛過去。我告訴你，他們睡得很酣。每隔幾年，又一批新的枕木鋪在鐵軌底下，火車從上面碾過；因此，如果一些人滿心快樂來乘坐火車在鐵軌上駛過，那肯定有另一些人在下面遭遇不幸，被碾壓過去。要是他們碾過一個夢遊者——一根錯位的多餘的枕木——吵醒了他時，他們會突然停車，為此大聲叫了起來，彷彿是在法庭上表示反對。我滿心高興發現，每隔五英里鐵路就有一隊養路工人，以保證那些枕木（沉睡者）平躺在路基（牀）上，這個事實本身說明，這些枕木（沉睡者）有時候會鬆動（再爬起來）。

我們為甚麼要生活得如此匆忙，如此浪費生命呢？我們還不如在捱餓之前乾脆餓死就罷了。常言道，及時縫上一針，日後省縫九針，可是今天他們就縫了一千針，只是為了省縫明日的九針[23]。至於這種做法，我們得不到任何效果。我們得了聖·維特斯[24]的狂舞病，不可能使我們的頭腦保持清靜。我要是在教區鐘樓下拉了幾下繩子，好像報火警似的，就是說，鐘聲還沒有大響起來，在康科德郊外農家的任何一個人——儘管今天早上藉口說過多少次他如何忙得不可開交——或者說，還有孩子、婦女，我敢說，肯定拋下手頭的工作，循着鐘聲跑過來，說實話，他們跑來的主要目的，不是從大火中搶救財物，八成是來作壁上觀，因為大火早已燒起來了，反正大家心裏知道這火不是自己放的——為甚麼不來看看大火是如何被撲滅的，如果不用費甚麼氣力的話，那就幫忙救救火；是的，哪怕教區禮拜堂本身着了火，恐怕也會是這樣。一個人吃過午飯，剛睡過半個小時午覺，醒來後抬頭就問："有甚麼消息沒有？"彷彿別人都在給他站崗放哨似的。有的人吩咐道，每過半個小時叫醒他，毫無疑問，也並沒有甚麼其他目的；稍後，作為回報，他們胡扯自己做的夢給別人聽。睡了一夜醒來，新聞之須臾不可離，如同早餐一樣。"請告訴我，這個地球上某某地方發生的有關某某人的新聞，好嗎？"——他一邊喝咖啡，吃麵包卷，一邊看報紙，得知這天早上瓦奇托河[25]上，有一個人的眼睛給挖掉了；可他從來不想一想，此時此刻，他就生活在世界這個深不可測的大黑洞裏，自己的一隻眼睛也早已失明[26]了。

就我來說，沒有郵局，我也能輕鬆應付。我想，只有極少的重要信息需要郵局傳遞。說得更確切些，我一生中至多也只收到過一兩次信是值得我花那郵資的——這還是我多年前寫過的話。通常，一便士郵資的制度，其目的是你正正經經給一個人一便士，就得到了他的想法，結果呢，你得到的往往是一個玩笑。我敢說，我從來沒有在報紙上讀到過任何難以忘懷的新聞。如果說我們讀到有一個人遭到攔劫了，或者說被謀殺了，或者說死於非命了，或者說一幢房子給火燒了，或者說一條船沉沒了，或者說一艘輪船爆炸了，或者說一頭母牛在西部鐵路上給撞死了，或者說一隻瘋狗被殺掉了，或者說入冬後出現一羣蝗蟲——那我們就不用再讀其他甚麼玩意了。一條就夠了。如果說你對原則早已瞭如指掌，你為甚麼還要去管多如牛毛的實例及其應用呢？在哲學家看來，一切所謂的新聞，全是閒扯，編輯新聞和閱讀新聞的都是一些喝茶聊天的老婦人。然而，不少人對這種閒扯樂此不疲。前幾天，我聽說有那麼多人蜂擁到一家報館，想打聽最新收到的國外消息，擠碎了報館的幾個大玻璃窗——那條消息，我倒是認真思考過，腦筋靈活一點的人肯定在十二個月前或者十二年以前就可以寫好它。比方說西班牙，只要你知道如何不時將堂‧卡洛斯和公主[27]‧堂‧彼得羅和塞維利亞和格拉納達這些字眼，寫得恰如其份就可以了——自從我讀報以來，這些字眼也許有了一點變化——如果沒有其他樂事可供報導時，不妨扯一扯鬥牛吧，這可是千真萬確的新聞，就西班牙的現狀或衰敗向我們作了出色的報導，如同報上這個標題底下那些最簡潔明瞭的報導一模一樣。至於英國呢，來自那個地方的最新要聞，幾乎還是 1649 年的革命；如果你早已知道英國穀物每年平均產量的歷史，那你再也用不着關心這類事了，除非你僅僅為賺大錢做投機生意。如果有人不看報就能下斷語，那麼，國外說真的沒有發生過甚麼新鮮的事，即使是法國革命也不例外。[28]

何謂新聞！要知道甚麼是萬古長青的事情，那才是最重要的。"蘧伯玉（衛大夫）使人於孔子。孔子與之坐而問焉。曰：夫子何為？對曰：夫子欲寡其過，而未能也。使者出。子曰：使乎，使乎。"伯引自《論語·憲問》。在週末，昏昏欲睡的農夫們的休息日裏——星期日正是含辛茹苦的一週的結尾，不是新的一週嶄新壯觀的開始——傳教士偏偏向他們耳朵裏灌輸的不是冗長乏味的佈道，而是用力發出驚雷般的吼聲："停——停住！為甚麼看上去很快，其實卻慢得要死呢？"

　　偽善和謬見被推崇為最健全的真理，現實卻成了虛懸幻象。如果說人們都尊重現實，不為幻夢所欺，那麼，我們的生活與現在的生活相比，將是其樂無窮，猶如"天方夜譚"。如果我們只尊敬那種不可避免的和有權利生存的事物，那麼，音樂和詩歌將會在街頭激起迴響。只要我們從容和聰明就會看出，唯有偉大而優秀的事物方可永久而絕對地存在——些微的恐懼和些微的樂趣只不過是現實的影子罷了。現實總是令人振奮，令人崇敬。人們閉目微睡，任憑各種假像欺騙，到處確立和鞏固日常生活的例行習慣，其實後者仍然建立在純粹虛幻的基礎之上。兒童模仿成年人活動做遊戲，比成年人更清楚認識到生活的真正規律與關係，成年人虛度一生，但自以為比兒童聰明得多，因為他們有經驗，也就是說，他們有過失敗的經驗。我在一本印度的書裏面讀到："有一位王子，從小被趕出了他出生的城市，由一個樵夫收養，就在這樣的環境裏長大成人，一直自以為屬他生活其中的化外之民。他父親手下的一個大臣發現了他，告訴了王子他的身世。他對自己出身的錯誤想法終於得以冰釋，他知道自己原來是一個王子。所以，"這位印度哲學家接下去說，"由於身處環境的緣故，這個人對自己出身產生誤解，直到某個聖潔的老師向他說明真相，這時他方才知道自己是婆羅門 [29] 我發覺，我們新英格蘭的居民過着這種普通生活，是因為我們的視野還穿透不了事物的表象。我們當似是而非的東西是真實的東西。如果有一個人走過這個村鎮，看到的只是現實，那麼，你不妨想一想，米爾德姆街 [30] 將會走向何處？如果他給我們描述他在那處看到的種種現實，那麼，我們對他描述的那個地方恐怕就認不出來了。看一看禮拜堂，或者縣府大樓，或者監獄，或者商店，或者住宅，在真正凝視它們之前，你倒說說看，它們真的是甚麼樣，反正在你的描述中它們都會化為烏有。人們尊重遙遠的真理，是在現成體制之外，在最遙遠的星辰後面。在亞當之前，在最後那個人之後上帝創造了亞當和夏娃之後才開始有了人類。因此，亞當是人類的先祖 [31]。永恆中確實存在真理和崇高。然而，所有這些時代、地點、和事件，都在此時此地 [32]。上帝之偉大已在此時此刻達到極致，斷不會隨着時代消逝而顯得更神聖。我們只有永遠不斷融入和開挖我們周圍的現實，才能懂得甚麼是崇高，甚麼是高貴。宇宙經常順應我們的觀念；不管我們走得快還是走得慢，反正軌道已給我們鋪好了。讓我們畢生懷有這種設想吧。詩人或藝術家從未有過如此美好高尚的設想，但至少他的某些後代會將它付諸實現。

讓我們像大自然那樣從容不迫度過一天，莫讓掉在軌道上的硬果外殼和蚊子翅膀而造成出軌。讓我們黎明即起，吃或者不吃早餐，心平氣和，泰然自若；讓人來人往，讓鐘聲響起，讓孩子們啼哭 —— 決心好好過日子。為甚麼我們要認輸，隨波逐流呢？讓我們不要飲食無度，佳餚珍饌就像淺灘，有着可怕的激流和漩渦。闖過了這一險關，你就平安無事，剩下的是下山的路了。莫讓神經鬆弛，借助黎明的活力，朝另一個方向起航，就像尤利西斯荷馬史詩《奧德賽》裏的英雄人物，為了抵制海上女妖塞壬 (Siren) 美妙歌聲的引誘，讓人綁自己在桅桿上，避免了上當受騙、人船俱亡的慘劇 [33] 一樣，綁自己在桅桿上。如果火車頭拉響了汽笛，就讓它拉響吧，直到它的響聲沙啞。如果鐘聲響起，我們為甚麼要拔腿就跑？我們還要思考一下，聽聽它們像是甚麼樂曲。讓我們安下心來工作，涉足於全球泛濫的污泥濁水一般的輿論、偏見、傳統、謬見和表象之間，穿越巴黎、倫敦、紐約、波士頓、康科德、教堂、國家、詩歌、哲學與宗教，一直來到一處堅硬的底層和牢固的基石，我們可以叫做現實，現實就在這裏，沒錯；你可以在這個支點[34]之上，在山洪、冰霜與火焰之下，開始在這個地方建造一道牆，或者建立一個國家，或者為求安全豎起一根燈柱，或者一個測量儀器，不是尼羅河水位測量儀器，而是一個現實測定器[35]，讓未來的各個時代可以知道，虛假和表象有如山洪般積聚下來，該有多麼深。如果你直立着，面對事實，你就會看到事實的兩面都閃爍着陽光，好像這是一柄古代阿拉伯人使用的雙刃短刀，感覺到它那利刃正在剖開你的心臟和骨髓，於是你便欣然告別人生[36]。生也好，死也好，我們渴求的僅僅是現實。如果我們真的一瞑不視了，就讓我們聽聽自己喉嚨裏發出的咯咯聲，感覺到四肢冰冷吧；如果我們還活着，就讓我們忙自己的事去吧。

時間只是可供我垂釣的小溪流。我飲用的是小溪裏的水；但我一邊飲用，一邊看着小溪底的沙土，發覺它是多麼淺呀。溪水悄悄流去，然而永恆長存。我會盡情痛飲；我會尋找到佈滿鵝卵石般星星的穹蒼。我連"一"都數不出來。我不認得字母表的第一個字母。我常引以為憾，覺得自己還不如初生時聰明了。智力是一把刀，它能洞察縫隙，剖開萬物的奧秘。我不希望自己雙手忙於可有可無的事情。我的頭腦是手和足的象徵。我覺得自己所有最佳才能都凝聚於此。我的本能告訴我，我的頭腦是一個開挖的器官，就像有些動物用牠們的鼻嘴和前爪挖洞，我要用它去挖自己的洞，穿過這些山巒，開闢自己的道路。我想，最富有的礦脈埋藏在這裏附近的地方。因此，利用占卜杖[37]，根據升騰的霧氣，我作出斷定：就在這裏我着手開礦[38]。

1　此處喻指因為管閒事而吃苦頭。

2　據考證，此處引自英國詩人考珀（William Cowper，1731—1800）的《也許是亞歷山大·塞爾柯克所寫的詩》。

3　阿特拉斯：古希臘神話中用肩膀扛着天的大力神，喻身負重擔的人。

4　梭羅意在説明不願做甚麼悶悶不樂的哀歎，他要使自己寫出的感受能對他人多少有點益處。作為全書的宗旨，梭羅在本書首次問世時，即將這一題詞印在卷首扉頁，以警示世人。

5　奧林匹斯山：據傳是眾神之家，意思是天堂樂園。

6　林肯：美國有許多個以林肯命名的村鎮。此處指馬薩諸塞州的林肯鎮，在康科德東面不遠。

7　康科德戰場：獨立戰爭中，北美人民第一次與英國交戰的戰場。此戰役發生於 1775 年 4 月 19 日。

8　韃靼人：泛指歐亞兩洲之間韃靼人居住地區，但無一定區域，因為韃靼族屬遊牧民族。

9　達摩達拉：亦即克利須那的別名，印度神話中三大神之一，毗瑟拿的第八化身。梭羅這段話引自印度敘事詩《哈利梵薩》。

10　這是英國詹姆斯一世時期一位無名詩人所寫的詩。梭羅可能引自托馬斯·伊萬斯（Thomas Evans）編《古民謠》（Old Ballads，1810）一書。

11　中國商代成湯王，又稱武湯，商代開創者。據《禮記·大學》記載，成湯王曾將上文刻於浴盆，用以自誡。也有人説出自湯之《盤銘》。

12　《吠陀經》：印度婆羅門教的經典，共四卷。意思是 "早晨是一天之中的最佳時辰。" 猶如中國諺語："一日之計在於晨。" 或説："萬知醒於晨。"

13　門農：古希臘神話中的人物，曙光女神奧羅拉的兒子，在著名的特洛伊戰爭中被渾身刀槍不入的阿喀琉斯殺害，宙斯卻又賜予他永生。

14　意思是普天之下盡是為生活而生活的人，而真正領會生活意義的人卻寥寥無幾。

15　意思是不要庸庸碌碌虛度一生。

16　斯巴達人：斯巴達，古希臘奴隸制城邦，古代斯巴達人素以生活簡樸、嚴謹、刻苦、耐勞而著稱。

17　遠引自《新英格蘭初級讀物》（The New England Primer）的宗教教義部份。這一段表達了梭羅對生活的看法及其進入樹林的目的。

18　我們早已變成人了：在希臘寓言中，有一個故事講到審判阿依庫斯曾勸他父親——主神宙斯變螞蟻為人。

19　天鶴：荷馬在《伊利亞特》第 3 卷中，比喻特洛伊人為與俾格米人作戰的天鶴。

20　這是梭羅的一句名言，強調生活不要奢侈，不要多為瑣事所累。

21　此處意思是許多事情要考慮。"一千零一"源自《一千零一夜》書名，形容數量極多。

22　此處是雙關語，"枕木"又比喻那些為修造鐵路賣命而又昏睡不醒、毫無覺悟的人。由此可見，梭羅對鐵路這一資本主義物質文明的標誌所懷有的不滿情緒，在本書中多處表達出來。同時，他對修造鐵路的勞工深表同情。

23　意思是事倍功半。比喻人們從事無謂工作，對人的精神毫無裨益。

24　聖‧維特斯：古代西西里島上的一個貴族之子，患有狂舞病，後被奉為這些瘋症的救主，並稱這些瘋症為聖‧維特斯舞病。

25　瓦奇托河：The Wachito River，又名 Ouachita，紅河的一條支流，源自阿肯色州，流入路易斯安那州。

26　傳說在美國肯塔基州的大山洞裏發現過無視力的魚類，梭羅在此將世界比喻為這種尚未探明的黑山洞，比喻這種人為洞中的盲魚，含有極大諷刺挖苦之意。

27　堂‧卡洛斯和公主：1839 年，西班牙斐迪南國王去世，堂‧卡洛斯和堂‧彼得羅兩人為王位展開了競爭，結果伊莎貝拉公主於 1843 年被封為西班牙女王。

28　意思是對一個不看報的人來説，國外並無甚麼新聞，連法國革命也等於沒發生過似的。

29　婆羅門：印度教有三位主神，梵或梵天（Brahma），又譯婆羅門，是創造之神，亦指眾生之本或智慧的象徵；毗瑟拿（Vishnu）是保護之神，濕婆（Siva）是毀滅之神。

30　米爾德姆街：當時康科德鎮上的商業中心。

31　此句用亞當（Adam）指人類誕生之前，用最後那個人（the last man）指人類消亡之後，旨在説明當今人們只重視遠古和遙遠的將來，而不重視現在。

32　意思是不必到過去或將來去尋求真理，真理就在眼前。

33　此處梭羅告誡人們像尤利西斯抵制塞壬一樣，不為七情六慾所動。

34　原文為法文 Point d'appui。

35　這是作者根據前者類比臆造的詞，意思是"現實測定器"，用來鑒別真偽。

36　意即一旦真理在握，死也甘心。

37　據稱可以用來探尋礦脈或水源等的一種叉形木杖。

38　此處表明作者隱居林湖之間的目的以及探求生活真諦的信念。

3
閱讀

擇業時如果考慮得周全一些，也許所有人大抵會做學生和觀察家，因為大家對兩者的性質和命運，不用說，都感興趣。為我們自己或者後代積累財富，成立家庭或者創建國家，或者甚至沽名釣譽，凡此種種，我們畢竟都是凡夫俗子；但在探究真理時，我們卻是不朽的，也不必害怕變故或意外。最古老的埃及或印度的哲學家，給神像撩開了一角面紗，那顫動搖晃的衣袍至今還往上撩着。我凝視着它如同當初那樣燦然榮光，因為當初顯得如此勇敢是附在他身上的我，而如今回顧這一幻覺的是附在我身上的他。衣袍上一塵不染；從神靈被顯示以來，時間並沒有流逝而去。我們真正在改進的，或者說可以改進的那個時代，既不是過去，又不是現在，也不是未來。

我的住處跟一所大學相比，不僅更適宜於苦思冥想，而且更適宜於認真閱讀。儘管我閱讀的書都在一般流通圖書館範圍以外，但是我受到在全世界流通的圖書的影響，卻比以往任何時候更多，那些書最早是寫在樹皮上，如今不時抄在亞麻布紙上。詩人米爾・卡瑪・烏丁・馬斯特[1]說："靜心打坐，任憑神思馳騁在心靈世界；我從書中得到了莫大好處。一杯美酒足以使人陶醉，我讀深奧學說如飲玉液瓊漿，其樂無比。"整個夏天，我將荷馬的《伊利亞特》放在桌子上，儘管只是偶然看上幾頁。起初，我手上有忙不完的工作，我既要造好房子，同時又要鋤豆子地，使我不可能讀更多的書。但以後可以讀得更多的期盼，始終支持着我。我在工作之餘讀過一兩本淺顯的談旅行的書，後來我自己都臉紅了，我不禁反躬自問，此時此刻，我究竟置身在何方。

　　學生可以閱讀希臘文的荷馬或埃斯庫羅斯[2]的原著，不會有放蕩或奢侈的危險，因為學生讀了原著，多少會仿效詩篇中的英雄人物，奉獻自己的清晨時間給他們的詩章。這些英雄詩篇，即使用我們的母語印出來，在當前日漸衰退的時代，也常常會變成一種僵死的文字；因此，我們必須勤勤懇懇尋找每個詞、每行詩的原意，以我們固有的智慧、膽識和氣量，細心琢磨出它們的弦外之音。現代廉價而多產的印刷業，儘管出版了那麼多翻譯作品，卻一點沒有使我們更接近那些古代的英雄作家。他們看上去依然寂寞，他們被印出來的文字跟從前一樣稀奇古怪。你年輕時花去珍貴的光陰，去學一種古代語言，哪怕學到幾個詞語，也是值得的，因為它們是從街頭巷尾的俚俗生活裏提煉出來的，具有恆久的聯想和激勵。農夫聽了幾個拉丁文詞語就記在心上，時常唸叨着，並非徒勞。有時候，人們說古典作品的研究，好像最終會讓位於更現代化的實用研究；但是，富於進取心的學生還抱着始至不渝的心來研究古典作品，不管它們是用甚麼文字寫出來的，也不管它們又是如何古老。古典作品乃是人類最高貴的思想的記載，捨此以外，還能是甚麼？它們是唯一的不朽的神諭，對大多數現代質詢都會作出哪怕是特爾斐[3]也從沒給予過的解答。也許我們不妨暫且不去研究大自然，因為她畢竟老了。讀好書，就是說，要讀實至名歸的理想的書，這是一種高尚的鍛煉，這種累得讀者筋疲力盡的鍛煉，超過當今時尚的任何運動鍛煉。它要求讀者如同運動員經受過的訓練那樣，幾乎畢生矢志不渝、苦心修煉。書本是經過審慎思考後寫出來的，所以閱讀原著如同寫作原著一樣，務必審慎、含蓄。即使能說原著所用的那個國家語言也還不夠，因為口語與書面語（亦即聽到的語言與閱讀的語言），兩者有顯著的差異；口語通常都是瞬息萬變，僅僅是用一種聲音，一種俚俗方言，幾乎有點野腔野調，我們多少有點拙口笨舌似的，從母親那裏不知不覺學會這種口語。至於書面語呢，它是在口語的基礎上漸漸成熟的經驗總結；如果說前一種是我們的母語，那後一種就是我們的父語，一種含蓄而又洗練的詞語，它的含意光靠耳朵還聽不出來，為此，我們必須重新投胎才能學會這種詞語。在中世紀，僅僅會說希臘語和拉丁語的老百姓，由於出身的偶然因素沒有資格讀天才們用這兩種語言寫成的作品；因為這些作品不是用他們知道的希臘語或拉丁語寫成的，而是用洗練的文學語言寫成的。希臘和羅馬更高貴的語言，他們還沒有學會，在他們看來，這些高貴的語言寫出來的書只不過是一堆廢紙，他們反而看重廉價的當代文學。但是，到了歐洲幾個國家獲得他們自己的語言，雖然粗俗，但很鮮明，達到他們的文學崛起的目的已是綽綽有餘，初始的學問也隨之復興，學者們能夠鑒別遙遠地方的古代珍藏了。過去羅馬和希臘的羣眾不能聽懂的作品，經過幾個世紀之後，已有少數學者在閱讀，而且至今也只有少數學者在閱讀。不管我們多麼讚賞演說家偶然迸發出的滔滔不絕的辯才，最高貴的書面語，通常還是隱藏在轉瞬即逝的口語之後，或者凌駕於轉瞬即逝的口語之上，如同繁星閃爍的穹蒼隱藏在轉瞬即逝的浮雲後面。繁星就在那裏，能看到它們的人就可以識讀它們。天文學家始至不渝在解釋它們，觀察它們。它們不會散發出像我們日常口語和模糊詞語的氣息。演講台上的所謂辯才，一般說就是文學習作中的修辭。演說家憑藉轉瞬即逝的靈感，向他面前的聽眾和那些能夠傾聽他的人演講；可是，作家需要更寧靜的生活，那些激發演說家靈感的人羣和事件，反而使他分神，所以說，他是向着人類的心智說話，向着任何時代一切能理解他的人說話。

難怪亞歷山大大帝[4]，古代馬其頓國王[5]，繼位後先征服希臘、埃及和波斯，後入侵印度，建立亞歷山大帝國。遠征時，還要在他的寶匣裏帶上《伊利亞特》。書面文字是文物珍遺中的精品。它比其他藝術品跟我們更親密，同時也更普及。它是最貼近生活本身的藝術作品。

它可以翻譯成各種文字，不僅供人們閱讀，實際上還可以朗誦，朗朗上口——不僅描摹在畫布上或者鐫刻在大理石上，而且從生活本身的話語中脫穎而出。古代人思想的象徵變成了現代人的言語。兩千個盛夏就像賦予希臘的大理石雕刻品一樣，已賦予希臘文學的豐碑更成熟的金燦燦的秋天色彩，因為它們將自己的靜謐、聖潔的氣氛遍及世界各地，保護它們不受時間侵蝕。書是世界的珍寶，各個國家都可以世代相傳。最古老、最優秀的書，自然應當放在每個家庭的書架上。它們可沒有甚麼理由求情，但當它們開導與激勵讀者時，讀者卻通情達理，不會拒不接受它們。它們的作者不論在哪個社會，都成了富有魅力的天然貴族，對人類產生的影響遠遠超過國王和皇帝。目不識丁，也許還看不起別人的商人，由於苦心經營獲得了他垂涎已久的閒暇和獨立，躋身於富有和時尚的階層，最後，他無可避免會轉向更高級，卻又高不可攀的天才和知識精英的世界，此時此刻，他才感到自身文化力量不足，自己的全部財富無非顯示虛榮和缺憾；於是，為了進一步證明自己還算頭腦清醒，他費盡苦心來讓他的子女們獲得他深感匱乏的知識文化，也就這樣，他成了一個家族的始祖。

那些沒有學會閱讀古典作品原著的人，對人類歷史知識肯定非常欠缺。顯而易見，這些古典作品一直沒有現代語的譯本，除非我們的文明本身可以當作諸如此類的譯本。荷馬至今還從來沒有用英文印行過，埃斯庫羅斯也沒有過，甚至維吉爾[6]也都沒有——這些大師的作品，寫得這麼優雅、這麼堅實、這麼壯麗，幾乎宛若晨曦；後來的作家，我們儘管如何讚賞他們的天才，但能與這些古典作家筆下的精美、完整、不朽的英雄詩篇相媲美的，就算有，也是寥寥無幾。那些從來不知道它們的人，談的只是莫要再提到它們。等我們有了學問和才識，能夠閱讀它們、欣賞它們時，他們的這些話也就很快忘掉了。當我們稱之為古典作品的遺產，以及比古典作品更古老、更古典，卻又鮮為人知的各國經典著作積累得越來越多時，梵蒂岡教廷裏堆滿了《吠陀經》、《阿維斯陀古經》[7]和各種《聖經》，以及荷馬、但丁和莎士比亞作品，而且後繼的世紀不斷將它們的勝利紀念品提供給世人公開討論的機會，到了此時此刻，那個時代才真的是富麗輝煌。有了這麼一大堆精品，也許我們就有最終登上天堂的希望。

偉大詩人的作品，迄今人類還沒有讀懂呢，因為唯有偉大的詩人才能讀懂它們。閱讀這些作品的水平，只是像眾人觀望星辰，至多是從星象學的角度，而不是天文學的角度去觀察研究。大多數人學會閱讀，僅僅為了得到一點方便，有如他們學會阿拉伯數字，只是為了記賬，免得做生意時上當受騙；對於閱讀作為一種高尚的智力練習，他們就知之甚少，甚至一無所知；但是，從高尚的意義上來說，唯有這樣才算是閱讀，絕不是像奢侈品那樣吸引我們的閱讀，也不是使我們更高貴的官能昏昏欲睡的閱讀，而是恰恰相反，我們不得不踮起腳尖去閱讀，奉獻我們最警覺、最清醒的時光給閱讀。

我想，我們認識字母以後，就該閱讀最好的文字作品，而不是永遠重複唸 a 以及單音節的詞，像四五年級的小學生，一輩子坐在最低年級最前排的座位上。大多數人只要自己能夠閱讀，或者聽別人閱讀，就心滿意足了，或許他們還堅信有了一本好書《聖經》裏的智慧也不差，於是，他們在生命的剩餘歲月裏所謂的輕鬆閱讀中，浪費才能，無所事事並白白度過餘生。我們的流通圖書館裏，有一部多卷本的作品，名叫《小讀物》，我想恐怕是我沒有去過的一個小鎮的名字。有那麼一些人，就像鸕鷀和鴕鳥，各種各樣食物都能消化，甚至在暴食一頓葷菜之後，照樣也消化得了，因為他們不讓東西白白遭到浪費。如果說別人是供應這種飼料的機器，那麼，他們就是閱讀這種飼料的機器。他們讀過了九千個關於西布倫和賽弗羅尼亞的傳說故事，說他們如何相愛，過去從來沒有人像他們那麼相愛過，而且他們真正相愛的過程也不是一帆風順——反正不管怎麼說，他們如何相愛，絆倒在地，再站起來，繼續相愛！某個可憐的倒霉鬼如何爬到了教堂的尖頂上，但願他從來沒有爬到鐘樓上面就好了；現在，既然他毫無必要便爬到了尖頂，這位興高采烈的小説家卻用力敲起鐘來，讓全世界的人都趕過來聽，哦，老天哪！看那個小子如何下來！依我看，全球小説世界裏有的是這類向上爬的英雄人物，他們還不如把這些人物寫成風信雞好了，如同他們過去常把英雄人物置身於星座之中一樣，讓風信雞在那裏不停旋轉，直到生鏽為止，莫讓它們下地來胡鬧，打擾老實人。下一次，這位小説家敲鐘時，就算那座禮拜堂燒掉了，我也照樣巍然不動。《踮起腳尖單足跳》，"一部中世紀傳奇故事，是《鐵特爾—托爾—譚》的著名作者的新著，按月連載；購者摩肩接踵，欲購從速。"讀着這一切，他們滿懷有如原始人的好奇心，眼睛睜得像盤子似的，而且胃口特別好，也用不着擔心有損胃壁，猶如一個四歲大的小孩坐在板櫈上，看兩美分一本燙金封面的《灰姑娘》——可是，他們讀後，反正我看得出，他們在發音上、語氣上、重音上，都沒有甚麼長進，在題旨的提煉或修飾上也沒有學到甚麼技巧。閱讀的結果是視力模糊，生死攸關的循環凝滯，一切智能衰退，彷彿蛻了皮似的。這類薑汁麵包，差不多每個烤箱裏每天都在烤出來，而且烤得比純正小麥麵粉或者黑麥加粗玉米粉做的麵包更賣力，同時也更對路適銷。

　　那些最好的書，即使是所謂的好讀者，也不閱讀。我們康科德的文化又算是甚麼？甚至英國文學中最優秀的作品或者説頂級的好書，儘管作品裏面的單詞大家都能讀懂，也能拼寫，可是這個小鎮上除了極少例外，人們對這些好書就是沒有興趣。就是在大學裏讀過書、算得上受過所謂文科教育的人，不管在這裏或者別處都一樣，對英國經典作品實際上也是知之甚少，或者説一無所知；至於記載人類智慧的書籍，比方説，古代經典著作和各種聖經，只要願意了解它們的人都很容易得到，可惜只有極少數人肯下力氣去閱讀。我認識一個中年伐木工人，訂閱了一份法文報紙，他說不是為了看新聞（因為他對新聞不屑一顧），而是為了"讓自己不斷練練法語"，因為他出生在加拿大；我問他，在這個世界上，他覺得自己能做的最好的事是甚麼，他回答說，除了法語外，也學好英語。受過大學教育的人，一般說來所做到的，或者想做的，也就是這樣，他們訂閱英文報紙就是出於這個目的。一個人剛剛讀過一本也許是最好的英文書，可他能尋找到幾個可以一起對這本書交談交談的人呢？或者假定說，他剛剛讀完一部希臘文或者拉丁文的經典作品，即使所謂的文盲都知道要對它讚揚一番；但他卻尋不到一個可以一起聊聊的人，就只好對它保持沉默了。一位大學教授如果擅長破解希臘文中各種疑點，也就相應擅長破解一位古希臘詩人的才智和詩篇中深奧之處，並且相應將這種情投意合的同感，傳授給那些靈敏和滿懷豪情的讀者；可惜這樣的教授在我們的大學裏確實絕無僅有；至於神聖的經文，或者說人類的各種聖經，這個鎮上又有誰能一一為我道來道來它們的名字呢？大多數人都不知道，唯獨希伯來這個民族擁有一部經文。任何一個人，為了拾到一枚銀幣該有多花工夫；可是這有的是勝過黃金的文字，那是古代最聰慧的人說出來的，其價值是歷代智者都向我們證實過的 —— 殊不知我們學的只不過是一些簡易讀物、識字課本和班級點名記分冊，離校後讀的是"小讀物"和專門給孩子和初學者看的故事書；我們的閱讀，我們的交談和思想，水平非常之低，跟小人國裏侏儒倒是很相配。

我倒是巴不得結識一些比康科德本土生出的更聰明的人，他們的名字在這裏幾乎都沒有聽說過。難道說我會聽到過柏拉圖的名字，卻從來不去讀他的書嗎？好像柏拉圖是我的同鄉，我卻從來沒見過他 —— 好像他跟我比鄰而居，我卻從來沒聽到過他說話，或者從來沒有聽到他那智慧的雋語。但是實際情況又如何呢？柏拉圖的《對話錄》，包含着他的不朽思想，就擱在書架上，我從來沒讀過它呢。我們是教養不良，粗俗無知的文盲；文盲有兩種：一種是我鎮上目不識丁的老鄉，一種是只讀過兒童作品和適合極低智力讀物的老鄉，這兩種文盲究竟有甚麼顯著區別，我承認，我還看不出來。我們應該像古代聖賢一樣優秀，但我們首先要知道他們是如何優秀的。我們是一羣小山雀，在智力的飛躍中只比日報專欄稍微高出一點。

並不是所有的書都像它們的讀者一樣愚鈍。書裏面的文字也許就是針對我們的境況而說的，我們要是果真聽到了，並且有所感悟的話，那麼，它們會比清晨或春天更有利於我們的生活，而且還有可能為我們揭開事物的新面目。有多少人因為讀了一本書，從而開始了人生的新時代。一本書既能解釋我們的奇蹟，又能向我們揭示新的奇蹟，這本書也許就是為我們而存在的。目下許多説不出來的事情，我們也許會發現在別處已經給説出來了。這些問題使我們感到困惑和不知所措，也同樣讓所有聰明人碰到過；一個都沒有給漏掉，每一個人都根據自己的能力，用自己的話和自己的生活，對這些問題作出回答。再説，有了智慧，我們將學會寬宏大量。康科德郊外某農場，有一個孤獨的僱工，曾有過第二次出生和特殊的宗教經歷，因為他相信自己由於信仰的緣故，進入了靜穆莊重和遺世獨立的境界，也許他會覺得上面的話是不真實的。但是好幾千年以前，瑣羅亞斯德[8]就走過了同樣的道路，也有過同樣的經驗；然而，瑣羅亞斯德很有靈性，知道這是普遍現象，因此善待眾鄰居，據説甚至還在人間發明並首創了拜神活動。那麼，就讓那位孤獨的僱工謙謙虛虛與瑣羅亞斯德親密交談吧，並在所有聖賢的寬容思想影響下，與耶穌基督本人親密交談吧，讓"我們的教會"垮掉吧。

我們誇口説，我們屬19世紀，正在邁着比哪個國家都要快的步伐前進。可是想一想這個村鎮為自己的文化所做的又何其微不足道。我可不想去恭維我鎮上的鄉友們，也不想他們來恭維我，因為這樣一來，我們誰都不會有長進。我們應當像公牛那樣需要刺激 —— 受驅趕 ——

才會快跑。我們已有一個相當像樣的公立學校 [9] 可惜僅僅為嬰兒開設的；不過，冬天就有個處於半饑餓狀態的呂克昂學府 [10]，近來還有根據政府建議開辦一個小小的圖書館，除此以外，卻沒有我們自己的學院。我們花在肉體的食糧或者肉體的病患上的錢，要比花在精神食糧上的錢多得多。現在該是我們創辦不同凡響的學校的時候了，一個個村莊應該都成為大學的時候了，村裏老年居民 —— 如果說他們確實那麼富裕的話 —— 就有閒暇成為各大學裏的研究員 —— 可以在晚年進行大學文科研究。難道說世界上永遠只有一個巴黎（大學）或者一個牛津（大學）嗎？難道學生們不可以寄宿在這裏，在康科德的藍天底下接受文科教育嗎？難道我們不可以出資聘請一位阿伯拉爾 [11] 來給我們講學嗎？天哪！我們盡是忙於餵牛、開店，好長好長時間沒上學校了。我們的教育慘遭忽視。村鎮在某些方面應該取代歐洲的貴族的地位。它應該是美術的守護者。它富有得很。它欠缺的就是寬宏大量和優雅。在農場主人和商人覺得重要的那些事情上，它肯一擲千金，而對更有知識的人認為更有價值的事，如果要它出錢，它卻認為那是烏托邦的空想。感謝好運或者政治，這個村鎮花掉一萬七千塊錢造了一幢鎮公所，但要它培育生動活潑的風趣，宛如貝殼裏面的蚌珠，就算過了一百年，它也不肯花這麼多的錢。為了冬天開辦呂克昂學府，每年募捐一百二十五塊錢，其實比鎮上任何同樣數目的籌款都要花得更有意義。我們生活在 19 世紀，為甚麼不該享受 19 世紀提供的種種好處呢？我們的生活為甚麼還過得這樣鄉下氣呢？如果我們看報紙，為甚麼不跳過波士頓的閒談，馬上訂閱世界上最好的報紙呢？ —— 不要吮吸"中立派系"報紙的奶頭，或者咀嚼新英格蘭這裏的"橄欖枝" [12]。讓各種學術團體來我們這裏作報告吧，我們將要看看他們是不是真的知道一點甚麼。我們為甚麼要讓哈珀兄弟圖書公司和雷丁出版公司 [13] 代替我們選擇讀物呢？這就好比趣味高雅的貴族，在他周圍的一切必然有利於自己的文化修養 —— 比方說，天才——學問——風趣——書籍——繪畫——雕塑——音樂——哲學的工具,等等;那就讓村鎮也這樣吧——不要只請一個教師、一個牧師和一個司事,不要只辦一個教區圖書館,不要只選三名市政委員,就算萬事大吉了,因為我們清教徒前輩移民[14],就是仰仗以上這些人物,在荒涼的岩石上捱過了寒風凜冽的冬天。集體行動是符合我們制度的精神;我堅信隨着我們經濟狀況日益興旺發達,我們的財力一定會比貴族更雄厚。新英格蘭可以出資聘請世界上的哲人賢達來教育開導她,要他們膳宿在這裏,讓我們完全摒除粗野的鄉氣。這就是我們想要的不同凡響的學校。讓我們擁有高貴的村鎮居民,而不是貴族。如果必要的話,我們寧可在河上少造一座橋,多繞一些路,但在我們周圍黑暗無知的深淵上,至少架起一座拱橋吧。

章註

1　據說是 18 世紀波斯詩人。

2　埃斯庫羅斯,Aeschylus,公元前 525—公元前 456,古希臘三大悲劇作家之一,據說寫過 80 多個劇本,現存僅 7 個,其代表作是《被縛的普羅米修斯》和《阿伽門農》。

3　古希臘兩城市,前者有阿波羅神示所,後者有宙斯神示所和多多那。

4　亞歷山大大帝:Alexander the Great,公元前 356—公元前 323。

5　馬其頓國王:公元前 336—公元前 323。

6　維吉爾:Virgil,公元前 70—公元前 19,古羅馬詩人,作品有《牧歌》19 首及《農事》4 卷,代表作是《埃涅阿斯紀》;他的作品對歐洲文藝復興和古典主義產生了巨大影響。

7　古波斯瑣羅亞斯德教,中國古籍中稱祆教,俗稱拜火教的聖書。

8　瑣羅亞斯德:Zoroaster,公元前 628—公元前 551,在中國古籍中稱 "蘇魯支",古波斯瑣羅亞斯德教 (亦即祆教) 創始人,據傳他 20 歲時離家隱修,後對波斯多神教進行改革,創立祆教。

9　美國公立學校,一般包括中小學部,但有時僅有小學幼兒部的體制。

10　呂克昂學府:古希臘亞里士多德在雅典創辦的學府,現在一般指演講場所。

11 阿伯拉爾:Pierre Abelard,1079—1142,中世紀法蘭西經院哲學家、邏輯學家和神學家,他的《神學》一書被指控為異端而遭焚毀。

12 "橄欖枝":一份衛理公會週報。

13 哈珀兄弟圖書公司和雷丁出版公司,此處指設在紐約和波士頓兩地的出版商。

14 清教徒前輩移民,指 1620 年到達北美創立普利茅斯殖民地的英國清教徒。

聞籟

然而如果我們局限在書本範圍，儘管這些書是經典精品；我們讀的只是一種特殊的書面語言，它們本身無非是方言土話；我們就有忘掉另一種語言的危險，那是一種所有事物不靠比喻就能說出來的語言，唯獨它最豐富，也最標準。發表的東西倒是很多，但印出來的卻很少。從百葉窗裏透進來的亮光，只要百葉窗全給打開了，就再也沒人記得了。任何一種方法或訓練，也都無法替代永遠保持警覺的必要性。一門歷史，或者哲學，或者不管選得如何精練的詩歌，或者是極好的社會，或者是最令人豔羨的生活常規，如果跟永遠着眼於可預見之物的準則相比，又都算得上甚麼呢？你樂意僅僅做一個讀者，或者是一個學生，還是做一個預言家？不妨預測一下你的命運，看一看你的面前是甚麼，就直接邁向未來吧。

第一個夏天，我沒有讀書，我鋤豆子地去了。不，我做的常常比這個還好呢。有時候，我真捨不得奉獻眼前美好的時光給任何工作，不管是腦力工作，還是體力工作。我喜歡給自己的生活留出更多空間。有時候，夏天一清早，慣常洗過澡之後，我就獨坐在灑滿陽光的門口，從日出一直到正午，出神冥想，置身於松樹、山核桃樹和漆樹叢中，四下一片孤寂和寧靜，唯有鳥兒在近處歌唱，或者悄悄掠過我的小屋，直到夕陽餘暉照在我的西窗上；或者遠處的公路上，觀光客車馬的轔轔聲隱約可聞，這時我才不禁想起了流光易逝。在這些季節裏，我就像夜間的玉米一樣在成長，它們比任何手作的工作都要神妙得多，事實上，不但無損於我的生命健康，反而使我延年益壽。我才悟出了東方人所謂玄思和賦閒是甚麼意思了。其實，我並不在乎韶光的流逝。[1] 白晝走在前頭，彷彿為了照亮我的工作；剛才還是早上，可是看吧，一晃眼就是晚上，令人難忘的事並沒有完成。我可不是像鳥兒似的歌唱，我是在默默笑看着自己的好運紛至沓來。麻雀落在我門前的山核桃樹上拼命囀鳴，而我呢，有時也會暗自發笑，要不然就遏制住自己的笑聲，生怕也許牠會從我的巢中聽到。我心目中的日子，並不是指一個星期裏面的哪一個日子，沒有用異教徒的神祇來命名的[2]，也沒有被分割成一個小時，一個小時，讓座鐘的滴嗒聲使你煩躁不安；因為我的生活就像普里[3]印第安人，據說普里人的"昨天、今天和明天只用一個詞，他們用手所指的方向來表示三者的不同含義，比方說，用手指向後面表示昨天，指向前面表示明天，指向頭上表示今天"。這在我鎮上的鄉友們看來，毫無疑問，純屬無稽之談；但是，如果讓花鳥按牠們的標準來估量我的話，那我應該說是無懈可擊的。人必須尋找自我需求，相信這話吧。順應自然的日子是非常平靜的，很少會指責他的好逸惡勞吧。

有一些人為了娛樂消遣只好外出上劇院，與人交際應酬，相形之下，我在自己的生活方式裏至少就有這麼一點好處：我的生活本身已成了我的娛樂，而且還歷久常新。它是一個多幕劇，沒有結局。如果說我們確實想要過上好日子，按照我們學到的最新最佳的方式來管理生活，那麼，我們定不會被百無聊賴所困擾。緊緊跟隨你的天賦，它會時時刻刻給你展示一個嶄新的前景。做家務是一種令人愉快的消遣。屋子裏地板髒了，我就早早起來，一口氣全部家具搬到屋外草地上，牀和牀架疊成一堆，往地板上一灑水，再撒上一些湖裏的白砂，稍後用一把掃帚擦洗得白白淨淨；等村民們剛一吃過早飯，太陽已經曬得我屋子裏乾透時，我就可以搬家具回去，而我的沉思默想幾乎沒有中斷過。我很高興看到，我的全部家當在草地上很搶眼，疊成了一個小垛堆，活像吉卜賽人行李似的；而我的那張三條腿桌子，置放在松樹與山核桃樹底下，桌子上的鋼筆和墨水我全都沒有取走。它們看樣子也高興到屋外去，還不樂意搬回去呢。有時候，我心裏真巴不得在它們上頭支起一頂帳篷，我就安坐在那裏，看着太陽映照在它們上頭，聽聽微風吹拂着它們，真的太有意思了；熟悉的家具在屋外看上去要比屋子裏更耐人尋味。小鳥落在附近的樹枝上，永久花[4]長在桌子底下，黑莓的藤蔓纏繞着桌子腿；松果、栗子以及草莓的葉子俯拾即是。彷彿它們這些形態就這樣轉化為我們的家庭用具，桌椅、牀架子——因為我們的家庭用具原先就來自這些草木之間。

我的小屋坐落在一個小山坡上，緊挨着一大片樹林的邊緣，四周圍長滿幼小的北美油松和山核桃樹，離湖大約六桿[5]遠，有一條狹窄的小路從山腳下直通湖邊。我的前院裏，長着草莓、黑莓、永久花、狗尾草、一枝黃花、矮橡樹、沙櫻、烏飯樹和落花生。臨近5月底，沙櫻[6]在小路兩側綴滿了嬌嫩的花朵，短短的花梗周圍宛如一簇簇傘狀花叢，入秋後沉甸甸垂着又大又好看的櫻桃，形成花環似的在閃閃發光。感謝大自然的恩賜，我品嚐過這些櫻桃，儘管並不好吃。漆樹[7]在我屋子周圍瘋長，第一季度就長高了五六英尺，拱起了我砌好的一堵矮牆。她那闊大、羽狀熱帶樹葉片，望過去儘管有點怪，但還是招人喜愛。暮春時節，碩大的蓓蕾突然從彷彿死掉的枯枝上冒出來，像變魔術似的長成了淡雅嫩綠的柔軟枝條，直徑倒有一英寸；有時候，我坐在窗子跟前，由於她們不經意快速生長，樹杈不堪重負，我會聽到哧嚓一聲，一根鮮嫩的樹枝有如一把扇子冷不防墜落，其實這時一絲風都沒有，是給它自己的重量壓斷了。8月間，漫山遍野的漿果，在開花時節吸引了許多野蜜蜂。漿果也漸漸染上了鮮豔的天鵝絨般的深紅色，柔軟的枝條同樣因為不堪重負而給壓斷了。

今年夏天的一個午後，我坐在窗子邊，一羣鷹在我的林中空地上空來回盤旋；野鴨子在拼命疾飛，三三兩兩映入我的眼簾，或者閒不住地落在我的屋子後面白皮松枝頭上，當空叫喚；一隻魚鷹在波平似鏡的湖上，啄了一圈漣漪，叼走了一條魚；一隻水貂悄悄從我門前的沼澤地中溜出來，在湖岸邊逮住了一隻青蛙；蘆葦鳥常在這裏那裏飛落，莎草實在不堪重負，也都給壓彎了；在最後的半個小時裏，我聽到了火車轟隆轟隆的響聲，一會沉寂下去，一會又響了起來，就像鷓鴣[8]翅膀在撲動拍打着似的，從波士頓帶觀光客到鄉間來。我可不像那個孩子與世隔絕，聽說，那個孩子被送往這個村鎮東頭的一個農夫家，但他確實太想家，沒多久就出逃，又回到了自己家裏，這時他的鞋後跟都給磨破了。他從來沒見過這樣沉悶而又偏僻的地方；那裏的老百姓全跑光了；老天哪，你甚至連口哨聲都聽不見！我懷疑馬薩諸塞州現在還有沒有一個這樣的地方 —— 我們的林子真的成了一個靶子，

> 給飛箭似的鐵路所擊中，
> 寧靜的平原上和諧之音，
> 原來就是 —— 康科德。[9]

　　菲奇伯格鐵路離我住處南邊大約一百桿處與湖邊毗連。通常我沿着它的堤道走到村裏去，在某種程度上說，我就是通過這條路才跟社會有了聯繫。貨運列車上來回跑全程的那些人，常常向我點頭打招呼，彷彿我是他們的老相識，畢竟過往看見我的次數太多了，他們顯然以為我是個僱工；那可以了，我就算是個僱工吧。反正我也很樂意在地球軌道上的某個路段當一名養路工人。

　　不管寒冬酷暑，火車頭的汽笛聲穿過我的樹林，好像一隻盤旋在農夫院子上空的蒼鷹在尖聲叫喚，告訴我有許多浮躁不安的城市商人正在來到這個村鎮的周圍，或者說，有富於冒險精神的鄉村商人正在從相反

方向來到這裏。他們來自同一條地平線，於是彼此大聲發出警告，讓對方閃開讓道，這種警告聲音有時候兩個村鎮都聽得到。鄉村哪，看，你們的雜貨已送到；老鄉哪，你們的糧食已送到！如今沒有哪個農人還能獨立生活，敢對它們說一個"不"字。於是，鄉下人的哨子叫起來了，這就是你們付給它們的代價！像長長的攻城槌[10]的原木，以每小時二十英里的速度向城牆衝過去，裏面座椅多得不計其數，疲憊不堪、負擔沉重的城裏人都可以入內就座了。鄉村置備了如此巨大笨重的厚禮，向城市送去了座椅。印第安人山上長滿漿果的烏飯樹全給採伐殆盡，盛產越橘的草地也被耙平，果實都運到城裏去了。棉花上來了，布匹下去了；絲上來了，毛織品下去了；圖書上去了，可是寫作的智力卻下降了。

我看到那火車頭，拖着長長一排車廂，像行星運轉似的往前駛去，或者不妨說，像一顆彗星，看上去它的軌道不像可以轉回來的曲線，觀看的人不知道它按照哪種速度、朝着哪個方向駛去，還會不會再折回到這軌道上來；火車頭噴出的水蒸氣，如同一面旗幟，綴着金環銀環，飄浮在後面，就像我看到過懸浮高空的許多羽絨般的雲朵，一大塊、一大塊徐徐舒展，熠熠生輝——彷彿這個周遊四方的半人半仙、吞雲吐霧的怪物，馬上會把夕陽西沉時的天空當作火車的號衣似的。我聽到這匹鐵騎吼聲如雷，使羣山響起了回聲，它的鐵蹄震撼着大地，鼻孔裏不時噴火吐煙（我可不知道，在新的神話中，人們會收進甚麼樣的飛馬與火龍），看來大地終於添了新的一族，不愧為大地的居民。如果這一切確實都像看上去的那樣，人們通過役使風、土、水、火四大要素，達到崇高的目的，該有多好！如果飄浮在火車頭上空的雲是創英雄業績時灑下的熱汗，或者說像懸浮在農田上空的雲一樣惠及蒼生，那麼，四大要素和大自然本身都會樂意為人類效勞，做人類的護衛者。

我遠望清晨時份列車通過時的心情，如同我眺望日出時一模一樣。日出倒也不見得會比列車更準時。火車正在駛往波士頓，長長的一條雲帶在它後面延伸，越升越高，升上穹蒼，一瞬間遮住了太陽，並讓我遠處的田野隱沒在一片陰影中，儼然一列天上火車，而近旁的那列擁抱大地的小火車，只不過是矛槍上的小小倒鈎罷了。今年冬季裏有一天早上，那匹鐵騎的廄主起身得早，借着山間星光餵飼它，開始套車，而且那麼早就生起火來，給它體內供熱，讓它及時上路。反正做這種事，就像老一輩那樣簡單就可以了！遇上積雪很深時，人們給它穿雪鞋，用巨大的鐵犁在羣山之間辟開一條路，直達沿海地區；而在上面行駛的列車就像一部播種機，把所有浮躁不安的人們和價格浮動的商品，當作種子撒在了鄉間。這匹火駒整天這樣在鄉間飛駛，只有主人歇息時才停下來。子夜時份，我也會被它的鐵蹄聲和哼哧哼哧的噴氣聲所驚醒，這時，它正在遠處森林峽谷裏，碰到了冰雪交加等險情，直到晨星初現時才回到馬廄，殊不知既沒有休息，也沒有打個盹，又馬不停蹄地上路了。要不然在傍晚時份，我聽見它在馬廄裏釋放出白晝過剩的精力，使自己的神經鬆弛下來，肝腦也靜下來一兩個鐘頭，好讓那鐵騎合起眼迷睡了。但願這項事業能持之以恆、毫不疲倦，而又英姿勃勃、威風凜凜，該有多好！

　　遠離城鎮、人跡罕至的一些森林，過去唯有獵戶大白天才進入過，如今那些燈火輝煌的特等客車，在漆黑的夜裏風馳電掣般駛去，坐在裏面的人們卻一無所知；此時此刻正停靠在村鎮或者城市的某個燈光燦爛的火車站，有上流社會人士雲集在那裏，下一站卻停靠在迪斯默爾沼澤[11]，嚇跑了貓頭鷹和狐狸。列車的離站、到站，如今成了鄉村日常生活裏的頭等大事。它們來來去去，既定期而又準時，汽笛聲很遠就聽得見，農夫們常常據此來校準鐘錶，這麼一來，一個管理完善的機制使整個國家管理得井然有序。自從發明了火車以來，人們在遵守時刻方面不是有所改進嗎？人們在火車站裏說話和思想的節奏，不是比在驛站裏面更快了嗎？火車站裏彷彿有着通上了電流的氣氛。火車站所創造的種種奇蹟，使我感到驚奇；原先我以為，我的一些鄰居應不會搭乘如此快捷的交通工具到波士頓去，可是現在鐘聲一響，他們卻都到了站台上。仿照"鐵路方式"辦事，現在已成了口頭禪；有關權威機構屢屢提醒人們不要挨近鐵路道軌，對於這種真心誠意的告誡還是值得記取的。這種事既不能向鬧事羣眾宣讀"取締鬧事法"勒令散去，也不能向騷亂羣眾朝天開槍。我們已經創造了一個命運女神阿特洛波斯[12]，那是永遠不閃開避讓的。（不妨給你的火車頭命名為"阿特洛波斯"號吧。）人們一看公告就知道，幾點幾分將有哪些弩箭射向羅盤上某一個具體地點；反正它從不干預別人的事，而孩子們上學則走另一條專線。因此，我們生活得更有把握了。我們就這樣人人都可以培養成威廉・退爾[13]的兒子了。空中有的是看不見的弩箭。每一條路都是通向命運之路，只有你自己的路例外，那就可以了，還是走你自己的路吧。

　　我之所以對商業嘖嘖稱讚，是因為它有進取心、有勇氣。它不會兩手十指交錯地緊握着向朱庇特祈禱。我看見這些人每天在忙着做生意，不管怎樣都有膽識和滿足的表現，做得比他們想像的多得多，説不定比他們精心設計的還要出色呢。在布埃納維斯塔[14]前線能堅守半個小時的那種英雄氣概，固然我也覺得很感動，但是，更讓我深深感動的，還是在鏟雪機裏過冬的人們那種堅定、愉快的精神；他們不僅具有拿破崙認為最難得的凌晨三點鐘打仗的勇氣，而且還不肯早早休息，硬要頂到暴風雪停住之後，要不然在他們的鐵騎的筋骨都給凍僵之後，他們這才躺下睡覺。這天大清早，特大風雪還在肆虐，簡直冷得人們的血液快給凍結，我從他們呼出的水汽凍結後形成的霧堤裏，聽到火車頭發出被蒙住了的鐘聲，宣告列車開來了，沒有誤點，根本不管來自新英格蘭北部的暴風雪百般阻擋；我看到了那些鏟雪人披雪掛霜，他們正低着頭仔細察看那鏟雪板底下翻起來的，可不是雛菊和田鼠洞穴，而是像內華達山脈的巨礫，堪稱天外之物。

商業是出乎意料地自信、莊重、機靈、有進取心，而且還根本不知疲倦。它所採用的方法都很自然，乃是許多充滿幻想的事業和感情用事的實驗所不可企及，因此才獲得出色的成功。一列貨車打從我身邊轟隆轟隆地駛過，我不由得頓覺心曠神怡，我聞得到從長碼頭到香普蘭湖一路上貨物散發出來的氣味，使我想起了異國他鄉，想起了珊瑚島、印度洋、熱帶地區，乃至於廣袤無邊的環球世界。我看到了棕櫚葉，來年夏天，不知有多少新英格蘭淺黃色髮絲的頭上會戴着它；我還看到了馬尼拉的大麻、椰子殼、舊繩索、黃麻袋、廢鐵和鏽釘子，就在此時此刻，我覺得自己更像一名世界公民了。這一車子的破船帆要是拿去造紙、印書，也許會使閱讀更容易，也更為有趣呢？有誰能夠像這些破船帆那樣繪聲繪色寫下自己驚濤駭浪的歷史呢？它們就是根本不用改正的校樣。緬因州森林裏的木材從這裏運走，因為有些木材已經運走了，或者被鋸成板料，上次水漲時沒有出海的木材，每一千根漲了四塊錢，松木、雲杉和雪松 —— 質量分為一等、二等、三等和四等，但不久前木材總共才只有一個質量標準，價格常在熊、駝鹿和北美馴鹿的價位之上，波動不定。稍後，轟隆轟隆駛過的是托馬斯頓[15]石灰，第一流貨色，將被運往遙遠的山區讓它逐漸熟化。至於這一袋袋的破布，真可以說五顏六色，質地好壞都有，乃是棉花和亞麻落到了最慘的境地，也是衣着穿戴的最終下場 —— 它們的圖案時下再也沒人嘖嘖稱讚了，除非是在密爾沃基[16]，因為那些色彩搶眼的衣物，英國的、法國的，或者美國的印花布、方格布、平紋細布等等，既有富人的，也有窮人的，都是從四面八方集攏來，將要變成一種顏色的紙，或者僅僅色彩深淺不一的紙，說不定在那紙上面會寫出一些真實生活的故事，有的寫上層社會，有的寫下層社會，不過全是根據事實來寫的！這一節悶罐車散發出鹹魚的腥味，強烈的新英格蘭商業味道，讓我回想到大淺灘[17]和漁業的情景。鹹魚 ——誰沒有見過？徹頭徹尾是為了芸芸眾生醃製的，決不會使它變質，讓持續蒙恩加爾文神學[18]的聖人們都感到臉紅。有了鹹魚，你可以掃街、鋪路、砍劈柴；卡車司機本人與他的貨物也好拿它來遮陽避雨——還有商人在商鋪開張時懸掛一條鹹魚在店門上當招牌，正如某個康科德商人做過的一樣，到頭來連老主顧全都不確定它究竟是動物、菜蔬，還是礦物，不過它依然潔白像雪花呢。要是你放牠入鍋裏煮，煮出來的準是一條味道好極了的鹹魚，可供週末晚餐時食用。接下來是西班牙的皮革，依稀可辨那牛尾巴舉向空中還在旋轉，有如這些公牛當初奔馳在西班牙本土大草原一模一樣——一種執拗的典型，證明一切與生俱有的缺憾是如何沒得希望和不可救藥啊。說實話，在我了解一個人的脾性後，我承認，在目前生存狀態下，我並不指望它變好或者變壞。正如東方人所說的："一條狗尾巴可以加熱、燙平，用帶子綁住，花費了十二年精力，到頭來它的本性還是改不了。"類似牛尾巴這樣根深蒂固的本性，唯一的根治辦法，就是把它們製成膠汁，我相信通常它們都可派這樣的用場，發揮黏性的作用。這裏有一大桶糖蜜或者白蘭地，即將運往佛蒙特州卡廷斯維爾市，交給約翰·史密斯先生，格林山區的商人，他是給鄰近本人林中空地的農夫們來辦進口貨的，此刻也許他站在艙壁上面，心裏捉摸着近期到岸的幾批貨物，會如何影響他的貨價，現在告訴他的顧客們，說他急切期望下一趟火車會運來第一流貨色，其實，這話在今天早上以前，他給他們唸叨過已有二十遍呢。甚至還在《卡廷斯維爾時報》上登過廣告。

這批貨物運走了，另一批貨物運來了。我被一陣颼颼聲驚醒，於是放下書本，抬眼只見一些長長的松樹，好像插上翅膀飛過了格林山區和康涅狄格州；

這些松樹是在遙遠的北方砍下來的，飛箭似的在十分鐘內穿過了城鎮，人們還來不及看上一眼，它就成為一根桅桿，豎立在大旗艦上。[19]聽吧！運牲畜的車開來了，裝着千山萬嶺的牛羊，甚麼天上的羊圈啦、馬廄啦、牛欄啦，甚麼手持牧杖的放牧人啦，趕着羊羣的小牧童啦，除了山裏牧場以外，全都來了，它們好像被 9 月裏秋風從山上吹下來的落葉在打轉。空中充滿牛羊的咩咩聲，公牛們在猛撞亂擠，彷彿正在駛過的是一座放牧牛羊的山谷。那隻老的帶頭羊只要鈴鐺一響，高山真的像公羊似的在歡躍，小山崗有如小山羊在蹦跳。列車有一節車廂都是放牧人，此刻和他們放牧的牛羊幾乎平起平坐，他們雖然下了崗，可還是手持那根沒有用處的牧杖，好像它就是他們司職的標誌。但是，他們的牧羊狗上哪裏去了？這對牧羊狗來說，可是大潰散呀；牠們完全被拋開了，牠們的嗅覺也不靈了。我彷彿聽到牠們在彼得博羅山後面狂吠不已，或者在格林山區西坡上喘着氣奔走呢。牠們不會跟着牛羊一塊被宰割。牠的職責也到盡頭了。牠們的忠誠和機靈現在不管用了。牠們心灰意冷回窩去了，也許乾脆豁出去，與狼和狐狸結盟。你的牧羊人生涯就這樣隨風而去了。但是，鐘聲響了，我要離開軌道，讓列車駛過去 ——鐵路依我看是甚麼呢？

> 我不去張望
> 它的盡頭在何方。
> 它填高一些溝壑，
> 又給燕子築好堤岸，
> 它讓黃沙滿處飛揚，
> 又叫黑莓隨地生長。

可是我穿過鐵路，就像我走過樹林裏的小道。我不會讓火車的黑煙、蒸氣和嘶嘶聲污染了我的眼睛與耳朵。

如今，列車已經遠去了，躁動的世界也隨着列車遠去了，湖中的魚再也感覺不到火車的隆隆聲，我卻感到份外孤寂。漫長的午後，也許只有偶然從遠處公路上隱隱約約傳來的一輛車或是一組車馬的輕微響聲，才會干擾我的沉思吧。

有時，趕上星期天，順風的時候，我聽到鐘聲，來自林肯、阿克頓、貝德福或者康科德的鐘聲，聽起來柔和悅耳，儼然是自然的旋律，迴蕩在曠野上，真美極了。在遙遠的樹林上空，這種旋律平添了一種顫動的微弱聲響，彷彿地平線上的松針就是豎琴上的琴弦，正在輕輕撥弄着似的。凡此種種音響，哪怕在最遠處，只要聽得見，都有一種同樣的效果，勝過七弦琴上的顫音，就像迢迢遠方的山脊，由於大氣介於中間，被抹上了淡藍色，望過去格外令人悅目。我覺得這次傳來的是一種在微風中越傳越悠揚的旋律，與樹林裏每一片葉子和松針喁喁私語後，風又吸收部份聲音，經過變調在一座山谷迴響之後又傳到了另一座山谷。這種迴響在某種程度來説，就是初始的聲音，具有神奇的魅力。它不僅重複了鐘聲裏值得重複的部份，而且部份還有着樹林裏的聲音；以及林中仙子低吟的昵語和樂音。

傍晚，樹林盡頭、遠處的地平線上，傳來牛的哞哞聲，很甜美動聽，開始時我會誤認為是某些滑稽説唱團[20]在演唱，因為有時我聽到過他們唱的小夜曲，也許此刻他們正好吟遊在山谷之間；可是聽着聽着，我很快失望了 —— 失望之餘，我還是略感欣慰 —— 因為那聲音漸漸拖長，變成了像牛叫那種廉價原始的音樂。我這樣説絕不是在挖苦那些年輕人，而是表示我對他們的歌唱很欣賞，我説，我分明聽得出他們的歌聲與哞哞聲差不多，不過，説到底，兩者無疑都是天籟，你説是不是？

夏天有過一些日子，每天傍晚七點半，火車很準時駛過以後，三聲夜鶯唱過半個小時的晚禱曲，就落在我門前的樹樁上，或者落在我的屋脊上。每天晚上，日落以後，在某個特定時間的五分鐘內，牠們就開始鳴叫，幾乎跟座鐘一樣準確。我利用難得的機會，漸漸熟悉了牠們的習慣。有時，我聽到同時有四五隻三聲夜鶯，在樹林各個不同地點啼唱，偶然一隻鳥兒唱的比另一隻鳥兒差了一小節，而且離我又是那麼近，我不僅聽得出每一個音符之後的咯咯聲，而且時常聽到一種獨特的嗡嗡聲，就像一隻飛蠅落進了蜘蛛網，只不過比飛蠅的響聲稍微高一些。有時候，一隻三聲夜鶯會從好幾英尺遠的樹林飛過來，繞着我飛來飛去，就像被一條繩子拴住了似的，說不定是我挨着鳥蛋太近了吧。牠們徹夜通宵時斷時續不斷啼唱，而且常在黎明前和黎明即將來臨之際，牠們的歌唱又跟過去一樣富於極大樂感。

其他鳥兒靜下來時，叫梟開始鳴叫，像哭喪婦似的發出的嗚 —— 嚕 —— 嚕。那種淒叫聲，頗有本·瓊生的遺韻 [21]。聰明的子夜女巫！牠不像詩人們筆下 tu—whit tu—who 那麼真實和呆板，不過，嚴肅來說，那是一支異常蕭穆的墓畔小曲，像一對自殺的戀人在陰曹冥府的樹林裏，不知怎地想起了生前戀愛的苦與樂，少不得彼此安慰一番。然而，我特別愛聽牠們的哀鳴，牠陰慘慘的應答，沿着樹林一側不停囀鳴；有時，讓我聯想到音樂和鳴禽；彷彿那就是音樂飽含淚水的陰暗面，不得不歌吟的悔恨和哀歎。牠們都是一些墮落者的幽靈，低落的情緒，憂鬱的預感，以前牠們曾經有人的形態夜遊四方，只做黑暗勾當，如今牠們早已罪孽昭著，牠們吟唱哀歌，祈求贖罪。牠們使我全新感覺到，我們共同居住的大自然真是豐富多彩，兼容並包。哦 —— 喔 —— 喲 —— 喲 —— 喲 —— 我根本還沒出生 —— 生 —— 生 —— 生 —— 過！湖的這一邊，有一隻夜鶯歎道，在焦灼的絕望中來回盤旋，在灰溜溜的橡樹上尋找新的棲息處。稍後，湖的另一邊，傳來了迴響：我根本還沒出生 —— 生 —— 生 —— 生 —— 過！那迴響充滿着發顫的真摯感情；甚至從遙遠的林肯那邊的樹林也隱隱約約傳來迴響 —— 還沒有出生 —— 生 —— 生 —— 生 —— 生過！

此外還有一隻啞啞鳴叫的貓頭鷹向我唱小夜曲呢。在近處聽，也許你會覺得這是大自然中最憂鬱的鳴叫聲，彷彿牠想讓這種聲音凝聚人們臨終之前的呻吟，並使它永遠留在牠的歌吟之中 —— 這是凡人彌留之際留下可憐而又微弱的遺音，他留希望在身後，在進入黑黝黝的幽谷時像動物一樣嚎叫，還帶着活人的抽泣聲，由於某種咯咯聲很動聽，但聽着聽着反而更可怕 —— 我想模擬那種聲音時，不覺發現自己一開始唸出了這咯字音，正好表明：一切健康勇敢的思想都已壞疽時，一個人的心靈達到了膠凝似的發黴變質階段。它使我想起了盜屍鬼、白癡和瘋子的嚎叫。可是此時此刻，從遠處的樹林傳來了一聲回應，由於離得遠些，聽起來倒是真的很悅耳 —— 呼 —— 呼 —— 呼 —— 呼啦 —— 呼；說實話，那種聲音只會給人帶來許多愉快的聯想，不管聽它的時候，是白天還是夜晚，是夏天還是冬天。

可喜的是我這裏有貓頭鷹。讓牠們為人們做些白癡般的瘋狂嚎叫吧。這種聲音最適宜於晝光照不到的沼澤地和幽暗的樹林，使人聯想到大自然中還有一個幅員遼闊而尚待開發的領域，人類至今依然沒有發現。牠們代表全然的朦朧狀態和人人都有的沒得滿足的思想。太陽整天照在一些原始的沼澤表面上，這裏只見雲杉林立，松蘿地衣長滿樹身，小鷹在上空來回盤旋，黑頭山雀在常春藤裏面嘰嘰喳喳，野鴨子和野兔子則在底下潛行；可是此時此刻，一個更陰鬱、更合適的白晝來臨了，一種不同的生物已經甦醒過來，在那裏充份表達了大自然的意圖。

夜深以後，我聽見遠處車輛從橋上開過，發出轟隆隆的聲音 —— 這種聲音在夜間聽起來顯得格外遙遠 —— 我還聽到了犬吠聲，有時我能聽到遠處牛棚裏傳來一頭憂鬱的母牛的哞哞聲。與此同時，環湖岸邊震盪着牛蛙的叫聲，牠們是冥頑不靈的古代酒鬼和縱酒歡鬧之徒的精靈，依然不知悔改，在牠們冥河般的湖上放聲高唱 —— 但願瓦爾登湖上凌波仙子們原諒我作這樣的比喻，因為這裏儘管沒有水生植物，但青蛙遍地都是 —— 牠們倒是樂於遵循古老宴席上狂歡亂叫的規則，雖然牠們的聲音越發沙啞了，顯得一本正經，於是嘲笑歡樂，美酒也失去了醇味，僅僅成了灌飽牠們腹部的液體，朦朧醉意不會淹沒往昔的記憶，只會使牠們的肚子脹飽，頓覺沉甸甸、脹鼓鼓的。那隻牛蛙下巴支在心形葉子上，好像在垂涎的嘴角底下掛了一塊餐巾，牠在北岸底下豪飲了一口過去看不起的水酒，就向後傳遞酒杯，同時連聲吆喝道：特爾 —— 爾 —— 爾 —— 烏恩克，特爾 —— 爾 —— 爾 —— 烏恩克，特爾 —— 爾 —— 爾 —— 爾 —— 烏恩克！這一聲口令馬上從遠處的水面重複後又傳了過來，那是另一隻職位稍低的牛蛙心滿意足喝下一口酒後發出同樣的口令；這一聲酒令在湖邊繞了一周，司酒令的牛蛙很滿意，大聲喝道：特爾 —— 爾 —— 爾 —— 烏恩克，於是，每一隻牛蛙依次重複着同樣的聲音，一直傳遞給那隻喝得最少、漏水最快、肚子最癟的牛蛙，傳遞中一點沒出錯；稍後，酒令聲又一遍遍往下傳遞，直到太陽驅散晨霧為止，這時只有那隻長老牛蛙還沒有喝醉跌進湖裏，[22] 所以說，既有爛醉狀態，又有跳入湖裏的動感。而且時不時喊着特爾 —— 爾 —— 爾 —— 烏恩克，等待回應，但到頭來還是徒勞。

我可說不定，在我的林中空地上聽過公雞報曉，我覺得養隻小公雞還是值得的，哪怕僅僅當牠為鳴禽，為了聽聽牠的打鳴也好。公雞從前是印第安人的野雞，在所有鳥類中，牠的鳴叫聲當然最出色，要是牠們還沒有被馴養成家禽的話，牠們的鳴叫聲很快會成為我們森林中最有名的聲音，勝過鵝的嘎嘎聲和貓頭鷹的哀鳴聲；然後，不妨想一想吧，當公雞嘹亮的啼唱停歇時，母雞就會快快樂樂咕咕叫來填補這個空當！難怪人類將這種鳥兒列入家禽類呢 —— 更不必提雞蛋和雞腿了。冬天的早上，漫步在羣鳥繁衍生息的樹林裏，聽聽野公雞在枝頭鳴叫，那麼清脆又嘹亮，方圓好幾英里以內，大地為之震響，其他鳥兒微弱的鳴叫聲通通給淹沒了 —— 你可想而知！牠會使整個國家處於戒備狀態。誰不會早點起牀，一天比一天起得更早，直到他變得說不出來的健康、富有與聰明呢？全世界的詩人在讚美他們本國鳴禽的同時，全都讚美過這種異國他鄉鳥兒的樂音。全世界哪個地方對勇敢的雄雞全都相宜。牠甚至比本地產的禽鳥要略勝一籌。牠歷來體質很好，音色洪亮，精神永不衰萎。即使航行在大西洋和太平洋上的水手，也都會被牠的啼唱聲所喚醒；殊不知牠那嘹亮的啼聲，卻從來沒有使我從睡夢中醒來。我沒有養狗、貓、牛、豬，也沒有養母雞，也許你會說我這裏缺失家畜的聲音；其實，我這裏也沒有攪拌奶油的聲音，沒有紡車的聲音，甚至沒有水壺煮沸時的聲音，沒有咖啡壺的嘶嘶聲，更沒有孩子們的哭鬧聲等等給我一些慰藉。一個抱殘守缺的人，也許就這樣發了瘋，乃至於鬱鬱悶死。牆裏面連老鼠都沒有，因為牠們通通餓死了，或者寧可說，從來就沒有被誘餌所吸引過 —— 只有松鼠在屋頂上和地板下走動，三聲夜鶯落在屋脊上，藍色的鳥在窗下尖叫，兔子和土撥鼠在屋底下竄動，叫梟或者貓頭鷹棲在屋子後面，野鵝或者愛笑的潛水鳥掠過湖面，此外還有狐狸會在夜間吠叫。甚至雲雀或黃鸝，這些溫和的鳥兒，從來都還沒有造訪過我的林中空地。院子裏沒有公雞的啼唱，也沒有母雞的聒噪，你會說，那根本不像個院子！但是一無遮攔的大自然，直接延伸到了你的窗子跟前。一片新生的樹林在你的窗下，野黃櫨樹和黑莓藤蔓爬進了你的地窖；挺拔的北美油松因無生長空間，觸碰到屋子的木板而嘎吱嘎吱作響，它們的根鬚也延伸到宅基地下頭。大風刮來的，不是天窗或者窗簾，而是你屋後面松樹的殘枝斷杈，或者連根拔起的松樹，可供燃料之用。大雪中不是沒有通向前院大門的小路 —— 而是根本沒有門 —— 沒有前院 —— 沒有通往文明世界的路！

章註

1 籟：此處指自然界發出的聲音。中國古詩中有"萬籟此俱寂，但餘鐘磬聲"詩句。亦可參見《莊子・齊物篇》。

2 英文中一個星期裏的每一天，都是以某個神的名字演變而來的，比如，星期二，Tuesday 由 Tiu's day 演變而來，是陰暗神提爾 (Tiu) 的名字；又如星期三，Wednesday 由 Woden's day 演變而來，是戰神瓦丹（Woden）的名字等等。總之，除了星期六來自古羅馬農神薩圖恩（Saturn）以外，星期二、三、四全部來自古代斯堪的納維亞神話，故被梭羅稱為異教徒。

3 普里：此處指巴西印第安人，附錄引文摘自菲菲夫人的《一位女士周遊世界》。

4 永久花：花朵乾枯後色狀均不變的植物，尤指某些蠟菊屬植物。

5 桿：美國長度單位。1 桿約有 5.5 碼。

6 沙櫻：拉丁文學名 Cerasus pumila。

7 漆樹：拉丁文學名 Rhus glabra。

8 鶉雞：拉丁文學名 Tetrao umbellus。

9 康科德：在英文中和諧之音和康科德是同一個單詞 —— 文中和諧之音和，真是一語雙關，由此可見梭羅寫書的初衷。引詩作者為梭羅好友詩人錢寧。

10 攻城槌：古代西方一種攻城的兵器，此處原木比喻早期火車車廂均用原木製成。

11 迪斯默爾沼澤：位於弗吉尼亞州東南部和北卡羅來納州東北部沿海平原上，幾乎無法越過，逃亡的奴隸經常藏身此地。

12 命運女神阿特洛波斯：Atropos，古羅馬神話中的命運三女神之一，司職剪斷生命之線。

13 威廉・退爾：William Tell，瑞士傳說中反抗奧地利統治的英雄人物，為爭取民族獨立而鬥爭，被迫用箭射放在他兒子頭上的蘋果，結果獲得成功，兒子安然無恙。

14 布埃納維斯塔：墨西哥一地名，1847 年曾經是戰場。

15 托馬斯頓：地名，位於南緬因州。

16 密爾沃基：美國威斯康星州東南部一港口城市，瀕臨密歇根湖。

17 大淺灘：北美紐芬蘭島東南廣闊的大西洋淺灘，為世界大漁場之一。

18 蒙恩加爾文神學：所謂持續蒙恩，指上帝的預定選民註定會持續蒙受恩典直至得救。

19 引自英國著名詩人約翰・彌爾頓（1608—1674）的《失樂園》。

20 滑稽説唱團：在美國，有些白人飾黑人作滑稽演唱活動。

21 本・瓊生：Ben Johnson，1572—1637，英國著名詩人與劇作家，與莎士比亞齊名。

22 梭羅在本書中常用一語雙關手法，使文章更生動，富有活力。此處仿英文成語 under the table，意思是爛醉，或醉後不省人事。

5

離羣索居

這是一個多美的傍晚，全身只有一種感覺，每個毛孔都浸透喜悦。我以出奇的自由，在大自然裏走來走去，已與大自然渾然一體。我脱去外衣，只穿襯衫，漫步在多石的湖邊，天氣雖有涼意，多雲又有風，我也沒有發覺有甚麼特別誘人的景物，但周圍一切於我可以説異常相宜。牛蛙的聒噪迎來了黑夜，吹皺了湖水的微風傳來了三聲夜鶯的囀鳴聲。檀木和楊樹枝葉搖曳多姿，我豈能無動於衷，幾乎連氣都喘不過來？然而，就像湖水一樣，我心中寧靜只有一些漣漪，而沒有激起波濤。晚風吹起的一些微波，依然像波平似鏡的湖面一樣，離暴風雨還遠着呢。雖然天色已黑，風還在樹林裏呼呼作響，波浪還在拍岸，一些動物還在用自己的樂音，為另一些動物催眠。沒有十全十美的寧靜。野性十足的動物並沒有安歇下來，這時正在捕捉獵物呢；狐狸、臭鼬、兔子，這時也在田野上、森林裏遊蕩着，一無畏懼。牠們是大自然的巡夜人 —— 是連接生機盎然的白晝的一個環節。

我回到屋裏，發現已有好幾位訪客來過，他們都留下了自己的名片，有的是一束鮮花，有的是一個常春藤編的花環，有的是用鉛筆在一片黃色胡桃木葉子上或者小木片上留下的名字。他們難得入林一遊，常拿樹林裏的小玩意，放在手裏一路把玩，離去時，有的故意有的出於偶然，就留在寒舍。有一位剝了柳樹皮下來，編成了一枚戒指，丟在我的桌子上。我外出時訪客有沒有來過，我總能知道，不是折斷樹枝或者青草彎斜了，就是地上有他們的鞋印，一般來説，根據他們留下的一些雪泥鴻爪，比方說，有的丟下一朵花，有的抓來一把青草卻又給扔掉了，哪怕是遠到半英里開外的鐵路邊上才扔掉呢；或者有的人抽雪茄或者煙斗，人去了煙味還不散，反正我都能說出他們的性別、年齡或者性格。豈但如此，我往往能根據煙斗的香味，推斷出六十桿開外的公路上，有一個觀光客打從那裏經過。

我們周圍的空間，一般來說很寬敞。我們的視線不會就在咫尺之間。茂密的樹林並不是就在我們家門口，湖泊也是如此，通常都是隔着一塊空地，由於我們經常使用，對它很熟悉，我們還佔有了它，用柵籬圍了起來，彷彿向大自然要求收回來似的。如此浩瀚無比、幾個平方英里內人跡罕至，但是遭人類遺棄的大森林，我憑甚麼要據為己有呢？我的鄰居離我最近也有一英里之遙，而且，除非登臨小山頂上，在我住處方圓半英里以內，不管從哪個方向看，都看不見一所房子。我的視域全給樹林包圍起來了；抬眼遠望，只見一邊是與湖接界的鐵路，另一邊是一道沿着林地公路的圍欄。但從大體上說，我住的地方就像在大草原上一樣孤獨。這個地方離新英格蘭，就像離亞洲或者非洲一樣遙遠。實際上，我倒是有我自己的太陽、月亮和星星，還有一個完全屬我自己的小天地。入夜以後，從來不會有觀光客從我屋子跟前經過，或者叩響我的門，我真的就像混沌初開時最早的那個人或者最後的那個人；除非到了春光明媚的季節，經過漫長的嚴冬間隔之後，有些人會從村裏來這處釣鱈魚 —— 說白了，在瓦爾登湖裏，他們釣得更多的是他們自己的天性，不外乎用黃昏給魚鈎權當誘餌罷了 —— 不料他們很快就偷偷離去了，通常魚簍子裏幾乎一無所獲，卻"把整個世界留給了黃昏與我"整源自英國詩人格雷[1]的名詩《墓園挽歌》。，而黑夜的核心從來還沒有被任何人類鄰居褻瀆過。我相信，人們一般說來還是有點害怕黑夜的，儘管巫婆全給吊死，基督教和蠟燭也都給引進來了。

不過，有時候，我會切身感受到，在大自然中不論任何場合，都能跟最甜蜜、最溫柔、最天真和最鼓舞人的朋友結交，乃至於對憤世嫉俗的可憐人和最憂鬱的人也不例外。凡是生活在大自然之中，心智還健全的人，就不可能會有極度的憂鬱。對於健康而無邪的耳朵，暴風雨無非是風神埃俄羅斯 [2] 式的音樂罷了。任何事情確實無法迫使一個簡單而勇敢的人產生一種低俗的悲哀。我在享受四季給予的友情時，我相信，不管甚麼事情都不能使生活成為我的累贅。濛濛細雨滋潤了我的豆子地，讓我今天留在家裏，但我並不因此感到討厭、發愁，反而還覺得很好呢。下雨天，固然我不能下地鋤豆子，可是，下了雨遠比我鋤地更有價值。如果說雨總是下個不停，使地裏種子和低窪地的馬鈴薯都泡爛了，那對高地上的草還是有好處的，既然如此，豈不是對我也有好處。有時候，我拿自己跟別人作比較，看來天上諸神對我特別垂青，比我應得的還要多呢；彷彿我有一張證書和保單在他們手上，而別人卻沒有，因此，我得到了上天特殊的指引和保護。我可不是在恭維我自己，不過，很可能倒是他們在吹捧我。過去我從來沒有感到孤獨，或者換句話說，絲毫沒有被孤獨感壓抑過，不過有一次，那是在我進入樹林幾週之後，我有過一段時間懷疑，對於一種寧靜而健康的生活來說，有個近鄰互相交往是不是必須的。獨處不是令人愉快的事情。與此同時，我又意識到自己的情緒有一點失常，不過好像我也預知自己會恢復正常。我正在冥思苦想之際，紛紛細雨飄落下來了，我突然意識到，與大自然默默一來二往，沒承望會如此甜美、如此友好，在每一滴淅瀝的雨聲中，在我屋子周圍每個聲音和每個景點中，都有一種無窮無盡和難以表述的友情，有如一種支援我的氣氛，使我原先與人毗鄰而居的念頭已經一無可取，從此，我再也不曾有過那種想法。每根細小的松針都富有同情心，彷彿漸漸長大，成了我的朋友。我清楚意識到，即使在我們通常稱之為野蠻、沉悶的地方，都有某種與我有緣的感覺，而且，與我最親近的血緣、最富有人情味的，並不是一個人或一個村民，因此，從今以後，不管身在何方，我再也不感到陌生了——悲慟使哀傷的人過早衰竭；

> 生者在塵世間，來日無多，
> 托斯卡的美麗女兒啊。[3]

　　我某些最美好的時光，是在春秋兩季持續暴風雨時，上午或午後，我困在屋裏，聽着暴風不停咆哮和大雨瓢潑之聲，卻給了我些微慰藉；暮色早早四合，迎來了一個漫漫長夜，其間就有千絲萬縷思緒彷彿及時生根，徐緩舒展開來。來自東北角的滂沱大雨，使村裏每幢房子都經受了考驗，女僕們手提拖把和水桶，站在門口攔截大水進屋，這時我坐在小屋門背後，那是唯一的一道門，至此我才深深體會到它有力地保護了我。在一場大雷雨中，閃電擊中了湖對岸的一棵高大的北美油松，自上而下劈出一道螺旋形狀的凹槽，很顯眼而又勻稱，有一英寸多深，四五英寸寬，就像你在手杖上開的凹槽一模一樣。前天，我從它那裏經過，一抬眼就看到了那個標記，我不禁大吃一驚，那是八年前一個嚇人的、不可抗拒的霹靂留下來的痕跡，現在看上去比從前要清晰。人們常跟我唸叨說：「我想，你在那裏一定會感到很孤獨，總想和人們更接近一些吧，特別是在下雨、下雪的日日夜夜裏。」我按捺不住很想就這樣回答：——我們居住的整個地球，充其量只不過是宇宙中小小的一個點。那邊的天空那顆星星，連我們的天文儀器還根本估量不出它有多大，你想想，它上面的兩個相距最遠的居民又能有多遠距離呢？那我怎麼會覺得孤獨呢？我們這個地球難道不也是在銀河系嗎？你提的這個問題，我覺得並不是最重要的問題呀。甚麼樣的一種空間，才會隔開人與人，讓他感到孤獨呢？我發覺兩條腿不管怎麼用力走，也不能讓兩顆心挨得更近些。我們的住處最想靠近的是甚麼地方？當然不是人多的地方，甚麼車站啦、郵局啦、酒吧啦、禮拜堂啦、學校啦、雜貨店啦、烽火山啦、五點區啦 [4]，因為這些地方人羣雜沓 —— 而是更樂意接近我們生命不竭之源泉 —— 大自然，我們從自己全部經歷中發現，我們的生命源自大自然，就像長在水邊的柳樹，它的根鬚也向水邊延伸一樣，人的天性不同，因此情況也殊異，不過，聰明的人就是在這樣的地方挖他的地窖……有一天晚上，在去瓦爾登湖的路上，我趕上一位鎮上鄉友，他已積攢了所謂的"一筆很可觀的資產" —— 雖然我對此從來還沒有正面了解過 —— 他趕着兩頭牛到市場去，問我怎麼會心血來潮，全放棄了生活中那麼多的安逸。我回答說，我非常確信，我真的很喜歡這樣的生活；我說這話可不是鬧着玩的。就這樣，我回家上牀安歇了，撇下他在黑暗泥濘中朝着布萊頓走去 —— 或者說，朝着光明城 [5] 走去 —— 說不定他在清晨某個時刻就會趕到那處了。

對一個死者來說，任何覺醒或者復活的前景，不管在甚麼時間、甚麼地點，都是無足輕重。也許會發生這種情況的地點總是相同的，對我們的感官來說有着難以形容的歡欣。我們大多數人都拿一些無關的、倏忽的枝節當作大事去做。實際上，它們才是使我們分心的原因。離萬物最近的是創造一切的力量。其次挨近我們的，是最莊重的法則在不斷起作用。再次挨近我們的，是創造我們出來的那個工匠 [6]，而不是我們僱用的工匠，雖然我們特別喜歡跟他嘮叨。

> "鬼神之為德，其盛矣乎！"
> "視之而弗見，聽之而弗聞，體物而不可遺。"

"使天下之人，齋明盛服，以承祭祀，洋洋乎如在其上，如在其左右。" [7]

我們都是一種試驗的對象，我對這種試驗還頗感興趣呢。在這種情況下，難道說我們乾脆離開這個充滿流言蜚語的社會 —— 用自己的思想來鼓舞我們自己就不行嗎？孔子説："道不孤，必有鄰。"誠哉斯言。

有了思考，我們就會心智健全，歡欣若狂。通過心靈有意識的努力，我們就可以超然獨立於各種行動及其後果之外；世間萬物，不管好壞，都像激流似的從我們身邊逝去。我們還不是渾然一體融合於大自然之中。也許我是急流中的一塊浮木，或者就是從高空俯瞰它的因陀羅[8]。看一場戲很可能感動我；另一方面，一件看似與我更休戚相關的真事，卻未必能感動我。我只知道我自己是作為一個人而存在；也可以說，就是反映我的思想和情感的舞台；我很清楚自己有一種雙重人格，因此，我可以遠遠看待自己，就像看待別人一樣。不管我的經驗該有多麼生動有力，我都意識到自我的一部份在批評我，在某種程度上説，卻又不是自我的一部份，而是一個旁觀者，並不分享我的經驗，而至多只是注意到我的經驗；這就像他再也不是你，也不可能是我。等到人生的戲 —— 也許是一齣悲劇 —— 一演完，觀眾也就散場了。就觀眾來説，它是一種虛構，僅僅是一件充滿想像力的作品。有時候，這種雙重人格極其容易使別人很難跟我們做鄰居、交朋友。

我發現一天之中大部份時間獨處，是有利身心健康的。有人做伴，就算是最好的伴，沒多久也會感到厭倦、無聊。我愛獨處。比孤獨更好的伴，我從來還沒有發現過。我們到了國外與人交往，大抵比留在自己家裏更孤獨。一個人在思考或者工作的時候，總是獨自一個的，讓他樂意在哪裏就在那裏。孤獨不能用一個人跟他的同伴們隔開多少英里來衡量。劍橋學院擁擠的小屋裏，真正勤奮學習的學生，就像沙漠裏的苦行僧一樣孤獨。農夫可以整天在田地裏或者樹林裏獨自做工，一就鋤草鬆土，一就砍伐樹木，絲毫不感到孤獨，因為他有做不完的工作；但是等到他晚上回到家裏，卻不會獨自留在屋子裏，任憑自己胡思亂想，而是非得到"看得到老鄉"的地方去樂一樂，而且，照他的想法，那是對他一整天孤獨的補償；因此，他暗自納悶，學生怎麼就能日以繼夜獨自留在屋子裏，一點都不覺得煩悶和"憂鬱"；不過他並沒有明白，儘管學生留在自己屋子裏，他卻也是在他的田地裏工作，在他的樹林裏砍樹呢，有如農夫在他的田地裏和樹林裏一模一樣；隨後，學生也要尋求同樣的娛樂消遣，尋求同樣的社交活動，儘管這些活動形式也許會更濃縮些。

社交活動通常沒有多大價值。我們相聚時間十分短暫，來不及從對方那裏獲得任何新的有價值的東西。我們每日三餐會面時，彼此之間只不過重新嚼嚼我們固有的那種陳舊、發霉的奶酪味道。我們不得不同意這麼一套規則，亦即所謂的禮儀和禮貌，務使這種經常的會晤彼此都能包涵些，以免公開發生衝突。每天晚上，我們相聚在郵局、在聯誼會、在篝火周圍；我們住得太擠，互相干擾，彼此之間說話吞吞吐吐，我想，就這樣，我們互相之間失去了一些敬意。當然，所有重要而開心的聚會，倒也不見得非要天天舉行不可。想想工廠裏那些女工 —— 她們絕對不會獨處，就是做夢，她們也不孤獨呢[9]。如果說一平方英里以內只有一個居民，正如我住的地方一樣，那也許就會好得多呢。一個人的價值並不在於他的皮膚，我們不必非得與之接觸。

我聽說過，有一個人在樹林裏迷了路，他又餓又累，倒在一棵樹底下快要斷氣了，由於極度虛弱，他那病態的想像力，讓他看到周圍全是奇形怪狀的幻象，還都信以為真，這麼一來，他的孤獨也就隨之消失了。同樣，只要身心健康，孔武有力，我們可以從類似的、更正常、更自然的社交活動中不斷感到欣慰，從而知道我們從來不是孤獨的。

我屋裏就有許多同伴，特別是在早晨，還沒有人來探訪的時候。讓我先作幾個比較，也許有的可以描述出我的一些境況。我並不覺得比湖中大聲喧嘩的潛水鳥更孤獨，而且，我也不覺得比瓦爾登湖本身更孤獨。我倒想問問，那孤獨的湖又有誰做伴？可是，在它水天一色的湖上，並不是藍色的魔鬼，而是藍色的天使。太陽是孤獨的，除非天上烏雲密佈時，有時候看上去好像有兩個太陽，不過有一個是假的。上帝是孤獨的——但是魔鬼呢，他倒是一點也不孤獨；他就有許多弟兄；他還有一大隊人馬。我不見得比牧場上一朵毛蕊花或者蒲公英更孤獨；或者換句話說，我也不見得比一片豆葉子、一棵酢漿草、一隻馬蠅，或者一隻大黃蜂更孤獨。我也不見得比磨房溪、風信雞、北極星、南風、4月間的陣雨、1月裏的融雪，或者新居第一隻蜘蛛更孤獨。

在漫長的冬日夜晚，滿天飛雪，大風在林中呼嘯，早年開拓者、原先的主人，偶然會過來看看我，據說當年他開挖過瓦爾登湖，並用石頭圍起來，環湖還栽上了松樹；他給我講過往的軼聞，以及新近的永生的故事；就這樣，我們兩人不管怎樣度過一個歡樂的夜晚，傾心交談，很開心，而且還滿心歡喜交換了一些看法，即使並沒有蘋果和蘋果酒助興——這個絕頂聰明又幽默的朋友啊，我非常喜愛他，他知道的秘密，甚至比戈菲或華萊 [10] 還要多呢。雖說人們都說他已死了，可誰都說不出他給掩埋在哪處。此外，還有一位老太太住在我家附近，人們八成都見不到她，有時候，我倒是喜歡到她那座芳香四溢的百草園去散步，採摘一些藥草，聽聽她講述的寓言故事，因為她具有舉世罕見的稟賦，她的記憶可以追溯到遠比神話更悠久的時代，善於引經據典，説出每個寓言的來歷，是根據哪個事實而來的，因為這些事一件件、一樁樁都在她小時候發生過的。這位臉色紅潤、精力充沛的老太太，不管甚麼天氣、甚麼季節，她總是興高采烈，説不定她會比她的子女們活得還要長呢。

太陽、風雨、夏天、冬天——大自然的純真和恩惠是難以描述的——它們永遠提供這麼多健康、歡樂，還有這麼多同情，它們始終給予我們人類，而且如果説有人為了正當理由而感到悲傷，那麼，整個大自然都會為之動憐：太陽就會黯然無光，風會像人們一樣嗚咽歡息，雲端會淒然落淚，樹木會在仲夏季節枯萎落葉，披上了喪服。難道我不該和大地有心靈感應嗎？難道我自己的一部份，不也是綠葉和菜蔬滋長的土壤嗎？

是甚麼藥丸使我們保持健康、寧靜和滿足的呢？不是我的或者你的曾祖父的藥丸，而是我們的曾祖母大自然的萬能草藥，她仰仗這些草藥而青春永駐，她的壽命比同時代那麼多"老派爾"[11]，她靠消滅脂肪維持健康。我們有時看到淺長的黑色大篷車上拉來許多藥瓶子，裏面裝的是江湖郎中蘸着冥河水和死海的水製作而成的藥水；而我的靈丹妙藥，就是讓我深深吸上一口純淨的清晨空氣。清晨的空氣啊！如果説人們在一天的源頭喝不到這種泉水，那我們就要裝它們進瓶子裏，拿到店鋪裏去，賣給這世上那些早上來不及訂購的人們。但是請記住，就算在最冷的地窖裏，它也只能保存到正午，你還要早早打開瓶蓋，然後隨着曙光女神奧羅拉的腳步西行。我並不崇拜健康女神許革亞[12]，這位老草藥醫神埃斯科拉庇俄斯的女兒，在紀念碑上，她總是一隻手抓住一條蛇，另一隻手拿着一隻杯子，有時候那條蛇會喝杯子裏的水。我寧願崇拜朱庇特的司酒赫柏[13]，她是朱諾[14]和野萵苣的女兒，她能使天上諸神和人類返老還童。也許她是地球上唯一健壯、健康、健全的少女，不論她走到哪裏，那裏就是明媚的春天。

章註

1　格雷：Thomas Gray，1716—1771 的名詩《墓園挽歌》。此處引用著名學者卞之琳先生的譯文，詳見王佐良編《英國詩選》，上海譯文出版社 1988 年版。

2　風神埃俄羅斯：古希臘神話裏的風神。

3　引自詹姆斯・麥克弗遜的《奧西安》（1762）中的詩句。

4　烽火山在波士頓，五點區在紐約，都是人口密集的居住區，前者為富人區，後者為窮人區，但人口擁擠是共同特點。

5　光明城：此處又是一語雙關，因為布萊頓（Brighton）和光明城（Bright）在拼寫與發音上相近之故。

6　工匠：此處指上帝。

7　詳見《中庸》。

8　因陀羅（古代印度神話中大地之神和風暴之神，司雷雨，戰勝敵人。）

9　當年麻省不少紡織廠僱用一些女孩子，讓她們住在工廠集體宿舍，擁擠
　　不堪。

10　戈菲或華萊：戈菲（William Goffe，1605—1679）與華萊（Edward Whalley，
　　1607—1675）均為審判並對查理一世行刑的法官。在英國大革命中，他們
　　是克倫威爾的得力將領，後逃往美國新英格蘭。

11　"老派爾"：全名托馬斯・派爾（Thomas Parr），據說是英國的老壽星，活了
　　3個世紀（1483—1653），以"老派爾"著稱於世，詩人約翰・泰勒曾寫詩讚
　　美過他。

12　許革亞：Hygeia，古希臘神話中的健康女神。

13　司酒赫柏：Hebe，古羅馬神話中的青春和春天女神。

14　朱諾：Juno，古羅馬神話中的天后，主神朱庇特之妻。相傳她吃了過量野
　　萵苣，就生下了赫柏。

6

來客

我想，我跟大多數人一樣很喜歡交際，而且隨時做好準備，像水蛭似的吸引住任何一位血氣方剛的上門人客。我自然不是隱士，我要是有事去酒吧，那我很可能比那些泡酒吧的常客要等的時間還要長呢。

我的屋裏備有三把椅子：一把獨處時用，兩把給友人來訪時坐，三把交往活動時用。要是來客很多，始料所不及，也還是三把椅子招待他們，不過，通常他們都在屋裏站着，節省空間。巴掌大的一個小房間，居然能容納那麼多男男女女，真的令人吃驚。有一次，在我的屋頂下，來了二十五個或者三十個靈魂，外加他們的軀體，可我們在分手時，常常還不覺得互相之間挨得那麼近。我們有許許多多房子，不管公家財產的還是私人財產的，照例都有多得簡直數不清的房間，寬敞的廳堂和儲藏名酒與和平時期軍需品的地窖，依我看，住在裏面的人好像只不過是寄生在屋裏的一些蛙蟲。當看到在特雷蒙、阿斯托或米德爾塞克斯酒店門前，侍應生通報來客時，活像一隻滑稽可笑的老鼠從賓客經過的遊廊那裏爬出來，轉眼間又鑽進走道上的窟窿裏。使我感到很驚訝。

我的屋子這麼小，有時也有一些不便之處，那就是說，我們高談闊論重大思想時，客人和我互相之間很難保持適當距離。你的思想需要足夠的空間，方可準備揚帆啟程，按照一兩條航線航行，最後到達目的港。你那思想的子彈萬萬不可打偏、跳飛，這樣才能以穩當準確的方式，直達聽者的耳朵裏，要不然它就會從聽者的腦袋旁邊擦過。再說，我們的句子也需要空間，便於漸次展開，排列成行。個人，就像國家一樣，必須有合適的、寬闊的天然邊界，乃至於有一個相當大的中立地帶。我發現跟友人隔湖交談，真的是一種奢華的享受。在我的屋子裏，我們互相挨得太近，説話反而聽不清楚——可是我們又不能讓話音壓得太低，要不然別人就聽不到；這就像你扔了兩顆石子進去平靜的水面，因為石子挨得太近，彼此的漣漪都給攪亂了。如果我們僅僅是慣於大聲聒絮的人，那麼，我們不妨站得更近些，緊緊挨在一起，感受到彼此的呼吸，倒也沒有甚麼；可是，如果我們講話很含蓄，富於思想性，那麼，我們最好還是互相隔開得更遠一點，它們分別是在波士頓、紐約、康科德的有名酒店。以便我們的活力和朝氣有機會散發出去。我們中間每個人都有一些不可言傳、只能意會的話語，要是喜歡與之進行最親密的交流的話，那麼，我們不僅要默不作聲，而且身體往往還要隔開得遠些，使我們怎樣也聽不到對方的聲音才好。按照這個標準，大聲説話只是為了方便那些耳背的人；不過有許多美好的事情，如果大聲叫，那我們就怎樣也表述不出來。只要談話的聲調開始越發崇高、莊嚴時，我們就會漸漸移後椅子，移得遠遠的，移到對面屋角落裏的牆根前，到了那時候，常常就覺得房間不夠大了。

不過話又説回來，我“最好”的房間，我的客廳，就是屋後那片松樹林，隨時準備接待來客，而且太陽幾乎很難得照到地毯上。入夏以來，貴賓來訪時，我就帶他們上那裏去。有一位不可多得的管家早已打掃過地板，還給家具撢去了塵土，樣樣東西都執拾得井然有序。

如果來客只有一位，有時他便跟我共進便餐，我們一邊交談，一邊攪動玉米粥，或者看着一塊麵包在火上漸漸膨脹、漸漸烤熟，反正兩人話語聲不絕於耳。萬一客人來了二十個的話，就在我的屋裏歇息，用餐一事只好免談了，也許我有足夠兩個人吃的麵包，無奈這時候吃飯彷彿成了一種已經戒掉的習慣，我們自然而然去禁食了。這從不會使人覺得怠慢客人，反而是一種處理最妥當、考慮最周到的辦法。物質生活受到耗損，通常急需加以補救，但非常出奇的是，在當時卻滯後了，好在生命的活力還能堅持過去。就這樣，不管來二十個人，還是一千個人，我照樣都能接待；如果說有人看到我正好在家裏，離開我屋子時卻餓着肚子，不免感到十分掃興，那麼有一點他們會肯定，至少我也是愛莫能助。建立更好的新風俗習慣，取代舊的風俗習慣，原本一點不難，儘管許多管家對此表示懷疑。你的聲譽好不好，並不取決於你是否請客吃飯。就我來說，我不時拜訪別人，我從來都沒有被甚麼克耳柏洛斯[1]驚嚇過，倒是設宴款待我的人反而使我退避三舍；我想，這是一種非常客氣兜着圈子的暗示，要我往後再也別去麻煩他。我想，以後我再也不去這些地方了。我自豪的是，有一位客人在一張權充名片的黃澄澄胡桃木葉子上，留下了斯賓塞[2]的幾行詩，我就不妨拿它來做我的陋室銘——到了那裏，他們擠滿了小屋子，

> 不尋求那裏原來沒有的娛樂；
> 休息勝過宴會，一切悉聽尊便。
> 崇高的心靈就是最能心滿意足。

後來擔任普利茅斯殖民地的總督溫斯洛[3]，偕同一個夥伴，安步當車穿過森林，對馬薩索伊特[4]作禮節性的訪問。他們到達馬薩索伊特的棚屋時又累又餓，受到馬薩索伊特酋長的熱情款待，可是那一天卻隻字未提進餐一事。黑夜來臨，不妨援引他們自己的話來說："他讓我們睡在他自己與妻子的牀上，他們睡在一端，我們睡在另一端，這牀僅僅用木板搭成，離地一英尺高，上面鋪了薄薄的一條席子。他手下的兩個部屬，因為沒有地方睡，也擠在我們身邊；本來我們一路上已經夠勞累，沒期望在這裏下榻，竟然讓我們更勞累不堪。"次日，馬薩索伊特"帶

來兩條他捕獲的魚"，就有鯿魚的三倍那麼大；"兩條魚就放在水裏煮，至少有四十個人等着分而食之。不管怎樣大多數人都吃到了。兩夜一天，我們只吃了這麼一頓飯；要不是我們兩人中間的一個人買了一隻鶉雞，我們一路上風塵僕僕，簡直像在禁食。"他們一來沒食物可吃，二來因為"野人們的野蠻歌聲（他們經常就這樣唱着歌不知不覺睡着了）"也睡不好覺，生怕自己說不定也會暈倒了，因此，他們趁自己還有點力氣走路時就動身趕回家去。說到住宿，確實虧待了他們，雖然他們所碰到的諸多不便，無疑已屬款待貴賓的禮遇；不過，就吃東西一事來說，依我看，印第安人所做的真是極妙的一招。他們自己也是一點吃的都沒有；他們倒是很聰明，知道向客人一再道歉也代替不了食物；所以，他們就乾脆勒緊褲帶，隻字不提了。後來，溫斯洛又去拜訪了他們，真巧，趕上他們豐收季節，因此再也不存在食物匱乏了。

至於人，差不多到哪裏都有的。我在林中居住期間，接待過的客人比我一生中任何時候還要多；我的意思是說，我雖然獨居森林，但依然不乏知音。我在林中接待過幾個朋友，林中的環境比任何地方要好得多。不過，很少有人是為了一點小事來找我的。在這方面，由於我住得離鎮很遠，僅僅這一段距離就使我朋友被篩選了出來。如今，我已退隱到孤獨的汪洋大海深處，雖然還有許多社會河流匯合入海，但就我的需求來說，只有最優良的沉積物麇集在我周圍。此外，還有地球另一面尚待探索、尚待開化的各種證物，也隨之漂流到了我跟前。

今天早上，要不是一位真正荷馬式或者帕菲拉格尼亞[5]式的人物，還會有誰光臨我的小屋呢——他的名字，真的是名如其人，富有詩情畫意，可惜我不能如實寫在這裏——一個加拿大人，專門伐木，製造標桿，一天能給五十根標桿鑿出洞眼來；他的狗逮住了一隻土撥鼠，於是，他就拿牠來做他的最後晚餐。他也聽說過荷馬其人其詩，而且，"要不是因為有了那幾本書，"他真的"不知道怎樣打發下雨天"，儘管許多個雨季過去了，也許他根本還沒有讀完過一本書。他那遙遠的老家教區內，有個牧師懂得希臘文，曾經教過他讀《聖經》裏面的詩篇；現在我就得給他翻譯了，他手裏拿着那本書，阿喀琉斯在責備愁容滿面的帕特洛克勒斯 [6] 下面引用的是荷馬《伊利亞特》中的一段詩。：——

"帕特洛克勒斯，你為甚麼哭得淚汪汪，像一個小女子似的？"
—— 要不你從畢蒂亞那裏聽到甚麼消息？
據說阿克托之子麥諾提俄斯還活着，
愛考斯之子帕琉斯也在密耳彌冬人那裏，
他們不論誰死了，我們都會心痛如絞。

他說，"寫得真好。"在他腋下夾了一大捆白色橡樹皮，是他這個星期天早上替一個病人撿的。"我想，今天做這種事，總不會有甚麼壞處吧。"他說。他覺得荷馬是一位大作家，儘管荷馬的詩裏寫了些甚麼，他並不知道。比他更簡單、更像白紙一張的人，恐怕很難覓到了。罪惡與疾病，已給世人思想上投下了如此陰暗的色彩，但在他看來，彷彿根本不存在似的。他大約二十八歲左右，十二年前，他離開加拿大和他父親的家，到美國來打工，想賺點錢買個農場，也許是在他老家買吧。他是從最粗糙的模子裏鑄出來的；身材壯實而不太好動，但舉止還算文雅，粗脖子曬得黑黝黝的，頭髮也烏黑而又亂蓬蓬，藍眼睛有些昏昏欲睡、沒精打采，不過偶然卻會發出富有表情的閃光來。他頭上戴着一頂扁平的灰色布帽子，身上披着一件骯髒的原色羊毛大衣，腳蹬一雙長筒牛皮靴。他是吃肉大王，經常用一個鐵皮桶，帶上他的午飯，走過我的屋子，到兩英里開外去工作 —— 因為他整個夏天都在砍伐樹木 —— 他帶的都是冷肉，常常是冷土撥鼠肉；他的腰帶上用繩子掛着一隻粗製陶罐頭，裝着咖啡，有時他還會讓我喝一口。他很早就過來了，穿過我的豆子地，不緊不慢，悠悠閒閒去工作，很像北方佬。他工作不想傷了自己元氣，即使賺到的錢只夠吃住，他也滿不在乎。他經常在灌木叢裏擺下飯菜，萬一他的狗在半路上抓到一隻土撥鼠，他就往回走一英里半路，煮熟土撥鼠，放在他借宿的房子地窖裏；不過在這以前，他曾經思索過半小時，想想能不能浸土撥鼠在湖裏直到天黑——反正對於這類問題，他就是喜歡長時間來回思考。一大早，他路過的時候總會說："這裏有的是鴿子啊！以後我不用每天去做工啦，我只需要打獵，擔保想吃肉就有肉吃啦！——甚麼鴿子啦，土撥鼠啦，兔子啦，鶉雞啦——我的天哪！一星期的肉食，我擔保一天就捕捉完成。"

他是一個熟練的伐木工人，整日癡迷於砍伐樹木這門工藝。他貼着地面將樹木齊根砍倒，這麼一來，日後新長出來的樹苗會更茁壯，雪橇也可以從樹頭上滑過去；他不是先砍去一大半樹根，再用繩子將整棵大樹拉倒，而是砍大樹直到它只剩下細細的一根，或者薄薄的一片，最後只需要用手一推，大樹就倒下了。

他之所以使我感興趣，是因為他是那麼安靜，那麼孤寂，而內心又是那麼快樂；兩眼流露着喜悅和滿足的神情。他的歡聲笑語中沒有摻雜其他成份。有時候，我看到他在樹林裏砍伐樹木，他會笑吟吟跟我打招呼，那種心滿意足的氣氛簡直沒法形容。儘管他英語講得也很好，但他跟我打招呼時用的卻是帶着加拿大腔調的法語。我走到他身邊時，他會放下手頭的工作，抑制住內心的喜悅，躺在被他砍倒的松樹邊。他剝下松樹裏層的樹皮，捲成小球，放它在嘴裏，一邊咀嚼，一邊說說笑笑。他渾身真有用不完的精力，有時碰到想着想着不知怎的引他發笑的事，他就會哈哈大笑，倒在地上連着打滾。眼看着他周圍的樹木，他會大聲叫道：——"我的天哪！在這裏砍砍樹，我已開心死啦；天底下最好的樂事我也不稀罕。"有時候，他閒下來了，就會帶着小手槍，整天這樣在樹林裏，一邊四處走走，一邊以固定的間隔時間鳴槍向自己致敬，盡給自己尋開心吧。入冬以後，他生了火，中午時份就在火上用小壺熱他的咖啡，他坐在一根原木上頭吃午餐時，無冠山雀有時會飛過來，落在他的胳臂上，啄着他手裏的馬鈴薯；他說他"很喜歡身邊有些小東西"。

在他身上最發達的乃是陽剛之氣。論體力和健碩，他可以跟松樹和岩石稱兄道弟。有一次，我問他做了一天工作，到了夜裏覺不覺得很累；他露出一本正經的神情，回答說："天知道，我活了大半輩子，從來就沒覺得累過。"反正在他身上，智力亦即所謂的"靈性"還在沉睡中，就像嬰兒時一樣。他接受過只採用天真的、無效的方式進行的教育，天主教神甫就是採用這種方式來開導土著；而採用這種方式，小學生永遠達不到有自我意識的境界，僅僅達到了信任和崇敬的程度，這個孩子並沒有經過培養而長大成人，他依然還是個小孩罷了。大自然創造他時賦予他健壯體魄，使他樂天知命，並在各方面尊敬他，信任他，做他的後盾，這樣他就可以像孩子一樣，一直活到七十歲。他生性率真，不諳世故，因此，就用不着正正經經來介紹他，猶如你大可不必向鄰居介紹土撥鼠一樣。他要慢慢認識自己，就像你要慢慢認識自己一樣。他不會裝腔作勢。他工作，別人給他錢，這就幫助他不愁溫飽；但他從來不跟人們交換看法。他是那麼單純，而且天生卑微 —— 如果說胸無大志的人可以叫做卑微的話 —— 這種卑微在他身上既不是明顯的品質，也不是他自己能意想得到的。聰明一點的人，在他心目中，幾乎成了天上諸神。如果你告訴他，這樣的一個大人物正要駕到，那麼，他彷彿覺得如此至關重要的事肯定跟他不相干，用不着自己去瞎操心，還不如乾脆忘掉他就算了。他從來沒有聽到別人讚揚過他。他特別尊重作家和傳教士。他們的言傳身教使他驚歎不已。我告訴他，說我寫過不少作品，他想了好半天，以為我是在說寫字，因為他自己也能寫一手好字。有時候，我看見他寫老家教區的名字在公路旁雪地上，字體很漂亮，還標上正確的法語重音符號，由此我才知道他曾經從這裏走過。我問他是不是想過寫下自己心裏的感想。他說他曾給不識字的人唸過和寫過一些來往信件，但從來沒有試過寫自己的感想 —— 不，他寫不了，他不知道開始應該先寫點甚麼，這真的要他的命，寫的時候還要留意切勿拼錯了單詞！

我聽說，一個知名的聰明人兼改革家問過他，他願不願意這個世界發生變革；不料，他卻驚訝得哈哈大笑，因為這個問題他過去從來沒有考慮過，"不，這個世界我很喜歡呢。"哪個哲學家跟他閒聊一下，一定會得到許多啟發。在陌生人看來，他彷彿對人情世態一竅不通；然而，有時候，我在他身上卻看到了一個我前所未見的人，我真不知道，他是像莎士比亞那樣聰明，還是像小孩一樣單純天真；我也不知道他是富有詩人的才氣呢，還是極為愚笨。一個鎮上的鄉友告訴我，說他看見他頭戴一頂緊繃繃的小帽，悠閒地穿過村莊，還吹着口哨，令人不由自主想起一個假扮的王子。

他只有一本歷史書和一本算術書，他特別擅長算術。歷史書在他看來是一部大百科全書，他認為裏面包含了人類知識的精華，事實上也確實如此。我喜歡問問他對當前種種改革問題有何看法，對此他從來都能作出最簡單、最實際的回答。反正這樣的問題，他過去從沒聽說過。沒有工廠，他行不行？我問他。過去他一直穿的就是家庭手工織的佛蒙特灰布，他說，還不是很好嘛。那麼沒有茶和咖啡，他行嗎？除了水，這裏還供應甚麼飲料呢？他說，他常常在水裏泡鐵杉葉子，他覺得熱天喝它比水還要好呢。我問他沒有錢，行不行呢，他舉例說明錢給人帶來的便利，他的表述富於哲學意味，竟然跟貨幣起源和和一拉丁文 Pecunia[7] 的詞源不謀而合。如果說他的家產是一頭牛，現在他想到商店裏去買些針線，可是每次買這麼一點針線，都要拿牛的一部份去做抵押，他就覺得既不方便，又很難辦到。他可以替許多制度作辯護，比哲學家還高明，因為他的說法都跟他本人直接有關，他指出了它們盛行起來的真正理由，他並沒有胡思亂想出甚麼其他理由。有一次，聽了柏拉圖關於人

的定義 —— 沒有羽毛的兩足動物 —— 還聽說，有人拿來一隻公雞，拔掉了牠全部的毛，管牠叫做"柏拉圖的人"，他當即說明，公雞膝蓋的彎曲方向不一樣，這是人與公雞的一個重大區別。有時，他會大聲叫道："我很喜歡聊天啊！天哪，我可以一直聊上一天呢！"有一次，我已有幾個月沒見過他了，問他對今年夏天有沒有新的想法。"老天啊，"他說，"一個像我這樣工作的人，要是他有過一些想法，而且又能念念不忘的話，那他就一定會做得不錯。也許跟你一起鋤地的人想要和你比試一下；天哪，那你就要全副心思撲在鋤地上，心裏想的只是雜草。"在這種場合，有時候他會搶先問我有沒有甚麼改進。入冬後有一天，我問他是不是常常感到很滿足，希望在他的內心能有一種東西，來取代外部的牧師，達到更高的生活目的。"滿足啦！"他說，"有人滿足於這件事，有人滿足於另一件事。有人已經要甚麼就有甚麼，也許會滿足於背烤着火，肚子頂着餐桌，一整天坐着，我的天啊！"可是，哪怕我使盡花招，我怎麼也沒找到他看待事物時所持的教會觀點；彷彿在他心目中的最高境界，就是簡單方便，有如你指望野蠻人會察覺到的那樣；這一點，實際上，大多數人都是如此。如果我建議他不妨改進一下生活方式，那他只是回答說，太晚了，來不及啦，毫無遺憾的表情。但是話又說回來，他徹底信奉忠誠，以及諸如此類的美德。

從他身上可以察覺到，有某種確實存在的獨創性，不管它多麼微乎其微，而且，我偶然還發現過他在獨自思考，表達自己的意見，真是難得見到，我很樂意在哪天跑上十英里路去觀察這種現象，這無異於重溫一下許多社會制度的起源。雖然他有時遲疑不決，也許還不能有棱有角地表達他自己，但是，他在話語之間常常隱含一種不俗的見解。不過話又說回來，他的思想非常原始，而又沉浸於他那粗獷不羈的生活之中，雖然要比僅僅有學問的人思想更有出息，但還沒有成熟到值得報導的程度。他說過，在生活的最底層，儘管他們出身低微，而又目不識丁，說不定也不乏天才人物，他們總是有自己的見解，從不裝作自己甚麼都知道的樣子；人們都説瓦爾登湖深不見底，他們就像瓦爾登湖一樣，儘管也許有些渾濁不清。

許多觀光客偏離遊覽路線，特意過來看看我和我的室內擺設，而且還為登門造訪找個藉口，説是要討一杯水喝。我告訴他們，我喝的是湖裏的水，用手指着湖，還借一把舀水勺給他們。我雖然離羣索居，但每年仍免不了有人來看我，我想，大抵在每年 4 月 1 日左右，人人都想出門到郊外遊覽吧；我無論怎樣交了好運，儘管我的來客裏面有一些稀奇古怪的人物。來自濟貧院或者別處的弱智族，也跑來看我；不過，我總是竭力使他們全部智力都施展出來，向我説出心裏話；在這種場合，智力往往成了我們談話的主題；我也從中獲益匪淺。説實話，我發現他們裏面有些人倒是很聰明的，一點不比所謂教會執事濟貧助理或者市鎮管理委員會成員遜色；我覺得現在該是他們互相易位的時候了。説到智力，我認為弱智與大智並沒有多大區別。有一天，一個頭腦簡單但人很隨和的貧民特地過來看看我，過去我倒是常常見到他和另外一批人，彷彿當作柵籬一樣，站在或坐在田地兩端的穀物容器上 [8] 照顧着牛和他自己不至於走失，這一次，他卻表示自己要像我一樣生活。他流露出非常單純、真實，以及遠遠超出了，或者還不如説低於一般所謂的“自卑”神情，告訴我説他自己“缺乏才智”，“缺乏才智”就是他説的原話。上帝打造他成了這副德行，可是他認為上帝關心他，就像關心別人一樣。“我一向就是如此，”他説，“從我小時候起，我就是這個樣子；我腦筋從小就不管用，我跟其他孩子不一樣；我的腦子可不靈啦。這是上帝的旨意，我想。”而他就在我跟前，證實了他説的話沒錯。我覺得他是一個很玄乎的謎。我難得碰上這樣一個大有希望的人 —— 他説的話是那麼單純，那麼誠懇，那麼真實。説真的，他越是顯得謙卑，反而越是高貴。起初我並不知道，這是一種聰明策略取得的結果。這麼看來，在這個弱智貧民所建立的真實而又坦率的基礎上，我們的交談倒是可以達到比跟智者交談還要好的效果。

我還有一些來客，通常不被認作城市貧民，其實，他們應該都算是貧民，而且不管怎麼說，他們理應稱作世界貧民；這些來客籲求的不是你的殷勤好客，而是你的樂善好施；他們焦急期盼着你的幫助，他們一開始就說明來意，他們已經痛下決心，就是說，他們絕不幫助自己了。我要求來客別餓着肚子來看我，雖然說不定他們有世上最好的胃口，也不管他們又是如何得來的。慈善事業的對象，不是來客。儘管我又開始張羅自己的事，回答他們的問話不免越發冷淡，越發怠慢，怎料有些客人還是不明白他們的訪問早已結束了。候鳥遷移的季節，來我這處訪問的，智力程度殊異的人幾乎都有。有些人智力較高，他們就不知道該如何加以運用；一些逃亡的奴隸，一舉手、一投足，活生生像仍在種植園裏似的；他們有如寓言中的狐狸，時時聽到獵犬在追蹤牠們，苦苦哀求地直望着我，彷彿在說：—— 哦，基督徒，你會送我回去嗎？這些人裏面，有一個真正逃亡的奴隸，我幫着引導他朝北極星的方向逃去。有的人只有一個心眼，就像帶着一隻小雞的母雞，或者像帶着一隻鴨子的母鴨；有的人私心雜念特別多，腦裏亂糟糟，就像那些要照料百隻小雞的老母雞，個個都在追逐一隻小昆蟲，每天在晨露中肯定都會丟失一二十隻 —— 到頭來都變得羽毛蓬亂，遍體疥癬；有的人光有想法而沒有長腿，像一條智力不俗的蜈蚣，使你渾身起雞皮疙瘩。有人建議不妨置備一本簽名簿，供來訪者留下自己的名字，就像懷特山[9]那處一樣；可是，天哪！我的記性非常好，用不着那個玩意。

我不能不注意到我的來客有一些特點。少男少女和少婦通常好像很喜歡到樹林裏去。他們看湖水，看野花，消磨時光。一些商人，乃至於農場主，他們想到的只是孤獨和生意經，認為我住得不是離那裏太遠，就是離這裏太遠，實在諸多不便；儘管他們說過，他們偶然也喜歡到樹林裏走走，其實，一望可知，他們並不喜歡。那些焦灼不安的人，他們的時間通通拿去謀生或者維持生活；那些上帝不離口的牧師，彷彿拿這個話題當成他們的專利品，因此對所有其他意見也就難以容忍了；醫生、律師以及那個不安份的女管家，在我外出時，她會窺探我的碗櫥和牀鋪—— 要不然某某太太怎麼會知道我的牀單就沒有她家的牀單乾淨呢？—— 還有那些年輕人，再也不算年輕了，他們卻認為跟着各行各業的舊路走，這才最保險，他們都說我當前生活境況不會有多大好處。就是了！問題正好就在這裏。體弱多病的以及膽子小的人，不管年齡、性別如何，想得最多的是疾病、意外和死亡；在他們看來，生活似乎充滿了危險—— 其實，只要你不去想這想那，又哪來危險不危險呢？—— 他們認為一個謹小慎微的人應該精心選擇最安全的地區，因為在那裏，有一位 B 醫生 [10] 可以隨叫隨到。在他們看來，"村莊"按字面來講，就是一個 Com 叫"隨到"。在他們看英文 Community[11]，意思是共同抵禦的聯盟，你不妨想一想，他們連去採摘烏飯樹漿果時都要帶藥箱。這就是說，一個人活着總會有死亡的危險；只是由於此人活着跟死去無甚差別，這種死亡的危險因而也就相對地減少了。一個人在家中閉門靜坐，其實，跟外出跑步一樣都有危險。最後，還有一種人，他們自命為改革家，所有來客裏面就數他們最討厭，他們還以為我一直在歌唱—— 這就是我親手修造的屋子；這就是住在我造的屋子裏的人；可是他們並不知道第三行詩是—— 正是這些傢伙煩死了住在我造的屋子裏的人。我不怕捉小雞的兇鷂，因為我沒有飼養小雞；但是我怕捉人的兇鷂。

撇開最後這種人，我還有一些更令人愉快的來客。孩子們來這裏採摘漿果，鐵路工人穿着乾淨的襯衫，星期天早上來散步，漁夫和獵戶、詩人和哲學家，總而言之，一切老老實實的朝聖者，為了自由的緣故，全都來到樹林裏，他們真的拋了村莊在身後，我已準備好歡迎詞："歡迎，英國人！歡迎，英國人！"據說這一歡迎詞，就是當年英國清教徒移民抵達普利茅斯時，薩莫塞特部落印第安人所說的。因為過去我跟這一個民族打過交道。

章註

1　克耳柏洛斯：古希臘神話中，保衛冥府入口處，有三個頭的猛犬，名叫克耳柏洛斯。

2　斯賓塞：Edmund Spenser，1552—1599，英國著名詩人，以長詩《仙后》著稱於世，他詩歌藝術的卓越成就對後世英國詩人產生了深遠影響。

3　溫斯洛：Edward Winslow，1595—1655，北美普利茅斯殖民地的開拓者，後來連任三屆該殖民地總督，1620年乘"五月花"號船移居新英格蘭，為英國清教徒移民領袖之一。

4　馬薩索伊特：Massasoit，1580—1661，北美萬珀諾亞格印第安人首領，各部落的大酋長，1621年白人乘"五月花"號船抵達普利茅斯後，他與移民訂立和平協議，彼此友好相處，直至他逝世。

5　帕菲拉格尼亞：古希臘的一個邊區村落，瀕臨黑海之濱，小亞細亞北部。

6　洛克勒斯：古希臘神話中人物，在特洛伊戰爭中被赫克托耳殺害，後來阿喀琉斯為他復仇。

7　詞根 Pecus：原意是"牛"，作者由此引出以下例子。

8　原文為蒲式耳 bushel，與中國舊時農村的笆斗大致相似。

9　懷特山：美國阿巴拉契亞山脈的一部份，位於新罕布什爾州北部，其主要山峯以美國歷屆總統的名字命名，故有"總統之峯"的美譽。

10　B醫生：此處指康科德的一位名叫約西亞・巴特利特（Josiah Bartlett）的醫生。

11　Community：意思是村莊或社區，有時也譯"共同體"。在拉丁文裏，com意思是"共同"，munity 意思是"抵禦"。

種豆

這時，我種下的豆子，一排排地加在一起就有七英里長，急需要鋤草鬆土，因為最終一批還沒有播完，頭一批種的豆子卻長大得驚人，的確是不好再延宕下去了。這種在赫拉克勒斯看來純屬區區小事，做得如此投入，如此富有自尊心，究竟有甚麼意義，我可不知道。久而久之，我愛上了我種下的一排排豆子，其實，我也要不了那麼多豆子。它們讓我眷戀着大地，因此我有無窮力量，就像安泰[1]一樣。可是，我為甚麼要種豆子呢？只有天知道。整個夏季，非常出奇的是，我就是這樣忙碌在大地表層的這片土地上，原先只長委陵菜、黑莓和狗尾草之類，還有味甜野果子和好看的花，現在卻只長豆子了。我從豆子那裏能學到些甚麼，而豆子又能從我這裏學到些甚麼呢？我珍愛它們，給它們鋤草鬆土，從早到晚照顧着它們，這就是我在白天的工作。它們的葉子寬大，很好看。我的助手就是滋潤這片乾旱地塊的露水和雨水，地塊本身含有一定的肥力，但大部份卻是貧瘠和枯竭的。我的敵人是昆蟲，在冷天，八成是土撥鼠。土撥鼠吃光了我一英畝中四份之一的豆子。可是話又說回來，我又憑甚麼權利鏟掉狗尾草，毀掉它們自古以來的百草園呢？反正剩下的豆子，過不了多久，就會茁壯成長，足以應對新的敵人。如今，我還清晰地記得，我四歲那年從波士頓遷移到我這個家鄉，穿過這些樹林和這個地塊，來到了這個湖邊。這是銘刻在我記憶裏最久遠的景象之一。今天晚上，我的笛子喚醒了蕩漾在這個湖上的迴聲。松樹林依然屹立在那裏，都比我的歲數要大得多呢；或者說，有的松樹已被砍掉了，我就用它們的根來煮飯，新松樹卻在四周圍長出來，在初生嬰兒眼裏別有一番景象。在這片牧場上，從同一叢多年生根部，長出了幾乎清一色的狗尾草，甚至我最後還給我小時候夢境中神話般的風景披上了盛裝。要知道我來到這裏後所產生的影響，不妨看看這些豆子葉、玉米大葉子和馬鈴薯藤蔓就可以了。

我種了大約兩英畝半高地；由於這個地塊的樹木約在十五年前遭到砍伐，我自己挖出了兩三考得[2]的樹樁，也就沒有施過任何肥料；但在夏天，我鋤地時挖出過一些箭頭來，由此可見，遠在白人開墾土地之前，一個已經消失了的民族曾經定居在這裏，而且還種植過玉米和馬鈴薯，因此，在某種程度上來說，為了好收成，他們已經使地裏肥力消耗殆盡。

土撥鼠和松鼠還沒有來得及跑過大路，或者說太陽還沒有冉冉升上那片矮橡樹林之前，我就開始在我的豆子地裏除掉那些高傲的雜草，並用泥塊壓在它們上頭，儘管農夫們反對我這麼做——但我還是奉勸諸位，趕在晨露未消去之前，盡可能完成你所有工作。大清早，我光着腳工作，像一個雕塑家在沾滿晨露的碎沙土裏擺弄着泥巴，但過了一會，太陽直曬得我腳上起了水泡。太陽照着我給豆子鋤草鬆土，在黃沙高地上，在長十五桿的一排排綠油油豆苗裏，慢慢來回走動，一端連着一片矮橡樹林，到時我會在那裏歇一會涼，另一端通向一塊黑莓地，我每鋤一個來回，青翠的漿果顏色不知怎的就會變得更深一些。鋤掉雜草，給豆稈周圍培上土，鼓勵我種下的豆苗快點生長，讓這塊黃土地以豆葉和豆花，而不是以苦艾、蘆管、狗尾草來表達它那夏日情思——這就是我的日常工作。因為我既沒有牛馬相助，也沒有僱短工或者童工幫忙，更沒有採用改良農具，我做的工作非常慢，這麼一來我就跟豆子相處得格外親近。反正用手工作，哪怕到了做苦工份上，也許絕對算不上賦閒的最壞形式吧。它含有一種萬古不滅的真諦，對學者來說，乃是一種堪稱典範的成果。對那些走過林肯和韋蘭德一路西行、不知去向的觀光客來說，我就是一個勞苦的農夫[3]；他們悠閒地坐在馬車上，兩個肘子擱在膝蓋上，韁繩鬆散地下垂像花飾一樣；我呢，株守家園，只跟泥巴打交道的鄉下人。但是用不了多久，他們既不會看到，也不會想到我的家園了。大路兩旁有很長一段路，只有這塊地才是耕地，因此，他們也就特別留意。有時，在這塊地裏耕作的人會聽到觀光客更多說三道四的話，其實並不是存心說給他聽的，他們評頭論足地說："豆子種晚了！豌豆也種晚了！"——因為別人已開始鋤地了，我還在下種——可我這個牧師下鄉種地的人，卻根本還沒想到過這些呢。"玉米嘛，老兄，只能算飼料；玉米只能算飼料。""他住在那裏嗎？"那個身穿灰色上衣、頭戴黑色圓頂禮帽的人說；於是，那個臉相難看的農夫喝住他那聽話的老馬問道："犁溝裏沒得肥，你在這裏做甚麼？他就建議我不妨撒一點爛泥屑粒，或者廢料，或者草木灰，或者灰泥都行。可是，眼前有兩英里半長犁溝，只有一把鋤頭替代馬車，用兩隻手在工作——說到其他甚麼車和馬，我打從心裏就反感——而爛泥屑粒離這裏很遠才有呢。車轔轔，馬蕭蕭，觀光客打從這裏經過，拿我的豆子地和他們一路上所見過的莊稼，扯高嗓門來比較，這才讓我知道我在農業世界中的地位了。原來這塊地沒有列入科爾曼先生[4]的報告。不過，順便說一下，大自然在更荒涼的、未經人類改良的地頭上所產出的穀物，有誰去估算出它們的價值呢？英格蘭乾草的收成，倒是有人細心地稱過重量，乃至於它的濕度、矽酸鹽和碳酸鉀，也都一一計算過；但是，在所有山谷、林中窪地、牧場和沼澤地裏，都生長着豐富而又多種多樣的穀物，只不過是人們還沒有去收割罷了。我的豆子地，彷彿介於野地與被開墾的土地之間；猶如有的國家是開化了，有的國家是半開化，還有的國家則是蠻荒或者野蠻的，我種的地塊堪稱半開化，雖然這不是從壞的意義上來說的。那些豆子快樂地回到了我栽培它們的野生的原始狀態，我的鋤頭還給它們演奏

了一支瑞士牧歌[5]

離這裏不遠，有一棵白樺樹，樹頂上有一隻棕鶇 —— 有人喜歡叫牠做紅歌鶇 —— 在歌唱，唱了一早上，很高興跟你做伴，要是你的地塊不在這裏，牠就會飛到另一個農夫的地上。你在下種時，牠就會給你助興，唱道：“點種，點種 —— 蓋土，蓋土 —— 往上拽，往上拽。”反正這裏種的不是玉米，就算有像牠這樣的敵人在一旁，也還是挺安全的。也許你會暗自納悶，牠這一連串繞口令，牠這個業餘的帕格尼尼[6]在單弦或者二十根弦上演奏的樂曲，跟你種的豆子又有甚麼關係。可是，你寧願聽牠唱下去，也不去濾掉灰燼或者灰泥。這是最便宜的一種頂級肥料，我完全相信。

我用鋤頭在地頭上翻出新土時，不知怎的，翻出了遠古時代在這一片藍天底下居住過、卻沒有歷史記載的民族所遺留的灰燼，他們打仗和狩獵時用過的小型器具，都在當今盛世重見天日。它們和其他天然石塊摻雜在一起，有些石塊上留有印第安人用火燒過的痕跡，有些是烈日暴曬留下的印記，還有一些陶器和玻璃碎片，是近代拓荒者帶來的。我的鋤頭碰撞石塊時會叮叮噹噹作響，這好聽的響聲在樹林和半空中回旋飄蕩，有它跟我做伴，我的工作即時產生了無法估量的收穫。我鋤的不再是豆子，而且鋤豆子的也不是我；當時我不免為之感動、憐憫而又驕傲地記起來 —— 如果説我還記得不錯的話 —— 我的朋友們都到城裏聽清唱劇去了。在那陽光燦爛的下午，夜鶯在我頭頂上空盤旋 —— 有時，我的工作會持續上一天 —— 它好像是在我眼裏的一粒沙，或者説在天空眼裏的一粒沙，它時不時嘩的一聲尖叫，向下俯衝，彷彿天空一下子被扯破了，最後被扯成了碎布一樣，但穹蒼卻依然天衣無縫似的；只見滿天空都是小精靈，它們在光禿禿的沙土地上，或者在山頂的岩石上產卵，卻很少有人看見它們；它們優美、纖長，好像湖上皺起的漣漪，又像被風一吹、飄浮在空中的樹葉；大自然裏有的是這樣的親緣吧。鷹是波浪的空中兄弟，牠在波浪之上一邊掠飛，一邊察看，牠那翩躚空中的翅膀，像在應酬着大海那原始的、還不會飛的翼尖。或者有時候，我看見一對鷂鷹在高空盤旋，一上一下交替翻飛，一近一遠如影隨形，彷彿牠們是我自己的思想的化身。或者說我給一羣野鴨子吸引住了，眼看着牠們從這座樹林飛向另一座樹林，帶着一點嗡嗡響的顫音，匆匆飛去；或者說，有時候，我的鋤頭從腐爛的樹根底下挖出了一條花斑蠑螈[7] 看牠那模樣枯萎不堪的、又古怪、又醜陋，頗有埃及和尼羅河的痕跡，卻又跟我們是同一個時代的。我傍着鋤頭歇息時，這些天籟美景不管在地上哪個地方，我都聽得到、看得見，乃是其樂無窮的鄉間生活的一部份。

趕上節慶日，城裏禮炮齊鳴，傳到樹林裏如同打氣槍似的，一些軍樂聲偶然也會這麼傳過來。遠在城外的豆子地裏，在我聽來，那大炮的響聲彷彿是馬勃菌在爆裂；萬一有軍隊出動，而我又一無所知，有時我整日恍然若失，感到地平線那裏在發癢，像得了病似的，彷彿馬上會發疹子，一就是猩紅熱，一就是馬蹄瘡，直到後來和風吹過田野，吹到韋蘭德公路，很快給我帶來了"民兵"的信息。遠處隱隱約約傳來了嗡嗡聲，聽起來好像誰家的蜜蜂在傾巢出動，鄰居們依着維吉爾的辦法，拿出家裏面最響亮的器皿叮叮噹噹敲了起來，召喚牠們回蜂房去。直到那叮噹之聲聽不見了，嗡嗡聲也隨之消失，最宜人的和風也不會再帶來甚麼好消息，我才知道他們已安全引回最後一隻雄蜂到米德爾塞克斯蜂房，此時此刻他們就全副心思撲在蜂房裏面滿滿的蜂蜜上了。

我感到驕傲，知道馬薩諸塞州的自由和我們國家的自由已安如磐石；於是，我回過身來又去鋤地時，懷着一種難以表述的自信及愉快的心情，繼續我的工作，泰然自若地對未來充滿了希望。

當有好幾支樂隊同時在演出時，那聽起來彷彿整個村莊就成了一個大風箱，所有房舍交替在喧囂之中，好像一會鼓起來，一會又癟掉了。但有時候，傳到樹林來的樂曲，卻是真正崇高和激動人心的，還有那歌頌英名的喇叭聲，而我不知怎的覺得自己彷彿真的要揰死一個墨西哥人[8]過過癮呢——這些區區小事，我們為甚麼總要容忍呢？——我在四處尋找土撥鼠和臭鼬，很想顯一顯我的騎士精神。這些軍樂旋律聽起來好像遠在巴勒斯坦，我想起了十字軍在地平線上行進，震得村莊上空的榆樹梢頭都微微搖曳和顫動。這是了不起的一天；儘管林中空地上空和平日裏一樣，還是一望無際的穹蒼，反正我看不出有何差別。

我種下豆子以後，總是跟豆子打交道，久而久之，就積累了不俗的經驗，那不外乎是下種啦、鋤地啦、收割啦、挑揀啦、脫粒啦、出售啦，諸如此類——所有工作就數最後一種特別棘手——也許我還要加上一個"吃"，因為我先要嚐嚐豆子的味道。我下了決心，要對豆子了解透徹。豆子正在生長的時候，我常常從清晨五點鐘開鋤，一直到中午收工。剩下的時間，一般就忙其他事去了。不妨想一想，一個人與各種雜草打交道，互相之間居然會這樣親密，你說怪不怪——這類事說起來很麻煩，反正工作的時候，不用說，麻煩多多——毫不留情地搗毀雜草的纖弱組織——用鋤頭仔細區分出良莠好壞，先通通除掉這種草，然後小心翼翼培養另一種草。那是羅馬苦艾草——那是豬獾草——那是酢漿草——那是蘆葦草——揪住它，往上拔，然後翻過根鬚，在烈日之下暴曬，別讓根鬚留在陰涼處，要不然它就翻個身豎立起來，過不了兩天又會長得碧綠，活像韭蔥似的。一場持久戰，對方不是鶴，而是雜草，有太陽和雨露助陣的這些特洛伊人[9]豆子每天看見我肩扛鋤頭來救它們，痛殲它們的敵人，使戰壕裏面填滿了枯死的雜草。許許多多身強力壯、趾高氣揚、比戰友們高出整整一英尺的赫克托耳[10]，全都倒斃在我的武器跟前，滾進塵土裏去了。

夏日裏，我同時代的人裏面，有些人在波士頓或者羅馬，獻身於美術，另一些人則在印度苦思冥想，還有一些人在倫敦和紐約做生意，而我卻跟其他新英格蘭的農夫們在一起，致力於農事。這倒不是說我想要吃豆子，因為我這個人天性上屬畢達哥拉斯[11]派，至少在種豆一事上確實如此，不管這些豆子能煮成粥，或者用於投票[12]，或者拿去換大米；也許將來有一個寓言作家用得着，哪怕僅僅是為了比喻和表達，算了，反正總要有人在地裏工作。總的來說，這是一種難得的娛樂消遣，要是持續時間太長，也許就會浪費時光了。雖然我沒有給豆子地施過肥，也沒有鋤掉周圍的全部雜草，但我對鋤草鬆土總是很賣力，到頭來也還得到了回報。"說真的，"正如伊夫林所說的，"任何混合肥料或是其他甚麼肥料，都比不上用鐵鏟不停地鋤草鬆土。""土地，"他還在其他地方補充着說，"尤其是新鮮泥土，裏面有某種磁力，可以吸引鹽、能量或者美德（你叫做甚麼也無妨），賦予活力給土地，因此，我們就靠圍繞土地的一切工作，來養活我們自己；一切糞肥和其他穢物只不過是這種改良的替代品罷了。"再說，這是一塊閒置土地，早已耗盡肥力，變得非常貧瘠，正在享受安息日；或者就像凱內爾姆·迪格比爵士[13]想到過的，它已從空氣中吸收了"生命的元氣"。我收穫了十二蒲式耳豆子。

　　不過，人們抱怨說科爾曼先生的報告裏主要談鄉紳農場主人的昂貴試驗。為了更詳盡起見，我列出我的開支——

鋤頭一把 0.54 元

犁地、耙地、開溝 7.50 元（費用太貴）

豆種子 3.125 元

馬鈴薯種子 1.33 元

豌豆種子 0.40 元

蘿蔔種子 0.06 元

柵籬白線 0.02 元

耕馬和三小時短工 1.00 元

收穫時僱用車馬 0.75 元

共計 14.725 元

我的收入 [14] 來自：

售出九蒲式耳十二夸脫豆子 16.94 元

五蒲式耳大馬鈴薯 2.50 元

九蒲式耳小馬鈴薯 2.25 元

草 1.00 元

莖 0.75 元

共計 23.44 元

盈餘（就像我在別處說過）8.715 元

以上就是我種豆經驗的結果。大約在 6 月 1 日，種下那種常見的小小白色豆子，每行長三英尺，間距十八英寸，排列成行，都是精心挑選新鮮的、渾圓的、沒有摻雜的種子。首先要注意提防蟲害，沒有出苗的空檔要補種。然後注意提防土撥鼠，因為要是地上沒遮沒擋的話，嫩葉子一長出來，土撥鼠一到，那裏就會啃得清光；再說，嬌嫩的捲鬚一竄出來，土撥鼠馬上注意到，就像松鼠一樣在那裏坐得筆直，啃光全部蓓蕾和嫩豆莢。不過，最要緊的是，如果你想躲開霜凍，使作物能賣個好價錢，那麼，你就得盡量早點收割；這樣一來，也許你就可以免受很大損失。

我還獲得以下更多有益的經驗。我自言自語道，下一個夏天，我可不想花費那麼大的氣力去種豆子和玉米，而是要播種諸如誠實、真理、簡樸、信仰和純真這一類種子，只要這些種子還沒有失落，我就要看看它們會不會在這片土地上生長，能不能以較少的勞力與肥料來養活我自己，因為它的肥力肯定沒有消耗到不令這些莊稼長得不好。唉！我就是這樣跟自己說的；可是，現在又一個夏天過去了，而且一個又一個夏天全都過去了。我不得不告訴你，讀者啊，我所播種的種子，如果說它們確實是那些美德的種子，都通通給昆蟲吃光了，或者說喪失了它們的活力，所以也就沒有抽芽生根。一般來說，人們只能像他們的父輩一樣勇敢，或者說一樣膽怯。這一代人務必在新年來臨時種下玉米和豆子，就像印第安人幾個世紀前所做的，同時又教會了第一批移民那樣做的一模一樣，彷彿這是命裏註定似的。前幾天，我看見一個老人用鐵鍬正在挖洞，至少挖了七十次，但他自己並不打算躺在裏面，真讓我大吃一驚！新英格蘭人為甚麼不可以嘗試一下新的生意？不該過份看重他的穀物、他的馬鈴薯和草料，還有他的果園——何不去種植其他農作物？我們為甚麼偏要這樣關心豆種，而根本不關心一代新人呢？我前面提到過那些品德，我們都認為要比其他產品更珍貴，但是它們大部份已經煙消雲散了，如果說我們看到一個人，發現那些品德卻在他身上紮根、生長，這時我們真的應該感到滿意和歡欣呢。如今沿着大路來了這麼一些深奧莫測而又不可言喻的品德，比方說真理或正義，儘管它們數量極少，然而品種卻是新的。我們的駐外大使們應該奉命寄回諸如此類的種子到國內，而我們的國會應該幫忙分發那些種子到全國各地種植。我們對真誠千萬不要拘禮。我們千萬不要用我們的卑劣行為來互相欺騙、互相凌辱、互相排斥，如果說已有了高貴與友誼的核心的話。我們相見時不應該就這樣忙忙碌碌。大多數人我根本沒見過，因為他們好像沒有時間；他們在為自己的豆子而忙呢。我們可不要跟這種單調乏味的人打交道，他們歇息時靠在鋤頭上或者鐵鍬上，彷彿是一根拐棍，而不是一隻蘑菇，但僅有一部份破土而出，有點豎立起來，像燕子飛落下來，在地上行走似的——說話時，他不時將翅膀舒展，展翅欲飛時，卻又收攏起來。[15] 這麼一來，我們懷疑莫不是在跟一個天使對話呢。麵包不見得總是給我們滋養；但麵包對我們總是有好處，讓我們的關節不會僵硬，使我們肢體柔軟，心情愉快，乃至於我們不知道受到甚麼病痛時，認識到人類或大自然的寬宏大量，分享到任何純淨和崇高的歡樂。

古代的詩歌和神話，至少使我們聯想到，農事曾經是一種神聖的藝術；可惜我們對它往往操之過急，掉以輕心，乃至大不敬；我們的目標不外乎擁有大農場、大豐收。我們沒有節慶日，沒有列隊祈禱，沒有慶典儀式，也沒有耕牛展示大會以及所謂的感恩節。本來農夫就是通過這些形式來表示他這個職業的神聖意義，或者藉以追溯農事的神聖起源。現在引誘他的卻是酬金和酒宴了。他供奉祭品的神祇，不是穀神刻瑞斯[16]和塵世的主神朱庇特，而是陰曹冥府的財神普路托斯[17]。我們誰都擺脫不了貪婪、自私和卑劣的習慣，視土地為財產，或者換句話說，視土地為獲得財產的主要手段，因此，風景變得蕭殺，農事跟我們一起被貶損，農夫們過着最卑微的生活。他對大自然的了解，跟強盜對大自然的了解如出一轍。卡托說，農業的利潤是特別虔誠和正當的（maximeque piusquaestus），按照瓦羅[18]的說法，古羅馬人"以同一個名字稱呼地母和刻瑞斯，認為從事耕作的人過着一種虔誠和有益的生活，認為只有他們才是農神薩杜恩王[19]的的遺民"。

我們常常忘了，太陽照在我們的耕地上，跟照在草原和森林上毫無二致。它們都反射和吸收太陽的光線，前者只是太陽每日運轉時美妙圖畫中的一小部份。在太陽看來，大地全都耕耘得如同花園一樣。因此，我們就要相應地滿懷信任和寬宏大量的情懷，接受它的光與熱的恩澤。我珍視豆種和當年的秋收，那又怎麼樣呢？這片寬闊的土地，我守望了這麼長時間，寬闊的土地並不認為我是主要的耕作者，而是撇開我，目光轉向給它澆水、讓它發綠、對它很近乎的各種影響要素。這些豆子結出的果實，並不是由我一人收穫。它們有一部份不就是為土撥鼠生長的嗎？麥穗[20]，不應該是農夫唯一的希望；它的核或者穀物[21]，也不是它產出的全部。那麼，我們的莊稼怎麼會收成欠佳呢？難道說我們不應該為雜草的豐盛而感到高興嗎？因為雜草的種子不也是鳥兒的食糧嗎？至於大地的產出能不能填滿農夫的穀倉，相對地說，也就是無傷大雅的事。真正的農夫犯不着焦灼不安，就像那些松鼠對樹林裏今年結不結栗子根本不放在心上一樣；真正的農夫每天完成自己的勞動，並不要求地裏產出的成品全都歸他所有，他心裏想的是，他奉獻出的不僅是他的第一個果子，而且還有他的最後一個果子。

章註

1　安泰：Antaeus，古希臘神話中的人物，力大無比，只要身體不離開土地，就能百戰百勝，後被赫拉克勒斯識破，將他舉至空中捏死。

2　考得：cord，木材的計量單位，通常為 128 立方英尺，約 3.6246 立方米。作者在書中多處使用英制，以此說明美國受英國殖民地影響很大，同時告誡國民應盡快建立本國計量制度。

3　原文為拉丁文 agricola laboriosus。

4　科爾曼先生：Henry Colman，1785—1849，當時麻省的農業專員。

5　瑞士牧歌：原文為法文 Rans des Vaches。

6　帕格尼尼：Niccolo Paganini，1782—1840，著名意大利小提琴家和作曲家，其創作與演奏藝術舉世聞名。

7　花斑蠑螈：古代西方神話中的火怪形像，又稱火蜥蜴、火蛇或火精。

8　墨西哥人：由此可見，作者雖然離羣索居，但依然關心天下大事，寫這段話時，很可能是在美國發動侵略性的美墨（墨西哥）戰爭期間。

9　特洛伊人：古希臘神話，描寫特洛伊城被埃及人圍攻，埃及人因久攻不下，就將一隻木馬棄於城外，特洛伊人誤以為圍兵撤走，便拖木馬進城內，木馬肚子裏的埃及士兵乘夜逃出，襲擊特洛伊城成功。

10　赫克托耳：古希臘神話中的英雄人物，即前面譯注中圍攻特洛伊城的英雄，後被阿喀琉斯殺害。

11　畢達哥拉斯：Pythagoras，公元前 582 — 公元前 507，古希臘哲學家、數學家和畢達哥拉斯教團的創始人，提倡禁慾主義，認為數是萬物的本原，促進了西方數學和理性哲學的發展。據說畢氏本人是不吃豆子的。

12　投票，沒想到一個半世紀前的北美，也像中國舊時農村選舉時讓選民們用豆子來投票，計算出候選人獲得的選票數。

13　凱內爾姆·迪格比爵士：Sir Kenelm Digby，1603—1665，英國海軍軍官和作家，宮廷大臣，曾率領私掠船在今土耳其伊斯肯德倫擊沉法國船隻，著有《論肉體的本質》等哲學著作。

14　收入：patrem familias vendacem, non emacem esse oportet：原文為拉
丁文，源自卡托《鄉村篇》，意思指一家之主應善於銷售，不該只顧進貨。

15　詩句引自英國宗教詩人誇爾斯（Francis Quarls，1592—1644）的《牧羊人
的神示》第 5 首頌歌。

16　穀神刻瑞斯：古羅馬神話中的人物，為穀物和耕作的女神。

17　財神普路托斯：古羅馬神話中的財神。

18　瓦羅：公元前 116 — 公元前 27，古羅馬學者和諷刺作家，著作甚豐，現僅
存《論農業》等書。

19　農神薩杜恩王：Saturn，古羅馬神話中的農神，相當於古希臘神話中的克洛
諾斯。

20　麥穗：拉丁文學名 spica，古拉丁文裏是 speca，源自 spe，意思是 "希望"。

21　核或者穀物，granum，源於 gerendo，意思是 "生產"。

8
村莊

鋤草鬆土之後，上午也許看看書，要不然寫點甚麼，通常我在湖裏再洗個澡，游過一個小水灣，不管怎樣洗掉我工作後一身污垢，或者說消去了讀書留下的最後一道皺紋；下午我就絕對自由了。每天或者隔天，我就走到村裏去，聽聽那些沒完沒了的閒言碎語，有些是口口相傳的，有些是各報互相轉載的，如果採用順勢療法小劑量接收，真的是令人耳目一新，有如枝葉蕭瑟，青蛙啾鳴似的。正如我漫步在樹林裏，愛看鳥兒和松鼠一樣，我漫步在村裏，也愛看大人小孩；可是我在村裏面聽到的不是陣陣松濤，而是車轔轔的喧囂聲。從我的小屋朝一個方向看去，只見河邊草地上有塊地方，麝鼠在那裏出沒無常；在那邊地平線上，榆樹和懸鈴木樹陰下，有一個村莊，那處都是大忙人，讓我覺得奇怪的是，彷彿他們原本就是草原犬鼠，一就各自蹲在洞穴口，一就竄到鄰家去閒聊。我經常到村裏觀察他們的生活習慣。依我看，這個村莊活像一個龐大的新聞編輯室；在村莊的一邊，給它撐門面的，就像當年斯達特街上的里丁出版公司，人們經營乾果或者葡萄乾，或者食鹽和粗麵粉，以及其他雜貨。有些人對頭一種商品，亦即新聞，胃口特別大，消化能力特別強，他們可以一輩子坐在通衢大街上一動也不動，聽那些新聞慢慢地沸騰起來，然後竊竊私語，像地中海的季風衝着他們吹過去，或者說，好像吸入了乙醚，只管產生局部麻醉，對疼痛全無感覺了——要不然有些新聞聽起來往往讓人覺得痛苦的——但對人們意識還是毫無影響。我在村裏四處漫步時，一排排這樣的活寶屢見不鮮，或者坐在梯子上曬太陽，身體稍微前傾，兩眼時不時露出色迷迷的表情，不停東張西望；要不然兩手插在口袋裏，身體靠在穀倉牆頭上，有如女像柱似的，彷彿就靠它來支撐那座穀倉。他們素常總是留在戶外，這陣風裏面有些甚麼都聽得出來。這些都是頭一道碾磨得最粗糙的磨坊，所有的閒言碎語首先在這裏粗粗消化一遍，方可倒入室內比較精細的給料漏斗裏。我觀察到村裏最富活力的是食品雜貨店、酒吧間、郵局和銀行；此外，就像機器中必不可缺的配件，擺在適當地方，照例有一座鐘、一尊大炮和一輛救火車；為了充份發揮男人們的潛力，村舍全是按巷子面對面排列，這樣一來，每個觀光客勢必受到夾道鞭打，村裏男女老少都好揍他一頓。斯達特街[1]那些住在離巷口最近的人們，最先看到別人，也最先被人看到，又是第一個出手揍觀光客的人，不用說，為了他們的地段付出了最高昂的代價；住在村外的零散家庭，在他們那裏開始出現一段段很長的豁口，觀光客可以越牆而過，或者走進小道，就這樣溜之大吉。因此，這些人所付的土地稅和窗戶稅[2]也就微乎其微。為了招徠觀光客，四處裏都懸掛着幌子；有的幌子一看就令他胃口大開，比方說，小酒店和酒窖裏的食店；有的幌子迎合顧客喜好，比方說，綢布衣裝店和珠寶店；還有一些幌子，專門瞄準頭髮，或者腳丫子，或者裙子，比方說，理髮店、鞋店或者裁縫店。此外，還有更嚇人的是，他們總是邀請你挨家逐戶地探訪，在這些場合，少不了有一大批看熱鬧的人。在大多數情況下，我都能奇蹟般地化險為夷，或者我勇往直前，毫不猶豫向着目的地走去，這一招真值得向那些受到夾道鞭打的人推薦；或者讓我全副心思放在崇高的事上，就像奧菲士[3]，"彈着他的七弦琴，高聲歌唱天上諸神的讚美詩，將塞壬[4]的聲音都淹沒，從而轉危為安。"有時候，我突然出走，誰都不知道我到哪裏去了，因為我平素不大拘禮，在圍柵的豁口前絕不會總是遲疑不決。我甚至還習慣突然闖到別人家裏去，別人照例會很好招待我，就在了解一些要聞以及最新精選的新聞以後，知道某些已經平息下去的事態、戰爭與和平的前景，以及世界各國能不能持久地團結一致等等，我便抄着後面小路滑脚溜掉，又遁入樹林裏去了。

每當我在城裏留得很晚，自己才動身回到黑夜之中，特別是在漆黑一團、風暴驟起的夜晚，我從一個明亮的鄉間客廳或者演講廳揚帆起航，肩上扛着一口袋黑麥或者印第安粗玉米粉，直奔我在樹林裏溫馨的港灣，外頭一切都給紮得很結實，腦裏裝滿歡樂思想，直接來到了甲板下，只讓那個外部的我掌着舵，要不然趕上一帆風順的時候，我乾脆連舵全給拴住了，這是十分愉快的。"我在航行的時候，"在船艙的火爐邊，我不知怎的心中湧起許多令人欣慰的思緒。雖然我遇到過許多次駭人的風暴，但不管是甚麼天氣，我從來沒有失事過，也從來沒有洩氣過。就是在平常的夜晚，樹林裏也都要比大多數人所想像的更黑暗。在伸手不見五指的夜晚，我不得不經常抬起頭來，看看小路上頭樹與樹之間的縫隙，以便認清我走的路徑；而且走到了沒有車轍的地方，我還要用我的兩脚來探索我剛踩出來模糊不清的小道，要不然用我的雙手摸摸我熟悉的樹木來辨別方向，比方說，從兩棵松樹之間穿過，它們的間距就不會超過十八英寸。有時候，趕上漆黑一片而又悶熱潮濕的夜晚，我就這樣很晚才回到家，兩眼看不見的道路，我只好用脚丫子來探路，一路上懵懵懂懂，彷彿做夢似的，直到我伸出手去打開門閂，這才算清醒過來，卻怎麼都回想不起來，這一步一步自己是怎麼走回來的，我想，也許我的身體，在它的主子丟棄它以後，還會尋找到回家的路，好像用不着幫忙，手總是摸得到嘴巴一樣。有好幾次，有個來客很難得等到了晚上，趕上這天夜色漆黑得出奇，我不得不領他到屋後面的那條車道上，指給他看他要去的方向，並且關照他，給他領路的是他的脚，而不是他的眼睛。一個黑黝黝的夜晚，我就這樣指點過兩個湖上垂釣的年輕小伙子上路。他們兩人住在離樹林大約一英里以外，不用說，摸熟門路。殊不知過了一兩天，他們之中的一個人告訴我，說他們在自己的住所附近來回走動了大半夜，直到天光大亮才回到了家，中間下了幾場大雨，樹葉都濕透，他們自然被淋得渾身濕透。我聽說，有許多人就算行走在村裏小道上也都會迷路，因為那天夜裏特別黑，像一塊黑布，正如俗語所說，可以用刀子一塊塊割下來。有些人住在郊區，趕着馬車到城裏去採購，只好在那裏投宿過夜；有些紳士和女士們出門訪客，才走了還不到半英里路，只好用他們的兩腳來探路，連甚麼時候該拐彎都不知道。不管在甚麼時候，在樹林裏迷路，都是一種驚人、難忘的寶貴經歷。暴風雪刮起時，哪怕是在大白天，走在一條熟悉的舊路上，也會暈頭轉向，不清楚哪條路通往村莊。儘管他知道自己在這條路上走過成千次，可是路上的特徵就是一點都記不得，反而覺得陌生的，好像是西伯利亞的一條路呢。入夜以後，困惑當然更是說不盡、道不完。我們平日裏隨意漫步時，經常地，雖然又是無意識地，像領航員一樣，根據某些熟悉的燈塔和海角往前駛行；我們萬一偏離了自己慣常的航線，腦海裏仍然留下了鄰近某些海角的印象；除非我們完全迷路了，或者換句話說，轉了個身——因為你在這茫茫大地上，只要閉上眼睛轉一個身，肯定會迷失方向——我們這才領略到大自然的浩瀚和奇詭了。不管是睡着了，還是心不在焉，每個人醒來時，都要經常不斷了解羅盤上指針的方向。除非我們迷了路，或者換句話說，除非我們失去了這個世界，我們這才開始發現我們自己，認識到我們的處境，以及我們各種聯繫的無限內涵。

頭一個夏季快要結束時，有一天下午，我到村裏鞋匠那裏取一隻鞋子，我被捕了，坐了大牢，因為正如我在其他地方說過的 [5] 我沒有繳稅，或者換句話說，不承認這個國家的權威，因為這個國家在參議院門前當男人、女人和兒童為牛羊一樣買賣。我為了其他事才到樹林裏去。可是，不管一個人走到哪裏，他們那些骯髒機構就跟到那裏，追蹤他，抓住他，只要他們能夠做到，總要強制他回到屬他們那個絕望的共濟會式的社會中去。誠然，我本來可以強烈地進行抵抗，多少會有一些效果，我本來也可以"像殺人狂似的"反對社會；但我寧可讓這個社會"像殺人狂似的"來反對我，反正這個社會已是絕望的一方了。不過話又說回來，第二天我就被釋放了，拿到了我那隻修補過的鞋子，及時返回林中住處，還在美港山上大啖一頓烏飯樹藍色漿果。我從來沒有受到任何人的騷擾，只有那些代表國家的人除外。除了那張存放我的文稿的寫字枱以外，我既不上鎖，也不上閂，更沒有給我的門閂和窗戶釘過一顆釘子。反正不管白天也好，黑夜也好，我從來不鎖門，儘管我有時出門一連好幾天；乃至於第二年秋天，我去緬因州樹林裏住過兩個禮拜也沒有鎖門。但是，我的小屋卻備受人們尊敬，勝過有大隊士兵守衛在我的屋子四周。疲憊的漫遊者可以到我這裏休息，圍着火爐取暖，而文學愛好者不妨翻看我桌上的幾本書，聊以自娛，要不然那些富好奇心的人，會打開我的碗櫥，看看我的午餐剩下些甚麼，預測晚餐又將如何。雖然各階層有很多人都來過瓦爾登湖，不過我並沒有因此感到諸多不便，甚麼東西也沒有丟失過，只缺了一本小書，那是一卷荷馬的作品，也許這書皮燙了金遭人眼紅，我相信這是我們兵營裏一個大兵拿走的。我深信，如果人人都像我當時那樣過簡樸的生活，那麼偷竊和搶劫也不會發生。之所以發生這樣的事，蓋因社會上存在貧富不均。蒲柏[6]翻譯的荷馬作品，會很快得到適當的傳播——

Nec bella fuerunt，

Faginus astabat dum scyphus ante dapes.

世人只要山毛櫸碗時

就不再會有戰事。

子為政，焉用殺。子欲善，而民善矣。

君子之德風，小人之德草。草上之風，必偃。[7]

章註

1 斯達特街：美國波士頓的金融中心，有時也譯州府街。

2 窗戶稅：英王威廉三世創設，將巨大戰爭開支轉嫁於民，當時北美移民常為抗稅泥封窗戶，反對宗主國斂錢苛政。

3 奧菲士：古希臘神話中的人物、詩人和歌手，善彈七弦琴，彈奏時，猛獸俯首，頑石點頭。

4 將塞壬：古希臘神話中的人物，半人半鳥的女海妖，以美妙的歌聲蠱惑過往的海員，讓駛近的船隻觸礁沉沒。

5 因為正如我在其他地方説過的，此處指梭羅的著名文章《消極反抗》。該文曾引起極大反響。

6 蒲柏：Alexander Pope，1688—1744，英國著名詩人，擅長諷刺，善用英雄偶體，尤以翻譯荷馬史詩《伊利亞特》和《奧德賽》著稱。

7 引自《論語·顏淵》。

9
湖

有 時候，我對人際交往和閒言碎語，乃至於我所有鄉友全都膩
透了，於是，我就去比我慣常住所更遠的西邊漫遊，進入這
個鄉鎮人跡更罕至的地域"新的樹林和新的牧場"；要不然，夕陽西沉
時，在美港上以黑果和烏飯樹藍色漿果充當晚餐，隨後再撿起一些漿果
來，以備好幾天食用。這些果實的真正美味，是採購它們的買主和出售
它們的種植者不會品嚐到的。要想品嚐它們真正的味道，只有一個辦
法，可惜很少有人採用過。你要是真想了解黑果的美味，不妨問問牧童
或者鷓鴣。從來沒有採摘過烏飯樹藍色漿果的人，自以為品嚐過它們的
美味，這可是一種常見的錯誤。正宗的黑果從來沒到過波士頓，儘管它
們都長在波士頓的三座山上，但在當地卻鮮為人知。在運往市集時，這
種果子的芳香和精髓，連同它那鮮豔色澤一起耗損殆盡，卻成了人們果
腹的食品。只要永恆的正義還在人世間，地地道道的黑果就不會從鄉村
的山上運到城裏去。

完成一天的鋤地工作後，我偶然也會跟某個無耐性的朋友做伴；
此人一早就來湖邊垂釣，靜悄悄的，一動也不動，像一隻鴨或者一片漂
浮的樹葉，而且，實行過形形色色的人生哲學之後，並在我來到之前，
他大抵已得出了結論：他屬老派的修道院住院修士[1]。有一位年紀稍大
的人，是個極好的漁夫，各種木工工作樣樣精通，他見到我搭建的房子
給漁民提供方便，覺得很高興；我看見他坐在我門口打理釣絲，同樣也
很高興。我們偶然會一起泛舟湖上，他坐在小船的這一端，我坐在小船

的另一端；無奈我們之間很少說話，因為近年來他耳朵聾了，不過他偶然突然哼起一首聖詩來，卻與我的人生哲學不謀而合。我們的神交完全是一種扯不斷的和諧融洽，回想起來比真的用話交談更令人神往。我在找不到人說話的時候，照例用槳把叩打自己的船舷，發出陣陣迴響，在周圍的樹林裏激起一圈圈傳得越來越遠的聲浪，好像動物園裏管理員激起野獸吼叫聲一樣，最後，每個樹木蔥蘢的峽谷和山坡全都在發出咆哮似的。

在暖洋洋的傍晚時份，我常在小船上吹笛子，看見鱸魚一直在我周遭游來游去，彷彿被我的笛子聲迷住似的。月光在螺紋條狀的湖底徐緩移動，湖底山林的殘缺倒影隱約可見。早先，我不時有點獵奇似的來到這湖上，都是在夏天黑幽幽的夜間，跟一個朋友在水邊生了一堆篝火，認為火光也許會吸引住魚羣，我們又用掛滿誘餌的釣線捉了些鱈魚；我們就這麼釣呀釣的直到夜深時份，從高角度向天空拋出燃燒中的木頭，它們像衝天焰火，從高處墜落湖裏，嗡的一聲巨響就熄滅了，一瞬間我們完全處於黑暗之中，只好摸索着行走。就這麼一邊摸黑行走，一邊吹吹口哨，我們終於又來到人們三五成羣的地方。可是現在，我在湖岸上已有了自己的家。

有時候，我就在村裏某個客廳等到這家人都歇息去了，方才返回樹林，多半是為了第二天的飯食問題，因為深更半夜我常在小船上、月光下垂釣幾個鐘頭魚，聽貓頭鷹和狐狸在唱牠們的小夜曲，還不時聽到近處不知名鳥兒的尖叫聲。這些經歷對我來說彌足珍貴、難以忘懷——在水深四十英尺處拋了錨，離岸約有二三十桿遠，有時好幾千條小鱸魚和銀色小魚團團圍住了我，在月光下用牠們的尾巴使湖面上出現了漣漪；於是，我用一根亞麻釣線，跟深居在四十英尺水下、常在夜間出沒的神秘魚兒在默默傳神；或者有時候，我乘着夜間輕柔的微風在湖上漂遊，小船後面拖上六十英尺長的釣線，時不時感到釣線在輕輕抖動，表明一個生命正在釣線那端覓食，渾然摸不清楚在那邊這個愣頭愣腦的玩意目的何在，所以也不能立時讓自己拿主意。到了最後，你慢慢往上拉釣線，兩手交替去拉呀拉的，看，一條魚（此處尤指盛產於美國東部的雲斑。）一邊吱叫着，一邊全身扭動着給拉到了半空中。特別是在漆黑的夜間，正當你神思馳騁、漫無邊際之時，卻感覺到了這微弱的顫動，打斷了你的夢想，連結你和大自然在一起，豈不奇怪！那就像我接下來會向空中拋出釣線，如同我將釣線往下拋向密度不比空氣更大的水裏去一樣，這麼一來，我彷彿用一個釣鈎卻捉到了兩條魚似的。

瓦爾登湖的風景只好算粗線條，儘管很美，還說不上壯觀；不經常光臨或者不在湖邊居住的人，對它也不是特別關注；然而，瓦爾登湖以它的深邃純淨著稱於世，值得對它詳盡描述一番。原來它是一口清澈而黛綠的井，半英里長，周長一又四份之三英里，面積約有六十一英畝半；松樹和橡樹林中央，有一股終年井噴的泉水，除了雲霧和蒸發以外，根本看不到它的入水口和出水口。周圍的山巒陡然聳立，高出水面四十到八十英尺，雖然在東南角高達一百英尺，在東端更高達一百五十英尺，綿延大約四份之一英里或者三份之一英里。它們清一色都是林地。我們康科德境內的水域，至少具有兩種顏色，一種老遠就望得見，而另一種更接近原色，在近處才看得出。第一種更多取決於光線，隨着天色而變化。在天氣晴朗的夏天，從不遠處看去，湖面呈現蔚藍色，特別在水波蕩漾的時候，而從很遠的地方望過去，全是水天一色。趕上暴風雨的天氣，水面有的時候呈現深石板色。不過，據説海水在大氣層中看不出有甚麼變化的情況下，卻是今天藍，明天綠。白雪皚皚時，我看到過我們這河裏，水和冰幾乎都是草綠色。有人認為藍色是"純淨水的顏色，不管它是流動的水，還是凝固的冰"。反正直接從小船上看湖面，倒是看得出非常不一樣的顏色。瓦爾登湖一會藍，一會綠，哪怕是從同一個視角看過去。瓦爾登湖位於天地之間，自然兼具天地之色。從一個山頂上望過去，它映現出藍天的色彩，而從連岸邊的沙你都看得到的近處看，它卻呈現出先是淡黃色，繼而淡綠色，同時逐漸加深，終於變成了全湖一致的黛綠色。在有些時候的光線下，哪怕是從山頂上往下俯瞰，毗鄰湖岸的水色也是鮮靈靈的綠色。有人認為，這是草木青蔥返照的緣故，但在鐵路軌道沙壩的映襯下，湖面依然是綠幽幽的；等到春天還沒有葉茂成蔭，這時湖光山色也不外乎是天上的湛藍色與沙土的黃褐色掺在一起的結果，堪稱瓦爾登湖彩虹般的色彩。入春以後，湖上冰層因受從湖底折射上來的、又透過土層傳來的太陽熱量而變暖，於是首先被融化，在中間仍然凍結的冰凌周圍，形成了一條狹窄的小河。正如我們的其他水域一樣，每當天色晴朗、水波瀲灩之時，水波表面會從合適角度映出藍色天空，或者由於糅合了更多亮光，如果稍微遠一點望過去，湖面彷彿呈現比天空本身更深的湛藍色；此時此刻，泛舟湖上，從各個不同的角度觀看水中倒映，我發現了一種無與倫比、不可名狀的淡藍色，有如浸過水或者閃閃發光的絲綢和利劍青鋒，卻比天空本身更具天藍色，它與水波另一面原有的黛綠色交替閃現，只不過後者相對來說顯得有點渾濁罷了。那是一種玻璃般綠裏泛藍的色彩，跟我的記憶裏一樣，有如冬日夕陽西沉時，從雲層裏呈現一片藍天。反正舉起一玻璃杯水，往亮處看，它裏面好像裝着空氣，一樣沒有顏色。眾所周知，一個大玻璃盤略帶一點綠色，據玻璃製造廠說，是由於玻璃"體厚"的緣故，但同樣都是玻璃，小塊的就沒有顏色了。至於瓦爾登湖該有多少水量，才會泛出綠色，我倒是從來沒有驗證過。人們直接俯視我們河水，河水是烏黑或者深棕色，而且如同大多數湖裏的水一樣，會給洗湖浴的人擦上一點淡黃色；但是瓦爾登湖水卻比水晶更純淨，使洗湖浴的人軀體潔白有如大理石一般，而且奇怪的是，此人的四肢給放大了，同時也給扭曲了，產生了一種駭人的效果，值得米開蘭基羅[2]好好研究呢。

　　湖水如此晶瑩剔透，一眼就看得到二十五英尺或者三十英尺深的湖底。你光腳踩水，可以看見許多英尺深水下，有成羣的鱸魚和銀色小魚，它們也許只有一英寸長，但是前者一道道的橫着花紋倒也很容易辨認出來，你會覺得牠們必定是苦行修煉的魚種，才到那裏尋找生計的環境。好幾年前的冬天裏，有一次，我在冰層上鑿洞釣狗魚，我上岸時扔我的斧頭回冰層去，不料，彷彿神差鬼使似的，只見那柄斧頭在冰層上滑出四五桿遠，正好掉進一個冰窟窿裏面去了，那處水深二十五英尺。我出於好奇心，伏倒在冰層上往那個冰窟窿裏面看一看，只見那柄斧頭側向一邊，斧柄朝天豎起，隨着湖水的脈動來回擺動，要是我不去打擾它的話，它說不定會在那裏就這樣直立下去，晃呀晃呀，隨着時光流逝，直到斧柄爛掉為止。我就在斧頭的上方，用我帶來的冰鑿又鑿了一個窟窿眼，用我的刀砍下我在近處尋到的最長的一根白樺樹枝，枝頭上打了一個活結套，隨後小心翼翼放它下去，套住斧柄上凸起的一塊疙瘩，用繫住白樺樹枝的一根繩子往上拉，就這樣拉那柄斧頭上來了。

湖岸由一長條好似鋪路用的滴溜滾圓的白色石子築成，除了一兩處小小沙灘以外，在許多地方都非常陡峭，縱身一躍正好落到沒頂深的湖水中；要不是湖水晶光鋥亮得出奇，你一定看不見湖底，除非湖底在對面升了起來。有人認為，瓦爾登湖是湖深沒有底的。湖水不論在哪處也不渾濁，偶然觀湖的人還以為湖底根本連水草都沒有，至於看得見的草木，除了不久前被水淹過的、原本不屬湖的那些小小草地以外，哪怕是再仔細查看，也確實看不到菖蒲或燈芯草，連一朵百合花都沒有，不管是黃色還是白色的，至多只有一兩片心形葉和河蓼草，說不定還有一兩片眼子菜；反正置身水中的人也許根本看不出來；這些水生植物，好像如同它們賴以生長的湖水一樣潔淨、晶瑩透亮。岸石延伸入水有一兩桿遠，湖底就是清一色的沙了，只有在最深的地方通常會有一點沉積物，也許經歷許多個秋季樹葉飄落、沉澱腐爛的緣故，甚至在仲冬時節，鮮綠水草也會隨着鐵錨一起浮出水面。

往西大約兩英里半，一個叫九畝角的地方，我們還有一個類似這樣的湖，那就是白湖。雖說方圓十幾英里以內的湖泊十之八九我都很熟悉，但我還沒有見過第三個湖水質比井水更純淨。這湖水也許古往今來各民族全都飲用過、讚賞過、測量過，隨後也就相繼消失了，唯有這湖水依然碧綠澄清。一個春天都沒有間斷過！說不定在亞當和夏娃被逐出伊甸園的那個春天早晨，瓦爾登湖早就存在了，甚至就在那個時候，隨着薄霧彌漫和南風拂面而來的是一場濛濛春雨，打破了湖上的平靜，飛來了成羣的鵝和鴨，牠們全然不知道亞當和夏娃被逐出伊甸園一事，覺得能有這樣純淨的湖水，牠們早就心滿意足了。即使在那個時候，這個湖已開始時漲時落，湖水碧綠澄清，呈現出今日的色彩，彷彿具有藍天的特徵，成為世上獨一無二的瓦爾登湖和天上露珠的蒸餾器。誰知道，有多少無人記得的民族文學作品稱這個湖為卡斯塔利亞泉[3]？要不然在古代神話中的黃金時代，又有多少山林水澤的仙女們曾在這裏居住過？這就是康科德冠冕上的第一顆滴水寶石。

不過，率先來到瓦爾登湖的人，說不定留下了他們的足跡。我因發現陡峭的山坡上有一條逼仄的小路而感到驚訝，環繞湖邊，甚至還通過湖邊被砍伐過的茂密樹林。這條小路的走勢有時忽上忽下，有時跟湖沿卻又若即若離，也許和這裏的人類一樣古老，是由當地土著獵戶一步一步踩踏出來；此後，今日這塊土地的居住者就時不時不知不覺在上面行走。入冬以後，剛下過一場小雪，你站在湖中央望過去，這條小路顯得特別清晰，猶如一道連綿起伏的白線，不但沒有被雜草和枝條遮蓋住，哪怕在四份之一英里開外的許多地方，還是呈現得特別顯眼。可是一到夏天，就算你站在近處，也不見得能看清楚。在某程度上說，看上去好像白雪用清晰的白色隆雕翻印它出來了。說不定這裏有一天會興建別墅，裝飾庭院，但願類似這樣的一些痕跡能保留下去。

湖水時有漲落，但不管它有沒有規律或者週期，都是無人知曉，儘管有許多人慣常都會不懂裝懂。一般説，湖水冬天高，夏天低，這和大氣的潮濕乾燥並沒有相應關聯。我還記得，倘若跟我住在湖邊時相比，湖水甚麼時候落下去一兩英尺，甚麼時候漲上去一兩英尺，甚麼時候又會漲上去至少五英尺。有一條狹長的沙洲直接延伸到湖中，沙洲一邊的湖水非常深，離主岸六桿遠，大約在 1824 年，我在這沙洲上煮過一鍋海鮮雜燴濃湯，時隔二十五年，要想再煮也是不可能了；另一方面，我已告訴過我的朋友們，説幾年之後，我常駕着小船到隱蔽在樹林幽深處的小灣裏去釣魚，離他們知道的湖岸才不過十五桿遠，但現在那處早已變成了一片草地。他們聽後總是不大相信，可是湖水兩年來不斷在上漲；現在，1852 年的夏天，比我住在那裏時高出了五英尺，或者換句話説，相當於三十年前的水位高度，豈不是又可到那塊草地上釣魚了。從外表看，水位落差有六七英尺；可是從周圍羣山流下來的水量並不大，水位上漲一定跟影響深處泉源的原因有關。就在同年夏天，湖水又開始回落了。引人注目的是，湖水這種時漲時落，不管它有沒有週期性，好像都需要許多年方能完成。我曾經觀察到一次湖水上漲和兩次湖水部份回落，我估算再過十二年或者十五年，湖水又會回落到我過去所了解的低水位了。東端一英里的佛林特湖，因湖水流入和流出而時有漲落，那些介於兩者之間的小湖，則和瓦爾登湖的水情大致相仿，近來也和後者一樣漲到了它們最高水位。根據我的觀察，白湖的水位也是如此。

瓦爾登湖時漲時落，間隔時間很長，至少起到這樣一種作用，湖水處於這種很高的水位，已有一年左右，儘管環行走不易，但從上次漲水以來，沿湖長出來的灌木叢，以及諸如北美油松、白樺樹、橙木、大齒楊等等樹木通通給沖走了，等到水位再次回落時，就留下光禿禿的湖岸；因為瓦爾登湖跟許多湖泊和每天水位有漲落的河流不一樣，水位最低時，湖岸偏偏最乾淨。臨近我房子的湖邊，一排高達十五英尺的北美油松全被沖走，好像用杠桿給掀翻似的，從而止住了它們向湖岸擴展；

這些樹木軀幹的大小，表明上次湖水上漲到這種高度以來已經多少年了。通過這種漲落，瓦爾登湖對湖岸擁有了主權，因此，湖岸彷彿被剃光了鬍子，使那些樹木不能憑藉所有權來侵佔湖岸。這些瓦爾登湖的嘴唇上一莖鬍子也都長不出來。湖水時不時舔着自己的下巴。湖水漲高時，橙木、柳樹和槭樹淹沒在水中的樹根周圍，都浮起大量纖維似的紅色根鬚，長達幾英尺，高出地面三四英尺，拼命來保護它們自己；我知道湖岸那一帶有一些高高的烏飯樹灌木叢，通常不結果子，但在這種條件下倒是會結出豐碩的漿果來。

這湖岸怎麼會被鋪砌得如此整整齊齊，難免有人百思不得其解。我鎮上的鄉友們都聽說過這麼一個傳說，歲數最大的人們也告訴過我，說他們年輕時就聽說過，古時候印第安人曾在這裏一座小山上舉行一次帕瓦儀式[4]，那座小山一下子升高，聳入穹蒼，有如現在這湖，深深沉入大地一樣；根據他們的說法，他們做了許許多多褻瀆神靈的事，儘管這些罪行印第安人從來都沒有做過，可是正當他們鬧得這麼厲害的時候，這座小山東搖西晃起來，突然下沉，只有一個上了年紀的女人逃了出來，她的名字叫做瓦爾登，於是，瓦爾登湖就這樣照她的名字叫開了。有人推想，小山撼動時，這些山石從山坡上滾下來，形成了今日的湖岸。反正有一點完全可以肯定的是，以前這裏沒有湖，而現在有了一個湖；這個印第安人的傳說，與我前面提到的，那位古代原住民所說的不矛盾，因為此人清晰記得，他初來該地時，帶着一根神杖，只見一片薄薄霧氣從草地上升騰起來，那根榛木神杖自始至終指着下方，於是決定在這處挖一口井。至於那些岸石，許多人仍然認為，倘若歸諸羣山波動的原因，也未必能解釋清楚；不過據我細心觀察，這同一種石頭在周圍的山上顯然俯拾即是，因此，人們不得不用這些石頭在離瓦爾登湖最近的鐵路兩側築起護牆；再說，湖岸越陡峭的地方，石頭也越多；可惜的是，這對我來說再也不是甚麼神秘兮兮了。反正我已尋到了鋪砌石頭的人。如果説瓦爾登湖這個名字不是來源於某一個英國地名 —— 比方説，薩夫倫・瓦爾登[5]的話，那麼，你就不妨想想，這個湖原來叫做"圍而得"而湖此處原文 walledin[6]，意思是"用牆圍起來"。

　　這個湖依我看就是一口現成的井。一年之中有四個月，湖水冷冰冰，如同湖水一年到頭純淨一樣；我猜想這時候湖水就算不是鎮上最好的，至少也是跟其他湖一樣好。入冬後，凡是暴露在空氣中的水，都要比避寒保暖的泉水和井水更冷些。我從下午五點鐘一直坐到次天中午，亦即 1846 年 3 月 6 日，寒暑表上溫度有時是華氏 65 度，有時是華氏 70 度 —— 部份是由於照在屋頂上的陽光的緣故吧 —— 湖水放在我屋裏的溫度是華氏 42 度，或者換句話説，比從村中最冷的一口井裏剛汲取上來的水還低一度呢。同一天，沸泉的水溫是華氏 45 度，亦即經測試過的各種水中最溫暖的度數，不過，據我所知，到了夏天，這算是最冷的水了，因為這時候淺層不流動的地表水，並沒有和它混合在一起。再説，在夏天，瓦爾登湖因為很深，所以從來不像大多數暴露在陽光下的水那樣變得很暖和。在最暖和的天氣裏，通常我放一桶水在地窖裏，讓它在夜裏冷卻下來，一直保持到第二天；儘管有時我也到鄰近的泉水去汲水。過了一個星期，水還像剛舀上來時一樣好，一點水泵的氣味都沒有。要是有人夏天到湖邊露營一週，只要在他帳篷陰涼處深埋一桶水達幾英尺，肯定用不着冰塊這類奢侈品了。

　　人們在瓦爾登湖裏捉過一些狗魚，有一條重達七磅，姑且先不談另有一條魚飛快逃跑時，帶走了一卷釣線；漁夫沒有看到牠，估計至少也有八磅重；曾捉到的還有鱸魚和鱈魚，其中有的每條重達兩磅以上；還有銀色小魚、鯿魚[7]或者太陽魚，數量很少的歐鯿，以及一兩條鰻魚，有一條重達四磅 —— 我之所以説得特別詳細，是因為一條魚的身價通常以重量為標準，而這兩條鰻魚卻是這裏我聽説過的，一種獨一無二的鰻魚——此外，我還模糊記得一條小魚，長五英寸，兩側銀灰色，脊背泛綠，從牠的特徵上看有點像鰷魚，我在這裏提到牠，主要為了聯繫起事實和寓言。不過話又說回來，這個湖裏並不盛產魚類。狗魚雖說不算多，卻成了這個湖的一大驕傲。有一次，我趴在冰層上，看到狗魚至少有三種類型：一種又長又扁，鐵灰色，很像從河裏捉到的那樣；一種金燦燦的，泛着綠色閃光，在很深的水域裏，乃是這裏最常見的魚；還有一種是金黃色，形狀和前一種相似，只是兩側有深褐色斑點或者黑色斑點，間雜着一些淡血紅色斑點，活像鮭鱒魚。這種魚按拉丁文學名稱為 reticulatus（網狀）不夠貼切，還不如叫做 guttatus（斑斕）為好。這些魚全是肉質結實，看上去比牠們的模子要重得多。銀色小魚、鱈魚和鱸魚，還有所有棲息在這個湖裏的魚類，確實要比生長在其他江河湖泊裏的魚類更乾淨、更漂亮、更結實，因為這裏的湖水更純潔，人們一眼就能區別牠們。也許很多魚類學家可以利用牠們來培育新品種。這個湖裏還有一些品種乾淨的青蛙和烏龜，以及數量極少的淡菜；麝鼠和水貂也在這裏留下了牠們的痕跡，偶然一隻周遊四方的香龜都會到此一遊。有時候，我一大早推船離岸時，不知怎的會驚動那夜間藏身在船底下的大香龜。春秋兩季，鵝鴨成羣，往往在這裏出沒；白肚皮的燕子[8]在湖上輕輕掠過，還有一些斑鷸[9]整個夏天只在石頭湖岸上"晃來晃去"。有時候，我還會驚動棲息在湖邊白皮松枝頭上的一隻魚鷹；但我不知道海鷗有沒有來過這裏，如同牠們常去美港一樣。潛水鳥到這裏來至多每年一次。現在常到這裏來的，全是一些不同凡響的動物。

趕上風平浪靜的天氣，你坐在小船上，可以看到湖的東頭沙灘附近那一帶，水深八英尺至十英尺，還有在湖的別處，也可以看到一些圓形堆垛，高約一英尺，直徑六英尺，由比雞蛋還小的圓石疊成，周圍全是光滑的沙。起初你會納悶，這是不是印第安人故意在冰層上堆疊這些圓石，等到冰層融化時，就一起沉到了湖底；可是，這些圓石疊得太整齊匀稱，有些圓石顯然也太新鮮，不像人工堆疊。它們與河裏找到的石頭一模一樣；反正這裏既沒有胭脂魚，也沒有七鰓鰻，我可弄不清楚那些圓石堆由哪些魚疊起來。也許牠們就是銀色小魚的窩吧。這些圓石堆給湖底平添了幾分令人喜歡的神秘感。

湖岸錯落有致，一點都不單調。在我心目中，西岸是犬牙交錯的深水灣，北岸較為險峻，而南岸呈扇貝形，很漂亮，一連串岬角互相交疊，不由得使人想到岬角之間還有好些人跡罕至的小水灣。湖水邊沿聳立的羣山之間有一個小湖，從小湖中央放眼四望，你會欣賞到在森林映襯下，從未有過的絕妙美景；因為森林映在湖面的倒影，不但形成了最佳風景，而且，迂迴曲折的湖岸，也成為它最自然、最宜人的邊界線。這裏與板斧砍出來的林地不一樣，與毗鄰湖邊的耕地也不一樣，既無斧鑿的痕跡，又無不完美之感。樹木享有充份空間可向水滲擴展，每棵樹都衝着這個方向伸展出最富活力的枝杈。在這裏，大自然編織了一道天然花邊，一眼望去，從湖邊低矮的灌木叢蜿蜒向上，一直望到那些參天樹木。在這裏，你看不見有甚麼人工痕跡。湖水沖洗堤岸，有如一千年前一模一樣。

湖 —— 在天然景色中最美、最富表情的就數它了。它是大地的眼睛；人們觀湖，可以估量出他自己天性的深淺。湖畔的水生樹木，彷彿是給它鑲了邊、修長的睫毛，而四周樹木蔥鬱的羣山和峭壁，則是它懸挑的濃眉了。

9月間的一個下午，風平浪靜，薄霧迷蒙，湖對岸的輪廓顯得模模糊糊，此時此刻，站在湖的東頭平坦的沙灘上，我方才恍然大悟，"湖面如鏡"這種説法究竟從何而來。你要是倒轉頭來看湖，湖就像一條最精緻的薄紗懸掛在峽谷上空，在遠方松林的映襯下閃閃發光，一層層分隔開大氣。你會覺得，你可從它底下衣不沾濕地走過去，一直走到湖對面的羣山那裏，而掠過湖面的燕子，也可在湖上棲息。有時候，那些燕子果真向它俯衝下來，好像一時失誤，稍後才恍然大悟。你朝西頭湖岸抬頭望去，不得不舉起兩手遮住自己的眼睛，擋開地道的陽光和從水中反射上來的陽光，因為這兩種陽光同樣亮得耀眼；你要是用挑剔的眼光，在這兩種亮光之間審視湖面，就會看到它真的波平如鏡了；此外只見一些貼水掠飛的昆蟲，遍佈整個湖面，彼此錯開相同間距，在陽光下飛來飛去，在水面上產生最美的閃光；也許有時還有一隻鴨在梳理自己的羽毛，或者，正如我前面說過的，有一隻燕子貼水低飛，快要碰到水面似的。也許從遠處望去，一條魚兒在半空中畫出了一道三四英尺的弧線，在牠躍出水面時映出一道閃光，在牠鑽進水裏時又映出了一道閃光；有時候，這一道銀光閃閃的弧線還會整個顯現出來；要不然，也許有一根薊草漂浮在湖的甚麼地方，魚兒衝它一躍，湖面上也會激起一圈圈漣漪。這時，湖面像融化的玻璃，冷卻了但還沒有凝結，裏面絕無僅有的塵埃也顯得純潔優美，可謂白璧的微瑕。你經常會看到一片更光滑、更幽暗的水域，彷彿有一張看不見的蜘蛛網，截然分開它和其他水域，成為水中仙子在那裏憩息的水柵。你從山頂上可以俯看到，幾乎所有水域都有魚兒在跳躍；在這波平似鏡的水面上，只需要一條狗魚或者銀色小魚在捕食一隻小昆蟲，就會攪亂整個湖面的平靜。真厲害，這麼簡單的一件事，卻顯現得這麼精巧 —— 這種魚類傷生害命的事終必敗露 ——我從很遠就清晰看到一圈圈直徑為六七桿的波浪形在四周圍擴散。你還會看見一隻水蝽[10]在平滑水面上不停歇地滑過了四份之一英里；牠們在水面上輕輕犁出了波紋，兩道分叉線形成了明顯的漣漪，可是長足昆蟲在水面上滑行，卻不會留下看得見的漣漪。湖面上一掀起波浪，長足昆蟲和水蝽連影子都見不着了。但是，趕上風平浪靜的日子，牠們就會離開自己的避風港，好像探險似的，憑着一時衝動，打從湖邊出發，一直往前方滑行，直到滑完全程為止。入秋後晴朗的一天，坐在高高山頭的樹樁上，沐浴在溫煦陽光裏，俯瞰瓦爾登湖的湖景，仔細捉摸那一圈圈漣漪，不停雕刻在有着天空和樹木倒影的水面上，要不是這些漣漪在晃動，連水面也都看不見呢——這真是令人舒心的快事啊！在這麼浩淼的水面上，甚麼干擾都沒有，即使有一點，很快就會緩解消失，讓人安靜下來，好像在湖邊汲取一壺水，顫動的水波流到了岸邊，一切復歸平靜。魚兒從水中躍起，小昆蟲落到了湖裏，不外乎通過一圈圈漣漪和優美的線條表述出來，好像這是泉水不斷在向上震顫、井噴。是牠的生命在輕輕搏動，是牠的胸脯在上下起伏。那是歡樂的激動，還是痛苦的戰慄，全都說不清楚。湖上好一派安謐的氣象啊！人類的勞動如同在春天裏，又在閃閃發光。是啊，每片葉子、每根枝條、每顆石子、每張蜘蛛網，到了午後時份都在閃閃發光，宛如春天早晨它們身上沾滿的露珠似的。船槳或者小昆蟲的每個動作，也都會發出閃光；聽那船槳的欸乃聲，該有多美啊！

趕上九月、十月裏這麼一天，瓦爾登湖儼如十全十美的森林明鏡，四周鑲上圓石子，依我看，這些圓石子十分珍貴，可謂稀世之寶。說不定地球上再也沒有一個湖，會像瓦爾登湖這樣純美，同時又這樣浩渺。遠自天上超凡脫俗的水啊！它不需要護欄。多少個民族來了又去了，都沒有玷污過它。它是一面石頭砸不碎的鏡子，它的水銀永遠不會消退，它的鑲邊金飾大自然還在不斷修補呢；風暴、塵垢，都沒法使它永遠光鮮的表面黯然失色——這一面鏡子，凡是不潔之物落在上面立時會沉下去，被太陽底下的霧氣揮去塵埃，洗刷乾淨——這是一塊拂塵布——往上面呵一口氣也都留不住，只管自己直升到高空，宛如懸浮在湖上的朵朵白雲，同時又清晰地倒映在湖面上。

泱泱的湖水，讓空中的精靈出沒無常。它不斷從天上接受新的生命和旨意。它實質上在天地之間充當媒介。大地上只有草木隨風搖曳，而水自身卻被風吹起一圈圈漣漪。從一縷或者一片閃光裏，我看得出風在輕輕吹拂。我們能夠仔細俯視湖的表面，真是匪夷所思。說不定我們將來終究也會像這樣仔細俯視天空的表面，發覺一個更玄妙的精靈從它上面掠過呢。

10 月的後半個月，嚴霜降臨，長足昆蟲和水蟲終於銷聲匿跡；再往後到了 11 月，風平浪靜的日子裏，通常湖面上絕不會被甚麼玩意激起漣漪來。11 月的一個下午，持續好幾天的暴風雨終於停了下來，但天上仍然陰雲密佈，霧氣迷濛，我觀察到瓦爾登湖上光滑得出奇，連湖面都很難辨認出來；它雖然反射不出 10 月裏光豔豔的色彩，卻映照出了周圍羣山在 11 月間的暗淡色調。我盡可能輕輕划着小船過湖，可是我的小船激起的波紋卻一直擴散到我看不見的遠方，使湖裏的倒影泛出彎彎曲曲的形狀。我抬眼觀望湖面，隱隱約約看見遠處星星點點的微光閃爍不定，就像一些在水上掠過的昆蟲，躲過嚴霜之後卻在那裏紮起堆來了，或者說，也許湖面過於光滑，連泉水從湖底往上井噴，也依稀可見。輕輕蕩起雙槳，來到了那些地點，我吃驚地發覺，四周全是數不盡的小鱸魚，大約有五英寸長，在碧綠的湖水裏呈深銅色，牠們在湖中嬉戲，經常躍到水面上來，激起一圈圈漣漪，有時還會留下一些小小泡沫。在如此透明、好像無底、映現雲彩的湖水中，我好像乘着氣球懸浮在空中，鱸魚們則游來游去，依我看，如同飛翔或者盤旋似的，牠們儼然是一羣鳥兒從我的下方或左或右穿過，牠們的鰭有如全部撐開的風帆。瓦爾登湖就有許多這樣的水族，顯然牠們要在嚴冬還沒有落下冰簾、遮住牠們頭上廣闊的陽光之前，充份利用一下這個短暫季節；有時，牠們給湖面呈現出些許細紋模樣，好像只是一絲微風拂過湖面，或是灑下幾滴雨點罷了。我漫不經心地漸走漸近時，牠們大吃一驚，突然拍擊湖水，搖着尾巴激起了水花來，好像有人拿着一根刷子似的枝條在擊水，眨眼間牠們都躲到湖水深處去了。最後，湖上一起風，霧靄漸濃，浪開始翻滾，鱸魚們比前時躥得更高，魚身很快躥出了水面，形成上百個黑點，三英寸長。有一年，即使遲至 12 月 5 日，我還看到水面上有一些水花，以為一眨眼就要下大雨了，空中霧氣彌漫，我匆匆坐到划槳的位置上，向着家直接划去；這時好像雨已經越下越大了，雖然我臉頰上還絲毫沒有感覺到，但我估計自己肯定會淋成落湯雞了。竟不知那些水花突然連影都看不見了，原來水花是鱸魚們激起來的，我的划槳聲嚇得牠們潛入深水裏去了，我目睹牠們成羣消失得渺無影蹤；就這樣，我衣不沾濕地度過了這天下午。

將近 60 年前，有一位老人，經常在森林周圍已是漆黑一片的時候光臨湖邊，他告訴我說，那些年他有時還看到湖上很熱鬧，鴨子和其他水禽在湖中戲水，許多老鷹在來回盤旋。他是來這裏釣魚的，划着一隻他在岸邊尋到的破舊獨木舟。這獨木舟由兩棵白皮松中間鑿空打造在一起，首尾兩端都給砍成方方正正。它那個樣式很難看，但是管用，已經許多年了，後來進了水才泡爛，也許就沉到湖底去了。他不知道那小船是誰家的；算了，它就算屬於瓦爾登湖吧。老人常常絞山核桃樹皮當作他的錨鏈。還有一個在革命前就住在湖邊的老人，跟他談過這湖底有一個鐵箱子，老人還看過呢。有時候，那個鐵箱還會漂浮到岸上來；不過，你要是一挨近它，它就又下沉到深水裏去，立時渺無影蹤。聽到那隻破舊的獨木舟的來歷，我很高興，它替代了那種印第安人的獨木舟，儘管兩者木材相同，但是前者做工稍微好看一些；說不定它原先只是岸邊的一棵樹，後來倒伏在湖水裏，漂浮過二三十年，成為最適合在這湖裏行駛的船隻了。記得我起初觀察湖水深處時，就看到湖底隱隱約約躺着許多許多巨大樹幹，也許是從前被大風刮倒，要不然是最後一次遭砍伐被人扔在冰層上，因為那時節反正木材很不值錢；殊不知如今這些樹幹十之八九都不見影了。

我頭一次在瓦爾登湖上划船時，環湖全是茂密、高大的松樹和橡樹林，在湖的一些小水灣裏，葡萄藤蔓爬過了湖沿的樹木，形成了一個個涼亭，小船可以從它底下穿過。形成湖岸的那些羣山很陡峭，那裏有很多參天樹木，你要是從西邊往下俯瞰，這裏看上去就像一座圓形劇場，可供某些林中仙子演出。年輕的時候，我就在那處消磨過許多時光；我像風一樣隨心所欲，漂浮在湖面上，划了我的小船到湖中央，自己仰臥在座位上，在一個夏天的上午，似夢非夢，半眠半醒，等小船撞着了沙灘，我方才驚醒過來，於是站起來，看看命運之神將我推向甚麼樣的湖岸了；在那些日子裏，賦閒乃是最誘人的事業，它的產出也最豐富。我讓許多個上午都悄悄溜走，覺得還是這樣消磨掉一天當中最珍貴的時間較好；因為，就算我沒錢，但我卻有陽光明媚的時光和涼爽歇夏的日子供我盡情享受；我沒有浪費更多時光在工場裏或者在教師的講台上，對此我也並不後悔。可是，自從我離開湖岸以後，伐木者對樹木越發亂砍濫伐，往後許多歲月裏，再也不能在林間小道上徜徉了，也不可能從枝杈之間偶然看到湖水了。我的繆斯女神[11]要是從此沉默了，對她也是情有可原。樹林全給砍光了，你還能指望鳥兒們歌唱嗎？

湖底的樹幹、古老的獨木舟和環湖幽深的樹林，如今都見不着了，村民們就連湖座落在哪處也不知道，他們想的不是來這湖裏沐浴和掬飲，卻要把它的水 —— 這至少也該像恒河一樣聖潔的水啊 —— 通過管道引進到村裏去，好讓他們洗碟刷盤！只需要拔去一個軟塞，或者擰一下水龍頭，就用到了瓦爾登湖的水！這像魔鬼的鐵馬，它那震耳欲聾的巨響，整個村鎮上都聽得見，它的腳丫已經攪渾了沸泉，再說，也正是它，吞噬了瓦爾登湖畔所有樹林。這匹特洛伊木馬，肚裏藏了成千個人，全是經商的希臘人琢磨出來的！這個國家的勇士，摩爾府上的摩爾[12]在哪裏？應該迎頭趕到"底普卡特"[13]，將復仇的長矛對準這個驕橫害人精的肋骨直捅進去吧。

不過話又說回來，據我所知，各種特色中，或許就數瓦爾登湖的特色最好，保持它的純潔性，也是令人叫絕。許多人都被比喻為瓦爾登湖，但這一美譽只有少數人受之無愧。儘管伐木者先後大片大片砍光了環湖的樹，愛爾蘭人在湖邊搭建了他們的陋屋，鐵路已經侵佔了湖的邊緣地帶，冰商還來這裏鑿取過冰塊，但瓦爾登湖本身並沒有變化，依然是我年輕時目睹過的湖水；變化了的反而是我自己。瓦爾登湖裏有過數不盡的漣漪，恆久不變的波紋卻一道也沒有。瓦爾登湖永遠年輕，我可以停下來站在湖畔，看一隻燕子俯衝下來，將一隻小昆蟲從湖面上叼走，如同在往日裏一模一樣。今夜，我不禁又觸景生情，彷彿我幾乎沒有跟它朝夕相見長達二十多年之久，這就是瓦爾登湖，多年以前我發現的那同一個林中之湖；去年冬天在湖邊砍掉了一個樹林，今年春天又一個樹林就會傍湖拔地而起，依舊生機勃勃；同樣的思緒如同在往日裏一樣從湖面上噴湧上來 —— 這對湖本身與湖的創造者來說，是同樣源源不絕的歡樂和幸福，是的，對我來說可能也是如此。不用說，瓦爾登湖是一位勇士的傑作，他絕不會耍狡猾！他親手圍住了這湖水，在他的思考中使湖水得以深化和澄清，並在他的遺囑中將它傳給了康科德。我從它的湖面上看到了同樣的倒影活靈活現；我差不多要說：瓦爾登，是你嗎？

> 我絕對不會夢想
> 去雕飾一行詩；
> 唯有住在瓦爾登湖旁，
> 我方可走近上帝和天堂。
> 我是圓石堆砌的湖濱
> 上面輕輕地吹過的風；
> 在我的掌心裏
> 是湖裏的水和沙，
> 湖最幽深的勝地
> 高臥在我的思緒裏。

火車從來沒有停下來觀賞一下瓦爾登的湖光山色；不過，我猜想火車上的司機、司爐和司閘員，還有那些持有月票的旅客，他們倒是常常看在眼裏，其實，觀賞瓦爾登湖的景色，就數他們最地道。司機在夜間開車並沒有忘記它，或者說，司機的天性並沒有忘記它，而在大白天，司機至少會對靜謐、純潔的湖光山色投以一瞥，就算它僅僅是驚鴻一瞥，也足以沖洗乾淨斯達特街[14]和發動機上的污垢。有人提議不妨叫瓦爾登湖水為"聖水一滴"。

我已說過，瓦爾登湖的進水口和出水口都是看不見的，但它一邊和佛林特湖遙相呼應，間接地連在一起，佛林特湖水位比較高，有一連串小湖從那裏流過來；它另一邊又顯然直接和康科德河連在一起，而康科德河水位較低，也有一連串類似的小湖從中穿過，在某個地質時期也許河水泛濫過，只需要稍微開挖一下 —— 無奈上帝禁止開挖 —— 它還是可以流到這裏來。如果說瓦爾登湖像林中隱士一樣莊敬自重地生活了那麼長時間，從而獲得如此神奇的純潔，那麼，佛林特湖較為不潔的湖水一旦和瓦爾登湖水渾在一起，或者換句話說，瓦爾登甘美的湖水遭白白浪費掉，流入了海洋，誰能不為之感到惋惜呢？

佛林特湖或稱沙湖，位於瓦爾登湖以東一英里的林肯附近，是我們這裏最大的湖和內海。佛林特湖湖面浩瀚，據說佔地一百九十七英畝，湖中漁產也更豐富；不過，水位比較淺，水質也不太純。穿過樹林散步往那裏去，常常是我的一大消遣。哪怕是僅僅感受一下那吹拂在臉頰上令人痛快的清風，僅僅看看此起彼伏的水波，僅僅追懷一下海員們的生活，那也不算是虛此一行吧。入秋後起風的日子裏，我去過那裏拾栗子，那時堅果都掉在水裏，又給水波沖到了我腳跟邊；有一次，我正沿着蘆葦叢生的岸邊爬行，鮮靈活潑的浪花飛濺在我臉上，我碰見了一條破船的殘骸，船舷沒有了，在燈芯草叢裏幾乎給人留下只有一個平底的印象；不過，船的模型還是輪廓分明，彷彿是一大塊爛透了的墊板，依然有棱有角。這是人們在海岸上可以想像到令人印象深刻的船骸，還包含耐人尋味的寓意。這個時節，湖岸上不外乎是腐質土壤，很難看出真面目來，到處長滿了燈芯草和菖蒲。這個湖北端的湖底沙灘上，漣漪留下的痕跡，常常使我讚賞不已；湖底受到水的壓力變得異常堅硬，涉水者走在上面就更有具體感受；單行生長的燈芯草呈波浪形條紋，跟湖底的漣漪痕跡合轍，一排又一排，彷彿波浪栽植了它們。在那裏，我還發現許多奇形怪狀的球體，分明由細草或者根鬚，也許還有穀精草組成，其直徑從一英寸半到四英寸，倒是很完美的圓形物體。這些球體在湖底沙灘淺水裏來回沖蕩，有時還被湖水捲到了湖岸上。它們一就是鐵硬的草團，一就是中間帶着一點沙。開始時，你也許會說，它們是被波浪衝擊而成的，如同鵝卵石一模一樣；但是，最小的球體僅有半英寸長，儘管質地粗糙跟大的球體相同，但它一年之中只要一個季度就長大成形了。再說，我還懷疑，波浪所起的作用，不是在打造，而是在損壞早已抱成團的物體。這些球體一旦乾透了，它們的形狀依然可以保存相當長的時間。

佛林特湖！我們給它起的名字，沒想到會如此醜陋呀。邋邋遢遢、傻裏傻氣的農夫，竟然在這水天一色的湖中開墾農場，惡狠狠糟蹋湖岸，令它不堪入目，他憑甚麼權利用自己的姓氏命名它？好一個不知羞恥的吝嗇鬼，天底下他最愛的是一塊美元或者一枚閃亮的分幣的反光，從中他可以看到自己那張厚黑的臉；他甚至看棲息在湖上的野鴨子為入侵者；由於長期慣常貪婪掠奪，他的手指已經變得彎曲而又尖硬，就像哈比¹⁵ 的鷹爪 —— 因此，這個湖名我覺得很不順心。我到那裏去，不是去看他，也不是去聽人談論他；他從來沒有看過這個湖，也沒有在這個湖裏洗過澡；他從來沒有喜愛過這個湖，從來沒有保護過這個湖，從來沒有說過這個湖的一句好話，更沒有感謝過創造了這個湖的上帝。給這個湖命名，還不如乾脆採用在湖中戲水的魚兒的名字，在湖上出沒無常的飛禽或者走獸的名字，或者傍湖生長的野花的名字，或者用一個他們的身世和湖的來歷交織在一起的野人，乃至於野孩子的名字；不要採用他這個人的姓氏，因為除了同他意氣相投的鄰居或者立法機構發給他一張契約以外，他對這個湖並沒有所有權 —— 他這種人心裏想的只是這個湖值多少錢；他在湖上的出現，說不定只會使環湖灘地橫遭災禍；他這種人只會使湖周圍的土地潛力全給耗盡；他這種人唯一感到遺憾的是，這裏不是盛產英格蘭乾草或者越橘的草場 —— 在他的眼裏，這確實沒有甚麼可補償的 —— 所以，只要湖底的淤泥可以賣錢，他認為，即使排乾湖水也行。反正湖水再也不會叫他的水磨轉動，他也並不覺得觀賞湖上景色是一種莫大榮幸。對他的生活，以及他那個樣樣東西明碼標價的農場，我是不屑一顧的；他這種人會拿風景，甚至還有他的上帝，到市場上去拍賣，只要他從中有利可圖；其實，他到市場上去，說白了，就是為了他那個上帝；在他的農場上，甚麼玩意都不會長出來；他的地裏長不出穀物，他的草場上見不到花兒，他的果樹上不結果實，反正長出來的是金元；他喜愛的並不是他的果子的美；他覺得他的果子只有變成了美元，這才算成熟了。算了吧，反正我安於窮雖窮、其實真富的生活。農夫們越是貧困，越是得到我的敬意和關注 —— 貧困的農夫們。虧它還是個模範農場！農場裏的房子，就像糞堆上長出來的真菌，住屋啦、馬廄啦、牛棚啦、豬圈啦，不管是乾淨的，還是不乾淨的，全都連在一起！人就像畜生似的擠在裏面！勝過一大塊油漬，散發出糞肥和奶酪摻和在一起的氣味。在一個高度文明的社會階層裏，連人的心腦都給浸成了糞肥！彷彿你到教堂墓園去種馬鈴薯！原來模範農場就是這個德行。

不，不；如果說最優美的景點要冠以人名，那就不妨採用最高貴的精英人物的名字。讓我們的湖擁有真正的名字，至少要像伊卡羅斯海[16]那樣，在那裏，一次"勇敢的嘗試"至今仍在海上迴響着。

鵝湖，湖不太大，座落在我去佛林特湖的路上；美港是康科德河的一個大水灣，據說面積大約有七十英畝，在西南角一英里處；白湖，約有四十英畝，離美港有一英里半之遙。這些就是我的湖鄉。這幾個湖，連同康科德河，成了我的水上特區；日以繼夜，年復一年，我送去的那些穀物都給它們碾成了粉。

自從伐木者、鐵路和我，玷污了瓦爾登湖之後，最誘人的湖，哪怕不是最美麗的湖，堪稱林中瑰寶，在我們這裏所有的湖裏面，也許就數白湖了——好一個可憐的湖名，由於它太平凡吧，它的得名不管源於水質極其純潔，還是源於沙的顏色。反正不管從哪個方面來說，白湖與瓦爾登湖乃孿生兄弟，只不過稍微小一些。它們相似之處非常多，你會說它們在地底下一定是連在一起的。白湖也有同樣的圓石湖岸，湖水也是同樣的顏色。正如瓦爾登湖，趕上熱得邪門的酷暑天氣，透過樹林，俯瞰湖中一些水灣（它們雖然算不上很深，但因湖底的反光，染上了一層色彩），白湖的水也平添了一種霧濛濛淡綠的，抑或是海綠的色彩。多年前，我常去那裏採沙，用小車運回來做砂紙，後來我還繼續不斷地去過那裏。有一個常去白湖的人提議，不妨叫它做“綠湖”就可以了。也許還可以稱它為“黃松湖”，理由如下：大約在十五年前，你會看到一棵油松的樹梢頭，不斷往外伸向深水的上空，離湖岸竟有許多桿遠呢。這種松樹並不是甚麼名貴品種，但在這附近一帶都稱之為黃松。有人甚至還認為白湖原先下沉過，從前在這裏有過一片原始森林，這棵黃松就是其中的一棵。我發現，甚至遠在 1792 年，在馬薩諸塞州歷史學會藏書館裏，就有一位公民寫過一部《康科德地形圖志》，這位作者談到了瓦爾登湖和白湖後，補充着說：“白湖的水位很低時，在湖心那裏可以看到，有一棵樹，樹根雖然在離湖面有五十英尺的深處，但看上去彷彿生長在目前所在的地點；樹梢頭已被摧折殆盡，被摧折之處直徑據測算有十四英寸。”1849 年春天，我和一個住在薩德伯利、離湖最近的人閒聊，他告訴我，正是他在十年或許十五年以前拽出這棵樹的。就他記憶所及，這棵樹離湖岸有十二桿或者十五桿遠，那處水深約有三十英尺或者四十英尺。正是嚴冬季節，他上半天在湖上鑿冰，決定午後請鄰居們幫忙，拽出這棵老黃松樹。他先在冰層上鋸開了一條通道，直接通向湖岸，隨後用一頭牛拔起它，再拖到了冰層上；殊不知這工作還沒多大進展，他就大吃一驚地發現，這棵樹卻是樹根朝天，枝條的根茬反而朝下，那小的一端在沙質的湖底牢牢紮了根。那大頭的直徑約有一英尺，他原先指望能尋到一根可開出上等鋸材的原木，沒料到它已經極為腐爛，只配當作劈柴生火，如果説拿它來做燃料的話。當時，他的雜物屋裏面還有一點木頭。那上頭還有斧痕和啄木鳥的喙痕呢。他認為，那可能是湖岸上的一棵死樹，後來被大風刮倒在湖裏，樹頂被水浸透了，樹底部份還是很乾燥的，份量又很輕，因此浮上了水面，倒栽着沉了下去。他父親年屆八旬，記不起那棵樹甚麼時候不在那裏。現在湖底依然可以看到一些很粗的原木，由於湖面上水波不斷在蕩漾，它們看上去就像碩大無朋的水蛇在游動似的。

白湖很少讓船隻玷污過，因為湖裏可引誘漁夫的生物少得可憐。既沒有潔白的百合（因為它需要污泥），也沒有常見的菖蒲；在純淨的湖水中，稀稀落落地點綴一些藍幽幽的菖蒲，它們都是從沿岸四周湖底石灘上彷彿一躍而起似的。到了 6 月間，蜂鳥就來這裏探訪，那藍幽幽的葉片和藍幽幽的花朵，特別是它們在湖中的倒影，與海藍色的湖水顯得格外和諧。

白湖與瓦爾登湖是大地上的兩大塊水晶，"光之湖"。如果説它們是永遠凝固的、小得可以拿捏的東西，也許它們早被奴隸們帶走，如同寶石一樣，點綴在帝王頭上了；殊不知它們是液體，煙波浩淼，永遠惠及我們和我們的子子孫孫。可惜我們自己並不賞識它們，卻去追求甚麼科依諾爾 [17] 大鑽石。它們定是太純潔，以至沒有甚麼市場價值，而且它們不含污垢。倘若跟我們的生命相比，它們不知道該有多美啊！倘若跟我們的性格相比，它們不知道還要透明多少呢！我們從來沒聽說它們有過甚麼微瑕。倘若跟農家門前鴨子在戲水的池塘相比，它們不知道該有多美啊！看，潔淨的野鴨子到這裏來了。大自然啊，還沒有一個居民能欣賞她呀。鳥兒連同牠們的彩羽和歌喉，與鮮花可謂琴瑟和諧，但是又有哪個少男少女能與大自然的粗獷華麗之美息息相通呢？大自然遠離塵囂，獨自欣欣向榮。還胡扯甚麼天堂！你玷污了大地。

章註

1　修道院住院修士：此處也是梭羅慣用的一語雙關手法。英文為 coenobites，意思是 "修道士"，如果我們稍加注意這字的發音，就會發現 "See, no bites"，意思是 "你看，沒有魚上釣"。

2　米開蘭基羅：Michelangelo， 1475—1564，意大利文藝復興時期雕塑家、畫家、詩人和建築學家，代表作有雕塑《大衛》、《摩西》和壁畫《最後的審判》等。

3　卡斯塔利亞泉：古代神話傳說中位於帕納薩斯山的一座泉，被認為是詩歌藝術靈感的泉源。

4　帕瓦儀式：北美印第安人祈求神靈治病或保佑戰鬥和狩獵等勝利而舉行的一種儀式，通常伴有巫術、盛宴和舞蹈等。

5　薩夫倫·瓦爾登：Saffron Walden，英國名城劍橋以南一城鎮。

6　意思是 "用牆圍起來"，發音與 Walden 相似，故中譯文湖名亦按音譯。

7　鯿魚：拉丁文學名 Leuciscus pulchellus。

8　白肚皮的燕子：拉丁文學名 Hirundo bicolor。

9　斑鷸：拉丁文學名 Totanus macularius。

10　水蚊：拉丁文學名 Gyrinus。

11　繆斯女神：古希臘神話中掌管文學藝術，特別是詩歌的女神。

12　摩爾：據傳，摩爾是古代英國傳説中的屠龍英雄人物。

13　"底普卡特"：原文為 Deep Cut，意為深深砍下去。

14　斯達特街：即麻省首府波士頓市內一條大街，以金融中心著稱於世。

15　哈比：古希臘、古羅馬神話中一個怪物，他的臉及身軀似女人，而翼、尾和爪似鳥，殘忍、貪婪和掠奪成性。

16　伊卡羅斯海：伊卡羅斯為古希臘神話中的一個人物，雕塑家戴達勒斯的兒子，與其父雙雙以蠟翼黏身飛離克里特島，因為飛得太高，蠟翼被陽光融化，墜落愛琴海而死。

17 科依諾爾：原產自印度的一顆大鑽石，重 191 克拉，1849 年後被英國奪走，成為英王王冠上的寶石。

10
貝克農場

有時，我漫步到松樹林，松樹林聳立着像寺院，或者像海上裝備齊全的艦隊，樹枝像波濤起伏，又像漣漪閃閃發光，看到那麼柔和蒼翠的濃蔭，德魯伊特們也會擯棄他們的橡樹林，專程來到這些松樹林下頂禮膜拜了；有時，我漫步在佛林特湖畔的雪松樹林，那些參天大樹上掛滿了灰白色的藍莓，樹幹越長越高，移植到瓦爾哈拉殿堂前倒是十分相宜；而杜松的藤蔓盤繞交錯，果實累累遍地；有時，我漫步來到沼澤地帶，只見白杉上倒懸着花彩似的松羅地衣，滿地都是傘菌，它們是沼澤地眾神的一張張圓桌子，而份外美麗的香菌則點綴在樹根周圍，像蝴蝶、像彩貝，也像植物峨螺；那裏長着石竹和山茱萸，紅色的橙木漿果活像小精靈的眼珠；就算是最堅硬的樹木，也會給蠟蜂啃成累累凹痕而毀掉；而野冬青的漿果，真美極了，令人看了流連忘返；還有許多其他不知名的野生禁果，也都是光豔奪目，十分誘人，味道太好了，凡夫俗子是從沒嚐過的。我一次又一次去接觸的，不是哪一位學者，倒是在這一帶十分罕見的一棵棵不同凡響的樹木，它們遠遠聳立在牧場中央，或者生長在樹林或者沼澤地的深處，或者生長在小山岡頂上。比方說，黑樺木，我們就有一些漂亮的標本，直徑達二英尺。與黑樺木同一綱目的，還有黃樺木，披着寬大的金色外衣，跟黑樺木一樣散發着香味。還有山毛櫸，長得那麼潔淨脫俗，全身呈現美麗的地衣色彩，所有細部全都完美無缺；這一種樹，除了散在各處的標本，在這一帶我知道唯有這樣小小的一片樹林，樹身倒是相當可觀，據說還是那些被附近山毛櫸堅果引誘過來的鴿子所播下的種子呢；你一劈開這種樹木，只見銀色的顆粒閃閃發光，煞是好看。此外，還有椴樹、鵝耳櫪樹[1]，我們這裏只有一棵生長得很好。還有一些可以作桅桿的高聳松樹，以及一棵可以做木瓦的樹；一棵不同凡響的鐵杉，矗立在樹林裏宛如一座寶塔。我還可以列舉出許多其他樹木。不管嚴冬酷暑，這些都是我必去朝覲的聖地。古代凱爾特人中一批有學識的人，擔任祭司、教師、法官或巫師、占卜者等。據說，他們崇拜橡樹林。北歐神話中諸神兼死亡之神奧丁接待戰死者英靈的殿堂。

有一次，說來也真巧，我站在一道彩虹的拱座裏，只見這條彩虹貫通大氣的底層，給周圍的草葉點染了色彩，使我一下子眼花繚亂，彷彿我正在透視一個五彩繽紛的水晶體，這裏隨即成了一個光之湖，一瞬間，我活像在虹光之湖裏的一頭海豚。那彩虹要是持續的時間長一些，說不定會使我的事業和生命異彩紛呈了吧。我行走在鐵路堤道上時，常對我影子周圍的那個光輪感到驚訝，自以為是上帝的一名選民了。有一個來訪者告訴我，在他面前的那批愛爾蘭人，他們的影子周圍就沒有光輪，只有生於斯、長於斯的土著才有呢。本梵努托‧切利尼[2] 在他的回憶錄裏告訴我們，在聖安琪羅城堡囚禁期間，做了一個可怕的噩夢或者幻覺之後，無論在早上和晚上，都有一團燦爛的光芒出現在他的頭影上，不管他是在意大利，還是在法國，而且，要是在草上有露珠時，那光輪也就更明顯，說不定這跟我說過的是如出一轍的現象，在大清早顯得尤其清楚，不過，在其他時間裏，乃至於在月光之下，也是這樣。這固然是一種常見現象，但很少被人注意到，而像切利尼那樣驚人的想像力，就足以構成迷信的基礎。此外，他還告訴我們，他只是指點給極少數人看的。不過話又說回來，那些意識到自己得天獨厚的人，難道說真的就是卓犖冠羣嗎？

有一天下午，我穿過那片樹林，去美港釣魚，以彌補一下我光吃蔬菜所引起的營養不足。我路上穿過快樂草地，它隸屬於貝克農場，從前有個詩人就歌唱過這麼一塊隱退勝地，詩的開首是——

> 入口是一片宜人的田野，
> 在長滿苔蘚的果樹之間，
> 一條泛紅小溪在涓涓地流，
> 麝鼠卻在水邊忽閃忽現，
> 還有鮮蹦活跳的鱒魚，
> 也在水中盡情游來游去。

　　我在入駐瓦爾登湖之前，倒是考慮過去那裏居住。我曾經在那裏"鈎過"樹上的蘋果，跨躍過那條小溪，嚇跑過麝鼠和鱒魚。那些下半天，時間好像長得不得了，超過我們壽命的一大半，其間會發生許許多多事情；就是這麼一個下半天，時間早已過半，我才動身。走到半路，碰到一場大雨，我只好在一棵松樹底下站了半個小時，頭上堆滿樹丫枝，再用一塊手絹來遮擋雨水；到最後，我已站在齊腰深的水裏，正要拿眼子菜來碰碰運氣呢，突然之間，我發現自己置身於一塊烏雲底下，雷聲開始轟隆作響，我別無選擇，只好洗耳恭聽了。天上諸神定然自以為了不起，我想，居然用這樣叉形的閃電，來打擊一個手無寸鐵可憐的釣魚人。於是，我趕緊直奔最近的那個小屋去躲一躲，那小屋離哪條大路都有半英里路遠，不過離湖倒反而近得多了，何況很久以來沒有人在那裏住過——這裏是一位詩人所造，

> 在他的風燭殘年，
> 眼看這簡陋的小木屋，
> 也有倒塌的險象。[3]

繆斯女神講過的寓言就是這樣。但我卻發現當下住在這裏的一個愛爾蘭人，名叫約翰·菲爾德，還有他妻子和幾個孩子；那個臉大的男孩子已能幫父親做點工作，此刻跟着父親從沼澤地奔回家躲雨，來到那個臉上有皺紋、像先知一樣的圓錐體腦袋的嬰孩跟前，那嬰孩則坐在父親的膝蓋上，就像坐在貴族的宮殿裏，從他那個潮濕又捱餓的家裏好奇地直望着陌生人，不用説，這是嬰孩的特權，他卻不懂得自己是貴族世家的最後一代，是當今世界的希望、引人矚目的中心，而並不是甚麼約翰·菲爾德可憐的、捱餓的小孩。我們一起坐在漏雨最少的屋頂底下，而屋外，雷聲隆隆，大雨滂沱。從前，我曾在這裏坐過不知多少次了，那時節，載着他們一家漂洋過海到美國來的那艘船，恐怕還沒有造好吧。約翰·菲爾德，一望可知，是個誠實、勤勞，但又無可奈何的人；他妻子倒是很潑辣，總在高高的爐子那裏忙着做飯；看她那張臉圓圓的、油膩膩的，露着胸脯，仍然夢想着總有一天改善一下她的境遇；儘管她手裏一刻不離小拖把，但哪裏都看不出它有甚麼效果。雞羣也進了屋裏躲雨，好像家裏人一樣在屋裏面走來走去，反正牠們太像人類，我想，就算烤熟了，味道也不見得好極了。牠們站在那裏，直盯住我的眼睛，或者故意來啄一啄我的鞋子。就在這時候，我主人講自己的身世給我聽，説他如何給鄰近的一個農場主人在“沼澤地”裏工作，用鐵鍬（或者沼澤地專用的鐵鋤）翻耕一片草地，報酬是每一英畝地十塊錢，並且可使用施過肥的土地一年；又説他那臉大、身型小的兒子，一直在父親身邊快樂地工作，一點不知道他老爸這一筆買賣該有多麼倒霉。我試圖用我的個人經驗幫助他，告訴他，説他是我的近鄰之一，説我也不外乎來這裏釣釣魚，看起來是個流浪漢，和他本人一樣自謀生計；我還告訴他，我住在一個狹窄但明亮潔淨的屋裏，屋的造價一點也不高於他每年租用這種陋屋的租金，如果他願意的話，他也可以在一兩個月內，給自己造一座宮殿；我平素不喝茶，不喝咖啡，不吃牛油，不飲牛奶，

也不吃鮮肉，因此，我就用不着為了得到這些去工作；再者，我工作不
太吃力，用不着吃得很多，所以，我的吃食費用也是微不足道；可是他
呢，因為他一開始就要飲茶、喝咖啡，吃牛油、喝牛奶、吃牛排，那他
就不得不拼命工作，來償付這些吃食開支，而且，他越是拼命工作，就
越是要拼命吃喝，以彌補他體力上的消耗——結果呢，他的開支越來越
大，而開支越來越大，要是長此以往，確實難以承受，因為他總是要設
法得到滿足，結果他的一生就這樣耗掉在這筆買賣中；殊不知他還是認
為到美國來是賺的，在這裏，你每天可以喝到茶、咖啡和吃肉類呢。其
實，那唯一真正的美國是這樣一個國家：在這裏，你可以自由追求這麼
一種生活模式，即使沒有這些照樣也行，而且，在這裏，國家並沒有強
迫你去支持蓄奴制，去供養戰爭，以及為了間接或者直接用於諸如此類
的事而付出額外費用。原來我帶有目的來跟他說這些話，好像他就是一
個哲學家，或者換句話說，他願意成為一個哲學家。我倒是很樂意讓地
球上所有草地依然處在荒蕪狀態，如果說那就是人類開始為自己贖罪的
結果。一個人不見得讀了歷史，才悟出甚麼東西對他自己的文化最有裨
益。可是，老天哪！一個愛爾蘭人的文化，從心理上來說，就是用一種
沼澤地專用的鋤頭去開創自己的事業。我告訴他，既然他在沼澤地裏工
作，他就需要加厚靴子和結實的衣服，要不然這些衣靴一下子就給弄髒
了、磨爛了；而我穿着輕便的鞋和薄薄的衣服，還不到他所花的錢的一
半，說不定他認為我穿扮得活像一個紳士（其實並非如此）；我倒是可以
在一兩個鐘頭以內，不費吹灰之力，僅僅作為一種消遣，就能釣到很多
魚兒，夠我吃上兩天，或者賺到夠多的錢，可供養我一個多星期。如果
說他和他一家願意過簡樸生活，夏天他們可以全家都去拾烏飯樹漿果，
不管怎樣也是一件樂事。聽了我這番話，約翰長歎了一聲，而他的妻子
雙手叉腰，兩眼直瞪着，他們兩個人看起來都在思忖，他們有沒有足夠
資金開始過這種生活，或者說，他們有沒有足夠運算能力使它付諸實

現。在他們看來，這好比張帆航行少不得航位測算，可是他們弄不清楚該怎樣才能到達他們的港口；因此，我估計他們仍然會按照他們的方式生活，勇敢面對生活，竭盡全力應對着，他們沒有能耐採用最精銳的楔子，自然也楔入不了生活的巨大立柱，將它一一劈開後用精細手工刻上花紋——他們想到的是將就着應對生活，就像人們應對棘手問題一樣。可是，他們卻在極端不利條件下拼搏——過日子，約翰·菲爾德，天哪！不會計算，註定一敗塗地。

"你釣過魚嗎？"我問。"哦，釣過，我休息的時候，倒是常常釣過一些；我還釣到過很棒的河鱸魚呢。""你用的是甚麼魚餌呢？""我用魚蟲釣銀色小魚，再用銀色小魚作誘餌來釣河鱸。""好啊！，你現在就去釣魚，約翰。"他妻子說，臉上露出希望的閃光；可是，約翰卻遲疑不定。

這時，陣雨已經過去了，東邊樹林上空映現一道彩虹，預示着一個美好的夜晚；於是，我就起身告別。到了門外，我又轉過身來，向他們要一杯水喝，希望看看他們這口井的水質，完成我對周遭住家的調查；可是，天哪！這井底竟然是個淺灘，裏面盡是流沙，繩子扯斷了，水桶也壞得沒法修補。就在這時候，我找出灶間用的一隻杯，杯裏的水，好像蒸餾過了，經過一番磋商，拖了好長時間，才傳遞到了那口渴的人手上——還沒有涼下來，更沒有澄清呢。我想，這裏的人就是靠這種稀湯水來活命的；於是，我巧妙地將塵埃抖落在水底，為了主人真誠殷勤的招待，我閉上眼，一飲而盡。在諸如此類的場合，我可一點也不拘禮節的。

雨後，我離開了愛爾蘭人一家，大步又向湖邊走去。我涉水走過一些僻靜的草地，泥坑與沼澤地的洞穴，也走過不少荒野的地塊。我那種匆匆去釣狗魚的心情對我這個讀過中學、上過大學的人來說，一下子顯得可有可無；不過，我一下了山，直奔一抹紅霞的西邊，一道彩虹懸在我兩肩之上，隱隱約約有一種叮噹聲，透過潔淨的空氣，傳入我的耳際，這時，我又不知道從甚麼地方，聽到我的守護神好像在跟我說話似的——你要天天去遠處釣魚打獵——越遠越好，地域越廣越好——你就在許多小溪邊休息，在許多人的圍爐邊休息，莫要擔驚受怕。你在花樣年華時，要感念你的造物主。你要在黎明前就一無牽掛地起來，追求冒險去吧。讓正午看見你在其他一些湖邊，入夜後，你就四海為家。天底下沒有比這裏更開闊的田野，也沒有比這裏更珍貴的獵物。按照你的天性，粗獷地成長吧，就像那些莎草和歐洲蕨，它們絕不會變成英格蘭的乾草。讓雷聲隆隆吧；它要是毀掉農夫們的莊稼，那又怎麼樣？那可不是派給你的苦差。別人逃到車裏和雜物屋裏躲雨，你不妨就躲在烏雲底下吧。你要謀生，靠的不是自己的手藝，而是自己的消遣。盡情享受大地的樂趣吧，可千萬不要佔有大地。人們由於缺乏進取心和信心，勢必依然故我，一輩子就像奴隸那樣買進賣出。

啊，貝克農場！大自然中最艷麗的景觀
是一線天真無邪的陽光。……
農場周邊都圍上了籬柵，
誰也不會跑去縱情歡樂。……
你平素從不跟人們爭辯，
沒有哪個問題難得倒你，
你身穿樸素的褐色工作服，
像頭一次見到時一樣馴良。……
來吧，你們愛也好，
來吧，你們恨也好，
聖鴿的子女們，
和州裏的蓋伊·福克斯[4]

還有種種陰謀詭計

　　懸掛在粗硬的橡木[5]上！

　　只有入夜以後，人們才乖乖從毗鄰的田地或者市集街上回到家裏，聽聽家裏耳熟能詳的迴聲。他們的生命力日漸脆弱，這是因為它沒有吐舊納新吧；晨昏時份，他們的影子到達比他們每天的腳步還要遠的地方。我們每天應該從遠方、從奇遇、危險和發現中，帶着新經驗和新性格回家轉。

　　我還沒有到達湖邊，沒期望約翰・菲爾德卻在新的衝動之下趕過來了。他的腦袋已開了竅，太陽落山前不去沼澤地工作了。不過話又説回來，他，這個可憐蟲，只釣到一兩條魚，我卻釣到了一長串魚，他説這就是他的運道；可是，我們互換了在小船上的座位，運道也跟着易了位。可憐的約翰・菲爾德啊！——我相信，他是不會讀到這些話的，除非他讀過後會有長進——他想在這個原始的新國家裏，按照缺乏獨創性的古老鄉村模式來生活——用銀色小魚作誘餌釣鱸魚上來。有時候，這是很棒的魚餌，我承認。憑他自己所有的見識，他還是一個窮人，生來就窮，繼承了愛爾蘭的貧困和貧困生活，繼承了他那亞當的老奶奶和沼澤地耕作方式，因此，不管是他還是他的子孫後代，在當今世界裏都無法崛起，除非他們泡在沼澤地裏的蹼足後跟，穿上一雙有翼涼鞋。

章註

1　鵝耳櫪樹：拉丁文學名為 celtis occidentalis，亦即假榆樹。

2　本梵努托・切利尼：Benvenuto Cellini，1500—1571，意大利文藝復興時期雕塑家和作家，他的回憶錄是一部名著。

3　以上兩處詩句轉引自美國作家錢寧（W. E. Channing，1780—1842）的《貝克農場》，錢寧是美國基督教公理會自由派牧師，主張神學人文化，反對蓄奴、酗酒、貧困和戰爭。

4　蓋伊・福克斯：Guy Faux，1570—1606，英國天主教徒，為英國火藥陰謀案（1605）的主犯，在直通英國議會大廈的地下室埋下炸藥，陰謀炸死詹姆士一世，事敗後被處死。英文中 Faux（福克斯）意思是 "虛假偽善"，此處又是梭羅善用雙關語的實例之一。

5　此處暗喻絞刑架，因絞刑架全由粗硬原木製成。

11
更高的法則

我手裏提着一串魚，拖着釣竿，穿過樹林回家的時候，天已黑下來了，我瞥見一隻土撥鼠從我的小徑溜過去，頓時感到一陣野性喜悅的刺激，恨不得將它生擒活捉，一口吞了下去。這倒不是我當時饑腸轆轆，而不外乎是牠所代表的那種野性罷了。我在湖上生活時有過一兩次，發覺自己像一隻半饑半飽的獵犬，在樹林裏面狂奔，非常放縱，來尋找一些我可以吞食的野味，不管是哪種野味，反正我都吞得下去。就算最野蠻的場景，我都莫名其妙變得熟悉起來。我發現，至今仍然發現，自己內心深處有一種本能，想過一種更高級的生活，亦即所謂精神生活，對此大多數人都有同感；但我還有另一種本能，想歸入原始階層，過一種野性生活。我對這兩種本能都很尊重。我之熱愛野性，並不亞於熱愛善良。釣魚寓有野性和歷險，對我來說，至今仍然情有獨鍾。有時候，我希望能過一種粗獷的生活，就像動物似的度過自己的一生。也許正因為我年紀很輕時就釣魚打獵，我才和大自然有了最親密的交往。漁獵很早就引我們進入大自然，讓我們置身於大自然景色之中，要不，就憑那個年齡，我們恐怕很難對大自然熟悉起來。漁民、獵戶、樵夫等人，在田野和森林裏度過他們的一生，從某種特殊意義上說，他們本人已成了大自然一部份，他們在工作之餘，經常觀察大自然，其心情之樂觀，甚至超過那些期盼接近大自然的哲學家和詩人。大自然並不害怕展現自己給他們看。旅行者到了大草原上，自然成了獵人，在密蘇里河和哥倫比亞河上游，就成為一名捕獸者，而在聖瑪利亞大瀑布，則成了一個漁民。說穿了，他們充其量只不過是一個旅行者，學到的也僅僅是二手貨，一知半解，算不得甚麼權威。我們最感興趣的是，科學報告裏已向我們闡明了通過實踐或者本能所發現的一切，因為唯有這樣的報告才具有真正的人性，或者換句話說，才是人類經驗的記述。

有人以為住在北方的人娛樂很少，因為他們的公眾假期不太多，大人和孩子的遊戲也不像在英國玩的那麼多，這種看法就錯了，因為我們這裏有着更原始，但又獨一無二的娛樂，比方說，打獵和釣魚等等，還沒有讓位給前者呢。差不多跟我同時代的每個新英格蘭孩子，在十歲和十四歲之間，肩上都扛過獵槍；跟英國貴族的專有保留地不一樣，他們打獵和釣魚的地域不受限制，有的甚至比野蠻人的還要遼闊無邊。所以，北方佬不經常到公共場所去玩樂，也就不足為奇。但是，當前正在發生變化，倒不是因為人們日益具有人性，而是因為獵物在日益銳減，說不定獵戶才是獵物們最了不起的朋友，保護動物協會也一概不能例外。

再說，我在湖邊時，有時釣釣魚，不外乎換換我的口味罷了。其實，就像世間最早捕魚為生的人們一樣，我真的出於需要才去釣魚的。不管我以人性的名義反對捕魚，那都是虛假的，涉及更多的是我的哲學思考，而不是我的感情問題。現在我只談捕魚問題，因為我對打鳥早就有不同的看法，來這樹林之前，我索性賣掉了獵槍。倒不是我比別人缺失多少人性，而是因為我一點意識不到自己有甚麼惻隱之心。我既不憐憫魚兒，也不憐憫誘餌。這已是習以為常了。說到打鳥，在最後幾年裏，我扛着獵槍打獵去，我的藉口是我在研究鳥類學，我尋覓的也僅僅是新的或者珍稀鳥類。但是，我承認，現在我開始覺得，要研究鳥類學，還有比這更可取的方式。這就需要更仔細注意觀察鳥類的生活習慣，就憑這麼一個理由，放下獵槍，我也心甘情願。儘管有人從人性角度出發加以反對，我還是不得不懷疑，有沒有同樣有價值的娛樂可以取代打獵這些活動；我的一些朋友經常焦灼不安，他們對自己的孩子特別操心，問我：是不是應該讓他們的孩子打獵，我的回答是：應該 —— 我記得這是我所受教育中最好的一部份 —— 讓他們成為獵人，雖然他們早先只是運動員，如果可能的話，到最後也許會成為一名身強力壯的獵人，這麼一來，以後他們會知道，在這裏或者在任何一個原野上都沒有足夠獵物，可供他們捕殺了 —— 得人如得獵物和魚 [1] 因此，直到今日，我倒贊同喬叟筆下那個修女的看法，她說："還沒有聽到老母雞說過獵人並不是聖潔之人。"喬叟 [2] 在個人和種族的歷史上，都有過這麼一個時期，獵人成了"最好的人"，阿爾貢金人 [3] 就是這樣稱呼過他們的。對於從來沒有開過槍的孩子，我們不能不表示憐憫；因為他的教育不幸被忽視了，他已不再富有人情味。對於那些癡迷於打獵的青年人，我也說過與此相同的話，相信日後他們長大成熟後也就不再樂此不疲了。沒有人在度過他那糊塗的童年之後，還會濫殺任何生物，因為生物跟人類一樣，也具有生存的權利。兔子陷入絕境時，會大聲呼喊就像一個孩子似的。我警告你們，母親們，我的同情並不總有那種仁慈特徵。

以上是年輕人如何通過打獵接近森林的最常見情況，以及他們身上最富有本色的一部份。他們到森林去，開始時是一個打獵和釣魚的人，到後來，如果說他心裏已萌生仁慈種子的話，他總會發現自己正確的目標，也許他會做一個詩人，或者說成為一個博物學家，將獵槍和釣竿置諸腦後。在這方面，芸芸眾生還很稚嫩，而且一直總是很稚嫩。在有些國家裏，愛打獵的牧師並不是罕見之事。諸如此類的牧師，說不定會成為一隻好的牧羊犬，但卻難以成為好牧人 [4]。我曾仔細思考，對如今唯一平淡無奇的行業感到驚訝 —— 先撇開伐木、鑿冰等等行業不談 —— 能使我鎮上的眾鄉友，不管是在鎮上做老爸的還是當兒子的，在瓦爾登湖上流連了整整半天的，顯然只有釣魚這一行不會例外。一般來說，他們並不認為：他們很幸運，他們也不枉來此一遊，除非他們釣到了長長一串魚，雖然他們借此機會，還可以盡情欣賞湖上景色。也許他們還要去湖上垂釣一千次，這種對釣魚的膚淺見解才會沉到湖底，讓他們的目的得以淨化；但是，毫無疑問，這樣一種淨化過程還要無時無刻不在繼續進行。州長和他的議員們對瓦爾登湖的記憶已是模糊不清，因為他們還是在童年的時候去湖上釣過魚。如今，他們歲數太大，身價又高，不好再去釣魚了，因此，他們永遠不會領略到垂釣的樂趣。不管怎麼說，反正最後他們還是指望到天堂去呢。如果說他們要立法，那大抵是對湖上准予垂釣的魚鉤數目作出規定；可是，他們不知道，這麼一來卻使湖光山色大煞風景，立法反而成了魚餌呢。由此可見，即使在文明社會裏，處於胚胎狀態的人，也需要經過一個漁獵者的發展階段。

近年來，我不止一次發現，只要一去釣魚，我的自尊心就減少一點。我試過了一次又一次。我有釣魚技巧，就像我的夥伴們一樣，這是我生來就會釣魚的本能，竟不知這種本能在我心中時不時復甦。等我釣過魚之後，我卻又後悔早知道還是不去釣魚的好。我認為我的想法並沒有錯。這是一種隱隱約約的暗示，就像黎明前的曙光似的。毫無疑問，我的這種本能，卻是屬造物中層次較低的一種；反正我對釣魚的興趣在逐年遞減，雖然人性乃至於智慧不見得有所增加；如今，我根本就不去釣魚了。可是，我知道，如果我生活在荒原上的話，我還會抵禦不住誘惑，變成一個一本正經的漁人和獵手。再說，這種飲食和所有肉類，基本上是不潔淨的，我開始懂得，哪裏來的那麼多家務工作，哪裏來的那麼多苦差事，每天要穿戴整潔而又體面，保持居室溫馨，沒有惡臭髒亂景象，那開支不知該有多大啊！好在我一身數役，既是屠夫、雜役、廚師，又是大吃大喝的男子，所以，我說的這些話，全都來自異常完整的經驗。其實，我之所以反對吃獸肉，是因為牠不乾淨；再說，就算我自己釣到的魚兒，經過清洗、烹煮，並且吃過以後，好像也並沒有給予我很多營養。反正是微不足道，又沒有必要，當然，得不償失啦。一小塊麵包和幾片馬鈴薯，就足以果腹，既不麻煩，又無污物。我就像許許多多同時代人一樣，許多年來已很難得吃葷腥，或茶或咖啡等等；這倒不是因為我已找出了它們的負面影響，而是因為它們跟我的想像力格格不入。我對葷腥的反感並不是經驗引起的，而是出於一種本能。粗茶淡飯[5]的生活，在許多方面來看，反而顯得更美；雖然我從來沒有做到這樣，但至少也做到了使我的想像力滿意。我相信，每個人要是真心誠意使自己更高級或富詩意的官能保持最佳狀態，那就要特別自我克制，戒絕葷腥與暴食豪飲。昆蟲學家認為這是一個意味深長的事實，我在柯爾比和斯彭塞[6]的著作裏讀到："有些昆蟲處於完美狀態，雖有進食器官，卻從來沒有使用過。"他們把牠概括為"一個普遍的法則，幾乎所有處於這種狀態的昆蟲，進食要比牠在幼蟲期少得多。貪食的毛蟲變成了蝴蝶……貪婪的蛆變成了蒼蠅"，只要得到一兩滴蜂蜜，或者一點其他甜汁就滿足了。在蝴蝶翅膀底下的腹部，牠的幼體形狀至今還依稀可見。這就是誘發牠以蟲為食的奧秘所在。大肚漢乃是還處於幼體狀態的人；有些國家還處於幼體狀態，是一些沒有幻想或者沒有想像力的國家，只要看一看他們的大肚子，全都暴露無遺。

飲食烹製既要如此簡單、清潔，又具有想像力，這可真不容易；不過，我想，我們體內固然需要滋養，想像力同樣需要滋養，所以說，這兩者應該同時兼顧。這也許不難做到。適量吃些水果，我們不必因此使自己的胃口感到難堪，也不會阻撓我們最有價值的追求。但是，你的餐盤裏要是添加了額外佐料，對你來說無異於毒藥。錦衣玉食的生活是毫無意義的。大多數人要是在親手精心烹製主餐（不管是葷腥還是素食）時給人看到，不免會感到難為情，其實，像這樣的主餐，每天別人都在給他們準備好了。反正這種情況不改變，我們哪有甚麼文明可說，就算是紳士淑女，也不是地地道道的男人女人。當然，這使人聯想到應當有所改變才好。為甚麼想像力與肉類和脂肪是不可調和的，這用不着多問，反正你心裏有數就可以了。說人是一種食肉動物，難道這不就是一種譴責嗎？沒錯，指靠獵取其他動物，可以使他活下來，實際上的確也活下來了，但這是一種很慘的方式 —— 也許任何一個抓過兔子、宰過羔羊的人都知道這一點 —— 如果有人能教導人類只吃不是殺生葷腥，但又更有利於健康的食物，那他就會被尊稱為人類的救星。不管我個人實踐的成果如何，我一點都不懷疑：這是人類命運的一部份，在人類發展循序漸進過程中，必然戒除食用葷腥的習慣，就像野蠻人與較文明的人交往頻繁以後，逐漸戒除各部落間人吃人的習慣一樣。如果說有人聽了他的天良發出的最微弱、卻持續不斷的暗示（當然，都是真實可靠的），那他也未必看得清楚這暗示會引他向甚麼樣的極端，乃至於發瘋狀態；但是，隨着他的毅力與信念越發增強，他要走的路就在眼前了。一個健康的人覺得要反對的理由，雖然很微弱，卻又充滿自信，最終一定會戰勝人們的種種爭論與習俗。通常人們從來不會聽從自己的天良，除非那天良將他引入歧途的時候。雖然造成的結果是體質衰弱，但是，也許誰都不會說，這樣的結果是令人遺憾的，因為這樣一種生活符合了最高原則。如果說你滿懷喜悅之情迎接白晝與黑夜，生活就像鮮花香草一樣芳香四溢，而且更有彈性，更像繁星，更不朽 —— 那就是你的成功。於是，整個大自然都向你表示慶賀，而你一時也有理由為自己祝福。收益和價值越來越大，就越難使人們領情。我們很容易懷疑它們是不是真的存在。我們很快就忘掉了它們。它們是極高級的現實。也許是最驚人、最真實的各種事實，在人與人之間從來就沒有交流過。我日常生活中的真正收穫，好比晨昏之時天上色彩，觸摸不到，難以言傳。我得到的是一點塵埃，我抓住的僅僅是一段彩虹罷了。

然而，就我來說，我從來不是特別過於拘謹；如果必要的話，有時候，一隻油炸老鼠我也會吃得津津有味。我很高興自己好久以來一直喝白開水，要問原因嘛，這就像我最喜歡的是大自然的天空，而不是大煙鬼的天堂如出一轍。我願意始終保持頭腦清醒，而醉酒的程度卻是無窮無盡。我相信，水是聰明人唯一的飲料；酒並不是甚麼高貴飲品；不妨想想，一杯熱咖啡毀掉一個早晨的希望，一杯茶毀掉一個溫馨的傍晚！啊，我受到咖啡和茶誘惑後，竟然一落千丈，不堪回首！甚至音樂也可以使人癡迷沉醉。就是諸如此類小小不能説出來的原因，毀掉過希臘和羅馬，日後也會毀掉英國和美國。一切醉人佳品之中，誰不願意更陶醉在他呼吸的空氣之中呢？我覺得，我之所以極力反對長時間玩命似的工作，這是因為像這樣工作迫得我也會玩命似的吃喝。可是不瞞你説，如今我在這些方面也不如從前那麼認真了。我很少將宗教氣氛引向餐桌，我也不期求甚麼保佑；倒不是因為我比從前更聰明了，不管這該有多遺憾，我還是不得不坦白承認，隨着歲月流逝，我已變得更粗俗而冷漠。也許這些問題，就像大多數相信詩歌的人一樣，只是在年輕時才會考慮到。我的實踐"哪裏都看不見"，但我的意見都寫在這裏了。不過，我並不自以為是《吠陀經》裏説的那種特權人物，"凡是篤信無所不在的天神之人，都可以食用一切生存之物，"這就是説，用不着問他吃的是甚麼，又是誰給他準備好的；從《吠陀經》所説的情況中，也可以看到，就像一個印度的詮釋家所説的，吠檀多將這種特權限定在"危難之時"。

有時候，雖然沒有胃口，卻照樣大快朵頤，誰曾沒有這種經歷呢？由於通常説的味覺，我在思想上得到了感悟，於是，在味覺的啟發之下，我坐在小山坡上吃過一些漿果，以便滋養我的天性，一想到這些，我就覺得激奮不已。曾子曰："心不在焉，視而不見，聽而不聞，食而不知其味。"[7] 能品味出食物真正味道的人，絕對不是一個老饕；反過來説，一個老饕也絕不會品味不出食物的真正味道。一個清教徒也許吃起黑麵包屑粒來，胃口之特佳，就像一個市政委員在大啖甲魚一模一樣。玷污他的不是入口的食物，而是進食時的胃口。要害不在於質量，也不在於數量，而是在於貪圖口腹之樂；如果説進食不是為了維持我們的生命，也不是為了激發我們的精神生命，那就僅僅是為了養活我們體內的饞蟲罷了。如果說獵人愛吃香龜、麝鼠以及其他類似野味，那麼，美女非常喜愛小牛蹄凍肉或者來自海外的沙丁魚，他們可以說都是半斤八兩，不分高下呢。獵人到他的磨坊湖邊去，美女去拿她的凍肉罐頭。令人驚訝的是：他們，或者說你和我，怎麼會過這種卑鄙如畜生般的生活，只會吃吃喝喝？

我們整個一生，注重道德的程度令人驚訝。善與惡之間，從來都沒有瞬間的休戰。善是獨一無二的、永遠不虧本的投資。豎琴音樂在全世界奏響，它因堅持彈奏以善為主題的樂曲而激動人心。豎琴彷彿成了宇宙保險公司的旅行推銷員，宣傳它的法則，我們小小的善心是我們所付的保費。雖然年輕人到最後變得漠不關心，但宇宙的法則卻不會漠不關心，而是永遠站在最敏感的人這一邊。聽一聽西風中的譴責之聲吧，聽不到譴責的人才是不幸的。我們只要撥動一根弦，移動一個音栓，那迷人的寓意就會滲透到我們心靈裏去。許多不堪入耳的聲音，傳開去特別遠，聽起來有點像音樂吧，對於我們卑賤的生活來說，不僅是一種傲然絕妙的諷刺。

我們意識到，我們體內有一種獸性；我們崇高的天性正在昏昏欲睡之際，它就會醒過來了。它是一隻貪圖感官享受的爬行動物，也許沒法全部徹底清除乾淨；好像一些昆蟲，哪怕在我們生活安康時，它們也會鑽入我們體內。也許我們可以躲開它，卻改變不了它們的本性。我們擔心的是，說不定它們也相當健康；也許我們也可以說很健康，但是未必純潔。前幾天，我拾到一塊野豬的下顎骨，雪白壯實的牙齒和獠牙，可以看出動物也有牠的健康和活力，與精神上的截然不同。這種獸類之興旺發達，指靠的不是節制和純潔，而是其他方式。孟子曰：“人之所以異於禽獸者幾希，庶民去之，君子存之。”[8]。如果說我們已經達到了至純境界，有誰知道那會導致何種生活方式呢？如果說我知道有這麼一個絕頂聰明的人，能教我至純之道，那我一定馬上去找他。"控制好我們的情慾和身體的外在器官，多多行善，就像《吠陀經》上説的，乃是心靈上接近天神所必不可少的。"不過，這種精神暫時能夠滲透和控制體內每種器官和功能，將外部最粗俗的感官享受轉化為至純與虔誠。生殖能力一放縱，就會淫糜成風，使我們很不潔淨，如果加以節制，即會使我們精力旺盛而受到激勵。貞潔是人類綻放中的花朵；所謂天賦、英雄主義、神聖等等，不外乎是它開花後結出的果實。至純之道一旦開通，人們馬上有如潮湧，奔向上帝。我們時而受到至純鼓舞，時而又因不潔感到沮喪。確信自己體內的獸性一天天消亡，神性一天天增長的人，就是福份不淺。也許人人只好引以為恥，因為他身上還摻雜着低劣的獸性。我深恐我們只不過是一些神或者説半神，就像農牧之神福納斯和薩梯福納斯[9]那樣，是神與獸的結合，貪婪好色的生物，而且，在某種程度來説，我們的生命本身就是我們的恥辱——他呀多開心，分派羣獸各得其所，

心中塵念全無，就像砍伐後的林地。

****

他能驅使馬、羊、狼以及一切獸類，

在獸類跟前，他自己還不算蠢驢，

不然，人不僅無異於羣豬倌，

而且，還要充當那妖魔鬼怪，

使它們狂妄肆虐，越來越壞。[10]

所有的淫蕩，儘管形式各異，都是一樣東西；所有的至純，也都是一樣東西。一個人不管是吃吃喝喝，男女同居，睡覺淫蕩，其實都是一回事。它們只有一個慾念，而我們只要看到一個人在做這件事，就會知

道此人是怎樣一個好色之徒。不潔與至純是絕不能平起平坐。蛇在洞穴的這一端捱了打，就會在洞穴的另一端露面。你要保持貞潔，那就必須節制。甚麼是貞潔呢？一個人如何才知道他是不是貞潔？反正他是不會知道的。我聽說過這種德行，但不知道它究竟是些甚麼。我們只是道聽途說、人云亦云罷了。智慧和至純源自力行；愚昧和淫蕩則源自懶惰。就學生來說，淫蕩乃是一種智力上懶惰的陋習。一個不潔的人，一般說來，就是一個懶鬼，他坐在火爐邊取暖，俯臥着曬太陽，一點也不累，卻總是歇着。若要避免不潔和一切罪孽，你就要努力工作，哪怕是打掃馬廄都行。本性是很難克服的，但是本性必須克服。如果說你並不比異教徒更純潔，如果說你再也不能否定自己，如果說你還不夠虔誠，那你就算是個基督徒，又有甚麼用呢？我知道，有許多被認作異教的宗教制度，他們的清規戒律使讀者感到羞愧，激勵讀者作出新的努力，說白了，只不過是奉行儀式罷了。

其實，我並不願意說這些事，這倒不是因為這個話題難於啟齒 —— 我不在乎我使用了淫詞穢語 —— 而是因為我一講這些事，無異於使我的不潔曝了光。有時，我們會毫無忌憚般談論淫慾的這種形式，而對另一種形式卻緘口不語。我們生怕有失自己身份，所以簡直不能談論人類天性的必要功能。在更早的那幾個時代，在某些國家，談到每種功能都令人肅然起敬，而且每種功能都由法律規定。印度的立法者甚至對待區區小事也照樣不厭其煩，雖然這種做法也許跟現代人的趣味有很大差異。他教人如何吃、如何喝、如何同居、如何大便、如何小解，諸如此類，提高了這些猥陋事情的等級，不再視為過於瑣碎，因此也就裝模作樣，避而不談。

每個人都是一座寺院的建築師，這寺院就是他的身體，按照純屬他自己的方式向神頂禮膜拜，即使他去雕鑿大理石，也離不開自己的寺院。我們都是雕刻家和畫家，我們使用的材料就是我們的血肉和骨骼。

崇高的品行使人的風貌立時變得高雅，而卑劣或者淫蕩則又會使人立時淪為禽獸。

　　9 月間的一個夜晚，約翰・法默完成了一天勞累的工作後，坐在自己家門口，腦內多少還在惦念着他的工作。洗澡之後，他坐了下來，不管怎樣讓自己腦筋休息一會。那天夜晚相當冷，他的左鄰右里都擔心會有霜凍來襲。他剛開始思考沒多久，就聽到有人在吹笛子，那笛子的聲音跟自己的心情倒是很和諧。這時，他心裏仍然在惦念自己的工作，不用説，他思慮重重；儘管他一直在動腦筋，而且還違心地在構想和策劃之中，但他卻覺得已經無關緊要了，充其量不過是他肌膚上的碎屑不時往下脱落。然而，他聽到的那笛子吹的樂曲，來自跟他工作那處截然不同的環境，卻傳入了他的耳際，使他身上某些沉睡着的官能甦醒過來。那笛子聲輕柔悠揚，彷彿使他所居住的城市街道、村莊和國家不翼而飛了。有一個聲音對他説 —— 既然你有可能過一種頂級生活，為何還留在這裏，過這種低賤的苦日子？同樣的星星照耀的不是這裏，而是別處的田野 —— 可是話又説回來，問題是如何走出這種困境，真的移居到那裏去？盡他所能想到的，不外乎是新的苦行修煉，讓他的心靈融入自己的肉體，再來救贖它，而且對待自己也越來越尊敬。

章註

1　參見《聖經・新約全書・馬太福音》第 4 章 19 節：耶穌對他們説："來跟從我！我要叫你們得人如得魚一樣"。

2　喬叟：Geoffrey Chaucer（1343—1400）英國詩人，用倫敦方言寫作，使其成為英國文學的語言，代表作為《坎特伯雷故事》，反映 14 世紀英國社會生活面貌，體現了人文主義思想。此詩句引自該書，但梭羅説錯了，這兩行詩是教士説的，並不是修女説的。

3　阿爾貢金人：居住在加拿大渥太華河河谷地區，屬阿爾貢金語族的印第安人。

4　好牧人：即基督耶穌的稱號。

5 譯者譯作“粗茶淡飯”不外乎順應中國習慣說法，意思是“飲食宜粗淡，忌精細”，事實上，梭羅說過自己不飲茶，請讀者見諒。

6 柯爾比（William Kirby 1759—1850）、斯彭塞，William Spence 1783—1860，均為英國昆蟲學家，兩人合著《昆蟲學概論》（共四卷），舉世聞名。

7 詳見《禮記·大學》。

8 詳見《孟子·離婁下》。

9 農牧之神福納斯和薩梯福納斯：農牧之神，古羅馬神話中一個半人半羊的形象；薩梯，森林之神，古希臘神話中，具人形而有羊的尾、耳和角等，性嗜嬉戲，好色。

10 多恩：John Donne（1572—1631）英國詩人，是玄學派代表人物，上述詩句引自他所寫的《致愛·赫伯特爵士》一詩。

12
鳥獸若比鄰

有時候，我常跟一個朋友結伴釣魚，他從城的那一端過來，穿過村莊來到我屋裏，我們兩人一起釣魚去，這倒跟請客吃飯一樣，是一種交際應酬罷。

隱士我暗自納悶，當今世界在做些甚麼。三個小時裏，連香蕨木上的蟬叫，我都沒有聽見。鴿子都在鴿棚裏打盹 —— 撲棱聲也沒有。此刻，在樹林外頭吹響的，是不是農場主人的午休號角聲呢？僱工們收工回來，吃煮熟的鹹牛肉、蘋果酒，還有玉米粉麵包。人們為甚麼要這樣自尋煩惱呢？人不吃不喝，也就用不着工作。我不知道他們的收成有多少。誰會住到這種地方來，那狗汪汪叫得使人根本不可以好好想事情呢。哦，還有，家務工作！在這明亮的大白天，要擦亮該死的門上銅把手，還要擦浴缸！看來還是乾脆沒有家的好。算了，不妨住在一個空心樹洞裏；那麼一來，晨訪和晚宴通通給免掉了！住在樹洞裏，反正只有啄木鳥的啄木聲啦。哦，那裏人羣雜沓；那裏太陽暴曬，熱得邪門；依我看，他們這些人太世故了。我從泉水邊打水喝，廚架上還有一塊焦黃的麵包 —— 聽！我聽到樹葉在沙沙作響。莫非是村裏哪隻餓狗在四處亂轉覓食嗎？要不然就是那隻迷了路的豬，據說還在樹林裏，反正雨後我還看過牠的爪印。牠匆匆奔過來了；連我的漆樹和多花薔薇都顫動起來了 —— 哦，詩人先生，是你嗎？你覺得當今世界怎麼樣？[1] 詩人看這些雲，懸浮長空，多美！這是我今天看到最美麗的景致。像這樣的雲彩，古畫裏沒有，在異國他鄉也沒有 —— 除非我們到了西班牙海岸觀景。那才是地地道道的地中海藍空。我想，我不管怎樣總要過日子吧，今天肚子也還沒有填補過，那我就不妨釣魚去。這才是詩人的真功夫呢。也是我學得好的唯一手藝。來吧，我們兩人一起釣魚去。

隱士恭敬不如從命。我那塊焦黃的麵包很快就要吃完了。我樂意馬上跟你一起走，不過，我那苦思冥想正在結束之中。我想，反正我快要接近尾聲了。算了，讓我獨處一會吧。不過，為了兩相不誤，你不如先去挖挖魚餌，好嗎？這裏附近很難挖到蚯蚓，因為這裏的泥從來沒有施過肥；蚯蚓一族眼看着都快絕種了。挖蚯蚓這玩意，幾乎和釣魚一樣有趣，只要你的胃口不太刁鑽，今天你就可以獨享。我奉勸你帶上鏟子，到那邊花生地裏挖，就是你看見狗尾草在搖擺的地方。我想，我敢向你擔保，你只要在草根底下好好找一找，就像除雜草一樣，每翻起三塊草皮，擔保挖到一條蚯蚓。要不然，你乾脆走遠些，那也不算是不聰明，因為我發現，好魚餌幾乎跟遠距離成正比。

隱士獨白。讓我想想看；我想到哪裏去了？我以為，我已接近心智的這個框架；這個世界處在這種角度。我是應該上天堂呢，還是去釣魚？要是我的苦思冥想馬上結束了，難道還會有這麼一個美妙的機會嗎？剛才我差不多已經和萬物的精髓渾然一體了，那是我一輩子都還沒有過的呢。我生怕自己的思想不會回來了。只要管用，我也樂意吹吹口哨，召它回來。當初思想向我們泉湧而至時，卻說：我們會想到它，這算聰明嗎？我的思想一點痕跡都沒有留下，我再也找不到自己的思路。我此刻在想的是甚麼呢？這一天可真夠一頭霧水的。我還是來想想孔子的三句話，也許能恢復剛才的思路。我不知道那是悶悶不樂呢，還是初露頭角的狂喜。記住，機會是從來只有一次的。

詩人怎麼啦，隱士，是不是太快了呀？我已挖到了整整十三條，此外還有幾條缺頭少尾的，或者太小的；不過，小的鈎鈎小魚還可以；牠們拴在魚鈎上很不顯眼。村裏那些蚯蚓，太大了；銀色小魚飽餐一頓，還碰不到那串肉的鐵鈎子呢。

隱士，我們這就動身吧。我們要不要去康科德呀？要是水位不太高，不妨就去那裏玩個痛快。

構成這個世界的，為甚麼偏偏就是我們看到的這些事物？為甚麼人類與之毗鄰而居的，只有這麼一些獸類呢？看來這個縫隙，普天之下只有老鼠能夠來填補！我思索着，皮爾佩公司[2]算是充份利用動物，可以說達到了極致，因為他們都是馱獸，在某種程度上說，負載着我們的一部份思想。

我屋裏出沒無常的老鼠，並不是常見的，據說是從外國引進的那種，而土生土長的野老鼠，村裏面反而看不到。我抓了一隻送給一位著名的博物學家，引起他極大興趣。我造房子的時候，有一隻老鼠在我的房子底下築窩，我的樓板還沒鋪好，刨花也沒有掃出去，只要一到午餐時刻，牠就定時跑出來，啄食我腳跟下的麵包屑。說不定過去這隻老鼠從來沒見過人，所以一來二去，就跟我非常熟，在我的鞋和衣服上爬來爬去。牠可以不費吹灰之力，往上一躥，就爬到屋的四壁，活像一隻松鼠，連動作也都非常相似。到後來，有一天，我讓胳膊肘支在櫈子上頭，牠一下子爬上我的衣服，循着我的衣袖，繞着我盛放晚餐的紙包來回打轉；接着，一會我拿那包東西過來，一會又推開去，反正躲躲閃閃，和牠一起玩起躲躲貓[3]的遊戲來；最後，我用拇指和食指夾住一塊奶酪，可以了，牠就索性過來坐在我的掌上啃起奶酪來了，啃完以後，活像一隻蒼蠅似的，擦擦牠的臉和爪，然後揚長而去。

沒多久，一隻東菲比霸鶲來到我的小木屋築窩，還有一隻知更鳥，為了尋求庇護，也來到屋邊的一棵樹上棲居。到了 6 月間，鷓鴣 —— 本是一種羞答答的鳥兒 —— 也帶着牠的幼雛，經過我的窗戶跟前，從屋後的樹林繞到屋前，像一隻老母雞似的咯咯呼喚牠的孩子們，看牠那副模樣，可以證明牠的確是林地母雞。你只要一走近牠們，母雞就發出一個信號，牠們突然四處散開，彷彿給一陣旋風捲走了；牠們也活像枯枝敗葉一樣，許多觀光客常常會一腳踩在一窩雛鳥上，只聽見老鳥起飛時呼的一聲，急急呼喚着，聽上去像貓叫似的，要不然會看見老鳥在鼓動翅膀，吸引觀光客的注意力，也就用不着再對牠們的周圍左顧右盼，有時候，母鳥會在你跟前連地滾，打轉，使牠的羽毛蓬亂不堪，讓你一時間看不出它究竟是一種甚麼樣的鳥兒。幼雛一動不動地蹲在地上，常埋自己的頭在樹葉底下，只聽母鳥從遠處發出的信號，就算你走近了，牠們也不會再亂跑，讓自己暴露無遺。

說不定你還會一腳踩在牠們身上，或者兩眼直望着老半天，也沒有發現牠們。有過那麼一次，我讓牠們留在我的掌上，牠們依然只聽從牠們母鳥的信號和牠們的本能，還要蹲在原地，一點不害怕，也不顫抖。這種本能如此完美，有一次，我又放牠們到樹葉上，其中一隻不小心摔倒在一邊，我發現，牠在十分鐘之後跟其他幼雛一樣，還是保持原來的姿勢。鷓鴣的幼鳥不像大多數幼雛那樣不長羽毛，若跟其他小鳥相比，牠們倒是長得更豐滿完美，乃至於更早熟。牠們睜大了寧靜的眼睛，明顯露出成熟而天真的表情，確實令人難忘。全部才智彷彿從牠們的眼睛裏反映出來，不僅使人看到的是幼雛的純潔無瑕，而且還有由經驗洗練過的智慧。這樣的目光不是鳥類與生俱有的，而是跟牠映現的天空一樣久遠。這樣的瑰寶森林裏絕無僅有。觀光客不見得會經常看到如此清澈的一口井。無知或殘忍的獵戶常常在這樣的時刻用槍擊斃牠們的父母，使這些無辜的幼雛成為四處覓食的猛獸或者猛禽的犧牲品，或者漸漸混入跟牠們非常相似的枯枝敗葉中一起爛掉。據說，這些小鷓鴣如由母雞孵化出來，牠們稍受一點驚嚇，立即四散逃走，就這樣失蹤了，因為牠們永遠也聽不到母親召集牠們的呼喚聲。以上這些就是我的母雞和小雞啊。

值得注意的是，有多少生物粗獷不羈地隱居在樹林裏，有時到村鎮附近覓食為生，只有獵戶猜得着牠們藏身在哪裏。水獺在這裏過着多麼僻靜的生活啊！水獺長到四英尺高，就像一個男孩子，也許還沒有人見過呢。過去，我在屋後面的樹林裏看過一頭浣熊，就是現在夜裏，說不定仍然聽得見牠們的吼叫聲。通常，我上午耕種之後，中午在陰涼處休息一兩個小時，接着用午餐，然後在泉水邊讀一點書，這股泉水是一片沼澤地和一道小溪的源頭，打從離我的農地大約半英里遠的布里斯特山腳下涓涓地流淌着。到達這泉水邊，需要穿過一片片野草叢生的低窪地，那裏長滿了小油松，隨後進入沼澤地附近一個比較大的樹林。在那裏，樹蔭環繞，幽靜極了，一棵濃陰蔽日的白皮松底下，還有一塊乾淨而又堅實的草地，不妨稍事歇坐。我在這裏挖出了泉眼，砌成一口井，蓄滿清澈的淡水，可以打滿一桶水，井水也不會渾濁；仲夏時節，我幾乎每天都到這裏來取水，因為這個時候湖水是最熱的。山鷸也來這裏，帶着它的幼雛，在爛泥地裏尋覓昆蟲，隨後又飛過泉邊上空，離雛鳥約一英尺高，而小山鷸成羣結隊在下面奔跑；但在最後發現我時，母鳥撇開牠的幼雛，在我身邊一圈圈打轉，挨着我也越來越近，直到只有四五英尺時，卻佯裝翅膀或兩腿折斷了，引開我的注意力，好讓小山鷸趁機逃生，其實，那一批幼雛早已撒腿逃跑，按照老山鷸的指令，排成單行，發出微弱的吱吱叫聲，穿過了沼澤地。或者換句話說，這時我已看不見那隻母鳥，只不過聽見小鳥們吱吱叫。斑鳩們也飛落在這座泉水邊，或者在我頭上柔軟的白皮松枝丫之間來回穿梭；或者，還有紅松鼠從最近的樹枝上一躍而下，對我特別親熱又好奇。你只要在樹林裏某個引人入勝的景點閒坐一會，也許所有林中棲居者會輪流登場，在你面前一一亮相。

我還是一些不太和諧事件的見證人。有一天，我走出門，到我的木棧——或者說得更確切些，是我的一堆樹樁頭那裏去——這時，我看見兩隻大螞蟻，一隻渾身通紅，另一隻體型特別大，差不多有半英寸長，是黑得很難看的，牠們正在互相兇毆，一交手，不管是哪一隻也誓不罷休，只是拼命搏鬥着，角力着，就在那堆小木片裏面不停歇地來回打滾。再往遠處一看，我驚奇地發現，小木片堆裏面到處都是這樣的角鬥士，這不是決鬥，而是一場戰爭，一場兩個蟻族之間的戰爭，紅螞蟻總是跟黑螞蟻惡鬥，往往還是兩隻紅的對付一隻黑的。在我的木料場裏，滿坑滿谷都是密耳彌多涅人 [4] 已死和垂死的，紅色的和黑色的，比比皆是。這是我親眼目睹過的唯一的一場戰役，也是我在激戰猶酣之時親歷其境的唯一的一個戰場；紅色的共和派為一方，黑色的保皇派則為另一方。交戰雙方都投入了這一場殊死戰，可惜我甚麼響聲也沒有聽見，反正人類士兵根本都沒有打過這樣的硬仗。我看見在明媚的陽光下，小木片成堆的小山谷裏，有一對鬥士拼命抱住不放，準備從現在正午時份，一直打到夕陽西沉，或者換句話說，乾脆打到命歸陰曹。那隻小小的紅螞蟻，卻像老虎鉗似的死死咬住了敵人的腦袋，並且滿地翻滾，用力啃齧敵人觸鬚的根，其實，另一根觸鬚早已給咬斷了；就在此時此刻，那隻更壯實的黑螞蟻卻將紅螞蟻從一邊到另一邊地搖來搖去，我湊過去，仔細一看，只見紅螞蟻有幾個部位都給咬掉了。牠們互相廝打，比叭喇狗 [5] 來得更兇悍。雙方一點都沒有退讓的意向。顯然，牠們的戰鬥口號是："不戰勝，毋寧死。"就在酣戰之際，這個小山谷旁邊走來一隻單身的紅螞蟻，一望便知，牠格外亢奮，一就是牠打死了一個敵人，一就是還沒有投入這場戰役；看上去倒是像後者，反正從肢體上看，牠還不是斷臂缺腿的；牠母親已關照過牠一就手持盾牌回來，一就躺在盾牌上由別人抬回來 [6] 也許牠就是又一個阿喀琉斯，獨自怒火中燒，此刻趕來拯救他的好友帕特洛克勒斯 [7] 或者說替他雪恥復仇來了。牠遠遠看到，這是一場力量懸殊的戰鬥 —— 因為黑螞蟻的體型幾乎是紅螞蟻的兩倍 —— 牠急如星火地奔了過來，就在離那兩隻螞蟻半英寸遠的地方站崗，稍後，看準了時機，向那隻黑色鬥士猛撲過去，開始攻擊黑螞蟻的右前腿根，任憑敵人也攻擊自己的肢體上哪一個部位；三個鬥士為了求生就這樣死纏在一起，彷彿發明了一種新型吸引力，使所有其他鎖鍊和水泥全都相形見絀。這時，要是看到牠們雙方各自都有管樂隊，安置在某些顯眼的小木片上，演奏牠們各自的國歌給那些形勢險峻的鬥士鼓勵士氣，給那些垂死的鬥士莫大的激勵，那我也不會覺得驚奇了。我自己都為之激動不已，彷彿牠們儼如人類一樣。你越是這麼想，越是覺得螞蟻和人類之間本來無甚區別。至少，姑且撇開美國歷史不談，在康科德的歷史上，確實還沒有哪種惡戰的記錄，可以跟這種蟻戰相提並論，不管從參戰的人員數量來說，還是從他們所表現的愛國熱忱和英雄氣概來說。論參戰人員和殘殺的程度，這不僅是一場奧斯特利茨戰役[8]，或者說是一場德累斯頓戰役[9]。康科德之戰又算甚麼！愛國者一方有兩名捐軀，路德·布朗夏爾也受傷了！為甚麼在這裏，每隻螞蟻都是一位布特利克[10]民兵，開火！為了上帝，開火！"——成千上萬士兵都面臨着戴維斯和霍斯默的命運。這裏沒有一個是僱傭兵。我毫不懷疑，牠們很像我們的祖祖輩輩，是為道義而戰，而不是為了免繳他們區區三便士的茶葉稅；這次戰役的結果，對參戰的雙方來說，都是生死攸關，令人難忘，至少像我們的邦克山戰役[11]一樣。

我特別詳細描述了三隻螞蟻在小木片上的殊死搏鬥，我拿那塊小木片回家去，放在窗台上，用一個大水杯罩住，以便了解戰果如何。用顯微鏡觀看那隻最先提到的紅螞蟻，我看到儘管牠猛啃敵人的前腿附近，又咬斷了敵人剩下的蟻鬚，牠自己的胸脯卻全部被黑色武士的利齒扯破了，所有內臟暴露無遺。回頭再看那黑色武士的胸甲，顯然很厚實，因而穿刺不透；這個受難者的眼睛的黑色球晶，流露出一般只有打硬仗才會激發出來的兇光。牠們在那個大水杯底下搏鬥了半個多小時，等到我再看時，那黑色士兵已使兩個敵人身首異處，那兩個還活着的小小首級，披掛在牠的兩側，好像是披掛在牠馬鞍兩側的、嚇人的戰利品，只是明擺着牠們依然跟剛才那樣緊緊地咬住對方不放；那隻黑螞蟻儘管觸鬚全都沒有了，腿也只剩下一點，牠好像還想作一困獸鬥似的；我真不知道牠身上其他創傷該有多少，但牠總是想扔掉那兩個小小首級；最後，過了半個小時，牠總算大功告成了。我一舉起大水杯，牠就一瘸一拐地從窗台上爬了過去，經過這回戰鬥，牠能不能存活下來，在某家傷殘退役軍人院裏度過餘生，那我就不得而知了；反正我想，從今以後，牠就算拼命賣力，也不會有多大出息。我一直不知道究竟是哪一方取得了最後勝利，也不知道這場戰爭的起因是甚麼；但一直在那一天時間裏，我滿懷激動和痛苦，覺得彷彿在家門口目睹了一場鮮血淋漓、慘不忍睹的人類戰爭。

柯爾比和斯彭塞告訴我們，螞蟻的戰役素來為人們稱道，戰役的日期也有記載；但是他們説，在近代作家中，唯有胡伯 [12] 好像是親眼目睹過螞蟻大戰。他們説：“埃尼斯‧西爾維烏斯：教皇庇烏二世 [13] 曾非常詳盡描述一場，在一棵梨樹上大螞蟻和小螞蟻之間展開的惡戰。”接下來，他補充着説：“此戰發生於尤金尼斯第四 [14] 在位期間，著名律師尼古拉斯‧庇斯托里恩西斯親歷戰事，對這場戰爭的全過程作了極其忠實的描述。”奧勒斯‧瑪格努斯也記述過一次類似的戰爭，結果小螞蟻打了勝仗，據説是掩埋牠們自己士兵的屍體，但對龐大的敵人暴屍不埋，任憑鳥兒啄食。此事發生於暴君克里斯蒂安二世被逐出瑞典之前。至於我親眼目睹的這場螞蟻之戰，發生於波爾克 [15] 任職期間，亦即《韋伯斯特逃亡奴隸法案》[16] 通過之前五年。

村裏有許多老牛，本來只好在儲存食品的地窖裏追趕香龜，如今卻背着牠的主人，拖着牠那笨重的軀體到樹林裏玩耍；牠一會嗅嗅老狐狸的洞穴，一會聞聞土撥鼠的地洞，當然，一無所獲。説不定牠是被雜種狗引進來的，這種狗體型瘦小，動作靈活，常在林中穿來穿去，林中鳥獸至今還會情不自禁對牠感到恐懼 —— 這時，老牛遠遠落在嚮導後面，像一頭犬牛似的向躲在樹上仔細觀察的一隻小松鼠狂吠一陣，隨後慢慢走開，牠那笨重軀體壓彎了樹枝，但牠還自以為在追蹤迷了路的跳鼠呢。有一次，我看見一隻貓竟在湖的石岸邊徘徊，因為牠們通常很少離家走得那麼遠。我和貓都大吃一驚。可是，整天這樣躺在地毯上的家貓，到了樹林裏倒顯得像在家裏一樣舒適自在，看牠那鬼鬼祟祟的狡猾樣子，足以證明：牠比林中常住居民還要入鄉隨俗。有一次，我在樹林裏拾漿果，碰上了一隻貓，帶着好幾隻小貓咪，這些小貓咪還是野性未泯，都像牠們母親那樣拱起背，惡狠狠般衝着我吐口水。好幾年前，我還沒有來林中居住的時候，離湖最近的林肯某農場主人家裏，亦即吉里安·巴克先生府上，就有過一隻所謂"長翅膀的貓"。1842 年 6 月，我特地去拜訪她[17]，她像平時一樣，上樹林裏獵食去了。她的女主人告訴我，這隻貓是一年多前，大約在 4 月間，來到這裏附近，最後由她們家收留；還說那隻貓渾身深棕灰色，脖子底下有一個白點，白蹄子，毛茸茸的大尾巴，活像狐狸尾巴；入冬以後，皮毛長得又厚又密，在她兩側垂下來，形成了十到十二英寸長、二英寸寬的毛髮，她的下巴底下好像長着一個暖手筒，上頭的毛比較鬆散，下頭卻板結得像毯子似的；到了春天，這些附屬品全都掉了。他們給了我那隻貓的"一對翅膀"，我至今還保存着。好像這一對翅膀上並沒有薄膜。有人認為，這隻貓有部份血統是飛松鼠，或者其他甚麼野生動物，這倒也不是不可能，因為，根據博物學家的說法，貂和家貓交配，會產生這一多育雜種。這倒是不失為一種好貓，如果說我養貓的話；因為既然一位詩人的馬可以插翅飛奔，詩人的貓為何就不可以長出雙翅來呢？

秋天，潛水鳥[18]像往常一樣來了，在湖裏褪毛、戲水，我還沒有起牀，就聽到牠們的狂笑聲，在樹林裏迴響着。聽說潛水鳥要來了，米爾達姆那裏獵戶集合起來，有的坐車，有的步行，三三兩兩，帶上專利獵槍、尖頭子彈，還有望遠鏡。他們像秋天的樹葉，穿過樹林沙沙作響，追尋一隻潛水鳥，至少也有十個獵手。有些人守望在湖的這邊，有些人則在湖的另一邊，因為這種可憐的鳥兒不可能在各處同時出現；潛水鳥如在湖岸這邊鑽自己的頭到水裏，肯定會在湖岸那一邊冒上來。不過，時下 10 月小陽春的風吹起來了，使樹葉沙沙發響，湖面上微波蕩漾，潛水鳥再也聽不見、看不到了，雖然牠的敵人們還在用望遠鏡掃視湖上，槍聲一直在樹林裏迴響着。看那水波大起大落，怒拍着湖岸，跟所有水禽站在一起，我們的獵手們只好回到村鎮上、店裏去，照常做自己沒有做完的事。不過，他們得逞的時候也還是很多的。大清早，我上湖裏去打水，經常看見這種氣宇不凡的鳥兒游出我的小水灣，相距只有幾桿遠。如果我想坐船追上它，看看牠到底如何耍花招，那牠就會以頭栽入水中，全都沒跡可尋，這麼一來，我再也見不到了，有時候，直到當天下午後一段時間，牠才會出現。不過在水面上，我還是比牠強。通常它總是在雨中逃走的。

10 月間，一個風平浪靜的下午，我操着雙槳，在湖的北岸划船，因為正是在這樣的日子裏，潛水鳥才會浮現在湖面上，像馬利筋草絨毛似的；我掃視着湖面，卻見不到潛水鳥的蹤影，不料，突然之間卻出現了一隻，從岸邊直接向湖心游去，在我前面僅有一兩桿之遠，狂笑了幾聲，卻使自己曝了光。我揮槳追了上去，牠一下子鑽進水裏就不見了，等牠再浮出水面時，我跟牠挨得更近了。牠又一次潛入水中，可是我估錯牠的方向，這一次，牠再浮出水面時，離我已有五十桿之遙，我們之間距離拉得這麼遠，乃是我失誤所造成的；牠又放聲大笑了半天，這一次笑得顯然更有理由了。牠靈活的動作如此俏皮，就算離牠五六桿的地方，我怎麼也都達不到。每一次，牠浮出水面，東張西望，冷靜地測算水域和陸地，明顯在選擇牠的路線，以便牠浮出水面時，正好是水域最開闊、離船也最遠的地方。牠作出決定後，立即付諸實行，居然如此之快，實在令人吃驚。轉眼之間，牠已將我誘入湖上最寬闊的水域，從那裏我就沒法追逐牠了。牠腦內正在想一件事的時候，我也竭盡全力猜度牠的想法。這真是一場絕妙的遊戲，一個人與一隻潛水鳥在波平似鏡的湖面上見高低。突然之間，你對手的棋子在棋盤底下消失了，問題是你要知道牠下次在哪裏出現，就放你的棋子在離牠最近的地方。有時候，牠會出其不意地在你對面浮出水面，顯然是從你的船底下直接潛水過去的。牠可以鑽進水裏很長一段時間，而且一點也不累，等牠游到很遠時馬上又潛入水中；這時，任憑你智謀超人也猜度不出，在這深不可測、波平似鏡的湖裏哪個地方，牠會像一條魚兒似的急速潛游，因為牠畢竟有時間，也有能力到這湖底最深處探索。據說，在紐約一些水深八十英尺的湖裏捉過潛水鳥，只不過是被捕捉鮭魚的鉤子鉤住的 —— 可是瓦爾登湖始終比那些湖還要深呢。魚兒們見了這個來自異域的不速之客，居然能在牠們族羣中間游來游去，肯定驚訝不已！不過話又說回來，看來牠深諳水性，在水底擇路游走跟在水上一樣駕輕就熟，甚至於游得比在水上還要快呢。有過一兩次，我看見牠浮出水面時激起一圈漣漪，牠的頭剛探出來四處張望了一下，一瞬間，又鑽入水中全都不見了。我覺得我既可以估計出牠下次從哪裏出現，也不妨放下划槳，等牠再次浮出水面，豈不是兩全其美嗎？因為我瞪着兩眼朝一個方向凝視水域時，牠卻一次又一次地在我背後怪笑，不由得使我嚇一大跳。但是，為甚麼牠如此狡詐蒙混了我以後，每次浮出水面，就必定喧笑一陣，從而使自己暴露無遺呢？難道說牠那潔白的胸脯還不夠引人矚目嗎？我想，牠確實是一隻傻傻的潛水鳥。通常我都聽得見牠浮上來時的拍水聲，據此也就知道牠在哪裏。可是，一個鐘頭過去之後，牠似乎還是照舊那麼活蹦亂跳，隨心所欲般潛入水裏，而且游得比一開始時還要遠呢。牠一浮出水面，卻又安詳地游開去了，只見牠那胸脯上的羽毛一點都不皺亂，那是全靠自己的蹼腳給撫平了的，實在令人吃驚。牠經常發出的都是魔鬼般的笑聲，有點像水禽的叫聲；但是，有時牠偶然成功躲開我，游到了很遠的地方才浮出水面，發出一陣綿長的怪叫聲，聽起來根本不像鳥叫，倒更像是狼嚎；也好像一頭野獸，嘴鼻貼在地面上咻咻叫。這就是潛水鳥的聲音——這種最狂野的聲音，也許在這一帶從來還沒有聽過，卻在樹林裏迴響。我想：牠在嘲笑我徒勞無功，同時又相信自己會情急智生。此時此刻，天色陰沉沉，但湖面上卻很平靜，牠的叫聲我雖然聽不見，但依然看得見牠在那處劃破水面。牠那潔白的胸脯，還有，天上一絲微風都沒有，湖水又很平靜，這一切對牠來說都是不利的。最後，牠在五十桿處浮出水面後，發出了長長的一聲吼叫，彷彿呼喚潛水鳥之神來救援牠，頃刻之間，東邊果然起風了，吹皺了湖水，滿天空都是霧濛濛的細雨，當時，我印象很深，好像潛水鳥的祈禱有了回應，牠的神對我光火了；於是，我就撇開牠，讓牠遠遠消失在波濤翻滾的湖面上。

秋天裏，我就會一連幾個鐘頭，觀看野鴨神出鬼沒般游來游去，牠們始終據守着湖中央，遠遠躲開獵人；反正這些把戲，恐怕牠們也用不着到路易斯安那州牛軛湖操練吧。牠們不得不起飛時，偶然飛到一定高度，來回盤旋於湖的上空，像天空中的點點黑斑，居高俯瞰，別處的江河湖泊，盡收眼底；我想，牠們早已飛到那些地方去了，牠們斜穿過四份之一英里遠的開闊地，飛到了一個比較不受干擾的地方；可是，牠們飛到瓦爾登湖的中心，除了安全以外還有些甚麼呢，我就不得而知了，除非牠們熱愛這一泓湖水，跟我熱愛的緣由如出一轍。

13

室內取暖

10月間，我去河邊草地採摘葡萄，滿載而歸，我覺得除了果腹以外，葡萄最可貴的就是它色澤芳香。在那裏，我也很喜歡越橘，那小小的蠟寶石，垂掛在草葉子上，勝過珍珠般亮晶晶，紅豔豔，我倒是沒有採摘過，但農夫們卻用可怕的釘齒耙集攏它們，使平整的草地亂成一團；他們只是按每個蒲式耳多少美元價錢，隨隨便便估算一下，就販賣這些草地上的掠奪物到波士頓和紐約去；這些葡萄命裏註定要被製成果醬，滿足城裏面熱愛大自然的人們的口味。屠夫們還在大草原上的野草裏，一邊耙，一邊收集野牛舌草，至於這些野牛舌草是否被扯爛、枯萎，他們也就一概不管。小檗的果實光彩奪目，也僅僅是讓我一飽眼福；不過，我採集過不少野蘋果，用文火煮一煮，味道不錯，這倒是當地領地主人和觀光客還沒有想過的呢。栗子熟了，我就儲存半蒲式耳，準備過冬。在那個金秋季節裏，漫步於林肯那處一望無際的栗子林，確實讓人心曠神怡——可惜如今這些栗子樹卻長眠在鐵道底下了——那時節，我肩上挽着一個布袋，手裏提着一根開刺果的棍棒，因為我總是等不到霜凍，就在枯葉的沙沙作響和紅松鼠跟鳥聒噪的古怪聲中，去那裏閒逛。有時，我還偷吃過牠們啃過一半的堅果，因為牠們挑選過的刺果裏面，確實有大塊果肉。偶然，我也會爬上果樹，去搖晃它們的果實，我屋後也長栗子樹，有一棵大得差不多遮蓋了我的屋，等到開花時節，就像一大束鮮花，連左鄰右里都是香氣四溢，但是樹上的果實，八成都給松鼠和鳥吃掉了；一大早，鳥三五成羣飛過來，趁着栗子還沒有落地，就啄破果皮吃掉了。這些樹我通通讓給了牠們，自己到離此處更遠的樹林裏去，那處倒是清一色的栗子樹。這些堅果，照它們的實情看，堪稱麵包的理想代用品。不過也許還可以尋到許多其他代用品呢。有一天，我在挖魚餌時，發現了成串的野豆[1]，是土著居民的馬鈴薯，一種神奇的果實，我就開始懷疑，莫不是我小時候挖掘過，並且還吃過呢，正如別人告訴我的，反正以後我再也沒有夢見過了。過去，我常常看見它那捲曲的紅天鵝絨似的花朵，傍着其他植物梗子，卻不知道與它還是同梗同莖呢。可惜開荒種地，已使它差不多要絕種了。野豆味甘，口感很好，很像經過霜凍的馬鈴薯味道。我發現煮野豆要比烤味道更好。這種塊莖彷彿是大自然冥冥之中的一種默默的許諾，要在未來某些時期栽培她自己的兒女，就在這裏讓他們過簡樸溫飽的日子。在當今耕牛肥育、麥浪翻滾的時代，這種不起眼的野豆，儘管它一度還作為某個印第安人部落的圖騰，卻早已被人遺忘了，至多也只有它開花時的藤蔓還能見得到；不過，要是讓原始的大自然重新在這裏統治，那些嬌嫩的、奢侈的英國穀物，説不定會在無數仇敵跟前銷聲匿跡。毋須人們操心，也許烏鴉甚至會送最後一顆玉米種子回到西南方，印第安人的上帝的大片玉米地裏，據説以前烏鴉就是從那裏帶種子過來的；不過，現在幾乎瀕臨絕跡的野豆，不怕霜凍和蠻荒，以後也許還會復甦，證明自己是土生土長的，重振它那作為狩獵部落的食物的昔日雄風。印第安人的穀物女神和智慧女神，想必就是野豆的發明者和賜予者；只要詩歌開始在這裏佔上風，野豆的葉和成串的堅果，説不定就會在我們的藝術作品裏得到表現。

到了9月1日，我已看到湖對面的一個岬角上，離湖不遠有兩三棵小楓樹變紅了，在那三棵分了岔的白楊之下。啊，她們的色彩講述了多少個故事！一個星期又一個星期，每棵樹的性格漸漸凸現出來，她盡情欣賞自己有如明鏡一樣的湖面倒影。每天早上，這個畫廊的經理取下牆上的舊畫，換上一些新畫，新畫更鮮亮，色彩和諧，美極了。

10 月裏，黃蜂們數以千計飛臨我的住所，好像是來過冬，落腳在我窗戶裏和上面的牆上，有時候會嚇得一些來客不敢進門。每天早上，牠們總有冷得凍僵了的，我就掃牠們到屋外去，但我並沒有花費心力來除掉牠們；不僅如此，牠們肯屈駕寒舍，我甚至還覺得榮幸之至呢。牠們雖然跟我睡在一起，但從來沒有傷害過我；後來，牠們漸漸地見不到影了。我不知道牠們鑽進了甚麼縫隙裏面，為的是躲避嚴冬和難以描述的寒冷吧。

到 11 月，如同那些黃蜂一樣，最後進入冬居之前，我常到瓦爾登湖的東北岸邊去，在那裏，陽光從油松林和石岸反射過來，無形之中形成了湖畔火爐；只要你還能做得到，曬太陽暖暖身體，確實要比家裏圍爐取暖更愜意，也更有利於健康。夏天好像是一個離去的獵人，卻留下了還在發光的餘燼；而我就這樣靠這些餘燼取暖過冬。

當我砌好煙囪的時候，對泥水匠工作總算入了門。我使用的是舊磚，先要用瓦刀刮乾淨它，這麼一來，我對磚頭和瓦刀的特徵就有了更深了解。那些舊磚上頭的灰漿，已經五十年了，據說年代越久越牢固；不過，以上這些話，人們喜歡這麼說，也不管它究竟對不對。這樣的說法本身隨著年日越久，也變得越牢固，需要用瓦刀狠狠刮，不斷刮才能刮乾淨舊磚上這個未卜先知的老話。美索不達米亞有許多村莊，都是用質量非常好的舊磚頭砌造的；從巴比倫廢墟裏撿來的，舊磚上頭的水泥更古老，也許更牢固吧。不管怎麼樣，那把純鋼瓦刀的鋼刃特別堅硬，經得起那麼多猛砸，一點不捲刃，真讓我吃驚。我的磚頭原本來自一座舊煙囪，雖然我沒見過上面有尼布甲尼撒二世 [2] 的名字，我盡可能多撿出些壁爐用的磚塊來，這樣既省工，又不會浪費。我用湖邊尋找到的石頭填塞壁爐四周磚頭之間的空隙，並用湖邊的白沙土製成供我使用的灰漿。壁爐作為屋裏最要緊的一部份，令我在壁爐上花最多時間。說真的，我做得非常仔細，雖然一大早我就從地上開始砌磚，到晚上才壘起了離地幾英寸高，夜裏我拿它當枕頭，但我記得我並沒有睡歪了頸；而過去我倒是常有的毛病。大約就在這段時間，我邀來了一位詩人，在這裏住了半個月，因為房間狹窄，令我好不尷尬。他隨身帶來了自己的刀，其實我也有兩把，我們常常用刀來回捅進地裏的辦法，將刀擦得乾乾淨淨。他還幫過我做飯，眼看着我的壁爐方方正正，結結實實，漸漸壘高起來，我心裏很高興。我就這樣想，雖說進度慢了一點，據說壽命反而很長呢。煙囪在某程度來說，是一個獨立結構，拔地而起，穿過屋頂，直衝雲霄；甚至在燒掉了屋以後，煙囪有時依然聳立着，它的重要性和獨立性顯而易見。那時接近夏末。現在卻是 11 月了。

北風一起，湖水才開始變冷，還要一連幾個星期，風不停歇地刮着，湖水才會結冰，因為這個湖太深了。我頭一次在晚上生火時，還沒有給屋內板壁抹上灰漿，煙從煙囪裏溢出的情況特別好，因為板壁之間縫隙多得很。我就在這雖然寒冷但通風良好的房間裏，度過了幾個愉快的夜晚，四周全是毛糙的、帶節疤的棕色木板，上面的椽子還連着樹皮呢。我屋後抹過了灰漿，我不由得格外喜歡自己的屋，我不得不承認，住在這樣的屋裏，自然也格外舒服。人們居住的每個房間，難道不應該頭頂得很高，高得給人產生朦朦朧朧的感覺，入夜以後看得見一些椽子四周，火光投射的影子在跳躍嗎？這些影子的形態，要比壁畫或者其他最昂貴的家具，更能激活人們的幻想和想像力。現在第一次入住我的屋，不妨這麼說，我已開始利用它來取暖，同時又可以遮擋風雨了。我還尋到兩個舊柴薪架，讓木柴再也不會傍靠爐壁了。眼看着我造的煙囪後面積累的黑灰，真是好不高興，因此，我撥弄起爐火來，也比平常更賣力，感到更滿足了。我的住處又窄又小，我很難在屋裏產生迴音；但是，當作單身房間使用，跟鄰居們隔得也很遠，似乎顯得又大了一些。一幢房子的整個魅力全都集中在一個房間；它是廚房、是臥室、是客廳又是儲藏室；凡是父母或者孩子，主人或者僕人，住在一幢房子裏，不管他們得過甚麼樣的滿足，我通通享受到了。卡托說，一家之主 (patremfamilias) 一定要在他的鄉間別墅擁有，要一連幾個星期，風不停歇地刮着，湖水才會結冰，因為這個湖太深了。我頭一次在晚上生火時，還沒有給屋內板 pectare，et rei，et virtuti，et gloriae erit[3]，也就是說，"一個儲油存酒的地下室，還有許許多多儲物木桶，以後如遇艱難日子，也就有備無患；這樣對他會有好處、有功效，而且值得自豪。"我在自己的地下室裏儲存了一桶馬鈴薯，大約兩夸脱[4]豌豆，包括摻雜在豌豆裏面的象蟲。我的架子上，還有一點大米，一罐糖漿，以及黑麥和印第安玉米粉各一配克[5]。

有時候，我夢見過一幢可容納很多人的大房子，它在一個黃金時代拔地而起，建房材料經久耐用，也沒有華而不實的裝飾，但它只有一個房間，一個寬敞、簡陋、實用、頗具原始氣氛的廳堂，沒有天花板，或者說沒有抹過灰漿，僅有光禿禿的椽子和檁條，支撐着頭頂上低矮的天棚——遮擋雨雪倒是很管用；在那裏，你一跨過門檻，向那俯臥着的古代農神行禮之後，桁架中柱和桁架雙柱[6]彷彿起立接受你的敬意；這是一幢空洞洞的房子，你在裏面必須綁火炬在長桿子上才能看得見屋頂；在那裏，有人可以住在壁爐邊上，有人在窗子的凹室裏，有人在高背椅子上，有人在廳堂的這一端，有人則在廳堂的那一端，有人甚至跟蜘蛛一起在上面的椽子上，反正只要他們願意就可以了；這麼一幢房子，你一推開大門，就能長驅直入到達廳堂，一切繁縟禮節都全免了；在那裏，疲憊不堪的觀光客不妨盥洗、進餐、聊天、睡覺，用不着出門遠行；狂風暴雨之夜，你最期盼到達的，正是這麼一個棲身之處，裏面一切家用必需品應有盡有，何況又沒有家務之累；在那裏，廳堂裏所有金銀財寶，你絕對能一覽無遺；每件常用物品全都掛在木釘子上；在那裏，既是廚房，又是配餐室、客廳、臥室、儲藏室也是閣樓；在那裏，你能看得見諸如木桶、梯子這類必需品，還有像碗櫥之類用起來很方便的東西；你還聽得見水壺在沸騰，你要向給你做飯的火灶和給你烤麵包的爐子致敬；在那裏，必不可缺的家具和器物成了主要的裝飾物；在那裏，洗過的衣物不用晾在外面，爐火不熄滅，女主人也不會嗔怒；廚師到地下室時，有時也許請你打開活板門，這樣你也不必用腳去踩，就知道地上哪裏是牢實的，哪裏是虛空的。一幢房子像鳥巢似的全部向外敞開，讓人一目了然，你可以從前門進去，從後門出來，卻看不見住在裏面的人；在那裏，就算做客人，照樣享受到一切自由待遇，不是被棄絕於它八份之七以外的地方，關在一間特殊的斗室裏，還關照你，說甚麼賓至如歸等等——其實幽禁了你。現在主人決不會邀請你到他的壁爐邊去，而是叫來泥水匠給你在走廊裏面另砌一個火爐，所謂"殷勤招待"乃是一種跟你保持最大距離的訣竅。說到烹飪，竅門自然很多，多得彷彿他想要毒死你似的。我知道我到過許多人的府邸，本來很可能被他們依法着令我離去的，但我並不知道自己去過許多人的家裏；如果說我走到了像我所描述過的巨宅裏，我倒是不妨身穿舊衣去拜訪過着儉樸生活的皇帝和皇后；但是，如果說我萬一在現代宮殿裏被逮捕，那麼，我真恨不得學會掉頭偷走。

　　看來我們的社交語言已失去了它的全部活力，完全退化為閒聊；我們的生活如此遠離它的符號，它的隱喻和借喻又顯得如此牽強附會，可以說，只好通過滑道和升降梯來傳遞了；換句話說，客廳離廚房和作坊太遠了。就算進餐，通常講的也不過是進餐的大話罷了。好像唯有野蠻人住的地方跟大自然和真理挨得太近了，反而可以向他們借用比喻似的。遠在"西北邊陲"或者"馬恩島"又稱"人島"，位於愛爾蘭海上的一個島嶼。的學者，他又怎麼會知道廚房裏說的是甚麼彬彬有禮的語言呢？

　　但是話又說回來，我客人裏面只有一兩個還不算膽小，留下來和我一起喝玉米麵粥；可惜他們一看見危機顯露時，就匆匆落荒而逃，好像危機會震塌這屋似的。結果呢，反正熬好了那麼多玉米麵粉，這屋依然屹立着。

直到天氣真的冰冷了，我才開始抹灰漿。為了這件事，我划着小船從湖的對岸運回更潔白、更乾淨的沙，反正有了小船這種運輸工具，必要時，就算去的地方更遠，我也絕對樂意。就在這時候，我屋裏每面牆都釘上了木板條，從高處一直到齊牆根。釘木板條時，我很高興，只要一錘釘下去，就牢牢釘死釘子。我一心追求的是，要從木板條上乾淨利落地抹灰漿到牆頭上。我忽然想起了一個自大傢伙的故事，此人身穿優質衣服，總是在村裏東逛西蕩，給工人們出主意。有一天，他心血來潮，想用實幹取代空談，於是，他捲起衣袖，拿起一塊灰漿工用的木板，用瓦刀裝上灰漿，做得總算沒出差錯，稍後，他得意揚揚地望了一下長長的木板條，不管三七二十一就抹了灰漿上去，不料整團灰漿馬上掉在他那氣呼呼的胸脯上，真丟臉啊。我對抹灰漿倒是十分欣賞，因為它既經濟，又方便，有效抵禦了寒氣，而且抹過後又顯得那麼光潔好看。我也了解到泥水匠很容易遭到各種意外事故。我因發現那些磚塊乾渴得很厲害而感到驚奇，我還來不及抹平灰漿，水份早給磚塊吸乾了；更令我驚奇的是，為了新砌一個壁爐，我真不知道耗去多少桶水呢。前一個冬季，我將我們大河裏尋到的珠蚌貝殼[7]燒製成少量石灰，為了準備做實驗；因此，我也就知道我的材料是從哪裏來的。若我樂意的話，説不定我在一兩英里以內，可以找到上等的石灰石，親自動手燒製。

　　就在這時候，陽光最照不到、最淺的小水灣裏已經結了一層薄冰，比整個湖面結冰早了好幾天，乃至於幾個星期。第一塊冰特別耐人尋味，也顯得特別完美；它質地堅硬，呈淺黑色而又透明，這對觀察淺水處的湖底來説是一個絕佳機會。你不妨全身趴倒在一英寸厚的冰面上，像一隻掠水蟲似的，慢慢琢磨研究湖底，離你才不過兩三英寸，勝過玻璃後面的一幅圖畫，不用説，這時水始終是平靜的。湖底的沙上有很多溝槽，一些生物在溝槽上爬過來，又循着原路爬回去；至於殘骸到處可見，全是白石英細顆粒形成的石蠶殼。也許那些溝槽就是它們留下來的，因為你發現在那些溝槽上有它們的殘殼，儘管這些溝槽又深又寬，不是它們一蹴而就。但冰凌本身是最耐人尋味的事物，因此，你務必把握時機去琢磨研究它。你要是在結冰後那個早上來仔細觀察它，就會發現那些驟眼看起來好像在冰凌裏面的氣泡，實際上依附在冰面上，還有更多氣泡正從水底不斷泛上來；再說，這冰凌相當堅實而又發暗，所以，你才可以透過它看到了水。這些氣泡的直徑，有些是 1 英寸的八十份之一，有些是 1 英寸的八份之一，它們非常清楚，非常美麗，透過冰凌，你可以看見你的臉孔映照在氣泡上。每一平方英寸裏面，也許就有三四十個氣泡。還有一些氣泡已經在冰凌裏面，狹小的，橢圓的，垂直的，大約半英寸長，呈圓錐體，頂尖朝上；如果說是剛才結成冰的冰凌，常常會有細小氣泡，一個浮在另一個上頭，望過去宛如一串珠子似的。不過，冰凌裏面的氣泡，並沒有像附着在冰凌底層的氣泡那麼多，也沒有那麼明顯。有時候，我常常往冰凌上扔一些石子，試試看冰凌有多大力度，那些砸破冰面的石子會連空氣也帶了進去，在冰凌底下形成特別大而又特別顯眼的氣泡。有一天，我過了四十八小時後，再回到老地方去，發現這些稍大的氣泡依然完美如初，儘管那裏又結上了厚達一英寸多的冰凌，因為從一塊冰凌旁邊的裂縫裏，我看得清清楚楚。不過，前兩天，天氣很暖和，好像小陽春似的，那冰凌就不怎麼透明了，呈現出湖水的深綠色，而湖底有一點渾濁，呈現灰白色，冰凌比前時厚了兩倍，卻沒有過去那麼結實，因為氣泡受熱後大大膨脹，積聚在一起，打亂了原來的格局；它們不再是一個浮在另一個上頭，倒是像從一個袋裏倒出來的銀幣，一個個堆壓在一起，或者說，就像一些薄片似的，彷彿填補一些細微的裂縫。冰凌之美早已無影無蹤，再想琢磨研究湖底，已是為時太晚。出於好奇，很想知道，在新近結成的冰凌中，那些大氣泡佔着甚麼位置，於是，我鑿取了一塊含有中型氣泡的冰，讓它翻個身，底面朝天。新結的冰凌是在那個氣泡周圍和底下形成，所以，氣泡就在兩塊冰的中間。它完全處在底下的冰層，但又貼近上層冰凌，扁平形，或者說，也許有點像扁豆形狀，圓邊，深四份之一英寸，直徑四英寸；令我驚奇的是，我發現正對着氣泡的底下，冰凌融化很有規則，好像倒置的茶碟形狀，中間高度為八份之五英寸，水和氣泡之間有一條薄薄的分界線，薄得幾乎還不到八份之一英寸；這條分界線裏許多地方，小氣泡往下爆裂，也許在最為巨大、直徑為一英尺的氣泡底下，根本就沒有冰凌了。我由此可以斷定，我頭一次看到附在冰凌底下的無數小氣泡，這時也在冰塊裏面結了冰，每個小氣泡在不同程度上在冰凌底下起了類似取火鏡的作用，要使冰凌融化殆盡。這些小氣泡就是微型氣槍，讓冰凌融化時爆裂有響聲。

最後，冬天真正來到了，我那抹牆的工作剛完，狂風開始在我屋子周圍呼嘯，彷彿直到此刻它才被允許呼嘯似的。一夜又一夜，鵝羣在黑暗中伴隨着尖叫聲、拍翅聲，笨拙而又緩慢地飛過來，甚至大地上已鋪滿白雪之後還會飛過來，有些落在瓦爾登湖上，有些低低掠過樹林，飛向美港，打算去墨西哥。有好幾次，已是十點鐘或者十一點鐘，我從村裏回家，忽然聽見一羣鵝或者一羣鴨在走動，在我屋後湖沼邊上，踩着樹林裏的枯葉，四處覓食；牠們匆匆離去的時候，那領頭鵝的低喚聲還隱約可聞。1845 年，[8] 11 月 25 日起，大地全是皚皚白雪，我突然被冬日雪景包圍住了。我萬般無奈，只好躲進自己的小窩，真想在屋裏和心裏點燃起一簇旺亮的火堆。這時，我去戶外的差事，就是到森林裏去尋找枯木，然後手提或者肩扛回家轉，或者有時候，胳臂底下分別夾住一棵枯死的松樹，就這樣拖到我的雜物屋裏。這棵枯樹曾經是昔日森林圍柵，有過多麼風光的歲月，如今讓我拖着它相當花工夫。我獻它給火神伏爾甘古 [9] 為祭，因過去它已獻給護界神特爾米努斯 [10] 為祭，這是多麼意味深長的一件事啊，據說人類晚飯的由來是這樣的，當初有人到雪地裏去狩獵，不，你不妨可以這麼說，去偷燃料，拿去燒晚飯的！他的麵包和肉果然都很香噴噴呢。我們大多數村鎮，在森林裏都有各種木柴和廢木料，足夠人們生火，可是當前它們卻沒有給人們帶來溫暖，而且，有人還認為，它們會妨礙幼林的生長。湖上還有一些漂來的木材。夏天，我發現過一排油松原木[11]紮成的木筏，是當年愛爾蘭人造鐵路時釘在一起的。這裏面有一部份，我已經拖到了湖岸上。在湖裏浸泡過兩年多，隨後高地上又晾了六個月，它是頂級好木材，儘管部份吸水太多，還沒有完全乾透。冬天裏，有一天，我就這樣聊以自娛：我將這些木頭一根根從湖上拖過去，差不多有半英里遠，一根十五英尺長的原木，一端擱在我肩頭上，另一端搭在冰凌上，就像溜冰似的一路滑行過去；要不然，我用樺樹條捆起了好幾根木頭，隨後，用一根長一點的、頭上帶鈎的樺木棍或者橙木棍鈎住它，從湖上拽過去。這些木料完全被水浸泡過，沉甸甸像鉛塊，可是，它們不僅耐燒，而且火苗特別旺；不，我覺得，正因為湖裏浸泡過，這些木頭才更好燒，彷彿經過水裏浸泡過的松脂，在燈籠裏更好燒一樣。

吉爾平[12]描述英格蘭的林中居民時說："有些人已侵佔了土地，於是，在森林的邊界就這樣築了圍柵，造了房子。""古代森林法認為，這是一個嚴重的侵害行為，應當以侵佔公地的罪名給予重罰，因為這使飛禽恐懼，森林受害。"不過，我對野味和森林的保護要比獵人和樵夫更關注，彷彿我自己就是護林官一樣。如果說森林有一部份給燒掉了，哪怕是我自己不小心造成的，我也會感到創巨痛深，要比領地主人悲痛得更持久，也更難得到安慰；不，還有呢，就算樹木是領地主人自己砍掉的，我照樣會感到痛心。我倒是希望我們的農場主人們在砍伐一片森林時，也能感受到某種恐懼，就像古羅馬人在神聖的森林[13]裏，為了讓多些陽光透進來，砍掉少些樹木，以免長得更稀疏時所感受到的那種恐懼，這是因為古羅馬人相信那片森林已奉獻給某些天神。古羅馬人先是贖罪，然後祈禱，不管你是男神還是女神，這片森林是專門奉獻給你們的，請賜福給我和我的一家，以及子子孫孫吧。

　　值得注意的是，即使在當今時代，在這個新的國家，林木畢竟還是極有價值，這種價值要比黃金的價值更久遠，也更普遍。我們已經有了許多發現和發明，但還沒有哪個人走過一堆木料時能無動於衷。林木對我們來說，就像對我們的撒克遜和諾曼祖輩一樣是彌足珍貴的。如果說當年他們是用木材做弓箭，那麼，如今我們就用木材來做槍托。三十多年前，米紹[14]就說過，在紐約和費城，木頭燃料的價格"跟巴黎質地最好的木料價格幾乎相同，有時也許還會超過，儘管這個巨大的首都每年需要三十多萬考得的木材，周圍三百英里的平原上又都是耕地"。在我們這個鎮上，木材價格差不多在持續上漲，唯一的問題是，今年的木材價格比去年究竟要上漲多少。機械工人和商人親自出馬到森林裏來，不為別的，肯定是參加木材拍賣會，甚至願出高價，獲得伐木者離場之後撿取零星木料的權利。不知有多少歲月流逝而去了，人們總是到森林裏面尋尋覓覓，不外乎就是燃料和藝術的材料；新英格蘭人、新荷蘭人、凱爾特人、農場主人和羅賓漢、古迪·布萊克和哈里·吉爾[15]，來自世界各地的王子和農民，以及學者和野蠻人，大家同樣要到森林拿幾根木頭去生火取暖、做飯。就算是我，絕對也少不了它的。

　　每個人看着自己的柴火堆，都會喜形於色。我喜歡在窗前堆起我的柴火堆，劈柴劈得越多，越能勾起我對自己愉快工作的回憶。我有一把擔保沒人會要的舊斧頭，冬閒時，我就坐在屋裏向陽那邊，用它來砍我從種豆地裏挖出來的那些樹樁頭。就像我犁地時租用的馬車主人預言過的，這些樹樁頭給過我兩次溫暖，一次是我劈它們成柴片的時候，另一次是它們着火燃燒的時候，反正再也沒有其他燃料能發出比它更多的熱量來。至於那把斧頭，有人勸我拿到村裏鐵匠那裏去"蘸火"；但我是自己給它"蘸火"的；而且，還從樹林裏尋到一根山核桃木給它裝上斧把，用起來就更順手了。雖說這斧頭很鈍，但至少很好用吧。

兩三片油脂松木，不僅是一大珍寶。想想如今大地深處還秘藏着不知多少這種引火燃料，真的是匪夷所思了。前幾年，我經常到光禿禿的山坡上進行"勘探"，從前，那裏有過一片油松林，我還刨過一些油脂松樹根莖出來。它們幾乎是堅固不可摧毀的。那些樹樁頭，至少也有三四十年了，樹心裏面還很好，儘管邊材已經腐朽了，那厚厚的樹皮，在離樹心四五英寸處，形成一個圓環，與地面接齊。你帶上斧頭和鏟對這種礦藏進行勘探，順着那黃色牛油脂肪骨髓一樣的儲藏物一直挖下去，或者説，就像你挖到了大地深處中的金礦礦脈一樣。但是，通常我是用樹林裏的枯樹葉來引火的，那還是我趕在下雪前就儲存在雜物屋裏的。青翠的山核桃木劈成細細的棍子，伐木者在樹林裏宿營時，常拿它來引火。這種引火柴，我時不時總要儲存一點。村民們遠在天邊生火的時候，我的煙囱裏也會冒出嫋嫋的青煙來，讓瓦爾登峽谷裏各種山野居民都知道，我是醒着的——

> 雙翼輕盈的青煙，伊卡羅斯之鳥，
> 往上升騰，你的羽翼將會融化掉，
> 悄無聲息的雲雀，黎明的信使啊，
> 盤旋在屋舍上空，當作自己的窩；
> 　要不然你是逝去的夢，子夜時
> 　迷幻的身影，撩起你的衣裙；
> 　長夜裏給星星披上了面紗，
> 　白日裏遮住了亮光和太陽；
>
> 去吧，我的薰香，從圍爐這裏飛起，
> 請求天上諸神，寬恕這明亮的火焰。

那碧綠的硬木剛剛劈開，儘管我生火時用得很少，我覺得它卻比其他木料更便宜。有時，我在冬日午後，爐火很旺的時候，外出去散步，過了三四個鐘頭回到家時，火苗依然在閃閃發光。我出門之後，我的屋總也不算是空蕩蕩的，彷彿我留下了一位愉快的管家似的。住在這小屋裏的是我和爐火；一般來說，我這位管家真是忠實可靠。怎料有一天，我還在屋外劈木柴，突然想到該去窗口看上一眼，看看屋裏會不會着了火；在我的記憶中，唯獨這一次讓我為這種事特別心煩；就這一看，不好了，一小點火花燒着了我的牀鋪；我立刻趕緊進屋去撲滅了火，還好它只燒掉巴掌大的一小塊。不過，我的屋方位很好，陽光充足，可避風雨，屋頂又很低，所以，後來在任何一個冬日午後，我差不多都熄滅掉爐火。

鼴鼠在我的地窖裏做窩，啃掉了馬鈴薯的三份之一；牠們甚至利用我抹牆剩下來的一些毛髮和牛皮紙，給自己搭了一個舒適的小窩鋪；因為哪怕是最富野性的動物，也跟人類一樣，眷戀舒適和溫暖；也正因為牠們如此小心翼翼築起了窩，牠們才能安然越過寒冬存活下來。我有一些朋友說，彷彿我到樹林裏來，就是存心讓自己給凍成雪條呢。野獸僅僅在一個避風處搭上一個小窩鋪，靠自己的體溫來取暖；可是，發現了火的人類，關了空氣在一個寬敞房間裏取暖，反正他不是靠自己的體溫來取暖，而是當那個房間為自己的牀鋪，在那個房間裏面，他可以安之若素，用不着穿上很厚的衣服，在冬天就像夏天那樣暖和，通過窗可讓陽光照進室內，點了燈如同白晝延長一樣。他就這樣比本能超前了一兩步，省出時間來從事美術創作。當我長時間置身於狂風之中，全身就開始麻木，可是，我有一次到我家中溫馨的氣氛裏，馬上就神清氣爽，延年益壽。說實話，就這一點來說，即使身居豪宅的人也沒有甚麼好吹噓，我們也不必自尋煩惱，揣測甚麼人類最後如何毀滅。只要北方刮來稍微強勁一點的狂風，隨時都可以切斷他們的生命線。我們常常用"寒冷的星期五"和"大雪天"來計算日子；反正星期五更冷一點，或者雪下得更大些，人類在地球上的生存，恐怕就會告一段落。

　　第二年冬季，為了節省起見，我改用一個很小的火爐，因為這片森林畢竟並不是歸我所有；但這個小火爐不像敞開的壁爐那樣總是火苗很旺。那時候，烹飪八成不再富有詩意，僅僅是一個化學過程罷了。在使用火爐的日子裏，人們很快就忘掉從前自己跟印第安人一樣，在餘燼裏面烘烤過馬鈴薯。火爐不僅佔地方，熏得滿屋煙霧騰騰，連火苗都看不到，我覺得自己好像失去了一位伴侶似的。你在火光中總是能看到一張臉龐。傍晚時份，人們在工作之餘，兩眼凝望着火苗，會使白晝積存的俗世雜念一一得到淨化。可是我再也不能坐下來守望火苗了，有一位詩人所寫的深中肯綮的詩句，使我充滿了新的力量——

明亮的火焰啊，你是生活的映像，
你可愛可親之情，別捨不得給我。
如此光芒迸射，莫非是我的希望？
入夜如此低沉，難道我氣運不旺？
你平素深受人們歡迎和愛戴，
緣何被逐出我們廳堂和爐台？
難道你一生太沉湎於幻想，
不給芸芸眾生一點光亮？
難道你那神秘的光芒不是在
跟我們的心靈神交？心照不宣？
是的，我們安全又強健，因為此刻
坐在火爐邊，沒有黑影在晃動，
也沒有歡樂傷悲，只有一圍火
溫暖我們的手足——希望並不高；
有了它這密集又實用的一堆火，

在它身旁的人不妨閒坐打盹，

別害怕從幽暗中遊蕩過來的鬼魂，

古樹火光忽明忽暗似的跟我們對話。¹⁶

章註

1　野豆：拉丁文學名 Apios tuberosa。

2　尼布甲尼撒二世：公元前 627—公元前 562，巴比倫國王，曾侵佔敘利亞和
　　巴勒斯坦，攻佔並焚毀耶路撒冷，將大批猶太人驅逐至巴比倫，在位時修建
　　巴比倫城和空中花園。

3　此處是拉丁文。

4　夸脫：穀物等容量單位，約 8 蒲式耳。

5　配克：穀物等容量單位，約 8 夸脫或 2 加侖。

6　此處原文為 King and queen posts，光從字面看，意思是"國王和王后柱"。

7　珠蚌貝殼：拉丁文學名 Unio fluviatilis。

8　瓦爾登湖在 12 月 22 日夜間第一次全部凍封，而佛林特湖和其他水位較淺
　　的湖和康科德河早在十天前就冰封了；1846 年冰封的日子是 12 月 16 日；
　　1849 年大約在 12 月 31 日；1850 年大約在 12 月 27 日；1852 年是 1 月 5
　　日；1853 年是 12 月 31 日。

9　火神伏爾甘古：羅馬神話中火與鍛冶之神，亦稱火神。

10　護界神特爾米努斯：古羅馬神話中保護界標之神，亦稱護界神了。

11　油松原木：樹皮還留着。

12　吉爾平：William Gilpin，1724—1804，英國作家，他走遍英倫三島，對他
　　的遊歷給予詩一般的描述，其文風為後人仿效。

13　古羅馬人在神聖的森林：拉丁文為 Lucum conlucare。

14　米紹：1746—1802，法國植物學家。

15　哈里·吉爾：此處指英國著名詩人華茲華斯（William Wordsworth 1770—
　　1850）的名詩《古迪·布萊克和哈里·吉爾》裏的一些人物。

16　引自美國田園詩人胡珀，Ellen Sturgis Hooper 1812—1848 的名詩《柴火》。

原住民，冬日來客

我經歷過幾次愉快的暴風雪，在爐邊度過了一些歡暢的冬日夜晚，大雪在外面瘋狂打轉，甚至蓋過了貓頭鷹的尖叫聲。幾個星期以來，我外出閒逛時連一個人都沒碰見過，除了偶然來樹林裏伐木的人，用雪橇拖木柴回村裏去。不過話又說回來，倒是大風大雪唆使了我，在樹林最深的積雪中開出一條小路，因為有一次我穿過樹林時，大風吹了橡樹葉到我踩踏出來的腳印裏，它們留在裏面吸收了陽光，融化了積雪，這麼一來，我不僅腳下有了乾爽的路面可走，而且入夜以後，它們那黑糊糊的線條就給我引路。至於人與人之間的交往活動，我不得不想起了樹林裏那些原住民。我們鎮上有許多人都還記得，那些原住民的歡聲笑語，曾在我小屋附近那條大路上迴蕩，我小屋四周全是樹林，這裏那裏點綴着他們的小花園和小屋，不過，那時節繁茂的樹木遮擋得比現在更嚴實。有些地方，我自己都記得，松樹的枝杈會同時刮破輕便馬車的兩側，婦女和孩子們不得不單獨步行到林肯去，經過這處不免有些心裏害怕，往往還要跑上一段路。雖然大體上說，這只是一條通往鄰村不起眼的小道，或者換句話說，是專供伐木工人行走的小道，但由於它當年萬種風情，倒是給觀光客帶來更多情趣，並在他們的記憶裏久久縈繞不去。如今，從村莊到樹林，中間有一大片空曠的田野，那時這條小道打從槭樹林的沼澤地穿過，路基底下全是原木，直至今日，在眼前這條塵土飛揚的公路下面，毫無疑問，仍然看得到它們的殘跡；這條公路是從斯特拉頓，亦即現在的濟貧院農場，直接通往布里斯特山。

加圖・英格拉哈姆就住在我的豆子地東邊，公路的對面；他是康科德村鄉紳鄧肯・英格拉哈姆老爺的奴隸，這位老爺給他的奴隸造了一間屋，允許他住在瓦爾登樹林裏 —— 我在這裏提到的加圖，不是尤蒂卡的那個加圖，而是康科德的這個加圖。有人說他是畿內亞人。有少數人還記得他那個核桃林裏有一小塊地，他培育核桃樹成樹林，等到他歲數大了，打算派上用場了；怎料到頭來還是落到了一個年紀輕輕的白人投機者手裏。反正現在他還有一間同樣狹小的房屋。加圖跡近湮沒的地窖洞口還依稀可見，但早已鮮為人知，因為旁邊有一排松樹擋住了它，人們就算走過，也都看不見。如今，那裏長滿了光潔的漆樹[1]，最原始品種的黃花[2]，也長得很茂盛。

在我土地的邊角上，離鎮更近些，有一個黑人婦女名叫齊爾法，住在小小一間房屋裏，她在那裏替鎮上的人織亞麻布。她有一副特別好的嗓子，她那嘹亮的歌聲在瓦爾登樹林裏迴響着。後來，在 1812 年戰爭中，她的房屋被英國兵 —— 這是一夥憑誓獲釋的俘虜兵 —— 放火燒掉了；當時，幸好她不在家，但她的小貓、小狗和老母雞通通給燒死了。她過的艱苦生活，簡直不像是人過的。一個常來樹林漫步的人記得，有一天中午，他路過齊爾法的家門口時，聽見她衝着沸騰的水壺喃喃自語道 ——“你們全是屍骸，屍骸啊！”我在橡樹林裏，還看到了磚頭呢。

循着公路下行，靠右邊，布里斯特山上，住着布里斯特・弗里曼，“一個心靈手巧的黑人，”他一度是卡明斯鄉紳家的奴隸 —— 當年布里斯特栽培的蘋果樹，至今仍在那處，現已長成很大的老樹了，我覺得它們結出的果實，口感依然是地道的野蘋果味道。不久前，我在老林肯墓園裏看到他的墓誌銘，在他的墓碑附近，是一些無墓主姓名，亦即從康科德撤退時倒下的英國擲彈兵的墳墓 —— 他墓碑上寫的是“西皮奧・布里斯特”阿非利加努斯[3]“一個有色人種”，好像他已褪了色似的。我從墓碑上知道，上面還特別強調他是在甚麼時候死去；這僅僅間接告訴我他曾經飽嚐過塵世況味罷了。和他住在一起的是他的妻子芬達，她殷勤好客，會替人算命，總讓人聽了很開心——身型大、圓圓的、黑黑的，比黑夜裏哪個孩子還要黑，這麼一個黑黝黝的肉球，在康科德真可以說空前絕後。

沿着小山再往下走，靠左邊，在樹林的古道上，是斯特拉頓家族莊園的地界；他們家的果園一度遍及布里斯特山的所有山坡，可惜老早就被油松所吞沒，只剩下一些殘株，它們的老根上至今還長出很多枝繁葉茂的野樹來。

離鎮更近些，在大路的另一邊，恰好在樹林的邊沿上，你就來到了布里德的地方；這個地方因為有過一個妖怪而出了名；雖然這個妖怪在古代神話中沒有明確記述，但它在我們新英格蘭人生活中卻扮演着很顯眼、很驚人的角色，就像任何一位神話人物一樣，總有那麼一天，應該有人給他寫一部傳記似的；最初，他是喬裝打扮成一個朋友，或者一個僱工，沒多久就洗劫並殺害了主人全家老小——真是新英格蘭一大怪；但歷史想必還沒有一一記述這裏上演過的所有悲劇；不妨讓時間從中斡旋，給這些悲劇清除一些哀痛，添上一點蔚藍色彩吧。有一個最含糊不清的傳說，說這裏從前有過一家小酒店；還有一口井，就是這井水加在路人的飲料裏特別好喝，並使他的坐騎很快恢復活力。在這裏，人們互相打個招呼，聽聽新聞，然後各自上路。

布里德的小屋雖然早就沒有人居住了，但在十二年前還矗立在那裏。它跟我的小屋大小差不多，那是一個總統大選的夜晚，如果說我沒有記錯的話，是幾個淘氣小男孩放火燒掉它的。當時我住在村莊邊上，還在捧讀戴夫南特[4]的《龔迪伯特》出了神，那年冬天，我得了渴睡症——順便說一下，我不知道這毛病是不是遺傳的，反正我有一個叔父，連刮鬍子的時候都會睡着，因此，每逢禮拜日不得不下地窖去摘掉馬鈴薯上的芽，就是讓自己保持清靜，守他的安息日；要不就是因為我想精讀查爾默斯[5]的《英國詩選》，一首也不跳過去，結果導致了昏睡。這部詩選簡直征服了我的神經[6]。我讀着讀着腦袋越來越垂了下來，火警鐘聲突然響了，救火車飛也似的趕了過來，衝在前頭的是一羣大人和孩子，而我跑在最前面那幫人裏面，因為那條小溪我縱身一躍就過去了。我們都以為着火地點遠在樹林南邊 —— 以前我們都去救過火的 —— 甚麼穀倉啦，店鋪啦，或者甚麼住宅啦，或者是所有這一切通通着了火。"是貝克家的穀倉着火了。"有人大聲叫道。"是考德曼的住宅着火了。"另一個人很有把握地説。隨後，鮮亮的火苗升上了樹林上空，彷彿屋頂塌了下去，我們全部人都大聲高喊着："康科德，快快來救火呀！"馬車急如星火般駛去，車上擠滿了人，説不定裏面還有保險公司經紀人，反正不管有多遠，他們是哪處有火就往哪處趕的；可是，救火車的鈴聲不時在後面響起來，越來越慢，越來越穩當，落在大夥的最後面，就像事後人們竊竊私語的，也許正是他們這幫人先放了火，再去報警的。就這樣，我們繼續往前趕，像真正的理想主義者，不相信自己感官提供的證據，直到在大路上拐彎時，我們聽見了劈哩啪啦的爆裂聲，真的感受到牆那邊傳過來的熱度，這才突然醒過來，老天哪！我們就在火場裏。火場倒是近了，我們的熱情反而涼下來了。開始，我們打算澆一個蛙塘裏的水到大火上去；但後來還是隨它燒下去，這小屋已經燒得差不多，救也是枉費。於是，我們圍着救火車停下來站着，互相推推拉拉，通過喇叭筒表達我們的觀點，或者壓低聲音，談到世人目睹過的所有大火災，包括巴斯考姆家的商號失火在內，而在我們自己一些人之間，卻想到：如果我們自己的"老爺船"[7]及時趕到，旁邊又有一蛙塘的水，也許我們可以將最後這場駭人的大火變成另一場大洪水的。最後，我們一點惡作劇都沒作就全部撤退，回去睡大覺。我呢，回去就看《龔迪伯特》。不過，説到《龔迪伯特》，序言裏面有一段話，説機智就是靈魂的火藥 —— "大多數人不懂得機智，就像印第安人不懂得火藥。"這段話，我可不敢苟同。

次天晚上，大約在同一時刻，我穿過田野，正好走過那裏，突然聽見一陣低沉的哭泣聲。我摸黑走近一看，發現這個人我認識，他是這個家族唯一的倖存者，繼承了這一家人的善與惡，只有他還記掛着這場大火，這時趴在地上，眼看着地窖的斷垣殘壁還在冒煙的餘燼喃喃自語，如同往常一樣。他整天在河邊草地那處工作，但凡有時間也會抽空過來，看看他祖先的老宅，他自己的青春歲月就是在那裏度過的。他經常趴在那個地窖上，從各個角度、各個方位，輪番地仔細察看，彷彿那石板裏面藏着他還記得的金銀財寶，其實，如今甚麼都尋覓不到，只有一堆堆碎磚和灰燼。房子早已蕩然無存了，他眼前看到的只是一片廢墟。此刻我來到他面前所隱含的同情，不管怎樣使他得到不少寬慰。他指給我看已被覆蓋住的那口井，天色已黑了，盡可能去看看；真是謝天謝地，那口井是絕對燒不掉的；他沿着牆根摸索了大半天，總算尋到了他老爸親手製作並且親手架起來的井水提取裝置，摸摸那鈎住盛滿水的井桶往上提的鐵鈎或者鐵扣 —— 如今，他抓得住、摸得着的，也僅僅是這個東西了 —— 他要我相信它是一個非同尋常的"提水裝置"。我就摸了它一下，後來我差不多每天出去散步時，總會過去看看它，因為它上面還懸掛着一個家族的興衰史。

在左邊，就在看得見水井和牆邊丁香花的今天那塊空地上，納廷和勒·格羅斯曾經在這裏住過，不過都回林肯那裏去了。

比以上這些地方更遠的樹林裏，離湖最近的地方，陶工韋曼擅自佔用一塊地；平日他給鎮上的人製作陶器，還讓自己後代繼承他的手藝。他們活在世上可以說很不寬裕，只是默許他佔住這塊地；縣裏治安官[8]常常跑來收稅，也總是白跑一趟，"扣押一件破玩意，"例行工事罷了，我看過他的賬目，除此以外確實身無長物。仲夏時節，有一天，我正在鋤地，有一個人駕着一輛滿載陶器的馬車去趕集，到了我的地旁邊，他就勒馬停了下來，向我打聽有關小韋曼的情況。很久以前，小韋曼向他

買過一個陶輪 [9]，他很想了解一下小韋曼現在怎樣了。過去我在經文裏讀到過陶工的泥坯和陶輪，但從來沒有想過我們所用的陶器，就在今天看得見水井和牆邊丁香花的那塊空地上，或者說就像長在樹上的葫蘆一樣，所以，聽説在我的街坊裏面，有人從事這種塑造藝術，我心裏很高興。

在我之前，這些樹林裏最後一位居民，是愛爾蘭人休·誇爾 [10]，借住在韋曼的屋子裏 —— 人們叫他誇爾上校。據説他以一名戰士身份，參加過滑鐵盧戰役。如果今天他還活着，本來我應該讓他重上戰場，一顯身手。他在這裏是靠挖溝過活。拿破崙去了聖赫勒拿島；誇爾來到了瓦爾登樹林裏；據我所知，他是一個悲劇人物。他很講究風度，就像見過世面的人似的，他説起話來特別彬彬有禮，那是你從沒有聽到過的。到了仲夏時節，他身上還披着一件厚大衣，因為他患着震顫性譫妄症，連臉色都紅得像抹上胭脂似的。我入住樹林後不久，他就死在布里斯特山腳下的大路上，所以，在我的記憶中沒有他這個鄰居。他的房子還沒拆掉以前，他朋友都當它為"凶宅"而退避三舍，我反而實地走訪過。只見他那些舊衣服都已穿得皺皮疙瘩，就像他本人似的，亂堆在那張高高隆起的木板牀上。擱在壁爐上的，是他的破煙斗，而不是一隻在泉水邊打破了的碗。布里斯特泉水永遠也不會成為他死亡的象徵，因為他向我坦白承認過，他儘管早就聽説過布里斯特泉水，卻一輩子都沒見過；黏滿塵埃的紙牌，甚麼方塊、黑桃和紅心、老 K 等等，滿地都是。一隻黑色小雞沒讓遺產管理人捉去，它的羽毛烏黑得像黑夜，一聲不響，默默等待列那 [11] 它依然棲息在隔壁房間裏面。房子後面花園的輪廓，至今依稀可見，那裏草木種下以後一次都沒有鬆過土、除過草，因為主人患病後全身一直在震顫，不過如今已到了收穫時節了。園裏長滿了羅馬苦艾和叫化草，而叫化草的果實都黏附在我的衣服上。一張土撥鼠毛皮新近剝下來，緊繃在房子後面，這是他最後一件滑鐵盧的戰利品；反正如今他再也不稀罕甚麼溫暖的毛皮帽子或者手套了。

　　現在，地上只有一個淺坑，還讓人看得出這些舊宅的遺址，地窖裏的石塊已被掩埋，草莓、紫莓、榛子灌木叢，以及漆樹，全都生長在陽光燦爛的草皮那邊；一些油松或者多節的橡樹，已從往昔煙囪那個角落裏長了出來。當年門前石階那裏，也許還有一棵芳香的黑樺樹在搖曳呢。有時，水井的凹坑至今還能依稀可見，原先這裏有過泉水，如今只有乾枯無淚的野草；要不就是這家族最後一個人離去時，從草地裏搬來一塊石板，將水井深深蓋住了 —— 反正早晚總會被人發現。掩蓋起水井 —— 想必是令人傷心的事，淚泉隨之汩汩地噴湧。這些地窖的凹坑，好像被遺棄的狐狸窩、舊洞穴，全是往昔人類沸騰生活留下的遺跡，當時他們用不同形式和不同方言討論過何謂“命運、自由意志、絕對的預知”等問題，但是，據我所知，他們討論的結果不外乎是“加圖和布里斯特扯過羊毛”，這差不多就像極有名的哲學流派的歷史一樣發人深省。

　　大門、門楣和門檻消失了一個世代以後，丁香花樹至今依然枝繁葉茂，每到春天，鮮花怒放，香氣四溢，喜愛沉思的觀光客都會前去採摘；過去是孩子們在前院的小小土地上親手栽下和呵護過的 —— 如今卻落到了杳無人跡的草場頹垣邊上，讓了位置給一些新拔地而起的樹林 —— 這些丁香花樹就是這個家族唯一的倖存者，也是這個家族最後的孑遺。黑黝黝的孩子們根本想不到，他們在住宅陽光照不到之處，插下只有兩個芽眼的細枝，經過他們天天澆水，就這樣深深紮下了根，沒期望活得比孩子們的歲數還大，而且活得比在後面給它遮蔭的大宅本身壽命更長，甚至比大人們的花園和果園發展的歷程更悠久，在他們長大、去世後又過去了半個世紀，丁香花樹卻悄悄講他們的故事給一個孤獨漫遊者聽 —— 丁香花開得好美，而且，芳香四溢，宛如在第一個春天裏開放一模一樣。丁香花那種依然嬌嫩、淡雅和歡快的色彩，深深印在我腦海裏。

不過話又說回來，這個小村莊按理說是大有可為的好幼苗，為甚麼它卻倏忽消失，而康科德還留在原地呢？難道說它不具備自然資源優勢——比方說，水源不足嗎？啊，深深的瓦爾登湖，清涼的布里斯特泉——常喝這些水有益於健康，該有多好，可惜人們根本沒有加以利用，只不過用它去稀釋他們的杯中物。他們都是清一色酒徒。為甚麼就不能讓編籃子、紮馬廄掃帚、織席子、烤玉米、織麻布、製陶器等行業在這裏生意興隆起來，使荒原像玫瑰一樣燦爛盛開，使子子孫孫能繼承他們祖先的田地呢？貧瘠的土壤至少也能防止低地的退化。天哪！這些原住民的記憶，竟然根本沒能使這裏的山山水水增添光彩！也許大自然會再次考驗，讓我做第一個移民，使我去年春天造的小屋成為這村裏最古老的住宅。

我不知道我住宅基地上從前有沒有人造過房子，讓我遠離那個建造在古城廢墟上的城市吧，因為這種城市是利用廢墟建成，以墓地造花園。那裏的土地已經泛白，而且已經受到詛咒，而且在還沒有採取必要措施之前，說不定大地本身也會給毀掉。我就這樣回首前塵，追懷往事，彷彿使原住民重歸樹林，然後自己才安然入睡。

寒冬季節，我很難得有客人來。積雪最深的時候，往往一個星期或者半個月，都沒有一個人走近我的小屋，但我生活得很舒服，就像大草原上的一隻老鼠，或者牛羊和家畜似的，據說牠們埋在積雪中間很長時間，即使沒有吃的東西，也照樣存活下來；或者說像本州薩頓鎮早期移民那一家人，1717 年刮起那場大雪時，這個移民本人正好外出，不料他那個小茅屋全給大雪覆蓋了，只見煙囱裏冒出來的熱氣在積雪中融化成一個窟窿，被一個印第安人發現，這才使一家人得救了。不過，對於我呢，至今沒有哪個友好的印第安人表示過關注；其實，對他來說也沒有必要，因為這小屋主人總是守在家裏呢。很大的雪啊！聽着，多愉悦！農夫們沒法駕着驢馬去樹林和沼澤地了；他們不得不砍倒自家門前的那些綠蔭樹；積雪變得越來越硬時，他們還要到沼澤地去砍樹，等到來年開春時一看，沒想到砍樹那塊地方，竟然離地面有十英尺高呢。

積雪最深時，從公路到我小屋的那條小路，約有半英里路長，也許可用一條彎彎曲曲的虛線標出來，每兩個圓點之間都有很大空檔。要是有個多星期裏，天氣穩定，我來來去去的時候，總是邁着同樣數目的步履，同樣大小的步伐，故意找準我獨個踩出來的足跡走路，精確得就像一副圓規——原來冬天就這樣使我們循規蹈矩走舊路呢——不過，這些足跡裏常常映現穹蒼著自己的蔚藍色。但不管是怎樣的天氣，都阻撓不了我去散步，或者外出，因為我經常為了踐約起見，在最深的雪地裏步行八或者十英里，去跟一棵山毛櫸，或者一棵黃樺樹，或者松樹林中的一個老朋友相會；積雪和冰凌壓彎了松樹的枝椏，樹梢頭顯得更尖峭，因而變成了冷杉似的；有時候，我踩着近兩英尺深的積雪，舉步維艱向高高的山頂走去，每走一步，都像另一場暴風雪衝我頭頂上撲過來；有時候，我索性用雙手和膝蓋在雪地裏爬行、拼搏，反正當時連獵戶全都回去過冬了。有一天下午，我興緻勃勃觀察一隻胸部有褐色斑紋的大林鴞[12]，牠棲息在一棵白皮松低矮的枯枝上，緊挨着樹幹，恰好是在大白天，我站的地方離它還不到一桿遠。當我走動時，兩腳踩雪的聲響，牠是聽得見的，卻看不清我。我讓兩腳在雪地裏踩得猛響時，只見它的脖子就伸了出來，脖頸羽毛豎立起來，眼睛也睜得大大的；但牠的眼瞼卻很快又閉上，開始打起盹來了。我觀察牠半個小時之後，自己也有點睡眼惺忪，看牠就這樣兩眼半睜半閉着，棲息在那裏，像一隻貓，或者換句話說，像貓長了翅膀的兄弟。牠的眼瞼之間只留着一道窄縫，這樣，牠和我就保持了一種半島狀的關係吧；牠就這麼兩眼半睜半閉，從夢幻中往外觀望，極力想知道我是甚麼人：是一個模糊不清的物體，抑或是遮住牠視線的一顆塵埃。最後，也許是某個更大聲響，也許是我越走越近的緣故，牠就顯得很不自在了，在棲枝上懶洋洋轉了個身，彷彿牠的美夢給攪亂了而很不耐煩似的。於是，牠展翅起飛，穿過松樹林，將牠的翅膀舒展到了令人始料不及的極致，但我卻一點響聲都聽不見。就這樣，牠不是靠視力，而是憑藉牠對周邊環境的靈敏感覺，在松樹枝椏之間飛來飛去，彷彿牠的羽毛都是極其敏感，能在昏暗中摸索自己的飛行路線。於是，牠終於找到了一個新的棲枝，也許牠就會在那裏安靜等待牠的白晝到來。

我從橫貫草地長長的鐵路堤岸上走過時，一陣砭人肌骨的寒風迎面刮來，因為它只有到了這裏，刮起來才算最痛快淋漓；反正冰霜猛打我的左頰，儘管我是一個異教徒，我也還是照樣將右頰送了過去[13]從布里斯特山上來的火車道上，也好不了多少。反正我還是要到鎮上去，就像一個友好的印第安人，漫山遍野的積雪在瓦爾登路兩側有如牆壁似的堆積起來，只需半個小時，風雪定會掩蓋了行人的足跡。我回來的時候，就在新形成的積雪裏跟蹌掙扎過，西北風很匆忙在大路一個急拐處積存了粉狀白雪，那裏連一隻兔子的足跡都看不到，更不用說一隻草地老鼠的些許足跡了。但不管怎麼說，即使在寒冬季節，我也還看過暖和而鬆軟的沼澤地上，野草和臭菘依然永久常綠，一些耐寒飛禽有時偶然會來這裏，等待大地回春呢。

有時候，雖說冰天雪地，我傍晚散步回來，會發現樵夫從我家裏走出來的深深腳印，在壁爐上頭還有他削好的一堆碎木片，屋裏充滿他抽煙的味道。或者，在一個星期天的下午，如果碰巧我在家，聽得見一個精明的農夫踩雪時唞嚓唞嚓的腳步聲。他是一個長臉的農夫，大老遠穿過樹林，找上門來拉關係，閒談聊天；他是少數"在自家農場"種莊稼的人之一；他身上穿的不是教授的長袍，而是一套工作服，他說話時動不動會援引教會或者國家的那些仁義道德，就像他從牲口棚裏拉出一車糞肥似的。我們談到了原始時代的簡樸生活，那時候，人們在冷得反而有精神的天氣裏，圍坐在一大堆篝火邊，個個頭腦清醒；如果說沒有其他甜點助興，那我們就不妨拿自己的牙齒來試一試，聰明的松鼠老早丟掉許多堅果，因為那些堅果雖然外殼很厚，其實往往都是空心的。

有一位詩人 [14] 頂着駭人的暴風雪，踩着深不可測的積雪，大老遠趕到寒舍來作客。哪怕是一個農夫、一個獵戶、一個大兵、一個記者，乃至於一個哲學家，都有可能給嚇退了；但是，甚麼也不能嚇住一個詩人，因為他的一切都從純粹的愛出發的。他的來來去去，有誰能預測呢？他的職業就像醫生，哪怕上牀睡覺了，也隨時被叫喚出門應診去。我們使這個小屋裏歡聲笑語不絕於耳，而且許多輕聲細語的清醒的談話也在迴響着，這就彌補了瓦爾登谷地很久以來的沉默。相形之下，百老匯 [15] 也會顯得冷清而又荒涼了。我們兩人不時縱聲大笑，也許是因為剛才脫口而出的一句妙語，要不就是因為正要說到的一則笑話。我們一邊喝稀粥，一邊談論許多"嶄新"的人生哲學，而這碗稀粥卻將宴飲之樂和哲學所必需的頭腦清醒融合在一起了。

我可忘不了，我在湖邊最後的一個冬天，還有一個深受歡迎的來客 [16]，有一次，他穿過樹林，頂着雨雪，摸黑趕來，後來從樹叢裏瞥見了我的燈光，於是跟我一起度過幾個漫長冬夜。最後一批哲學家裏面的一位 —— 康涅狄格州推他向世界 —— 早先他是兜售康涅狄格州的商品，後來，據他自己所說，就兜售他的頭腦了。他至今依然在兜售頭腦，讚揚上帝，貶損世人，唯獨他的頭腦能結出果實，就像堅果裏面有果肉一樣。我想，他必定是當今世界上還活着最虔誠的人裏面的一個。他的話語和態度始終表明，一切事物都比別人所瞭解的好得多；而由於時代在演進，也許他會成為感到失望的最後一個人。現在他還沒有甚麼冒險行動。雖然當今人們不怎麼理會他，但是他一旦旗開得勝，大多數人意想不到的法則就見效了，一家之主和統治者們都會來向他求教的 —— 看不到清澈的人是多麼盲目啊！[17] 人類的一個真正朋友，幾乎也是人類進步的唯一朋友了。一個古老的凡夫俗子，還不如說是一個不朽之人，懷着不倦的耐心與信念，闡明深深印在人身上的形象，他們的上帝實際上只是一些殘碑斷碣罷了。他既親熱又聰明，體察孩子、乞丐、瘋子、學者，他對各種思想兼容並蓄，還常常使它博大精深。我想，他應該在世界大道上開設一家旅館，各國哲學家都可以來投宿，他的招牌上應該寫上："賓至如歸，役畜免進。凡有閒暇、心境平和、熱切地尋求正道的人，請進來。"在我認識的人裏面，也許就數他神智最健全，怪主意也最少；他昨天是甚麼樣，明天也還是甚麼樣。從前，我們兩人一起漫步、聊天，完全將俗世凡塵置諸腦後；因為他沒有向世上任何制度起過誓，是個生來自由自在的性情中人。不論我們轉身走向何處，好像天地都渾然一體了，因為他使湖光山色顯得更美麗。一個身穿藍衣服的人，他覺得最合適的屋頂，就是映現他心境寧靜的穹蒼。我看不出他怎麼會死去；大自然還捨不得他呢。

　　我們各自攤開思想來談，就像拿木片出來晾乾似的；我們坐了下來削木片削得尖尖的，一邊試試我們的刀鋒，一邊欣賞那些松木中清晰的黃色紋理。我們如此虔敬地輕輕涉水而過，或者說我們如此平平穩穩地攜手並進，因此，我們思想中的魚既沒有從小溪中被嚇跑，也不害怕在岸邊垂釣的人，而是快活地游來游去，宛如西邊天空上飄過的浮雲，那五光十色的雲團在那裏時而形成，時而消散。在那裏，我們做作業，考訂神話，潤飾寓言，構建空中樓閣，因為大地上提供不了良好基地。了不起的觀察家！了不起的預言家！跟他思想交流不僅是新英格蘭夜譚啊！啊！我們，隱士和哲學家，還有我提到過的那個老移民——我們三個人——就這樣侃侃而談，談得我的小屋彷彿在不斷膨脹、搖晃；我可不敢說，在每一個直徑為一英寸的圓圈上，要承受這種氣氛重達多少磅的壓力；小屋已裂開了縫，以後就得填塞很多東西，才能防止洩漏——反正這類填絮我早已準備足夠了。

　　此外，還有一個人[18]，我和他在他的村舍裏一起度過久久難忘的

"美好時光"，而他也不時到我的小屋來；除此以外，我在這裏再也沒有跟其他甚麼人有交往了。

反正不管到哪裏都一樣，有時我也期盼過那些必不會來的客人。毗瑟拿·普納那印度教的主神之一 説："傍晚時份，主人始終要守在院子裏，等上擠完一頭乳牛的時間 —— 或者時間更長些，如果説他樂意的話 —— 鵠候客人到來。"我常常恪盡這種好客的職守，等上很長很長時間，足夠擠完一羣乳牛，無奈我總是沒看見一個人從城裏走來。

章註

1　漆樹：拉丁文學名 Rhusglabra。
2　黃花：拉丁文學名 Solidago stricta。
3　"西皮奧·布里斯特"阿非利加努斯 (Scipio Africanus，公元前 237—公元前 183)，古羅馬將軍，入侵非洲。他的名字 Scipio 與布里斯特 Sippio 相近，他的姓 Africanus 與非洲 Africa 同一個字根，亦與布里斯特是黑人有關。—— 他倒是有資格叫做西庇奧·阿非利加努斯的。
4　戴夫南特 (Sir William Davenant，1606—1668) 英國詩人，劇作家兼劇院經理，著有喜劇《眾才子》、假面劇《愛之神殿》和詩集《馬達加斯加》等，創作英國第一部公演歌劇《圍攻羅得島》，有莎士比亞 "精神之子" 美譽。
5　查爾默斯 (Alexander Charmers，1759—1834) 是英國劇作家。
6　原文 Nervii，原指公元前 57 年被凱撒打敗的一個北方歐洲部落，而梭羅寫到此處，意思是查爾默斯的詩選征服了他的神經系統，可謂一語雙關。
7　老爺船：指行動緩慢的救火車。
8　縣裏治安官大多由民選產生。
9　陶輪：也叫拉坯輪，陶工使用的一種踩動腳踏板時能旋轉的水平盤。
10　如果寫成科爾也無妨。
11　狐列那：寓言和民間故事中狐狸的名字；列那狐指中世紀法國敘事詩《列那狐的故事》中的著名形象。
12　大林鵰：拉丁文學名 Strix nebulose。
13　參見《聖經·新約全書》，書中要求基督徒，別人打你的左臉，你還將右臉送上去，藉以化解矛盾，所以，梭羅在此處有 "異教徒" 的説法。
14　此處指詩人錢寧。
15　百老匯：紐約劇場等娛樂場所集中之地，以繁華熱鬧聞名全球。
16　來客：指阿爾科特 (Amos Bronson Alcott)，美國超驗主義哲學家和教育家。

其女乃是美國文學名著《小婦人》的作者。

17　此句引自托馬斯‧斯托勒（Thomas Storer）所寫的《托馬斯‧華斯萊傳》（1599）。其中 Serenity 一詞，意思是"清澈、安詳、平靜、晴朗"，但在大寫時，詞義為"尊貴的閣下"，由此可見，梭羅在此使用該詞，頗有一語雙關之深意。

18　此處指美國著名作家愛默生（Ralph Waldo Emerson， 1802—1882），梭羅的鄰居、朋友、導師，對梭羅一生影響極大。

19　毗瑟拿‧普納那印度教的主神之一，守護神。

15
越冬鳥獸

各個湖裏通通凍成堅冰時，不僅有了通往許多地點的嶄新捷徑，而且，從湖面上環視周圍熟悉的景色，也有了新的視野。從前，我常常蕩舟於佛林特湖上，還在湖面上溜過冰，但我穿過大雪覆蓋後的湖面時，意料之外覺得它顯得那麼寬闊，那麼陌生，使我不由得想起了巴芬灣[1]。舉目四望，只見林肯的羣山屹立在皚皚白雪的平原上，我已記不起往昔自己在那裏駐足過的一些地方；在冰凌上確實分不出遠近，漁夫牽着他們的狼狗慢慢走着，活像是捕海豹的獵戶，或者像愛斯基摩人似的；或者換句話說，在霧沉沉的天氣裏，如同神話傳說裏的生靈忽隱忽現，我真弄不清楚他們究竟是巨人呢，還是侏儒。我晚上到林肯去演講時，走的就是這條路，反正從我的小屋到演講室之間，我既不走其他的路，也不路過誰的家門口。在途中要經過鵝湖，那處是一羣土撥鼠的棲居地，牠們的小窩棚在冰凌上高高隆起，我路過時卻沒見過一隻土撥鼠在外頭。瓦爾登湖跟其他幾個湖一樣，通常積不了雪的，至多只有零碎的一層薄冰漂浮在湖面上。等到別處積雪平均達到將近兩英尺深時，我倒是可以在瓦爾登湖面上優閒散步，而村民們卻被圍困在自己的街區裏。這裏，遠離村裏的街道，很難聽得見雪橇上鈴鐺響聲，我在冰凌上又滑雪、又溜冰，彷彿置身於一個被踩平了的巨大鹿苑之中，那裏矗立着橡樹和肅穆的松樹，它們不是被大雪壓得低低的，便是倒掛着一根根冰柱。

冬天的夜裏，就算白天也一樣，我常聽到遠處傳來貓頭鷹的叫聲，淒涼卻又悅耳，這種聲音彷彿是冰凍的大地用合適的琴撥彈奏時發出來的，正是地地道道的瓦爾登樹林的土話 [2]，儘管這鳥兒鳴叫時我從來沒見過，但後來我對這種叫聲倒也耳熟能詳了。冬夜，我一推開門，往往就聽見牠那"嗚呼——嗚呼——嗚呼——嗚啦——嗚呼"的叫聲，聽上去很響亮，而且頭三個音節的發音，有點像在打招呼"你——好"似的；或者，牠有時只是不斷發出"嗚呼——嗚呼"的叫聲；初冬時節，有一天夜裏，湖裏還沒有完全結冰，大約九點鐘左右，一隻野鵝嘎嘎嘎地大叫，嚇了我一跳；我剛進家門，又聽見牠們掠過我屋頂時的拍翅聲，就像一陣風暴打從樹林裏穿過似的。牠們越過湖面，向美港飛去，見到我的燈光，好像不敢逗留，領頭鵝一路上總是發出節奏分明的叫喚聲。突然之間，有一隻貓頭鷹從離我很近的地方，發出非常刺耳並令人發顫的叫聲；這種叫聲在樹林裏居民中，我從來沒聽過，卻不時回答了那隻野鵝的叫聲，彷彿發了狠，讓這個來自赫德遜灣的入侵者曝光和獻醜，牠的叫聲越來越大、越來越響亮，還是那麼一副土腔土調："嗚呼——嗚呼"，看起來非逐它們出康科德的藍空不可。在這深更半夜，你來驚擾我那神聖不可侵犯的城堡，究竟是甚麼意思？你以為我一到夜裏這個時刻睡着了，就沒有你那樣的肺活量和嗓門嗎？"波嗚——嗚呼，波嗚——嗚呼，波嗚——嗚呼！"這種讓人震顫不止的噪音，我真的還從來沒聽到過呢。不過，你要是耳朵特別靈，能夠審辨音素，那就能從中聽得出有一些十分和諧的音素，類似這樣的音素，原野上倒是從來沒有看過，也還沒有聽過呢。

　　我還聽得見湖上冰凌發出窸窸窣窣的聲響，湖是和我一起睡在康科德這張牀上的大夥伴，好像在牀上總是靜不下來，只好翻來覆去，同時，還要為腸胃氣脹、再三做噩夢而發愁；要不是這樣，我會被嚴寒凍裂地面時的巨響驚醒，彷彿這時有人趕着一套馬車，不知怎的撞着了我的家門，我一早起來，定神一看，地上果真有了一道大裂縫，四份之一英里長，三份之一英寸寬。

有時候，在明月皎潔的夜晚，我聽見狐狸爬過雪地，尋覓鷓鴣或其他甚麼飛禽，像森林裏的惡狗一樣發出妖魔般刺耳的吠叫聲；牠們彷彿火急萬分，或者說想表現些甚麼，拼命追求光明，借此立刻變成犬獒，到街上自由自在地奔跑；如果說我們考慮到各個時代演進歷程，難道野獸中間不是像人類一樣，也存在着一種文明嗎？我反而覺得牠們像穴居的原始人，仍然在捍衛着牠們自己，等待學我們變形的那一天。有時候，一隻狐狸會被我的燈光引誘，走到我窗戶跟前，像吠叫似的衝我發出一聲狐狸的詛咒，隨即轉身溜走。

通常紅松鼠[3]會在天濛濛亮時吵醒我，因為牠在屋頂上跑來跑去，在屋內四壁爬上爬下，好像牠從樹林跑出來，為的就是叫醒我。過冬的時候，我會把八成還沒有成熟的甜玉米穗撒在我門前的雪地上，稍後，我興致勃勃地觀察被引誘來的各種動物競相爭食的場面。從黃昏到夜深，兔子常來這裏飽餐一頓。紅松鼠整天這樣來來去去，牠那種機靈敏捷真的給我莫大樂趣。開始的時候，有一隻紅松鼠小心翼翼走近去，穿過低矮的橡樹叢，在雪地上四處跑跑停停，像一片隨風飄舞的樹葉，忽然往這個方向躥出去好幾步遠，速度快得出奇之餘也耗廢不少精力，牠"快步迅跑"那種匆匆的樣子簡直令人難以想像，似乎牠是不惜孤注一擲似的；一會牠又往那一邊跑出去好幾步遠，但每一次絕不超過半桿遠；看牠又突然停了下來，擺出一個滑稽亮相，接着翻了一個筋斗，令人莫名其妙，彷彿整個宇宙的眼睛全都定格直盯住牠似的 —— 因為一隻松鼠的所有動作，哪怕是在最孤寂、最幽靜的大森林深處，也像一個跳舞女郎會吸引住那麼多的觀眾 —— 可惜那麼多的時間浪費在它磨磨蹭蹭，不斷來回兜圈，要不然牠早就跑完全程了 —— 我從來沒見過一隻松鼠是一步又一步地直接走過去的 —— 這時，牠又突然停了下來，眨眼間，牠早已躥上了一棵小油松的樹頂，隨後旋緊了牠的發條似的，責罵着所有想像中的觀眾，同時，牠既像個人在獨白，又像在跟整個宇宙對話 —— 箇中緣由，我一點猜不出來，我想，或許連牠自己也不見得知道吧。最後，牠不管怎樣挨近了玉米穗，從裏面選好合意的一個，還是那樣蹦蹦跳跳，按着原來很不固定的三角形路線，直躥到我窗前那個木柴堆上，到了那裏，牠就眼定定直望着我，而且等了幾個小時，時不時為自己辦新的玉米穗，開始時狼吞虎嚥亂啃一通，扔掉啃過一半的玉米芯。後來，牠越來越挑三揀四，拿牠的食物玩耍，僅僅淺嚐一下玉米粒。牠用一隻爪抓住玉米穗擱在柴火棍上，但一不小心掉在地上，牠露出一種茫然不知所措的滑稽表情，低下頭看着那玉米穗，好像懷疑那掉下來的玉米穗是不是也有生命，拿不定主意，該不該再撿起它，或者另叼一個新的，或者乾脆走開算了；牠一會想到那玉米穗，一會又聽聽風聲中有甚麼動靜。就這樣，這個隨性的小傢伙一上午糟蹋了許多玉米穗；最後，牠抓起了一個長一點、粗一點，比牠大很多的玉米穗，不管怎樣牠拖住玉米穗，朝着樹林走去，就像一隻老虎拖着一頭大水牛，同樣照着原來路線，左拐右彎，走走停停，還拖着玉米穗，真夠累的；牠覺得彷彿這個玉米穗太沉重，動不動掉在地上，於是，牠讓玉米穗循着垂直線與地平線之間對角線方向移動，不管怎樣，硬要拉它回去 —— 好一個輕浮古怪的傢伙 —— 牠就這般拖它到自己的棲居地，也許是在四五十桿遠一棵松樹的頂上；後來，我總會在樹林裏發現那些到處亂扔的玉米芯。

最後，鳥來了，牠們刺耳的尖叫聲早就聽到了；牠們在八份之一英里之外，小心翼翼飛過來，從這一棵樹不動聲息飛到另一棵樹，越飛越近，撿起了松鼠們掉在地上的玉米粒。隨後，牠們落在一棵油松的樹枝上，匆匆吞下玉米粒，不料玉米粒太大，哽在喉嚨口，差點噎死；牠們費了很大氣力，才吐了玉米粒出來，接着花上個多小時，用牠們的尖喙啄呀啄的，好不容易啄碎了玉米粒。牠們分明是一幫盜賊，我對牠們一點好感都沒有。至於松鼠呢，雖說牠們一開始有點羞羞答答，之後動起手腳時卻像在拿屬於自己的東西似的。

就在這個時候，飛來三五成羣的山雀，銜起松鼠們掉在地上的屑粒，飛到了最近的樹枝上，用爪抓住屑粒，用小小尖喙啄開，彷彿那是樹皮裏面的一隻小昆蟲，直到屑粒被啄得又細又小，能從牠們纖細的喉嚨裏咽下去。每天都有一小羣類似這樣的山雀，到我柴火堆前享受一頓午餐，或者到我的門前來啄食屑粒，歡蹦亂跳，發出微弱的喞啾聲，好像草叢裏冰柱的丁零聲。要不然牠們發出“得、得、得”的叫喚聲，或者更難得的是，在有幾分春天氣息的日子裏，牠們從樹林邊上發出夏日常見類似彈琴的“菲—比”的鳴叫聲。久而久之，牠們竟然跟我熟悉起來，後來有一隻鳥兒落在我捆抱進來的柴火上，無所畏懼啄起那些細小枝條。有一次，我在村中園子裏鋤草，忽然一隻麻雀落在我肩上，逗留了一會，此時此刻，我覺得自己特別風光，哪怕我佩戴過甚麼榮譽肩章，也都沒法與之相比。一來二去的，松鼠們最後都跟我很熟了，偶然走近時，甚至會從我鞋上踩過去。

大地上一直不再是素裹銀裝，冬天也接近了尾聲，積雪已開始在南山坡和我的柴火堆上融化，這時，鳥早晚從樹林裏飛出來，到這裏覓食。在樹林裏，不管你走到哪一邊，鳥都會拍打着翅膀忽然飛出來，抖落上面枯黃樹枝上的積雪，在陽光中飛濺的雪花就像金燦燦的塵埃似的；原來這種勇敢的鳥兒根本不怕冬天。牠們常常會被積雪覆蓋，據說：“有時在飛行中還會一頭紮進軟綿綿的雪堆裏，藏身在那裏長達一兩天之久。”落日偏西時，牠們會飛出樹林，到曠野裏啄食野蘋果樹上的“嫩芽”，所以，我還常在那裏嚇得牠們慌忙飛走。每到傍晚，牠們都會定時落在某些慣常棲息的樹上，狡猾的獵人正在那裏守候牠們，這時緊挨着樹林的遠處果園也都會遭了殃。我很高興，反正鳥兒不管怎樣都能找到可吃的東西。牠們以啄芽、飲晨露為生，本來就是大自然自己的鳥兒。

在昏暗的冬天早晨，或者在短暫的冬天午後，有時候，我會聽到一大羣獵犬狂吠，遏制不住自己追腥逐臭的本能，正在樹林裏搜索，圍獵的號角時不時吹響，證明獵人就緊跟在後面。獵犬的狂吠聲在樹林裏再次響起，但並沒有狐狸躥到湖邊的開闊地，那夥獵人也沒跟上來，對他們的亞克托安 [4] 窮追不捨。說不定在黃昏時份，我看到獵戶回來了，正在尋找旅館過夜，只見他們的雪橇後面拖着一條狐狸尾巴，就算是他們的戰利品吧。人們告訴我，說狐狸只要躲在冰凍的地底下，肯定萬無一失，或者說，狐狸只要向前直奔，獵狐犬休想追得上牠；但是，遠遠拋離那批獵犬在後的狐狸，停下來歇口氣，豎起耳朵聽着，直到獵犬們又追上來了，這時，狐狸卻繞着圈子中途折回自己的老窩去，怎料，獵戶們正好在那裏守候着。不過，有時候，狐狸會偶然發現好幾桿遠有一堵牆，於是縱身一躍，躥到了牆的另一邊，似乎牠知道狐臭一遇到水就沒有了。有一個獵人告訴我，說有一次，他看見一頭被獵犬猛追的狐狸，一下子躥到了瓦爾登湖，湖裏冰凌上恰好有淺淺的一層水，牠跑了半程路，又折回到了原先的湖岸上。沒多久，獵犬們匆匆趕到了，可是這裏卻怎麼都聞不到狐臭了。有時候，一羣獵犬會互相不停追逐，繞着我的小屋打轉，一邊追逐一邊狂吠，根本不理我，彷彿患上某種瘋狂症，反正怎麼也都阻止不了牠們一直互相追逐。就這樣，牠們總是繞着圈追逐，沒多久終於找到一隻狐狸的新蹤跡，因為哪怕只有一絲狐狸的蹤跡，聰明的獵犬也絕不會輕易放棄的。有一天，一個來自列克星敦的人到我的小屋來打聽他那匆匆離去的獵犬的下落，他本人一直在找牠，已有一個星期了。不過，我想，就算我將一切向他和盤托出，恐怕他也不能完全明白，因為我每次打算回答他的問題，他都打斷了我，說："你在這裏做甚麼呀？"他丟掉了一隻狗，卻找到了一個人。

有一個老獵戶，說起話來總是乾巴巴的；他每年照例來瓦爾登湖洗一次澡，總是在湖水最暖熱的時候，還會順便過來看看我，告訴我，說許多年以前，有一天下午，他只帶一支獵槍，到瓦爾登樹林裏去巡邏；他正行走在韋蘭德路上時，忽然聽見獵犬們的吠叫聲越來越近，過不了多久，一頭狐狸躍過沿牆躥到了大路上，一瞬間又躍過了另一道沿牆，從大路上逃跑了；他馬上舉槍射擊，無奈絲毫沒有碰着牠。從後面不遠處來了一隻老獵犬，帶着牠的三隻幼犬，全力追擊，各自在搜尋，轉眼卻又消失在樹林裏。下午後半晌，他正在瓦爾登南邊密林裏休息，忽然聽見獵犬遠遠朝美港方向，繼續追捕狐狸所發出的叫聲；牠們正衝着這處過來，牠們的吠叫聲在整個樹林裏迴響，彷彿越來越近，一會從威爾草地傳過來，一會又從貝克農場傳過來。他絲毫不動，停了下來，站在那裏半天，一直在聆聽牠們的音樂之聲，這在獵戶的耳朵裏聽起來真美極了。這時，狐狸突然出現了，輕快地穿過林中小徑，牠的響聲已被樹葉深表同情的颯颯聲所遮蓋，只見牠一會反應特快，一會又安靜下來，守住陣腳，牠的追捕者遠遠給拋在後面；稍後，牠躍上了樹林裏的一塊岩石，直着身體坐下來，聽聽動靜，後背卻朝着那個獵人。一瞬間，後者被惻隱之心所掣肘；然而，他的這一個閃念卻轉瞬即逝。反正說時遲，那時快，他一舉起獵槍，砰的一聲——那隻狐狸立時被擊斃，從岩石上滾落到地上。那獵人還在原地守候，傾聽獵犬的聲響。牠們還在四處追逐，這時，牠們惡魔般的狂吠聲在鄰近樹林裏所有小徑的上空迴響着。最後，那頭老獵犬突然映入獵人眼簾，牠用鼻亂嗅着地面，好像着了魔似的朝天大聲吠叫，稍後就直奔那塊岩石；怎料牠一看見那隻死狐狸就突然停止追獵，彷彿受了驚嚇，噤若寒蟬，繞着死狐狸一聲不響來回打轉；牠的幼犬一隻隻先後趕來了，像牠們的母親一樣，這眼前的啞謎也使牠們一聲不響。此後，那獵人走了過去，站在牠們中間，這啞謎才算揭開了。獵人剝下狐狸的毛皮，牠們靜靜等着，稍後，跟在狐狸尾巴後面走了一會，最後又折回樹林裏了。當天晚上，一位韋斯頓的鄉紳到那個康科德的獵戶的小屋裏，打聽他那些獵犬的情況，還告訴他說這幾隻獵犬離開韋斯頓樹林，各自追捕獵物，已有個多星期了。康科德的老獵戶把自己所知道的告訴了他，還要送狐皮給他；但是，那位鄉紳卻謝絕了，隨即告辭離去。那天夜裏，老獵戶沒有找到他的獵犬，不過次天就知道，牠們過了河，在一個農夫家裏宿了一夜，還在那裏飽餐一頓，一大早便離去了。

給我講這個故事的獵人，還記得有一個名叫山姆·納丁的人，常在美港岸礁那裏獵熊，拿着熊皮到康科德村裏換朗姆酒 5 喝。獵熊人告訴他，說他在那裏甚至還見到過一隻駝鹿呢。納丁養了一條很有名的獵狐犬，名叫布爾戈因 —— 他卻讀成了"布金" —— 給我講故事的老獵戶，經常去借納丁那條獵狐犬。鎮上有一個做生意的老頭，他既是老闆，又是鎮上文書兼代表。在他的"流水賬"裏，我看到了以下記載：1742 年至 1743 年 1 月 18 日，"約翰·梅爾文，貸方，一隻灰狐狸，兩角三分"；現在這種事在這裏已見不到了；在他的流水賬裏，1743 年 2 月 7 日，赫澤吉亞·斯塔拉頓，貸方，"半張貓皮，一角四分半"；不用說，是一張野貓皮，因為斯塔拉頓從前當過中士，參加過法蘭西之戰，不會為連野貓也不如的獵物去借錢。那個年代也有人以獵取鹿皮得到貸款的，每天都有鹿皮出售。有一個人至今還收藏着此地附近獵殺得到，最後一隻鹿的鹿角。還有一個人告訴我他的叔父參加一次狩獵活動的詳情。過去，此地獵戶人數眾多，日子過得快快樂樂。我至今還記得，有一個瘦骨嶙峋的人，名叫寧錄 6，他在路邊隨手摘一片樹葉，就能用它吹奏出一些歌曲來，如果我沒有記錯的話，甚至比狩獵的號角還要粗獷、好聽呢。

子夜時份，皓月當空，有時我路上會碰到好些獵犬，牠們都在樹林裏東奔西竄，卻會閃開，給我讓路，彷彿有點害怕似的，站在灌木叢裏不發一聲，直到我走過去才出來。

松鼠和野鼠為了我儲存的堅果爭吵不休。在我的小屋周圍有幾十棵油松，直徑從一英寸到四英寸都有，去年冬天全給老鼠啃過 —— 牠們覺得那好像是一個挪威式的冬天，因為雪下的時間很長，積雪又很厚，牠們不得不混雜大量樹皮和其他食物。這些樹木還可以活着，入夏後看來長得還很茂盛，其中有好些樹木居然長高了一英尺，雖然被啃去了一圈樹皮；怎料又過了一冬，這些樹卻全都死了，無一例外。説來也真怪，小小一隻老鼠竟然能吃掉整整一棵大樹，牠不是自上而下一口口啃的，而是繞着樹幹一圈圈啃的；不過話又説回來，為了讓樹木之間長得稀疏些，也許這還是必要的，不然的話，樹木常常會長得密不透風。

野兔子[7]是最常見的。有一隻兔子在我的小屋底下過了整整一個冬天，跟我僅僅隔了一層地板；每天早上，我剛開始走動，牠就匆匆離去，嚇了我一跳 —— 砰、砰、砰，牠由於慌不擇路，連腦袋都撞到了我的地板底柱上。傍晚時份，牠們常到我家門前踅來踅去，啃着我扔掉的馬鈴薯皮，牠們跟地面的顏色如此相近，在牠們靜止不動時，兩者簡直難以識別。有時，在暮色蒼茫之中，我的窗戶底下有一隻紋風不動的小兔子，突然映入眼簾，忽然又倏地不見了。晚上，我一打開門，牠們吱的一聲四散逃竄。反正跟我那麼近，它們只會使我為之動憐。有一天晚上，一隻兔子留在我家門口，離我僅僅兩步遠，一開始就渾身發抖，硬是不肯離去，好一隻可憐的小東西，瘦骨嶙峋、破耳朵、尖鼻子、短尾巴、細爪子，看上去好像大自然再也沒有甚麼更高貴的品種，只剩下牠這隻醜八怪。牠那大大的眼睛看起來還年輕，但不健康，幾乎像得了水腫似的。我往前走了一步，哦，只見牠運用彈跳力，縱身一躍，牠的身體和四肢以優美姿態伸展開來，就躥過了雪地，一瞬間使樹林介乎我和牠自己中間了 —— 這充滿野性自由的筋肉，體現了大自然的活力和尊嚴。牠之所以長得修長，並不是沒有緣由的。那是牠的天性使然。[8]

鄉下要是沒有野兔子和鷓鴣，那還算是甚麼鄉下呢？牠們土生土長，是最簡單的動物；屬古老的目科動物，不論在古代和現代都很出名；

與大自然有同樣色彩，同樣實質，與樹葉和大地又有最近的親緣——牠們互相之間更有親緣；牠們不是長翅膀，便是長腿腳。兔子和鷓鴣要是突然不翼而飛了，你很難覺得牠們是一種野性未馴的動物，反而會看作大自然的一部份，完全就像颯颯作響的樹葉一樣。不管發生甚麼樣的革命，鷓鴣和兔子肯定會繁衍生息下去。如果說森林被砍掉了，樹苗和灌木叢還會長出來給牠們藏身，牠們就會繁殖得比過去更多。連一隻兔子都養不活的鄉下，說實話，必定是窮鄉僻壤。我們的樹林裏有的是這兩種動物，每一片沼澤地上，都會看到鷓鴣和兔子在走動，可惜沼澤地的四周，牛仔們往往會用樹枝圍上了柵籬，還用馬鬃設置陷阱。

章註

1　巴芬灣：位於格陵蘭島和加拿大的巴芬島之間。

2　原文是 lingua vernacula（拉丁文），意思是"方言"或"土話"。

3　紅松鼠：拉丁文學名 Sciurus Hudsonius。

4　亞克托安：古希臘神話中的一個獵手，因看狩獵女神狄安娜沐浴，被狄安娜變成一頭牝鹿，最終被他自己的獵犬撕成了碎片。

5　朗姆酒：英美人愛喝的一種甜酒。

6　寧錄：《聖經》中的一個英勇獵戶，後來以寧錄一詞泛指獵人。

7　野兔子：拉丁文學名 Lepus Amerlcanus。

8　拉丁文學名：Lepus，源自 Levipes，有人認為是"蹄疾如飛"的意思。

16

冬日瓦爾登湖

我度過了一個寂靜的冬夜，醒來時依稀記得彷彿有人向我提問，比方說，甚麼啦 —— 怎麼啦 —— 在甚麼時候 —— 在甚麼地方？睡夢中我很想一一回答，結果還是徒勞。但是，黎明時份，萬物片刻不可離的大自然，臉呈寧靜、滿意的神情，直望着我那寬大的窗戶，她的唇邊倒是看不出在提問。我意識到了那道答題，意識到了大自然和天光大亮。大雪深深覆蓋着幼松點染的大地，我的小屋所在的小山坡，似乎在說：前進吧！大自然並沒有提問，對我們凡夫俗子的提問一概不予回答。她很早就下過決心了。"啊，王子，我們兩眼充滿崇敬傾慕，並在凝思默想，將這宇宙間奇妙多變的景象傳達給靈魂。毫無疑問，黑夜掩蓋了這光輝創造的一部份；然而，白晝來了，給我們顯示了這一傑作，從大地一直延伸到浩茫的穹蒼。"

然後，該是我忙早上的工作去了。首先，我拿了一把斧頭和提桶，外出找水去，但願不是在做夢吧。度過一個寒冷的雪夜以後，找水還真少不得有一根占卜杖才好。平日裏湖面水波蕩漾，對一絲微風都很敏感，常常映現出閃光和倒影；但一到每年冬天，湖裏冰凌結得很堅實，深達一英尺或者一英尺半，就算是最沉重的馬車都能承受得住；也許大雪覆蓋得跟冰凌一般深，你很難識別是在湖上還是在平地上。像周圍羣山中的土撥鼠，牠閉着眼進入冬眠，可以長達三個月或者三個月以上。站在大雪覆蓋的平原上，好似在羣山中的一塊草場，我先要穿過一英尺深的雪地，接下來是一英尺厚的冰凌，在我腳下開一個窗口，跪了下來喝水，俯瞰水下魚兒們寧靜的廳堂，那裏充滿了柔和的亮光，好像透過一塊磨砂玻璃窗照進去的，亮閃閃的細沙湖底和夏天的時候一模一樣；在這裏，常年水波不興，始終是一片靜謐，就像黃昏時琥珀色的天空，這倒是跟水中居民的冷靜而和順的氣質息息相通。天空在我們的腳下，也在我們的頭上。[1]

大清早，經過霜凍後顯得格外寒冷，人們帶上釣竿和午餐便當，拋釣線到雪地下面來釣狗魚和鱸魚；這一班野腔野氣的人，看來不像是他們的城裏人，他們本能地採用其他生活方式，相信其他權威，他們就這樣來來去去，縫合起許多城市部份，要不然，這些城市互相之間還是毫無關聯的。他們穿着厚實的粗絨大衣，坐在湖邊乾枯的橡樹葉上吃午餐，他們一說到自然知識總是頭頭是道，就像城裏人會矯揉造作一樣聰明。他們從來不求教書本，他們的動手能力大大地超過他們所掌握的並可傳授的知識。他們做過的許多事，據說至今還沒有人知道。這裏就有一位，常用大鱸魚作誘餌去釣狗魚。你看着他的木桶好不奇怪，就像看到了夏日裏的湖，彷彿他鎖好夏天，藏它在自己家裏，或者說他知道夏天已躲藏到哪裏去了。請問，隆冬季節，他怎麼會捕到這麼多魚呢？哦，地上到處凍了冰，但他從爛木頭裏尋到昆蟲，所以，他擔保能釣得到那麼多魚。他的生活原本就是在大自然裏度過的，比博物學家[2]的研究還要深入得多；他本人就是博物學家研究的對象。博物學家用刀輕輕揭去苔蘚和樹皮，從裏面尋找昆蟲；但他只需要一斧頭下去，就劈開樹芯，但見苔蘚和樹皮一下子飛得老遠老遠。他就靠剝樹皮為生。這樣的人就有權釣魚，我很喜歡看到大自然在他身上顯靈呢。鱸魚吃蟎蟲，狗魚吃鱸魚，漁夫吃狗魚；生物等級中所有空隙就是這樣給填滿的。

霧沉沉的天氣裏，我沿湖散步，有時看到一些比較粗獷的漁夫所採用的原始方式，我覺得很有趣。冰淩上有許多個小窟窿，各自相距四五桿遠，離湖岸也有那麼遠吧，也許他就在小窟窿上面擱一些橙樹枝，拴住釣線的一端在一根樹枝上，以免被拉下水去，再在冰一英尺多遠處，將鬆散的釣線掛在橙木的一根樹枝上，上面繫一片乾枯的橡樹葉，只要這釣線被拽了下去，就說明魚已上鈎了。這些橙木樹枝在迷霧中時隱時現，間距相等，你沿湖走着走着，走過一半的時候，就可以見到了。

啊，瓦爾登湖的狗魚！我看見牠們躺在冰凌上時，或者，我從漁夫在冰凌上開鑿小小的一口井裏看到牠們的稀世之美，常常使我驚歎不已，彷彿牠們是寓言裏的神秘之魚，在城市街道上，乃至於樹林裏都是見不着的，而且在我們康科德的生活中，也像見不着阿拉伯半島一模一樣。牠們具有一種亮麗奪目、超凡脫俗的美，這種美使牠們與灰白色的鱈魚和黑鱈相比，竟有天壤之別，可是後兩種魚在我們城市街道上卻是響噹噹的。牠們沒有松樹那麼綠，也沒有岩石那麼灰，更沒有穹蒼那麼藍，依我看，牠們的色彩，很可能是舉世無雙，像花朵，像寶石，牠們儼然是珍珠，是瓦爾登湖水中生物凝結的晶核或者水晶。不用說，牠們是地地道道的瓦爾登湖；在這個動物王國中，牠們本身就是一個個小小瓦爾登，好一個瓦爾登派 [3]，令人吃驚的是牠們卻在這裏被人捕捉——這種金翠色大魚原本暢遊於泱泱深水之中，遠離瓦爾登大路上轔轔聲響的馱畜、輕便馬車和鈴聲叮噹響的雪橇。這種魚我在市場上從來沒見到過；如果上市的話，牠保證能夠吸引住人們的眼球。牠們只要身體痙攣似的扭動幾下，即時抖掉牠們濕漉漉的鬼相，就像一個凡夫俗子，雖然時限未到，卻已進入了天堂。

那消失已久的瓦爾登湖的湖底，我真恨不得它早點恢復，所以，在1846 年初，趁湖裏冰凌還沒融化之前，帶上羅盤、測鏈以及測深繩，我就對它仔細進行了勘探。至於這個湖到底有沒有湖底，歷來眾說紛紜，當然也都是一些無稽之談罷了。令人奇怪的是，人們自己既沒有測量過湖底，卻長期以來相信它是無底之湖。我在這裏附近一次散步中就曾經到過兩個所謂的"無底之湖"。許多人相信，瓦爾登湖一直通到了地球的另一邊。有的人趴在冰凌上老半天，透過那夢幻似的媒介物向下俯視，也許還看得眼裏水波蕩漾，又因害怕胸部着涼，就匆匆下了結論，說他們確實看見了許許多多巨大的窟窿，"裏面可以填塞大量乾草，"如果真的有人下去填塞的話；這裏無疑就是冥河的源泉，地獄的入口。還有一些人，從村裏拉來一個標重"五十六磅"的鐵疙瘩和滿滿一車子繩索，但他們並沒有探測到湖底；因為他們把這個"五十六磅"鐵疙瘩擱在一邊，將繩索全都慢慢放下水裏去，結果還是徒勞，怎麼也不夠長去到這神奇而深不可測的湖底。我可以切實告訴我的讀者，瓦爾登湖有一個緊密得合乎常理的湖底；湖的深度雖然深得非同尋常，但也並非不合常理。我只需要用一根釣鱈魚線，線頭上拴一塊一磅半重的石頭，扔到湖水中，很容易就能測出它的深度，因為石頭落到湖底後缺乏浮力，再往上提要費更大氣力，所以，石頭甚麼時候離開湖底，我必定能說得十分精確。湖的最深處，正好是一百零二英尺；也許還要加上後來上漲的湖水五英尺，總共是一百零七英尺。水域如此迫窄，卻有這樣的深度，確實相當可觀，但是，光憑想像力，你也絕不能再減去它的一英寸。如果說所有的湖都很淺，那又會怎麼樣？這不會在人們心靈上產生影響嗎？我真心感謝瓦爾登湖，這麼深，這麼純潔，可以作為一種象徵。既然有人相信無限，就必定有人相信有些湖是無底的。

有一個工廠主人聽說我測出了湖的深度，認為這不是真實的，因為根據他所熟悉的堤壩來判斷，湖底細沙沒法堆積在如此陡峭的坡度上。但是，即使是最深的湖，跟它們的水域相比，也沒有大多數人所想像的那麼深，而且，要是排乾湖水，再來看一看，也不會成為深不可測的谷地。它們不像羣山之間的杯狀物；而瓦爾登湖從它的面積來說，確實深得出奇，但從湖中心的垂直剖面來看，也不過像一個淺盤那麼深。大多數湖泊，排乾了水，就呈現出一片草地，並不比我常常見到的那麼低窪。威廉·吉爾平在描寫景色時既令人讚歎，而又十分準確，站在蘇格蘭法恩湖灣[4]的岬角上，他是這麼描述的："一個鹹水灣，六七十英尋深，四英里寬，大約五十英里長，羣山環抱。"他又評論說："如果說我們能在洪水泛濫之前，或者在受到天災之前，或者在大水鯨吞之前就看到了它，那麼，它定然是一個非常駭人的缺口啊！"

> 高高隆起的羣山啊！
> 谷底卻又那麼低，
> 龐大的河牀，寬闊而又深沉。[5]

我們已經看到從垂直剖面來看，瓦爾登湖只是一個淺盤，可是，如果我們拿法恩湖灣的最短一條直徑，按照相應比例來估算瓦爾登湖，那麼，瓦爾登湖看來還要淺四倍呢。法恩湖要是排乾湖水，它的缺口所增加的駭人程度，原來也不過如此罷了。毫無疑問，許多山谷好像笑吟吟似的，一直伸展到玉米地裏，正好成為大水退去之後這麼一個"駭人的缺口"，雖然這還要有地質學家的遠見和洞察力，才能使那些沒有料想到的居民相信這一事實。凡是特別好奇的眼睛，在地平線的小山上，常常可以發現一條原始湖的堤岸，平原後來就算升高了，也沒有必要去掩蓋它們的來歷。但是，經常在公路上工作的人都知道，大雨過後看一看哪裏有泥水，就最容易發現低窪地了。這意味着，只要允許想像力稍微放縱一下，就要比大自然下潛得更深，升起得更高。因此，人們會發現海洋的深度若跟它的面積相比，也許是淺得微不足道了。

我已通過冰層測量過瓦爾登湖水的深度，現在我就可以確定湖底的形狀，這比測量沒有結冰的港灣，可能還要準確得多，總的說來，湖底整齊勻稱，使我驚訝不已。湖底最深處有好幾英畝地都是平整的，幾乎勝過所有風吹日曬、被犁過的耕地。舉個實例來說，我隨便挑選了一道線，在三十桿以內，深淺不同程度不超過一英尺；一般說來，毗鄰湖心一帶，不管向哪個方向移動，我都可以預先算出，每一百英尺的變化，大約在三四英寸以內。有人常說，哪怕是像這樣平靜的細沙湖底還有許多又深邃、又危險的窟窿，但是如有這種情況，湖水早已填平了湖底全部的坑窪。湖底整齊勻稱，與湖岸以及毗鄰山脈保持着一致性，真是如此完美，即使在湖對岸，照樣能測量遙遠的岬角，而且只要觀察一下對岸，也可以確定它的走向。岬角成了沙洲和淺灘，溪谷和山峽成了深水和峽灣。

我按照十桿比一英寸的比例，繪製了一幅湖的全圖，在一百多處標明它的深度，我發現了這一驚人的一致性。注意到標明湖水最深處的地方顯然位於這幅全圖的中心，我用一根尺子在全圖最長的地方豎着畫了一道線，又在最寬的地方橫着畫了一道線，我竟然發現，這兩道線恰好在湖水最深處相交了，儘管湖中心幾乎是平坦的，但湖的輪廓卻遠不是整齊勻稱，最長的線和最寬的線是通過測量湖灣才得出來的。我自言自語道，有誰知道，這是不是暗示海洋的最深處與湖泊或者水塘的情況如出一轍呢？這一規則是不是也適用於高山，使高山與山谷可看成相對？我們知道，一座山在它的最狹處，不見得就是它的最高點。

五個湖灣裏面有三個，或者換句話說，所有我測量過的湖灣裏面，它們的出口處都有一個沙洲，裏面湖水比較深，看來這沙洲的走向不僅向內陸擴大水域，而且還向深處擴大水域，形成了一個盆地或者獨立的湖，兩個岬角的走向正好表明了沙洲的這一進程。每一個海港的入口處，也都有一個沙洲。湖灣的入口處，寬度大於長度，沙洲裏面水也要比盆地裏面的水更深些。既然已經洞悉湖灣的長度和寬度、周圍湖岸的特性，你幾乎擁有足夠資料，可以列出一個公式來，對所有情況均可適用。

根據這次經驗，我就在湖水最深處觀察它的平面輪廓和湖岸特性，查看一下我測量結果的準確性如何；我還繪製了一幅白湖的平面圖。

白湖佔地面積約有四十一英畝，跟瓦爾登湖一樣，湖中沒有島嶼，也沒有任何看得見的入水口或者出水口。由於最寬的線和最窄的線挨得非常近，就在這裏，兩個遙遙相望的岬角也越來越近，而兩個相對的沙洲卻相距越來越遠；我在最窄的線上標上一個點，但仍然落在與最長的線的交點上，作為湖水最深處的標誌。果然發現這最深處離這個點不到一百英尺，比我原定的方向再遠一點，深度只有一英尺，換句話說，是六十英尺深。當然，如果說有一道溪澗流過，或者說，湖中有一個島嶼，問題就會更錯綜複雜了。

如果說我們了解大自然的一切法則，那我們需要的只有一個事實，或者說是有關一個實際現象的描述，就可以舉一反三，得出許多各具特色的結論來。現在我們知道的只有很少幾個法則，我們的結論往往無濟於事；當然，這並不是由於大自然雜亂無章，或者毫無法則可循，而是因為我們在計算時對某些基本原理一無所知。我們對法則與和諧的認識往往局限於我們已知的少數事例；但為數更多的法則，看似矛盾實則互相呼應，可惜卻未被我們察覺，正是這些法則產生一種無比神奇的和諧呢。各種特殊的法則，其實來自我們的觀點，這就像觀光客在遊山過程中，始終移步換景，目不暇給，儘管山的形狀絕對來說只有一個，但它的側影卻是不知其數。你即使劈山鑿洞，也不能窺見它的全貌。

根據我的觀察，湖的情況對行為準則倒是同樣適合。這就是平均律。這麼一種雙徑規則，不僅指引我們觀察天體中的太陽，指引我們觀察人心，而且就一個人特殊的日常行為和生活潮流整合後的長度和寬度，也可以畫上兩道線，通向他的湖灣和入水口，那兩道線的交叉點就是他性格的最高點或者最深處了。也許，我們只要知道他的湖岸走向和他的周圍環境，就可以知道他的深奧和深藏不露的底蘊了。如果說他的四周羣山環繞，湖岸險峻，山峯聳立，並在他胸中有反映，那麼，他也必然會體現出同樣的深度。但是，低淺平滑的湖岸，就說明此人在其他方面也很膚淺。在我們的身體上，一個明顯突出的額頭，表明有一種相應的思想深度。此外，我們身上每一個凹進去的入口，彷彿都有一個沙洲，或者說一種特殊傾向；每一個凹口都是我們短暫的港灣，我們滯留在那裏，部份被陸地包圍起來。這些傾向並不離奇古怪，它們的形態、大小以及方向，其實都是湖岸的岬角，亦即古時候地勢升高的軸線所確定的，這個沙洲因暴風雨、潮汐或者洪水而漸漸增高，或者因水位回落而浮出水面時，起先這只不過是湖岸的一種傾向，其中卻孕育着一種思想，後來又從海洋分隔開來，成為一個獨立的湖，思想在這裏確立了它自己的地位，也許由鹽水變成了淡水，變成了淡水海、死海，或者說是一個沼澤。每個人來到塵世間，我們可不可以說，就是這麼一個沙洲已經升到了水面上呢？的而且確，我們都是一些可憐的航海家，我們的思想大體上說，時而靠近、時而遠離沒有港口的海岸駛行，至多只能跟稍微有點詩意的小小港口打交道，要不然駛往公共大港的入口，進入科學的枯燥碼頭，在那裏，它們僅僅整修一下以適應當今世界，沒有甚麼自然潮流能使它們保持獨立性。

至於瓦爾登湖的出入口，除了雨、雪和蒸發，我甚麼都沒有發現，雖然用溫度錶和線繩，說不定可以找到出入口；因為凡是水流入湖的地方，也許湖水夏天最涼，入冬後又最暖和。1846 年至 1847 年間，採冰人在這裏開鑿冰塊，有一天，送到岸上的冰塊卻被囤冰商所拒收，因為冰塊太薄，與其他冰塊疊在一起不夠厚；採冰人由此發現，一個小地塊內凍結的冰塊，要比別處薄二三英寸，他們推想此處說不定是個入口處。他們還指給我看另一個他們所謂的"漏洞"，瓦爾登湖在一座小山下漏入鄰近一片草地，他們讓我站在一塊冰凌上，隨即推了我過去看看。那是一個小小的洞穴，水深有十英尺；不過，我可以保證，這個小小漏洞不用堵上，除非日後發現更大的漏洞。有人覺得，如果說確實存在這麼一個"漏洞"，而且又和草地確有聯繫的話，那也是不難證明的，只要在洞口撒上一些帶色的粉末或者木屑，再放過濾器在草地的泉水邊上，就一定可以截住水流帶過來的小小屑粒。

我在勘察的時候，十六英寸厚的冰凌，在微風吹拂下，也會像湖水一樣波動。眾所周知，冰凌上頭是不能用水準儀測量的。我在岸上放置水準儀，對準冰凌上一根有刻度的木桿進行測量。儘管冰凌似乎跟湖岸緊密相連，但在離岸一桿遠的地方，冰凌最大的波動幅度就有四份之三英寸了。在湖的中心，波動幅度也許還更大呢。我們的儀器要是再精密一些，說不定還能測出地殼的波動，誰知道呢？我將測量儀的兩條腿支在岸上，第三條腿支在冰凌上，再從第三條腿的視角觀察時，冰凌上稍微有一點波動，在湖對岸一棵樹上就會出現好幾英尺的差別。我為了測量水深，開始鑿洞，由於積雪很深，壓得冰凌沉了下去，所以積有三四英寸的水；但是，湖水很快流進這些窟窿裏去，形成很深的溪澗，一直流了兩天，全磨光了周圍的冰凌，湖面變得乾爽了，即使這不是主要原因，至少也算是基本原因；因為，水流進去了，冰凌隨之升高，浮上了水面。這有點像在船底上鑿了一個洞眼，讓水流出去。後來，這些窟窿冰凍了，接着下了雨，最後又結了冰，使整個湖面形成一層鮮亮光潔的冰凌，裏面呈現雜色斑駁的優美網絡，有點像蜘蛛網，你也不妨叫它做冰玫瑰花結，那是來自四面八方的水流向湖中心的渠道形成的。有時，當冰凌上佈滿了淺淺的水潭，我會看到自己的兩個影子，一個在冰凌上，另一個在樹木或山坡的倒影裏，兩者互相疊映。

1月間，天氣依然寒冷，冰雪既厚又堅實，深謀遠慮的地主已從村裏來到湖上鑿冰，為的是準備夏天冰鎮飲料用的冰塊；現在還只是1月份——人們身穿厚大衣、戴着皮手套，許多事情都還沒有安排，但是他呢，卻預料到7月裏的酷熱和口渴，他這份超前的精明實在令人折服，甚至於感到可悲！也許他今生沒有積攢過甚麼錢財，好讓他來世享用他的冰鎮夏季飲料吧。他鑿破、鋸開堅實的湖上冰凌，掀掉魚兒們的屋頂，使魚兒賴以生存的冰凌和空氣，給鐵鏈和椿子緊緊拴住，就像捆木頭一樣，趁着冬日裏晴好天氣，一車又一車拉走冰凌，儲存在通風的地窖裏，讓冰凌在裏面靜待酷暑來臨。拉冰車從城市街道上走過，遠望過去，彷彿晶體的穹蒼似的。這些鑿冰的都是一班快活的人，有説有笑，工作有如玩耍似的。每當我來到他們中間時，他們常常邀我站在下面拉鋸，跟他們一起鋸冰。

1846 年到 1847 年冬天，來了上百個“極北樂土之人”[6]，那天早上，他們蜂聚似的來到我們的瓦爾登湖，好幾輛大車上拉來了笨重的農具，比方説，雪橇、犁耙、條播機、鍘草機、鏟子、鋸子、耙子等等，每人捎上一把雙股叉，像這樣的農具在《新英格蘭農業雜誌》或者《農事雜誌》上都沒有描述過呢。我不知道他們是不是來為冬天的黑麥播種，或為新近從冰島引進的其他種子播種。我並沒有看到肥料，我猜度他們會像我一樣，覺得這裏土層很厚，休耕時間也夠長了，大概只打算淺耕一遍吧。他們説，有一個躲在幕後的鄉紳，想讓自己的錢成倍往上翻，據我所知，此人資產大抵已有五十萬了。如今，為了他的每一塊美元上再往上疊一塊美元，他就在這砭人肌骨的大冷天裏，來剝瓦爾登湖唯一的一件外衣，不，是它唯一的一層皮呀！他們説做就做，有的犁地，有的耙地，有的開溝，一切井然有序，好像他們硬要打造這裏為一個示範農場似的；不料，等我睜大眼睛，看看他們往溝裏播點甚麼種子時，我身邊那班人便開始用鈎子鈎住這處女地的沃土，突然拋出已鈎住的東西，一直拋到了沙地上，或者説水裏了——因為那是特別鬆軟的泥巴——那一點沒錯，那裏所有土地全是這樣的——稍後裝上雪橇就拉走了。於是，我猜想，他們必定是在沼澤地裏挖泥炭。就這樣每天來來去去，伴隨着火車頭奇怪的尖叫聲，來往於北極的某個地方，我覺得他們像是一羣來自北極的雪雞。不過話又説回來，有時候，瓦爾登湖這位印第安女人也會來個報復：一個僱工走在他那一夥人的後面，不小心滑到了一條通往陰曹冥府的裂縫裏去了，看他剛才還是那麼驍勇無比，一瞬間只剩下九份之一的生命；他的體溫幾乎消失殆盡，能到寒舍避難，他覺得真是喜出望外，而且還承認這火爐功德無量；或者說，有時，堅硬的凍土會使鐵犁上的鋼齒，不是給砸斷就是使鐵犁陷在溝裏，不得不從凍土裏刨它出來。

　　說實話，每天有上百個愛爾蘭人，在北方監工的帶領下，從劍橋來到這裏開鑿冰塊。他們將冰凌切割成一個個方塊，那方法是人盡皆知，毋庸贅述。這些冰塊用雪橇拉到湖岸邊，很快拖到一個儲冰平台上，再用馱馬拉的抓鈎、滑輪和索具，對準排列整齊，像一桶一桶麵粉那樣，一塊一塊地疊起來，好像在給一座聳入雲霄的方塔打下堅實的塔基似的。他們告訴我，做得好的話，一天可以挖到一千噸，那是大約一英畝地的出產吧。你看，深深的車轍和固定支架的"搖籃洞"，在冰凌上如同在陸地上一樣到處可見，這是雪橇在同一條軌道上來回滑動的結果，而馱馬總是在挖成木桶似的冰槽裏面吃燕麥。他們就這樣在露天放置冰塊，堆成一個冰垜，高達三十五英尺，六七桿，以此長度為邊的正方形，在外面鋪襯一層乾草，與空氣隔絕；因為即使不算是特別冷的風，照樣能穿透冰垜，從而出現很大的裂縫，以至這裏那裏都支撐不住，冰垜到頭來就會倒塌的。最初，這冰垜看上去很像一座巨大的藍色城堡，或者說像瓦爾哈拉殿堂（瓦爾哈拉，北歐神話中奧丁神接見戰死者英靈的殿堂。）但是，人們開始用粗糙的草皮去填塞冰塊縫隙，外面披掛着冰霜、冰柱時，它看上去倒是像一個歷盡滄桑、長滿苔蘚的灰白色廢墟，原由藍色大理石建成，亦即冬神的寓所，那個我們常在年曆上看到的老人——是他的陋屋，彷彿他老人家打算跟我們一起避暑似的。據他們估算，這堆冰塊裏面有百份之二十五到達不了目的地，百份之二或百份之三會在車上耗損掉。不管怎麼說，這個冰垜絕大部份的命運與主人的初衷正好適得其反；因為，要不就是這些冰塊不像預期那樣好保存，裏面含有比平常更多的空氣，要不就是其他原因，反正這些冰塊從來都到達不了市場上。這堆冰垛是在 1846 年到 1847 年冬天疊起來的，估計儲量一萬噸，最後又覆蓋了乾草和木板；第二年 7 月間，蓋子被揭開而一部份冰塊被取走，剩下的暴露在驕陽底下，這年夏天和翌年冬天全都安然度過，直到 1848 年 9 月還沒有完全融化掉。不用說，大部份冰塊就這樣回歸瓦爾登湖。

瓦爾登湖的冰凌像湖水一樣，近看是綠的，但遠看卻是美麗的藍色，與四份之一英里開外河上的白色冰凌，其他一些湖裏僅僅是淡綠的冰凌，一眼就能區別開來。有時候，從鑿冰人雪橇上有一大塊冰掉在村裏大路上，躺在那裏一個星期，像一大塊翡翠，引起所有過路行人的興趣。我注意到瓦爾登湖有一個部份的水是綠的，但一結了冰，哪怕從同樣的視角看去，它卻變成了藍色。因此，在湖周邊的一些低窪地，有時入冬後積滿綠的水，跟瓦爾登湖水一樣，可是改天冰凍過後卻變成了藍色。說不定這湖水的藍色和冰凌的藍色，是因為它們所包含的光線和空氣所造成，而且，最透明的地方，色彩也最藍。冰凌是沉思中最耐人尋味的主題。他們告訴我，說他們有一些冰塊在富來喜湖的冰庫裏儲存已有五年之久，至今依然十分完好。一桶水為何很快就會發臭，而結了冰卻可以永遠保持甘美呢？人們常說，這就好比是情感與理智之間的差別吧。

就這樣，我一連十六天，從我的窗口看到上百個人在忙碌，像繁忙的農夫似的，成羣結隊，牽着車馬，帶上全套農具，如此的熱鬧畫面，我們在年曆的扉頁上倒是屢見不鮮的。每當我憑窗遠眺的時候，我常常想起雲雀和收割者的寓言，或者播種者的故事，以及諸如此類的故事傳說。如今，他們全都走了，也許過了三十多天以後，我又會憑窗遠眺純海綠色的瓦爾登湖水，湖水映現出雲彩和樹木，將它蒸發的水汽無聲無息升上天際，一點都看不出有人在那裏流連過的痕跡。也許我會聽到一隻孤獨的潛水鳥，鑽自己的頭到水裏和梳理羽毛時的喧笑聲；或是會看到一個孤獨的漁夫，駕着一葉小舟，他的身影映現在水波裏；可是不久前，上百人還曾在那裏忙着工作呢。

因此，看來在查爾斯頓和新奧爾良，以及馬德拉斯、孟買和加爾各答，那些熱得喘不過氣來的居民們，好像會在我的水井邊啜飲呢。清晨，我才智飛靈，沉浸在《福者之歌》印度著名經典《摩訶婆羅多》的一部份，以對話形式闡明印度教教義。這麼令人驚歎的天體演化的哲學裏，自從這部經典問世以後，聖賢們的時代也早已逝去；相形之下，我們近代世界及其文學似乎顯得多麼微不足道；我懷疑那種哲學是否僅僅涉及往昔的生存狀態，它的崇高風格離我們的理念又何其遙遠。我放下了書本，走到我的井邊去打水，可是，我的天哪！我在那裏遇到了婆羅門教的僕人，梵天、毗瑟拿和因陀羅的僧侶，此人還打坐在恆河邊上他的寺院裏念《吠陀經》，要不然就帶着他的餡餅皮和水罐，棲息在一棵大樹底下。我遇見他的僕人過來給主人汲水，我們的水桶好像在同一口井中碰在一起。純淨的瓦爾登湖水，已經和恆河的聖水摻在一起了。乘着順風，這水波流過了亞特蘭蒂斯[7]和赫斯珀里得斯[8]這些傳說中的島嶼，像漢諾[9]環航似的，飄過德那第島和蒂多爾島[10]，以及波斯灣的入口，在印度洋的熱帶風中匯合在一起，最後在亞歷山大也僅僅聽說過的一些港口登陸。

章註

1　引自印度史詩《摩訶婆羅多》。
2　此處博物學家尤指直接觀察動物與植物的科學工作者。
3　瓦爾登派：梭羅在此又是一語雙關，指的是大約 1170 年出現於法國南部的一個基督教派別，參加過宗教改革運動。又譯韋爾多派。
4　蘇格蘭法恩湖灣：位於蘇格蘭高地地區南部，為遊覽勝地。
5　引自英國著名詩人彌爾頓《失樂園》第 7 卷 288-290 行。

6 古希臘神話中，居住在陽光普照、北風不到和四季常春之地的人，被稱為
"極北樂土之民"。

7 亞特蘭蒂斯：傳說中的島嶼，據說位於大西洋直布羅陀海峽以西，後沉入
海底。

8 赫斯珀里得斯：古希臘羅馬神話中金蘋果園所在地。

9 漢諾：古代迦太基航海家。

10 蒂多爾島：今屬印度尼西亞。

17
春

由於鑿冰人大量採冰，通常會使湖面提前解凍；因為湖水在颳起大風時，即使在嚴寒，都能消融它周圍的冰凌。可是那一年，瓦爾登湖並非如此，因為冰凌才消融，很快又重新結冰，以至比之前更厚實。這個湖從來不像附近其他湖很早就融冰，因為湖水要比後者深得多，而且又沒有溪澗從湖中穿過，來融化或沖走冰凌。我從來沒見過它在冬天會融冰，除了 1852 年到 1853 年冬天，那時許多湖都經歷了嚴峻考驗。瓦爾登湖通常在 4 月 1 日左右融冰，比佛林特湖和美港要遲一個星期或者十天，從北岸與淺水域開始融化，而這些地方本來也是最先開始結冰的。跟附近任何水域相比，它更能顯示出這個季節的絕對進度，幾乎不大受到溫度瞬息萬變的影響。3 月間，持續好幾天的嚴寒，也許會推遲其他湖解凍融冰的時間，可是瓦爾登湖的溫度，卻幾乎不斷增高。1847 年 3 月 6 日，溫度錶插入瓦爾登湖中心，顯示溫度在華氏 32 度，亦即為冰點；湖岸附近在華氏 33 度。在這同一天，佛林特湖中心溫度在華氏 32 度半；離湖岸十二桿遠的淺水處，冰厚一英尺的水下，溫度則為華氏 36 度。在佛林特湖，深水域和淺水域溫度相差華氏 3 度半，事實上，這個湖八成都是比較淺，這就可以說明它為何比瓦爾登湖融冰要早得多。這個時候，在最淺處凝結的冰凌，要比湖中心的冰凌薄好幾英寸。仲冬時節，湖中心最暖和，那裏的冰凌也最薄。同樣，入夏以後，在湖邊蹚水而過的人全知道，靠近湖岸的水該有多暖和，只不過三四英寸深，不過稍遠點，深水處的水面卻比靠近湖底的水還要暖和。

到了春天，太陽不僅使空氣和大地的溫度增加，它的熱量還透過一英尺厚，或者比一英尺更厚的冰凌，在淺水處湖底折射上來，因此湖水也變暖了，冰凌底下開始逐漸融化；同時，由於太陽直接照射在融化了的冰層上頭，使它變得凹凸不平，釋放出氣泡，而氣泡又上下散開，直到冰層全都形成一個個蜂窩狀的物體，最後突然在一場春雨中消失殆盡。冰凌跟樹木一樣，也有它的紋理。冰塊開始融化，或者形成類似"蜂窩"的時候，不管它處於甚麼位置，氣泡和水面上的東西都是成直角的。如有岩石和原木從水底下靠近水面，水面上的冰凌就會變得很薄，經常被折射過來的熱量融化掉；我還聽説過，有人在劍橋一個木製淺池裏做試驗，儘管冷空氣在下面循環，使上面下面都有冷空氣循環，但從池底折射上來的陽光熱量，還是大大抵消了這一有利因素。仲冬時節，一場暖雨融化了瓦爾登湖的冰雪，在湖中心留下一塊發暗或者透明堅硬的冰，這時湖岸周邊，大約有一桿或者一桿多寬處，會出現長長一排易碎，卻又更厚的白冰，那也是反射上來的熱量所造成的。此外，還有我早就説過的，在冰層裏面的氣泡本身起了類似聚光鏡的作用，融化了底下的冰凌。

這一年四季的現象，天天在湖上層出不窮，只是規模較小。每天早上，一般説來，淺水要比深水暖得更快些，雖然説到底也暖不到哪裏去，但是每天晚上，淺水也會比深水冷卻得更快些。一天就是一年的縮影。黑夜是冬天，晨昏是春天和秋天，正午是夏天。冰凌的坼裂聲表示溫度的變化。1850 年 2 月 24 日，度過了一個寒冷的夜晚，我迎着怡人的晨光到佛林特湖去，打算在那裏逗留一天。讓我感到驚訝的是，當我用斧頭砍冰凌時，那響聲就像敲鑼打鼓一樣，周圍好幾桿遠都聽得到，或者換句話説，彷彿我敲打的是一面繃緊了的鼓。太陽升起以後大約一個鐘頭，湖感受到從山上斜射過來的陽光熱量，就開始隆隆發響；湖就像一個剛睡醒了的人，伸一伸懶腰，打了個哈欠，響聲越來越大，持續了三四個鐘頭。到了正午，它打了一個盹；傍晚時份，隆隆聲又響了，因為太陽在收回它的影響。天氣正常的時候，湖會極其準時鳴放它的黃昏禮炮。但在一天的正午時份，坼裂聲四起，空氣的彈性又比較差，湖完全失去了共鳴，即使敲擊湖面，恐怕連魚和土撥鼠聽了都不會發愣的。漁夫説，"湖上的雷鳴"嚇得魚兒都不敢上鈎。這湖並不是每天到了傍晚都會雷聲大作，我也説不定甚麼時候你會聽到它的雷鳴。反正天氣裏有哪些細微變化，也許我看不出來，但湖倒是感受到了。誰想到這麼寒冷、這麼皮厚的龐然大物，居然會如此敏感呢？當然，湖也有它自身的規律，遵循這規律才會雷聲大作，就好比花蕾到了春天定然綻開一樣。大地復甦，到處生機盎然。最大的湖對大氣的變化那麼敏感，就像寒暑表管柱中的小小一滴水銀似的。

吸引我住到樹林裏來的，就是我可以有閒暇，有機會看看春回大地的全部歷程。湖上的冰凌終於開始出現蜂窩狀，我從那裏走過，後腳跟都會陷進去。霧、雨、越來越暖和的陽光，漸漸融化了積雪；白晝顯然越來越長；我覺得我不用給柴火堆添料都足夠過冬，因為這時再也用不着旺火取暖。我密切注視着春天的最早信號，聽聽一些飛來的鳥兒偶然發出的啁鳴聲，或者有斑紋松鼠的吱吱聲，因為牠儲存的食物想必此刻快要耗盡了，或者看看土撥鼠從牠的越冬窩裏，毫無畏懼鑽出來。3月13日，我已聽到藍色鳴鳥、歌雀和紅翅鶇在歡唱後，湖上冰凌差不多還有一英尺厚呢。天氣越來越暖，冰凌還沒有給湖水沖掉，也不像河裏的浮冰那樣漂了起來，雖然離湖岸半桿處，冰凌已經融化，但在湖中心的冰凌依然呈現蜂窩狀，被湖水所浸透，因此，在六英尺厚的冰凌上，你仍然可以踩着走過去呢。怎料到了第二天晚上，也許大霧剛過去，又下了一場暖洋洋的春雨，冰凌就完全不見了，跟霧一起不知不覺消失了。有一年，我穿過湖中心才五天，冰凌就完全無影無蹤了。1845年，瓦爾登湖第一次完全融冰，是在4月1日；1846年，是在3月25日；1847

年，是在 4 月 8 日；1851 年，是在 3 月 28 日；1852 年，是在 4 月 18 日；1853 年，是在 3 月 23 日；1854 年，大約是在 4 月 7 日。

我們生活在這麼一個冷熱極為懸殊的氣候圈裏，河與湖的融冰，天氣的穩定，凡是與兩者有關的每一件事，我們都會特別感興趣。天氣越來越暖和的時候，住在河邊的人，夜裏會聽到冰凌的坼裂聲，那嚇人的轟鳴像大炮一樣，彷彿冰凌的鎖鏈完全給斷裂了，不到一兩天，只見它倏然消融殆盡。就像鱷魚從泥沼中鑽了出來，大地也隨之震顫不已。有一位老人，觀察大自然，真可以說細緻入微。他對大自然的一切運作，似乎獨具慧眼，料事如神，彷彿他還在孩提時代，大自然就上過造船台，而他也幫着安裝過她的龍骨 —— 如今，他已長大成人，他要是活到瑪土撒拉 [1] 的歲數，恐怕也很難獲得更多自然知識了 —— 他告訴我，入春後有一天，他提着槍坐上了小船，打算去打一兩隻野鴨子，但聽到他對大自然的運作還表示驚奇時，我不由得大吃一驚，因為我本來覺得大自然與他之間已無甚麼秘密可言了。那時，草地上還有冰凌，但河裏的冰凌早已蕩然無存，他坐上了小船，從他的住地薩德伯里一路暢通，直達美港湖，在他意料之外，看見這裏十之八九還覆蓋着堅硬的冰凌。那一天很暖和，看見湖上還有那麼多冰凌，他驚駭不已。甚麼野鴨子都沒看見，他在北岸藏起小船，或者說，湖中一個小島的背後。他獨自躲到南岸的灌木叢裏，等待野鴨子到來。離湖岸四桿的地方，冰凌都已融化了，湖面光滑暖和，湖底一片泥濘，野鴨子喜愛的正是這種地方，他心裏想着，過不了多久，野鴨子定會飛過來的。他已有一個多鐘頭安靜臥在那裏，忽然聽見一陣低沉、似乎非常遙遠的聲音，但聽起來又特別莊重，給人印象很深，跟他往日裏聽到過的聲音截然不同；那聲音逐漸高揚，不斷加強，彷彿它將會有一個響徹天地的難忘的尾音，一陣沉悶的、匆匆的聲響，在他聽來，就像一大羣飛禽馬上要棲落在這裏似的。於是，他抓起了槍，一躍而起，心情亢奮極了。可是他發現，真的叫他驚呆了：原來就在他臥伏的時候，整整一大塊冰凌已開始活動，漂浮到了岸邊，他剛才聽到的聲音，就是冰凌邊緣碰撞湖岸的聲音——開始，冰凌邊緣還是輕輕啃動着、碎裂着，但到後來卻沿着小島周圍不斷往上翻騰，冰凌的碎片飛濺到一定高度，方才復歸於平靜。

最後，太陽的光線直射大地，暖風吹散了霧和雨，湖岸上的積雪也融化了。太陽驅散迷霧之後，面向明暗交錯、褐白相間的風景微微一笑；而在薰香似的濛濛煙霧中，觀光客從一個小島尋路到另一個小島，沉醉於成千條溪澗流水奏鳴的樂曲聲中，這些溪澗的脈管裏，冬天的血液暢流不息，也隨之悄然逝去。我到村裏去，照例要穿過鐵路，見到融冰後的泥沙從鐵路兩側陡坡深溝流下去，如此罕見的壯觀，對我來說，不僅是一種莫大驚喜，雖然自從鐵路發明以來，想必用合適材料新建起來的鐵道路基，也大大增加了。那材料就是沙，粗細程度不同，而且異彩紛呈，通常還要摻上少量泥土。當霜凍在春天——以至在冬天融雪的日子裏出現時，沙開始像火山熔岩似的從鐵路陡坡流下來，有時還穿透積雪而流了出來，泛濫於以前從沒有沙的地方。數不清的小溪流縱橫交錯，展現出一種混合產物，部份服從水流的規律，部份卻遵循植被的法則。沙往下流淌的時候，看上去就像多汁的樹葉或者藤蔓，而且往外噴灑出一堆堆軟漿，竟有一英尺或者一英尺多深，你在俯瞰時會覺得它們很像某些苔蘚，有鋸齒狀的、有條裂狀的、有鱗甲狀等菌體；或者會想起珊瑚、豹掌或者鳥爪、腦子、肺葉或者腸子，以及各種各樣的排泄物。這真的是一種奇形怪狀的植被，它們的形態和色彩，我們看過，在青銅器皿上有所仿造，這麼一種建築學上常見的葉飾，要比葉形裝飾、菊苣、常春藤、藤蔓或者其他植物的葉子更古老、更典型；在某些情況下，也許將註定成為未來地質學家難解的一個啞謎呢。整個深溝給我印象很深，彷彿它是一座岩洞，連同它的鐘乳石全都呈現在陽光之下。這些沙真是豐富多彩，令人賞心悅目，包括鐵各種不同的顏色：棕色、灰色、淡黃色，以及淡紅色。這麼一大塊的流沙達到路基腳下的排水溝時，就平鋪開來，形成了淺灘；個別小溪流失去了它們的半圓錐形狀，慢慢變得越來越平坦、越來越寬闊似的，如果說還是濕漉漉時便會匯合在一起，最終形成一塊幾乎平展的沙灘，但依然豐富多彩，非常好看，你還可以從中看出植物的原始形態的痕跡；最後，它們到了水中變成了堤岸，就像河口上形成的那些沙洲一樣，那些植物形態終於消失在湖底粼粼波紋中。

整個堤岸高度從二十英尺到四十英尺，有時堤岸的一側或兩側，都被一大塊、一大塊這種葉飾，或者說，春天裏常有細沙開裂的縫隙所覆蓋，往往長達四份之一英里。這種沙葉飾之所以引人注目，就在於它倏然就躍入眼簾。我在路基的一面看到的是毫無生氣的側面 —— 因為太陽總是先照在一面的 —— 另一面卻是在一個鐘頭以內造成如此豐富多彩的葉飾；我不由得深受感動，彷彿奇怪地意識到，我已站在創造了世界和我的那個藝術家的實驗室裏 —— 來到了他仍在繼續創造的現場，看到了他正在路基那邊大顯身手，而且精力異常充沛，使他的鮮活構思隨處可見。我覺得好像自己跟地球的內臟更接近了，因為這種流沙所形成的葉狀團塊，倒是跟動物的內臟一模一樣。從這些流沙裏面，你會發現一種有植物葉子的預感。難怪大地常常依託葉子為其形，並以這樣的理念勞其神。原子早已認識到這一法則，據此成果豐碩。懸掛在枝頭的葉子，在這裏看見了自己的原型。不管地球也好，還是動物也好，它們的內部都有一張濕潤的、厚實的"葉子"。這個詞特別適用於肝、肺和脂肪葉，它的希臘文字源 λειβω，英文為 labour，拉丁文為 lapsus，是"漂流"，或者"向下流淌"、"流逝"的意思；λοβο 流，拉丁文為 globus，英文 bobe（葉）；英文 globe（地球）的意思；還有 lap（重疊）的意思；flap（垂下物）的意思，以及許多其他詞語，從外表來看，是一張薄薄乾枯的葉，英文是 leaf，甚至字母 f 和 v 的發音，也是擠壓發出的音質粗糙的 b。葉 (lobe) 的詞根是 lb，柔軟的 b 音（是單葉片的，或者 B，是雙葉片的），流音 l 在後面，推動 b 音。地球 (globe) 一詞的 glb 中，g 這個顎音對喉部的功能尤為意味深長。鳥兒的羽毛和翅膀，也是葉，只是更乾爽、更單薄罷了。所以，你可以從泥土裏笨拙的蠐螬，預見到牠變成在空中翩躚的蝴蝶。我們這個地球不斷超越自己，不斷改變自己，在自己的軌道上撲動翅膀。甚至冰凌也是從精細如水晶一樣的葉開始的，彷彿它已流進了一個個模子，而後者正是印在湖水這面鏡裏水中植物的葉。整整一棵樹只不過是一片葉，河流是更大一些的葉，它們的葉質和大地交錯在一起，鄉鎮和城市則是它們葉腋上的蟲卵。

太陽偏西時，沙停止流淌，但到了次天早晨，這些溪流就又開始流淌，而且一條一條叉了開來，形成了數不清的支流。也許你從這裏會看到血管是如何形成的。只要你仔細觀察，就會看到從最先融化的主體中流出一條軟化的沙流，它的頂端像水滴，和圓圓的手指頭相似，盲目向下慢慢尋路流淌，隨着太陽越升越高，變得很熱，很濕潤，後來那流淌最快的部份，八成順從最呆滯的部份也會遵循的法則，終於跟後者分道揚鑣，形成自己的一條迂迴曲折的渠道，或者換句話說，一條動脈，從中可以看到，有一道銀色溪流，像閃電般在發光，從軟漿似的葉或者枝杈的階段進入了另一個階段，而且還不時被流沙吞沒。沙在流動時井然有序，使自己神速而又完美，利用沙團提供最佳材料，在渠道兩側形成尖尖的邊緣。江河的發源地就是這樣。河水中含有矽的物質，也許就是骨骼系統，在更精細的泥土和有機物中，即是肌肉纖維或者細胞組織了。人是甚麼，還不就是一團融化的泥土嗎？人圓圓的手指頭，只不過是凝結了的一種滴狀物。手指和腳趾從融化中的軀體裏流了出來，達到自己的極限。在更適宜於生長發育的環境中，誰知道人體會擴展到甚麼樣子呢？人的手掌難道不就是一張撐開了的棕櫚葉[2]，有葉片和片脈嗎？耳朵不妨可以想像為一種苔蘚，拉丁文為 umbilicaria，垂在頭的兩邊，也有葉片，或者說還有滴狀物。嘴唇——字源是 labium，大抵來自 labour（勞動）這個詞——是在洞穴似的嘴巴上下兩邊的重疊物或者懸垂體。鼻子，一望可知，是一個凝縮的滴狀物，或者說，鐘乳石。下巴是一個更大的滴狀物，臉上的滴水全在這處匯合。臉頰是一面斜坡，從眉毛滑下臉龐，由顴骨支撐住。植物葉片上每塊圓圓的葉片，也是一個濃稠的正在流淌的滴狀物，儘管有大有小；葉片是葉的手指；它有多少葉片，就會向多少個方向流動，如有更多熱量，或者受到其他適宜於生長發育的影響，它就會流動得更遠了。

由此看來，這面斜坡以圖例闡明了大自然所有運作的原則。大地的創造者只得到葉片一項專利權。有哪一個商博良[3]能為我們破譯這種象形文字，讓我們終於可以翻開新一頁呢？這種現象比豐饒多產的葡萄園更讓我感到亢奮。不錯，它是有點分泌排泄的性質，反正甚麼五臟六腑等等，好像地球從裏往外全給揭示出來；不過，這至少表明，大自然也是有腸臟的，而且還是人類的母親。這是從凍土裏結出來的霜花；這就是——春天。就像神話先於符合韻律的詩歌，它是先於青山綠水的春天，先於姹紫嫣紅的春天。我可不知道還有甚麼可以蕩滌冬天的霧霾和消化不良。它使我相信，大地依然是在被子和寬鬆衣帶包裹之中的嬰兒，它小小的指頭向四處伸展。那光禿禿的額頭上長出了稚嫩的鬢髮。天地間原本沒有甚麼無機之物。路基上佈滿葉飾圖案，如同火爐裏的熔滓，說明大自然內部"正是一片旺火"。大地不僅是死氣沉沉的歷史裏面，其中的一個片段，像一本書那樣一頁一頁層層交疊，讓地質學家和考古學家去研究，它是活生生的詩歌，像樹上的葉，先於花朵，先於果實——它不是一個化石的地球，而是一個活生生的地球；相形之下，一切動植物的生命，只不過是寄生在大地這一個了不起的生命中心上。它那劇烈的搏動能使我們的殘骸從墳墓裏給拽了出來。你可以熔化你的金屬，澆鑄它們到你能打造出最美的模子裏；它們卻從來沒有使我激動過，從來沒有像這大地熔化後所形成的圖樣令我亢奮不已。不僅是它，而且任何制度都像陶工手上的泥巴，可塑性很強。

沒多久，不僅僅是在堤岸上，而且在每座小山、每個平原和每塊低窪地裏，都有霜花從地裏冒出來，好像一頭穴居的四足動物從冬眠中醒來，在音樂聲中尋找海洋，或者換句話說，遷徙到雲中其他地方去。溫言軟語的融化之神，卻比手執大鎚的雷神托爾[4]更具力度。前者善於緩緩融化，而後者只會亂砸一通。

地上積雪已部份消融，一連幾天很暖和，地面比較乾爽了，這時，不妨拿新年伊始剛露出來最早的柔嫩景象，同熬過嚴冬的蒼勁植物那莊重之美比一比，倒是別有一番情趣 —— 長生草、一枝黃花、芹葉太陽花，以及那些淡雅的野草，往往比她們在夏日裏顯得更鮮明有趣，好像她們的美，非得飽經寒夜摧殘之後才達至成熟似的；即使是羊鬍子草、香蒲、毛蕊花、狗尾草、絨毛繡線菊、白色繡線菊，還有其他硬莖植物，這些都是招待最早飛來的鳥兒取之不盡的穀倉 —— 是很不錯的雜草，至少也是大自然披上寡婦穿的全黑喪服罷[5]，特別是羊毛草禾束似的拱頂吸引住我；它將夏天帶到我們的冬日記憶裏來了，那種形態是藝術所喜愛仿效的，而且在植物王國裏，這些形態就如同天文學在人類心目中已有的預兆一樣有着相同關係。它是一種比古希臘或者古埃及更古老的風格。冬日裏的許多現象，使人想起了難以描述的柔嫩纖細的雅致。我們常聽到有人描寫這個冬日之王為一個粗野狂烈的暴君，其實，他倒是以戀人的脈脈溫情使夏日的秀髮鮮豔倍增。

春天臨近，我正坐下來讀書或者寫作時，紅松鼠來到了我的屋子底下，牠們成雙成對地直接到我的腳下，嘰嘰喳喳，唧唧咕咕，或者有時長嘶短鳴，出奇的是，那聲音非常古怪，我還從沒聽見過呢。我跺了幾腳，牠們的叫喚聲反而更響，彷彿牠們瘋狂的搗亂早已置畏懼於度外，對人類的勸阻滿不在乎了。你們別再 —— 嘰哼、嘰哼地叫了。牠們對我的斥責充耳不聞，或者一點都沒感受到我斥責的力量，反而撒潑罵人似的，真讓我拿牠們沒法呢。

第一隻報春的麻雀！這一年在從來沒有如此年輕的希望中開始！從局部光禿禿的、濕漉漉的田野裏，隱隱約約地傳來了銀鈴般的啁啾聲，那是藍色鳴鳥、北美歌雀和紅翅鶇在歡叫，彷彿冬天最後的雪花飄落時的丁零聲。在這麼一個時刻，歷史、編年史、傳說，以及一切文字記載的啟示錄，都算得上甚麼？小溪在向春天唱讚美詩和三部重唱歌曲。沼澤地的鷹低低地掠過草地，已在尋覓頭一批甦醒過來的纖弱的生物。融雪的滴水聲，漫山遍谷都聽得到，各個湖裏的冰凌在迅速消融。小草像春火似的燃遍了半山腰——春天的雨帶來了一片新綠，新綠從來沒有如此年輕的希望中開始！從局部光禿禿的、濕漉漉的田野裏，隱隱約約地傳來了銀鈴般的啁啾好像大地發出滿腔熱量，迎候太陽的回歸；那火苗的色彩不是黃的，而是綠的——那是青春永駐的象徵，那草葉啊，好像一條長長的綠色緞帶，從草地裏流向夏天，不錯，被霜凍攔阻過，但倏忽又往前推進，豎起去年乾草的嫩莖，讓新的生命從底下長出來。它慢慢生長，宛如小溪從地下緩緩滲出來似的。它差不多跟小溪渾然一體，因為在適宜作物生長的六月天裏，小溪乾涸了，草葉就成了它們的渠道，不知多少年以來，牛羊都在這條常綠的小溪裏飲水，而且，刈草人還會及時來收割用來過冬取暖的草料。因此，我們人類的生命即使滅絕，只要根還在，就仍會長出永恆的綠葉來。

瓦爾登湖冰凌正在迅速消融中。湖的西北兩側，有一條兩桿寬的運河，流到東頭會更寬一些。偌大一片冰從主體上裂開了。我聽到北美歌雀在湖邊灌木叢裏吟唱——歐利特、歐利特、歐利特——吉潑、吉潑、吉潑、吉、喳——吉、威斯、威斯、威斯。牠也是在幫着冰凌坼裂呢。冰凌邊緣的大幅度曲線，該有多麼漂亮啊，它與湖岸的曲線多少有所呼應，卻又顯得齊整得多！最近以來有過一陣子，天氣異常寒冷，冰凌堅硬得出奇，上面都有波紋，就像宮殿裏的地坪似的。但是，風陡然朝東邊吹去，掠過渾濁的冰層，直到吹皺了遠處鮮活的水面。看着這緞帶似的湖水在陽光下閃閃發光，真是讓人好不喜歡。光滑的湖面上洋溢着歡樂和青春，彷彿它在訴說湖中魚兒們的歡樂，以及湖岸上細沙的歡樂——好像是魚鱗片上發出的一片銀色的光輝，整個湖儼然都成了一條歡蹦亂跳的魚。冬天和春天的對比，就是如此。但是，我在前文已經說過，這一個春天，湖上開始凍得更慢呢。

從暴風雪和冬天轉換到平靜而溫煦的天氣，從昏暗和懶怠的時刻轉換成明亮而富有彈性的時刻，這是萬物稱頌、難以忘懷的轉捩點。最後，變化彷彿是一蹴而就似的。突然之間，一股春光透了進來，充滿我的小屋子，雖然已近黃昏時份，冬天的雲堆依然懸掛在天際，雨雪之後的水珠正從屋簷滴落下來。我抬眼眺望窗外，看！昨天那裏還是灰沉沉、冷絲絲的冰湖，此時此刻卻是一泓透明的湖水，平靜而充滿希望，勝過夏日裏的黃昏時份，在湖的胸脯上襯映出夏日裏暮色蒼茫的天空，這樣的景致雖然暫時還看不見，但它彷彿已跟遙遠的地平線心心相印了。我聽到有一隻知更鳥在遠處鳴叫，我覺得好幾千年以來彷彿還是頭一次聽到似的，即使再過好幾千年，牠的鳴叫聲我也不會忘掉——它還是那麼甜美，那麼富有活力，跟從前一模一樣。啊，黃昏時份的知更鳥，在新英格蘭的一個夏日倏忽消逝的時刻！但願我能覓到牠棲息過的丫枝！我指的是它呢；我指的是那根丫枝呢。至少這不是 Turdus migratorius [6] 吧。我屋子周圍的油松和橡樹叢，好久以來總是垂頭喪氣似的，此刻它的很多特性突然恢復了，看上去更鮮亮，更青翠，更挺秀，更有活力，彷彿經過雨水洗滌，很靈驗，恢復了元氣。我知道再也不會下雨了。只需要看看森林中的任何一根丫枝，是的，看看你的柴火堆，你就可以知道冬天究竟過去了沒有。天色越來越暗淡，一羣野鵝低空掠過樹林時發出的唳聲，嚇了我一大跳，因為牠們像疲累的旅行者一樣，從南邊的湖上飛過來，不免姍姍來遲，只好抱怨不迭，互相安慰。我站在門口，聽得到牠們撲棱翅膀的聲音；牠們衝我的小屋子飛來時，突然發現了我的燈光，喧叫聲才戛然而止。牠們盤旋數圈，飛落在湖上。於是，我轉身進屋，關上門，在樹林裏度過我的第一個春宵。

清晨，我從門口透過薄霧觀看野鵝，只見牠們在五十桿遠的湖中央來回游弋；牠們是那麼多，那麼喧鬧，瓦爾登湖彷彿成了一個供牠們戲水的人工湖。可是，我站在湖岸上時，忽聽見領頭鵝發出一聲信號，牠們馬上拍翅起飛，排成行列，在我頭頂繞了一圈，總共二十九隻，直接向加拿大飛去了；牠們的領頭鵝不時發出嗔聲，彷彿通知牠們到比較渾濁的湖中吃早餐似的。一大羣野鴨子也同時飛了起來，緊跟着那些喧鬧的兄弟們，飛往北方去了。

一個星期以來，我常聽見一隻孤雁在晨霧中來回盤旋、摸索、嗔叫，尋覓牠的夥伴；牠們就棲居在樹林裏，牠的嗔叫聲越來越響，連樹林都難以承受。到了 4 月間，就可以見到鴿子，三五成羣地掠過天空，到一定時候，我聽得見聖馬丁鳥在我的林中空地啁啾，看來鎮上未必有那麼多的聖馬丁鳥，讓我這裏也可以有一兩隻吧。我想，聖馬丁鳥是一種古老的飛禽族，遠在白人到來以前就棲息在洞穴裏。在幾乎所有氣候宜人的地區，烏龜和青蛙都是這個季節的先驅和信差；鳥兒一邊歌唱一邊飛翔，羽毛在空中閃閃發亮；各種植物拔地而起，花兒盛放，和風吹拂，彷彿糾正了南北兩極之間的輕微擺動，使大自然保持了平衡。

每一個季節，對我們來說，似乎都是妙不可言，因此，春天的來臨，就像鴻蒙初闢，宇宙創始，黃金時代到來了——

Eurus ad Auroram, Nabatheaque regna recessit，
Persidaque, et radiis juga subdita matutinis. [7]

東風退卻到奧羅拉和納巴泰王國[8]，
退卻到波斯和在晨光之下的山嶺。

****

人誕生了。究竟是造物主為了創始
更美好的世界，用神的種子創造人；
還是大地剛剛從高高的穹蒼墜落，
卻保留了同一個上天的一些種子。

一場細雨過後，小草長得越發青翠欲滴。同樣，我們展望前景，只要有美好的思想注入，就會越發光明。如果我們總是活在當下，對眼前每一件事都善於利用，就像小草沾上一點露水也承認對自己有影響；別將時間浪擲在彌補錯失的機遇上，還認為我們在盡自己的職責；那麼，我們應該說是幸福的。春天已經來臨，可是我們還在冬天徘徊不前。在一個令人愉快的春天的早晨，人間的一切罪惡都得到了寬赦。這就是罪惡消亡的日子。陽光如此溫暖人心，即使壞人說不定也會回頭。我們自己恢復了純真，自然也能看到我們鄰居的純真。也許你知道你的鄰居昨天是一個小偷、一個酒鬼，或者是一個色鬼，不是憐憫他就是鄙視他，從而對這個世界感到絕望；可是，陽光照亮了這個世界，溫暖了這個春天的第一個早晨，重新創造了這個世界，你會碰見他正在安靜地工作，只見他衰竭、淫逸的血管裏溢滿平靜的歡樂，祝福新的日子來臨，像嬰兒似的天真感受到春天的影響，於是，他的一切差錯你都忘掉了。他不僅置身於一種善意的氣氛之中，甚至還有一種神聖的氣味，也許在盲目而又徒勞地表現，好像是一種新生的本能；不久，南邊山坡上再也沒有庸俗的玩笑聲在迴響。你會看到他那多節瘤的樹皮上，有些天真可愛的嫩枝條正在用力抽芽，嘗試另一個年代的生活，那麼柔嫩、那麼鮮活，就像幼樹苗一樣。他甚至還進入過他的上帝的歡樂天地呢。為甚麼獄卒還不打開他的牢門——為甚麼法官還不撤銷他手頭的案子——為甚麼傳教士也不讓會眾離去！這是因為他們不服從上帝給予他們的暗示，也不接受上帝自由地賜予眾人的寬恕。

"牛山之木嘗美矣，以其效於大國也。斧斤伐之可以為美乎？是其日夜之所息，雨露之所潤，非無萌蘗之生焉。牛羊之從而牧之，是以若彼之濯濯也。人見其濯濯也，以為未嘗有材焉，此豈山之性也哉。"

"雖存乎人者，豈無仁義之心哉。其所以放其良心者，亦猶斧斤之於木也。旦旦而伐之，可以為美乎？其日夜之所息，平旦之氣，其好惡與人相近也者幾希？則其旦晝之所為，有梏亡之矣。梏之反覆，則其夜氣不足以存，夜氣不足以存，則其違禽獸不遠矣。人見其禽獸也，而以為未嘗有才焉者，是豈人之情也哉。"[9]

"首先建立的是黃金時代。這個時代，沒有人強迫它，沒有法律，卻自動地保持了信義和正道。在這個時代裏沒有刑罰，沒有恐懼；金牌上也沒有刻出嚇人的禁律；沒有喊冤的人羣心懷恐懼觀望着法官的面容；大家都生活安定，不必怕受審判。當時山上的松柏還沒有遭到砍伐，作成船隻航海到異鄉；除了自己的鄉土，人們不知道還有甚麼外族。……四季常青，西風送暖，輕拂着天生自長的花草。"[10]

4月29日，我在九英畝角橋附近的河岸上釣魚，站在搖曳的野草與柳樹根邊，在這裏土撥鼠出沒無常。我聽到了一種獨特的咯咯聲，有點像孩子們用手指耍弄木棍時發出的聲音，這時，我抬頭一看，但見一隻非常小但很俊秀的鷹，活像夜鶯一樣，一會打水花似的直沖雲霄，一會又翻筋斗似的落了下來一兩桿，就這樣輪番升降，顯示牠那翅膀的潛力，活像陽光下亮閃閃的一條緞帶，或者說，比貝殼裏閃光的珍珠還漂亮。這種景象使我想起了獵鷹訓練術，以及這一項運動所顯示的何等高貴的情致和詩意。依我看，不妨叫牠做"灰背隼"[11]：儘管我並不在乎牠的名字。牠那飄飄欲仙的飛翔，我是從來還沒有目睹過。牠不像蝴蝶一樣翩翩起舞，也不像蒼鷹那樣凌空翱翔；牠是在田野上空，充滿驕傲自信地飛着遊玩似的；牠發出怪叫聲，越飛越高，牠一次又一次瀟灑而又優美地俯衝下來，像風箏似的一個翻身，隨後在高空的翻騰中恢復過來，彷彿牠從來沒有在大地上落腳過。看來牠在浩茫宇宙之中沒有甚麼伴侶——總是獨自在嬉戲長空——牠只需要黎明和太空，這才是牠唯一的玩伴呢。牠並不是很孤獨，倒讓牠底下的整個大地顯得很孤獨。孵養牠的母親去了哪裏？牠的親屬、牠的父親都去了九霄雲外？牠是空中來客，牠和大地似乎僅有這麼一點點關係，那就是有過一個鷹卵，不知甚麼時候在岩縫裏面孵化出來——或者換句話說，莫非牠那故土的鳥巢，是在雲中一隅，由彩虹邊緣和夕照長空所構成，再用從大地上升起輕柔的仲夏霧靄作陪襯嗎？牠的猛禽窩，此刻還在懸崖似的雲堆裏呢。

此外，我還捉到許多罕見的銅色魚，看牠們的色彩，金黃銀白，交相輝映，望過去很像一串串珍珠。啊！不知有多少個開春第一天早晨，我深入過這些草地，從一個小圓丘蹦跳到另一個小圓丘，從一個柳樹根蹦跳到另一個柳樹根，這時，荒野的河谷和樹林沐浴在如此純潔、如此明媚的日光裏，如果死者就像有人所說的，只不過在墳墓裏面打盹，此時此刻，恐怕他們也會醒過來。永生不朽，用不着甚麼更有力的證據了。萬物都應該生活在這樣的日光裏。死啊，你的毒鈎在哪裏？死啊，你得勝的權勢在哪裏？[12]

我們村莊周圍要是沒有尚待探索的森林和草地，我們的鄉村生活就會死氣沉沉。我們需要原生態來激勵自己——有時跋涉在潛伏着麻和鷺鷥的沼澤地，聽聽沙錐鳥的叫聲；聞一聞颯颯作響的莎草，草叢裏面只有一些更野、更孤獨的飛禽在築窩，還有水貂肚皮貼地在爬行。就在我們熱切地探索和熟悉一切事物的同時，我們卻要求萬物都是神秘的，從來沒被探索過的；要求大地和海洋處於極其原生態，從來沒被勘察過、測量過，因為它們都是深不可測的。我們對大自然絕不會感到膩煩。我們看到無窮無盡的活力，看到巨大的提坦[13]力大無比般的形象，看到海岸上航船的殘骸，看到荒原上活樹與枯樹並存，看到雷鳴雨雲，看到一連下了三週、引發洪水泛濫的暴雨，定必會感到精神振奮。我們必須看到自己的極限被突破，到從未漫遊過的地方去自由地生活。雖說腐肉使我們作嘔、洩氣，但見禿鷲從啄食腐肉中獲得健康和力量，我們倒是頗感高興。通往我屋子的小道旁邊有一個坑，裏面有一匹死馬，有時候，我只好繞道而行，特別是在陰沉沉的夜間，但牠卻使我深信，大自然的胃口很好，而又非常健康，這就算是我從中得到的補償吧。我愛着大自然充滿了如此眾多的生物，甚至還經受得住無數生靈之間互相捕食與殘殺犧牲；我愛着纖嫩的生物像果肉似的，一氣不吭地給壓榨掉了——蒼鷺一口吞掉蝌蚪，烏龜和蟾蜍在大路上被車輪碾死，有時候，簡直血肉橫飛！既然這麼容易碰到意外事故，我們必須看到這是人們對此不大重視。聰明人得出的印象是：世間萬物天真無邪。毒藥到頭來不見得有毒，創傷也未必會致命。憐憫是很靠不住的。它必定是轉瞬即逝。它所懇求的必不會是一成不變。

5月初，橡樹、山核桃樹、槭樹以及其他樹木，才從湖周圍的松樹林裏發芽抽枝，它們像陽光似的使湖光山色顯得格外光豔，特別是在陰天，彷彿太陽穿透了迷霧，給滿山坡灑下了淡淡的亮光。5月3日或者4日，我在湖裏看見一隻潛水鳥，在這個月的頭一個星期裏，我聽到了三聲夜鶯、棕嘲鶇、威爾遜鶇、美洲小鶪、棕雀，以及其他鳥兒的鳴叫聲。歌鶇的鳴叫，很早以前我就聽見過了。東菲比霸鶲頻頻來到我的窗門前往屋子裏窺探，看看好不好在我的小屋子裏築窩；牠一邊在查看我屋裏的情況，一邊在空中撲棱着翅膀，收緊爪子，彷彿牠全身讓空氣支撐住似的。沒多久，北美油松硫黃似的花粉就鋪滿了湖面，以及岸邊亂石堆和朽木林，因此，你可以毫不費力地收集到滿滿一桶花粉。這就是我們聽人說起過的所謂"硫黃雨"。甚至在迦梨陀娑的劇本《沙恭達羅》

裏，我們就讀到：＂蓮花的金粉染黃了小溪。＂就這樣，四季更迭，到了夏天，我們可以漫遊在越長越高的青青草叢中。

我第一年在林中的生活就此告一段落，第二年跟它如出一轍。1847年9月6日，我最終離開了瓦爾登。

章註

1　瑪土撒拉：《聖經・舊約全書・創世記》中以諾之子，據傳活了969歲。

2　棕櫚葉：梭羅在此處一語雙關，因為英文中棕櫚（palm），還可作＂手掌或手心＂解釋。

3　商博良（Jean Francois Champollion，1790—1832）是法國歷史學及埃及學的專家。根據刻有希臘文字、埃及象形文字及通俗文字的羅塞塔石碑銘文而譯出的象形文字。

4　雷神托爾：古代北歐神話中的雷神，亦即主神奧丁的兒子。

5　全黑喪服罷：梭羅在這裏又是一語雙關，英文 weeds 既是野草或雜草，也指寡婦穿的全黑喪服。

6　Turdus migratorius：拉丁文，候鳥的意思。

7　Persidaque, et radiis juga subdita matutinis：拉丁文，意思即是緊隨其後兩行詩的中譯文。

8　納巴泰王國：西南亞古代阿拉伯王國，位於今約旦西部。

9　引自《孟子・告子》。

10　引自奧維德《變形記》第一章，著名學者楊周翰先生譯，作家出版社1958年版。

11　灰背隼：英文 Merlin，音譯＂墨林＂，中世紀傳說中的魔術師和預言家，亞瑟王的助手。

12　這兩句話引自《聖經・新約全書・哥林多前書》第15章55節。

13　提坦：古希臘神話中提坦眾巨神之一，天神烏拉諾斯與大地女神蓋婭之子。

18

結束語

有人得了病，醫生會明智地建議他不妨換換空氣和環境。
謝天謝地，這裏並不意味着整個世界。七葉樹不會生長在新英格蘭，嘲鶇的鳴叫聲這裏也很難聽得到。野鵝倒是比我們更具有國際性；它在加拿大吃早餐，到俄亥俄州吃午飯，然後在南方的牛軛湖梳理自己的羽毛過夜。甚至野牛，在某種程度上，也能緊隨着季節更迭，先在科羅拉多牧場上吃草，直到黃石公園有了更綠、更鮮美的青草在等候牠時為止。然而，我們認為，如果說我們的農場將柵欄通通拆掉，疊起了石牆來，我們就給自己的生活定下了界限，我們的命運也就選定了。你要是被選為鎮上文書，那麼，今年夏天你就去不了火地島；不過，你倒是可以到地獄烈火國去。宇宙比我們看到的還要廣闊得多呢。

然而，我們應該像好奇的旅行家一樣，經常到我們的船尾看看景色，而不要像愚蠢的水手那樣，一路航行中自己只顧低頭撿用來填船縫的麻絮。地球的另一面，不外乎是我們同類的家。我們的航行只不過是繞了一個大圈，而醫生開的藥方無非是治治皮膚病罷了。有人急急趕到南非去追捕長頸鹿，其實，他應該獵捕的肯定不是這樣的獵物。你說，一個人能花多少時間去追捕長頸鹿啊？獵捕沙錐鳥和土撥鼠，也是很稀奇罕有、很好玩的事；但我相信，射向自我倒是不失為更高貴的一項娛樂——你的視野一轉向自己的內心，會發現

在你心中就有一千個地方

還沒被發現。那你去那裏旅遊，
就會成為家庭宇宙誌的專家。[1]

　　非洲意味着甚麼？── 西方又代表甚麼？在地圖上，不也是我們
自己心中一片空白嗎？儘管一旦被發現，它會像海岸一樣黑糊糊的？難
道要我們去發現時，是尼羅河的源頭，或者尼日爾河的源頭，或者密西
西比河的源頭，或者我們大陸上的西北走廊嗎？難道說這些就是跟人類
休戚相關的問題嗎？難道說失蹤的僅僅是弗蘭克林爵士[2]一人，所以他
妻子就該十萬火急趕去尋找他嗎？格林奈爾[3]先生知不知道自己身在何
處？還不如爭當芒戈・帕克[4]，成為路易斯[5]、克拉克[6]和弗羅比歇[7]這
樣的探險家，探討你自己的河流和海洋；探索你自己的南極或北極地區
吧 ── 必要時，船上不妨裝足罐頭肉，維持自己的生命；還可以堆起
空罐頭，堆得很高，當作標誌用。難道說發明罐頭肉僅僅為了保存肉類
嗎？不，你得爭當一個哥倫布，去發現你內心的新大陸和新世界，開闢
新的航道，不是為了做生意，而是為了溝通思想。每個人不僅是一國之
主，相形之下，沙皇的帝國只不過是蕞爾小國，是冰凌遺留的一塊小疙
瘩。然而，有的人毫不莊敬自重，卻能奢談愛國，為了少數人的利益而
犧牲大多數人的利益。他們喜愛的是給自己造墓的土地，而對賦予自己
軀體以活力的精神卻無動於衷。所謂愛國僅僅是他們頭腦裏造出來的
幻想罷了。南太平洋海島探險遠征[8]，不論聲勢、耗資都是如此浩大，
究竟意味着甚麼，其實，只是間接承認了這麼一個事實：在人們的精神
世界裏，同樣存在大陸和海洋，每個人只是這個精神世界裏的一個半島
或者一個島嶼，但他還沒有去探索，卻坐在一艘政府的大船裏，經過寒
冷、風暴和吃人族的地域，航行了好幾千英里，帶上五百名水手和僕役
來伺候他，這比獨自一人去探索內心的海洋、大西洋和太平洋，畢竟要
容易得多 ──

Erret, et extremos alter scrutetur Iberos.

Plus habet hic vitae, plus habet ille viae.

讓他們漫遊去，考察異邦澳大利亞人，

我懂得更多的是神，他們懂得更多的是路。[9]

　　滿世界跑去桑給巴爾[10]清點貓科動物，很不值得。可是話又說回來，如果說你沒事可做，這種事也不妨偶一為之。也許你真的找到了一些"西姆斯洞"姆西姆斯[11]由此終於進入內心世界。英國、法國、西班牙和葡萄牙，黃金海岸[12]和奴隸海岸[13]。全都面對內心的世界，雖然從那裏出發，毫無疑問，可以直航印度，卻沒有哪一艘船敢於駛往看不見陸地內心的海洋。儘管你學會了各種方言，認同了各國風俗習慣，儘管你會比一切旅行家都走得更遠，又能適應一切氣候與水土，讓斯芬克司[14]氣得一頭撞到石頭上，那也還要聽從那位古代哲學家的箴言：去探索你的內心世界吧。這就用得着眼力和大腦。只有敗將和逃兵才去打仗，開小差的懦夫才會應募入伍。現在就開始探索，向西遠征吧，這就不會在密西西比河或者太平洋逗留，也不會到古老的中國或者日本去，而是一往直前，好像經過大地的一條切線，不管寒暑晝夜，日沒月落，毫不間斷直到最後地球消失。

　　據說，米拉波[15]攔路搶劫過，為的是"驗證一下，有人正式違抗社會上最神聖的法律，究竟需要多大決心"。後來，他聲稱："大兵打仗時需要的勇氣，只有攔路搶劫的一半。"——"榮譽和宗教永遠阻攔不了考慮周到和堅定不移的決心。"一般來說，米拉波其人其事頗具鬚眉氣概；但又很無聊，即使還算不上十惡不赦。一個比較清醒的人會發覺自己屢屢"正式違抗"所謂"社會上最神聖的法律"，因為他要聽從更神聖的法律，根本用不着超越常規，也已經驗證了他的決心。其實，他不必對社會採取這樣一種態度，只要順從他自己認可的法律，保持自己原有的態度，這樣他就絕對不會跟公正政府對抗的，如果說他碰得上這麼一個政府的話。

我離開樹林就像我入住樹林一樣，都有充份的理由。也許我覺得，似乎還有好幾種生活方式可供選擇，我不該在這樣一種生活方式上花費更多時間。值得注意的是，我們很容易不知不覺習慣了某種生活方式，陳陳相因，久而久之，給自己踩出了一條舊路來。我住在那裏還不到一個星期，我的腳底下就踩出來了一條小道，從我家門口一直通往湖邊；自此以後已有五六年了，這條小道至今依然清晰可見。說真的，我想，別人也走過這條小道，所以一直保持暢通無阻。大地的表面是柔軟的，人們一走過就會留下蹤跡；同樣，人的心路歷程也會留下蹤跡。不妨想一想，人世間的公路已給踩得多麼坑坑窪窪，塵土飛揚，傳統和習俗又形成了多麼深的車轍！我不願意枯坐在船艙裏邊；我覺得還不如乾脆站在世界的桅桿和甲板前面，因為從那裏，那羣山之間月色溶溶的美景，我可以看得更真切。那時我再也不想回到船艙下面去了。

我至少從我的試驗中悟出了這麼一點心得：一個人只要充滿自信，朝着他夢想指引的方向前進，努力去過他心中想像的那種生活，那他就會獲得平時意想不到的成功。他會把某些事情置諸腦後，越過一道看不見的界限，在他周圍與內心深處確立一些人人懂得而更自由的新法規來；要不，舊的法規加以擴充，並從更自由的意義上獲得有利於他的新詮釋，而他就可以獲得高一等生靈的資格生活。他的生活越是簡單，宇宙的法則也會顯得越簡單，孤獨將不成其為孤獨，貧困將不成其為貧困，懦弱也將不成其為懦弱。如果你造了空中樓閣，你是不會徒勞的；樓閣本該造在空中。現在已是給它們打下基礎的時候了。

英國和美國提出了一個荒唐可笑的要求，那就是：你說話非得讓他們聽得懂。無論是人也好，還是傘菌也好，都不會變得如此。好像那種要求還很重要，沒有他們也就沒有人理解你了。彷彿大自然支持的是僅僅這麼一種理解模式：它養得起四足動物，卻養不起鳥兒，養得起爬行動物，卻養不起飛禽，連耕畜都聽得懂的"噓、吁"的吆喝，倒是成了非常好的英語。彷彿唯有傻裏傻氣，反而萬無一失似的。我的主要擔心是，也許我的表達還不夠過火，也許沒有突破我日常經驗的狹隘局限，因而沒法將我深信的真理表達得一清二楚。至於過火嘛！這倒是要看你處於甚麼場合。遷徙中的水牛到另一個緯度去尋找新的草場，就不會像擠奶時的乳牛一腳踹翻奶桶、躍過牛欄、緊迫它的小牛犢那樣來得更過火吧。我想到某些沒有忌諱的地方去説説話；就像一個清醒的人跟其他一些清醒的人那樣説話。因為我相信，就算為真實的表達奠定基礎，我離誇大其詞還差得遠呢。有誰聽過一段音樂後就擔心自己説話永遠會誇大其詞嗎？為了未來或者可能發生的事，我們的生活應該過得相當隨意，不受約束，而我們的原則也不妨顯得模糊不清，就像我們的陰影對着太陽也會不知不覺像滲着汗似的。我們言辭裏真實性變化無常，不斷暴露剩下的論述不夠充足。它們的真實性會轉瞬易變，只有其字面標記得以留存。表達我們的信仰和虔誠的話語是很不確切的；然而，對出類拔萃的人來説，它們猶如乳香，意味深遠，芳香四溢。

為甚麼我們總是使我們的認識降低到最愚笨程度，還要讚美它為常識呢？最常見的感受是人們睡覺時的感覺，他們是用鼾聲表達出來。有時，我們往往將難得的聰明人和笨蛋歸為一類，因為我們只能欣賞他們的聰明的三份之一。有人偶然起個大早，就對迎晨紅霞諸多挑別。我聽説，他們認為，迦比爾[16]的詩歌有四種不同的意義：幻覺、精神、才智和吠陀經典的通俗教義；但在我們這裏，要是有人在作品中接納不止一種的詮釋，那麼，人們就會藉口抱怨不迭。英國正在下大力防治馬鈴薯腐爛，難道就不能下大力醫治大腦腐爛嗎？大腦腐爛現象，實在更普遍，因而也更致命啊。

我並不是説，我已達到晦澀的境地，但是，如果説在我這些書頁裏發現的致命差錯不比從瓦爾登湖冰凌上發現的更多的話，那我就感到自豪了。南方的買家極不喜歡瓦爾登湖冰凌的藍色，往往看成是泥漿造成的，其實，這才是它純潔無瑕的證明；他們反而喜歡劍橋的冰凌，白花花的，但有一股草腥味。人們所喜愛的純潔，就像籠罩大地的霧靄，而不是凌駕於霧靄之上的藍色太空。

有人在我們耳邊嘀咕着說，我們美國人以及一般意義上的現代人，倘若跟古人相比，甚至跟伊麗莎白時代的人相比，都不過是智力上的侏儒。但是，這話是甚麼意思？一條活狗畢竟勝過一頭死獅吧。一個人屬侏儒族，難道就活該去上吊，而不能成為侏儒裏面身型高的一個嗎？讓每個人都管好自己的事情，力求成為名副其實的萬物之靈。

我們為何如此急於求成，如此鋌而走險呢？如果說有人跟不上他的同伴們，也許這是因為他聽到的是另一種的起點。讓他踩着自己聽到的音樂節拍走路，不管這節拍是怎樣，或者換句話說走得該有多遠。至於他該不該像蘋果樹或者橡樹那麼迅速就成熟，這並不重要。他該不該把他的春天變成夏天呢？如果說我們要求的條件還不具備，我們可以用來取代的，又算是怎樣的現實呢？我們不要因為虛空的現實而一敗塗地。難道我們要下大力氣在自己的頭頂上建造一片藍色玻璃似的天空，建成後我們還要抬眼凝望那個地地道道的遙遠太空，彷彿前者並不存在似的？

庫魯城裏有一個藝術家，他喜好追求完美。有一天，他突然想做一根手杖。他覺得，一件作品之所以不完美，時間是個因素，但凡一件完美的藝術作品，時間是在所不惜的。於是，他自言自語道：哪怕我這輩子其他事情都不做，我這根手杖也要做得十全十美。他馬上直奔森林去，凡是不合適的木材決不採用；他就這樣尋找木料，一根一根挑選起來，哪一根都沒選中，這時他的朋友漸漸離開了他，因為他們工作一直做到老，一個個都死掉了，但他直到此刻一點還不見老呢。他一門心思，抱定宗旨，而又異常虔誠，不知不覺之中讓他永保青春。因為他決不向時間妥協，時間只好靠邊站，留在遠處歎息，徒呼奈何。他還沒尋覓到完全適用的材料，但是庫魯城已成了一片廢墟；於是，他就坐在一個土堆上剝樹皮。他還沒有給手杖勾畫出合適的形狀來，坎大哈王朝卻壽終正寢了，他用手杖的尖頭在沙土上寫下了那個種族最後一個人的名字，回頭繼續自己的工作。等他把那手杖磨平拋光時，卡爾帕 [17] 已經不再是北斗星了；在他還沒有給手杖安上金箍和鑲嵌寶石的頭飾之前，梵天 [18] 睡醒過已有好幾次了。可是我緣何還要提到這些事情呢？因為等他的作品最後完成了，那手杖突然之間在他眼前一亮，變得無比光艷奪目，終於成為梵天所有創造物中最完美的珍品，讓藝術家大吃一驚。他在製造手杖時創建了一種新的制度，一個完美和公正協調的新世界；在這個世界裏，古老的城市和王朝雖已消失，但取代它們的是更漂亮、更輝煌的城市和王朝。現在，他看到自己腳跟邊堆滿刨花，依然是嶄新的，覺得就他和他的工作而言，時間的流逝只不過是一種幻覺，其實時間並沒有流逝，就像梵天腦子裏閃過的火花星子，點燃了凡夫俗子頭腦裏的火絨似的。他挑選的材料是至純精美，他的藝術也是爐火純青，結果怎麼能不神奇呢？

我們可以使事物美觀，但到最後都不會像真理那樣使我們受益。唯有真理持續令人滿意。我們大多數人並不是得其所哉，而是處於一種虛假位置上。由於我們天性脆弱，我們設定一種情況，擺了自己進去，這麼一來，我們同時處於兩種情況之中，要走出來就難上加難了。清醒時，我注重的只是各種事實，亦即實際情況。說你要說的話，而不是你該說的話。任何真理都要比虛偽好。補鍋匠湯姆·海德站在絞刑架上，有人問他有沒有甚麼話要說。"轉告裁縫師傅們，"他說，"在縫第一針之前，記住線頭上打一個結。"而他朋友們的祈禱，倒是早給忘掉了。

不管你的生活多麼卑微，那也要面對它過下去；不要躲避它，也不要貶損它。生活畢竟還不像你那麼要不得吧。你最富的時候看上去倒像窮鬼。只愛挑剔的人，就算到了天堂，也總會吹毛求疵。熱愛你的生活吧，哪怕是很貧困。即使在濟貧院裏，説不定你也會有一些快活、激動、極其開心的時光。夕陽照在濟貧院的窗上，跟照在富豪家的窗上一樣亮閃閃；那門前積雪同在早春時一樣融化掉。我想，一個人只要心地寧靜，即使身在濟貧院，也會像在宮殿裏一樣心滿意足，思想愉快。鎮上的窮人，依我看，往往過着人世間最獨立不羈的生活。也許正是因為他們太了不起，所以受之無愧。多數人認為，他們根本用不着鎮裏來扶持；實際上，他們常常靠不正當的手段來養活自己，這應該説是很不光彩的。要像園中芳草和聖人[19]那樣安於清貧吧。你何苦去找新的花頭，不管是衣服，還是朋友。改變舊的，回到那裏去。萬物是恆久不變；變的是我們。你的衣服可以賣掉，但你的思想要留住。上帝會看到，你並不需要社交。如果説我整天這樣關在閣樓上一個角落裏，像一隻蜘蛛似的，但我只要自己有思想，這個世界依我看還是一樣大。哲學家説："三軍可奪帥也，匹夫不可奪志也。"[20]不要急着尋求發展，讓自己受到屢被耍弄的影響；這些全是瞎胡鬧。卑微像黑暗，會透露出天國之光。貧窮和卑微的陰影團團圍住我們"可是看吧！天地萬物擴大了我們的視野。"人們經常提醒我們，如果説上天賜克洛索斯[21]的巨富給我們的話，我們的宗旨仍然一定不會變，我們的方法實質上也不會變。再説，如果你受到貧困的限制，比方説，你連書報都買不起，其實，你也只不過限制在最有意義、最具活力的經驗之中；你被迫跟盛產糖和澱粉的物質領域打交道。貧困的生活最溫馨。你必定不會去做無聊事情。下層的人不會因為對上層的人心胸寬大而遭受損失。多餘的財富只能購買多餘的東西。而靈魂的必需品，是用錢也買不到的。

　　我生活在鉛牆的角落裏，它的成份裏注入一點鉛銅合金。經常在我午休的時候，有一種嘈雜的叮叮噹噹聲從外面傳到我的耳際。這是我同時代人的噪音。我的鄰居告訴我，說到他們和一些知名的紳士淑女的奇遇，還有他們碰到過的甚麼重要人物；怎料我對這等事就像對《每日時報》的內容根本不感興趣。他們的興趣和談吐多半是有關穿着打扮和舉止風度；反正呆頭鵝總歸是呆頭鵝，不管你怎麼打扮牠。他們向我講到加利福尼亞和得克薩斯，講到英國和印度，講到某某大人——講到佐治亞州或者馬薩諸塞州，所有這一切，全是過眼煙雲，我差點像馬穆魯克[22]老爺一樣從他們的院子裏逃走。我很高興擺正自己的定位——不喜歡耍滑頭，擺架子，招搖過市，出盡風頭，即使我可以跟宇宙造物主走在一起，我也不樂意——不樂意生活在這個躁動不安、神經緊張、熙熙攘攘、瑣屑無聊的十九世紀，而是喜歡站着或坐着冥思苦想，任憑這個十九世紀流逝而去。人們在慶祝些甚麼？他們都是籌備委員會成員，隨時期盼聽其他人演說。上帝僅僅是這一天的主席，韋伯斯特[23]是他的演說家。那些最強烈吸引我的東西，只要言之有理，我就喜歡對它們仔細考量，琢磨研究，並且朝它們靠近——而不會拉住磅秤橫桿，試圖使它們的份量輕一些——不會假設一種情況，而是要按照它的實際情況辦事；走在我能走的唯一小路上，因為走在這種小路上，任何力量也都阻攔不住我。基礎還沒有紮穩就去跳拱門，不會令我稱心如意。我們還是別玩這危險的遊戲。甚麼事都要有一個硬實的基礎。我們在書裏讀到，有個旅行家問一個孩子，他前面的沼澤地裏是不是有一個硬實的底部。那個孩子回答說是有的。怎料，轉眼之間，旅行家的馬卻齊肚地往下陷了進去，於是，他就對那孩子說："我聽你說的，這個沼澤地裏有個硬實的底部。""沒錯，底是有的，"孩子回答說，"不過現在你還沒有達到它的一半深呢。"社會的沼澤地和流沙也都是這樣；不過箇中奧妙，只有活到老的孩子才懂得，也只有在極其難得的巧合中，說了或做了自己想的事，那才好呢。有人傻得往板條和灰漿的牆裏面釘釘子，我才不會這樣做；因為做過這類事，我肯定夜夜睡不好覺。給我一把錘子，讓我摸一摸牆板上頭的紋路。灰漿是靠不住的。釘子要釘到實處，釘得牢實，你夜裏醒來想想自己這工作也保證滿意——就算繆斯女神給喚來了，你也不會覺得難為情。這樣做，上帝才會幫你的忙，也唯有這樣做，你的忙上帝才幫得上。打進去的每一顆釘子，都應該是在宇宙這台機器裏的又一顆鉚釘，這樣你才能繼續發揮作用。

最好給我真理，而不是愛情、金錢、名聲。我坐在一張擺滿珍饈美酒的餐桌前，受到阿諛逢承的招待，可是那處唯獨沒有真誠和真理；我離開這張怠慢的餐桌，依然饑腸轆轆。如此的招待，簡直冷若冰霜。我想倒是用不着再用冰塊冰鎮起它們。他們告訴我這酒的年代和酒的美名；但我想到了一種更陳、更新、更純的酒，一種更美名遠揚的佳釀，反正他們那處是沒有的，花錢也買不到。風格、住宅、庭院和"娛樂"，在我的心目中，都是可有可無的。我訪問過一個國王，他讓我在客廳裏等着，從他舉手投足來看，好像不大懂得招待客人似的。鄰近我的住處，有一個人住在空心樹洞裏面。他的舉止談吐倒是頗具真正的王者風度。我要是去訪問他，受到款待該會好得多吧。

我們要在門廊裏坐多久，恪守無聊的陳規陋俗，讓任何工作都變得荒謬之至？好像一個人每天一開始都要叫苦不迭，僱了一個人來給他種馬鈴薯；午後帶着事先想好的種種許願，出去實踐基督徒的溫順和愛心！不妨想一想中國的自大和人類停滯不前的自滿吧。這一代人托庇餘蔭，慶幸自己成為名門望族的最後遺民；在波士頓、倫敦、巴黎和羅馬，想到它那綿綿瓜瓞似的歷史，它還沾沾自喜在訴說着自己在藝術、科學和文學上取得的進步。各種哲學學會的記錄，關於偉人的公開頌詞俯拾即是！好人亞當在思考自己的美德。"是的，我們作出了偉大的業績，唱起了神聖之歌，它們將是不朽的"——也就是說，只要我們牢記它們。古代亞述[24]的學術團體和偉人——現在他們都在哪裏呢？我們是多麼年輕的哲學家和實驗家啊！我的讀者裏面，還沒有一個是活過完整的一生的。在人類生活中，這些也許僅僅是早春季節吧。如果説我們已有過七年之癢²⁵，可我們還沒有見過康科德的十七年蝗蟲²⁶。我們所熟悉的僅僅是我們賴以生存的地球上的一層薄殼，大多數人都沒有潛入過地下六英尺深，也還沒有躍過離地六英尺高。我們都不知道自己身在何方。再説，我們差不多有一半時間都在酣睡。但是，我們卻自以為很聰明，在地球上建立了一種秩序。真的，我們是深刻的思想者，我們是志存高遠的精靈！我站在森林覆被²⁷上，看到松針之間爬行的一條蟲，極力躲避我的視線，於是，我反躬自問，為甚麼它會有這些謙遜思想，藏起頭來躲避我；也許我是它的恩人，告訴牠的族羣一些可喜的信息；這時，我想到了那個更偉大的恩人與智者，也正在俯視我儼然像條蟲呢。

新奇事物源源不絕湧入當今世界，我們卻可以容忍不可思議的愚鈍。我只需要提示一下，在最開明的國土上，我們至今還在聽甚麼佈道就夠了。這裏面有諸如歡樂和悲哀之類的字眼，但它們都是讚美詩裏的疊句，用鼻音哼唱的，其實我們所相信的還是平庸和卑微。我們以為我們只要換一下衣服就可以了。據説，不列顛帝國很大，而且名聲很好；而美國則是一流的強國。我們不相信每一個人背後都在潮起潮落，這潮水能使不列顛帝國像小木片似的漂浮起來，如果説每個人心裏記住這個的話。誰知道下一次還會有甚麼樣的十七年蝗災呢？我生活所在的這個世界的政府，不像英國政府那樣，在晚宴之後喝酒閒聊中就可以構建起來。

我們體內的生命好似大河裏的水。也許今年河水漲得很高，人們從來沒見過，淹沒了乾旱的高地；甚至這一年説不定還是多事之秋，會淹死我們所有的麝鼠。我們居住的地方不見得總是在旱地上。我遠遠看到，深入內地的河岸在古代，遠在科學還沒有記錄它們的洪災之前，就受到河流的沖刷。每個人都聽説過在新英格蘭盛傳的那個故事：有一條健壯、美麗的蟲，從蘋果木舊餐桌的一塊乾爽的活動面板裏爬了出來。

怎料這張餐桌放置在農家廚房裏已經六十多年了，先是在康涅狄格州，後來到了馬薩諸塞州——可是那個蟲卵遠在六十多年前蘋果樹還活着時，就存活在樹裏面，至少也有好幾年了，反正從樹的年輪上是看得出來的；只聽得這蟲在裏面啃咬幾個星期，蟲卵也許受到水壺的熱氣才孵化出來的。聽了上面這個故事，誰能不感受到復活和不朽的信心隨之得到增強呢？它的卵子蟄伏在一層又一層的木頭芯裏，在枯死的社會生活裏埋伏了幾個世代，開始是在生青碧綠的活木材裏，後來活木材漸漸風乾變成墳墓似的硬殼——也許這時牠在木頭裏已啃咬好幾年了，讓坐在喜慶餐桌前的一家人聽到響聲，大吃一驚——誰知道，那美麗的、長着翅膀的生命，從社會最不起眼、別人贈送的家具裏破繭而出，終於享受牠完美的夏日生活！

我並不是説這一切約翰或者喬納森[28]都能認識到的。但是，僅靠時光的流逝，絕對到不了拂曉，這就是那個早晨的特性。遮住我們兩眼的亮光，對我們無異於黑暗。唯有我們清醒的時候，天光才大亮。天光大亮的日子多着呢。太陽才不過是一顆晨星罷了。

章註

1　引自哈賓頓（William Habbington）《致尊敬的奈特爵士》的詩句。

2　弗蘭克林爵士（Sir John Franklin，1786—1847）是英國探險家，海軍少將，率領官兵 130 餘人，遇難於西北航道的探險中。

3　格林奈爾（Henry Grinnell，1799—1874）是紐約富商，曾資助尋找遇難的弗蘭克林等一批人。

4　芒戈・帕克（Mungo Park，1771—1806）蘇格蘭探險家，兩次勘查非洲尼日爾河道，著有《非洲內地旅行》。

5　路易斯（Meriwether Lewis，1774—1809）和克拉克（William Clark，1770—1838）是美國探險家，兩人率隊進行首次直達太平洋西北岸橫貫大陸的考察活動。

6　克拉克（William Clark，1770—1838）。

7　弗羅比歇（Sir Martin Frobisher，1535—1838）是英國航海家。

8　此處指 1838 新的航道，美國海軍對南太平洋和大西洋的探險遠征。

9　引自古羅馬詩人克勞迪恩（Claudian，370—404）的《維羅納的老人》一詩。梭羅的英譯將 "西班牙人" 誤譯為 "澳大利亞人"。請讀者注意。

10　桑給巴爾，今日坦桑尼亞東北部。

11　姆西姆斯（John Symmes，1780—1829）是英國人，曾論證地球是空心的。

12　黃金海岸：西非國家加納舊稱。

13　奴隸海岸：今西非貝攏灣沿岸一帶，因西方殖民者由此大量販運非洲黑人至美洲為奴而得名。

14　斯芬克司：古希臘神話中長翅膀的獅身女怪，傳說常叫過路行人猜謎，猜不出者即遭殺害。在埃及現存獅身人面（或羊頭，或鷹頭）巨像。

15　米拉波（Counte de Mirabeau，1749—1791）是法國大革命時期君主立憲派領袖之一，是演說家和政治家。

16　迦比爾（Kabir）：印度神秘派詩人，曾試圖融合印度教和伊斯蘭教精華，形成簡易瑜伽，成為迦比爾道、錫克教以及許多教門的先驅。

17　卡爾帕（Kalpa）：梵文意思是 "劫"；古印度傳說世界經歷若干萬年毀滅一次，重新再生，這一週期稱為一劫。

18　印度教主神之一，為創造之神，亦指眾生之本。

19　聖人：此處原文 sage，又指鼠尾草類植物。

20　哲學家說："三軍可奪帥也，匹夫不可奪志也。" 引自《論語・子罕》。

21　克洛索斯：Croesus，公元前 6 世紀，呂底亞末代國王，斂財成巨富。

22　馬穆魯克：Mameluke，原指 1250 年到 1517 年統治埃及的軍人集團的成員，出身奴隸，後來泛指奴隸。據傳 1811 年在埃及一次大屠殺中，有一個馬穆魯克老爺翻牆跳到馬上，得以逃命。

23　韋伯斯特（Daniel Webster 1782—1852）是美國政治家和演說家。

24　亞述：古代東方一奴隸制國家，位於亞洲西部。

25　此詞為英美謔詞，指夫婦間結婚 7 年後常出現互相厭倦和不忠實的趨勢。

26　蝗蟲：暗指災星、老饕之類人物。

27　覆被：即指包含枯枝落葉等腐殖質形成的森林覆被。

28　約翰、喬納森都是英美人常用姓名，此處分別指英國人與美國人。